GOTREK & FELIX
THE FIRST OMNIBUS

A WARHAMMER OMNIBUS

WILLIAM KING

GOTREK & FELIX

THE FIRST OMNIBUS

BLACK LIBRARY

A Black Library Publication

Trollslayer copyright © 1999, Games Workshop Ltd.
Skavenslayer copyright © 1999 Games Workshop Ltd.
Daemonslayer copyright © 1999 Games Workshop Ltd.
A Place of Quiet Assembly, Kineater and *Mind-stealer* first appeared in
Gotrek & Felix: the Anthology copyright © 2012 Games Workshop Ltd.
Death and Glory first appeared in Warhammer Armies: The Empire
copyright © 1993 Games Workshop Ltd.
The original version of the Gazetteer first appeared in *Inferno! 36*
copyright © 2003 Games Workshop Ltd.
All rights reserved.

Blood Sport has not previously appeared in print.

Updated Gotrek & Felix Gazetteer by Lindsey D le Doux Priestley.

With thanks to Rob Clarke and Angela McIntosh for the
original version of the Gotrek & Felix Gazetteer.

This omnibus edition published in Great Britain in 2013 by
Black Library,
Games Workshop Ltd.,
Willow Road,
Nottingham, NG7 2WS, UK.

10 9 8 7 6 5 4 3 2 1

Cover illustration by Winona Nelson.
Map by Nuala Kinrade.

See Black Library on the internet at

www.blacklibrary.com

Find out more about Games Workshop
and the world of Warhammer at

www.games-workshop.com

Printed and bound by CPI Group (UK) Ltd, Croydon, CR0 4YY

This is a dark age, a bloody age, an age of daemons
and of sorcery. It is an age of battle and death, and of the
world's ending. Amidst all of the fire, flame and fury
it is a time, too, of mighty heroes, of bold deeds
and great courage.

At the heart of the Old World sprawls the Empire, the
largest and most powerful of the human realms. Known for
its engineers, sorcerers, traders and soldiers, it is
a land of great mountains, mighty rivers, dark forests
and vast cities. And from his throne in Altdorf reigns
the Emperor Karl Franz, sacred descendant of the
founder of these lands, Sigmar, and wielder
of his magical warhammer.

But these are far from civilised times. Across the length
and breadth of the Old World, from the knightly palaces
of Bretonnia to ice-bound Kislev in the far north, come
rumblings of war. In the towering Worlds Edge Mountains,
the orc tribes are gathering for another assault. Bandits and
renegades harry the wild southern lands of
the Border Princes. There are rumours of rat-things, the
skaven, emerging from the sewers and swamps across the
land. And from the northern wildernesses there is the
ever-present threat of Chaos, of daemons and beastmen
corrupted by the foul powers of the Dark Gods.
As the time of battle draws ever near,
the Empire needs heroes
like never before.

Claws

North of Here Lie The
Dreaded Chaos Wastes.

Erengrad.

Here Be Trolls...

Praag.

...nheim.

Middle Mountains.

Kislev

Kislev.

Wolfenburg.

Talabheim.

...ldorf.

The Empire

Nuln.

The
Moot.

Sylvania.
Dracken
-hof.

Karak Kad...

Zhufbar.

...s.

Averheim.

Black
Water.

Black Fire Pass.

...arak
Norn.

CONTENTS

TROLLSLAYER

GEHEIMNISNACHT

'After the terrible events and nightmare adventures
we endured in Altdorf, my companion and I fled
southwards, following no path more certain than
that chosen for us by blind chance. We took
whatever means of transport presented itself:
stagecoach, peasant cart, drayage wagon, resorting to
our own two feet when all else failed.

'It was a difficult and fear-filled time for me. At
every turning, it seemed, we stood in imminent
danger of arrest and either imprisonment or
execution. I saw sheriffs in every tavern and bounty
killers behind every bush. If the Trollslayer suspected
that things might have been otherwise, he never
bothered to communicate this information to me.

'To one as ignorant of the true state of our legal
system as I then was, it seemed all too possible that
the entire apparatus of our mighty and extensive
state might be bent to the apprehension of two
fugitives such as ourselves. I did not then have any
idea of quite how feebly and randomly the rule of
law was applied. It was indeed a pity that all those
sheriffs and all those bounty killers who peopled
my imagination did not, in fact, exist – for perhaps
then evil would not have flourished quite so strongly
within the boundaries of my homeland.

'The extent and nature of the evil was to become
very clear to me one dark evening after boarding a
southbound stagecoach, on what is perhaps the most
ill-omened night in our entire calendar...'

— From *My Travels with Gotrek, Vol. II*, by Herr Felix Jaeger
(Altdorf Press, 2505)

Damn all manling coach drivers and all manling women,' Gotrek Gurnisson muttered, adding a curse in dwarfish.

'You did have to insult the lady Isolde, didn't you?' Felix Jaeger said peevishly. 'As things are, we're lucky they didn't just shoot us. If you can call it "lucky" to be dumped in the Reikwald on Geheimnisnacht Eve.'

'We paid for our passage. We were just as entitled to sit inside as her. The drivers were unmanly cowards,' Gotrek grumbled. 'They refused to meet me hand to hand. I would not have minded being spitted on steel, but being blasted with buckshot is no death for a Trollslayer.'

Felix shook his head. He could see that one of his companion's black moods was coming on. There would be no arguing with him and Felix had plenty of other things to worry about. The sun was setting, giving the mist-covered forest a ruddy hue.

Long shadows danced eerily and brought to mind too many frightening tales of the horrors to be found under the canopy of trees.

He wiped his nose with the edge of his cloak, then pulled the Sudenland wool tight about him. He sniffed and looked at the sky where Morrslieb and Mannslieb, the lesser and greater moons, were already visible. Morrslieb seemed to be giving off a faint greenish glow. It wasn't a good sign.

'I think I have a fever coming on,' Felix said. The Trollslayer looked up at him and chuckled contemptuously. In the last rays of the dying sun, his nose-chain was a bloody arc running from nostril to earlobe.

'Yours is a weak race,' Gotrek said. 'The only fever I feel this eve is the battle-fever. It sings in my head.'

He turned and glared out into the darkness of the woods. 'Come out, little beastmen!' he bellowed. 'I have a gift for you.'

He laughed loudly and ran his thumb along the edge of the blade of his great two-handed axe. Felix saw that it drew blood. Gotrek began to suck his thumb.

'Sigmar preserve us, be quiet!' Felix hissed. 'Who knows what lurks out there on a night like this?'

Gotrek glared at him. Felix could see the glint of insane violence appear in his eyes. Instinctively Felix's hand strayed nearer to the pommel of his sword.

'Give me no orders, manling! I am of the Elder Race and am beholden only to the Kings Under the Mountain, exile though I be.'

Felix bowed formally. He was well schooled in the use of the sword. The scars on his face showed that he had fought several duels in his student days. He had once killed a man and so ended a promising academic career. But still he did not relish the thought of fighting the Trollslayer. The tip of Gotrek's crested hair came only to the level of Felix's chest, but the dwarf outweighed him and his bulk was all muscle. And Felix had seen Gotrek use that axe.

The dwarf took the bow as an apology and turned once more to the darkness. 'Come out!' he shouted. 'I care not if all the powers of evil walk the woods this night. I will face any challenger.'

The dwarf was working himself up to a pitch of fury. During the time of their acquaintance Felix had noticed that the Trollslayer's long periods of brooding were often followed by brief explosions of rage. It was one of the things about his companion that fascinated Felix. He knew that Gotrek had become a Trollslayer to atone for some crime. He was sworn to seek death in unequal combat with fearsome monsters. He seemed bitter to the point of madness – yet he kept to his oath.

Perhaps, thought Felix, I too would go mad if I had been driven into exile among strangers not even of my own race. He felt some sympathy for the crazed dwarf. Felix knew what it was like to be driven from home under a cloud. The duel with Wolfgang Krassner had caused quite a scandal.

At that moment, however, the dwarf seemed bent on getting them both killed, and he wanted no part of it. Felix continued to plod along the road, casting an occasional worried glance at the bright full moons. Behind him the ranting continued.

'Are there no warriors among you? Come feel my axe. She thirsts!'

Only a madman would so tempt fate and the dark powers on Geheimnisnacht, Night of Mystery, in the darkest reaches of the forest, Felix decided.

He could make out chanting in the flinty, guttural tongue of the Mountain Dwarfs, then once more in Reikspiel, he heard: 'Send me a champion!'

For a second there was silence. Condensation from the clammy mist ran down his brow. Then – from far, far off – the sound of galloping horses rang out in the quiet night.

What has that maniac done, Felix thought, has he offended one of the Old Powers? Have they sent their daemon riders to carry us off?

Felix stepped off the road. He shuddered as wet leaves fondled his face. They felt like dead men's fingers. The thunder of hooves came closer, moving with hellish speed along the forest road. Surely only a supernatural being could keep such breakneck pace on the winding forest road? He felt his hand shake as he unsheathed his sword.

I was foolish to follow Gotrek, he thought. Now I'll never get the poem finished. He could hear the loud neighing of horses, the cracking of a whip and mighty wheels turning.

'Good!' Gotrek roared. His voice drifted from the trail behind. 'Good!'

There was a loud bellowing and four immense jet black horses drawing an equally black coach hurtled past. Felix saw the wheels bounce as they hit a rut in the road. He could just make out a black-cloaked driver. He shrank back into the bushes.

He heard the sound of feet coming closer. The bushes were pulled aside. Before him stood Gotrek, looking madder and wilder than ever. His crest was matted, brown mud was smeared over his tattooed body and his studded leather jerkin was ripped and torn.

'The snotling-fondlers tried to run me over!' he yelled. 'Let's get after them!'

He turned and headed up the muddy road at a fast trot. Felix noted that Gotrek was singing happily in Khazalid.

Further down the Bogenhafen road the pair found the Standing Stones Inn. The windows were shuttered and no lights showed. They could hear a neighing from the stables but when they checked there was no coach, black or otherwise, only some skittish ponies and a peddler's cart.

'We've lost the coach. Might as well get a bed for the night,' Felix suggested. He looked warily at the smaller moon, Morrslieb. The sickly green glow was stronger. 'I do not like being abroad under this evil light.'

'You are feeble, manling. Cowardly too.'

'They'll have ale.'

'On the other hand, some of your suggestions are not without merit. Watery though human beer is, of course.'

'Of course,' Felix said. Gotrek failed to spot the note of irony in his voice.

The inn was not fortified but the walls were thick, and when they tried the door they found it was barred. Gotrek began to bang it with the butt of his axe-shaft. There was no response.

'I can smell humans within,' Gotrek said. Felix wondered how he could smell anything over his own stench. Gotrek never washed and his hair was matted with animal fat to keep his red-dyed crest in place.

'They'll have locked themselves in. Nobody goes abroad on Geheimnisnacht. Unless they're witches or daemon-lovers.'

'The black coach was abroad,' Gotrek said.

'Its occupants were up to no good. The windows were curtained and the coach bore no crest of arms.'

'My throat is too dry to discuss such details. Come on, open up in there or I'll take my axe to the door!'

Felix thought he heard movement within. He pressed an ear to the door. He could make out the mutter of voices and what sounded like weeping.

'Unless you want me to chop through your head, manling, I suggest you stand aside,' Gotrek said to Felix.

'Just a moment. I say: you inside! Open up! My friend has a very large axe and a very short temper. I suggest you do as he says or lose your door.'

'What was that about "short"?' Gotrek said touchily.

From behind the door came a thin, quavering cry. 'In the name of Sigmar, begone, you daemons of the pit!'

'Right, that's it,' Gotrek snapped. 'I've had enough.'

He drew his axe back in a huge arc. Felix saw the runes on its blade gleam in the Morrslieb light. He leapt aside.

'In the name of Sigmar!' Felix shouted. 'You cannot exorcise us. We are simple, weary travellers.'

The axe bit into the door with a chunking sound. Splinters of wood flew from it. Gotrek turned to Felix and grinned evilly up at him. Felix noted the missing teeth.

'Shoddily made, these manling doors,' Gotrek said.

'I suggest you open up while you still have a door,' Felix called.

'Wait,' the quavering voice said. 'That door cost me five crowns from Jurgen the carpenter.'

The door was unlatched. It opened. A tall, thin man with a sad face framed by lank, white hair stood there. He had a stout club in one hand. Behind him stood an old woman who held a saucer that contained a guttering candle.

'You will not need your weapon, sir. We require only a bed for the night,' Felix said.

'And ale,' the dwarf grunted.

'And ale,' Felix agreed.

'Lots of ale,' Gotrek said. Felix looked at the old man and shrugged helplessly.

Inside, the inn had a low common room. The bar was made of planks stretched across two barrels. From the corner, three armed men who looked like travelling peddlers watched them warily. They each had daggers drawn. The shadows hid their faces but they seemed worried.

The innkeeper hustled the pair inside and slid the bars back into place. 'Can you pay, Herr Doktor?' he asked nervously. Felix could see the man's Adam's apple moving.

'I am not a professor, I am a poet,' he said, producing his thin pouch and counting out his few remaining gold coins. 'But I can pay.'

'Food,' Gotrek said. 'And ale.'

At this the old woman burst into tears. Felix stared at her.

'The hag is discomfited,' Gotrek said.

The old man nodded. 'Our Gunter is missing, on this of all nights.'

'Get me some ale,' Gotrek said. The innkeeper backed off. Gotrek got up and stumped over to where the peddlers were sitting. They regarded him warily.

'Do any of you know about a black coach drawn by four black horses?' Gotrek asked.

'You have seen the black coach?' one of the peddlers asked. The fear was evident in his voice.

'Seen it? The bloody thing nearly ran me over.' A man gasped. Felix heard the sound of a ladle being dropped. He saw the innkeeper stoop to pick it up and begin refilling the tankard.

'You are lucky then,' the fattest and most prosperous-looking peddler said. 'Some say the coach is driven by daemons. I have heard it passes here on Geheimnisnacht every year. Some say it carries wee children from Altdorf who are sacrificed at the Darkstone Ring.'

Gotrek looked at him with interest. Felix did not like the way this was developing.

'Surely that is only a legend,' he said.

'No, sir,' the innkeeper shouted. 'Every year we hear the thunder of its passing. Two years ago Gunter looked out and saw it, a black coach just as you describe.'

At the mention of Gunter's name the old woman began to cry again. The innkeeper brought stew and two great steins of ale.

'Bring beer for my companion too,' Gotrek said. The landlord went off for another stein.

'Who is Gunter?' Felix asked when he returned. There was another wail from the old woman.

'More ale,' Gotrek said. The landlord looked in astonishment at the empty flagons.

'Take mine,' Felix said. 'Now, mein host, who is Gunter?'

'And why does the old hag howl at the very mention of his name?' Gotrek asked, wiping his mouth on his mud-encrusted arm.

'Gunter is our son. He went out to chop wood this afternoon. He has not returned.'

'Gunter is a good boy,' the old woman sniffled. 'How will we survive without him?'

'Perhaps he is simply lost in the woods?'

'Impossible,' the innkeeper said. 'Gunter knows the woods round here like I know the hairs on my hand. He should have been home hours ago. I fear the coven has taken him, as a sacrifice.'

'It's just like Lotte Hauptmann's daughter, Ingrid,' the fat peddler said. The innkeeper shot him a dirty look.

'I want no tales told of our son's betrothed,' he said.

'Let the man speak,' Gotrek said. The peddler looked at him gratefully.

'The same thing happened last year, in Hartzroch, just down the road. Goodwife Hauptmann looked in on her teenage daughter Ingrid just after sunset. She thought she heard banging coming from her daughter's room. The girl was gone, snatched by who-knows-what sorcerous power from her bed in a locked house. The next day the hue and cry went up. We found Ingrid. She was covered in bruises and in a terrible state.'

He looked at them to make sure he had their attention. 'You asked her what happened?' Felix said.

'Aye, sir. It seems she had been carried off by daemons, wild things of the wood, to Darkstone Ring. There the coven waited with evil creatures from the forests. They made to sacrifice her at the altar but she broke free from her captors and invoked the good name of blessed Sigmar. While they reeled she fled. They pursued her but could not overtake her.'

'That was lucky,' Felix said dryly.

'There is no need to mock, Herr Doktor. We made our way to the stones and we did find all sorts of tracks in the disturbed earth. Including those of humans and beasts and cloven-hoofed daemons. And a yearling infant gutted like a pig upon the altar.'

'Cloven-hoofed daemons?' Gotrek asked. Felix didn't like the look of interest in his eye. The peddler nodded.

'I would not venture up to Darkstone Ring tonight,' the peddler said. 'Not for all the gold in Altdorf.'

'It would be a task fit for a hero,' Gotrek said, looking meaningfully at Felix. Felix was shocked.

'Surely you cannot mean–'

'What better task for a Trollslayer than to face these daemons on their sacred night? It would be a mighty death.'

'It would be a stupid death,' Felix muttered.

'What was that?'

'Nothing.'

'You are coming, aren't you?' Gotrek said menacingly. He was rubbing his thumb along the blade of his axe. Felix noticed that it was bleeding again.

He nodded slowly. 'An oath is an oath.'

The dwarf slapped him upon the back with such force that he thought his ribs would break. 'Sometimes, manling, I think you must have dwarf blood in you. Not that any of the Elder race would stoop to such a mixed marriage, of course.'

He stomped back to his ale.

'Of course,' his companion said, glaring at his back.

Felix fumbled in his pack for his mail shirt. He noticed that the innkeeper and his wife and the peddlers were looking at him. Their eyes held something that looked close to awe. Gotrek sat near the fire drinking ale and grumbling in dwarfish.

'You're not really going with him?' the fat peddler whispered. Felix nodded.

'Why?'

'He saved my life. I owe him a debt.' Felix thought it best not to mention the circumstances under which Gotrek had saved him.

'I pulled the manling out from under the hooves of the Emperor's cavalry,' Gotrek shouted.

Felix cursed bitterly. The Trollslayer has the hearing of a wild beast as well as the brains of one, he thought to himself, continuing to pull on the mail shirt.

'Aye. The manling thought it clever to put his case to the Emperor

21

with petitions and protest marches. Old Karl Franz chose to respond, quite sensibly, with cavalry charges.'

The peddlers were starting to back away.

'An insurrectionist,' Felix heard one mutter.

Felix felt his face flush. 'It was yet another cruel and unjust tax. A silver piece for every window, indeed. To make it worse, all the fat merchants bricked up their windows and the Altdorf militia went around knocking holes in the side of poor folks' hovels. We were right to speak out.'

'There's a reward for the capture of insurrectionists,' the peddler said. 'A big reward.'

Felix stared at him. 'Of course, the Imperial cavalry were no match for my companion's axe,' he said. 'Such carnage! Heads, legs, arms everywhere. He stood on a pile of bodies.'

'They called for archers,' Gotrek said. 'We departed down a back alley. Being spitted from afar would have been an unseemly death.'

The fat peddler looked at his companions then at Gotrek, then at Felix, then back at his companions. 'A sensible man keeps out of politics,' he said to the man who had talked of rewards. He looked at Felix. 'No offence, sir.'

'None taken,' Felix said. 'You are absolutely correct.'

'Insurrectionist or no,' the old woman said, 'may Sigmar bless you if you bring my little Gunter back.'

'He is not little, Lise,' the innkeeper said. 'He is a strapping young man. Still, I hope you bring my son back. I am old and I need him to chop the wood and shoe the horses and lift the kegs and–'

'I am touched by your paternal concern, sir,' Felix interrupted. He pulled his leather cap down on his head.

Gotrek got up and looked at him. He beat his chest with one meaty hand. 'Armour is for women and girly elves,' he said.

'Perhaps I had best wear it, Gotrek. If I am to return alive with the tale of your deeds – as I did, after all, swear to do.'

'You have a point, manling. And remember that is not all you swore to do.' He turned to the innkeeper. 'How will we find the Darkstone Ring?'

Felix felt his mouth go dry. He fought to keep his hands from shaking.

'There is a trail. It runs from the road. I will take you to its start.'

'Good,' Gotrek said. 'This is too good an opportunity to miss. Tonight I will atone my sins and stand among the Iron Halls of my fathers. Great Grungni willing.'

He made a peculiar sign over his chest with his clenched right hand. 'Come, manling, let us go.' He strode out the door.

Felix picked up his pack. At the doorway the old woman stopped him and pressed something into his hand. 'Please, sir,' she said. 'Take this. It is a charm to Sigmar. It will protect you. My little Gunter wears its twin.'

And much good it's done him, Felix was about to say, but the expression on her face stopped him. It held fear, concern and perhaps hope. He was touched.

'I'll do my best, frau.'

Outside, the sky was bright with the green witchlight of the moons. Felix opened his hand. In it was a small iron hammer on a fine-linked chain. He shrugged and hung it round his neck. Gotrek and the old man were already moving down the road. He had to run to catch up.

'What do you think these are, manling?' Gotrek said, bending close to the ground. Ahead of them, the road continued on towards Hartzroch and Bogenhafen. Felix leaned on the league marker. This was the edge of the trail. Felix hoped the innkeeper had returned home safely.

'Tracks,' he said. 'Going north.'

'Very good, manling. They are coach tracks and they take the trail north to the Darkstone Ring.'

'The black coach?' Felix said.

'I hope so. What a glorious night! All my prayers are answered. A chance to atone and to get revenge on the swine who nearly ran me over.' Gotrek cackled gleefully but Felix could sense a change in him. He seemed tense, as if suspecting that his hour of destiny were arriving and he would meet it badly. He seemed unusually talkative.

'A coach? Does this coven consist of noblemen, manling? Is your Empire so very corrupt?'

Felix shook his head. 'I don't know. It may have a noble leader. The members are most likely local folk. They say the taint of Chaos runs deep in these out of the way places.'

Gotrek shook his head and for the first time ever he looked dismayed. 'I could weep for the folly of your people, manling. To be so corrupted that your rulers could sell themselves over to the powers of darkness, that is a terrible thing.'

'Not all men are so,' Felix said angrily. 'True, some seek easy power or the pleasures of the flesh, but they are few. Most people keep the faith. Anyway, the Elder Race are not so pure. I have heard tales of whole armies of dwarfs dedicated to the Ruinous Powers.'

Gotrek gave a low angry growl and spat on the ground. Felix gripped the hilt of his sword tighter. He wondered whether he had pushed the Trollslayer too far.

'You are correct,' Gotrek said, his voice soft and cold. 'We do not lightly talk about such things. We have vowed eternal war against the abominations you mention and their dark masters.'

'As have my own people. We have our witch hunts and our laws.'

Gotrek shook his head. 'Your people do not understand. They are soft and decadent and live far from the war. They do not understand the terrible things which gnaw at the roots of the world and seek to undermine us all. Witch hunts? Hah!' He spat on the ground. 'Laws! There is only one way to meet the threat of Chaos.'

He brandished his axe meaningfully.

They trudged wearily through the forest. Overhead, the moons gleamed feverishly. Morrslieb had become ever brighter, and now its green glow stained the sky. A light mist had gathered and the terrain they moved through was bleak and wild. Rocks broke through the turf like plague spots breaking through the skin of the world.

Sometimes Felix thought he could hear great wings passing overhead, but when he looked up he could see only the glow in the sky. The mist distorted and spread so that it looked as though they walked along the bed of some infernal sea.

There was a sense of wrongness about this place, Felix decided. The air tasted foul and the hairs on the nape of his neck constantly prickled. Back when he had been a boy in Altdorf he had sat in his father's house and watched the sky grow black with menacing clouds. Then had come the most monstrous storm in living memory. Now he felt the same sense of anticipation. Mighty forces were gathering close to here, he was certain. He felt like an insect crawling over the body of a giant that could at any moment awake and crush him.

Even Gotrek seemed oppressed. He had fallen silent and did not even mumble to himself as he usually did. Now and again he would stop and motion for Felix to stand quiet, then he would stand and sniff the air. Felix could see that his whole body tensed as if he strained with every nerve to catch the slightest trace of something. Then they would move on.

Felix's muscles all felt tight with tension. He wished he had not come. Surely, he told himself, my obligation to the dwarf does not mean I must face certain death. Perhaps I can slip away in the mist.

He gritted his teeth. He prided himself on being an honourable man, and the debt he owed the dwarf was real. The dwarf had risked his life to save him. Granted, at the time he had not known Gotrek was seeking death, courting it as a man courts a desirable lady. It still left him under an obligation.

He remembered the riotous drunken evening in the taverns of the Maze when they had sworn blood-brothership in that curious dwarf-ish rite and he had agreed to help Gotrek in his quest.

Gotrek wished his name remembered and his deeds recalled. When he had found out that Felix was a poet, the dwarf had asked Felix to accompany him. At the time, in the warm glow of beery camaraderie, it had seemed a splendid idea. The Trollslayer's doomed quest had struck Felix as excellent material for an epic poem, one that would make him famous.

Little did I know, Felix thought, that it would lead to this. Hunting for monsters on Geheimnisnacht. He smiled ironically. It was easy to sing of brave deeds in the taverns and playhalls where horror was a thing conjured by the words of skilled craftsmen. Out here, though, it was different. His bowels felt loose with fear and the oppressive atmosphere made him want to run screaming.

Still, he tried to console himself, this is fit subject matter for a poem. If only I live to write it.

The woods became deeper and more tangled. The trees took on the aspect of twisted, uncanny beings. Felix felt as if they were watching him. He tried to dismiss the thought as fantasy but the mist and the ghastly moonlight only stimulated his imagination. He felt as if every pool of shadow contained a monster.

Felix looked down at the dwarf. Gotrek's face held a mixture of anticipation and fear. Felix had thought him immune to terror but now he realised it was not so. A ferocious will drove him to seek his doom. Feeling that his own death might be near at hand, Felix asked a question that he had long been afraid to utter.

'Herr Trollslayer, what was it you did that you must atone for? What crime drives you to punish yourself so?'

Gotrek looked up to him, then turned his head to gaze off into the night. Felix watched the cable-like muscles of his neck ripple like serpents as he did so.

'If another man asked me that question I would slaughter him. I make allowances for your youth and ignorance and the friendship rite we have undergone. Such a death would make me a kin-slayer. That is a terrible crime. Such crimes we do not talk about.'

Felix had not realised the dwarf was so attached to him. Gotrek looked up at him as if expecting a response.

'I understand,' Felix said.

'Do you, manling? Do you really?' The Trollslayer's voice was as harsh as stones breaking.

Felix smiled ruefully. In that moment he saw the gap that separated man from dwarf. He would never understand their strange taboos, their obsession with oaths and order and pride. He could not see what would drive the Trollslayer to carry out his self-imposed death sentence.

'Your people are too harsh with themselves,' he said.

'Yours are too soft,' the Trollslayer replied. They fell into silence. Both were startled by a quiet, mad laugh. Felix turned, whipping up his blade into the guard position. Gotrek raised his axe.

Out of the mists something shambled. Once it had been a man, Felix decided. The outline was still there. It was as if some mad god held the creature close to a daemonic fire until flesh dripped and ran, then had left it to set in a new and abhorrent form.

'This night we will dance,' it said, in a high-pitched voice that held no hint of sanity. 'Dance and touch.'

It reached out gently to Felix and stroked his arm. Felix recoiled in horror as fingers like clumps of maggots rose towards his face.

'This night at the stone we will dance and touch and rub.' It made as if to embrace him. It smiled, showing short, pointed teeth. Felix stood quietly. He felt like a spectator, distanced from the event that was happening. He pulled back and put the point of his sword against the thing's chest.

'Come no closer,' Felix warned. The thing smiled. Its mouth seemed to grow wider, it showed more small sharp teeth. Its lips rolled back until the bottom half of the face seemed all wet glistening gum and the jaw sank lower like that of a snake. It pushed forward against the sword until beads of blood glistened on its chest. It gave a gurgling, idiotic laugh.

'Dance and touch and rub and eat,' it said, and with inhuman swiftness it writhed around the sword and leapt for Felix.

Swift as it was, the Trollslayer was swifter. In mid-leap his axe caught its neck. The head rolled into the night; a red fountain gushed.

This is not happening, thought Felix.

'What was that? A daemon?' Gotrek asked. Felix could hear the excitement in his voice.

'I think it was once a man,' Felix said. 'One of the tainted ones marked by Chaos. They are abandoned at birth.'

'That one spoke your tongue.'

'Sometimes the taint does not show till they are older. Relatives think they are sick and protect them till they make their way to the woods and vanish.'

'Their kin protect such abominations?'

'It happens. We don't talk about it. It is hard to turn your back on people you love even if they change.'

The dwarf stared at him in disbelief, then shook his head.

'Too soft,' he said. 'Too soft.'

The air was still. Sometimes Felix thought he sensed presences moving in the trees about him and froze nervously, peering into the mist, searching for moving shadows. The encounter with the tainted one had brought home to him the danger of the situation. He felt within him a great fear and a great anger.

Part of the anger was directed at himself for feeling the fear. He was sick and ashamed. He decided that whatever happened he would not repeat his error, standing like a sheep to be slaughtered.

'What was that?' Gotrek asked. Felix looked at him.

'Can't you hear it, manling? Listen! It sounds like chanting.' Felix strained to catch the sound but heard nothing. 'We are close, now. Very close.'

They pushed on in silence. As they trudged through the mist Gotrek became ever more cautious and left the trail, using the long grass for cover. Felix joined him.

Now he could hear the chanting. It sounded as though it was coming from scores of throats. Some of the voices were human, others were deep and bestial. There were male voices and female voices mingled with the slow beat of a drum, the clash of cymbals and discordant piping.

Felix could make out one word only, repeated over and over until it was driven into his consciousness. The word was 'Slaanesh'.

Felix shuddered. Slaanesh, dark lord of unspeakable pleasures. It was a name that conjured up the worst depths of depravity. It was whispered in the drug dens and vice houses of Altdorf by those so jaded that they sought pleasures beyond human understanding. It was a name associated with corruption and excess and the dark underbelly of Imperial society. For those who followed Slaanesh no stimulation was too bizarre, no pleasure forbidden.

'The mist covers us,' Felix whispered to the Trollslayer.

'Hist! Be quiet. We must get closer.'

They crept forward slowly. The long wet grass dragged at Felix's body, and soon he was damp. Ahead he could see beacons burning in the dark. The scent of blazing wood and cloying sickly-sweet incense filled the air. He looked around, hoping that no latecomer would blunder into them. He felt absurdly exposed.

Inch by inch they advanced. Gotrek dragged his battleaxe along behind him and once Felix touched its sharp blade with his fingers. He cut himself and fought back a desire to scream out.

They reached the edge of the long grass and found themselves staring at a crude ring of six obscenely-shaped stones amid which stood a monolithic slab. The stones glowed greenly with the light of some luminous fungus. On top of each was a brazier which gave off clouds of smoke. Beams of pallid, green moonlight illuminated a hellish scene.

Within the ring danced six humans, masked and garbed in long cloaks. The cloaks were thrown back over one shoulder revealing naked bodies, both male and female. On one hand the revellers each wore finger cymbals which they clashed, in the other they carried switches of birch with which they each lashed the dancer in front.

'Ygrak tu amat Slaanesh!' they cried.

Felix could see that some of the bodies were marked by bruises. The dancers seemed to feel no pain. Perhaps it was the narcotic effect of the incense.

Around the stone ring lolled figures of horror. The drummer was a huge man with the head of a stag and cloven hooves. Near him sat a piper with the head of a dog and hands with suckered fingers. A large crowd of tainted women and men writhed on the ground nearby.

Some of their bodies were subtly distorted: men who were tall with thin, pin heads; short, fat women with three eyes and three breasts. Others were barely recognisable as once having been human. There were scale-covered man-serpents and wolf-headed furred beasts mingling with things that were all teeth and mouth and other orifices. Felix could barely breathe. He watched the entire proceeding with mounting fear.

The drums beat faster, the rhythmic chanting increased in pace, the piping became ever louder and more discordant as the dancers became more frenzied, lashing themselves and their companions until bloody weals became visible. Then there was a clash of cymbals and all fell silent.

Felix thought they had been spotted, and he froze. The smoke of the incense filled his nostrils and seemed to amplify all his senses. He felt even more remote and disconnected from reality. There was a sharp, stabbing pain in his side. He was startled to realise that Gotrek had elbowed him in the ribs. He was pointing to something beyond the stone ring.

Felix struggled to see what loomed in the mist. Then he realised that it was the black coach. In the sudden, shocking silence he heard its door swing open. He held his breath and waited to see what would emerge.

A figure seemed to take shape out of the mist. It was tall and masked, and garbed in layered cloaks of many pastel colours. It moved with calm authority and in its arms it carried something swaddled in brocade cloth. Felix looked at Gotrek but he was watching the unfolding scene with fanatical intensity. Felix wondered if the dwarf had lost his nerve at this late hour.

The newcomer stepped forward into the stone circle.

'Amak tu amat Slaanesh!' it cried, raising its bundle on high. Felix could see that it was a child, though whether living or dead he could not tell.

'Ygrak tu amat Slaanesh! Tzarkol taen amat Slaanesh!' The crowd responded ecstatically.

The cloaked man stared out at the surrounding faces, and it seemed to Felix that the stranger gazed straight at him with calm, brown eyes. He wondered if the coven-master knew they were there and was playing with them.

'Amak tu Slaanesh!' the man cried in a clear voice.

'Amak klessa! Amat Slaanesh!' responded the crowd. It was clear to Felix that some evil ritual had begun. As the rite progressed, the coven-master moved closer to the altar with slow ceremonial steps. Felix felt his mouth go dry. He licked his lips. Gotrek watched the events as if hypnotised.

The child was placed on the altar with a thunderous rumble of drum beats. Now the six dancers each stood beside a pillar, legs astride it, clutching at the stone suggestively. As the ritual progressed they ground themselves against the pillars with slow sinuous movements.

From within his robes the master produced a long wavy-bladed knife. Felix wondered whether the dwarf was going to do something. He could hardly bear to watch.

Slowly the knife was raised, high over the cultist's head. Felix forced himself to look. An ominous presence hovered over the scene. Mist and incense seemed to be clotting together and congealing, and within the cloud Felix thought he could make out a grotesque form writhe and begin to materialise. Felix could bear the tension no longer.

'No!' he shouted.

He and the Trollslayer emerged from the long grass and marched shoulder-to-shoulder towards the stone ring. At first the cultists didn't seem to notice them, but finally the demented drumming stopped and the chanting faded and the cult-master turned to glare at them, astonished.

For a moment everyone stared. No one seemed to understand what was happening. Then the cult-master pointed the knife at them and screamed; 'Kill the interlopers!'

The revellers moved forward in a wave. Felix felt something tug at his leg and then a sharp pain. When he looked down he saw a creature, half woman, half serpent, gnawing at his ankle. He kicked out, pulling his leg free and stabbed down with his sword.

A shock passed up his arm as the blade hit bone. He began to run, following in the wake of Gotrek who was hacking his way towards the altar. The mighty double-bladed axe rose and fell rhythmically and left a trail of red ruin in its path. The cultists seemed drugged and slow to respond but, horrifyingly, they showed no fear. Men and women, tainted and untainted, threw themselves towards the intruders with no thought for their own lives.

Felix hacked and stabbed at anyone who came close. He put his blade under the ribs and into the heart of a dog-faced man who leapt at him. As he tried to tug his blade free a woman with claws and a man with mucous-covered skin leapt on him. Their weight bore him over, knocking the wind from him.

He felt the woman's talons scratch at his face as he put his foot under her stomach and kicked her off. Blood rolled down into his eyes from the cuts. The man had fallen badly, but leapt to grab his throat. Felix fumbled for his dagger with his left hand while he caught the man's throat with his right. The man writhed. He was difficult to grip because of his coating of slime. His own hands tightened inexorably on Felix's throat in return and he rubbed himself against Felix, panting with pleasure.

Blackness threatened to overcome the poet. Little silver points flared before his eyes. He felt an overwhelming urge to relax and fall forward into the darkness. Somewhere far away he heard Gotrek's bellowed war-cry. With an effort of will Felix jerked his dagger clear of its scabbard and plunged it into his assailant's ribs. The creature stiffened and grinned, revealing rows of eel-like teeth. He gave an ecstatic moan even as he died.

'Slaanesh, take me,' the man shrieked. 'Ah, the pain, the lovely pain!'

Felix pulled himself to his feet just as the clawed woman rose to hers. He lashed out with his boot, connected with her jaw. There was a crunch, and she fell backwards. Felix shook his head to clear the blood from his eyes.

The majority of the cultists had concentrated on Gotrek. This had kept Felix alive. The dwarf was trying to hack his way towards the heart of the stone circle. Even as he moved, the press of bodies against him slowed him down. Felix could see that he bled from dozens of small cuts.

The ferocious energy of the dwarf was terrible to see. He frothed at the mouth and ranted as he chopped, sending limbs and heads everywhere. He was covered in a filthy matting of gore, but in spite of his sheer ferocity Felix could tell the fight was going against Gotrek. Even as he watched, a cloaked reveller hit the dwarf with a club and Gotrek went down under a wave of bodies. So he has met his doom, thought Felix, just as he desired.

Beyond the ruck of the melee, the cult-master had regained his composure. Once more he began to chant, and raised the dagger on high. The terrible shape that had been forming from the mist seemed once again to coalesce.

Felix had a premonition that if it took on full substance they were doomed. He could not fight his way through the bodies that surrounded the Trollslayer. For a long moment he watched the curve-bladed knife reflecting the Morrslieb light.

Then he drew back his own dagger. 'Sigmar guide my hand,' he prayed and threw. The blade flew straight and true to the throat of the High Priest, hitting beneath the mask where flesh was exposed. With a gurgle, the cult-master toppled backwards.

A long whine of frustration filled the air and the mist seemed to evaporate. The shape within the mist vanished. As one, the cultists looked up in shock. The tainted ones turned to stare at him. Felix found himself confronted by the mad glare of dozens of unfriendly eyes. He stood immobile and very, very afraid. The silence was deathly.

Then there was an almighty roar and Gotrek emerged from amidst the pile of bodies, pummelling about him with ham-sized fists. He reached down and from somewhere retrieved his axe. He shortened his grip on the haft and laid about him with its shaft. Felix scooped up his own sword and ran to join him. They fought through the crush until they were back to back.

31

The cultists, filled with fear at the loss of their leader, began to flee into the night and mist. Soon Felix and Gotrek stood alone under the shadows of the Darkstone Ring.

Gotrek looked at Felix balefully, blood clotted in his crested hair. In the witch-light he looked daemonic. 'I am robbed of a mighty death, manling.'

He raised his axe menacingly. Felix wondered if he were still berserk and about to chop him down in spite of their binding oath. Gotrek began to advance slowly towards him. Then the dwarf grinned. 'It would seem the gods preserve me for a greater doom yet.'

He planted his axe hilt first into the ground and began to laugh until the tears ran down his face. Having exhausted his laughter, he turned to the altar and picked up the infant. 'It lives,' he said.

Felix began to inspect the corpses of the cloaked cultists. He unmasked them. The first one was a blonde-haired girl covered in weals and bruises. The second was a young man. He had an amulet in the shape of a hammer hanging almost mockingly round his neck.

'I don't think we'll be going back to the inn,' Felix said sadly.

One local tale tells of an infant found on the steps of the temple of Shallya in Hartzroch. It was wrapped in a blood-soaked cloak of Sudenland wool, a pouch of gold lay nearby, and a steel amulet in the shape of a hammer was round its neck. The priestess swore she saw a black coach thundering away in the dawn light.

The natives of Hartzroch tell another and darker tale of how Ingrid Hauptmann and Gunter, the innkeeper's son, were slain in some hor-rific sacrifice to the Dark Powers. The road wardens who found the corpses up by the Darkstone Ring agreed it must have been a terrible rite. The bodies looked as if they had been chopped up with an axe wielded by a daemon.

WOLF RIDERS

'I cannot quite remember exactly how and when the
decision to head southwards in search of the lost
gold of Karak Eight Peaks was made. Alas, like so
many of the important decisions made during that
period of my life, it was taken in a tavern under
the influence of enormous quantities of alcohol.
I do seem to remember an ancient and toothless
dwarf mumbling about "gold", and I distinctly
remember the insane gleam which entered into my
companion's eyes when it was described to him.

'It was perhaps typical of my companion that on
no more than this slim provocation, he was willing
to risk life and limb in the wildest and most barren
places imaginable. Or perhaps it was typical of the
effect of "gold fever" on all his people. As I was
later to see, the lure of that glittering metal had a
terrifying and potent power over the minds of all of
that ancient race.

'In any event, the decision to travel beyond the
Empire's southernmost borders was a fateful one,
and it led to meetings and adventures the dreadful
consequences of which haunt me still...'

— From *My Travels with Gotrek, Vol. II*, by Herr Felix Jaeger
(Altdorf Press, 2505)

'Honestly, gentlemen, I don't want any trouble,' Felix Jaeger said sincerely. He spread his empty hands wide. 'Just leave the girl alone. That's all I ask.'

The drunken trappers laughed evilly. 'Just leave the girl alone,' one of them mimicked in a high-pitched, lisping voice.

Felix looked around the trading post for support. A few hardy fellows clad in the heavy furs of mountain men looked at him with drink-fuddled eyes. The store owner, a tall, stooped man with lank hair, turned and began stacking bottles of preserves on the rough wooden shelving. There were no other customers.

One of the trappers, a huge man, loomed over him. Felix could see the particles of grease stuck in his beard. When he opened his mouth to speak, the smell of cheap brandy overwhelmed even the odour of the rancid bear fat which the trappers covered themselves with against the cold. Felix winced.

'Hey, Hef, I think we got a city boy here,' the trapper said. 'He speaks right nice.'

The one called Hef looked up from the table against which he had pinned the struggling girl.

'Aye, Lars, right pretty he talks, and all that nice golden hair, like cornstalks. Could almost take him for a girl himself.'

'When I come off the mountains anything looks good. I tell you what: you take the girl. I'll have this pretty boy.'

Felix felt his face flush. He was getting angry. He hid his anger with a smile. He wanted to avoid trouble if he could. 'Come on, gentlemen, there's no need for this. Let me buy you all a drink.'

Lars turned to Hef. The third mountain man guffawed. 'He has money too. My luck's in tonight!'

Hef smirked. Felix looked around desperately as the big man advanced on him. Damn, where was Gotrek? Why was the dwarf never around when a man needed him? He turned to face Lars. 'All right, I'm sorry I interfered. I'll just leave you gentlemen to it.'

He saw Lars relax somewhat, letting down his guard as he advanced. Felix let him come closer. He watched the trapper spread his arms as if he were about to hug him. Felix suddenly jabbed his knee hard into Lars's groin. With a whoosh like a blacksmith's bellows, all of the air ran out of the big man. He doubled over with a whimper. Felix grabbed his beard and pulled the man's head down to meet his knee.

He heard teeth break, and the trapper's head snapped backwards. Lars fell on the floor gasping for breath and clutching at his groin.

'What in the name of Taal?' Hef said. The big trapper lashed out at Felix and the force of the blow sent him reeling across the room into a table. He tipped over a tankard of ale.

'Sorry,' Felix apologised to the drink's startled owner. Felix struggled to lift the table and hurl it at his assailant. He strained until he thought the muscles in his back would crack.

The drunk looked at him and smiled wickedly. 'You can't lift it. It's nailed to the floor. In case of fights.'

'Thanks for telling me,' Felix said, feeling someone grab him by the hair and slam his head into the table. Pain smashed through his skull. Black spots danced before his eyes. His face felt wet. I'm bleeding, he thought, then realised it was just the spilled beer. His head was smashed into the table a second time. As if from very far away he heard footsteps approaching.

'Hold him, Kell. We're gonna have us some fun for what he did to Lars.' He recognised the voice as belonging to Hef.

Desperately Felix jabbed backward with his elbow, ramming it into the hard muscle of Kell's stomach. The grip on his hair loosened somewhat. Felix tore free and he turned to face his assailants. With his right hand he frantically fumbled for the beer stein. Through a haze he saw the two gigantic trappers closing in. The girl was gone – Felix saw the door close behind her. He could hear her start shouting for help. Hef was loosening a knife in his belt. Felix's fingers closed over the handle of the stein. He lashed out and hit Kell square in the face with it. The trapper's head snapped around, then he spat blood and turned back to Felix, smiling moronically.

Fingers, muscled like steel bands, grabbed Felix's wrist. The pressure forced him reluctantly to drop the stein. Despite frantic resistance, Felix's arm was inexorably forced up his back by Kell's superior strength. The smell of bear fat and body odour was almost overpowering. Felix snarled and tried to writhe free but his struggles were fruitless.

Something sharp jabbed into his throat. Felix looked down. Hef brandished a long-bladed knife at his throat. Felix smelled its well-oiled steel. He saw his own red blood trickle down its central channel. Felix froze. All Hef had to do was lean forward and Felix would be walking in the kingdom of Morr.

'That was downright unfriendly, boy,' Hef said. 'Old Lars was only bein' affectionate and you had to go and bust his teeth. Now what you reckon we should do about that, we bein' his friends 'n' all?'

'Kill the thnotling fondler,' Lars gasped. Felix felt Kell push his arm further up his back until he feared it would break. He moaned in pain.

'Reckon we'll just do that,' Hef said.

'You can't,' the trader behind the bar whined. 'That'd be murder.'

'Shut up, Pike! Who asked you?'

Felix could see they meant to do it. They were full of drunken violence and ready to kill. Felix had just given them the excuse they needed.

'Been a long time since I killed me a pretty boy,' Hef said, pushing his knife forward just a fraction. Felix grimaced with the pain. 'Gonna beg, pretty boy? Gonna beg for your life?'

'Go to hell,' Felix said. He would have liked to spit but his mouth felt dry and his knees were weak. He was shaking. He closed his eyes.

'Not so polite now, city boy?' Felix felt thick laughter rumble in Kell's throat. What a place to die, he thought incongruously, some hell-spawned outpost in the Grey Mountains.

There was a blast of chill air and the sound of a door opening.

'The first one to hurt the manling dies instantly,' said a deep voice that grated like stone crushed against stone. 'The second one I take my time over.'

Felix opened his eyes. Over Hef's shoulders he could see Gotrek Gurnisson, the Trollslayer. The dwarf stood silhouetted in the door-way, his squat form filling it widthwise. He was only the height of a boy of nine years but he was muscled like two strong men. Torch light illuminated the strange tattoos that covered his half-naked body and turned his eye sockets into shadowy caves from which mad eyes glittered.

Hef laughed, then spoke without turning round. 'Get lost, stranger, or we'll deal with you after we've finished your friend.'

Felix felt the grip on his arm relax. Over his shoulder, Kell's hand pointed to the doorway.

'That so?' Gotrek said, stomping into the room, shaking his head to clear the snow from his huge crest of orange-dyed hair. The chain that ran from his nose to his right ear jingled. 'By the time I've finished with you, you'll sing as high as a girly elf.'

Hef laughed again and turned around to face Gotrek. His laughter died into a sputtering cough. Colour drained from his face until it was corpse-white. Gotrek grinned nastily at him, revealing missing teeth, then he ran his thumb across the blade of the great two-handed axe that he carried in one ham-sized fist. Blood dripped freely from the cut but the dwarf just grinned more widely. The knife in Hef's hand clattered to the floor.

'We don't want no trouble,' Hef said. 'Leastwise, not with a Trollslayer.'

Felix didn't blame him. No sane man would cross a member of that doomed and death-seeking berserker cult. Gotrek glared at them, then lightly tapped the hilt of his axe against the floor. While Kell was distracted, Felix seized the opportunity to put some ground between himself and the mountain man.

Hef was starting to panic. 'Look, we don't want no trouble. We was just funnin'.'

Gotrek laughed evilly. 'I like your idea of fun. I think I'll have some myself.'

The Trollslayer advanced towards Hef. Felix saw Lars pick himself up and start crawling towards the door, hoping to slip past the Trollslayer while he was distracted. Gotrek brought his boot down on Lars's hand with a crunch that made Felix wince. It was not Lars's night, he decided.

'Where do you think you're going? Better stay with your friends. Two against one is hardly fair odds.'

Hef had broken down completely. 'Don't kill us,' he pleaded. Kell, meanwhile, had moved away, bringing him close to Felix again. Gotrek had moved right in front of Hef. The blade of the Slayer's axe lay against Hef's throat. Felix could see the runes on the ancient blade glinting redly in the torchlight.

Slowly Gotrek shook his head. 'What's the matter? There's three of you. You thought they were good enough odds against the manling. Stomach gone out of you?'

Hef nodded numbly; he looked as if he was about to cry. In his eyes Felix could see a superstitious terror of the dwarf. He seemed ready to faint.

Gotrek pointed to the door. 'Get out!' he roared. 'I'll not soil my blade on cowards like you.'

The trappers scurried for the door, Lars limping badly. Felix saw the girl step aside to let them by. She closed the door behind them.

Gotrek glared at Felix. 'Can't I even stop to answer a call of nature without you getting yourself into trouble?'

'Perhaps I should escort you back,' Felix said, inspecting the girl closely. She was small and thin; her face would have been plain except for the large dark eyes. She tugged her cloak of coarse Sudenland wool about her and hugged the package she had purchased in the trading post to her chest. She smiled shyly up at him. The smile transformed that pale hungry face, Felix thought, gave it beauty.

'Perhaps you could, if it's not too much trouble.'

'No trouble whatsoever,' he said. 'Maybe those ruffians are still lurking about out there.'

'I doubt that. They seemed too afraid of your friend.'

'Let me help you with those herbs, then.'

'The mistress told me to get them specifically. They are for the relief of the frostbitten. I would feel better if I carried them.'

Felix shrugged. They stepped out into the chill air, breath coming out in clouds. In the night sky the Grey Mountains loomed like giants. The light of both moons caught on their snow-capped peaks so that they looked like islands in the sky, floating above a sea of shadow.

They walked through the squalid shanty-town which surrounded the trading post. In the distance Felix saw lights, heard lowing cattle and the muffled hoofbeats of horses. They were heading towards a campsite where more people were arriving.

Gaunt, hollow-cheeked soldiers, clad in tattered tunics on which could be seen the sign of a grinning wolf, escorted carts drawn by thin oxen. Tired-looking drivers in the garb of peasants gazed at him. Women sat beside the drivers with shawls drawn tight, headscarves all but obscuring their features. Sometimes children peeked out over the back of the carts to stare at them.

'What's going on?' Felix asked. 'It looks like a whole village on the move.' The girl looked at the carts and then back at him.

'We are the people of Gottfried von Diehl. We follow him into exile, to the land of the Border Princes.'

Felix paused to look north. More carts were coming down the trail, and behind them were stragglers, limping on foot, clutching at thin sacks as if they contained all the gold of Araby. Felix shook his head, puzzled.

'You must have come through Blackfire Pass,' he said. He and Gotrek had come by the old dwarf routes under the mountain. 'And it's late in the season for that. The first blizzards must already be setting in up there. The pass is only open in the summer.'

'Our liege was given until year's end to leave the Empire.' She turned and began walking into the ring of wagons that had been set up to give some protection from the wind. 'We set out in good time but there was a string of accidents that slowed us down. In the pass itself we were caught by an avalanche. We lost many people.'

She paused, as if remembering some personal grief.

'Some say it was the "Von Diehl Curse". That the baron can never outrun it.'

Felix followed her. On the fires sat a few cooking pots. There was one huge cauldron from which steam emerged. The girl pointed to it.

'The mistress's cauldron. She will be expecting the herbs.'

'Is your mistress a witch?' Felix asked. She looked at him seriously.

'No, sir. She is a sorceress with good credentials, trained in Middenheim itself. She is the baron's adviser in matters magical.'

The girl moved towards the steps of a large caravan, covered in mystical signs. She began to climb the stairs. She halted, hand poised on the handle of the door, then she turned to face Felix.

'Thank you for your help,' she said.

She leaned forward and kissed him on the cheek, then turned to open the door.

Felix laid his hand on her shoulder, restraining her gently. 'A moment,' he said. 'What is your name?'

'Kirsten,' she said. 'And yours?'

'Felix. Felix Jaeger.'

She smiled at him again before she vanished inside the caravan. Felix stood looking at the closed door, slightly bemused. Then, feeling as if he was walking on air, he strolled back to the trading post.

'Are you mad?' Gotrek Gurnisson demanded. 'You want us to travel with some renegade duke and his rag-tag entourage? Have you forgotten why we've come here?'

Felix looked around to see that no one was looking at them. Not much chance of that, he decided. He and the Trollslayer nursed their beer in the darkest recess of the trading post. A few drunks lay snoring on the trestle tables and the sullen glowers of the dwarf kept the casually curious at bay.

Felix leaned forward conspiratorially. 'But look, it makes perfect sense. We are heading through the Border Princes and so are they. It will be safer if we ride with them.'

Gotrek looked at Felix dangerously. 'Are you implying I fear some peril on this road?'

Felix shook his head. 'No. All I'm saying is that it would make our journey easier and we might get paid for our efforts if the baron could be persuaded to take us on as mercenaries.'

Gotrek brightened at the mention of money. All dwarfs are misers at heart, thought Felix. Gotrek appeared to consider for a second, then shook his head. 'No. If this baron has been exiled he's a criminal and he's not getting his hands on my gold.'

He ducked his head and looked around with paranoid shiftiness. 'That treasure is ours, yours and mine. Mostly mine, of course, since I'll do the bulk of the fighting.'

Felix felt like laughing. There was nothing worse than a dwarf in the throes of gold-lust.

'Gotrek, we don't even know if there is any treasure. All we've got to go on are the ramblings of some senile old prospector who claims to have seen the lost hoard of Karak Eight Peaks. Faragrim couldn't remember his own name half the time.'

'Faragrim was a dwarf, manling. A dwarf never forgets the sight of gold. You know the problem with your people? You have no respect for your elders. Among my people Faragrim is treated with respect.'

'No wonder your people are in such dire straits then,' Felix muttered.

'What was that?'

'Nothing. Just answer me this. Why didn't Faragrim return for the treasure himself? He's had eighteen years.'

'Because he showed proper fiscal caution–'

'Meanness, you mean.'

'Have it your way, manling. He was crippled by the guardian. And he could never find anybody he could trust.'

'Why suddenly tell you then?'

'Are you implying I am not trustworthy, manling?'

'No. I think he wanted rid of you, he wanted you out of his tavern. I think he invented the cock-and-bull story about the world's largest treasure guarded by the world's largest troll because he knew you would fall for it. He knew it would put a hundred leagues between you and his ale cellar.'

Gotrek's beard bristled and he growled angrily. 'I am not such a fool, manling. Faragrim swore to the truth on the beards of all his ancestors.'

Felix groaned loudly. 'And no dwarf has ever broken an oath, I suppose?'

'Well, very rarely,' Gotrek admitted. 'But I believe this one.'

Felix saw that it was no use. Gotrek wanted the story to be true, so for him it was true.

He's like a man in love, thought Felix, unable to see his beloved's frailties for the wall of illusions he has built around her. Gotrek stroked his beard and stared into space, lost in contemplation of the troll-guarded hoard. Felix decided to play his trump card.

'It would mean we wouldn't have to walk,' he said.

'What?' Gotrek grunted.

'If we sign on with the baron. We could hitch a ride on a cart. You're always complaining that your feet hurt. This is your chance to give them a rest.

'Just think about it,' he added enticingly. 'We get paid and you don't get sore feet.'

Gotrek appeared to contemplate this once more. 'I can see I'll get no peace unless I agree to your scheme. I'll go along with it on one condition.'

'What's that?'

'No mention of our quest. Not to anybody.'

Felix agreed. Gotrek raised one bushy eyebrow and looked at him cunningly.

'Don't think I don't know why you're so keen to travel with this baron, manling.'

'What do you mean?'

'You're enamoured of that chit of a girl you left here with earlier, aren't you?'

'No,' Felix spluttered. 'Whatever gave you that idea?'

Gotrek laughed uproariously, waking several slumbering drunks.

'Then why has your face gone all red, manling?' he shouted triumphantly.

Felix knocked on the door of the caravan he had been told belonged to the baron's master-of arms.

'Come in,' a voice said. Felix opened the door and his nostrils were assailed with the smell of bear fat. Felix reached for the hilt of his sword.

Inside the caravan, five men were crowded. Three Felix recognised as the trappers he had met the previous evening. Of the others, one was young, richly dressed and fine featured, hair cut short in the fashion of the warrior nobility. The other was a tall, powerfully built man clad in buckskins. He was tanned and appeared to be in his late twenties although his hair was silver grey. He had a quiver of black-fletched arrows slung over his back and a powerful longbow lay near his hand. There seemed to be a family resemblance between the two men.

'Thatsh tha bashtard,' Lars said through his missing teeth. The two strangers exchanged looks.

Felix stared at them warily. The grey-haired man inspected him, casually assessing him.

'So you're the young man who broke the teeth of one of my guides,' he said.

'One of your guides?'

'Yes, Manfred and I hired them last season to steer us across the lowlands, along Thunder River.'

'They're mountain men,' Felix said, stalling for time, wondering how much trouble he was in.

'They're trappers,' the well-dressed youth said, in a cultured accent. 'They cross the lowlands in search of game too.'

Felix spread his hands. 'I didn't know.'

'What do you want here?' Greyhair asked.

'I'm looking for work, as a hired blade. I was looking for the baron's master-of arms.'

'That's me,' Greyhair said. 'Dieter. Also the Baron's Chief Forester, Master of Hounds and Falconer.'

'My uncle's estate has fallen on rather hard times,' the young man said.

'This is Manfred, nephew and heir to Gottfried von Diehl, Baron of the Vennland Marches.'

'Former baron,' Manfred corrected. 'Since Countess Emmanuelle saw fit to banish my uncle and confiscate our lands rather than punish the real malefactors.'

He noted Felix's quizzical look. 'Religious differences, you know? My family come from the north and follow blessed Ulric. All our southern neighbours are devout Sigmarites. In these intolerant times it was all the excuse they needed to seize the lands they coveted. Since they were Countess Emmanuelle's cousins we get exiled for starting a war.'

He shook his head in disgust. 'Imperial politics, eh?'

Dieter shrugged. He turned to the mountain men. 'Wait outside,' he said. 'We have business to conduct with Herr…?'

'Jaeger. Felix Jaeger.'

The trappers filed past. Lars gave Felix a hate-filled look as he came abreast. Felix looked straight into his blood-shot eyes. Their gazes locked for a second, then the trappers were gone, leaving only the whiff of bear fat hanging in the air.

'I fear you have made an enemy there,' Manfred said.

'I'm not worried.'

'You should be, Herr Jaeger. Such men hold grudges,' Dieter said. 'You say you are seeking employment?'

Felix nodded. 'My companion and I–'

'The Trollslayer?' Dieter raised an eyebrow.

'Gotrek Gurnisson, yes.'

'If you want a job, you've got one. The Border Princes are a violent place and we could do with two such warriors. Unfortunately we cannot afford to pay much.'

'My uncle's estates are now poor,' Manfred explained.

'We do not require much more than bed, board and carriage,' Felix said.

Dieter laughed. 'Just as well really. You can travel with us if you wish. If we are attacked you'll have to fight.'

'We are employed?'

Dieter handed him two gold coins. 'You have taken the baron's crown. You are with us.' The grey-haired man opened the door. 'Now, if you'll excuse us, I have a journey to plan.'

Felix bowed to each of them and exited.

'Just a second.'

Felix turned and saw Manfred jump down from the caravan after him. The young noble smiled.

'Dieter is a brusque man but you will get used to him.'

'I'm sure I will, milord.'

'Call me Manfred. We are on the frontier, not at the Court of the Countess of Nuln. Rank has less meaning here.'

'Very well, milor– Manfred.'

'I just wanted to tell you that you did the right thing last night. Standing up for the girl, even if she is the servant of that witch. I appreciate it.'

'Thank you. May I ask a question?'

Manfred nodded. Felix cleared his throat. 'The name of Manfred von Diehl is not unknown among the scholars of Altdorf, my home city. As a playwright.'

Manfred beamed broadly. 'I am he. By Ulric, an educated man! Who would have thought to find one here? I can tell you and I are going to get along, Herr Jaeger. Have you seen Strange Flower? Did you like it?'

Felix considered his answer carefully. He had not cared for the play, which dealt with the degeneration of a noblewoman into madness when she found out that she was a mutant, devolving to beasthood. Strange Flower was lacking that open-hearted humanity to be found in the works of the Empire's greatest playwright, Detlef Sierck. However, it had been very topical in these dark days when the number of mutations was apparently increasing. It had been banned by Countess Emmanuelle, Felix remembered.

'It was very powerful, Manfred. Very haunting.'

'Haunting, very good! Very good indeed! I must go now, visit my ailing uncle. I hope to talk to you again before the journey is complete.'

They bowed and the nobleman turned and walked away.

Felix stared after him, unable to reconcile this amiable eccentric young nobleman and the brooding, Chaos-haunted images of his work. Among the cognoscenti of Altdorf, Manfred von Diehl was known as a brilliant playwright – and a blasphemous one.

By mid-morning the exiles were ready to leave. At the front of the long, straggling line, Felix could see a tired-looking, white-haired old man, clad in a cloak of sable skin and mounted on a black charger. He rode under the unfurled wolf banner that was held by Dieter. Beside him Manfred leaned over to say something to the old man. The baron gestured and the whole caravan of his people began to roll forward.

Felix felt a thrill pass through him at the sight of it all. He drank in the spectacle of the line of wagons and carts with their armed escort of mounted and armoured warriors. He clambered aboard the supply wagon that he and Gotrek had commandeered from a crabbed old servant dressed in baronial livery.

Around them the mountains jutted skyward like grey giants. Trees dotted their sides and streams ran like quicksilver down their flanks towards the source of Thunder River. Rain, mingled with snow, softened the harsh outline of the landscape and lent it a wild loveliness.

'Time to go again,' Gotrek moaned, clutching his head, eyes bleary and hung-over.

They rumbled forward, taking their place in the line. Behind them men-at-arms shouldered their crossbows, drew their cloaks tight about themselves and began to march. Their oaths mingled with the curses and the whipcracks of the drivers and the lowing of the oxen. A baby started crying. Somewhere behind them a woman began to sing in a low musical voice. The child's squalling quietened. Felix leaned forward, hoping to catch sight of Kirsten among the people trudging through the sleet towards the rolling hills that unfolded below them like a map.

He felt almost at peace, drawn in to all that human motion, as if he were being borne by a river towards his goal. He already felt part of this small itinerant community, a sensation he had not enjoyed for a long time. He smiled, but was drawn from his reverie by Gotrek's elbow in his ribs.

'Keep your eyes peeled, manling. Orcs and goblins haunt these mountains and the lands below.'

Felix glared at him, but when he gazed once more at his surroundings it was not to appreciate their wild beauty. He was keeping watch for possible ambush sites.

Felix looked back at the mountains. He was not sorry to be leaving those bleak highlands. Several times they had been assaulted by green-skinned goblins whose shields bore the sign of a crimson claw. The wolf-riders had been beaten back, but with casualties. Felix was red-eyed from lack of sleep. Like all the warriors, he had taken double stints on watch, for the raiders attacked at night. Only Gotrek seemed to be disappointed by the lack of pursuit.

'By Grungni,' the dwarf said. 'We won't see them again, not since Dieter shot their leader. They're all cowards without the big bully-boys to put fire in their bellies. Pity! Nothing beats the slaughter of a few gobbos for working up an appetite. Healthy exercise is good for the digestion.'

Felix gave him a jaundiced look. He jerked a thumb towards a covered wagon from which Kirsten and a tall middle-aged woman descended. 'I'm sure the wounded in that cart would disagree with your idea of healthy exercise, Gotrek.'

The dwarf shrugged. 'In this life, manling, people get hurt. Just be glad it wasn't your turn.'

Felix had had enough. He clambered down from the seat of the wagon and dropped off onto the muddy ground.

'Don't worry, Gotrek. I intend to be around to complete your saga. I wouldn't want to break a sworn oath, would I?'

Gotrek stared at him, as if suspecting a hint of sarcasm. Felix made his expression carefully bland. The dwarf took the idea of Felix's composition seriously; he wanted to be the hero of a saga after his death, and he kept the educated Felix around to make sure of it. Shaking his head, Felix walked over to where Kirsten and her mistress stood.

'Good day, Frau Winter. Kirsten.' The two women surveyed him wearily. A frown crossed the sorceress's long face, although no expression seemed to flicker in her hooded, reptilian eyes. She adjusted one of the raven's feathers pinned in her hair.

'What's good about it, Herr Jaeger? Two more men dead from

wounds. Those arrows were poisoned. By Taal, I hate those wolf-riders.'

'Where's Doctor Stockhausen? I thought he would be helping you.'

The older woman smiled – a little cynically, Felix thought.

'He's seeing to the baron's heir. Young Manfred got his arm nicked. Stockhausen would rather let good men die than have little Manfred injured.'

She turned and walked away. Her hair and cloak fluttered in the breeze.

'Pay no attention to the mistress,' Kirsten said. 'Master Manfred lampooned her in one of his plays. She's always resented it. She's a good woman really.'

Felix looked at her, wondering why his heartbeat seemed so loud and his palms so sweaty. He remembered Gotrek's words back in the tavern, and felt his face flush. All right, he admitted, he found Kirsten attractive. What was wrong with that? Maybe the fact that she might not be attracted to him. He looked around, feeling tongue-tied, trying to think of something to say. Nearby, children were playing soldiers.

'How are you?' he asked eventually.

She looked a little shaky. 'Fine. I was afraid last night, with the howling of the wolves and the arrows coming down, but now… Well, during the day it all seems so unreal.'

Behind them, from the wagon, came the groans of a man in agony. She turned momentarily to look, then hardness passed across her face and settled like a mask.

'It's not nice working with the wounded,' Felix said.

She shrugged. 'You get used to it.'

Felix was chilled to see that expression on the face of a woman her age. It was one he had seen on the faces of mercenaries, men whose profession was death. Looking around, he could see children playing near the cart of the wounded. One was firing an imaginary crossbow; another gurgled, clutched his chest and fell over. Felix felt isolated and suddenly very far from home. The safe life of poet and scholar he had left back in the Empire seemed to have happened to someone else a long time ago. The laws and their enforcers he had taken for granted had been left behind at the Grey Mountains.

'Life is cheap here, isn't it?' he said. Kirsten looked at him and her face softened. She linked her arm with his.

'Come, let's go where the air is cleaner,' she said.

Behind them the shrieks of the playing children mingled with the groans of the dying men.

* * *

Felix caught sight of the town as they emerged from the hills. It was late afternoon. To the left, the east, he could see the curve of the fast-flowing Thunder River and beyond that the mighty peaks of the Worlds Edge Mountains. South he could see another range of hills marching bleakly into the distance. They were bare and foreboding and something about them made Felix shudder.

In a valley between the two ranges nestled a small walled town. White shapes that could have been sheep were being herded through the gates. Felix thought he saw some figures moving on the walls, but at this distance he could not be sure.

Dieter beckoned for him to approach. 'You are fair-spoken,' he said. 'Ride down and make parlay. Tell the people there that we mean them no harm.'

Felix just looked at the tall, gaunt man. What he means, thought Felix, is that I am expendable, just in case the people aren't friendly. Felix considered telling him to go to hell. Dieter must have guessed his thoughts.

'You took the baron's crown,' he said plainly.

It was true, Felix admitted. He also considered taking a hot bath and drinking in a real tavern, sleeping with a roof over his head – all the luxuries that even the most primitive frontier town could offer. The prospect was very tempting.

'Get me a horse,' he said. 'And a truce banner.'

As he clambered up on to the skittish war-horse, he tried not to think about what suspicious people armed with bows might do to the messenger of a potential enemy.

A crossbow bolt hissed through the air and stuck quivering in the earth in front of the hooves of his steed. Felix struggled to control the animal, as it reared. At times like these he was glad his father had insisted that riding be part of the education of a wealthy young gentleman of means.

'Come no closer, stranger, or, white banner or no, I'll have you filled full of bolts.' The voice was coarse but powerful. Its owner was obviously used to giving commands and having them obeyed. Felix wrestled his steed back under control.

'I am the herald of Gottfried von Diehl, Baron of the Vennland Marches,' Felix called. 'We mean no harm. We seek only shelter from the elements and to renew our supplies.'

'Well you can't do that here! Tell your Baron Gottfried that if he's so peaceful he can march on. This is the freistadt of Akendorf and we want no truck with nobles.'

Felix studied the man who shouted at him from the gate tower. Beneath a peaked metal cap his face was keen and intelligent. He was flanked by two men whose crossbows were pointed unwaveringly at Felix. Felix felt his mouth go dry and sweat run clammily down his back. He was wearing his mail shirt but he doubted it would be much good against their quarrels at such close range.

'Sir, in the name of Sigmar, we seek only common hospitality...'

'Begone, boy, you'll get no hospitality in Akendorf nor in any other town in these lands. Not travelling with twenty armed knights and fifty men-at-arms.'

Felix wondered at the quality of scouts the freistadt must have, to know the numbers of their force so exactly. He saw the pattern of things in this land. The baron's force was too powerful for any local warlord to open his town gates to them. It would be a threat to any ruler's position in these isolated towns. Yet Felix doubted whether the baron's force was strong enough to take a walled fort against determined resistance.

'We have wounded,' he shouted. 'Will you at least take them?'

For the first time the man in the tower looked apologetic. 'No. You brought those extra mouths here. You can feed them.'

'In the name of Shallya, mistress of mercy, you must help them.'

'I must do nothing, herald. I rule here, not your baron. Tell him to follow Thunder River south. Taal knows, there is enough unclaimed land there. Let him clear his own estate or claim one of the abandoned forts.'

Felix dispiritedly brought his horse around. He was keenly aware of the weapons pointed at his back.

'Herald!' the lord of Akendorf cried. Felix turned in the saddle to look at him. In the fading light the man's face held a look of concern.

'What?'

'Tell the baron on no account to enter the hills to the south. Tell him to stay by Thunder River. I would not have it on my conscience that he ventured into the Geistenmund Hills unwarned.'

Something in the man's tone made the hairs on the back of Felix's neck prickle.

'Those hills are haunted, herald, and no man should dare them, on peril of his immortal soul.'

'They will not let us past their gates. It's that simple,' Felix concluded, looking round the faces that circled the fire. The baron gestured for him to sit down with a faint movement of his left hand, then turned his rheumy gaze to Dieter.

'We cannot take Akendorf, at least not without great loss of life. I am no expert on sieges but even I can see that,' the grey-haired man said. He leaned forward and put another branch on the fire. Sparks drifted upwards into the cold night air.

'You are saying we must continue on,' the baron said. His voice was weak and reminded Felix of the crackle of dry leaves.

Dieter nodded.

'Perhaps we should go west,' Manfred said. 'Seek out land there. That way we could miss the hills, assuming there is anything there to fear.'

'There is,' the trapper, Hef, said. Even in the cheery glow of the fire his features looked pale and strained.

'Going west is a foolish idea anyway,' Frau Winter said. Felix saw that she was glaring right at Manfred.

'Oh, how so?' he asked.

'Use your brain, boy. The mountains to the east are the haunt of goblins, now that the dwarf realm is sundered. So the best land will be that furthest away from Thunder River, safest from raids. It will be held by the strongest of the local rulers. Any place to the west will be better defended than Akendorf.'

'I know my geography,' Manfred sneered. He looked around the fire, meeting the gaze of every watcher. 'If we continue south we will come to Blood River, where the wolf-riders are thicker than worms in a corpse.'

'In every direction lies peril,' the old baron wheezed. He looked straight at Felix and his blue eyes were very piercing. 'Do you think that the Lord of Akendorf warned us to keep to the river simply to make us a tempting target for any raiding greenskins?'

Felix considered for a moment, weighing his judgement. How could he be expected to tell whether the man had been lying or not on the basis of a few minutes' conversation? Felix was acutely conscious that he would influence the destiny of everyone in the caravan by what he said. For the first time in his life he felt a vague glimmer of the responsibilities of leadership. He took a deep breath.

'The man seemed sincere, Herr Baron.'

'He was tellin' the truth,' Hef said, tamping some smokeweed into the bowl of his pipe. Felix noted the way the man's fingers played nervously with its stem. Hef leaned forward and pulled a twig from the fire, using it to light his pipe before continuing.

'The Geistenmund Hills are an evil place. Folk say that centuries ago sorcerers came out of Bretonnia, necromancers exiled by the Sun King.

They found the barrows of the folk who passed here in Elder days and used their spells to raise an army. Came very near to conquering the whole of the Border Princes afore the local lords made alliance with the dwarfs of the mountains and threw them back.'

Felix felt a shiver pass up his spine. He fought an urge to look back over his shoulder into the shadows.

'Folk say that the sorcerers and their allies retreated into the barrows. These were sealed with dwarf stonework and powerful runes by the victors.'

'But that was centuries ago,' Frau Winter said. 'Strong though their sorceries were, can they endure?'

'I don't know, mistress. But tomb robbers never return from the Geistenmunds. Some nights, unnatural lights can be seen in the hills and when both moons are full the dead lie unquiet in their tombs. They come to take the living so that their blood can renew the life of their dark lords.'

'Surely that is nonsense,' Dr Stockhausen said.

Felix himself was not so sure. The previous year on Geheimnisnacht he had seen terrible things. He pushed the memory back from his mind.

'If we go west we face certain peril and no surety of finding haven,' the baron said, his face made gaunt and angular by the underlight of the fire. 'South it is claimed we will find clear land, guarded though it may be by a sorcerous foe. I think we should brave the southward way. It may be clear. We will follow Thunder River.'

His voice held no great hope. He sounded like a man who had resigned himself to his fate. Does the baron court death, wondered Felix? In the atmosphere created by the trapper's dark tale Felix could almost believe it. He made a mental note to find out more about the von Diehl curse. Then he noticed the face of Manfred. The young noble was staring raptly into the fire, a look almost of pleasure on his face.

'I believe I have found the inspiration for a new play,' Manfred von Diehl said enthusiastically. 'That delightful story the trapper told last night will be its core.'

Felix looked at him dubiously. They were walking along the west side of the caravan, keeping between the wagons and the ominous, barren hills.

'It may be more than a simple trapper's tale, Manfred. There is some truth to many old legends.'

'Quite so! Quite so! Who should know that better than I? I think I shall call this play Where the Dead Men Walk. Think of it: silver rings clinking on bony fingers, the parchment skins of the restless dead glistening in the witchlight. Imagine a king who lies in state untouched by the worms and who rises every year to seek blood to prolong his shadowy reign.'

Looking at those brooding, blasted heights, Felix found it only too easy to imagine such things. Among the four hundred who followed Baron von Diehl, only three people dared enter the hills. During the day Doctor Stockhausen and Frau Winter would search among the mossy boulders on the rubble-strewn slopes for herbs. Sometimes they would encounter Gotrek Gurnisson if they returned late. The Trollslayer prowled the hillside by night, as if daring the powers of darkness to touch him.

'Think,' Manfred said in a conspiratorial whisper. 'Think of lying sleeping in your bed and hearing the soft pad of approaching feet and no breathing whatsoever except your own... You could lie there listening to your heart pound and know that no heartbeat tolled within the chest of the approaching–'

'Yes,' Felix said hurriedly. 'I'm sure it will be an excellent work. You must let me read it when it is complete.'

He decided to change the subject, tried to think of one that would appeal to this strange young man. 'I was thinking perhaps of writing a poem myself. Could you tell me more of the von Diehl curse?'

Manfred's face froze. His glittering look made Felix shiver, then Manfred shook his head and smiled and became his old affable self.

'There is little to tell.' He giggled lightly. 'My grandfather was a very devout man. Always burning witches and mutants to prove it. One Hexensnacht he roasted a pretty maid called Irina Trask. All his subjects came to watch, for she was a beauty. As the flames rose about her, she called on the powers of hell to avenge her, to bring death to my grandfather and the wrath of Chaos to his heirs and followers and all of their children. The darkness and its children will take you all, she said.'

He fell silent and stared gloomily towards the hills. Felix prompted him. 'What happened?'

'Shortly thereafter my grandfather was killed while out hunting, by a pack of beastmen. There was a quarrel amongst his sons. The eldest, Kurt, was heir. My father and his brother rebelled and ousted him. Some folk say that Kurt became a bandit and was killed by a warrior of Chaos. Others claim that he headed north and met a much darker fate.

'My father inherited the barony and married my mother, Katerina von Wittgenstein.' Felix stared at him. The Wittgensteins were a family with a dark reputation, shunned by normal society. Manfred ignored his stare.

'Uncle Gottfried became their warleader. My mother died giving birth to me, and my father disappeared. Gottfried seized power. Since then we have been dogged by ill-luck.'

Felix could see a figure approaching downslope. It was Frau Winter. She seemed to be in a great hurry. 'Disappeared?' Felix said distractedly.

'Aye, vanished. It wasn't until much later I found out what had happened to him.'

Frau Winter approached, glaring at Manfred. 'Bad news,' she said. 'I've discovered an opening on the hillside up there. It is barred by runes, but I sense a terrible danger lies beyond it.'

Something in her tone compelled belief. She swirled on down into the camp. Manfred glared daggers at her back.

Felix looked over at him. 'There is no love lost between you two, is there?'

'She hates me, has done ever since uncle named me heir. She thinks her son should be the next baron.'

Felix raised an eyebrow.

'Oh yes, didn't you know? Dieter is her son. He's my father's bastard offspring.'

Moonlight dappled the waters of Thunder River. It gleamed like liquid silver. Old gnarled trees hung over the banks at this point, reminding Felix of waiting trolls. Nervously, he looked about. There was something in the air tonight, he decided; a tension, a feeling that something was not right. He had to fight to control the sensation that somewhere something evil stirred, hungry for his life, for the lives of all the people of Baron Gottfried's entourage.

'Is there something wrong, Felix? You seem very distracted tonight,' Kirsten said.

He looked over to her and smiled, finding pleasure in her presence. Normally he enjoyed their nightly walks by the river but tonight foreboding came between them.

'No. Just tired.' He couldn't restrain a glance in the direction of the nearby hills. By the light of the moons the opening looked very like a gaping maw.

'It's this place, isn't it? There's something unnatural about it. I can feel it. It's like when Frau Winter does one of her dangerous spells. The hair on the back of my neck prickles. Only this is much worse.'

Felix saw terror surface in her face, then disappear again. She looked out over the water. 'Something old and evil dwells below those hills, Felix. Something hungry. We could die here.'

Felix took her hand. 'We're quite safe. We're still by the river.' His voice quivered and his words did not come across reassuringly. He sounded like a scared boy. They were both shaking.

'Everyone in the camp is afraid, except your friend Gotrek. Why is he so fearless?'

Felix laughed quietly. 'Gotrek is a Trollslayer, sworn to seek death to atone for some crime. He's an exile from his home, family and friends. He has no place in this world. He is brave because he has nothing to lose. He can only regain his honour by dying honourably.'

'Why do you follow him? You seem like a sensible man.'

Felix considered his reply carefully. He had never really questioned his motives that closely. Under the gaze of Kirsten's dark eyes it suddenly became important for him to know.

'He saved my life. We pledged blood-loyalty after that. At the time I did not know what the ritual meant but I've stuck to it.'

He had given the barest facts, the truth in a sense, but not an explanation. He paused and stroked the old scar on his right cheek. He wanted to be honest.

'I killed a man in a duel. It caused a scandal. I had to give up my life as a student, my father disinherited me. I was full of anger, got into trouble with the law. At the time I met Gotrek I had no goals, I was just drifting. Gotrek's purpose was so strong I just got sucked along behind him. It was easier to follow him than to start a new life. Something about his self-destructive madness appealed to me.'

She looked at him questioningly. 'It doesn't any more?'

He shook his head. 'What about you? What brings you along Thunder River?'

They approached a tumbled tree. Felix gave Kirsten a hand up onto the bole, then jumped up beside her himself. She smoothed the folds of her long peasant skirt, tucked a lock of her hair behind one ear. Felix thought she looked very lovely in the light of the twin moons, with the mist beginning to rise.

'My parents were vassals of Baron Gottfried's, serfs back in Diehlendorf. They indentured me to Frau Winter. They died back in the avalanche, along with my sisters.'

'I'm sorry,' Felix said. 'I didn't know.'

She shrugged fatalistically. 'There has been so much death along the way. I'm just grateful to be here.'

She was quiet for a long moment and when she spoke again her voice was soft. 'I miss them.'

Felix could think of nothing to say, so he kept quiet.

'You know, my grandmother never travelled more than a mile from Diehlendorf in her life. She never even saw the inside of that bleak old castle. All she knew was her hut and the strips of fields where she laboured. Already I've seen mountains and towns and this river. I've travelled further than she ever dreamed. In a way I'm glad.'

Felix looked at her. Along the shadowy planes of her cheeks he could see a teardrop glisten. Their faces were very close. Behind her, tendrils of mist drifted from the surface of the river. It had thickened quickly. He could barely see the water. Kirsten moved closer.

'If I hadn't come I wouldn't have met you.'

They kissed, unskilfully, tentatively. Lips barely brushed lips. Felix leaned forward and took her long hair in his hands. They leaned into each other, holding one another hungrily as the kiss deepened. Passionately their hands began to wander, exploring each other's bodies through the thick layers of clothing.

They leaned over too far. Kirsten screamed slightly as they fell off the tree trunk onto the soft wet earth.

'My cloak's all muddy,' Felix said.

'Perhaps you'd better take it off. We can lie on it. The ground's all wet.'

Under the shadow of the deathly hills they made love in the mist and moonlight.

'Where have you been, manling, and why are you looking so pleased with yourself?' Gotrek asked surlily.

'Down by the river,' Felix replied innocently. 'Just walking.'

Gotrek raised one bushy eyebrow. 'You picked a bad night just to go walking. See the way this mist thickens. I smell sorcery.'

Felix looked at him, feeling fear creep though his bones. His hand went to the hilt of his sword. He remembered the mist that had covered the moors around the Darkstone Ring a year before, and what it had hidden. He glanced over his shoulder into the darkness.

'If that's true we should tell Dieter and the baron.'

'I've already informed the duke's henchman. The guard has been doubled. That's all they would do.'

'What are we going to do?'

'Get some sleep, manling. It will be your watch soon.'

Felix lay down in the back of the wagon on top of some sacks of grain. He pulled his cloak tight about him. Try as he might, sleep was a long time coming. He kept thinking of Kirsten. When he stared at Morrslieb, the lesser moon, it seemed he could see the outline of her face. The mist grew thicker, muffling all sound except Gotrek's quiet breathing.

When sleep finally came, he dreamed dark dreams in which dead men walked.

In the distance a horse whinnied uneasily. A huge hand was clamped over Felix's mouth. He struggled furiously, wondering whether Lars had come back for revenge.

'Hist, manling! Something comes. Be very quiet.'

Felix came groggily to full wakefulness. His eyes felt dry and tired; his muscles ached from the mattress of sacks. He felt weary and lacking in energy.

'What is it, Gotrek?' he asked softly. The Trollslayer gestured for him to be quiet and sniffed at the air.

'Whatever it is, it's been dead a long time.'

Felix shivered and drew his cloak tight. He felt fear begin to churn in the pit of his stomach. As the meaning of the dwarf's words sank in, he had to fight to restrain the terror.

Felix peered out into the mist. It cloaked the land, obscuring vision at more than a spear's length. If Felix strained every sense he could just make out the wagon opposite. He cast a glance back over his shoulder, fearful that some frightful denizen of the dark might be creeping up behind him.

His heartbeat sounded loud in his ears and he remembered Manfred's words. He pictured bony hands reaching out to grab him and carry him off to a deep dark tomb. His muscles felt as if they had frozen in place. He had to struggle to get them to move, to reach for the hilt of his sword.

'I'm going to take a look around,' Gotrek whispered. Before Felix could argue or follow, the dwarf dropped noiselessly off the cart and vanished into the gloom.

Now Felix felt totally alone. It was like waking from one nightmare to find himself in a worse one. He was isolated in the dark and clammy mist. He knew that just outside the range of his perception hungry, uncanny creatures lurked. Some primitive sense told him so. He knew that to stir from the cart meant death.

Yet Kirsten was out there, sleeping in Frau Winter's carriage. He pictured her lying in bed as terrible pressure was exerted on the caravan's door and slowly the timber buckled inwards, to reveal–

He drew his blade and leapt from the cart. The soft thud of his feet rang as loud as the tolling of a bell to his fear-honed senses. He strained to pick out details in the mist as he moved through the outer ring of wagons to where he knew Kirsten was.

Every step seemed to take eternity. He cast wary glances about him, fearful that something was creeping up stealthily behind. He skirted pockets of deep shadow. He wanted to cry out loud to alert the camp, but something instinctively stopped him. To do so would be to attract the attention of the terrible watchers – and that would mean death.

A figure loomed out of the shadows, and Felix brought his sword up. His heart was in his mouth until he noticed the figure was wearing leather armour and a metal cap. A guard, he thought, relaxing. Thank Sigmar. But when the figure turned, Felix almost screamed.

Its face had no flesh. Greenish light flickered in its empty sockets. Age-rotten teeth smirked from the fleshless, lipless mouth. He saw that the helm which he had originally taken for a guard's was verdigrised bronze and inscribed with runes which hurt the eye. The smell of mould and rotten leather rose from the thing's tunic and tattered cloak.

It lashed out at him with its rusty blade. Felix stood frozen for a moment and then, acting on reflex, flung himself to one side. The thing's sword nicked his ribs. Pain seared his side. He noticed the movement of ancient tendons under the paper-thin skin of the hand which held the weapon. He countered with a high blow to the neck, his body responding with trained discipline even as his mind reeled in horror.

His blade crashed through the thing's neck with a cracking of severed vertebrae. His return blow chopped through its chest like a butcher's cleaver through a bone. The skeletal warrior fell like a marionette with its strings cut.

As if Felix's blows were a signal, the night came alive with shadowy figures. He heard wood splinter and animals scream in terror, as if whatever spell had held them mute was broken. Somewhere off in the night Gotrek Gurnisson bellowed his war chant.

Felix rushed through the mist, almost colliding with Dieter as he tumbled out of a wagon. The big man was fully dressed and clutched a hand-axe.

'What's going on?' he shouted, through the cacophony of screams.

'Attackers… dead things from under the hills,' Felix said. The words came out in jerky gasps.

'Foes!' Dieter shouted. 'To me, men. Rally to me!' He gave out a wolf-like war-cry. From about them came a few weak answering howls. Felix charged on, seeking Kirsten's home. From the shadowy gap between two wagons, figures leapt out, striking at him with long, wickedly curved blades.

He writhed aside from one and parried the other. Two more skeletal creatures leered at him. He chopped at one's leg. It fell over as his blade broke through the knee. Mind numbed with horror, he fought almost mechanically, leaping over the blow of the one on the ground then bringing his heel down to break its spine. Blows flickered between him and the other until he chopped it to pieces.

He saw two of the fiends battering though the door of Frau Winter's wagon just as he had feared. From inside came the sound of chanting, which he assumed was a prayer. He prepared himself to charge but his eyes were dazzled by a sudden blueish flash. Chain lightning flickered and a rank smell of ozone filled the air, overcoming even the stench of rot. When Felix's sight cleared he saw the charred remains of two skeletons lying near the caravan's steps.

In the doorway Frau Winter stood calm and unafraid, a nimbus of light emerging from her left hand. She looked over at Felix and gave him an encouraging nod.

Behind her was Kirsten, who pointed mutely over his shoulder. He whirled and saw a dozen undead warriors rushing towards him. He heard Dieter and his men run up to meet them. Then he joined the rush.

For Felix the night became howling chaos as he hacked his way round the camp in search of Gotrek. At one point the mist cleared and he pushed some quivering children under a wagon away from the bodies of their dead parents. The man lay in a night shirt, the woman close by, a broom handle clutched in one hand like a spear. Felix heard a sound and turned to face a skeletal giant bearing down at him. Somehow he survived.

Felix fought back to back with Dieter until they stood among a pile of mouldering bones. The battle surged away from him as the mist closed in and for a long moment he stood alone, listening to the screams of the dying.

A passing figure lashed out at him and they exchanged blows. Felix saw that it was Lars, a grin frozen on his face revealing missing teeth, terror froth foaming from his mouth. Berserkly he hacked at Felix. The man was mad with fear.

'Bathtard!' he hissed, chopping at Felix with a blow which would have felled a tree. Felix ducked underneath the blow and lunged forward, taking him through the heart. Lars sobbed as he died. Felix wondered how crazed Lars really had been. If the trapper had killed Felix it could have been blamed on the attackers. He returned to the fray.

He rounded a corner to find a score of undead warriors being driven back by the furious onslaught of Gotrek's axe. Blue chain lightning flickered and the area about him was suddenly clear. He looked about for Frau Winter to offer his thanks but she was gone, vanished into the mists. He turned to see Gotrek standing astonished, his jaw hanging open.

Sometime before dawn, their assailants retreated back towards the hills, leaving Baron von Diehl's warriors to contemplate their ruined wagons and the bodies of their dead.

In the early morning light, Felix watched warily as Gotrek inspected the rubble of the old stone arch. The stench of dank air and mouldering bones that came from within made Felix want to gag. He turned to stare down the hillside, to where the surviving exiles were building funeral pyres for the dead out of the remains of ruined wagons. Nobody wanted to bury them so close to the hills.

Felix heard Gotrek grunt with grim satisfaction, and turned to look at him. The dwarf was running his hand expertly along the broken stones with their faint webwork of old runes. Gotrek looked up and grinned savagely.

'No doubt about it, manling: the runes guarding the entrance were broken from the outside.'

Felix looked at him. Suspicion blossomed. He was very afraid. 'It looks as though someone has been giving the von Diehl curse a helping hand,' he whispered.

Rain lashed down from the grey sky. The cart rumbled southward. Beside the caravan the waters of Thunder River tumbled headlong towards their goal. The rain-swollen river constantly threatened to burst its banks. Felix jerked the reins; the oxen lowed and redoubled their efforts to move on the muddy ground.

Beside him Kirsten sneezed. Like almost everyone else, she was pale and ill-looking. The strain of the long journey and the worsening weather had made them all prey to disease.

No town would take them in. Armed warriors had threatened battle unless they moved on to untenanted land. The trail had become interminable. It seemed as if they had been riding forever and would never come to rest. Even the knowledge that someone in the train had freed the undead beneath the hills had ceased to be alarming, fading into cold suspicion when no culprit could be found.

Felix looked at Gotrek guiltily, expecting Kirsten's sneeze to produce his usual crass comments about human frailty, but the Trollslayer was silent, staring towards the Worlds Edge Mountains with a fixity of purpose unusual even for him.

Felix wondered when he would pluck up the courage to tell Gotrek that he wasn't continuing onwards with him, that he was settling down with Kirsten. He was worried about what the dwarf's reaction would be. Would Gotrek simply dismiss it as another example of human faithlessness – or would he turn violent?

Felix felt miserable. He was fond of the Trollslayer, for all his black moods and bitter comments. The thought of Gotrek wandering off to meet a lonely doom disturbed him. But he loved Kirsten and the thought of being parted from her was painful to him. Perhaps Gotrek sensed this and it was the reason for his withdrawn mood. Felix reached over and squeezed the girl's hand.

'What are you looking for, Herr Gurnisson?' Kirsten asked the dwarf. Gotrek did not turn to look at her but continued to stare longingly at the mountains. At first it seemed as if the Trollslayer would not reply but eventually he pointed to the outline of one cloud-swathed mountain.

'Karaz-a-Karak,' he said. 'The Everpeak. My home.' His voice was softer than Felix had ever heard it and it held a depth of longing that was heart-breaking.

Gotrek turned to look at them and his face held such a look of dumb, brute misery that Felix had to look away. The dwarf's crest of hair was flattened by the rain and his face was bleak and weary. Kirsten reached past to adjust Gotrek's cloak about his shoulders, as she would have done for a lost child.

Gotrek tried to give her his ferocious, insular scowl but he could not hold it and he just smiled sadly, revealing his missing teeth. Felix wondered whether the dwarf had come all this way just for that fleeting glimpse of the mountain. He noticed a drop of water hanging from the end of the Trollslayer's nose. It might have been a teardrop or it might just have been rain.

They continued southward.

* * *

'We can't leave them just yet,' Felix said, cursing himself for being such a coward.

Gotrek turned and looked towards the tumbled-down fortified mansion which they had found. He could see smoke rising in plumes from the chimneys of the recently cleared building.

'Why not, manling? They've found clear ground, cultivatable land and the ruins of that old fort. With a little work it should prove quite defensible.'

Felix strove desperately to find a reason. He was surprised that he was trying so hard to delay the moment when he had to tell Gotrek of their parting. The way Gotrek looked at him disapprovingly reminded him of his father at his sternest. He felt once more the need to make excuses, and he hated himself for it.

'Gotrek, we're only a hundred miles north of where the Thunder River flows into Blood River. Beyond that is the Badlands and a horde of wolf-riders.'

'I know that, manling. We'll have to cross there on our way to Karak Eight Peaks.'

Tell him. Just say it, Felix argued with himself. But he couldn't.

'We can't go just yet. You've seen the bodies we found in the mansion. Bones cracked for the marrow. The walls have been burned. Dieter has found the spoor of wolf-riders nearby. The place is not defensible. With your help, with the help of a dwarf, it could be made so.'

Gotrek laughed. 'I don't know why you think that.'

'Because dwarfs are good with stone and fortifications. Everyone knows that.'

Gotrek glanced back at the mansion thoughtfully. He seemed to be remembering a former life. A frown creased his brow and he rested his forehead against the shaft of his axe.

'I don't know,' he said eventually, 'that even a dwarf could make this place defensible. Typical human workmanship, manling. Shoddy, very shoddy.'

'It could be made safe. You know it could, Gotrek.'

'Perhaps. It has been a long time since I worked with stone, manling.'

'A dwarf never forgets such things. And I'm sure the baron will pay handsomely for your services.'

Gotrek sniffed suspiciously. 'It had better be more than he pays his mercenaries.'

Felix grinned. 'Come on. Let's find out.'

* * *

Unable to sleep, Felix got up quietly. He dressed quickly, not wanting to wake Kirsten. He gently rearranged the cloaks that they used as blankets about her so that she would not get cold, then kissed her lightly on the forehead. She stirred but did not awake. He lifted his sword from where it lay by the entrance of their hut and stepped out into the cold night air. Winter was coming, Felix thought, watching his breath cloud.

By the moons' light he picked his way through the cluster of hovels which lay in the lee of the new wooden walls surrounding the mansion. He felt at peace for the first time in a long while. Even the night-time noise of the camp was reassuring. The fort had been completed before the first snows; it looked as if the settlers would have enough grain to last the winter and seed a new crop in the spring.

He listened to the cattle lowing and the measured tread of the sentry on the walls. He looked up and saw that a light still gleamed in the window of Manfred's room. Felix thought about his convoluted destiny. Not a place I would ever have imagined myself settling down, a fortified village on the edge of nowhere. I wonder what my father would think if he could see me now, about to become a farmer. He'd probably die of mortification. Felix smiled.

It was exciting to be here. There was a sense of something about to begin, a community still taking shape. And I will have a place in shaping that community, he thought. This is the perfect place to start a new life.

He walked on towards the guard tower, where he knew he would find Gotrek. The dwarf was unable to sleep, restless and ready to move on. He liked to while away the night watches in the tower he himself had designed.

Felix clambered up the ladder and through the trapdoor in the floor of the guardroom. He found Gotrek staring out into the night. The sight of the dwarf made Felix nervous but he steeled himself, determined to tell the dwarf the truth.

'Can't sleep either, eh, manling?'

Felix managed a nod. When he had rehearsed his speech to himself it all had seemed simple. He would explain the situation rationally, tell Gotrek he was staying with Kirsten and await the dwarf's response. Now it was more difficult, his tongue felt thick and it was as if the words had stuck in his throat.

He found himself flinching inwardly at all the accusations he imagined Gotrek would make: that he was a coward and an oathbreaker; that this was the thanks a dwarf got for saving a man's life. Felix had to admit that he had sworn an oath to follow Gotrek and record his doom. Certainly, he had sworn it while drunk and full of gratitude to a dwarf who had just pulled him from under the hooves of the Emperor's cavalry, but an oath was still an oath, as Gotrek was wont to point out.

He moved over to stand beside the Trollslayer. They stared out over the ditch that surrounded the outer wall and which was sided with sharpened stakes. The only easy way over it was the bridge of earth that this tower overlooked.

'Gotrek…'

'Yes, manling?'

'You've built well,' Felix said.

Gotrek looked up and smiled grimly. 'We'll soon find out,' he said. Felix looked to where the Trollslayer pointed. The fields were dark with wolf-riders. Gotrek raised the alarm horn to his lips and sounded a blast.

Felix ducked as an arrow splintered into the wood of the parapet in front of him. He reached down and took a crossbow from the fingers of the dead guard. The man lay with an arrow through his throat. Felix fumbled for a quarrel and strained to cock the weapon. He eventually slipped a bolt into place.

He leapt up. Fire arrows flashed overhead like falling stars. From behind him came the stench of burning. Felix looked down from the parapet. Wolf-riders circled the camp as a wolf-pack circles a herd of cattle. He could see the green skin of the riders glistening in the light of their burning arrows. The flames highlighted their jaundiced eyes and yellowish tusks.

There must be hundreds of them, Felix thought. He thanked Sigmar for the ditch and the spikes and the wooden walls that Gotrek had made them build. At the time it had seemed needless labour and the dwarf had been roundly cursed. Now it seemed barely adequate provision.

Felix aimed at a wolf-rider who was drawing a bead on the tower with one pitch-soaked arrow. He pulled the trigger on the crossbow. The bolt blurred across the night and took the goblin in the chest. It fell backwards in the saddle. Its blazing arrow was launched directly into the sky, as if aimed at the moons.

Felix ducked back and reloaded. With his back to the parapet he could see down into the courtyard. A human chain of women and children carried buckets from the rain-barrels to the flaming hovels, struggling vainly to extinguish the fires. He saw one old woman go down and others flinch as arrows fell around them like dark rain.

Felix turned and fired again, missing. The night was filled with a cacophony of sound. The screams of the dying, the howling of wolves, the deadly cutting whisper of arrows and crossbow bolts. He heard Gotrek singing happily in dwarfish, and somewhere far off the baron's dry, rasping voice giving orders in a firm, calm voice. Dogs barked, horses whinnied in terror, children cried. Felix wished he were deaf.

He heard the scratching of claws on wood nearby and lurched to his feet. He looked over the parapet and almost lost his face. The jaws of a wolf snapped shut below him. The creature had leapt the ditch, ignoring the stakes which were covered by the bodies of its fallen comrades.

He smelled the stench of its breath as it fell, saw its rider hanging on grimly as it gathered itself for another spring. Felix let fly with a crossbow bolt. It thunked into the creature's chest, and the wolf fell. Its rider rolled clear and scuttled off into the night.

Felix saw Frau Winter climb up into the watchtower, to stand at Gotrek's shoulder. He hoped she would do something. In the howling chaos of the night it was impossible to tell, but Felix sensed that things were not going well for the defenders. The ditch seemed to be filling with the bodies of their attackers, and the guards were falling like flies to the incessant barrages of arrows in spite of the protection of the parapet.

When Felix looked again, he saw a group of heavily armoured orcs, bearing a sharpened tree trunk, racing towards the gate. A few crossbow bolts landed among them but others were deflected by the shields of those who ran alongside the rammers. He heard the juddering sound of the tree's impact on the gate.

Felix fumbled for his sword, preparing to leap from the walls into the courtyard and hold the gate. If it fell, all he could do was sell his life dearly; they were too badly outnumbered to delay the besiegers long. He felt fear twist in his gut. He hoped Kirsten was safe.

Frau Winter's calm, clear voice rang out. She chanted like a priest at prayer. Then the lightning came.

Searing blue light leapt through the night. The air stank of ozone. The hair on the back of Felix's neck prickled. He tried to watch as the lightning flashed among the ram-carriers. He heard them scream. Some danced back, capering like clowns, dropping the treetrunk. They fell to earth, bodies smouldering. The disgusting burned-meat smell of scorched flesh filled the air.

Again and again the lightning lashed out. Wolves howled fearfully, the hail of arrows slackened, the sickening smell increased. Felix looked at Frau Winter. Her face was drawn and pale, her hair stood upright. As her face alternated black and blue in the nightmarish flashes, she looked daemonic. He had not suspected any human being could wield such power.

The wolf-riders and the orc infantry retreated, howling in terror, to beyond the reach of those appalling thunderbolts. Felix felt relieved. Then he noticed, off in the distance, a glow of light.

He peered into the darkness, making out an old greenskin shaman. A red nimbus played around his skull, illuminating the wolfskin head-dress and the bone-staff he held in one gnarled claw. A beam of blood-coloured light flickered from his head and lashed out at Frau Winter.

Felix saw the sorceress moan and totter back. Gotrek reached out to support her. He watched her grimace in pain, her face a pale mask. She gritted her teeth, and sweat beaded her brow. She seemed to be locked in a supernatural contest of wills with the old shaman.

The wolf-riders rallied around their braver leaders. Cautiously they began to return, although their renewed attacks lacked the wild ferocity of their initial onslaught. All through the night the struggle continued.

In the first light of dawn, Felix approached Gotrek where he stood with Manfred, Dieter and Frau Winter. The woman looked weary beyond endurance. People crowded around her, gazing at her in awe.

'How are we doing?' Felix asked Gotrek.

'As long as she holds out, we can. If she can call the lightning.' Manfred looked at Gotrek and nodded agreement.

There was a commotion from the other side of the courtyard.

'Frau Winter, come quickly,' Doctor Stockhausen called. 'The baron has been gravely wounded. An arrow, maybe poisoned.' Wearily, the sorceress walked into the mansion. From the crowd Felix saw Kirsten move to help her. He smiled at her, glad they were both alive.

With a sound like sudden thunder, the gate rocked back on its hinges. Another blow like that and it will fall, Felix thought. He looked over at Gotrek who was testing the edge of his axe experimentally with his thumb. On this second night of the siege the Trollslayer was looking forward to the hand-to-hand combat to come. Felix felt a tug on his shoulder. It was Hef. The big man looked deathly afraid.

'Where is Frau Winter?' he asked. He nodded at the gate. 'That's no battering ram. That's the staff of that old devil. He'll have all our heads for his lodge afore the night's out unless the witch can stop him!'

Felix looked from Hef to the rest of the pitifully depleted band of defenders. He saw tired warriors; wounded men who could barely carry a sword, teenage boys and girls armed with pitchforks and other improvised weapons. From outside the howling of the wolves was deafening. Only Gotrek looked calm.

'I don't know where she is. Dieter went to get her ten minutes ago.'

'Well, he's takin' his time 'bout it.'

'All right,' Felix said. 'I'll go and get her.'

'I'll come with you,' Hef said.

'Oh no you won't,' Gotrek said loudly. 'I trust the manling to return. You'll stay here. The gobbos will pass this gate over our dead bodies.'

Felix made for the mansion. He knew that Kirsten was with the sorceress. If things went as badly as he feared, he would at least see her before the end.

He had barely reached the door when he heard a splintering sound from behind him and the heart-stopping crash of the gate falling in. He heard Gotrek bellow his war-cry, and the screams of terror from some of the warriors. Felix turned and saw a terrible sight.

In the gateway, mounted on a great white wolf, was the shaman. Around his head crackled a halo of ruddy light. It played from the tip of his bone staff, staining the faces of all around like blood. From the wall a quarrel flashed but it was turned aside by some force before it could hit the sorcerer.

Flanking the shaman were six mighty orcs, mail-clad, axe-armed and fierce. Beyond them was a sea of green faces and wolves. Gotrek laughed aloud and charged for them. The last thing Felix saw before he stepped inside was the Trollslayer running forward, axe held high, beard bristling, towards the source of that terrible light.

Inside, the mansion was strangely quiet, the roar of sound outside muffled by the stone walls. Felix ran through the corridor, shouting for Frau Winter, his voice ringing eerily in the quiet halls.

He found the bodies in the main hall. Frau Winter had been stabbed through the chest several times. Her clean, grey dress was red. She had a look of surprise on her face, as if death had taken her unawares. How had the goblins got inside? Felix thought crazily. But he knew no goblin had done this.

Another body lay near the door, stabbed through the back as she had struggled to open it. Not wanting, not daring to believe it, Felix advanced, heart in his mouth. Gently he turned Kirsten's body over.

He felt a brief flicker of hope as her eyes opened, then noticed the trickle of blood from her mouth.

'Felix,' she sighed. 'Is that you? I knew you'd come.'

Her voice was weak and blood frothed from her lips as she spoke. He wondered how long she had lain there.

'Don't talk,' he said. 'Rest.'

'Can't. Have to talk. I'm glad I came down Thunder River. Glad I met you. I love you.'

'I love you too,' he said, for the first time, then he noticed her eyes were closed. 'Don't die,' he said, rocking her gently in his arms. He felt her body go limp and his heart turned to ash. He laid her down gently, tears in his eyes, then he looked towards the door she had tried to open and cold fury filled him. Felix stood and raced down the corridor.

Dieter's body lay in the doorway to the baron's room. The side of the big man's head had been caved in. Felix pictured him rushing through the doorway in anger and being hit from the side by his prepared enemy.

Felix sprang over the body like a tiger, rolling as he hit the ground and leaping to his feet. He surveyed the room. The old baron lay in bed, a knife through his heart, blood soaking the bandages on his chest and the sheets of the bed.

Felix glared over at the chair in which Manfred sat, his gore-smeared sword red across his lap.

'The curse is fulfilled at last,' the playwright said in a tight voice that held the shrill edge of hysteria. He looked up and Felix shuddered. It was as if Manfred's face were a mask through which something else stared, something alien.

'I knew it was my destiny to fulfil the curse,' Manfred said as if passing the time of day. 'Knew it from the moment I killed my father. Gottfried had him imprisoned when he started to change. Locked him up in the old tower, took him all his food himself. No one else was allowed into that tower except Gottfried and Frau Winter. Nobody else went there until the day I did. Ulric knows, I wish I hadn't.'

He rose to his feet gripping the hilt of his sword. Felix watched him, hypnotised by his own hatred.

'I found my father there. There was still a family resemblance in spite of the way he had... changed. He still recognised me, called me "Son" in a horrid rasping voice. He begged me to kill him. He was too cowardly to do it himself. So was Gottfried. He thought he was doing my father a kindness, by keeping him alive. Keeping alive a mutant.'

Manfred began to edge closer. Felix noticed the blood dripping from his blade, speckling the floor. He felt dizzy and tired. The mad young aristocrat became the centre of his world.

'As I felt the old man's blood flow over my knife, everything changed. I saw things clearly for the first time. I saw the way Chaos taints all things, twisting and corrupting them as it had done to my father's body. I knew that I was his son and that within me, carried in my blood, was the mark of daemons. I was the agent of Chaos, spawn of its loins. I was a child of darkness. It was my destiny to destroy the von Diehl line. As I have done.'

He laughed. 'The exile was the perfect opportunity, hell-sent. The avalanche was mine, a good start. I thought I had failed when I released the undead and they didn't succeed in destroying my uncle and his followers. But now nothing can save you. Darkness will take you all. The curse is complete.'

'Not yet,' Felix said, his voice choked with hatred. 'You're a von Diehl and you're still alive. I haven't killed you yet.'

Insane laughter rang out. Once more Felix felt as if he was staring at some devil in human flesh.

'Herr Jaeger, you do have a sense of humour. Very good! I knew you would be amusing. But how can you slay the spawn of Chaos?'

'Let us find out,' Felix said, springing forward to the attack. Viperishly swift, Manfred's blade rose to parry then began the counter. Swordstrokes flickered like lightning between them. Steel rang on steel. Felix's sword-arm was numb from the force of Manfred's blows. The nobleman had the strength of a maniac.

Felix gave ground. Normally, cold fear of Manfred's insanity would have paralysed him but now he was so filled with rage and hate that there was no room for terror. His world was empty. He lived only to kill Kirsten's murderer. It was his one remaining desire.

Two madmen fought in the baron's chamber. Manfred advanced with cat-like grace, smiling confidently, as if amused by some mild witticism. His blade wove a web of steel that was slowly tightening around Felix. His eyes glittered, cold and inhuman.

Felix felt the stone of the wall at his back. He lunged forward, striking at Manfred's face. Manfred parried with lazy ease. They stood vis-a-vis, blades locked, faces inches from each other. They pushed with all their strengths, each searching for advantage. Muscles stood out in Felix's neck, his arm burned with fatigue as slowly, inexorably Manfred pushed back his arm, bringing his razor-sharp blade into contact with Felix's face.

'Goodbye, Herr Jaeger,' Manfred said casually.

Felix brought the heel of his boot down on Manfred's instep, crunching into the foot with all his strength and weight. He felt bone splinter, saw the nobleman's face twist in agony, felt the pressure ease. He brought his blade forward, slicing across Manfred's neck. The playwright tottered back and Felix's thrust took him through the heart.

Manfred fell to his knees and stared up at Felix with blank uncomprehending eyes. Felix pushed him over with his boot and spat on his face.

'Now the curse is fulfilled,' he said.

Mind clear and unafraid, Felix stepped out into the cold night air, expecting to find the wolf-riders and death. He no longer cared. He welcomed it. He had come to understand Gotrek thoroughly. He had nothing worth living for. He was beyond all fear.

Kirsten, I will be with you soon, he thought.

In the gateway he saw Gotrek, standing amidst a pile of bodies. Blood flowed from the dwarf's appalling wounds. He was slumped forward, supporting himself on his axe, barely able to keep upright.

Nearby Felix saw the bodies of Hef and the other defenders.

Gotrek turned to look at him and Felix could see that one eye was missing, torn from its socket. The dwarf staggered dizzily, fell forward and slowly and painfully tried to pull himself upright.

'What kept you, manling? You missed a good fight.'

Felix moved towards him. 'So it seems.'

'Damn gobbos are all yellow-eyed cowards. Kill their leaders and the rest turn tail and run.' He laughed painfully. 'Course… I had to kill a score or so of them before they agreed.'

'Of course,' Felix said, looking towards the pile of dead wolves and orcs. He could make out the wolf head-dress of the shaman.

'Damnedest thing,' Gotrek said. 'I can't seem to stand up.'

He closed his eye and lay very still.

Felix watched the small line of stragglers begin to trek northwards under the watchful eyes of the few remaining soldiers. Felix thought that they might be taken in by one of the settlements now that they were no longer being escorted by the baron's full force. For the sake of the children he hoped so.

He turned to the mass grave, the barrow in which they had buried the bodies. He thought about the future he had buried with them. He was landless and homeless again. He settled the weight of the pack on his shoulders and turned to look at the distant mountains.

'Goodbye,' he said. 'I'll miss you.'

Gotrek rubbed at his new eye-patch irritably, then blew his nose. He hefted his axe. Felix noticed that his wounds were pink and barely healed.

'There's trolls in those mountains, manling. I can smell them!'

When Felix spoke his voice was flat and devoid of all emotion. 'Let us go and get them.'

He and Gotrek exchanged a look full of mutual under-standing. 'We'll make a Trollslayer out of you yet, manling.'

Wearily the two of them set out towards the dark promise of the mountains, following the bright thread of Thunder River.

THE DARK BENEATH THE WORLD

'After the dire events at Fort von Diehl, we set off with heavy hearts towards the mountains and Karak Eight Peaks. It was a long, hard journey, one not made any easier by the wildness of the country that we passed through. The hunger, the hardships and the constant threat of marauding greenskins did little to improve my state of mind, and it may be that I was perhaps particularly susceptible when I first looked on the fading grandeur of that ancient ruined city of the dwarfs, lost amid those distant peaks for all those long ages. In any case, I now recall that I had a terrible sense of foreboding about what we would find there and, as was usually the case, my fears were to prove amply justified...'

— From *My Travels with Gotrek, Vol. II*, by Herr Felix Jaeger
(Altdorf Press, 2505)

A scream echoed through the cold mountain air. Felix Jaeger ripped his sword from its scabbard and stood ready. Snowflakes fell; a chill wind stirred his long blond hair. He threw his red woollen cloak back over his shoulder, leaving his sword arm unobstructed. The bleak landscape was a perfect site for an ambush; pitted and rocky, harsher than the face of the greater moon, Mannslieb.

He glanced left, upslope. A few stunted pines clutched the mountainside with gnarled roots. Downslope, to the right, lay an almost sheer drop. Neither direction held any sign of danger. No bandits, no orcs, none of the darker things that lurked in these remote heights.

'The noise came from up ahead, manling,' Gotrek Gurnisson said, rubbing his eye patch with one huge, tattooed hand. His nose chain jingled in the breeze. 'There's a fight going on up there.'

Uncertainty filled Felix. He knew Gotrek was correct; even with only one eye the dwarf's senses were keener than his own. The question was whether to stand and wait or push forward and investigate. Potential enemies filled the Worlds Edge Mountains. The chances of finding friends were slim. His natural caution inclined him towards doing nothing.

Gotrek charged up the scree-strewn path, enormous axe held high above his red-dyed crest of hair. Felix cursed. For once why couldn't Gotrek remember that not everyone was a Trollslayer?

'We didn't all swear to seek out death in combat,' he muttered, before following slowly, for he lacked the dwarf's sure-footedness over the treacherous terrain.

Felix took in the scene of carnage with one swift glance. In the long depression, a gang of hideous, green-skinned orcs battled a smaller group of men. They fought across a fast-flowing stream which ran down the little valley before disappearing over the mountain edge in a cloud of silver spray. The waters ran red with the blood of men and horses. It was easy to imagine what had happened: an ambush as the humans crossed the water.

In mid-stream, a huge man in shiny plate-mail battled with three brawny, bow-legged assailants. Wielding his two-handed blade effortlessly, he feinted a blow to his left then beheaded a different foe with one mighty swing. The force of his blow almost overbalanced him. Felix realised the stream bed must be slippery.

On the nearer bank a man in dark brocaded robes chanted a spell. A ball of fire blazed in his left hand. A dark-haired warrior in the furred hat and deerskin tunic of a trapper protected the sorcerer from two screaming orcs, using only a longsword held in his left hand. As Felix watched, a blond man-at-arms fell, trying to hold in entrails released by a scimitar slash to his stomach. As he went down, burly half-naked savages hacked him to pieces.

Only three of the ambushed party now stood. They were outnumbered five to one.

'Orcish filth! You dare to soil the sacred approach to Karak Eight Peaks. Uruk mortari! Prepare to die,' Gotrek screamed, charging down into the melee.

An enormous orc turned to face him. A look of surprise froze forever on its face as Gotrek lopped off its head with one mighty stroke. Ruby blood spattered the Trollslayer's tattooed body. Raving and snarling, the dwarf ploughed into the orcs, hewing left and right in a great double arc. Dead bodies lay everywhere his axe fell.

Felix half-ran, half-slid down the scree. He fell at the bottom. Wet grass tickled his nostrils. He rolled to one side as a scimitar-wielding monster half again his bulk chopped down at him. He sprang to his feet, ducked a cut that could have chopped him in two and lopped off an earlobe with his return blow.

Startled, the orc clutched at its wound, trying to stop the blood flowing down its face. Felix seized his chance and stabbed upwards through the bottom of the creature's jaw into its brain.

As he struggled to free his blade another monster leapt on him, swinging its scimitar high over its head. Felix let go of his weapon and moved to meet his attacker. He grabbed its wrists as he was overborne. Foetid breath made him gag as the orc fell on top of him. The thing dropped its weapon and they wrestled on the ground, rolling down into the stream.

Copper rings set in the orc's flesh scraped him as the thing sought to bite his throat with its sharp tusks. Felix writhed to avoid having his windpipe torn out. The orc pushed his head underwater. Felix looked up through stinging eyes and saw the strangely distorted face leering down at him. Bitterly cold water filled his mouth. There was no air in his lungs. Frantically he shifted his weight, trying to dislodge his attacker. They rolled and suddenly Felix was astride the orc, trying to push its head under the stream in turn.

The orc grabbed his wrists and pushed. Locked in a deadly embrace they began to roll through the freezing water. Again and again Felix's head went under, again and again he floundered gasping to the surface. Sharp rocks speared his flesh. Realisation of his peril flashed through his mind as the current and their own momentum carried them towards the cliff edge. Felix tried to break free, giving up all thoughts of drowning his opponent.

When next his head broke surface, he looked for the cloud of spray. To his horror it was only a dozen paces away. He redoubled his efforts to escape but the orc held on like grim death and they continued their downward tumble.

Maybe ten feet now. Felix heard the rumble of the fall, felt the distorted currents of the turbulent water. He drew back his fist and smashed the orc in the face. One of its tusks broke but it would not let go.

Five feet to go. He lashed out once more, bouncing the orc's head off the stream bottom. Its grip loosened. He was almost free.

Suddenly he was falling, tumbling through water and air. He frantically grabbed for something, anything, to hold. His hand smashed into the rock and he struggled for a grip on the slippery streambed. The pressure of the freezing water on his head and shoulders was almost intolerable. He risked a downward look.

A long way below he saw the valleys in the foothills. So great was the drop that copses of trees looked like blotches of mould on the landscape. The falling orc was a receding, screaming greenish blob.

With the last of his strength Felix flopped over the edge, pushing against the current with cold-numbed fingers. For a second he thought he wasn't going to make it, then he was face down on the edge of the stream, gasping in bubbling water.

He crawled out onto the bank. The orcs, their leaders dead, had been routed. Felix pulled off his sodden cloak, wondering whether he was going to catch a chill from the frigid mountain air.

'By Sigmar, that was well done! We were sore pressed there,' the tall, dark-haired man said. He made the sign of the hammer over his chest as he spoke. He was handsome in a coarse way. His armour, although

William King

dented, was of the finest quality. The intensity of his stare made Felix uneasy.

'It would seem we owe you gentlemen our lives,' the sorcerer said. He, too, was richly dressed. His brocaded robes were trimmed with gold thread; scrolls covered in mystical symbols were held by rings set in it. His long blond hair was cut in a peculiar fashion. From the centre of his flowing locks rose a crest not unlike Gotrek's, save for the fact that it was undyed and cropped short. Felix wondered if it was the mark of some mystical order.

The armoured man's laughter boomed out. 'It is the prophecy, Johann. Did not the god say one of our ancient brethren would aid us! Sigmar be praised! This is a good sign indeed.'

Felix looked over at the trapper. He spread his hands and shrugged helplessly. A certain cynical humour was apparent in the way he raised an eyebrow.

'I am Felix Jaeger, of Altdorf, and this is my companion Gotrek Gurnisson, the Trollslayer,' Felix said, bowing to the knight.

'I am Aldred Keppler, known as Fellblade, Templar Knight of the Order of the Fiery Heart,' the armoured man said.

Felix suppressed a shudder. In his homeland the Empire, the order was famed for the fanatic zeal with which they pursued their crusade against the goblin races – and those humans they considered heretics.

The knight gestured to the sorcerer. 'This is my adviser on matters magical: Doctor Johann Zauberlich of the University of Nuln.'

'At your service,' Zauberlich said, bowing.

'I am Jules Gascoigne, once of Quenelles in Bretonnia. Although that was many a year ago,' the fur-clad man said. He had a Bretonnian accent.

'Herr Gascoigne is a scout. I engaged him to guide us through these mountains,' Aldred said. 'I have a great work to perform at Karak Eight Peaks.'

Felix and Gotrek exchanged glances. Felix knew the dwarf would rather they travelled alone in search of the lost treasure of the ancient dwarf city. However, parting company from their chance-met companions would only arouse suspicion.

'Perhaps we should join forces,' Felix said, hoping Gotrek would follow his line of reasoning. 'We too are bound for the city of the eight peaks, and this road is far from safe.'

'A capital suggestion,' the sorcerer said.

'Doubtless your companion, he goes to visit his kin,' Jules said,

76

oblivious to the dagger-stare Gotrek gave him. 'There still is a small outpost of Imperial dwarfs there.'

'We had best bury your companions,' Felix said to fill the silence.

'Why so glum, friend Felix? Is it not a lovely night?' Jules Gascoigne asked sardonically, blowing on his hands to warm them against the bitter cold. Felix pulled his spare cloak up over his knees and extended his hands towards the small fire Zauberlich had lit with a muttered word of power. He looked over at the Bretonnian, his face turned into a daemonic mask by the firelight.

'These mountains are chill and daunting,' Felix replied. 'Who knows what perils they hide?'

'Who indeed? We are close to the Darklands. Some say that is the very spawning ground of orcs and all other greenskin devils. Also, I have heard tales that these mountains are haunted.'

Felix gestured towards the fire. 'Do you think we should have lit this?' From nearby came Gotrek's reassuring snores and the regular rhythmic breathing of the others.

Jules chuckled. 'It is a choice between evils, no? I have seen men freeze to death on nights like this. If anything attacks us, it is best that we have light to see by. The greenskins may be able to spot a man in the dark but we cannot, eh? No, I do not think the fire makes much difference. However, I do not think this is why you are sad.'

He looked at Felix expectantly. Without really knowing why, Felix told the whole sorry tale of how he and Gotrek had joined the von Diehl expedition to the Border Princes. Von Diehl and his retainers had sought peace in a new land and found only terrible death. He told of his meeting with his beloved Kirsten. The Bretonnian listened sympathetically. When Felix finished telling of Kirsten's death, Jules shook his head.

'Ah, it is a sorry world we live in, is it not?'

'It is indeed.'

'Do not dwell on the past, my friend. It cannot be altered. In time all wounds heal.'

'It doesn't seem that way to me.'

They fell into silence. Felix looked over at the sleeping dwarf. Gotrek sat like a gargoyle, immobile, eye shut but axe in hand. Felix wondered how the dwarf would take the scout's advice. Gotrek, like all dwarfs, constantly brooded on the lessons of the past. His sense of history drove him inexorably towards his future. He claimed that men had imperfect memories, that dwarfs' were better.

Is that why he seeks his doom, Felix wondered? Does his shame burn in him as strong now as at the moment he committed whatever crime he seeks to atone for? Felix pondered upon what it must be like to live with the past intruding so strongly into the present that it could never be forgotten. I would go mad, he decided.

He inspected his own grief and tried to recall it new-minted. It seemed that it had diminished by a particle, had been eroded by time and would continue to be so. He felt no better, knowing that he was doomed to forget, to have his memories become pale shadows. Perhaps the dwarfs' way was better, he thought. Even the time he had spent with Kirsten seemed paler, more colourless.

During his watch, Felix thought he saw a greenish witchlight high up on the mountain above them. As he stared he felt a sense of dread. The light drifted about as if seeking something. In its midst was a vaguely human form. Felix had heard tales of the daemons haunting these mountains. He looked over at Gotrek, wondering whether he should wake him.

The light vanished. Felix watched for a long time but he saw no further sign. Perhaps it had been an after-image of the fire or a trick of the light and a tired mind. Somehow he doubted it.

In the morning he dismissed his suspicions. The party followed the road round the shoulder of the mountain and suddenly a new land lay spread out before them under the steel grey, overcast sky. They looked down into a long valley nestled in a basin between eight mountains. The peaks rose like the talons of a giant claw. In their palm lay a city.

Huge walls blocked the valley's entrance, built from blocks of stone taller than a man. Within the walls, next to a silver lake, sat a great keep. A town nestled beneath it. Long roads ran from the fortress to lesser towers at the base of each mountain. Drystone dykes criss-crossed the valley, creating a patchwork of overgrown fields.

Gotrek nudged Felix in the ribs and pointed towards the peaks.

'Behold,' he said, a hint of wonder in voice. 'Karag Zilfin, Karag Yar, Karag Mhonar and the Silverhorn.'

'Those are the eastern mountains,' Aldred said. 'Karag Lhune, Karag Rhyn, Karag Nar and the White Lady guard the western approach.'

Gotrek looked at the Sigmarite respectfully. 'You speak truthfully, Templar. Long have these mountains haunted my dreams. Long have I wished to stand in their shadow.'

Felix looked down on the city. There was a sense of enduring strength about the place. Karak Eight Peaks had been built from the bones of mountains to endure until the end of the world.

'It is truly beautiful,' he said.

Gotrek looked at him with fierce pride. 'In ancient times, this city was known as the Queen of the Silver Depths. It was the fairest of our realms and we grieved its fall most sorely.'

Jules stared down at the massive walls. 'How could it have fallen? All the armies of all the kings of men could be stood off in these mountains. Those fields could feed the population of Quenelles.'

Gotrek shook his head and stared down into the city as intensely as if he were staring back into elder days.

'In pride we built Eight Peaks, at the zenith of our ancient power. It was a wonder to the world; more beautiful than Everpeak, open to the sky. A sign of our wealth and power, strong beyond the measure of dwarfs or elves or men. We thought it would never fall and the mines it guarded would be ours forever.'

The Trollslayer spoke with a bitter, compelling passion that Felix had never heard in his voice before.

'What fools we were,' Gotrek said. 'What fools we were. In pride we built Eight Peaks, sure of our mastery of stone and the dark beneath the world. Yet even as we built the city, the seeds of its doom were planted.'

'What happened?' Felix asked.

'Our quarrel with the elves began; we scourged them from the forests and drove them from the lands. After that who were we to trade with? Commerce between our races had been the source of much wealth, tainted though it was. Worse, the cost in lives was more grievous than the cost to our merchants. The finest warriors of three generations fell in that bitter struggle.'

'Still, your folk now controlled all the land between the Worlds Edge Mountains and the Great Sea,' Zauberlich said with a pedant's smugness. 'So claims Ipsen in his book *Wars of the Ancients*.'

The acid of Gotrek's laughter could have corroded steel. 'Did we? I doubt it. While we had warred with our faithless allies, the dark gathered its strength. We were weary of war when the black mountains belched forth their clouds of ash. The sky was overcast and the sun hid its face. Our crops died and our cattle sickened. Our people had returned to the safety of their cities; and from the very heart of our realm, from the place we imagined ourselves strongest, our foes burst forth.'

He stopped speaking and in the silence Felix imagined he heard the caw of some distant bird.

'From tunnels far below any we had ever dug, our enemies struck into the core of our fortresses. Through mines that had been the source of our wealth poured armies of goblins and rat-like skaven and things far, far worse.'

'What did your people do?' Felix asked.

Gotrek spread his arms wide and looked into their faces. 'What could we do? We took up our weapons and went again to war. And a terrible war it was. Our battles with the elves had taken place under the sky, through field and forest. The new war was fought in cramped spaces in the long dark, with dreadful weapons and a ferocity beyond your imagining. Shafts were collapsed, corridors scoured with fire-throwers, pits flooded. Our foes responded with poison gas and vile sorcery and the summoning of daemons. Beneath where we now stand we fought with every resource we could muster, with all our weapons and all the courage desperation brings. We fought and we lost. Step by step we were driven from our homes.'

Felix looked down at the placid city. It seemed impossible that what Gotrek described could ever have happened and yet there was something in the Trollslayer's voice that compelled belief. Felix imagined the desperate struggle of those long-ago dwarfs, their fear and bewilderment as they were pushed from the place they had believed was theirs. He pictured them fighting their doomed struggle with more than human tenacity.

'In the end it became obvious that we could not hold the city, and so the tombs of our kings and the treasure-vaults were sealed and hidden by cunning devices. We abandoned this place to our foes.'

Gotrek glared at them. 'Since then we have not been so foolish as to believe any place is secure from the dark.'

All through the long day, as they approached the wall, Felix realised how much the old structures had suffered. What, from a distance, gave the impression of ageless strength and sureness became, on closer inspection, just as ruined as the road upon which they travelled.

The curtain wall blocking the road into the valley was four times as tall as a man and passed between steep, sheer cliffs. Signs of neglect were obvious. Moss grew between the cracks of the great stone blocks. The stones were pitted by rain channels and mottled with yellow lichen. Some were blackened as if by great swathes of fire. A huge section of the wall had tumbled away.

His companions were silent. The desolation cast a pall over the whole party. Felix felt depressed and on edge. It was as if the spirits of antiquity watched over them, brooding over the tumbled remains of ancient grandeur. Felix's hand never strayed far from the hilt of his sword.

The cracked valves of the ancient gate had been wedged open. Someone had made a half-hearted attempt to clear the sign of the hammer and crown over eight peaks carved into the stone. Already the lichen was growing back into place.

'Someone has been here recently,' Jules said, studying the gates closely.

'I can see how you earned your reputation as a scout,' Gotrek said sarcastically.

'Stay where you are,' boomed out an unfamiliar voice. 'Unless you want to be filled with crossbow bolts.'

Felix looked up at the parapet. He saw the helmeted heads of a dozen dwarfs looking down through the battlements. Each pointed a loaded crossbow at them.

'Welcome to Karak Eight Peaks,' their grey-bearded leader said. 'I hope you have good reason for trespassing on the domain of Prince Belegar.'

Under grey-white clouds they marched through the city. It was like a scene from after the day of judgement when the forces of Chaos returned to claim the world. Houses had tumbled and fallen into the streets. A fusty, rotten smell came from many of the buildings. Evil-looking ravens cawed from the remains of old chimneys. Clouds of more of the gaunt, black birds soared above them.

The score of dwarf warriors accompanying them were constantly on the alert. They scanned the doorways as if expecting ambush at any moment. Their crossbows were loaded and ready. They gave every impression of being in the middle of a battlefield.

Once they halted. The leader gestured for silence. Everyone stood listening. Felix thought he heard a scuttling sound but wasn't sure. He strained his eyes against the early evening gloom but could see no sign of trouble. The company leader gestured. Two of the armoured dwarfs moved cautiously towards the corner and glanced around. The rest formed into a square. After a long, tense moment, the scouts gave the all-clear.

The quiet was broken by Gotrek's laughter. 'Scared of a few goblins?' he asked.

The leader glared at him. 'There are worse things than goblins abroad on nights like this. Be assured of it,' he said.

Gotrek ran his thumb down the blade of his axe, drawing blood. 'Bring them on,' he roared. 'Bring them on!'

His shout echoed once through the ruins before it was muffled and swallowed by the ominous silence. After that even Gotrek was quiet.

The city was larger than Felix had imagined; perhaps even the size of Altdorf, greatest city of the Empire. Most of it was ruined, devastated by ancient wars.

'Surely your own people did not cause all this damage. Some of it seems quite recent,' Felix said.

'Gobbos,' Gotrek replied. 'It is the curse of their kind that when they have no one else to fight they fight amongst themselves. Doubtless after the city fell it was divided up among various warlords. Sure as elvish treachery, they'd fall out over the division of spoils.'

'In addition there have been many attempts to recapture the city by my kin and men from the Border Princes. There's still a motherlode of silver down there.'

He spat. 'No attempt to hold the city has ever lasted. The dark has lain here. Where once the darkness has been can never again be truly free of it.'

They entered an area where the buildings had been partially repaired and which now seemed abandoned again. An attempt to re-colonise the city had failed, defeated by the sheer immensity of the ruins. Under the walls of the great keep, the dwarfs seemed more relaxed. Their leader grumbled the occasional order to keep alert.

'Remember Svensson,' he said. 'He and his men were killed while on the path to the great gate.'

The dwarfs immediately reverted to their stern watchfulness. Felix kept his hand near his sword.

'This is not a healthy place,' Jules Gascoigne whispered.

As soon as they were through it, the keep's great gate closed with a crash like the fall of towers.

The hall was bleak, its walls covered by threadbare tapestries. It was lit by strange glowing gems that hung from a chandelier in the ceiling. On a throne of carved ivory inlaid with gold sat an aged dwarf, flanked by lines of mailed, blue-tunicked warriors. He gazed down with rheumy eyes, his glance flickering from the Trollslayer to the humans. Beside the ancient, a purple-robed female dwarf watched the whole proceeding with a strange, serene intensity. From a chain around her neck dangled an iron-bound book.

Felix thought he detected strain in the faces of these dwarfs. Perhaps dwelling in the haunted and run-down city had sapped their morale. Or perhaps it was something more; they seemed constantly to look over their shoulders. They started at the slightest noise.

'State your business, strangers,' the aged dwarf said in a deep, proud, brittle voice. 'Why have you come here?'

Gotrek glared back at him loutishly. 'I am Gotrek Gurnisson, once of Everpeak. I have come to hunt troll in the dark beneath the world. The manling Felix Jaeger is my blood-brother, a poet and rememberer. Do you seek to deny me my right?'

As he said the final sentence Gotrek hefted his axe. The dwarfish soldiers raised their hammers.

The ancient laughed. 'No, Gotrek Gurnisson, I do not. Your path is an honourable one and I see no reason to stand in it. Although your choice of brethren is an ill one.'

The dwarf soldiers began to mutter amongst themselves. Felix felt baffled. It seemed as if Gotrek had broken some incomprehensible taboo.

'There is precedent,' the robed dwarfess said. The sounds of consternation stopped. Felix expected her to speak further, to expand on what she had said but she did not. It seemed enough to the dwarfs that she had spoken.

'You both may pass, Gotrek, son of Gurni. Be careful of the gate you choose into the dark and beware, lest your courage fail you.' His voice held no hint of concern, only bitterness and secret shame.

Gotrek nodded curtly to the dwarf lord and withdrew to the back of the hall. Felix gave his best courtly bow, then followed the Trollslayer.

'State your business, strangers,' the ruler continued. Aldred went down on one knee before the throne and the others followed suit.

'I have come on a matter concerning my faith and an ancient pledge of aid between your folk and mine. My tale is a complex one and may take some time to tell.'

The dwarf laughed nastily. Once again Felix sensed some secret knowledge that ate at the aged dwarf-lord. 'Speak on. We are rich in no other commodity but time. We can spend it freely.'

'Thank you. Am I correct in assuming that you are the same Prince Belegar who led the expedition to reclaim this city from the greenskins twenty years ago?'

Belegar nodded. 'You are correct.'

'Your guide was a dwarfish prospector called Faragrim, who found many secret ways back into the city below the Eight Peaks.'

Once again the old dwarf nodded. Felix and Gotrek exchanged looks. It had been Faragrim who had told Gotrek about the troll-guarded treasure beneath the mountains.

'Your expedition was accompanied by a young knight of my order, a companion of Faragrim in his adventuring days. His name was Raphael.'

'He was a true man and a foe of our enemies,' Belegar said. 'He went with Faragrim on his last expedition into the depths and never returned. When Faragrim refused to seek him, I dispatched runners but they could not find his body.'

'It is good to know you honoured him, although I am downcast to learn that the blade which he bore was lost. It was a weapon of power and of great importance to my order.'

'You are not the first who has come here to retrieve it,' the dwarf woman said.

Aldred smiled. 'Nevertheless I have sworn a vow to return the sword, Karaghul, to the chapter house of my order. I have cause to believe I will succeed.'

Belegar raised an eyebrow.

'Before setting out on my quest I fasted for two weeks and scourged my body with purgatives and the lash. On Sigmarzeit last I was favoured with a vision. My lord appeared before me. He said he looked with favour on my mission and that the time was near for the enchanted blade to be drawn again.

'Further – he told me that I would be aided in my quest by one of our ancient brethren. I interpret this as meaning a dwarf, for so are your people always referred to in the Unfinished Book. I beseech you, noble Belegar, do not oppose my mission. My brother Raphael honoured the ancient vow of our faith, never to refuse aid to a dwarf, when he fell. It would be a mark of respect to allow me to recover his blade.'

'Well spoken, man,' Belegar said.

Felix could see he was moved, as dwarfs invariably were by talk of honour and ancient oaths. Still there was a hint of bright malice in Belegar's gaze when he spoke again.

'I grant your petition. May you have more luck than your predecessors.'

Aldred rose and bowed. 'Could you provide us with a guide?'

Once again Belegar laughed and there was a strange, wild quality to his mirth. He cackled nastily. 'I am sure Gotrek Gurnisson would be prepared to aid a quest so similar to his own.'

Belegar rose from the throne and the robed woman moved to support him. He turned to hobble from the room. As he reached the rear exit of the chamber he turned and said, 'You are dismissed!'

From the window of the tower where the dwarfs had housed them, Felix looked down at the cobbled street. Outside snow had begun to fall in feathery flakes. Behind him the others argued quietly.

'I don't like it,' Zauberlich said. 'Who knows how vast an area lies below ground? We could search from now till the end of the world and not find the blade. I had thought the dwarfs guarded the blade.'

'We must trust to faith,' Aldred replied, calmly and implacably. 'Sigmar wishes the blade to be found. We must trust that he will guide our hands to it.'

An undertow of hysteria was evident in Zauberlich's voice. 'Aldred, if Sigmar wished the blade returned, why did he not place it in the hands of the three of your brethren who preceded us?'

'Who am I to guess the Blessed Lord's motives? Perhaps the time was not right. Perhaps this is a test of our faith. I will not be found lacking. You do not have to accompany us if you do not wish.'

Off amongst the ruins, Felix spied a cold green light. The sight of it filled him with dread. He beckoned for Jules to come over and take a look. By the time the Bretonnian arrived at the window there was nothing to be seen. The scout gave him a quizzical look.

Embarrassed, Felix looked back at the discussion. Am I going mad, he wondered? He tried to dismiss the green light from his mind.

'Herr Gurnisson, what do you think?' Zauberlich asked. He turned to beseech the Trollslayer.

'I will be going down into the dark anyway,' Gotrek said. 'It does not bother me what you do. Settle your own quarrels.'

'We have already lost three-quarters of the people we set out with,' Zauberlich said, glancing from Jules Gascoigne to Aldred. 'What purpose would it serve to throw away our own lives?'

'What purpose would it serve to give up, save to make our comrades' sacrifice meaningless?' replied the Templar. 'If we give up now their deaths will be in vain. They believed that we should find Karaghul. They gave their lives willingly enough.'

The Templar's fanaticism made Felix uneasy. Aldred talked too casually of men laying down their lives. Yet he also had a calm certainty that gave his words a compelling urgency. Felix knew warriors would follow such a man.

'You took the same oath as everyone else, Johann. If you wish to foreswear yourself now so be it, but the consequences will be on your own eternal soul.'

Felix felt a wry sympathy for the mage. He himself had sworn to follow Gotrek while drunk, in a warm tavern in a civilised city, after the dwarf had saved his life. Peril had seemed remote then. He shook his head. It was easy to swear such oaths when you had no idea of the consequences. It was another to keep them when the path led to dismal places like Karak Eight Peaks.

Felix heard approaching footsteps. There was a knock and the door creaked open to reveal the female dwarf who had stood beside Belegar in the throne room. 'I've come to warn you,' she said in her low, pleasant voice.

'Warn us about what?' Gotrek enquired curtly.

'There are terrible things loose in the depths. Why do you think we live in such fear?'

'I think you had better come in,' the Trollslayer said.

'I am Magda Freyadotter. I keep the Book of Remembering at the temple of Valaya. I speak with the voice of Valaya, so you will know that what I say is truth.'

'Accepted,' Gotrek Gurnisson said. 'Speak truth then.'

'In the darkness, unquiet spirits walk.' She paused and looked around at them. Her gaze rested on the Trollslayer and lingered.

'When first we came here we numbered five hundred, with a few mannish allies. The only perils we faced were the orcs and their followers. We cleared this keep and parts of the upper city as a prelude to reclaiming our ancient mines.'

'We made forays into the depths, seeking the vaults of our ancestors, knowing that if we could find them word would spread among the kinsfolk and more would flock here.'

Felix understood the strategy. Word of a treasure find would lure more dwarfs here. He felt a little guilty. It had brought himself and Gotrek.

'We sent expeditions into the depths in search of the old places. Things had changed from the ancient plans we memorised as children. Tunnels had collapsed, ways were blocked, foul new passages dug by orcs inter-connected with our own.'

'Did the dwarf Faragrim lead any of these expeditions?' Gotrek asked.

'Yes, he did,' Magda replied.

Gotrek looked at Felix. 'That much of what he claimed is true then,' the Trollslayer said.

'Faragrim was bold and sought deeper and further than all others. What did he tell you?'

Gotrek studied his feet. 'That he had encountered the mightiest troll he had ever seen – and fled.'

Dwarfs are not good at lying, thought Felix. It seemed impossible that the priestess could not tell he was hiding something. But Magda didn't appear to notice anything amiss.

Felix thought back to the night in distant Nuln, in the Eight Peaks tavern, when the awesomely drunken Faragrim had poured out his tale to Gotrek. The dwarfs had been so inebriated that they had even seemed to forget there was a human present and had talked excitedly in a mixture of Reikspiel and Khazalid. At the time Felix assumed the dwarfs were only attempting to outdo each other in telling tall tales. Now he wasn't sure.

'So that is what terrified him – we thought it was the ghosts,' Magda said. 'One day he returned from the depths. His beard had turned pure white. He spoke no word but simply departed.'

'You spoke of terrors in the depths,' Zauberlich interrupted.

'Yes. Our patrols below soon spoke of encountering ghosts of ancient kin. The spirits howled and wailed and begged us to free them from the bondage of Chaos. Soon our early successes were reversed. What dwarf can bear the sight of kinsmen torn from the bosom of the ancestral spirits? Our forces lost heart. Prince Belegar led a mighty expedition to seek the source of the evil. His force was destroyed by the lurkers in the depths. Only he and a few trusted retainers returned. They have never spoken of what they found. Most of our surviving folk departed to their homelands. Now barely a hundred of us are left to hold this keep.'

The colour drained from Gotrek's face. Felix had never seen the Trollslayer display such fear before. Gotrek could face any living creature boldly but this talk of ghosts had leeched away his courage. The worship of their ancestors must be very important to his people, thought Felix with sudden insight.

'I have warned you now,' the priestess said. 'Do you still wish to go below?'

Gotrek stared off into the fire. All eyes in the room were on him. Felix felt that if Gotrek abandoned his quest then even Aldred might give up. The Templar seemed convinced that the Trollslayer was the dwarf of his prophecy.

Gotrek clutched his axe so tightly that his knuckles were white. He took a deep breath. He seemed to will himself to speak. 'Man or spirit, alive or dead, I fear it not,' he said quietly in a voice that was not convincing. 'I will go below. There is a troll I have to meet.'

'Well spoken,' Magda said. 'I will lead you to the entrance of the realm below.'

Gotrek bowed. 'It would be an honour.'

'Tomorrow then,' she said and rose to go.

Gotrek held the door for her. After she had departed he slumped into the chair. He laid down his axe and clutched at the armrests as if he feared he would fall over. He looked very afraid.

A huge doorway gaped in the side of the mountain. Above it, rising from the rock, was a great window cut through the rock. The window was roofed with red-slate tiles, many of which had fallen in. It was as if a keep had been built and then sunk beneath the earth so that only the tallest parts protruded above the ground.

'This is the Silvergate,' Magda said. 'The Silverway runs to the Upper Granaries and the Long Stairs. I believe the Way is clear. After that, beware!'

'Thank you,' Felix said. Gotrek nodded to the priestess. Aldred, Jules and Zauberlich bowed. The men looked very sombre.

They began to check their lanterns and the supply of oil. They had plenty of provisions. All their weapons were oiled and ready.

Magda reached within the sleeves of her robe. She produced a tube of parchment and handed it to Gotrek. He unrolled it, gave it a quick glance and bowed from the waist until his crest touched the ground.

'May Grungni, Grimnir and Valaya watch over you all,' Magda said and made a peculiar sign of benediction over them.

'The blessing of Sigmar upon you and your clan,' Aldred Fellblade replied.

'Let's go,' Gotrek Gurnisson said. They hefted their gear and passed under the arch. Felix could see that it was marked with old dwarf runes that time had yet to erode.

As they passed below, they were cast into shadow and chill. Felix could not repress a shiver.

Light from the great window illuminated the way down into the gloom. Felix marvelled at the precision of dwarfish engineering. At the brow of the slope he turned and looked back. The priestess and her escort stood there. He waved to her and she raised an arm in farewell. Then they began the downward way and the lands above were hidden from view. Felix wondered if any of them would ever see daylight again.

* * *

'What did the priestess give you, Herr Gurnisson?' Johann Zauberlich asked. Gotrek thrust the document into the magician's hand.

'It's a map of the city copied from the master-map in the temple of Valaya the Rememberer. It covers all the ground that Prince Belegar's expeditions explored.'

By the light of the glowing crystals overhead the sorcerer inspected it, then scratched his head. Felix looked over his shoulder and saw only a scrawl of tiny runes connected with lines in different coloured ink. Some of the lines were thick, others were thin and some were dotted.

'It is like no map I've ever seen,' the mage said. 'I can't make head nor tail of it.'

Gotrek's lips curled into a sneer. 'I would be surprised if you could. It's written in the rune-code of the Engineers' Guild.'

'We are in your hands, Herr Gurnisson, and Sigmar's,' the Templar said. 'Lead on.'

Felix tried to count the number of steps he took but gave up at eight hundred and sixty-two. He had noted the passages leading off the Silverway and began to have some idea of the scale of the dwarf city. It was like the floating mountains of ice that mariners reported in the Sea of Claws. Nine-tenths of it was below the surface. The scale overwhelmed any of the works of man Felix had ever seen. It was a humbling experience.

The way passed many openings in the wall. Some were still partially bricked up. The brickwork looked recent. Something had chipped through it using very crude tools. There was a smell of rot in the air.

'Grain silos,' Gotrek explained. 'Used to feed the city in winter. Looks like gobbos have been at Belegar's stores though.'

'If there are any greenskins near, they will soon taste my steel,' Aldred Fellblade said.

Jules and Felix exchanged worried looks. They were not as keen as the Templar and the Trollslayer to get to grips with whatever dwelled down here.

Felix lost track of time but he guessed it was half an hour before they left the Silverway and entered a hallway as large as the Koenigspark in Altdorf. It was lit by great slots in the ceiling. Motes of dust danced in a dozen columns of light taller than the towers of Nuln. The sound of their steps echoed, disturbing strange shadowy, fluttering things that lurked by the ceiling.

'The Square of Merscha,' Gotrek said, in a voice that held a note of wonder. He gazed into the hall with a strange mixture of hatred and pride. 'Where Queen Hilga's personal troops turned and stood off an army of goblins a hundred times their number. They gave the Queen and many of the citizens time to escape. Never did I expect to lay eyes on it. Walk carefully. Every stone has been sanctified with the blood of heroes.'

Felix looked at the Trollslayer. He saw a new person. Since they had entered the city Gotrek had changed. He stood taller, prouder. He no longer cast furtive looks around and muttered to himself. For the first time since Felix had met him the dwarf seemed at ease. It's as if he's come home, thought Felix.

Now it's we men who are out of place, he realised, suddenly aware of the immense weight of stone which lay between him and the sun. He had to fight against the fear that the whole mountain, held in place only by the fragile craft of those ancient dwarfs, would fall in on him, burying him forever. He sensed the closeness of the dark, of the old places beneath the mountains that had never known daylight. The seeds of terror were planted in his heart.

He looked out across a square larger than any structure he had ever known and he knew that he could not cross it. Absurdly, far below the surface of the earth, he began to feel agoraphobic. He did not want to pass below that vaulted ceiling for fear that the artificial sky would fall. He felt dizzy and his breathing came in ragged gasps.

A reassuring hand fell on his shoulder. Felix looked down to see that Gotrek stood by him. Slowly the urge to run back up the Silverway passed and he felt some semblance of calm return. He looked back out over the square of Merscha, overcome with awe.

'Truly, yours are a mighty people, Gotrek Gurnisson,' he said.

Gotrek looked up at him and there was sadness in his eyes. 'Aye, manling, that we were, but the craft which created this hall is beyond us now. We no longer have the number of masons needed to build it.'

Gotrek turned and looked back into the hall, then, he shook his head. 'Ach, manling, you have some inkling of how far we have fallen. The days of our glory are behind us. Once we created all of this. Now we huddle in a few shrunken cities and wait for the end of the world. The day of the dwarf has gone, never to return. We crawl like maggots through the work of elder days and the glory of what once was ours mocks us.'

He gestured out at the hall with his axe, as if he wished he could demolish it with one blow.

'This is what we must measure ourselves against!' he bellowed. The startled men looked at him. The echoes mocked him. Somewhere among them Felix Jaeger thought he heard the sounds of furtive movement. When he looked towards the noise he could almost swear he saw winking amber eyes receding slowly into the dark.

As they progressed, the stone of the undercity took on a peculiar greenish tinge. They moved away from the lit hall into shadowy gloom, faintly illuminated by dim, flickering glowjewels. Occasionally Felix heard a tapping sound. Gotrek stopped and placed a hand against the wall. Out of curiosity Felix did the same. He felt a small, distant vibration pass through the stone.

Gotrek glanced at him. 'Gobbo wall-drumming,' he said. 'They know we're here. Best speed our pace to confuse any scouts.'

Felix nodded. The walls glittered like jade. He could see fat, red-eyed rats move away from the light. Their hides were pure black. Gotrek cursed and stamped at the nearest one but it evaded him.

He shook his head. 'Even here, so close to the surface, we see the taint of Chaos. It must be worse down below.'

They came to a stairway running down into the dark. Great columns had fallen away. Piles of masonry lay in a heap. The stair itself seemed crumbled. They disturbed a nest of flitterwings. The small bats took off like scraps of shadow and fluttered about. Uneasily Felix wondered how safe the stairs were.

They descended through galleries marked with the signs of orcish despoliation. Rats scuttled ahead of them from nests under broken stonework. Gotrek gestured for them to halt and stood sniffing the air. From behind them Felix thought he heard the sound of footfalls further up the stairs.

'I smell gobbos,' the Trollslayer said.

'They are behind us, I think,' Jules said.

'All around us,' Gotrek said. 'This place has been used as an orc road for many years.'

'What shall we do?' Felix asked, exchanging worried looks with Zauberlich.

'Push on,' Gotrek said, consulting the map. 'We're going the way we want to anyway.'

Felix glanced back. He suspected they were being herded into a trap. Things look bad, he thought. Our way back to the surface has been cut off already, unless Gotrek knows another route. The Trollslayer's expression assured him that Gotrek was giving no thought to such matters.

The dwarf glanced around worriedly as if expecting to see a ghost.

Their pursuers' footsteps came ever closer. From ahead, echoing through the galleries, they heard a bellow that was deeper and louder than any orc's.

'What was that?' Zauberlich asked.

'Something big,' Aldred said quietly.

Gotrek ran his thumb along the blade of his axe until a jewel of blood glistened on its blade.

'Good,' he said.

'It must be close,' Felix said nervously, wondering if his face was as ashen as the sorcerer's and the scout's.

'Hard to say,' Gotrek said. 'These tunnels distort sound. Amplify it too. It could be miles away.'

The roar came again and there was the sound of running feet, as if goblins scuttled to obey an order.

'It's closer this time,' Felix said.

'Calm yourself, manling. As I said, it's probably miles away.'

It stood waiting in the next hall, near the foot of the long stairway. They passed under an archway carved with skeletal daemons' heads and saw the beast: an immense ogre, half again as tall as and four times the bulk of Aldred. A crest of hair emerged from its scaly scalp. Like Gotrek's crest, it was dyed. Unlike Gotrek's, it was patterned in alternating black and white bands. A huge spiked arm-guard, its fist a long, wicked scythe, covered its right arm. An enormous spiked ball and chain dangled from its left hand. It looked like it could demolish a castle wall.

The creature grinned, revealing spiked metal teeth. Behind it hunched a company of goblins, green skins glistening. They clutched metal shields emblazoned with the emblem of the skull. Scabs and boils and pock marks marked their leering, ugly faces. Some wore spiked collars round their necks. Some had metal rings pinching the flesh of their torsos. Their eyes were red and without pupils. Felix wondered if this was another sign of the taint of Chaos.

He glanced around. To his right was tumbled masonry. It looked as if old dwarfish stonework had been brought down and cleared to make way for newer and cruder carvings. Iron chains were set in the wall near him. To the left was a great chimney carved so that the fireplace was the maw of a gaping daemonic head. Brownish blood stained the stone. Have we stumbled into some goblin temple? wondered Felix. Just what we need, a man-hungry ogre and a horde of goblin fanatics. Well, he consoled himself, at least things can't get any worse.

He felt a tap on his shoulder and turned to look back up the stairs. Down them poured another company of goblins led by a burly orc. In its left hand it clutched a scimitar and in its right it held a standard whose banner depicted a stylised representation of the tusked maw of the cursed moon, Morrslieb. Stuck on the top of the standard was an embalmed human head. Behind the bearer came more goblins armed with maces and spears and axes.

Felix looked at Jules. The Bretonnian gave a shrug. What a terrible place to die, thought Felix. For a long moment the three groups exchanged glares. There was a brief peaceful silence.

'For Sigmar!' Aldred cried, raising his great sword high and charging down the stairs with surprising nimbleness for a man garbed in plate.

'Tanugh aruk!' Gotrek bellowed, as he followed. Overhead, the glowjewels seemed to glow briefly brighter. 'Kill the goblin-scum!'

Felix brought his blade to the guard position. Beside him, Jules Gascoigne stood at the ready. The standard bearer glared at them but made no move to come closer. Felix was reluctant to attack the goblins up the staircase. It was a stand-off.

Behind him Felix heard the clash of weapons and the screaming of battle-cries. The foul orc reek was strong in his nostrils. Iron-shod feet rang on the stairs behind him. He whirled just in time to parry a mace swung with considerable force by a greenskin warrior. The force of the impact jarred up his arm.

He gritted his teeth and stabbed out. His blade cut a glittering arc through the gloom. The goblin skipped back and Felix almost overbalanced. He moved as rapidly as he could down the stairs, hampered by the uncertain footing.

'Jules, hold the stair!' he shouted.

'Anything for a friend.'

Felix pushed on after the goblin. He had some trouble pursuing his nimble foe over the broken ground. The gobbo stuck out its tongue and yelled tauntingly. Overcome by stinging anger, Felix rushed forward and tripped. He fell to his knees and rolled, feeling pain where he had skinned flesh from his knees. Something scurried over him. Tiny claws scratched him. I've disturbed a nest of rats, he thought. For a moment he was disorientated. As he struggled to his feet he caught sight of the tableau of the battle.

Gotrek chopped into the chest of his foe. Mail exploded outward from the goblin's breast where the huge axe impacted. Aldred Fellblade charged within the sweep of the ogre's huge wrecking ball and stabbed upward through the creature's stomach. Felix saw his blade protruding from the ogre's back. Goblins swept past Felix to get at the dwarf, their ancient foe. Just out of reach of the struggle, Johann Zauberlich produced a scroll and chanted a spell. A ball of fire appeared in his left hand. Black rats swarmed everywhere. Shadowy flitterwings swooped agitatedly.

Felix fought for balance. His gaze shifted to Jules Gascoigne on the stair, bravely standing off a number of heavily armed foes. He had already killed one but more entered behind another standard bearer.

Pain surged through Felix as a club smashed into his shoulder. Flashing silver stars filled his field of vision. He fell on his face, letting go of his sword. Above him stood the goblin, its club raised, a leer of triumph on its face. Move, damn you, Felix told his protesting limbs as the club whistled down. It loomed like the trunk of a falling tree, moving with painful slowness to the man's panic-honed senses.

At the last moment Felix rolled to one side and the club hit rock with a loud crack. Felix twisted and lashed out with one foot, sending the goblin flying. Desperately Felix fumbled for his sword, feeling huge relief as his fingers closed over its hilt.

He dived forward, impaling the goblin before it could rise. The thing cursed as it died. Suddenly a titanic flash blinded Felix. He reeled back, covering his eyes as an inferno erupted before him. Hot air washed over his face. The air stank of sulphur. I'm dead, dead and in hell, he thought. Then understanding filled his mind. Zauberlich had unleashed his fireball.

He looked around. Gotrek and Aldred were clearing a path through the demoralised goblins. Behind them rushed the scout and the wizard. Jules grabbed Felix by the arm.

'Come on!' he yelled. 'We've got to get out while they're confused.'

They ran on down the long corridor. From behind them came the sounds of continuing conflict.

'What's happening back there?' he yelled.

'Different gobbo tribes,' Gotrek cackled. 'With any luck they'll slit each other's throats while they fight to see who gets to eat us.'

Felix stared down into the chasm. Stars glittered in its depths. Aldred and Gotrek glanced back down the corridor. Jules prowled out onto the corroded metal bridge. The sorcerer, Zauberlich, leaned against a cast-iron gargoyle, panting heavily.

'I fear I was not intended for the adventurous life,' he gasped. 'My studies did not prepare me for all this strenuous exercise.'

Felix smiled. The sorcerer reminded him of his old professors. The only conflicts they ever fought were struggles over the correct interpretation of the finer points of classical poetry. He was surprised and ashamed to find himself so contemptuous of those old men. Once it had been his ambition to become just like them. Had the adventuring life changed him so much?

Zauberlich was inspecting the gargoyle curiously. Felix revised his opinion of the wizard. He only superficially resembled those elderly academics. None of them would have survived the road to Karak Eight Peaks. The fact Zauberlich's sorcery was so adroit spoke volumes about the man's determination and intelligence. Magic was no art for a weakling or a coward. It held its own hidden perils. Curiosity overcame Felix. He suddenly wanted to ask the sorcerer how he had become involved with the Templar.

'I think we must have lost the goblins,' Aldred shouted. He and Gotrek clumped towards the others. The questions Felix had been about to ask Zauberlich died on his lips.

As they crossed the bridge Felix sensed he would never get another chance to ask them.

They gazed down the long, dark corridor. For the first time the light from the glowjewels had failed. Felix had grown so accustomed to the dim greenish light that its sudden failure shocked him. It felt as if the sun had set in the middle of the day. Gotrek pushed on into the dark, seemingly oblivious to the lack of light. Felix wondered at how well the dwarf could see.

'Best break out the lanterns,' Gotrek said, shaking his head. 'The lights have been vandalised. Damn gobbos. Those jewels should have glowed forever but they just couldn't leave them alone. They can never be replaced now. The art has been lost.'

Jules prepared a lantern. Zauberlich lit it with a word. Felix watched them, feeling redundant until he heard Gotrek moan behind him. Felix turned to look.

Far down the corridor there was a faint greenishly glowing figure. It was an old bearded dwarf. Light poured from it and through it. It looked transparent, as tangible as a soap bubble. The ghostly figure wailed, a thin, reedy sound, and advanced towards Gotrek, arms outstretched. The Trollslayer stood transfixed. Terror overwhelmed Felix. He recognised the quality of the light. He had seen it before, on the mountainside and in the city above.

'Sigmar protect us,' Aldred muttered. Felix heard the Templar's blade ring as he pulled it from the scabbard.

Felix felt his hair stir as the ancient dwarf advanced. The air seemed cold. His flesh tingled. The figure's lips moved and Felix thought he heard a gibbering far-way voice.

Gotrek stirred and moved forward, axe held up as if to ward off a blow.

The ghost redoubled its frantic pleas. Gotrek shook his head as if he did not understand. The ghostly dwarf hurried to meet him, looking over its shoulder as if pursued by a distant, invisible enemy. Horror filled Felix. The ghost was falling apart. It was like a mist before a strong wind, parts of it just peeled away and vanished. Before Gotrek could reach it, it vanished entirely. As it went Felix heard a distant, despairing wail. It was the cry of a damned soul, vanishing into hell. As Gotrek returned Felix saw the stunned look on his face. The Trollslayer looked appalled and bewildered. A tear gleamed beneath his single eye.

They hurried down the darkened corridor. Even after they reached an area where the glowjewels gleamed again, no one seemed in a hurry to extinguish the lantern. For long hours thereafter the Trollslayer never said a word.

Felix was tempted to drink from a spring flowing into the ancient carved trough. He bent over the greenly glowing water when he felt strong hands knot his hair and pull him back.

'Are you mad, manling? Can you not see the water is tainted?'

Felix was about to object when Zauberlich looked down into the water and inspected the greenish glowing flecks. 'Warpstone?' he said, in a surprised tone.

Felix felt his blood run cold. All he had ever heard about the dread substance was that it was the pure essence of Chaos, sought after by evil alchemists in certain grisly tales.

'What did you say, mage?' Gotrek asked curtly.

'I think this could be warpstone. It has the greenish luminescence that certain scholarly tomes attribute to that unpleasant substance. If there is even a trace of warpstone in the water that might account for the high level of mutation hereabouts.'

'There are old tales of the skaven poisoning the wells,' Gotrek said. 'Would even they be so foul as to do it with warpstone?'

'I have heard it said that the skaven subsist on warpstone. Perhaps this served a dual purpose. It gave them sustenance and made the wells unusable by their foes.'

'You seem very knowledgeable in the ways of Chaos, Herr Zauberlich,' Felix said suspiciously.

'The doctor and I have hunted our share of witches,' Aldred Fellblade said. 'It's a task that obliges you to learn much strange lore. Are you implying any companion of mine could be tainted by such foulness as trafficking with the Ruinous Powers?'

Felix shook his head. He had no wish to cross a warrior as deadly as the Templar. 'My apologies for my unjust suspicions.'

Gotrek guffawed. 'No need to apologise. Eternal vigilance is necessary in all foes of the dark.'

Aldred nodded in agreement. It seemed the Trollslayer had found a kindred spirit.

'We had best move on,' Jules Gascoigne said, looking nervously back the way they had come.

'Best stick to drinking what we brought with us, manling,' Gotrek said as they moved off.

'What is this stuff?' Felix asked nervously. His question echoed off into the distance. Jules shone lantern light into the dark caverns. Giant, misshapen fungi cast long shadows against the white mould-covered walls. Spores drifted in the lantern's beam.

'Once we cultivated mushrooms for food,' Gotrek muttered. 'Now it looks like another victim of mutation.'

The Trollslayer marched into the room. His boots left prints in the sodden carpet of mould. Somewhere in the distance Felix thought he heard running water.

Foot-long splinters of whiteness detached themselves from the walls, enlarging as they came. They hurtled towards the startled adventurers. Gotrek chopped into one with his axe. It gave with a squishing sound. More and more splinters left the wall like a blizzard of giant snowflakes. Felix found himself surrounded by soft bloated bodies and fluttering wings.

'Moths!' Zauberlich shouted. 'They're moths! They're trying to get at the light. Kill it.'

It went dark. Felix had a last vision of Gotrek, his body covered in the giant insects, then he stood within a whirling snowstorm of wingbeats, his flesh crawling at the moths' touch. Then all was silence.

'Back out. Slowly,' Gotrek whispered, revulsion showing in every syllable. 'We'll find another way.'

* * *

Felix paused to look back down the long hallway, wishing that the glowjewels were brighter. He was convinced he had heard something. He reached out and touched the smooth cold stone of the wall. A faint vibration thrummed through it. Wall drumming.

He strained his eyes. In the distance he could make out vague shapes. One carried a huge banner with what seemed to be a human head on top. He pulled his sword from its scabbard.

'Looks like they found us again,' he said. There was no reply. The others had disappeared round the corner. Felix realised that they had kept marching when he paused. He ran to catch up.

Filled with dread, Felix opened one eye. He emerged from slumber. It was Gotrek's watch but he thought he heard eerie voices. He looked around the small chamber and his hair stood on end. His heartbeat sounded loud and fast in his ears and he thought that he was going to faint dead away. All power had fled from his limbs.

The strange green glow lit the area. It washed over the Trollslayer's haggard face, making him look like some ghastly zombie. Gotrek's shadow loomed huge and menacing on the wall. The entity from which the light emerged was on its knees in front of the Trollslayer, arms outstretched beseechingly. It was the ghost of some ancient dwarfish woman.

It was insubstantial and yet it had the presence of ages, as if it were a manifestation of the elder times made real. Its garb was regal and the face had once possessed authority. Its cheeks seemed sunken and the flesh seemed to have sloughed away and was pock-marked, like it was riddled with maggots. The eyes that lurked under cave-like brows were pools of shadow in which witch-lights burned. It was as if the ghost were being eaten away by some unworldly disease, a cancer of the spirit.

The aspect of the thing filled Felix with terror, and its suffering only intensified his awful fear. It hinted that there were things waiting beyond the grave from which even death was not an escape, dark powers which could seize a spirit and torment it. Felix had always been afraid of death but now he was aware that there were worse things. He felt himself on the edge of sanity, hoping for the release from this terrible knowledge that madness might bring.

Nearby Jules Gascoigne whimpered like a child enmeshed in a nightmare. Felix tried to avert his eyes from the scene being played out before him but could not; a compulsion lay on him. He was horribly fascinated by the confrontation.

Gotrek raised his axe and put it between him and the troubled spirit. Was it his imagination, Felix wondered, or did the runes that inlaid the huge blade glow with internal fire?

'Begone, abomination,' the Trollslayer rasped in a voice barely above a whisper. 'Depart, I am yet among the living.'

The thing laughed. Felix realised that it made no sound. He heard its voice within his head.

'Aid us, Gotrek, son of Gurni. Free us. Our tombs are desecrated and a terrible warping power rests within our halls.' The spirit wavered and seemed about to dissipate like mist. With a visible effort it maintained its form.

Gotrek tried to speak but could not. The great muscles in his neck stood out, a vein throbbed at his temple.

'We have committed no crime,' said the spirit in a voice that held ages of suffering and loneliness. 'We had departed to join our ancestral spirits when we were brought back by the desecration of our resting place. We were wrenched from eternal peace.'

'How can this be?' Gotrek asked, in a voice that held both wonder and terror. 'What can tear a dwarf from the bosom of the ancestors?'

'What else has the strength to upset the order of the universe, Trollslayer? What else but Chaos?'

'I am but a single warrior. I cannot stand against the Dark Powers.'

'No need. Cleanse our tomb of that which lies there and we will be free. Will you do this, son of Gurni? If you do not we shall not be able to rejoin our kin. We will gutter and vanish like candle-flames in a storm. Even now we fade. Only a few of us are left.'

Gotrek looked at the anguished spirit. Felix saw reverence and pity flicker across his face. 'If it is within my power, I will free you.'

A smile passed across the spirit's ravaged face. 'Others we have asked, including our descendant Belegar. They were too fearful to aid us. In you I find no flaw.'

Gotrek bowed, and the spirit reached out a glowing hand to touch his brow. It seemed to Felix as if sudden insight flooded into the Trollslayer. The ghost dwindled and faded as if receding to a vast distance. Soon it was gone.

Felix looked around at the others. They were all awake and gazing at the dwarf in astonishment. Aldred looked at the Trollslayer with something akin to reverence. Gotrek hefted his axe.

'We have work to do,' he said in a voice like stone grinding against stone.

* * *

Like a man in a trance, Gotrek Gurnisson led them down the long corridors in the depths below the old city. They passed into an area of wide, low tunnels lined by defaced statues.

'Greenskins have been here,' Felix observed to Jules Gascoigne next to him.

'Yes, but not so recently, my friend. Those statues were not broken recently. See the lichen growing on the breaks. I like not the way it glows.'

'There is something evil about this place. I can sense it,' Zauberlich said, tugging at the sleeve of his robe and peering around nervously. 'There is an oppressive presence in the air.'

Felix wondered whether he could sense it too or whether he was simply receptive to his companion's forebodings. They turned a corner and moved along a way lined by mighty stone arches. Strange runic patterns were carved between each archway.

'I hope your friend is not leading us into some trap laid by the Dark Powers,' the sorcerer whispered quietly.

Felix shook his head. He was convinced of the spirit's sincerity. But then again, he thought, what do I know of such things? He was so far beyond the realms of his normal experience that all he could do was trust to the flow of events. He gave a fatalistic shrug. Things were beyond his control.

'I hate to bother you, but our pursuers have returned,' Jules said. 'Why have they not attacked? Are they afraid of this area?'

Felix looked back towards the redly glowing eyes of the greenskin company. He made out the hideous standard.

'Whatever they were afraid of, they seem to have plucked up courage now.'

'Maybe they've been herding us here for sacrifice,' Zauberlich said.

'Yes, look on the bright side,' Jules said.

Eventually they passed over another chasm-bridge and into a further corridor lined with decorative arches. Gotrek halted at a particular huge open archway. He shook his head like a man waking up from a dream.

Felix studied the arch. He saw a great groove made for a barrier to slide along. On closer reflection, Felix thought that if the opening were closed it would be invisible, blending into the pattern of the way along which they passed. Felix lit his lantern, driving back the shadowy darkness.

Beyond the opening lay an enormous vault, lined on either side with great sarcophagi carved to resemble the figures of sleeping dwarfs of noble aspect. To the right were males, to the left females. Some of the tops of the stone coffins had been removed. In the centre of the chamber was a huge pile of gold and old banners mingled with yellowing, cracked bones. From the middle of the heap protruded the hilt of a sword, carved in the shape of a dragon.

Felix was reminded of the cairn they had built for Aldred's followers on the road to the city. A hideous stench came through the arch and made Felix want to gag.

'Look at all that gold,' the Bretonnian said. 'Why has no greenskin taken it?'

'Something protects it,' Felix said. A question crossed his mind. 'Gotrek, this is one of the hidden tombs of your people you spoke of, isn't it?'

The dwarf nodded.

'Why is it open? Surely it would have been sealed?'

Gotrek scratched his head and stood deep in thought for a moment. 'Faragrim opened it,' he said angrily. 'He was once an engineer. He would know the rune-codes. Ghosts only started appearing after he left the city. He abandoned the tomb to despoliation. He knew what would happen.'

Felix agreed. The prospector was greedy and would certainly have ransacked the tomb if he could. He had found the lost horde of Karak Eight Peaks. If that was true, then was the other part of his story true as well? Had he fled from the troll? Did he leave the Templar, Raphael, to fight the monster alone?

While they talked, Aldred entered the tomb and walked over to the treasure heap. He turned and Felix saw the look of triumph on the Templar's lean fanatic face.

No, get out, Felix wanted to shout.

'I have found it,' he cried. 'The lost blade, Karaghul. I have found it! Sigmar be praised!'

From behind the heap of treasure a huge horn-headed shadow loomed, twice as tall as Aldred, broader than it was tall. Before Felix had time to shout a warning, it tore off the Templar's head with one sweep of a mighty claw. Gore splashed the ancient stones. The thing lurched forward, pushing through the mound of treasure with irresistible power.

Felix had heard tales of trolls, and perhaps once this had been one. Now it was hideously changed. It had a gnarly hide covered in huge, dripping tumours and three enormously muscular arms, one of which terminated in a pincer claw. Growing from its left shoulder, like some obscene fruit, was a small, babyish head which glared at them with wise malign eyes. It chittered horridly in a language that Felix could not recognise. Pus dribbled down its chest from a huge leech mouth set below its neck.

The bestial head roared and the echoes reverberated through the long hall. Felix saw an amulet of glowing greenish-black stone hanging from a chain around its neck. Warpstone, he thought, placed there deliberately.

He did not blame Faragrim for running. Or Belegar. He stood paralysed by fear and indecision. From beside him he heard the sound of Zauberlich being sick. He knew warpstone had created this thing. He thought of what Gotrek had said about the long-ago war beneath the mountains.

Someone had been so insane as to chain warpstone to the troll, to deliberately induce mutation. Perhaps it was the rat-men, the skaven that Gotrek had mentioned. The troll had been down here since the war, a festering abomination changing and growing far from the light of day. Perhaps it was the desecration of their tombs by this warpstone-spawned monstrosity which had caused the dwarf ghosts to walk? Or perhaps it was the presence here of the warpstone, of pure undiluted Chaos.

The thoughts reverberated through his mind as the roar of the mad thing echoed through the vault. He stood unable to move, transfixed by horror, as the monster came ever closer. Its stench filled his nostrils. He heard the hideous sucking of its leech mouth. It loomed out of the gloom, its pain-wracked, bestial face hellishly underlit by its glowing amulet.

The troll was going to reach him and slay him and he could not make himself do anything about it. He would welcome death, having confronted this manifestation of the insanity of the universe.

Gotrek Gurnisson leapt forward between him and the monster, hunched in his fighting crouch. His shadow swept out behind him in the green light so that he stood at the head of a pool of darkness, axe held high, runes shimmering with witchfire.

The Chaos-troll halted and peered down at him, as if astonished by the temerity of this small creature.

Gotrek glared up at it and spat.

'Time to die, filth,' he said and lashed out with his axe, opening up a terrible wound in the thing's chest. The creature continued to stand there, studying the wound in fascination. Gotrek struck again at its ankle, attempting to hamstring it. Once again he drew green blood. The creature did not fall.

With blinding speed its huge pincer descended, clicking shut. It would have snipped off the Trollslayer's head if he had not ducked. The troll bellowed angrily and lashed out with a taloned hand. Somehow Gotrek managed to deflect it with a sweep of his axe. He avoided the hail of blows that rained down on him.

The Trollslayer and the troll circled warily, each looking for an opening. Felix noted to his horror that the wounds Gotrek had inflicted were knitting together again. As they did so they made a sound like slobbering mouths closing.

Jules Gascoigne rushed forward and stabbed the troll with his sword. The blade pierced the creature's leg and remained there. As the Bretonnian struggled to pull it out, the monster hit him with a back-handed sweep that sent him flying. Felix heard ribs break and the scout's head hit the wall with a terrible crack. Jules lay still in a spreading pool of his own blood.

While the creature was distracted, Gotrek leapt in and struck it a glancing blow to the shoulder. He sheared off the babyish head. It rolled over to near Felix's feet and lay screaming. Felix managed to put down the lantern, draw his sword and bring the blade down, chopping the head in two. It began to rejoin. He continued to hack until his sword was notched, blunted then broken from hitting the stone floor. He still could not kill the thing.

'Stand back,' he heard Zauberlich say. He leapt to one side. The air suddenly blazed. It stank of sulphur and burned meat. The tiny head was silent and did not heal.

As if sensing a new threat, the troll leapt past Gotrek and seized the sorcerer in its giant pincer. Felix saw the look of terror on Zauberlich's face as he was raised on high. Zauberlich struggled to cast a spell. A fireball erupted, and the shadows fled briefly. The monster screamed. With a reflexive action it closed the claw, chopping the mage in two.

The wizard fell to the ground, clothes blazing. Black despair overwhelmed Felix. Zauberlich could have hurt the thing, burned it with purifying fire. Now he was dead. Gotrek could only hack futilely at the troll but its Chaos-enhanced powers of healing made it all but invulnerable. They were doomed.

Felix's shoulders slumped. There was nothing he could do. The others had died in vain. Their quest had failed. The ghosts of the dwarfish rulers would continue to wander in torment. It was all futile.

He looked at Gotrek's sweating face. Soon the Trollslayer would tire and be unable to dodge the creature's blows. The dwarf knew this too, but he did not give up. A renewed determination filled Felix. He would not give up either. He looked over at the burning body of the sorcerer.

The fire had become more intense, more so than if simply the man's clothes were burning. Realisation dawned. Zauberlich had been carrying spare flasks of lantern oil in his coat. Swiftly Felix stripped off his pack and fumbled for an oil-flask.

'Keep it busy!' he yelled to Gotrek, unstoppering the ceramic bottle. Gotrek uttered a foul dwarfish curse. Felix flicked the flask at the monstrosity, showering it with glistening oil. The thing ignored him as it sought to pin down Gotrek. The dwarf redoubled his efforts, chopping away like a madman. Felix emptied a second flask over it and then a third, always keeping to the monster's blind side.

'Whatever you're going to do, manling, do it quickly!' the Trollslayer yelled.

Felix ran over and picked up his lantern. Sigmar, guide my hand, he prayed as he threw the lamp at the creature. The lantern impacted on its back, shattering and spreading burning oil. It ignited the fuel with which Felix had already doused the creature.

The troll screamed shrilly. It reeled back. And now, when Gotrek's axe fell, the wounds did not heal. The dwarf drove the blazing troll back to the pile of gold. It stumbled and fell.

Gotrek raised his axe high above his head. 'In the name of my ancestors!' the Trollslayer howled. 'Die!'

His axe came down like a thunderbolt, severing the creature's foul head. The troll died and did not rise again.

Gingerly Gotrek picked up the warpstone amulet with the broken shard of Felix's sword. Holding the thing at arm's length, he took it outside to throw into the abyss.

Felix sat, drained of all emotion, on top of one of the sarcophagi. Once more it comes to this, he thought, sitting among ruin and corpses after terrible conflict.

He heard Gotrek's running footsteps coming closer. Panting, the dwarf entered the chamber.

'The gobbos come, manling,' he said.

'How many?' Felix asked.

Gotrek shook his head tiredly. 'Too many. At least I have disposed of that tainted thing. I can die happy here amid the tombs of my ancestors.'

Felix went over and picked up the dragon-hilted sword. 'I would have liked to have returned this to Aldred's people,' he said. 'It would give some meaning to all this death.'

Gotrek shrugged. He glanced to the door. The archway was filled with green-skinned marauders, advancing behind their grinning moon banners. Felix slid the Sigmarite sword smoothly from its sheath. A thrilling musical note sang out. The runes along its blade blazed brightly. For a second the goblins hesitated.

Gotrek looked over at Felix and grinned, revealing his missing teeth. 'This is going to be a truly heroic death, manling. My only regret is that none of my people will ever get to hear of it.'

Felix looked back at the oncoming horde, positioned himself so that his back was to a sarcophagus. 'You don't know how sorry I am about that,' he said grimly, making a few trial swipes with the blade. It felt good, light and well-balanced, as if it had been made for his hand alone. He was surprised to find he was no longer afraid. He had gone beyond fear.

The standard bearer halted and turned to harangue his troops. None of them seemed to be anxious to be the first to meet the Trollslayer's axe or the glowing runesword.

'Get on with it!' Gotrek bellowed. 'My axe thirsts.'

The goblins roared. The leader turned and gestured for them to advance. They surged forwards as irresistibly as the tide. This is it, thought Felix, steeling himself, preparing to lash out, to take as many foes as he could into the lands of the dead with him.

'Goodbye, Gotrek,' he said and stopped. The goblins had halted and stood, looking panic-stricken. What's going on? Felix wondered. Cold green light streamed over his shoulders. He looked back and hesitated at the sight. The chamber was filled with ranks of regal dwarfish spirits. They seemed fierce and terrible as they advanced.

The goblin standard bearer tried to rally his troops but the ghostly dwarf lords reached him and touched his heart. His face drained of colour, and he fell, clutching his breast. The spirits surged into the goblins. Spectral axes flickered. Greenskin warriors fell, no mark upon their bodies. A hideous keening filled the air, a thin reedy imitation of dwarfish war-cries. The remaining tribesmen turned and fled. The ghostly warriors swept after them.

Felix and Gotrek stood in the empty vault, surrounded by the towering sarcophagi. Slowly the air in front of them coalesced. Tendrils of greenish light drifted back through the entrance, took dwarfish shape. The spirits looked different.

The ghost who had spoken to Gotrek earlier stood there. She had changed somehow – as if a terrible burden had been lifted from her ethereal heart. She regarded Gotrek.

'The ancient enemies are gone. We could not leave them to despoil our tombs now that you have cleansed them. We are in your debt.'

'You have robbed me of a mighty death,' Gotrek said almost sourly.

'It was not your destiny to fall here this day. Your doom is far greater and its time is approaching.'

Gotrek looked quizzically at the ancient queen.

'I may say no more. Farewell, Gotrek, son of Gurni. We wish you well. You shall be remembered.'

The ghosts seemed to coalesce into one cold green flame that glowed like a star in the darkness. The light changed from green to warm gold and then became brighter than the sun. Felix averted his eyes and still was dazzled. When his sight returned he looked upon the tombs. The place was empty except for himself and Gotrek. The dwarf frowned thoughtfully. For a long moment a strange expression gleamed in his one good eye, then he turned and looked upon the treasure.

Felix could almost read his mind. He was considering taking the wealth, desecrating the tomb himself. Felix held his breath. After long minutes, Gotrek shrugged and turn away.

'What about the others? Shouldn't we lay them to rest?' Felix asked.

'Leave them,' Gotrek said over his shoulder as he strode away. 'They lie among the mighty. Their bodies are safe.'

They stepped through the arch, and Gotrek paused to touch the runes according to the ancient pattern. The tomb was sealed. Then they made their way up through the old darkness towards the light of day.

THE MARK OF SLAANESH

'As money was in short supply, we decided to return to the Empire and seek gainful employment of some sort. Our return from Karak Eight Peaks was in no sense an easy one. The weather was atrocious, the land bleak and empty, and my companion's mood even more savagely unreasonable than usual. Where we had come south in relative comfort and safety as part as a large, escorted caravan, our journey northwards was accomplished with no aid from anyone, and no means of transport other than our own legs. The people of the few villages we entered were understandably wary of two armed strangers, and the provisions they sold us were expensive and not of the best quality.

'It was perhaps unreasonable of me to expect any sort of respite from this seemingly unending chain of terrible adventures when we returned to my homeland, for it seems the Trollslayer and I were destined to forever be encountering minions of the Dark Powers. Even so, I would scarcely have credited the extent of their sinister influence, had I not witnessed it with my own eyes. Furthermore, I was destined to wrestle with the forces of darkness alone for a period, for an odd fate befell the Slayer...'

— From *My Travels with Gotrek, Vol. II*, by Herr Felix Jaeger
(Altdorf Press, 2505)

'By Grungni! What was that?' Gotrek Gurnisson bellowed, turning and raising his enormous axe defiantly.

As the second slingstone whizzed by his ear, Felix Jaeger ducked reflexively. The sharp stone splintered against the flat face of the nearest boulder, leaving a scar in its grey-green lichen covering. Felix threw himself behind the rock and glanced back with scared blue eyes, looking for the source of the attack.

The valley at the foot of Blackfire Pass was quiet. He could see only rolling tree-girt hills rising to the towering mountains beyond. He silently cursed the great rocks that filled the valley, blocking his line of sight.

Suddenly movement caught Felix's eye. From high on his right, a tide of misshapen bodies teemed down the slope, dislodging a small avalanche of gravel and scree as they came. Shouting like maniacs, bestial figures leapt downhill towards him with the agility of mountain goats. The long, deep note of a hunting horn cut the air.

'No, not now,' Felix heard a voice whimper, and to his surprise, recognised it as his own. He was so close to civilisation. The long hard trail from Karak Eight Peaks to the southern borders of the Empire was nearly complete. He had fought goblins in the hills near the old dwarf city and skirmished with bandits prowling the ruins of Fort von Diehl. He had endured the cold heights of Blackfire Pass, shivered in the snow-covered trails leading to the old dwarfish routes under the peaks. He shuddered when he recalled the shadowy things that had lurked there and scuttled on many legs through the darkness. He had come so far and endured so much – and now he was within the borders of his homeland and still he was being attacked. It just wasn't fair.

'Stop cringing, manling,' boomed Gotrek's deep coarse voice. 'It's only a bunch of gods-forsaken mutants!'

Felix threw the dwarf a nervous glance, wishing he shared the Slayer's confidence. Gotrek stood boldly on the open valley floor, disdaining the cover of the rocks, his great axe balanced negligently in one mighty fist. He seemed completely unworried by the hail of sling-stones raising plumes of dust around his feet. An insane grin twisted his brutal features: unholy joy burned in his one good eye. Gotrek looked as if he was enjoying himself.

It was typical of the dwarf. The only time he seemed happy was in the thick of the fray. He had smiled when the goblins ambushed them, relishing the prospect of violence. He had actually laughed when the bat-winged monstrosities with a thirst for human blood and the faces of beautiful children had descended on them at the ford on Thunder River. The worse things looked, the happier the Slayer became. He welcomed the prospect of his own death.

Gotrek thumped his chest with his fist and roared: 'Come on! My axe thirsts. She has not drunk blood in weeks.' A slingstone whistled past his head. The Slayer did not even blink.

Felix thought Gotrek's squat, massive frame presented much less of a target than his own tall, spare form. He shook his head; his berserker comrade probably didn't take such things into consideration. Felix gave his attention back to their assailants.

They were indeed mutants; humans tainted and changed by the strange magic of Chaos. Some said this was because they had a trace of warpstone in their blood. Others said that they had been secret followers of the Dark, their appearance altered over time to reflect their inner corruption. A few sages maintained that they were innocent victims of a process of change overtaking all humanity. At that exact moment Felix did not care. He had a secret horror of the foul creatures which grew greater each time he encountered them. Fear filled him and provided fuel for murderous rage.

They were close enough now for Felix to distinguish individual members of the pack. The leader was a grossly fat giant with a belt of daggers stretched across his bulging belly. He was so obese that his body appeared to be made from dough. Great rippling folds of flesh bobbed up and down with each lumbering step. Felix was surprised that the earth did not shake under his monstrous tread. The leader's babyish grin revealed a multitude of chins and almost as many missing teeth as Gotrek's answering snarl. In one chubby hand he brandished a massive stone-headed mace.

Flanking the leader was a lanky creature taller than Felix. Its ear was notched from a vicious bite taken in some internecine squabble. A long thin strip of hair drooped like rotting lichen from atop its narrow, near-shaven skull. It howled a challenge as it raised its rusty scimitar high above its pointed head. Felix could see its incisors were fanged like a wolf's.

An elk-headed giant paused and raised a great curling horn to its lips. Another thunderous blast rang out across the blasted landscape, then the mutant let the instrument swing once more from the chain round its neck and continued to charge, head forward, antlers down.

Behind them came a ragged horde of surly-faced followers. Each bore some stigmata of Chaos. Many were marked with weeping sores. Some had the faces of wolves, goats or rams. Some had claws or tentacles or great bludgeons of bone instead of hands. One had its head protruding from its belly, its neck a mere stump. Another had a hump on its back in which a great mouth glistened. The mutants brandished a motley assortment of crude weapons; spears and clubs and notched scimitars scavenged from forgotten battlefields. Felix estimated the number of attackers as somewhere above ten and below twenty. They were not odds that he relished, even though he knew the Slayer's awesome physical prowess.

Felix cursed silently. They had been so close to escaping from the Black Mountains to the lowlands of the Empire's southernmost province. From the brow of the pass the previous evening Felix had made out the lights of a town of men. He had been looking forward that very evening to a warm bed and a cold jack of ale. Now fear coursed through his veins like ice-water; he must fight for his life again. Involuntarily he let out a little moan.

'Get up, manling. Time for some bloodletting,' Gotrek said. He spat a huge gob of phlegm onto the rocks at his feet and ran his left hand through the massive red crest of hair that rose above his shaven tattooed skull. His nose chain tinkled gently; a strange counterpoint to his mad rumbling laughter.

With a sigh of resignation Felix threw his faded red cloak back over his broad right shoulder, freeing his sword arm for action, then he drew his longsword from its ornate scabbard. Reddened dwarfish glyphs blazed along the length of the blade.

The mutants were close enough now for him to hear the soft slap of their unshod feet and individual words in their harsh guttural voices. He could see greenish veins in yellowish, jaundiced-looking eyes and count individual studs on the rims of leather shields. Reluctantly he raised himself from behind his cover and prepared to fight.

He glanced at Gotrek, and to his horror saw a slingstone impact on the dwarf's massive skull. He heard the crack and saw the Slayer sway. Fear filled the man; if the dwarf went down he knew he had no chance of survival against the swarm of assailants. Gotrek reeled but remained upright, then reached up and felt the wound that the shot had left. A look of surprise passed over his face when he saw the blood on his fingertips. It was replaced in an instant by an expression of terrible wrath. The Trollslayer let out a mighty roar and charged towards the cackling mutants.

His ferocious attack took them off guard. The fat leader only just managed to duck back as the Slayer's axe whistled past his head. His agility surprised Felix. With a terrible crunch the axe tore through the chest of the thin lieutenant and then lopped off the head of a second attacker. The backstroke tore through a leather shield and sliced away an attached tentacle.

Without giving them time to recover, Gotrek tore among them like a deadly whirlwind. The fat leader scuttled well out of the reach of the lethal axe as he gibbered orders to his followers. The mutants began to surround the dwarf, kept at bay only by the great figure of eight described by Gotrek's battleaxe.

Felix launched himself into the fray. The magical blade he had taken from the dead Templar Aldred felt as light as a willow wand in his hand. It almost seemed to sing as he clove a mutant's skull from behind. The runes glowed bright as it cut away the top of the head as easily as a butcher's cleaver cutting a joint of beef. The mutant's brains fountained messily forth. Felix grimaced as the jelly splattered his face. He forced himself to ignore his disgust and keep on hacking at another mutant. A shock passed up his arm as he rammed his blade underneath a mottled ribcage into the creature's rotten heart. He saw the mutant's eyes go wide with fear and pain. Its wart-covered face wore a look of horror and it whimpered what might have been a prayer or a curse to its dark god as it died.

Felix's hand felt wet and sticky now, and he adjusted his grip on the sword to keep it from slipping as he was attacked simultaneously from either side. He ducked the swing of a spike-headed mace and lashed to the right. His blade cut the cheek of a barrel-like mutant, severing the earflap of its leather cap. The helm slid forward on the creature's face, covering its eyes and momentarily obscuring its vision. Felix kicked it in the stomach with the toe of his heavy Reikland leather boot and it doubled over, foolishly presenting its neck for the stroke that beheaded it.

Pain flashed through Felix's shoulder as the mace caught him a glancing blow. He snarled and turned, driven to frenzy by the agony. The accursed one caught the look on his face and froze for a heartbeat.

It raised its weapon in what might have been a gesture of surrender. Felix shook his head and chopped the creature's wrist. Blood sprayed all over him. The mutant screamed and writhed, clutching at the stump of its arm, trying to staunch the flow of blood.

Everything seemed to be happening in slow motion now. Felix turned and saw Gotrek swaying like a drunk man. At his feet lay a pile of mangled bodies. Felix followed the slow sweep of the immense axe as it caught another victim, driving the ruined body back into two cringing foes. They fell in a tangled mass. His axe rose and fell in a bloody arc as Gotrek proceeded to hack them to pieces.

All vestiges of humanity and restraint fell away in a wave of blood-lust and fear and hatred. Felix leapt among the survivors. Swift as an adder's tongue the enchanted blade flickered, the runes growing brighter as it drank more blood. Felix barely felt the jar of impact or heard the howls of pain and anguish. Now he was a machine, intended only to kill. He gave no more thought to preserving his own life. Only to the slaughter of his foes.

As swiftly as it had begun it was over. The mutants were in retreat, fleeing as fast as their legs would carry them, their fat leader fleetest of all. Felix watched them go. As the last of them was beyond reach, he turned howling with frustrated murder-lust and began to hack up the bodies.

After a while, he began to shake. Noticing, as if for the first time, the terrible ruin which he and the Slayer had wrought, he bent double and proceeded to be sick.

The clear cold water of the stream ran red with blood. Felix watched it swirl away and wondered at how numb he felt. It was as if the chill of the water had seeped into his veins. He realised how much he had changed since he had fallen into Gotrek's company and he was not sure he liked it.

He remembered how he had felt after he had killed the student, Krassner, the very first to fall to his sword. That had been an accident during what had been supposed to be a boyish duel on the field behind Altdorf University. The blade had slipped and the man had died. Felix could remember the look of disbelief on his face and his own feeling of horror and tearful remorse. He had ended a life and he had felt guilty.

But that had happened to someone else, a long lifetime ago. Since then, since he had sworn to follow the Slayer on his doomed quest for a heroic death, he had killed and killed again. With each death, he had felt a little less remorse; with each death, contemplating the next one had become a little easier. The nightmares that had once afflicted him came no more to trouble him. The sense of waste and revulsion had left him. It was as if Gotrek's madness had infected him and he no longer cared.

Once, as a student, he had studied the works of the great philosopher, Neustadt. He had argued in his great opus De Re Munde that all living creatures had souls. That even mutants were sentient beings capable of love and worthy of life. But Felix knew he had obliterated them without a second thought. They had been enemies, trying to kill him, and he could feel no real remorse at their deaths, only a wonder at his own lack of feeling. He asked himself where the change had occurred and could find no answer.

Was this why he loathed the altered ones so? Was it because he could see the changes happening in himself and feared that they might have an external manifestation? He found his new coldness sufficiently monstrous to justify it. How could it have happened and when?

Was it after Kirsten, the first great love of his life, died at the hands of Manfred von Diehl? He did not think so. The process was more subtle; a strange alchemy had transmuted him down all the long leagues of his wandering. A new Felix had been born here in these harsh lands by the world's edge, a product of the bleakness of the place and the hardness of his life and too many deaths seen from too close.

He looked across at Gotrek. The Slayer sat hunched on a flat plate of rock that jutted out into the stream. A piece torn from Felix's cloak was wrapped round his head, the red wool blotched a deep black by the dwarf's dried blood.

Will I become like that eventually, Felix wondered, hopeless and mad and doomed, dying slowly from a hundred small wounds, seeking only a magnificent death to redeem myself? The thought did not disturb him – and that in itself was disturbing.

What had he lost and where had he lost it, Felix wondered, listening to the rush of the water as if it carried some coded answer. Gotrek raised his head and slowly surveyed the scene. Felix noticed that the patch had come away from his ruined left eye, revealing the scarred and empty socket.

Felix himself looked at the tangle of leafless trees and thorny scrub that surrounded them and the cold grey of the rock. He felt dwarfed by the dismal titanic shadow of the great snow-capped mountains and asked himself how they had come to this gods-forsaken spot so many miles from his home. For a second it seemed he was lost in the endless immensity of the Old World, that he had no point of reference in time or space, that he and the Slayer were alone in a dead world, ghosts drifting in eternity bound by a chain of circumstance forged in Hell.

Gotrek glanced over at him. Felix returned his gaze with a feeling almost of hatred. He waited silently for the dwarf to start gloating about his pointless futile victory.

'What happened here?' the Slayer asked.

Felix looked at him open-mouthed.

The land was greener now that they had left the mountains. The warm gold sun cast a mellow late afternoon light over the long coarse grass of the plains. Here and there patches of purple heather bloomed. Red flowers blossomed among the grass. Ahead of them, perhaps a league away, a great grey castle loomed above the flatlands, perched on the craggy hilltop. Beneath it Felix could see the walls of a town. Smoke drifted lazily skyward from its many chimneys.

He felt more relaxed. He estimated that they would reach the town before nightfall. Saliva filled his mouth at the thought of some cooked beef and fresh-baked bread. He was heartily sick of the dwarfish field rations they had picked up in the Border Princes; hard biscuits and strips of dried meat. Tonight, for the first time in weeks, he could lie safe beneath a real roof and enjoy the company of his fellow men. He might even sup some ale before retiring to bed. Tension began to ease out of him. He felt his shoulders relax and became aware of just how keyed up he had been during the journey, straining constantly to spot any hidden threat the dangerous mountains might conceal.

He glanced worriedly back at Gotrek. The dwarf's face was pale and he often stopped to look around them with a look of blank confusion, as if he could not recall quite why they were there, or what they were doing. The blow to the head had apparently taken a lot out of the Slayer. Felix could not tell why. In his time, he had seen Gotrek take a lot worse punishment.

'Are you all right?' he asked, half expecting the dwarf to snarl at him.

'Yes. Yes, I am,' Gotrek said, but his voice was soft and reminded Felix of an old man's.

After the cool, clear air of the mountains and the scented freshness of the plains, the town of Fredericksburg came as a shock to the senses. From a distance the high narrow houses with their red-tiled roofs and white-washed walls had seemed clean and orderly. But even the dim light of the setting sun could not conceal the cracks in the brickwork and the holes in the slate roofs.

The narrow, maze-like streets were piled high with garbage. Starving dogs wandered from pile of rotting vegetation to heap of ordure, defecating liberally as they went. The cobbled streets smelled of urine and mould and fat dripping into cooking fires. Felix covered his mouth with his hand and gagged. He noticed the red blotch of a fresh flea-bite just above his knuckles. Civilisation at last, he thought ironically.

Vendors had set out lanterns to illuminate the market square. Loose women stood in pools of red light near the doorways of many houses. The business of the day was over, the atmosphere of the place changed as folk came to eat and be entertained. Storytellers gathered little circles round their charcoal braziers and competed with conjurers who made tiny dragons appear in puffs of smoke. A would-be prophet stood on a stool under the statue of the town's founder, the hero Frederick, and exhorted the crowd to return to the virtues of an earlier, simpler time.

People were everywhere, their lively movements dazzling Felix's eyes. Hawkers tugged at his sleeve offering lucky charms or trays of small, cinnamon-scented pastries. Children kicked an inflated pig's bladder in the mouth of a narrow alley and ignored their mothers' cries to come inside out of the dark. Over their heads, ragged washing sagged on lines stretched from window to window across the narrow alleyways. Carts now empty of produce rumbled towards the draymen's yards, clattering over ruts and dislodging loose cobbles.

Felix stopped by an old woman's food stand and bought a piece of stringy chicken she had cooked over a charcoal burner. Warm juices filled his mouth as he gobbled it down. He stood for a moment trying to centre himself in the riot of colour and smell and noise.

Looking at the swarm of people he felt dislocated. Men-at-arms in the tabards of the local burgermeisters moved among the crowd. Richly dressed youths eyed the street-girls and exchanged quips with their bodyguards. Outside the entrance to the Temple of Shallya, beggars raised their scabrous stumps to passing merchants who kept their eyes carefully focused on the middle distance and their hands on their purses. Ruddy-faced peasants rolled drunkenly through the streets gazing in wonder at buildings more than a single storey high. Old women, heads wrapped in tattered scarves, stood on doorsteps and gossiped with their neighbours. Their wizened faces reminded Felix of sun-dried apples.

Fredericksburg was a mere hamlet compared to Altdorf, he told himself; there was no need to feel daunted. He had lived in the Imperial capital most of his life and never felt out of place. It was just that he had become used to the quiet and the solitude of the mountains. He was unused to feeling enclosed. Still, it should take him mere hours to adjust to being back among men.

Standing in the crowd he felt lonely, just one more face in a sea of faces. Listening to the babble of voices he heard no friendly words, just haggling over prices and coarse jokes. There was an energy here, the vitality of a thriving community, but he was not part of it. He was a stranger, a wanderer from the wilderness. He had little in common with these folk, who had probably never ventured more than a league from their homes in their lives. He was struck by how strange his life had become. He suddenly felt a tremendous longing to be at home, in the comfortable wood-panelled halls of his father's house. He rubbed the old duelling scar on his right cheek and cursed the day he had been expelled from university into a life of petty crime and political activism.

Gotrek wandered slowly through the marketplace, gazing stupidly at the stalls selling cloth and amulets and food, as if he did not quite understand what was going on. The Slayer's one good eye was wide and he seemed dazed. Disturbed by his comrade's behaviour, Felix took him by the shoulder and guided him towards the tavern door. A lazy-looking painted dragon beamed down at them from the sign above the door.

'Come on,' Felix said. 'Let's get a beer.'

Wolfgang Lammel pushed the struggling barmaid from his knee. In her attempt to resist his kiss, she had marred the high velvet collar of his jerkin with rouge from her cheeks.

'Begone, slut,' he told her in his most imperious voice. The blonde girl stared at him angrily, her face flushed beneath its inexpertly applied mask of powder and paint, annoyance distorting her peasant-pretty face.

'My name is Greta,' she said. 'Call me by my name.'

'I'll call you whatever I like, slattern. My father owns this tavern, and if you would keep the job you so recently acquired you'll keep a civil tongue in your head.'

She bit back a retort and hurried beyond his reach.

Wolfgang smirked. He knew she would be back. They always came back. Father's gold saw to that.

He brushed the rouge carefully from his clothing with one

well-manicured hand. Then he studied his bearded aquiline features in his small silver hand-mirror, checking to make sure none of the girl's make-up marred his soft white skin. He ignored the titters of his sycophants and the amused looks of the bully-boys he employed as his bodyguards. He could afford to. By virtue of his father's wealth he was the undisputed leader of the clique of fashionable young fops who patronised this tavern. From the corner of his eye he could see Ivan, the tavern keeper, scolding the girl. The man knew he could not afford to offend the owner's son and heir. He saw the girl bite back an angry rejoinder and begin to come back across.

'I'm sorry for marking your raiment,' she said in a soft voice. Wolfgang noticed the two points of colour on her otherwise pale cheeks. 'Please accept my most humble apologies.'

'Of course,' Wolfgang said. 'Since your clumsiness is exceeded only by your stupidity and your stupidity is exceeded only by your plainness, I must take pity on you. Your apology is accepted. I shall ask Ivan to deduct the cost of a new jerkin to replace the one you have ruined from your pay.'

The girl's mouth opened but she said nothing. Wolfgang knew that the jerkin cost more than the girl would earn in a month. She wanted to argue but knew it was futile. Ivan would have to side with him. Her shoulders slumped. Wolfgang noticed the way her bosom was revealed by her low-cut bodice and a thought occurred to him.

'Unless of course you would care to repay the debt in another way. Say... by visiting my chambers this evening at midnight.'

He thought at first she was going to refuse. She was young and fresh from the country and still held quaint ideas about virtue. But she was a thrall, one of the lowest classes of peasant owned by their liege lords. She had fled here to the town seeking escape from servitude. Losing her job would mean a choice between starving in the town or returning to her village and the wrath of her owner. If she lost her position here Wolfgang could see she never got another one. The realisation of her situation sank in and her head sank forward and she nodded once. The movement was so slight as to be almost imperceptible.

'Then get out of my sight until then,' Wolfgang said. The girl fled through the mass of his hangers-on. Tears ran down her face. Coarse jibes followed her.

Wolfgang allowed himself a sigh of satisfaction then downed another goblet of wine. The sweet, clove-scented liquid burned down his throat and filled his stomach with fire. He stared across at Heinrich

Kasterman. The fat, pock-faced young noble stopped stuffing his face long enough to give him an ingratiating grin.

'Nicely done, Wolfgang. Afore this night is out, you'll have introduced young Greta to the secret mysteries of our hidden lord. May I join you later? Take my turn?'

Wolfgang frowned as Heinrich made the secret sign of Slaanesh. Even his father's wealth might not protect him if it got around that he and several of his trusted comrades were followers of the Lord of Vice. He looked around to see if anyone had paid any attention to the fat fool's remark. No one seemed to have noticed. He relaxed. He told himself he was unjustifiably nervous. In truth he had become a little uneasy since the stigmata had appeared on his chest. The books assured him that it was a sign of special favour from their patron power, a mark that showed he was one of the Chosen. Even so, if a witch-hunter ever found out…

Perhaps it would be wisest to deal with the girl after he had his way with her this evening.

'Maybe. Well, that's tonight's amusement – but what shall we do till then to while away the long tedious hours in this dull, dull place?'

He could see no one worth tormenting. Most of the patrons were of similar status to himself, with their own bodyguards. In one corner sat an old man, plainly a sorcerer, leaning on a staff. The two corner booths were filled with cheery Sigmarite pilgrims. Only a fool would cross a mage and the pilgrims were too numerous to be easy prey. Torches flickered in the draught as the outer door opened.

'Or perhaps this evening's entertainment has just arrived.'

An oddly mismatched pair entered the Sleeping Dragon. One was a tall, gaunt blond-haired man, his bronzed and handsome face marred by a long scar. His clothing had obviously once been fine but was now stained and patched and tattered by long travel. From his dress he might have been a beggar but there was something about the way he carried himself, a nervous poise, that suggested he was not quite as down at heel as he seemed.

The other was a dwarf. A full head shorter than the man in spite of a great red crest of hair, he must nevertheless have outweighed the other by a considerable margin, judging from the great slabs of muscle which sheathed his big-boned frame. He carried an axe in one hand that a blacksmith might have strained to lift with two. His body was covered in strange tattoos. A crude leather patch covered one eye. Wolfgang had never seen his like before. The dwarf looked hurt and moved slowly. His gaze was blank and stupid and confused.

They moved to the bar and the man ordered two steins of beer. His accent and perfectly modulated High Reikspiel suggested an educated man. The dwarf set his axe down by the fire.

The man looked shocked, somehow, as if he had never seen this happen before.

The tavern had gone quiet, anticipating what Wolfgang and his cronies would say. Wolfgang knew that they had seen him bait newcomers before. He sighed; he supposed he had a reputation to maintain.

'Well. Well. Has the circus come to town?' he said loudly. To his annoyance, the two at the bar ignored him. 'You, oaf! I said: Has the circus come to town?'

The man in the faded red cloak turned to look at him. 'Would you be talking to me, sir?' he inquired in a soft, polite voice at odds with the level cold stare he directed at Wolfgang.

'Yes, you and your half-wit friend. Are you perhaps clowns with some travelling troupe?'

The blond man glanced at the dwarf, who continued to stare around in bemusement. 'No,' he said and turned back to his drink. The man had looked confused, as if he had expected a response from the dwarf and got none.

Nothing infuriated Wolfgang more than being ignored. 'I find you surly and rude. If you do not apologise, I think I shall have my men give you a lesson in good manners.'

The man at the bar moved his head slightly. 'I think if anyone here needs a lesson in politeness it is yourself, sir,' he said quietly.

The nervous laughter of the tavern's other patrons fanned the sparks of Wolfgang's anger. Heinrich licked his lips and slammed a clenched fist into one pudgy palm. Wolfgang nodded.

'Otto, Herman, Werner. I can no longer bear the odour of this tramp. Eject him from the tavern.'

Herman loomed over Wolfgang and rubbed one large knobbly knuckled fist through his unkempt beard. 'I don't know if this is wise, lord. Those two look tough,' he whispered.

Otto rubbed his shaven head, gazing at the dwarf. 'He has the tattoos of a Slayer. They're supposed to be vicious.'

'So are you, Otto. I don't keep you around for your wit and charm, you know. Deal with them.'

'I dunno,' Werner grumbled. 'It could be a mistake.'

'How much does my father pay you, Herman?' The big man shrugged in resignation and beckoned for the other bravos to follow him. Wolfgang saw him slip something hard and metallic over his fist. He leaned back in his chair to enjoy the show.

The blond man looked at the approaching bodyguards. 'We want no trouble with you, gentlemen.'

'Too late,' Herman said and swung. To Wolfgang's surprise, the stranger blocked Herman's punch with his forearm and then doubled the big man over with a blow to his ample paunch. The dwarf did nothing.

'Gotrek, help!' shouted the man, as the bodyguards raced towards him. The dwarf merely looked around bemusedly, flinching as Werner and Otto grabbed the young man's arms. He struggled viciously, sending Otto hopping with a kick to the shins and then butting Werner in the face. The burly bodyguard reeled back, clutching a profusely bleeding nose.

Karl and Pierre, two of Heinrich's hired louts, joined the fray. Karl caught the blond man on the back of the head with a chair and sent him sprawling. The others propped him up against the bar. Werner and Otto pinned him while Herman proceeded to take out his anger on the helpless stranger.

Heinrich winced every time a fist crunched into flesh. Wolfgang felt his own lips draw back in a snarl. He found himself panting with bloodlust. There was a real temptation to let Herman keep on hitting until the man was dead. He found his thoughts drifting to Greta. He was aroused. There was something about pain, particularly other people's, which appealed to him. Perhaps later he and the girl would follow this line of thought to its logical conclusion.

Eventually Wolfgang snapped out of it. The Reiklander was bruised and bloody when he signalled that he had seen enough and ordered him thrown into the street.

And still the dwarf did nothing.

Felix lay on a pile of garbage. Every part of his body ached. One of his back teeth felt loose. Something wet ran down the back of his neck. He hoped it wasn't his own blood. A plump black rat sat atop a mound of mouldy food and gazed at him ironically. Moonlight made its red eyes glitter like malevolent stars.

He tried moving his hand. He put it down to brace himself on earth, preparing for the monumental task of rising to his feet. Something squashed under his palm. He shook his head. Little silver lights flickered across his field of vision. The effort of movement was too much for him and he lay back on the midden-heap. It felt as soft as a warm bed beneath him.

He opened his eyes again. He must have fallen unconscious. He had no idea how long for. The greater moon was higher than it had been. Morrslieb, the lesser satellite, had joined it in the sky. Its eerie glow illumined the street fitfully. Mist had started to rise. In the distance a night-watchman's lamp cast a pool of sulphurous light. Felix heard the slow, painful movement of an old man's steps.

Someone helped him to his feet. A strand of long wavy hair tickled his face. Cheap perfume warred with the odour of refuse in his nostrils. It slowly filtered into Felix's brain that his benefactor was a woman. He began to slip and she struggled to support his weight.

'Herr Wolfgang is not a nice man.'

It was a peasant's voice, Felix decided. The words were pleasantly slurred and it had a husky, earthy quality. He looked up into a broad moon face. Large blue eyes gazed at him over high cheekbones.

'I'd never have guessed,' Felix said. Pain stabbed through his side as the tip of his scabbard caught in the garbage and the pommel of his sword connected with a tender patch of flesh under his ribs. 'My name is... ugh... Felix, by the way. Thank you for your assistance.'

'Greta. I work in the Sleeping Dragon. I couldn't leave you just lying in the street.'

'I think you should find a place with a better class of patron, Greta.'

'I'm starting to think that myself.' Her slightly-too-wide mouth smiled nervously at him. The moon's light caught the white of her powdered face, making it look pale and sickly. If it wasn't for the make-up she would be beautiful, he decided.

'I can't believe no one came out to see how you were,' she was saying.

The tavern door opened. Automatically Felix reached for his sword. The movement caused him to gasp with pain. He knew he would be helpless if the bravos set on him again.

Gotrek stood in the door, empty handed. His clothes were splashed with beer. His crest was flattened and bedraggled as if someone had given him a ducking in an ale cask. Felix glared at him. 'Thank you for your help, Gotrek.'

'Who is Gotrek?' the Slayer said. 'Are you talking to me?'

'Come on,' Greta said. 'We'd better get both of you to a healer I know. He's a little strange but he's got a soft spot for me.'

The office of the alchemist Lothar Kryptmann smelled of formaldehyde and incense and the weirdroot he chewed constantly. The walls were covered in racks containing jars of chemicals: powdered unicorn horn, quicksilver, quicklime and dried herbs. On a stand in a corner huddled a mangy, glittering-eyed vulture; it was bald in places with no feathers on one wing. It took Felix some time to realise it was stuffed. On the heavy oak desk, amid a pile of papers scrawled in a crabbed illegible hand, was a massive bottle containing the preserved head of a goat-horned beastman. A mortar and pestle served as an impromptu paperweight to stop the notes floating away in the draught from the lazily shuttered windows.

Torches flickered smokily in niches and sent shadows scuttling into the cold recesses of the room. Leather bound volumes titled in fading gold leaf displayed the names of the great natural philosophers. Many were stuffed untidily into bookshelves which had bent dangerously under their weight. Wax from a taper set in a porcelain saucer dripped onto the topmost volume. In the grate a small heap of lit coals crackled. Felix saw some half-consumed sheets of paper jutting sootily from the hearth. He decided the whole place would be terribly dangerous if ever a fire broke out.

Kryptmann took another pinch of herbal snuff, sneezed, then wiped his nose on the sleeve of his filthy blue robe, adding another mark to the runes sewn into it. He threw a tiny measure of coal onto the fire with a small brass shovel and turned to look at his patients.

The alchemist reminded Felix of nothing so much as the stuffed vulture in the corner. His bald head was framed by wings of unruly grey hair. A great beak of a nose jutted over thin, primly pursed lips. Pale grey eyes glittered brightly behind small pince-nez glasses. Felix saw that the pupils were huge and dilated, a sure sign that Kryptmann was addicted to hallucinogenic weirdroot. When the alchemist moved, his bulky robes flapped around his thin frame, and he looked like a flightless bird attempting to take off.

Kryptmann moved over and perched on the edge of his desk. He pointed at Felix with a long bony finger. Felix noticed that the nail had been bitten and a fine sediment of dirt lay beneath it. When he spoke, Kryptmann's voice was high and grating, as irritating as a schoolmaster drawing his fingers down a blackboard.

'Feeling better, my young friend?'

Felix had to admit he did. No matter how unprepossessing his appearance, Lothar Kryptmann knew his job. The unguents he had applied had already reduced the swelling of the bruises and the vile-tasting brew he had forced Felix to drink had caused the pain to evaporate like mist in the morning sun. 'You say that Wolfgang Lammel's bodyguards did this, Greta?'

The girl nodded. The alchemist tut-tutted. 'Young Wolfgang is a nasty piece of work. Still, "malum se delet", as it says in *De Re Munde*.'

'Perhaps in young Wolfgang's case, evil may indeed destroy itself. But I'm prepared to give it a helping hand,' Felix said.

'You understand Classical! Oh, that's excellent. I thought all respect for learning had died out in this benighted age,' Kryptmann said happily. 'Good. I'm only too pleased to have been able to help a fellow scholar. If only curing your friend were so simple. It will be almost impossible, I'm afraid.' He smiled dreamily. From the corner in which he sat, Gotrek stared back, his gaze as empty as a pit.

'Why exactly is that?' Greta asked. 'What's wrong with him?'

'It would seem that his mind has been disturbed by a blow to the head. His mnemonic lobes have been violently agitated and many memories have been shaken loose. He no longer knows quite who he is and his ability to reason has been impaired.'

Not that he ever had much of that, thought Felix.

'Moreover the humours which govern his personality have been thrown into a new configuration. I would imagine he had not been behaving quite like himself recently, has he, my young friend? I can see by his appearance that he is one of the cult of Trollslayers. They are not famed for their tolerance of pacifism.'

'True,' Felix acknowledged. 'Normally he would have torn those men's lungs out for insulting him.'

He noticed that Greta's broad pretty face brightened at the mention of violence towards his attackers and wondered what grudge she had to settle with them. Felix was forced to admit to himself that he had a yet more ignoble motive for wanting the dwarf cured: he wanted revenge on the men who had beaten him up. He knew it was unlikely he could exact it on his own.

'Is there nothing that can be done for him?' Felix asked, taking out his purse ready to pay for his treatment. Kryptmann shook his head sadly.

'Although... perhaps another blow to the head would help.'

'You mean just hit him?'

'No! It would have to be a powerful blow, struck in just the right way. It sometimes works but the chances are surely a thousand to one. It's possible that such a treatment would just make things worse, perhaps even kill the patient.'

Felix shook his head. He did not want to risk killing the Slayer. His heart sank. He was filled with a complex mixture of emotions. He owed the Slayer his life many times over and he was sorry for his state of bemusement and inability to remember anything, including his own name. It seemed wrong to leave the dwarf in such a state. He felt obliged to do something about it.

But on the other hand, ever since the drunken night when he had sworn to accompany Gotrek on his suicidal quest and record his end for posterity in an epic poem, he had had nothing but trouble. Gotrek's illness represented an opportunity to avoid keeping the promise. In his present state Gotrek seemed to have forgotten all about his doomed task. Felix could be free to return home and pursue a normal life. And perhaps it would be kinder to leave the dwarf like this, unaware of the crimes he had committed and the dark destiny that drove him to seek his doom.

But could he really abandon Gotrek to fend for himself with his present diminished faculties? And how would he get home to Altdorf across countless leagues of danger-infested wilderness and forest without the aid of the Slayer's mighty axe?

'Is there nothing else you can do?'

'Nothing. Unless…'

'Unless what?'

'No… it probably wouldn't work anyway.'

'What wouldn't work?'

'I have the formula for an elixir normally used by ageing magicians on the verge of senility. Among other things, it consists of six parts weirdroot to one part mountain sunblossom. It is said to be very good at restoring the humours to their proper configuration.'

'Perhaps you should try it.'

'If only I could, old chap. But sunblossom is rare and for maximum potency needs to be picked at the death of day on the highest slopes of Mount Blackfire.'

Felix sighed. 'I don't care what it costs.'

Kryptmann removed his glasses and polished them on the sleeve of his robe. 'Alas, you misunderstand me, young man. I do not seek some petty pecuniary advantage. I simply mean I have no sunblossom in stock.'

'Well, that's that then.'

'Wait,' Greta said. 'Mount Blackfire is not so far from here. The pass runs near its peak… Couldn't you go and pick some, Felix?'

'Go back into the mountains, at this time of the year, on my own? There are gangs of crazed mutants up there.'

'I never said it would be easy,' Kryptmann said.

Felix groaned and this time it was not simply with pain. 'Tomorrow. I'll think about it tomorrow.'

Kryptmann nodded sagely. 'I wouldn't recommend going back to the inn this evening. The temple of Shallya has a flophouse for indigents. You'll probably get a bed there for the night if you hurry. Now, about my fee. Given your obvious poverty I'll waive it if you bring me back a suitably large amount of sunblossom.'

Felix looked at his depleted purse and let his shoulders slump in defeat. 'Very well. I'll go.'

Gotrek sat and gazed blankly off into the distance. Felix wondered what was going on behind that one mad and empty eye.

Wolfgang Lammel lay drunk on his bed. From the Sleeping Dragon below came the muted sound of revelry. Even the thick Bretonnian rugs on the floor and the heavy, leaded Tilean glass in the windows could not entirely dampen it out. He drained the goblet of Estalian sherry in one gulp and stretched, enjoying the caress of satin sheets against his skin. With a nostalgic sigh he closed the old pillow-book from Cathay which had been his first purchase in that strange bookshop in Nuln. To tell the truth, he found the calligraphy rather simplistic now and the positions of the illustrated couples tediously unadventurous. Only one of them might have proved vaguely interesting, but where was one to acquire a Lustrian devil-python in Fredericksburg at this time of the year?

He rose from the bed and drew his silk robe tight about him to conceal the stigmata on his chest. He smiled; the garment had been a gift from the fascinating traveller Dien Ch'ing, a guest of the Countess Emmanuelle's, and another patron of Van Niek's Exotic Books and Collectibles Emporium. He and Wolfgang had spent an interesting evening together in the Beloved of Verena, the famed brothel on the grounds of Nuln University. Their discussions had been wide-ranging and covered many topics. The Celestial, as he styled himself, had proved to be knowledgeable in many esoteric philosophies and the hidden mysteries of many secret cults. In spite of his lack of interest in the finer points of the worship of Slaanesh, he had been a most stimulating companion – one of the many Wolfgang had met during his time in Nuln.

Wolfgang missed being at the university now. He deplored this tiny backwater town with its moon-faced peasant girls and its third-rate courtesans who had simply no imagination at all. He often regarded his time in Nuln nostalgically as a golden period of his life to which he could never really return. It had not quite been the education his father had imagined when he sent him away to the Empire's finest university, but it had been one in which Wolfgang had excelled as a pupil. His teachers had been among the most debauched rakes and gallants of the age. It was just a pity that he had not done quite so well at his more conventional studies. Eventually his tutors had written to his father acquainting him with what they considered to be the truth about him.

Wolfgang laughed aloud. The truth! If those wizened old men had the vaguest inkling of the real truth of his activities they would have sent for the witch-hunters. If his father had any idea of the real truth then he wouldn't be simply threatening to disinherit him; he would have him banished to the woods to join Heinrich's bloated cousin, Dolphus, the one who had just kept on eating until he resembled a blob of dough. Rumour had it that he was caught trying to toast his own mother's ear. Such stories showed the paucity of imagination of the local townsfolk.

What could such unimaginative people know about the worship of Lord Slaanesh, the true god of pain and pleasure? He picked up the small statuette beside his bed and studied it. The jade carving was almost perfect; it showed the hermaphrodite figure, naked except for a cloak swept wide to reveal its single breast. One arm beckoned the viewer enticingly; a faint smile of lasciviousness, or perhaps of contempt, flickered across its beautiful face. Wolfgang studied it with something like love. No, what could the petty money-grubbing fools know of the worship of a real god?

Their minds would have bent under the sanity-shattering impact of the secrets Wolfgang had learned in the catacombs beneath Nuln. Their feeble souls would have been blasted by the strange summonings which took place in the murder-houses of the Kommerzplatz. Not even in their wildest imaginings could they visualise what he had seen in the cemetery-bordello on the city's edge where mutant prostitutes serviced depraved noblemen at the so-called Night Circus.

Wolfgang had seen the truth: that the world was ending; that the Dark Powers gathered their strength; that man was a sick, depraved thing concealing his lusts behind a mask of propriety. He wanted nothing of such hypocrisy. He had turned to a god that offered ecstasy on earth rather than in an uncertain afterlife. He would know the ultimates of human life before the ending of all things. He smiled at the truths the wine had revealed to him. One more proof of the superiority of Slaanesh's way.

He replaced the pillow-book and statuette alongside his copy of Al-Hazim's *Secrets of the Harem*, took a stick of his special weirdroot from its jar, then pulled the panel of the secret alcove securely into place. It wouldn't do for Papa to make a surprise visit and find this stuff. He was close enough to disinheriting Wolfgang as things stood. Only the hope of marrying his only son to Heinrich's pig-like sister, Inge, kept the old man from cutting Wolfgang off without a penny. Still, his father did have one great virtue: he might be a boring, dour, penny-pinching old miser but he was an incurable snob.

It was the only reason he sent Wolfgang away to university; it was the only reason he gave him enough money to live like an Imperial courtier. He wanted the Lammels to marry into the nobility and Heinrich's family, although inbred and poor, were definitely that. Yes, his father dreamed that his grandson might one day have the ear of the Emperor. Just think what that could do for business, he would often exclaim.

The weirdroot tingled on Wolfgang's tongue. He wondered whether Kryptmann had added more warpstone as he had ordered. It gave the drug extra savour. He could picture the alchemist's pale, nervous face even now, warning him of the dangers of warpstone exposure. Still, his contacts in Nuln had provided him with some interesting information concerning the alchemist and so long as he knew Kryptmann's little secret he would do whatever he was told. It amused Wolfgang to see fear and hatred war on the old man's face. Perhaps it was time to trouble him for that poison – Papa had been getting rather tiresome of late.

The clock struck twelve and Wolfgang shivered. The weirdroot made the sound seem like the tolling of the temple bell of Altdorf. He glanced at the clock. It was shaped like the House of Sigmar, built to resemble a tall, gabled temple. The weirdroot blurred its outline and gave a strange animated quality to the little dwarfish figures who had emerged from within the machine's workings to strike the gong beneath its face.

The girl was late, Wolfgang realised. Perhaps it was excusable. Few people had access to clocks as precise as his. It was a work of art, precision-made by the finest dwarf craftsmen from Karak Kadrin. Still, the slut was late! He would make her pay for her tardiness later. His cupboard contained some of the finest orc-hide whips and some more sophisticated implements of pleasure.

He stumbled over to the fire, wine and weirdroot making him clumsy. For a final time he checked that the positioning of the bearskin rug was exactly right. He didn't know why he was going to such trouble for a peasant girl. But he knew that it wasn't for her he was doing it, it was for himself and his god. The more pleasure he granted himself, the better pleased the Lord of Hedonism would be.

He went to the window, pulled back the brocade curtains, and peered out through the thick dimpled glass panes. No sign of the girl. Wait – what was that? It looked like her coming down the street. Something nagged in his weirdroot-dulled brain. Shouldn't she be serving downstairs? What was she doing out at this time of night? The mist was thick, perhaps it wasn't her.

Anyway, what did it matter, just so long as she arrived? Wolfgang heard the stairs creak under a light tread. He was glad he had pestered Papa to let him have the chambers over the Sleeping Dragon now. It simplified life so much. He guessed his father had given in to his entreaties because, despite his protestations, Papa really didn't care to know what his heir was up to.

Wolfgang tottered over to the door. He felt himself becoming aroused in spite of the drink and the drugs. The weirdroot made him tingle all over. He had to admit that the girl had a certain peasant prettiness that might conceivably be described as alluring in the dim light. Soon he would introduce her to the mysteries of Slaanesh in the proper and approved manner.

There was a faint, tentative knock on the door. Wolfgang threw it open. Fingers of mist drifted in. Greta stood there wrapped in her cheap cloak.

'Welcome,' Wolfgang slurred, letting the robe slip from his shoulders to reveal his naked body. 'Look what I've got for you.'

He was gratified when her eyes went wide. He was less gratified when she opened her mouth to scream.

Felix awoke to the smell of boiling cabbage and the stink of unwashed bodies. Chill had seeped into his bones from the cold flagstones. He felt old. When he sat upright he discovered that the aches from his battering the night before had returned. He fought back tears of pain and fumbled for the soothing lozenges the alchemist had given him.

Light filtered down from the vaulted ceiling, revealing the bodies crowding the temple vestibule. Poor wretches from all over the town had come here to shelter from the cold night and had been locked in together. The great double doors were barred, although the people here had nothing to steal. Felix wondered at the precautions. The doors at the far side of the room, in front of which priestesses were setting up a trellis table, had also been barred. He had heard the heavy bolts being slid into place last night after the main door had been locked. He wondered if there were really people who would steal from the lowest of the low. From what he had seen so far of Fredericksburg, he guessed so.

Icons of the sacred martyrs gazed down with melancholy wooden eyes onto their shabby flock. Although cheaply and crudely made, they had been hung too high for anyone in the vestibule to reach without a ladder. So little trust in the world, he thought. It's so sad when the servants of Shallya must protect themselves from those they aid. Looking at the folk around him he thought it was indeed sad – but wise. These people looked rough.

An old man lay on the floor crying. In the night his wooden leg had come detached from the stump of his knee. Someone had either stolen it or hidden it. He crawled around frantically asking people if they had seen it. An elderly woman, her face ravaged by the pox, sat coughing into a blood-spotted handkerchief. Two youngsters barely into their teens lay huddled together for warmth on the floor. Where were their parents? Were they runaways or orphans? One sat up and yawned and smiled. She had tousled blonde hair and the hopefulness of youth. Felix wondered how long it would be until that was knocked out of her.

The old madman who had spent the night howling that the end of the world was coming had at last fallen asleep. His babbling about cancers at the world's edges and rats gnawing at the foundations of the mountains had worked their way into Felix's dreams and given him nightmares about the things he had seen beneath Karak Eight Peaks. Felix pulled his cloak tighter about himself and tried to ignore the stabbing pains which shrieked through his shoulder blades.

Around him beggars picked themselves up from straw pallets and, scratching at fleabites, shuffled towards the makeshift table at the far end of the temple vestibule. There, white-clad priestesses of the goddess ladled cabbage soup into wooden bowls from a huge brass tureen.

'Best hurry if ye want breakfast,' said a filthy old warrior with a cauliflower ear. The smell of rotgut alcohol on his breath was nearly overpowering. 'Tis first come, first served. The bounty of the merciful goddess isn't unlimited.'

Felix lay back and studied the cracked plasterwork of the ceiling. A mural of the goddess healing the five thousand at the river in Nuln was slowly flaking away in the damp. The doves that perched on her shoulder were nearly shapeless blobs. The sight of it brought back memories from his childhood.

He could remember his mother's last long illness, when she had gone to the temple to pray. He had been nine at the time and he and his brothers could not understand why their mother coughed so much or spent so much time at the temple. It had bored them being there – they had wanted to be outside in the sun playing, not stuck inside with the calm old white-garbed women and their interminable chanting. Looking back he understood now his mother's pale features and her quiet recital of the Penitent's Litany. He was surprised by the force of the memory and the pain of it, although it had been nearly thirteen years. He forced himself to sit upright, knowing that he had to get out of this place.

Gotrek lay on a bed of straw across from him, snoring loudly. In sleep his face had a peculiar innocence. The harsh lines eroded into his craggy features vanished, leaving him looking almost young. For the first time Felix wondered about the Slayer's age. Like all dwarfs he had about him an aura of self-assurance that suggested great experience. Certainly everything about the Slayer hinted that he had endured suffering enough for a human lifetime.

Felix wondered about the life-spans of dwarfs. He knew they were not near immortal, as elves were said to be, but they were long-lived. How old was the Slayer? He shook his head. It was another mystery. It was surprising how little he knew of his companion, for all the time that they had travelled together. Certainly, in his present condition Gotrek would be unable to provide him with any answers.

He poked the Slayer with the toe of his boot, noticing how scuffed the once-fine leather had become. He cast a glance around at the score of tramps and beggars who had lined up in front of the priestess and filled the air with the sound of hawking and coughing and spitting. He looked at the shabbiness of his surroundings and of his clothing and realised to his horror that he fitted in here. The priestess did not give him a second glance. He and the Slayer looked at home amidst the beggars.

He thought of Gotrek's desire to be remembered as an epic hero. Would he want this mentioned in the poem, Felix wondered? Had Sigmar or any of the other great heroes endured this?

Certainly the balladeers never mentioned it. In those tales everything always seemed clean and clear-cut. The only time Sigmar ever visited a flophouse was in disguise as part of some cunning plan. Well, he thought, perhaps when I work this episode into the tale that is how I will tell it. He smiled ironically when he thought of all the tales of wandering heroes he had read as a youth. Perhaps the other storytellers had made similar decisions. Perhaps it had always been this way.

The old woman coughed loudly and long. It seemed to go on forever, rattling within her chest, as if bones had come loose. She was thin and pale and obviously dying and just for a second, looking at her, Felix saw his mother's face – though Renata Jaeger had been finely clad and married to a wealthy merchant.

He looked once more at the mural of the goddess overhead and offered her a silent prayer for the healing of the Slayer and the soul of his mother. If Shallya heard she gave no sign. Felix prodded Gotrek once more.

'Come, hero. It's time to move. We must get out of here. We have mountains to climb and a long way to go.'

The tavern was nearly empty except for the innkeeper and a drunk in the corner still fast asleep, his body curled around the ashes of the fire. An old woman was on her hands and knees cleaning the wooden floor, her face obscured by the veil of grey hair falling across it. Gotrek's immense axe was still propped up by the fireside where he had left it.

In the daylight, filtering in through the small dimple-glass panes, the place looked completely different from the night before. The dozen tables that had initially appeared so welcoming looked abandoned. The cruel sun showed every scar and scratch on the bar top and revealed the dust on the clay grog bottles behind the counter. Felix thought he could see dead insects floating on the top of the ale barrel. Maybe they were moths, he decided.

No longer full of people, the tavern looked larger and more cavernous. The cloying scent of tallow candles and spitted, roasted meat filled the air. The place stank of stale tobacco and soured wine. The lack of babbling drunken voices made the place seem to echo when someone spoke.

'What do you two want?' the landlord asked coldly. He was a big man, running to fat, his hair swept sideways across his head to cover a bald patch. His face was ruddy and tiny broken veins showed in his nose and cheeks. Felix guessed he sampled too much of his own wares. Ignoring both the owner and the aching in his muscles, Felix walked over and picked up the axe. Gotrek stood where Felix had left him, gazing blankly around him.

Its weight surprised him. He could barely move it one handed. He shifted his grip so that he could use both hands to lift it and tried to imagine swinging it. He could not. The momentum of its massive head would have overbalanced him. Remembering how Gotrek could use it in short chopping strokes and change the direction of his swing in an instant, Felix's respect for the dwarf's strength increased greatly.

Moving it gingerly with both hands he studied the blade. It was made of star-metal, which resembled no steel of this earth. Eldritch runes covered the bluish-silver material. Its edge was razor keen, although Felix could never recall having seen Gotrek sharpen it. Having satisfied his curiosity he gave the axe to the Slayer. Gotrek took it easily in one hand, then turned it in his grip as if inspecting it to see what it was for. He seemed to have forgotten all about how to use it. It wasn't a good sign.

'I said, what do you want?' The landlord stared at them. Felix could tell that beneath his bluster he was nervous. His face was flushed and a faint moustache of perspiration was visible on his upper lip. The slightest of tremors was evident in his voice. 'We don't need your sort here. Coming in and causing trouble with our regular patrons.'

Felix went over and leaned on the bar, resting himself on folded arms. 'I didn't start any trouble,' he said softly. There was menace in his voice. 'But I'm thinking about it now.'

The man swallowed. His eyes shifted so that he was looking over Felix's head, but his voice seemed to gain some firmness. 'Hrmph… penniless vagabonds, come in from the wilderness, always causing trouble.'

'Why are you so afraid of young Wolfgang?' Felix asked suddenly. He felt himself getting angry now. He was not in the wrong. It was obvious that Wolfgang had some influence in this town and that the innkeeper was taking sides out of self-interest. Felix had seen such things before in Altdorf. He had not liked it there either. 'Why do you lie?'

The innkeeper put down the glass he was polishing and turned to look at Felix. 'Don't come in here to my own tavern and call me a liar. I'll throw you out.'

Felix felt the nervous flutter in his stomach he always got when he could see violence coming and was forewarned of it. He put his hand on the pommel of his sword. He wasn't really afraid of the innkeeper but in his weakened state he wasn't sure whether he could handle the big man. But his pride still smarted from the beating he had taken the night before and he wanted to pay back someone for it. 'Why don't you do just that?'

He felt a tug at his arm. It was Gotrek. 'Come on, Felix. We don't want any trouble. We've got to make a start for the mountains.'

'Yes, why don't you listen to your little friend and go, before I teach you a lesson in manners.'

He felt his feet slide and fail to gain traction as Gotrek dragged him irresistibly towards the door.

'Why is it that everyone I meet around here offers me a lesson in manners?' Felix asked as he was dragged outside.

Greta was waiting for them on a street corner near the gate. She stood beside a striped canvas stall that a pastry maker was erecting in anticipation of the day's custom. Her eyes had a puffed, swollen look as if she had been crying. Felix noticed a bruise on her neck where someone had gripped her very tight. The scratch of nail marks was present too. Her hair was in disarray and her dress looked torn, as if someone had tried to remove it in a hurry.

'What's wrong?' Felix asked. He was angry with the innkeeper still and it came out too abruptly. She looked at him as if she wanted to cry but her face became set and hard.

'Nothing,' she said. The streets were starting to fill with freemen farmers come in to sell eggs and produce. The early morning passers-by stared at them; the beaten-up youth and the distressed tavern girl. A night-soil collector's cart rumbled by. Felix covered his mouth against the stench. Gotrek just stared blankly at the cart's wheels as they rumbled past, fascinated.

'Did someone attack you?' he asked, trying to sound more gentle, now that he saw how upset she was.

'No. No one attacked me.' Her voice was empty of expression. He had seen similar looks on the faces of survivors of the Fort von Diehl massacre. Maybe she was in shock.

'What happened last night?'

'Nothing!'

The anger smouldering within him began to focus on her, her deliberate lack of communication making her a target for his barely suppressed fury. He realised how upset he was by the beating he had taken. He was upset not just because of the pain but because of his own feelings of helplessness. He fought not to take his anger out on her.

'What do you want from me then, Greta?' His voice had an angry bitter edge. He wanted to be about his business and have nothing to do with someone else's problems. Pain and tiredness and anger had impaired his ability to sympathise.

'You're leaving town, aren't you? Take me with you.' It was almost a plea, as close to an expression of emotion as she had come since the conversation started.

'I'm going into the mountains to get the sunblossom for Kryptmann. It will be dangerous. The last time I was there we met hordes of mutants. I can't take you now. But I'm coming back to get Gotrek cured. We'll be going north then. You can come with us then if you like.'

He did not really like the thought of taking the girl with them on the long, dangerous route to Nuln. He did not like either the risk or the idea of having to watch over her en route but he felt he owed her something, that he had to at least make the offer. Even if she was going to be a burden to them.

'I want to come with you now,' she said. She was close to tears. 'I can't stay here any longer.'

Again Felix felt the slow burn of anger and surprised himself with his own callousness. 'No. Wait here. We're just going to the mountain. We'll only be gone for a day. We'll come back for you. Looking out for Gotrek is going to be bad enough. I really can't take you with us now. It's too dangerous.'

'You can't leave me here, not with Wolfgang,' she said suddenly. 'He's a monster…'

'Go to Kryptmann's. He's your friend. He'll look after you till we get back.'

It looked like she wanted to say something more but she saw the unyielding expression on his face and turned and fled. The sight of her disappearing down the street made Felix feel guilty. He wanted to call out, to tell her to come back, but by the time he had come to that decision she was gone.

Felix shrugged and headed for the gate.

Felix was glad to leave the town behind him. Once out in the rolling fields, Gotrek shuffling blankly alongside him, he sniffed the clean air and felt free from the corruption and poverty of Fredericksburg. Looking at the peasants at work in their long strips of land, he was glad he was not like them, shackled to the earth and a life of backbreaking toil.

Entire families worked the long, curving, cultivated strips. He saw stooped women, babies slung in pouches across their shoulders, bending to pick the crops. As he watched he saw a man stand up and rub his back; his entire spine seemed to be curved, as if the long years of working the fields had permanently affected his posture. A swine-herd drove his bristle-covered pigs along the road in the direction of the distant village. From the unworked strips came the scent of excrement, fertiliser made from the town's night soil.

Felix lifted his gaze from the fields towards the distant horizon. Beyond the worked lands he could see the forest stretching to the mountains. In the daylight they were beautiful, mighty towers rising proud above the plain, piercing the cloud. They formed a barrier across the horizon, like a wall that the gods had raised to keep men out of the divine realm and penned within lands more suitable to them.

The peaks held the promise of silence and cold, of escape – of peace. Overhead a hawk soared, spread out on the thermals, a bright speck free from mortal concern. It drifted below the clouds and Felix saw it as a messenger of the mountains, part of their spirit; he wished that he could be up there with it, above the world of men, apart and free.

But even as he watched, the hawk swooped. Impelled by hunger or perhaps simple killing lust, it plummeted from the sky. A rabbit burst from the undergrowth and hurtled towards him frantically. The hawk struck it. Felix heard the crack of the animal's back breaking. Sitting atop its prey, the hawk gazed around with bright fierce eyes before it began to tear gobbets of flesh from the carcass.

He noticed the riders, oblivious to the damage their horses caused as their hooves churned the soil, thundering across the empty fields towards where the hawk had landed. He had been mistaken. The hawk was not a messenger of the mountains but part of the corruption about him, a wild thing trained to kill for sport.

Felix saw with a shudder that among the riders was Wolfgang, and the others were his cronies from the night before.

The juddering pace of the horse was almost too much to bear. Wolfgang felt sick, and not just from the after-effects of too much wine and too much weirdroot. He was nearly ill with fear. What had the girl seen when he removed his robe? Had she seen the mark of Slaanesh? By all the gods, if she had and she told someone, the consequences could be simply dreadful.

He wished he could remember more. He wished he had not indulged in such a potent mixture of alcohol and narcotic drugs. His head felt as if it were an egg and some daemonic chick was pecking its way out. Slaanesh take them both, he wished that Otto and Werner would return soon with news of the girl. He wished he could forget the awful moment when he woke up from his drunken swoon and realised that she was not there.

Where had she gone when she had broken free of his fumbled first attempt at an embrace and left him sprawled on his bed? His groin still hurt from her well-placed knee and the movement of the horse wasn't helping any. He would make her pay for that injury a thousand times over.

Where could she be hiding? She definitely wasn't in the common rooms of the tavern or in the single room shared by three barmaids. Had she gone to the temples to seek a priest and report him? The thought made him tremble.

Get a grip, he told himself. Think.

Damn Heinrich! When would the fat fool stop his infernal prattling? Was the only time he shut his mouth when he chewed food? It had been an awful mistake to come hawking this morning. It had not distracted him from his worries, as he had hoped. It had merely forced him to endure the torture of Heinrich's company.

At dawn Heinrich had shown up with his offer of sport. He had really been hoping for a sniff at the peasant girl but, of course, she had not been there. Now he assumed that Wolfgang wanted to keep her to himself and had her hidden away somewhere. All morning Wolfgang had been forced to tolerate his inane innuendos and schoolboy jokes. Pride kept him from asking his associate's aid in finding Greta. Wolfgang could not abide losing face to such a loathsome toady as Heinrich.

'Look, Wolfgang, there are those two vagabonds you had ejected from the tavern. Didn't the dwarf look stupid when Otto and Werner threw him in the ale barrel? Come, let us have some more sport.'

Heinrich led the procession of horsemen towards the two strangers. By chance the hawk, Tarna, had landed near them and sat ripping flesh from her prey. Typical of fat Heinie's birds to be eating, thought Wolfgang. The whole damnable family has trouble with their appetites, so why not their birds too?

He brought his steed to a halt as close to the blond-haired young man as possible. He got some slight satisfaction from watching him trying not to flinch as the massive beast loomed over him. The dwarf stepped back, obviously intimidated by the horse's bulk.

'Good morning,' Wolfgang said as cheerily as he could manage with his stomach heaving. 'Recovered, I see. We must have had equally rough nights. I trust you are not feeling so unsociable this morning.' Wolfgang glanced left and right at Heinrich's bodyguards just to let the worm know who was in control here.

Anger warred with common sense on the young man's face. 'I'm
fine,' Felix said eventually.

Wolfgang heard the strain needed for self-control in the man's
voice. The youth didn't like him, that was obvious.

'No need to worry about your girlfriend either. Wolfgang is taking
care of her.'

By Slaanesh! Heinrich was repulsive when he was being triumphant,
thought Wolfgang. Then what he had said percolated into Wolfgang's
brain. Yes, Greta had left the tavern just after the stranger had been
thrown out. And he had not seen her again until she had shown up at
his door. Perhaps Heinrich was not so stupid after all.

'What girlfriend?' The blond-haired man looked genuinely puzzled.
He rubbed the old duelling scar on his right cheek. A frown marred
his smooth brow.

'The lovely Greta,' Heinrich crowed. 'You must have thought she'd
taken a shine to you when she followed you out into the street. Maybe
you imagined her soft peasant heart had been warmed by your plight.
Well, she spent last night warming Wolfgang's bed.'

Wolfgang winced. If only it were true.

The tramp's hand moved to the pommel of his sword. It stayed
there, too, in spite of the fact that Heinrich's men had drawn their
weapons. With what looked like a habitual motion he glanced at
the dwarf. The dwarf had stopped inspecting the hawk. He glanced
blankly up at the men on horse. The axe was held loosely in his hands,
as if he didn't quite know what to do with it.

'We don't want any trouble,' the man said. He let his hand move
away from his weapon.

The bodyguards guffawed. Wolfgang wished his head didn't hurt
so much, so that he could think clearly. He badly wanted to ask the
youth if he had seen the girl but pride kept him from asking in front
of his cronies. He tried to see some way out of his dilemma but the
solution just would not come to him. Life could be so hard sometimes, he thought.

He consoled himself with the thought that the girl could not have
gone too far. If she was still in the town, Werner and Otto would
eventually find her. And if she had decided to risk her lord's wrath and
flee back to the peasant community she'd have to pass through these
lands. So a sweep of the area surrounding the town would soon reveal
her whereabouts. And this hawking party would provide a particularly
fine excuse for it.

And, he reasoned, no one had come looking for him so she could not have told anybody yet. Even if she did, would anybody believe her; a peasant drab accusing the son of the town's most influential merchant? He allowed himself a smile. It was nice to know that one could still be brilliant, even with a simply dreadful hangover.

'Come, Heinrich,' he said magisterially. 'Let us leave these two clowns to return to their circus. It's too fine a morning to waste time in conversations with louts.'

He applied his spurs gently to the flanks of his mount and fought down the diminishing waves of nausea as it moved. Now that he had reassured himself, all seemed almost well with the world. He promised himself that when the girl was found she would pay for subjecting him to such excruciating, and what was worse, boring, torment.

The hills rose to meet the peak, the swell of their long curves reminding Felix of waves. Above them the mountains rose, tier upon massive tier, to block the horizon with their snaggle-toothed bulk.

Felix had feared that he would have some difficulty in locating the trail to Mount Blackfire but the path was obvious. It was a simple spur on the one he and Gotrek had followed the previous day while making their descent from the foothills of the range.

The strain on the back of his thighs and in his calves began to tell as the pathway continued to rise. It had been carved into the flank of the mountain by the passing of countless feet. Felix wondered whether the alchemist had ever followed this route or whether it was a way that had been left by less human passers-by. Some of the signs that had been scratched into the rock were in the form of a crude eye; but whether they were warnings of the goblins' presence or territorial claim markers left by the greenskins themselves he could not tell.

Gotrek looked like he was enjoying the walk. He hummed a broken tune to himself and took the slope in his stride without any noticeable effort. He picked his way along the slippery path with no difficulty, finding footholds where Felix could see none. Soon the man found it easiest to follow in the dwarf's footsteps. Gotrek was in an environment he was adapted to and it seemed wisest to let him lead.

Sweat rolled down Felix's back and his breathing became heavy. He had thought himself toughened by the long trip from Karak Eight Peaks but the effort of climbing these hills was a sore one. The beating he had taken and the alchemist's treatment had worn him out. He was worried about his ability to handle the tough climb. It would be worse if the clouds made good on their threat of rain.

The harshness of the landscape, all jutting rocks and windswept ground, matched the bleakness of his mood. Felix seethed with hatred for Wolfgang Lammel. He resented the wealthy young merchant's easy cruelty and spoiled arrogance. In his days in Altdorf, Felix had known dozens like him but had never had to contend with being the object of their cruelty. His father's wealth and social status had shielded him from it. In his more honest moments, he was forced to admit that perhaps he too had once behaved a little like Wolfgang. Now he had seen injustice from the underdog's point of view and he did not like it.

He understood now why Greta had been so disturbed. He tried not to imagine what had happened between her and Wolfgang, but thoughts of Lammel forcing himself on the girl ran through his head and made him half-mad with fury. He swore that he would get Gotrek cured and make the brat pay. Cursing to himself he marched on. He fought down an urge to yell at the Slayer to stop his infernal humming.

Gotrek disappeared over the brow of a ridge. Felix swore as his feet slipped on the scree of the path and he fell, cutting his hand on the small stones. Pain stung him. He pulled himself up over the brow and found himself lying flat on soft turf.

Felix wondered why it was that sunblossom had to grow on the highest slopes just below the snowline; why couldn't it grow here in the foothills with all the rest of the blossoms? After a moment he shrugged. In his life he had found that few things were ever easy. Maybe the alchemists only used these ingredients because they were difficult to find, to increase the mystique of their art. He would not be in the least surprised if that were the case.

He sat up and took another lozenge to dull the throbbing pain in his head. It was going to be a long day.

Hardy evergreen trees lined the steep slopes of the narrow vale, like stubble on the upturned face of a giant. High to the right, a waterfall made a series of spectacular leaps over hundred-foot drops until it plunged into the small lake at the valley's centre. The mountains framed the valley and Felix had to crane his neck upwards to see their peaks. Looking down the vale was like looking down the sight of a crossbow, the eye focused by the line of grey peaks marching into the distance.

Here the pungent aroma of roses mingled with honeysuckle and bitterbriar. Tangled bushes fought with each other for space, the flower heads like the helmets of warring armies of colour. He wondered if there was any sunblossom present, then remembered what

Kryptmann had told him about where the magical ingredient had to be picked.

A flicker of movement attracted his eye as the head of a huge elk, as high at the shoulder as a man, emerged from bushes overlooking a ledge of rock fifty yards above him. It gazed down warily as if judging whether it was safe to come down for water. Felix eyed the mighty sweep of its antlers with respect.

As the clouds parted, shafts of sunlight illuminated the valley. The chatter of birdsong reached his ears and mingled with the muted roar of the falling water. He bent to pick up a pine cone, enjoying the scaly roughness of its serrated edges beneath his fingers.

For a moment the beauty of the scene held him enthralled. Even his thoughts of revenge on the merchant's son evaporated. He felt relaxed and at peace, and the pain of his beaten body temporarily vanished. He was glad he had seen this place, that all the steps of his long journey had brought him here. He knew he would be one of the few men who ever saw this valley. The thought pleased him.

The presence of the elk was right. It made the scene look like a perfectly composed landscape painting. Then it struck him that perhaps it was rather odd that the deer was raising a horn to its lips with a massive, suspiciously human-looking hand. Then a blast of sound echoed down the valley and before it had faded the knowledge filtered into Felix's brain that he had not seen the head of an elk. It was the head of an altered one.

He lobbed the pine cone in the direction of the lake and, pulling his cloak around him against the increasing chill, he hurried onward and upward after Gotrek. He looked around for signs of pursuit but saw none. Even the elk-headed mutant was nowhere to be seen.

Now Felix knew for certain that they were being followed. Looking back down the winding trail he could see their pursuers, a band of mutants. All that long afternoon as he and Gotrek had climbed the flank of the mountain they had gathered behind them. The way back to Fredericksburg was blocked.

He stopped and let his breathing and heartbeat return to normal. He tried to count the number of their pursuers but it was difficult. The early evening gloom caused the creatures to blend in with the grey of the rock face. Felix made the sign of the hammer across his chest and commended his soul to Sigmar.

He had always known he would die in some out-of-the-way place. His participation in the dwarf's quest made it inevitable. He had just not imagined it would be so soon. It was all so stupid. Gotrek would not even get his heroic doom. The Slayer was too busy staring blankly into space, oblivious to their danger.

At first it had been easy to pretend that nothing was happening; that the horn-blowing beast was but a solitary creature too scared to tackle two well-armed travellers. But as the day wore on, the signs had mounted to tell them it wasn't so.

When Felix had seen the cloven-hoofed tracks mingling with clawed human footprints in the mud surrounding a ford he had managed to dismiss them as old spoor, something to which he did not need to pay too much attention. Yet even then he had loosened his sword in its scabbard.

Sometime later, as Felix clambered his way ever upwards after Gotrek's uncaring back, he had caught sight of scuttling shapes keeping pace with them. They flitted from tree to tree on either side of the path. He had tried to get a closer look but the shadow under the pines had defeated even his keen eyes. All he was left with was the impression of tentacled figures keeping carefully from view.

His nerves had begun to fray. He felt like charging under the canopy of the trees and seeking his foes. But what if he lost the path? Or what if there were more than one or two of them? Vague suspicion had kept him inactive. He had pushed aside his fears and kept climbing.

It had become almost unbearable when he had heard the horn blast away to his right and it had been answered by a similar one from the other side of the trail. He knew then that the accursed ones were closing in, that they were gathering for the feast. He was tempted to make a stand then, to get it over with – but some impulse had kept him going up towards the snowline.

He told himself it was the urge to keep trying, not to give up in the face of certain doom that drove him onwards, but he was honest enough with himself to know that it was just fear. He did not want to meet the mutants; he wanted to postpone the inevitable end for as long as possible.

Now he stood on the ridge near the snowline and looked back down the trail and knew it was finished. Here, in this frigid, wind-swept, barren place, his life would end along with the day. There would be no revenge on Wolfgang, no homecoming in Altdorf, no epic poem for Gotrek.

He looked at the Slayer who stood nearby, watching the oncoming mutants, his axe drooping in his clumsy grip. Felix counted about ten of them. The one in the lead was a familiar gross fat giant. His heart sank even further. He had envisaged perhaps begging for mercy or offering the prospect of a ransom, anything that would extend his life. Surely, though, the obese giant would want his revenge for the slaughter of the previous day.

Wait – what was growing at his feet? Small yellow flowers grew in clumps of thin soil in the shelter of the ridge. As the sun began to sink he realised it was what he had been sent to find. It seemed like a very slim chance but...

Swiftly he plucked a few blossoms and thrust them at Gotrek.

'Eat them,' he commanded. The Trollslayer stared at him as if he were truly mad. Slowly a frown passed across his scarred face.

'Don't want to eat flowers,' he said in bemusement.

'Just eat them!' Felix roared. Like an abashed child, the Slayer shoved them into his mouth and began to chew.

Felix studied him carefully, hoping to see signs of some change in the dwarf, the sudden, miraculous return of his old ferocity stimulated by the supposed magical quality of the flowers. He could see none.

Well, it had been a faint hope anyway, he told himself.

The mutants were close now. Felix could see that it was definitely the survivors of the band which had previously attacked them. Gotrek spat out a cud of yellow and moved behind Felix.

Oh well, Felix decided, best to meet death with a sword in his hand. At least this way he would take one or two of the warp-spawned to Hell with him. As he unsheathed the sleek weapon, the fading sunlight caught the blade, and caused the runes to glow. Felix studied them as if for the first time. The approach of death made all of his senses keener. He appreciated the workmanship of those old dwarf craftsmen as he had never done before. He wondered what the runes meant, what their intricate symbolism signified. There was so much he would never know now and so much he wanted to find out.

The mutants had stopped not fifty paces away and their giant leader peered at Felix myopically. After a pause he cuffed the elk-headed mutant about the ear and advanced.

Felix wondered whether he should charge at the foul thing and hope to slay him. Perhaps that would break the morale of his confederates. Sword versus great stone club, he was sure he could win if only the others didn't intervene. With that thought some semblance of courage returned. There was some hope. He grinned a feral grin; fear had passed him and he almost started to enjoy the situation.

The leader paused ten paces from Felix; a great wobbling mound of fat, girded around with studded leather and many weapons. Waves of blubber cascaded from his chin like tallow melting on a candle. His huge hairless head was like a ball of meat with tiny holes poked in it for the eyes, nose and mouth. To the man's surprise he seemed quite nervous.

'I'm not fooled, you know,' the mutant said at last. His voice sounded like the tolling of a great bell. It boomed out from within his vast chest. He was so close that Felix could hear his phlegmy, wheezing breaths.

'What?' Felix said, bemused. Was this a trick?

'I can see through your plan. Trying to get us within range of your friend's axe, then slaughter us.'

'But–' The unfairness of the accusation mortified Felix. Here he was, standing waiting bravely for death and his disgusting opponent was claiming it was the other way about.

'You must think us complete idiots. Well, the warpstone didn't melt our brains along with our bodies. How stupid do you think we are? Your friend here pretends to be afraid but we recognise him. He's the one who killed Hans and Peter and Gretchen. And all the others. We know him and we know his axe and there's no way you're going to lure us within its sweep.'

'But–' Now that he had mustered his courage to make a brave last stand Felix felt cheated. He wanted to demand that they get on with their attack.

'I told Gorm Moosehead that I thought it was you, but he said "No". Well, I was right and he was wrong, and I didn't gather the clan just so you and your nasty friend could collect the bounty on mutant heads.'

'But–' Slowly it dawned on Felix what was happening. They had been reprieved. He forced his mouth firmly shut before it could betray him.

'No! You may think you're clever but you're not clever enough. This is one trap we're not going to fall into. We're too smart for you. I just wanted you to know that.'

So saying, the mutant leader backed slowly and cautiously away. Felix watched the foul band melt back into the gloom and only then did he let out his breath. He stood transfixed for a moment. The twilight on the nearby peaks was the most beautiful thing he had ever seen. He even rejoiced in the chill and the pain that throbbed in his hand. They were signs he was still alive.

'Thank you, Sigmar, thank you!' he shouted, unable to contain his joy.

'What are you shouting about?' Gotrek asked excitedly.

Felix resisted the sudden blinding urge to run him through with his sword. Instead he clapped the dwarf on the back. After a moment it struck him that they were stuck up here on the mountain until the morning. Even that thought was endurable.

'Quick, we must gather the flowers,' Felix said. 'The sun hasn't set yet!'

'Who is it?' Lothar Kryptmann called warily from inside, as Felix banged upon his door. 'What do you want?'

It was just early evening and Felix was surprised by the elaborate precautions with which the alchemist greeted them.

'It's me. Felix Jaeger. I'm back. Open up!' Was it just his imagination or did Kryptmann sound more than usually nervous, Felix wondered? He turned and looked down the street. Lights glowed through the chinks in shuttered windows. In the distance he heard the clip-clop of horses' hooves and the metalled wheels of a carriage on cobbles, heading towards the taverns of the town square. The wealthy out to play, he supposed.

'Hold on! Hold on! I'm coming.'

Felix stopped knocking. He coughed. Just his luck to have caught a chill on that pestilential mountain-top. He mopped the sweat of fever from his brow and drew his cloak tighter against the chill mist. He glared at Gotrek, who stood stupidly at the top of the steps leading down to the basement apartment, holding the flowers he had collected. As usual the Slayer showed no sign of illness.

Bolts snapped on the door. Chains were loosened. The door opened a little. Through the chink, light spilled out along with the pungent odour of chemicals. Felix pushed the door open despite the alchemist's resistance and forced his way within. He was surprised to see Greta standing in the room's other doorway. She had obviously been hiding in the other rooms.

'Do come in, Herr Jaeger,' the alchemist said tetchily. He stood aside to let Gotrek enter.

'Wolfgang is looking for you,' Felix said to the girl. She looked too scared to speak. 'Why?'

'Leave her alone, Herr Jaeger,' Kryptmann said. 'Can't you see she's terrified? She's had rather a nasty shock at the hands of your friend, Lammel.'

Swiftly Kryptmann outlined what Greta had seen when she ventured into the merchant's son's quarters the previous evening. Kryptmann was discreet about why she went but he mentioned the stigmata of Chaos she had noticed.

'I feared as much. I should have known when he made me add warpstone to his weirdroot. I would imagine that's when he started to develop the mark of the daemon.'

'You added warpstone to his weirdroot? Warpstone?'

'There's no need to look so shocked, my young friend. Its usage is not that uncommon in certain alchemical operations. Many respectable practitioners of my art make use of it in small doses. Why my old tutor at Middenheim University, the great Litzenreich himself, used to say…'

'I heard that Litzenreich was thrown out of the university for his experiments and that the Guild of Alchemists withdrew his license. There was quite a scandal. In fact, the last I heard he was an outlaw.'

'There is always malice among academics. Litzenreich was simply a man ahead of his time. I mean, look how long it took Eisenstern's theory that the sun goes round the earth to become commonly accepted. He was burned at the stake for claiming it originally.'

'Regardless of the philosophical merits of your argument, Herr Kryptmann, warpstone is a highly illegal and dangerous substance. If a witch-hunter was ever to hear–'

Kryptmann seemed to shrink in on himself. 'That's exactly what Wolfgang Lammel told me – though how he found out about my experiments is beyond me. I purchase the warp… the substance from a very small, very discreet emporium in Nuln. Van Niek's. I told him I didn't want to do anything illegal with it. All I wanted to do was learn how to transmute lead into gold – and warpstone is the very essence of transmutation.'

'So Wolfgang is about to find out, it would seem.' Try as he might, Felix could not keep an unseemly note of gloating from his voice. It was perfect. He would unmask the decadent swine as a mutant in front of the whole town. Thus would he repay him for the beating he had taken, and for what he had done to Greta too of course.

'You won't report me to the authorities, will you, my young friend? After all, I did treat your wounds. I promise that if you don't report me, I'll never have anything to do with warpstone again.'

Felix glanced at the scared alchemist; he had nothing against him and Kryptmann might well have learned his lesson about dealing in illegal substances. But there was still the problem of the man's bodyguards to deal with. Still, he had the answer to that too.

'Herr Kryptmann, if you can cure my associate, I assure you that I will forget all about what you've done.'

* * *

Felix toyed idly with the pestle and mortar while Kryptmann proceeded with his work. The pungent fumes filled the laboratory, rising from the pot in which the alchemist had reduced the sunblossom to a yellow sludge.

The cool stone of the pestle was somehow comforting. The tang of the sunblossom perfume was noticeable even through his blocked nose. He had taken another two of Kryptmann's healing lozenges and he felt slightly distanced from everything. He wished his head would clear, that all of the aches and pains would go away.

'Felix?' a soft voice said, bringing him back to reality.

'What, Greta?' He was still snappish. Human contact closed the distance between himself and the world, broke the barriers around him that Kryptmann's medicine had built against the pain. It brought his anger back into focus.

'What will Wolfgang's men do if they find me here?'

'Don't worry about it. Soon Herr Wolfgang will have worries enough of his own.'

'I hope so. It's good of Lothar to hide me from him. It's at terrible risk to himself. You know what Wolfgang's bodyguards can be like.'

Privately, Felix thought that the alchemist had hidden the girl simply to spite Wolfgang. He had no reason to love the merchant's son. Or perhaps it was guilt for providing Wolfgang with the warpstone which had altered him. Had he always been a sadistic monster, Felix wondered, or had that transformation only come recently, with the mark of Chaos?

Other questions flickered through his dulled mind. Why did his enemy feel the need to use warpstone in the first place? And what about the sinister rumours Greta had claimed to have heard about him? He pushed them away. He would probably never know the answers. One thing was clear, though; he would be doing everyone in town a tremendous favour by disposing of the fellow.

'No! Put that down. That's acid!' Kryptmann shouted at Gotrek suddenly.

The Slayer stopped rooting about amidst the various jugs and beakers on Kryptmann's bench. He looked as if he were about to drink from one large silver flask. Gotrek shuffled his feet and returned the container to its proper place.

Felix glanced around the laboratory. He had never been in one before. It all looked so very arcane and incomprehensible. The benches were covered in intricate structures of pipework and beakers. Distillation equipment covered nearly half of one table. Several racks of stoppered glass tubes were stacked against one wall. Each contained liquids of cobalt blue or lime green or blood red. Some contained many layers of multi-coloured sediment. On one wall hung a framed certificate. Even at this distance Felix recognised the crest of the University of Middenheim, famed throughout the Empire for its schools of magic and alchemy.

Charcoal burners heated flasks and pots containing various substances. Kryptmann moved briskly from one to another, stirring, adjusting temperatures and occasionally tasting with a long glass spoon. He opened a great cabinet and produced a large, padded, white gauntlet covered in scorch marks. He pulled it over his right hand.

'Not long now,' he said, picking up a heated flask and pouring it into the central pot. The mixture bubbled and hissed. He put a stopper on the second flask and shook it before uncorking it and pouring it into the mix. A great cloud of pungent green smoke billowed across the room. Felix coughed and heard Greta do the same.

As the smoke cleared he saw Kryptmann carefully emptying the contents of the third alembic into the mixture. With each drop, a tiny puff of different-coloured smoke arose. The first was red, the second blue, the third yellow. Each rose, a tiny expanding mushroom-shaped cloud of vapour reaching upward towards the ceiling.

The alchemist set down the alembic and adjusted the flame under the pot. He picked up a small hourglass and turned it upside down. 'Two minutes,' he said.

A sense of triumph filled Felix. Soon Gotrek would be cured and they would visit the Sleeping Dragon. He would take out all of the many tribulations he had suffered on Wolfgang Lammel's hide.

No sooner had the last grain of sand fallen from the top of the hourglass than Kryptmann removed the pot from the flames. 'All done!'

He beckoned for Gotrek to come over, then ladled out a measure into a small china bowl.

Felix saw that the inner rim was marked with red circles and astrological signs. He presumed these represented various levels of dosage. He was somehow reassured when the alchemist filled it to the very top, then handed it to Gotrek.

'Drink it all up now.'

The Slayer swilled it down. 'Ugh!' he said.

They stood and waited. And waited. And waited.

'How long should it take to work?' Felix asked eventually.

'Er, not long now!'

'You said that an hour ago, Kryptmann. How long exactly?' Felix's knuckles whitened as his grip on the heavy pestle tightened.

'I told you that the process was, well, uncertain. There were certain risks involved. Perhaps the sunblossom was not in prime condition. Are you sure you picked it exactly at the death of day?'

'How. Long?' Felix enunciated both words clearly and slowly, allowing the measure of his irritation to show in his voice.

'Well, I – actually it should have worked almost instantly, jolting the mnemonic nodes and humours back into their old configuration.'

Felix studied the Slayer. Gotrek looked exactly as he had done when they entered Kryptmann's lab.

'How do you feel? Ready to seek out your doom?' Felix asked, very softly.

'What doom would that be?' Gotrek responded.

'Per–perhaps we should try another dose, Herr Jaeger?'

Felix let out an inarticulate howl of rage. It was not to be borne. He had endured a severe beating from Wolfgang's men. He had climbed that mountain along unspeakably difficult paths. He had narrowly escaped death at the hands of hordes of bloodthirsty mutants. He was tired and cut and bruised and hungry. What was worse, he was coming down with a pestilential flux. His clothes were torn. He badly needed a bath. And it was all the alchemist's fault.

'Calm down, Herr Jaeger. There's no need to growl like that.'

'Oh, there isn't, is there?' Felix snarled. Kryptmann had sent him for the flowers. Kryptmann had promised that he would heal Gotrek. Kryptmann had spoiled Felix's plans for glorious revenge. He had gone through hell for naught, at the foolish instructions of a foolish old man who did not know his own foolish business!

'Perhaps I could make you a nice soporific potion to calm your nerves. Things will look so much better after a good night's sleep.'

'I could have died getting those flowers.'

'Look, you're upset. Quite understandably so – but violence will solve nothing.'

'It will make me feel a lot better. It will make you feel a lot worse.' Felix threw the pestle at the alchemist. Kryptmann leapt to one side. The implement smacked into Gotrek's head with a great crunch. The Slayer fell over.

'Quick, Greta! Send for the watch!' the alchemist babbled. 'Herr Jaeger has gone mad! Help! Help!'

Felix darted round the work bench after Kryptmann, toppling him off his feet with a flying tackle. It gave him a great sense of satisfaction to get his fingers round the alchemist's throat. He began to tighten his grip, smiling all the while. He felt Greta try to pull him off Kryptmann. Her fingers locked in his hair. He tried to shake her off. The alchemist's face started to turn an interesting shade of purple.

'Not that I have anything against senseless violence, manling, but why exactly are you strangling that old man?'

The granite-hard voice was harsh and cracked and held an undercurrent of sheer cold menace. It took Felix a second to realise just who had spoken. He let go of Kryptmann's throat.

'And who is he? And where are we? And why does my head hurt, by Grimnir?'

'The blow from the pestle must have returned him to his senses,' Greta said softly.

'I, ah, prefer to think it was the delayed effect of my brew,' Kryptmann gasped. 'I told you it would work.'

'What senses? What brew? What are you talking about, you old lunatic?'

Felix picked himself up and dusted himself off. He helped Kryptmann to his feet, picked up the alchemist's glasses and handed them to him. He turned to face Gotrek. 'What is the last thing you can remember?'

'The mutant attack of course, manling. Some snotling-fondler caught me on the head with a slingshot. Now how did I get here? What magic is this?' Gotrek scowled majestically.

'This will take a lot of explaining,' his companion said. 'So first let's get some beer. I know a friendly little tavern just around the corner.'

Felix Jaeger smiled wickedly to himself, and the two of them set off for the Sleeping Dragon.

BLOOD AND DARKNESS

'After we exposed the cultists of Slaanesh in
Fredericksburg, and incapacitated several of their
minions, we ventured back onto the road to Nuln,
leaving our former tormentors to the less than gentle
mercies of their fellows. I have no idea why we
settled on that mighty city as the terminus of our
travels, other than perhaps because of the fact that
my family had business interests there.

'During one roadside halt in a tavern, Gotrek
and I decided, perhaps foolishly in hindsight, that
we should avoid the main road. Inevitably, and
perhaps predictably, our drunken decision to take a
circuitous route through the forest led to disaster.

'In our desire to avoid any possible encounter with
the agents of law, we wandered far from the normal
haunts of man, and ended up deep in the forests, in
an area long thought to be the site of a Black Altar
of Chaos. Little did we suspect when we set out that
we would soon meet with startling proof of that dire
fane's existence, and also that we would soon do
battle with the most powerful of all of the followers
of Darkness we had yet encountered...'

— From *My Travels with Gotrek, Vol. II,* by Herr Felix Jaeger
(Altdorf Press, 2505)

When she heard the approaching footsteps, Kat concentrated on making herself smaller. She squeezed even more tightly into the tiny space between the stone blocks of the tumbledown building, hoping that the beasts had not come back. She knew that if they had, and they found her, this time they would kill her for certain.

She wriggled further into the shadowy recess until her back was against stone. The rock was still warm from the fire which had burned down the inn. She felt a small measure of safety. No adult could squeeze into so small a hiding place, certainly nothing as large as the beasts. But they could always reach in with their spears or swords. She shuddered when she remembered the one with tentacles instead of arms, imagining the long leech-mouthed limbs questing like great snakes to find her in the darkness.

She grasped the hammer-shaped amulet that old Father Tempelman had given her and prayed to Sigmar to deliver her from all snake-armed things. She tried hard to block out her last memory of the priest, fleeing down the street, carrying little Lotte Bernhoff. A horn-headed giant had impaled him with a spear. The weapon had pierced both Tempelman and the five-year-old, lifting them into the air as though they were weightless.

'Something terrible has happened here, manling,' a voice said. It was deep and gruff and harsh, but it did not sound like the feral snarling of a beast. The accent was foreign, as if Reikspiel were not the native tongue of the speaker. It reminded Kat of the strangers she had once served in the inn.

Dwarfs, Old Ingmar – who fancied himself a traveller because he had once been to Nuln – had called them. They had been short, not much taller than herself but far broader and heavier than any man. They had worn cloaks of slate grey and, though they had called themselves merchants, they carried axes and shields. They spoke sadly in low musical voices and when drunk joined the villagers in singing.

One had shown her a clockwork bird which flapped its metal wings marvellously and spoke in a metallic voice. She had begged bald-pated Karl, the innkeeper, to buy it for her but, though he had loved her like she was his own daughter, he had just shaken his head and continued to polish the glasses, saying there was no way he could afford such workmanship.

She shivered when she thought of what had become of Karl and fat Heide and the others in the inn who she had called family. She had heard screams as the bestial horde ravaged through the village led by the strange warrior in black armour. She had seen the lines of villagers being marched to the great bonfire in the village square.

'Perhaps we should leave, Gotrek. By the looks of it, this is not a healthy place to linger,' said another voice from close by. This one definitely belonged to a human, Kat decided. It was soft-spoken and gentle, with a cultured accent similar to old Doctor Gebhardt's. A brief spark of hope flickered in Kat's mind. There was no way a beast could sound like that.

Or was there? Like many other villagers who had grown up in the depths of the wild woods, Kat was familiar with the stories. Of wolves who looked like men until let in by unsuspecting villagers. Of children who looked normal until they grew up into hideous mutated monsters that slew their own families. Of woodcutters who had heard a child's cry in the deep forest at twilight and who went to investigate and never returned. The servants of the Dark Powers were devilish and clever, and found many ways of luring the unwary to their doom.

'Not until I've found out what happened here. By Grungni, this place is an abattoir!' The first voice spoke again, unnaturally loud in the silence.

'Whatever force could do this to a walled village could surely squash us like bugs. Look at the holes in the walls of the keep! Let us be away.' There was an undercurrent of fear in the cultured voice which echoed the terror in Kat's own breast.

Once again the memory of the previous night rose before her. It had begun with a great thunderclap of sound although the sky had been empty. She recalled the tolling of the alarm bell and the splintering of the gate. She recalled rushing to the inn door and seeing the beastmen pouring down the street, torching the village and putting everyone to the sword.

One huge figure with the head of a goat had lifted Johan the miller clean over its head and pitched him into a burning cottage. Little Gustav, Johan's son, had driven a pitchfork through its chest before being torn to pieces by two deformed creatures in beggars' clothes whose faces showed wattled crests and lizard-like skin. She wished she could forget the way they tore the gobbets of flesh from the corpse and stuffed them greedily into fanged mouths.

She remembered wondering why Count Klein and his soldiers had not come to defend them but when she gazed at the castle she knew the answer. The towers were ablaze. Silhouetted against the flames, figures dangled from the lord's gibbet. She guessed they were Klein's men.

Karl had forced her inside and barred the door, before stacking the tables in front of the entrance. Karl and Ulf the potboy and even Heide, Karl's wife, had clutched knives and other kitchen implements; a pitiful defence against the foul rabble that whooped and gibbered in the streets outside.

They had stood around, pale-faced and sweating in the flickering light of the flambeaux, while outside the sounds of killing and destruction continued. It had seemed like all their darkest fears has come true, that finally the monstrous, mythical forces lurking in the forest's heart had erupted forth to claim what was theirs.

For a time it seemed like the inn was going to be left untouched but then the door was knocked from its hinges by a mighty blow and several immense beastmen had pushed aside the piled furniture. Kat remembered so vividly the taste of the smoky air that accompanied the opening of the door.

With a whimpering cry, Ulf had charged the leading monster. It brought a huge club down on his head, splitting his skull and splattering brains about the room. Kat had screamed as the jelly-like material hit her face and slid down her cheek.

When she opened her eyes she looked into the face of death. Over her loomed a huge creature. It was man-shaped but goat-headed, its horns twisted to resemble a strange X-shaped rune. Ruddy fur covered its mighty body; Ulf's brains covered its massive club.

The beastman had looked down on her and she saw that it had no eyes, only a blank expanse of flesh where the sockets should have been. Even so, she somehow knew that it could see her as well as any sighted thing. Perhaps the circlet of desiccated eyeballs dangling from its neck gave it sight. It had inspected her with a puzzled expression, then reached down and touched her long black hair, running its finger through the white streak that ran from her forehead to the back of her neck. It shook its head and backed away almost fearfully.

Nearby Karl bled to death, whimpering piteously as he failed to staunch the blood pumping from the stump where his left hand had been. Kat couldn't see what was happening behind the tumbled table where two beasts had Heide pinned but she could hear the old woman's screams. She had fled out into the night.

And there she had met the beautiful white-faced woman who was mistress of the beasts. She was sitting astride a great red-eyed steed whose flesh was as black as her ornate armour. The woman looked at the destruction, her smile revealing fanged incisors drawn back over ruby-red lips. Her hair was long and black with a white strip running down the middle. Kat wondered whether it was the mark of Chaos – and whether that was the reason the beastman had spared her.

The woman held a black sword in one hand, runes glowed the colour of blood along its length. She noticed Kat and looked down at her. For the second time that night, the girl thought she was dead. The woman had raised her blade as if to smite her. Numbed with terror, Kat had just stood there looking up at her, her gaze had locked with the warrior's.

The woman paused as their eyes met. Kat thought she detected a faint glimmer of sympathy there. The woman mouthed the word 'No', and nudged her mount into motion with a touch of her spurs. She rode off down the street, not looking back. Kat noticed the bonfire and the beaten villagers being pushed towards it and scurried into hiding.

Soon the sound of bestial chanting rose over the village. The burnt meat smell of roasting flesh, both tantalising and sickening, filled the air. The hideous screams of the dying villagers filled the night.

Kat had hidden until morning, praying for the souls of her friends, praying she wouldn't be found. When the sun came up, the beasts were gone as if they had never been there. But the smoking ruins of the village, and the piles of charred skulls and cracked bones in the still-smouldering embers of the bonfire showed it had not been a nightmare.

Suddenly it was all too much for Kat. She started to cry with great choking sobs. Tears ran down her soot-blackened face.

'What was that, manling?' the deep voice said nearby.

Kat stifled her sobs as stealthy footfalls approached. Something blocked the sunlight in the entrance to her hiding place. She stared up at a man's face, framed by long golden hair. The eyes that looked at her were scared and tired and world-weary. A long scar marred the man's cheek. She found herself looking at the sharp point of a longsword. Faint markings were etched into the blade.

'Come out slowly,' he said. His soft, cultured voice was cold now and held no hint of mercy. Kat crawled slowly out into the daylight. She could tell she was near to death at this moment. Fear of the unknown had made the man desperate.

She stood up. The man was much taller than she was and dressed like a bandit. A shabby cloak of faded red wool was thrown back over his right shoulder, leaving his sword arm free. His clothes were stained and patched and very travel-worn. His high leather boots were cracked and scuffed.

He glanced around with an edgy wariness that seemed habitual.

'It's only a little girl,' he shouted over his shoulder. 'Maybe a survivor.'

The figure that stomped into view past the tumble-down remains of Frau Hof's bakery was just as terrifying in its own way as the beasts had been. It was a dwarf – but one which bore little resemblance to the travelling merchants Kat had known.

He stood halfway between Kat and the bandit in height but he was heavy, maybe as heavy as Jan the blacksmith had been and certainly more muscular. A patchwork of intricate tattoos covered his whole body. A huge crest of red-dyed hair rose over his shaven skull. A crude leather patch obscured his left eye and a gold chain ran from his nose to his left ear. In one ham-sized fist he carried the largest axe Kat had ever seen.

The dwarf glared at her belligerently. There was a sense of barely restrained wrath about him that was desperately frightening. He showed none of the obvious fear his companion did.

'What happened here, child?' he demanded brusquely in a voice like scraping stones.

Staring into that one mad, inhuman eye, Kat could think of no response. The man touched her gently on the shoulder.

'Tell us your name,' he said softly.

'Kat. Katerina. It was the beasts. They came from the forest, killed everybody. I hid. They left me alone.'

Kat found herself babbling the story of her encounter with the beast-men and the woman in the black armour to the astonishment of the two adventurers. By the time she had finished the dwarf looked at her wearily. His ferocious expression had softened a little.

'Don't worry, child. You're safe now.'

'I hate trees. They're like elves, manling,' Gotrek said. 'They make me want to take an axe to them.'

Felix Jaeger peered into the shadowy forest nervously. All around, the great trees brooded, ominous presences whose branches met over the trail, intertwined like the fingers of a giant at prayer, blocking out the sun until only a few solitary shafts of light illuminated the way forward. Moss covered the branches and the scaly bark of the trunks reminded him of the withered hides of dead serpents. A stillness as old as the vast primeval forest surrounded them, broken only by occasional stirrings in the undergrowth. The sound spread across the silence until it vanished as mysteriously as ripples from the surface of a pool. Here in the forest's ancient, evil heart no birds dared to sing.

He was forced to agree with Gotrek. He had never really liked woods, not even as a child. He had never shared his brother's passion for hunting. He had always preferred to be left at home with his books. Forests for him were scary places, the haunt of beastmen and trolls and nightmare creatures from darkest legend. They were the places to which those who showed the stigmata of Chaos were banished to. In their depths he had always pictured werewolves and witches, and ferocious struggles between mutants and other exiled followers of the Ruinous Powers.

Up ahead Gotrek vaulted the log which had fallen across the path, then turned and helped Kat to climb over it, easily lifting the child one-handed. Felix stopped in front of the obstruction, seeing that the bole was rotten and blotched with some strange fungus. Segmented insects scuttled along it, blindly burrowing into the reeking mould. Felix shuddered as he felt the damp wood under his hand, bracing himself for his jump. His boots almost slipped on the wet moss of the other side. He was forced to spread his arms to keep his balance. As he did so his fingers touched a cobweb stretched from the lower branches. He swiftly pulled his hand away and tried to brush off the sticky substance.

No, Felix had never liked forests. He had hated the summer retreats to his father's manor in the wood. He had detested the pine-walled house surrounded by the timberlands which provided the raw materials for Gustav Jaeger's drayage and shipping interests. By day it hadn't been too bad if he didn't stray far from the buildings, but by night his overactive mind peopled even the open, managed woodlands with a host of monstrous inhabitants. The goblins and daemons of his imagination found a ready home beneath the swaying trees.

He had at once envied and pitied the fur-clad woodsmen who kept his father's estate. He had envied them their bravery, seeing them almost as heroes facing the terrors of the untamed land. He had pitied them for having to live constantly on their guard. It had always seemed to him that anyone who lived in a settlement in the woods lived in the most precarious environments imaginable.

He could remember standing at his window and looking out into the green, and picturing it stretching away to the very end of the world, to those wastes where the foul minions of Chaos roamed. The strange noises and the clouds of fluttering moths attracted to the building's lights did nothing to diminish his unease. He was a child of the city, of Altdorf's urban sprawl. Getting lost in the woods was a nightmare, one that had recurred often in those long summer nights.

Of course it had been a joke: the Jaeger estate was ten leagues from Altdorf in the most cleared area of the Empire. The wood was thinned by ceaseless logging. It was tamed, cultivated land that bore no resemblance to the dense, tangled Drakwald in which he found himself now.

Gotrek paused suddenly and sniffed the air. He turned and looked back at Felix. Felix cocked his head to one side enquiringly. Gotrek made the sign for silence, frowning as if he were concentrating on hearing some distant sound. Felix knew that the dwarf's hearing and sense of smell were better than his. He waited expectantly. Gotrek shook his head and then turned to move on. Was the malign presence of the forest getting on even the Slayer's iron nerves?

What he had seen this morning was justification for anyone's fears. These woods did indeed shelter forces inimical to humankind; Kat's story confirmed it. He looked down at his hands and saw that they were trembling. Felix Jaeger thought himself a hard man but what he had seen in the ruined village would make even the hardest shudder.

Something had rampaged through Kleinsdorf like an irate giant through an anthill. The little village had been levelled with appalling malevolence and thoroughness. The attackers had not left a single building untouched, and no inhabitant save Kat had survived. The sheer senseless brutality of it astonished him.

He had seen things there that he knew he would see again in nightmares. A bonfire in the village square piled high with skulls. Fused ribs sticking out of the smouldering ash like unconsumed wood. Some had come from the skeletons of children. A disgusting scorched meat smell had filled his nostrils and he had tried to keep from licking his dry lips for fear of what the windblown ash might contain.

He had stood stunned in the silence and desolation of the ruined village. Everything about him was ash-grey or soot-black, save for the few fires which still flickered here and there. He had flinched in alarm as the roof collapsed on the devastated town hall. It had seemed like a dark omen. He had felt like a tiny atom of life in an endless empty desert. Slowly, a bit at a time, memory of that moment had etched itself into his brain.

High on the hill, the scorched walled castle stood, a stone spider clutching the hilltop with blasted stone feet. Before the gaping maw of its broken gate, hanged men dangled on gibbets, flies caught in its single-strand web. The village below was the playground of daemon children, idiot giants who had grown bored with their toy town and kicked it to flinders.

Little things filled the street. A broken pitchfork, its prongs crusted with dried blood. A temple bell lying half-melted in the rubble of the toppled church. A child's wooden rattle and a shattered cradle. The printed pages of the Unfinished Book, the Sigmarite testament, floating on the breeze. Trails in the dirty street where bodies had been dragged, all leading to the central fire. A beautiful dyed dress, never worn, lying incongruously untouched in the street. A human femur, cracked for marrow.

He had seen violence before but never on such a scale and never so wantonly mindless. Even the carnage at Fort von Diehl had been a battle, fought by opposing sides for their own reasons. This had been a massacre. He had heard of such slaughters but to confront the hard, tangible evidence was altogether different. The reality, the implication that such things could and did happen, had always happened, scared him. How could Sigmar, how could any of the gods, permit such things?

He was disturbed too that Kat had survived. Looking at the little girl walking in front of him, her shoulders slumped, her hair grimy and her clothing soot-stained, he wondered how she could have been allowed to live. That too made no sense – why had she, alone out of all the inhabitants of that sleepy community, been spared?

Was she a changeling, some slave of Darkness, luring them to their doom? Did he and the Slayer escort something evil towards its next set of victims? Normally he would have dismissed such a thought as utterly ridiculous; obviously she was just a frightened young child who had the good fortune to live where others had died. Yet here in the gloom of the deep forest such suspicion came easily. The stillness and silence of their surroundings worked on the nerves, and bred watchfulness and mistrust of strangers.

Only the Slayer seemed undisturbed by their predicament. He marched along boldly, avoiding the clutching tree roots that threatened to trip him, his easy pace eating up the miles. The dwarf moved with uncanny quietness for one so squat and heavy. In the shadows of the forest he seemed at home, somehow; he stood taller and looked more alert. His habitual slouch vanished, perhaps because his under-mountain dwelling people were adapted to darkness and the feeling of being enclosed. He never stopped, as Felix did, to survey the under-growth whenever he heard rustling. He seemed quite confident in his ability to discern any threat.

The young man sighed, remembering the arguments he had had to use to prevent the dwarf from investigating the village further. The girl had at least proved a useful excuse for moving on and seeking a place of safety, where they might find her refuge. It had been that and the possibility that the creatures might be marching on the next village that had convinced the Slayer to take the road to Flensburg.

Felix paused, bidden by some buried instinct. He stood quite still and strained to hear anything out of the ordinary. Perhaps it was just his imagination, but it seemed to him that the very stillness of the woods had a quality of menace about it. It hinted at the presence of old evils, biding their time, waiting for victims.

Anything could lurk in those long shadows and now he knew that something did.

It was getting colder. A slight deepening of the gloom hinted that night was falling above the shroud of leaves. Felix glanced back over his shoulder, dreading the silence but dreading the sound of pursuit more. When he looked round again, Kat and Gotrek had vanished, disappearing round a curve in the path. Somewhere in the distance a wolf howled. Felix hurried to catch up.

Felix looked across the campfire at the Slayer. Gotrek sat propped up against the fallen tree trunk, gazing into the depths of the fire, watching the flickering flames as if he could divine some mysterious truth in their depth. His hands toyed idly with the flints of his firemaker. Lit from below, the stark angles of his face looked as rough-hewn as the face of a granite cliff. The flickering of their fire made shadows chase each other across the planes of his cheeks. His tattoos were shadowy blotches, like the signs of the last stage of some terminal disease. Light caught the pupil of his one good eye. It glittered inhumanly in its socket, a star reflected in the depths of a shadowy pool. Close to him Kat lay still, her breathing regular, apparently asleep. Gotrek sensed Felix watching him and looked up.

'What ails you, manling?'

Felix looked away from the fire. The bright after-image of the flame ruined his night vision. Still, he scanned the shadows under the trees, looking for signs of hidden watchers. The image of the villagers of Kleindorf going to sleep with the forces of Chaos creeping up on them unawares came unbidden to his mind. He cast around for something to say, decided upon the truth.

'Actually I'm… I'm a little worried, Gotrek. For some strange reason what we saw in that village back there frightened me. The gods alone know why.'

'Fear is for elves and children, manling.'

'You don't really believe that, do you?'

Gotrek smiled. His few remaining teeth looked even yellower in the firelight. 'Yes.'

'You don't seriously expect me to believe that dwarfs are never afraid, do you? Or is it Slayers who never know fear?'

'Believe what you like, manling. That's not what I said, though. Only a fool or a maniac is never afraid; only a child or a coward lets his fear master him. It is the mark of a warrior that he masters his fears.'

'Didn't the destruction of that village frighten you? Aren't you afraid now? Something's out there, Gotrek. Something evil.'

The Slayer laughed. 'No. I am a Slayer, manling. Born to die in battle. Fear has no place in my life.'

Felix shook his head, unsure of whether Gotrek was mocking him. He was used to the dwarf's erratic mood swings and starting to suspect that there were times when the Slayer possessed something close to a sense of humour. Gotrek put his flints back into his pouch and grasped the handle of his axe.

'Rest easy, manling. There's nothing you can do for the dead, and if whatever killed them is fated to find us there's nothing you can do about that either.'

'Is that supposed to reassure me?'

Suddenly the atmosphere of camaraderie evaporated as swiftly as it had formed. Anger blazed in the dwarf's voice. 'No, manling, it is not. But believe this: if I find the killers, there will be a reckoning in blood. Such evil as we witnessed this day will not go unpunished.'

There was no trace of human feeling in Gotrek's voice now. Looking into the dwarf's alien eye, Felix saw the madness there, the inhuman molten violence waiting to erupt. Just for a second he believed the dwarf, shared his mad conviction that he could stand against the dark power that destroyed the village. Then he recalled the sheer scale of the havoc that had been wrought and the moment passed. No warrior, not even one as mighty as Gotrek, could withstand that. He shuddered and drew his cloak tighter about him.

To cover his anxiety, he leaned forward and tossed more wood on the fire. Little stalks shrivelled and caught ablaze. Sparks drifted lazily upward. Acrid smoke stung his eyes as the lichen-covered branches smouldered.

He wiped away the smoke tears and spoke to fill the silence. 'What do you know of the man-beasts? Do you believe the girl's story about them attacking the village?'

'Why not? The beasts have inhabited these woods since my people drove the elves out nigh on three thousand years ago. Many times in history huge hordes of them have marched forth to attack the cities of dwarf and man.'

Felix felt some wonder at the way the dwarf so casually alluded to events three thousand years ago. The war he referred to preceded the founding of the Empire and recorded human history by many centuries. Why had not human scholars paid more attention to the dwarfs when they compiled their records? The part of Felix which had been a student regarded the dwarf as a first-rate repository of obscure lore. He listened carefully, trying to memorise all that Gotrek said.

'I thought the beasts were simply mutants, human exiles devolved into man-beasts, altered by the power of warpstone. Certain of our learned professors claim as much.'

Gotrek shook his head as if despairing at the folly of mankind. 'Such mutants follow the hordes as lackeys or camp followers but the beastmen proper are a separate race, with origins back in the Age of Woe. They date from the time of the first incursions of Chaos into this world, from when the Dark Powers first ventured through the Polar Gates to trouble this sad planet. They may well be the first-born children of Chaos.'

'I have heard tales of them aiding human champions of Chaos. It is said they made up the bulk of the troops that assaulted Praag two centuries ago. Part of the great host driven off by Magnus the Pious.' Felix remembered to make the sign of the Hammer when he mentioned the Sainted One's name.

'That is not surprising, manling. Beastmen worship strength almost as much as they worship Chaos. The champions of the Ruinous Powers are among the greatest warriors to walk this world, Grimnir damn them! I hope the girl-child's tale is true and that I may soon face this black armoured she-devil. It would be a worthy trial of arms and if ordained, a worthy death.'

'That it would be.' Felix fervently hoped it would not come to that. Any circumstance he could imagine which involved Gotrek dying at the hands of the Chaos Warrior would surely involve his own demise fairly soon thereafter.

'And what of the girl?' he whispered. 'Do you think she is what she claims? Could she not be in league with the attackers?'

'She is only a child, manling. She has not the stink of the Dark about her. If she had, I would already have killed her.'

To his horror Felix noticed that Kat's eyes were wide open, and she studied the two of them fearfully. Their gazes met. Felix was ashamed to see such fear in the eyes of one who had already suffered so much. He got up and walked around the fire. He placed his worn cloak over her and wrapped it round her.

'Go to sleep,' he said. 'You're safe.'

He wished he could believe it himself. He saw that Gotrek's eye was closed but his axe was gripped firmly in one hand. Felix lay down on the leaves he had piled for bedding and for a long moment gazed upwards at the stars glittering coldly through the branches. He slept fitfully and old nightmares stalked him.

'You have failed, beloved,' the Daemon Prince Kazakital said calmly. He looked at her through his stolen eyes and Justine felt a shock pass through her to the core of her being.

She flinched, knowing well the punishments her patron could inflict when displeased.

Instinctively her fingers closed on the ruby pommel of her black war-blade. She shook her head. Her great mane of white-striped black hair swayed. She felt powerless. Even though she had a small army of beastmen within earshot, she knew they could not help her. In her master's presence no one could help her, no one. She was glad that the old beastman shaman, Grind, and his acolytes had withdrawn beyond the Black Altar after the summoning. She wanted no one to witness her discomfiture.

'Everyone in the village is dead. As we both desired,' she lied, knowing even as she did so that it was futile. Her ornate armour already felt clamped around her like a vice. Faint hints of pain tickled her nerve endings. If the daemon so desired she knew that she would soon swim in an ocean of agony.

'The child lives.' The daemon's beautiful voice remained flat, uninvolved, emotionless.

Justine tried to keep from looking at it, knowing the effect that the sight of it would have upon her. She knew that it would already have started to change the body of the sacrificial victim into something that more resembled its true form.

She gazed around. Overhead the two moons glared down in evil conjunction. Morrslieb, the Chaos moon waxed full. Mannslieb was at its smallest. For tonight and the next two nights, the power of Chaos would be strong in the land, strong enough to summon her daemonic patron from his hellish home in the realms beyond reality. Strong enough to let it possess the body of the man which they had offered up on its altar here in the deep woods.

Through the thick red cloud surrounding the altar she could see the campfires of her followers, the flames smudged by the sweet red mists that stained the night. They were tiny stars compared to the bright sun of the daemon's aura. She heard it shift its weight, recognised the leathery creak of the wings emerging from the corpse's back. She focused her attention on the impaled heads that flanked the altar. The pale faces of Count Klein and his son, Hugo, looked back at her. They brought back the memory of last night.

The old count had been a fighter. He had come to meet her in the courtyard wielding a spiked mace, half-garbed in hastily thrown-on mail. He had cursed her for a hell-damned whelp of darkness. She had seen the fear written on his face, as he saw the bestial horde of gors and ungors at her back, pouring through the shattered gate of his castle. She had felt almost sorry for the moustached old fool. She had always liked him. He had been worthy of a warrior's death and she had granted him it quickly.

The youth stood behind his father, pale faced with terror. He had turned and fled through the blood-soaked courtyard where her followers were slaughtering the half-awake men-at-arms. She had followed him easily, relentlessly, the black armour fused to her flesh granting her extra endurance as well as strength.

The chase through the darkened castle had ended in Hugo's bed-chamber, where she had always known it must. That, after all, was the place where it had all begun. He had bolted himself inside and howled for the gods to save him. She had splintered the door with one kick of her armoured foot and strode in like an avenging daemon.

The place looked much the same as she remembered it. The same huge bed dominated it. The same fine Bretonnian rugs covered the floor. The same stags' heads and hunting trophies filled the walls, along with the same pennants and weapons. Only Hugo had changed. The intense thin-faced youth had grown into a blubbery man. Sweat ran down his jowled cheeks. His face looked babyish even as the eyes squinted in terror. Yes, he had changed. Another might not have recognised him after so much time but Justine did. She would never forget his eyes, those glassy eyes which had followed her from the very first day she had arrived in the castle, over seven years before.

A long sword was grasped awkwardly in his pudgy paw. He raised it feebly and she effortlessly batted it aside, sending the blade spinning across into the corner. She put the point of her sword to his chest and pushed slightly. He had been forced to back away until he had tripped over the foot of the bed and lay sprawled on the sheets. The smell of excrement pervaded the air.

The bloated pink maggot wet his lips.

'You are going to die,' she said.

'Why?' he managed to gasp. She removed her helmet then. He moaned aloud as he recognised – at last – her face, her long distinctive hair.

'Because I told you that you would, seven years ago. Do you remember? You laughed then. Why are you not laughing now?' She pushed on her blade a little harder. Blood blossomed on the white silk of his shirt. He stretched out his hand in entreaty.

For the first time in years, tears of passion stung her eyes. She felt again the hot surge of rage and hatred. It raced through her veins and transformed her face into a mask. She pushed the sword down, revelling in the shock of impact and the clean slice of hell-metal through flesh. She leaned forward, pinning him to the bed where he had forced himself upon her seven years before. Once again blood stained the sheets.

She had surprised herself. After long years of planning so many, slow, deliberate, delicious tortures she had dispatched him with a single stroke. Revenge had seemed less important somehow. She had turned and left the chamber and went to oversee the sacking of the town. She had ignored the pleas of the two men that the beasts were raising on the gallows in one of their incomprehensible macabre jokes. It had been down there, in the village, that she had encountered the child.

She strove to forget the child.

'You should not have spared the girl, beloved.' The daemon allowed a hint of its anger to glitter in its voice. The promise of eternities of pain emphasised its every word.

'I did not spare the child. I left it for the beasts. I am not responsible for the slaying of every dreary village urchin.'

The lash of the daemon's words stung her. 'Do not lie, beloved. You spared it because you were too soft. For a moment you allowed mere human weakness to stay your hand, to push you from your chosen path. That I cannot allow. Nor can you, for if you change course now you have lost everything. Believe me, if you let the girl live, you will have cause to regret it.'

She looked up at it then and, as always, was struck by the thing's polished, chitinous, beauty. She saw its black armoured form, the brutally beautiful face glaring out from beneath the rune-encrusted helmet. She met its redly glowing eyes and saw its strength. It knew no weakness, no mercy. It was without flaw. One day she could be like it. It plucked the thought from her mind and smiled in apparent pleasure.

'You understand, beloved. You know the nature of our pact. The path of the Chaos Warrior is but a trial. Follow the path to the end and you will find power and immortality. Deviate from it and you will find only eternal damnation. Great Khorne rewards the strong but he abhors the weak. The battles we fight, the wars we wage are but tests, crucibles to burn out our weakness and refine our strengths. You must be strong, beloved.'

She nodded now, hypnotised by the beauty of its molten voice, seduced by the promise of knowing neither pain nor weakness, of being flawless, perfect, of allowing no chink in her armour for the horror of the world to seep through. The daemon reached out with one clawed hand and she touched it.

'An age of blood and darkness is coming, an era of terror and rage. Soon the armies of the four Great Powers will march forth from the polar wastes and the fate of this world will be decided with steel and dark sorcery. The winning side will own this world, beloved. To the victors will belong eternal dominion. This planet will be cleansed of filthy humanity. We shall remould everything in our own image. You can be on the victorious side, beloved, one of its privileged champions. All you must do is be strong and lend our lord your strength. Do you wish that?'

That moment gazing into the creature's burning eyes, hearing the silken persuasiveness of its voice she felt no doubt.

'Do you wish to join us, beloved?'

'Oh yes,' she breathed. 'Yes.'

'Then the child must die.'

Justine marched through the crowds of her followers to take her place on the carved wooden throne. She placed her bare blade across her knees, confronting the mightiest of her followers, the gors. The sword was a reminder to them all of how she ruled here, a naked symbol of her power. She had the favour of their daemon god and the expression of that favour was her might. The beastmen might not like it but they would have to tolerate it until one of them could, according to their primitive code, best her in single combat. And none would challenge her if they had any sense: they all knew of Kazakital's prophecy, made when she had been elevated to the ranks of the Chaos Warriors. They all knew what the daemon had said – that no warrior would ever overcome her in battle. They had all witnessed its truth. Yet they were beastmen, and challenging their leader was an instinct.

This night she almost hoped that one of them would try; the blood-lust was strong in her tonight as it always was after she confronted her patron. She glanced at what the beastmen rested upon: a huge tapestry she remembered once covering an entire wall. It depicted scenes of battle and hunting from Klein's family's past. Now it was covered in mud and leaves from the floor of the forest glade and the filth of the beastmen's own excrement. She would order it burned. She wanted nothing left to remind anyone of the Klein family.

Seeing the huge animal-headed forms of her followers lolling on Lord Klein's favourite possession was a reminder to her of how her world had changed since that fatal morning when she fled Hugo's chamber into the depth of the woods.

The scene that confronted her now was like something from the nightmare engravings of the mad artist, Teugen. Great horned animals clad in armour walked among the twisted trees of the darkened forest. They looked like an evil parody of the chivalric ideal, an upset in the natural order of things, as if the brutes of the forest had risen to oust upstart man. As one day they would. The servants of Chaos would send all the kingdoms of men toppling into the dust. She had made a small start here. It would grow. As word of her victories spread, more and more servants of Chaos would flock to her banner. Soon she would have a great army and all the might of the Empire would tremble. Somehow that prospect did not excite her as once it would have. Disgruntled, she pushed the thought aside.

She gazed on the captains of her future army and wondered what orders she should give them. She ran her measuring gaze over them, wondering when and from where the challenge to her leadership would come from. It could be from any of them. They were all gors, the largest and most powerful type of beastman, and the most violently ambitious.

She saw posturing Hagal, his goat-horns burnished with gold, his brilliant blond fur gleaming in the firelight. Of all the beasts who followed her she thought him most likely to challenge her, to instigate the Clashing of Horns. Her spies told her that it was he who grumbled most loudly around the campfires, complaining that it was unnatural to have a female lead them. He was the most surly, always questioning her orders but never to the point where she would have to initiate the challenge. At the moment, though, he was biding his time until perhaps she weakened. If it came to a fight now he knew that she would win.

Against Lurgar she would have been less certain of victory, had it not been for the prophecy; the great red-furred bull-head was the most savage of her warriors in battle, a blood-drinking berserker whose appetite for carnage was exceeded only by his hunger for man-flesh. He was a deadly fighter when battle madness came on him. She almost feared a challenge from him, but thought it unlikely unless someone put him up to it. The man-bull was too stupid to have much ambition and was content to follow any leader who promised him foes to face and food to eat. Not a leader himself, he would be the perfect tool for someone to rule from behind.

Beside him sat one who obviously thought so: the old shaman, Grind. For a beastman, Grind was clever, possessed of low cunning and much of what passed for learning among the warped ones. He could cast bones and read omens, talk to spirits and intercede with the Ruinous Powers. In the time before Justine came to power it had been he who made the sacrifice to the Daemon Prince, Kazakital. But the fat, white-maned bull was too old now to father many sons in the Great Rut and so could not become leader of the warband. Justine knew it didn't stop him from resenting her pre-empting his position of spiritual authority in the tribe or simply hating her for being female. Justine could not afford to underestimate him, that much she knew. The shaman was full of spleen and malice, and his words swayed many of the rank and file beasts in her army.

Tryell the Eyeless was no real threat; a great warrior of heroic stature but marked by warpstone. He had no eyes, yet he could see as well as anyone. As one who had been marked by Chaos he had a great fear of Justine, who he saw as specially favoured by it. He lived only to kill and add new eyes to his collection.

Then there was Malor Greymane, whose father she had killed to assume leadership of this horde. If the youngling felt any resentment he hid it well. He followed her instructions to the letter, fought well and exercised sound judgement. Often his plans were better than those of war-leaders twice his age. He was already a great warrior, although not yet come into the full strength of his prime. Let the others grumble that he was a member of the council only because of his friendship for her. She knew that some had even been whispering the abominable lie that, secretly, he was her mate. She knew that he had earned his place on merit and his position was justified by his prowess.

Of all those she commanded, she felt she could place a measure of trust only in the black-armoured Chaos Warriors that she had recruited in the Wastes, long before she had returned here. They were sworn to her service. In a way she wished they were here now, to provide her with a measure of support, but they were not. This evening they were off in the depths of the woods, performing their own rites, propitiating the daemonic engine which they crewed with blood and souls, making it ready for the hard battles to come.

The beastmen looked up at her expectantly, a half-circle of animal faces whose eyes held both human intelligence and inhuman lusts. She was suddenly glad that her blade was easily accessible. She felt isolated and out of place here. As always, before she began the council she felt a sense of anticipation. Would it happen now? Would the challenge come?

Justine wondered what orders she should give them. She had never thought past this point. The doubts that she had felt earlier returned, redoubled. She had lived for her vengeance. Now that it was achieved she felt empty. When she spoke to Kazakital it was easy to be firm of purpose, to feel allegiance to his cause. The Daemon Prince had an almost hypnotic effect on her. But when he wasn't there, doubt set in.

She wondered whether she wanted what he wanted. Her major purpose had been achieved with the death of Hugo.

It was simply the fulfilment of a long-held desire that left her feeling so, she told herself. For seven years she had been driven by her desire for vengeance. Now it had left her, snuffed out with the life of her tormentor. It was bound to leave a gap after so many years. She forced herself to concentrate, to feel the desire for power and immortality that came so easily in the presence of her daemonic patron. She managed to summon up a faint shadow of it. It was enough.

'We have destroyed our first victims,' she said to them, voice strong. 'But there is one survivor. It is ordained that she must die. Our master demands it.'

'Should find other man-places. Kill more,' Hagal said, glancing round with his golden eyes. 'Why worrying about one survivor?'

Grind tapped his wand of carved human thighbone on the flag-stones. 'Let them live. Spread word to others. With word comes fear. Fear is our friend.'

Always this constant testing, she thought. Always this constant circling and searching for a weakness. Even simple matters became minor skirmishes as the beasts sought to enhance their status at the cost of others. Their society was based on a hierarchy of strength; showing weakness, any weakness, diminished prestige.

'Because our lord demands it. Because red Kazakital, Chosen of Khorne, says we must.'

Malor turned his grey gaze on Grind and Hagal. 'And because our leader, Justine, demands it!'

'Who are you to question what our leader demands?' Tryell asked directly of Hagal. So the rumours of bad blood between them were true. Good. It strengthened her position.

'I do not question our leader. I question need to find single human when could find dozens more. Are you so anxious to find girl because you spared her last night?'

'Who told that?' Tryell said, too quickly. 'Do you seek challenge?'

Justine sensed that Tryell was trying to cover this up, not that she cared. She, too, had spared the girl. Or was this what Hagal was getting at? Was this a subtle criticism of her? It did not suit her to allow the fight to continue. If Tryell killed Hagal, fine; but if it went the other way she would have one less true ally among the beasts' leaders and she doubted if she could find a replacement.

'There will be no challenge,' she said softly, but loud enough to be heard by all present. 'Unless it is with me!'

The gathering fell silent, waiting to see if anyone would call her to the clashing of horns. She saw Grind lick his lips in anticipation. She locked glances with Hagal. For a moment he was tempted, she could tell. For a moment he met her gaze full on and the killing lust came into his eyes. His hand reached to rest on the pommel of his weapon. She smiled, hoping to goad him into making the call, but at the last he seemed to think the better of it and lowered his head.

'Good,' she said with finality. 'Tryell, take your warriors and find me the girl with hair like mine. Take trackers, search the area, find her and bring her to me. I will offer her to Kazakital myself. The rest of you assemble your forces. We will march on to the next human town and find merit by slaughtering more men.'

They nodded agreement and approval and rose to depart. Justine was left alone in the chill hall with her thoughts, wondering just what she would do when they brought the girl to her.

'Wake up, manling! Something's coming!'

Felix roused himself from sleep. Wisps of eerie dreams still shrouded his mind. He shook his head to clear it, and felt the ache in his neck and back from lying on the cold forest floor. Chill had eaten through the insulation of the leaves and leeched strength from his body. He rose slowly to his feet and rubbed the sleep from his sticky eyes. As quietly as he could, he unsheathed his sword and glanced around.

Gotrek stood nearby; a squat, massive statue frozen in the dim light of the fading fire. The red glow of the embers reflected from his axe blade. The dwarf carried a weapon of blood.

Felix looked at the sky. The moons were almost down. Good. Dawn was not far off.

'What is it?' he asked. His words caught in his throat and came out as a rasping whisper. He did not need the dwarf's posture of alertness to tell him something was wrong. There was an air of quiet menace about the wood that even he could feel.

'Listen!'

Felix listened. He strained his ears to pick up any unusual sounds. At first all he heard was the thumping of his heart.

He could hear nothing unusual, only the chirping of the night insects and the quiet rustle of leaves. Then, somewhere far off, so quiet he might only have imagined it, he heard the low muttering of voices. He looked over at the Slayer. Gotrek nodded.

Felix glanced around to see what had become of Kat. She was awake as well, sitting hunched up by the fire. Her eyes looked huge and scared in the firelight. Felix prayed for the sun to rise quickly. He turned from the fire and peered out into the shadows, resolving not to look back and spoil his night sight again.

'Kat, put more wood on the fire,' he said quietly. There was an almost overwhelming temptation to turn and see if she was obeying. He fought it and was relieved when he heard movement behind him and the crackling of wood catching light. Shadows raced away from the fire and the island of light in which they stood expanded to encompass the near forest. The trees looked like monochrome titans in the dim illumination.

Felix stood absolutely still. In spite of the chill, sweat ran down his spine and made his clothing clammy. His palms were slippery and it felt like strength was draining from his limbs. He felt an urge to flee from whatever approached.

It was definitely coming closer, making no attempt at stealth. He could hear heavy footsteps in the distance and once a short yelping bark of what sounded like pain. There was a tautening of the muscles in his stomach and a fluttering, excited feeling in his belly. The incautious approach of their foes spoke of overwhelming self-confidence. Was he about to meet the destroyers of Kleindorf?

Strangely he began to feel the urge to move in the direction of the noise, to investigate, to not simply stand here by the fire like a sheep waiting to be slaughtered. To calm himself he made a few experimental swipes with his sword. It hissed as it cut the air. The runes on its blade grew brighter as if in anticipation of the coming conflict. The loosening of his muscles and the readiness of his enchanted dragon-hilted blade relaxed Felix a little. A smile grafted itself to his lips. If he died here he would not die alone.

The confidence vanished as a chorus of howls echoed through the woods, erupting triumphantly from half a dozen bestial throats. In the pre-dawn gloom they were echoes from his nightmares. Things were out there – things he did not wish to face. Their pursuers knew they were close and were prepared to close in for the kill. Felix wanted to drop his blade and run. Strength ran from him like wine from a spilled goblet. Behind him Kat whimpered and he heard the sound of stealthy movement, as if she crept for cover.

'Steady, manling. They do that to frighten their foes. Weaken them for the kill. Don't let your fear master you.'

Gotrek's calm, rumbling voice was almost reassuring but Felix could not help but think that whatever happened would be an acceptable outcome for the Slayer. Either he would vanquish his foes or, more likely, he would find his heroic death. Felix wondered if perhaps now was the time to point out that if he himself did not survive there would be no one left to record it. His humour made him laugh a little. He heard the Slayer move closer.

Their pursuers were nearly on top of them. Felix could hear the sandy rasping of their tread upon the trail. They could not be more than a hundred paces away. He glanced around looking for cover. There was a patch of bushes under the largest of the trees. He wondered about the advisability of hiding among them and then leaping out from ambush. Or perhaps not leaping out at all and simply hoping that the Chaos spawn did not find him. He realised that for him it was a slender hope.

He pointed to the briar patch with the tip of his sword and whispered, 'Kat, hide yourself there. If anything happens to Gotrek and me, stay hidden!'

He was gratified to see the small figure rush over, throw herself flat on her belly and wriggle into the undergrowth. She might have some chance if the two of them fell.

How had they been found, he wondered? Was it simply ill luck – was this just a party of scouts which had stumbled upon them? Or was there some malevolent sorcery at work? Where Chaos was concerned you could never tell. For a moment he allowed himself the fantasy that it was all a mistake – that this was a party of merchants who would shelter them. But he knew that only the dead or their killers would take the night road from Kleindorf, and that thought made him shudder.

The sound of footsteps was so close now that he felt their pursuers must soon come into view. He wished that the dying moons would break free from cloud and grant him some more light. As if Sigmar had answered his prayer, there came a break in the cloud cover. He wished that it had not.

The eerie silver light of Mannslieb mingled with the blood-tinged glow from the witch-moon, Morrslieb. It washed down through the rents in the treetops and fell on the faces of their pursuers; aberrations from the wildest reaches of his nightmares.

To the fore was a leashed mutant. It crouched close to the ground, sniffing the trail. It was the maker of the snuffling sound Felix had heard. It had a hairless, dog-like face and a huge nose. A spiked collar around its neck was joined to a heavy steel chain, the other end of which was held by a mighty, goat-headed beast. It was enormously muscular and it had a leather cloak over its shoulders. There was a necklace of what appeared to be dried eyes around its neck. It had no eyes of its own, only a blank expanse of flesh where the sockets should have been. Yet it walked as if it could see perfectly. Felix wondered what trick of Chaos sorcery permitted that. In one hand it held an enormous spike-headed club around whose tip were smeared congealed substances the nature of which Felix preferred not to think about.

Behind came its lackeys: smaller versions cut from the same monstrous template; hunched muscular giants carrying spears and rusty swords. Bestial eyes glared from goat-heads and stag-heads, turned red by the firelight. Aside from their leader none bore any obvious stigmata of further mutation. The sight of them made Felix's flesh crawl.

The thought of what they had done in the village the night before filled him with both fear and rage.

The eyeless leader halted and gestured to his followers with one immense knuckled hand. They filtered into the clearing and formed a large half-circle facing the man and dwarf. Felix moved into his fighting stance, willing his muscles to relax as his fencing masters had taught him. He tried to clear his mind, to be calm, but facing these massive monsters it was impossible.

For long moments man and beast glared at each other across the shadowy clearing. Felix willed himself to meet the gaze of the nearest goat-head. I am going to kill you, he thought, hoping that he could intimidate the creature. Its animal mouth opened and its tongue lolled out. Faint flecks of foam appeared on its lips. It looked as if it were mocking him. Well, perhaps I won't then, thought Felix and smiled.

He wanted to look at Gotrek, to see what the Slayer was going to do, but dared not take his eyes off his opponents. He feared that they might attack with supernatural speed if he looked away. This was the worst of facing foes of unknown quality; who knew what they might be capable of?

The beasts held their position, as if uncertain what to do in the face of two undaunted opponents. They looked at each other as if amused or uncertain. Perhaps they were deciding who would have the first choice of their prey's flesh, Felix decided. It struck him as odd that things with such dire reputations as eaters of man-flesh should have the heads of herbivorous animals. Perhaps it was a joke of the Ruinous Powers.

'Ready, manling?' Gotrek sounded remarkably lucid for a berserk on the verge of battle, Felix thought. His deep voice was calm, even and held no hint of any emotion.

'As I'll ever be.' Felix tightened his grip on the hilt of his blade until it was almost painful. The muscles of his forearm went as rigid as steel bands. When he heard the Slayer's wild laughter he, too, charged forward to face the foe.

Kat wriggled under the bushes. She did not want to, but fascinated horror forced her to look out again. She knew the beasts were closing in. She could feel it. There was the same sense of presence in the air that there had been the previous night. She looked out at her two benefactors and felt sorry for them. They were going to die. They may have been frightening, but they had tried to help her and they did not deserve the death the beasts would give them.

She looked at Felix. His handsome features wavered between an expression of hopeless fear and one of wild exultation. She understood how that could happen. She had often felt the same way when Karl had driven too fast along the rutted road in his cart. A sort of tingly feeling, of being excited and scared and happy all at once. Felix didn't look very happy, though, which was the difference.

The dwarf did. His brutal features were twisted into a grim smile that revealed his missing teeth. Kat was sure that he noticed her looking at him, because he turned and winked in her direction. Either he was not afraid or he was a very good actor, she decided.

They both looked brave in their own way. And looking at their well-used weapons, she knew they must both be great warriors. The runes on Felix's sword glowed with an inner fire like some enchanted blade in a story. Gotrek's axe looked as if it could knock down a tree with one sweep. But in the end she knew it would not matter; they were doomed. The beasts would see to that.

Despite herself she gasped when they entered the clearing. The leader, the one who held the snuffling mutant on the end of his chain, was the same one who had spared her in the inn the previous evening. She knew he had come looking for her, just for her, to rectify his error. His followers were some of those she had seen rampaging through the village. They were all massive; taller than Felix, heavier than Gotrek. Seeing the two warriors standing by the fire she realised what an unequal contest it was. Man against monster; outnumbered and outmatched, they would have no chance.

For a second they stood frozen, facing each other. Caught up in the drama of the situation Kat forgot her own fears. She held her breath. Gotrek crouched like a great gargoyle, his axe held lightly in one hand. Felix stood in the classic pose of the fencer that she had once seen the noble Hugo use at practice. Massed against them were the misshapen beasts, slouching confidently, weapons at ease.

She heard Gotrek's rumbled 'Ready, manling?', and Felix's answering 'As I'll ever be.' She saw the Slayer run his thumb over the blade of his axe until a bead of blood glistened on its tip. She heard his mad laughter and saw him charge. Felix followed in his footsteps. Unable to watch them get cut down, she closed her eyes.

She heard a great crunch and a howl of pain. That was the dwarf, she knew. He was the first to die. She heard the ring of steel on steel and the hoarse grunts of exertion followed by more cries of pain. Felix had gone too. But still the sound of fighting went on, longer than she would have thought possible. But eventually the sound of battle faded, as she had known it would. Burned hollow with terror, she opened her eyes to face her fate.

Felix charged. Ahead of him he saw the Slayer leap to one side as a spear lashed out at him. Gotrek caught the shaft with his left hand and moved forward, sliding his grip along the spear's length, holding it immobile as he closed. Once within striking distance he lashed out with his axe, splitting the astonished beastman's skull like a melon. There was a crunch and a strangled howl of pain. Good, thought Felix; one less to worry about.

He engaged blade to blade with a scimitar-wielding monstrosity. His sword rang against it, notching the rusted steel of his opponent's weapon. The thing was strong but unskilled. With a life of its own, Felix's enchanted blade found its way through the creature's guard. Within a matter of seconds he had it bleeding from several small cuts. It let out an angry bellow and hewed at him with a stroke that could have cut Felix in half. He leapt back, parrying wildly. Sparks flew as the blades made contact. His arm felt numb from the impact.

He looked up into the beastman's face. Foam flecked its lips and madness danced in its eyes. It lashed out again, its blade a blurring arc. Reflexively Felix ducked beneath it and stepped forward, his blade skewering up. The beast's warm entrails poured out over his hands. It reeled back trying to hold in its intestines with one hand, whimpering like a stuck pig. The other beastman had recovered from the surprise of being attacked and leapt into the fray.

It charged forward, head down, spear aimed at a point six inches behind Felix's back. The beastman slipped on his companion's guts and fell at Felix's feet. The young warrior offered up a prayer of gratitude to Sigmar and beheaded it with one easy stroke. He turned, sword sweeping, and put the other one out of its misery.

Gotrek had disposed of his two lesser foes and was engaged in a duel with the beastman leader. The mutant-tracker was nowhere to be seen. It had fled. Looking at the scene of carnage Felix reconstructed what must have happened. The Slayer's sudden charge, two great rending strokes, the first of which had split a skull, the second of which had staved in rib cages. The eyeless beast was made of sterner stuff.

Axe and club flickered back and forth with sight-blurring speed. Sparks flew as starmetal bit into the steel studs covering the bludgeon's head. The beast was larger but slower. The impact of the Slayer's axe drove him back with every stroke. Felix wondered whether he should help Gotrek but decided against it. Gotrek wouldn't thank him and the possibility of being accidentally caught by a stroke of his axe was too frightening to contemplate.

The beast made a massive desperate swing at the Slayer's head. Gotrek skipped back out of reach and caught the head of the club in the curve of his axe blade. With a swift twist he jerked the weapon from the beastman's hand, disarming it.

The dwarf's face held an expression of cold fury such as Felix had never seen before. There was no mercy written there, only anger and grim determination. Gotrek struck it on the leg, knocking it over. Blood flowed from the tendon-cutting wound. The creature gave a shrill screech of pain and rolled over. As it did so, the ancient axe descended like that of an executioner. The eyeless beastman's head parted from his shoulders and the thing tumbled lifeless to the ground.

The Slayer spat on the corpse then shook his head as if in disgust. 'Too easy,' he said. 'I hope that Chaos Warrior is tougher.'

Privately Felix hoped they would never find out.

Felix marched along with a spring in his step. He was not tired, despite his lack of sleep the previous evening and the rough terrain through which they passed didn't daunt him. He breathed in deeply, enjoying even the still air and the musty forest scents. At least he was still capable of breathing.

He was still alive! The sun filtered down through the leaves, catching spinning motes of dust, making them dance like fairy lights. He wanted to reach out and collect a handful of them, as if it were some kind of magic powder. For a moment the forest was transformed; they moved through an enchanted grove where foot-high mushrooms sprouted in the shadow of the great trees. Just then they did not look sinister; they were a promise of the continuity of life.

He was still alive. He repeated it to himself like a mantra. He had passed through terror and come out the other side. His foes, the monsters who had wanted to kill him, were dead. And he was still here, to feel the sunlight and drink in the air and watch Gotrek and Kat pick their way downhill, feeling their way from stone to stone set in the mud of the steep and slippery trail.

His senses were keener and he felt more alive, more full of energy, than he had ever been. It was simply a joy to be there.

Webs glistened with early morning dew. Birds sang. All around the forest was pregnant with the stirrings of life. Small animals moved through the undergrowth. Felix paused to let a snake cross the path and made no attempt to kill it. This morning he had a feeling of how precious life was, how fragile.

The fight with the beasts had brought home to him how tentative his grip on living was, how easily the cord of his life could be severed. It could have been him lying cold in an unmarked grave, or more likely filling the stomach of the beastman. The difference had been some luck, a bit of skill and the correct use of his blade. It could all have gone so much differently. One mistake and he might not have been here to enjoy this glorious morning. He could be wandering in Morr's misty grey kingdom or pitched into the oblivion which some scholars claimed was the only thing after death.

He knew the thought should frighten him – but it did not. Here and now he was too happy. In his mind he replayed every stroke of the fight, remembered every move with something close to love. He felt exalted; he had matched himself against mighty foes and come away the master. The forest could not frighten him today.

He knew that the feeling was artificial; he had felt something like it before on many occasions after he had fought. He knew that it would fade and be replaced by a horror at and guilt about what he had done, but for the moment he could stop himself. He was forced to admit that, in a strange way, he had enjoyed the battle. The violence had appealed to something dark in him, something that he usually kept hidden even from himself. For a moment he felt he could almost understand those who followed the Blood God, Khorne, who were addicted to bloodshed, combat and excitement. There could be no greater thrill than gambling with your life. There was no stake higher, except perhaps your soul.

That thought stopped him. He could see that his thoughts had been leading him down the path of sin. Perhaps all those who sold themselves to the Ruinous Powers started this way, taking pleasure in their own dark side. He had seen where that road led, and so he let his mind veer.

Ahead Gotrek stooped to inspect some tracks in the mud. Perhaps, Felix speculated, he was too addicted to battle. Perhaps this was why he followed his peculiar vocation – perhaps it was as much for his own gratification as for the atonement of the sins he had committed. Why else would anyone follow such a strange path, that led down such dark roads? Perhaps the Slayer's motives were less noble and tragic than he pretended.

Felix sighed; he would never know. The dwarf was alien to him, the product of a different society with a different code of ethics, perhaps even a different picture of the world looked at through different senses. He doubted that he would ever understand Gotrek. Every time he felt close to it, the understanding eluded him. The dwarf was different – strong in ways that Felix could never hope to be, brave beyond sanity, seemingly oblivious to pain and weariness.

Was that why Felix followed him? Out of admiration and a wish to be like him? To have his certainty and his strength? Certainly his life would have been much different now if he had not sworn his oath to follow the dwarf that drunken night in Altdorf. Perhaps he would have been happier. On the other hand, he would not have seen half of what he had seen, for good or for ill. There were times when the Slayer seemed like his own personal daemon sent to upset his life and lead him to the darkness.

He made his way carefully down the slope, watching where he placed his feet, feeling the hard rocks under the thin leather soles of his boots. When he reached the bottom of the hill he saw what Gotrek and Kat were looking at. The path had divided at a fork. There was a league marker by the right hand way – not the usual stone slab left to mark the Empire's highways but a simple block cut from the trunk of a tree. Felix read it.

'We'll be in Flensburg in a couple of hours then,' he said.

'If it's still standing, manling,' Gotrek said and spat.

'I wish I was brave like you, Felix,' Kat said.

Felix surveyed the open glade. The woods were thinner here and there was evidence of logging. Stumps littered the forest floor. Tangles of vegetation grew round them. Here and there saplings sprouted. The air had a hint of the fresh smell of new-cut wood about it. In the distance he thought he could hear the roar of a river. Overhead, through the break in the branches, the sky was bright and clear and blue. Far to the east, though, they could all see great storm clouds gathering. Thunderclouds piled one on the other, huge, insubstantial moving mountains drifting ever closer. Another evil omen.

He glanced down at the girl. Her soot-covered face was serious. 'What did you say?'

'I said, 'I wish I was brave like you'.'

He laughed at that. Something about her openness and transparent desire to be liked touched him. 'I'm not brave.'

'Yes you are. Fighting those beasts was brave – like something a hero in a tale would do.'

He tried to picture himself as a hero from one of the sagas he had been fond of as a youth, a Sigmar or an Oswald. Somehow he couldn't quite manage it. He knew himself too well. Those men had been god-like, flawless. In fact Sigmar had become a god, the patron deity of the Empire he had founded. People like that never knew fear or doubt or venality.

'I was scared. I was only trying to stay alive. I'm not brave – Gotrek is.'

She shook her head emphatically. 'Yes, he is – but so are you. You were scared and fought anyway. I think that's why you're brave.'

She was completely serious. Felix was amused and not a little flattered. 'No one's ever accused me of that before.'

She turned and pouted, thinking he was making fun of her. 'Well I think you are, anyway. It doesn't matter what no one says.'

He stood a little taller and pulled his ragged cloak tight. Strange – he had become used to seeing Gotrek as the hero of an epic tale, the one he was supposed to write on the Slayer's death. He had never imagined himself as a part of that tale before. He had always pictured himself more as an invisible observer, a chronicler of the dwarf's exploits, unmentioned in the text. Maybe the child had a point. Maybe he should devote some space to his own adventures as well.

The Saga of Gotrek and Felix. No – My Travels with Gotrek. By Herr Felix Jaeger. He could picture it as a leather-bound book, printed in immaculate Gothic script on one of his father's printing presses. It would be written in Reikspiel of course, a popular work. Classical was too stuffy, the language of scholars and lawyers and priests. Maybe it would be read all across the Known World. He might become as famous as Detlef Sierck or the great Tarradasch himself.

He would put in all their various adventures. The destruction of the coven on Geheimnisnacht; their skirmishes with wolf riders in the land of the Border Princes. All the events leading up to the destruction of Fort von Diehl. Their ventures into the dark beneath the world. Their battles with the Horned Man and their journey through the plague pits below Altdorf.

He tried to imagine how he would portray himself in the story – of course he would be brave, loyal, modest. Reality began to intrude on his daydream almost immediately. Brave? Maybe. He had faced some scary situations without dishonour. Loyal? If he stuck with the Slayer until the end he would certainly be that. Modest? Unlikely, since how modest was it to include oneself in the saga of someone else's adventures? Perhaps it wasn't such a good idea after all. He would just have to wait and see.

'If you're not a hero and Gotrek is, why do you travel with him?'

'Why do you ask such difficult questions, little one?' Felix asked, hoping the Slayer couldn't hear. Gotrek had wandered far ahead across the glade, wrapped up in his own dour thoughts.

It was a difficult question, Felix decided. Why did he follow the Slayer? The simple answer was because he was sworn to. He had taken an oath that drunken night after the Slayer had pulled him out from underneath the hooves of the Emperor's cavalry. He was honour-bound to keep his promise. He owed the dwarf a debt for saving his life.

In the beginning he had thought that was why he had stuck by Gotrek, but now he had another theory. The dwarf had presented him with the perfect excuse to adventure, to see far places and dark things. Things that interested and excited him. He could have stayed at home and become a boring merchant like his older brother, Otto. He had never wanted that, had always rebelled against it. The Slayer's quest had provided him with a reason to leave Altdorf. One that he had used to rationalise his own wish to go anyway. Since then he had lived an extraordinary life, one not so very different from that of the hero of a saga. He no longer knew what he would do if he ceased to travel with Gotrek. He couldn't imagine going back to his old life.

'I'm damned if I know,' Felix said eventually.

The arrow hit the tree trunk beside Gotrek and stayed there, quivering. The Slayer glared around, sniffing the air and peering into the long grass. Had the beasts caught up with them again? Why had they not just shot them?

Felix looked at the black feathers attached to the shaft. It couldn't be beastmen, he thought. It didn't look like their type of weapon. Kat hadn't mentioned seeing any of them armed with bows. His skin crawled with the threat of danger. He strained his senses to hear any sound. All he could hear was the wind in the branches, the singing of birds and the sound of the distant river.

'That was a warning shot,' said a voice, coarse and untutored. 'Don't come any closer.'

Downwind, Felix thought, the archer is downwind. Very professional. The same thought undoubtedly occurred to Gotrek as he glared at where the words had come from.

'I'll give you a warning shot all right. Come out and face my axe,' he said. 'Are you warriors or weaklings?'

'Doesn't sound like a beastman,' another voice said, off to the left. It sounded hearty. There was a hint of mirth so great that it could not be kept in check, no matter how serious the situation.

'Who can tell – these are strange times. Certainly doesn't look like a man.' This from a woman somewhere behind them. Felix turned to look but could see nothing. The area between his shoulder blades crawled. He expected an arrow to plant itself between them at any moment.

Gotrek's voice was full of wrath. 'Are you implying that I could be of your weak race? I'll make you eat those words, human. I'm a bloody dwarf!'

'Perhaps you should restrain yourself until we can see our ambushers,' Felix whispered, then he shouted: 'Forgive my friend. He is a great enemy of the Ruinous Powers and takes insult easily. We are not beastmen or mutants, as you can undoubtedly see. We are simple swords for hire, en route to Nuln and work. We mean no harm to you, whoever you are.'

'He's fair spoken an' that's for sure,' the first voice said. 'Hold your fire, lads. Until I give the word.'

'Could be he's a sorcerer – they're said to be educated men,' the woman's voice said. 'Maybe the child's his familiar.'

'Nah, that's Kat from the Kleindorf Inn. She's served me often enough. I'd know that hair anywhere.' The jovial voice sounded thoughtful for a moment. 'Maybe they've kidnapped her. I hear there's a good market for virgin sacrifices in Nuln.'

Felix thought that things could easily turn very nasty here. These people sounded scared and suspicious, and it wouldn't take much to convince them to fill him full of arrows and question the child later. He wracked his brains looking for a way out. He hoped Gotrek could restrain his natural inclination to go diving headlong into trouble or they might both be finished.

'Is that you, Herr Messner?' Kat said suddenly.

Sigmar bless you child, thought Felix. Keep them talking. Every word spoken increases the human contact, makes it harder for them to think of us as faceless foes.

'Don't kill them. They protected me from the beasts. They're not warlocks or Chaos-lovers.' She looked up at Felix with bright eyes. 'It's Herr Messner, one of the old Duke's rangers. He used to sing me songs and tell me jokes when he came to the inn. He's a nice man.'

That nice man is probably only a few seconds from putting an arrow between my eyes, thought Felix. 'Kat's right. We did kill beasts. We may have to kill many more. They destroyed Kleindorf – they may be on the march right now. They're led by a warrior of Khorne.'

A large paunchy man emerged from the woods to Felix's right. He was garbed in leathers and a mottled cloak of green and brown. Felix was surprised. He must have looked at the man several times and never known he was there. He had a bow in one big hand but he did not point it at either Gotrek or Felix. His movements were uncannily quiet for such a big man.

He stopped ten paces from the side of the trail and stared at them as if measuring them. His face was battered and his grey hair thinning. His nose looked broken and flattened. He had cauliflower ears like an ageing prize-fighter. His eyes were as grey and cold as steel.

'Nah – you don't look like hellspawn an' that's for sure. But if you're not you've certainly picked a fine time to go wandering in the woods – what with every warped soul from here to Kislev on the move.'

'Then why are you here?' Gotrek asked. His face was dark, his anger barely held in check.

'Not that I have to answer your questions, mind, but it's my job. Me an' the lads keep an eye on things in these woods for the old Duke. An' I can tell you just now I don't like what I've been seein'.'

He rubbed his nose with his knuckles and stood staring at them. Felix tried to gauge the man. He sounded like a peasant but there was a keenness to his eye and a humour to his lazy drawl that suggested a clever man cunningly concealed. He looked slow to anger but Felix guessed that, once aroused, he would be a formidable foe. In his quiet way he was frightening. The way he stood casually facing the Slayer suggested one who was sure of his authority. Felix had seen his sort before – trusted retainers who had their lord's confidence and who often dispensed instant justice on their holdings.

'We are not your enemies,' Felix said. 'We are just passing on the Emperor's road. We want no trouble.'

The man laughed as if Felix had said something amusing. 'Then you're in the wrong place, lad. Something's got the old beastmen stirred up like I ain't seen them in a score of years. They've left a trail of destruction from wood to mountain an' from what you're saying they've done for Kleindorf as well. Pity – I always liked the place. What of Klein an' his soldiers? Surely they must have done somethin'.'

'Died,' Gotrek said and laughed caustically. The forester looked at him. Anger was in his eyes.

'Nah – there was the castle. That's been there nigh on six hundred years. Beasts never attack fortifications. Don't have the strategy. It's what's kept us alive in these cursed lands.'

'It's true. What Gotrek says is true,' Kat said. She sounded like she was about to cry.

'I'd watch out for the next village if I were you,' Gotrek said, then added sardonically, 'for sure.'

Messner turned and shouted into the forest: 'Rolf – head west an' see what you can see. Freda – round up the rest of the lads an' meet us in Flensburg. I'll take our friends there. Looks like things are about to turn nasty.'

The others didn't respond. Felix didn't even hear a rustle of the bushes but he sensed that their watchers were gone. He shivered. He had been standing so close to death and never even seen its deliverers. He felt his dislike for the woods returning; he preferred a place where a man could see danger approaching.

Messner gestured for them to follow him. 'Come on. You can tell me what you know along the way. By the time we get to Flensburg I want to know exactly what happened.'

An old man sat cross-legged on a rush mat near the door of a blockhouse, smoking a long curved pipe. He and a young boy were playing draughts with pebbles on a board scratched in the earth. He looked up from his game and eyed Felix with the finely honed suspicion of the woodsman for the stranger, before blowing out several lines of smoke rings into the air. Messner waved to him, a kind of curt salute, and the old man returned it with a convoluted gesture of his left hand. Was he warding off the evil eye, Felix wondered, or communicating in some sign language?

He studied the little town with interest, paying special attention to the burly men carrying large two-handed axes. Their faces were covered with multicoloured scar-tattoos. Their eyes were narrow and watchful. They stomped through the muddy streets in high fur-trimmed boots with all the arrogant assurance of a Middenheim Templar. Sometimes they paused to exchange gossip with the fat fur-hatted traders or to leer at a pretty nut-brown girl carrying pails from the river to the drinking water barrels.

A pot-bellied man shouted Messner over to inspect a pile of furs spread out on wicker mats in front of him. They were obviously the pick of some trapper's haul. Messner shook his head in a friendly manner and strolled on. He stopped only to let laughing barefoot children chase a pig in front of him.

They passed a smokehouse in front of which hung great hams and half carcasses of boar. The smoky smell of the meat made Felix's mouth water. Chickens hung by their necks from thongs attached to the eaves. Felix was reminded uncomfortably of the men hanging from the gibbet outside Kleindorf and he looked away again.

Messner wandered over to the house of a scribe and after a brief consultation took a brush and ink and inscribed something on a tiny piece of paper. Then they marched over to a coop outside one of the blockhouses in which were six fat grey pigeons. Messner rolled the paper up and put it in a steel ring. Then he reached into the coop and took out one of the birds. He ringed it, released it and watched with some satisfaction as it fluttered skyward.

'Well, duty done an' the old Duke warned,' he said. 'Maybe Flensburg will be safe yet.'

Felix thought it might be; it was certainly defensible enough and there must be nearly seven hundred people here. Flensburg lay near the bend of the river, and resembled a great logging camp more than a village or town. It was walled on two sides with a ditch and a wooden palisade. The curve of the river protected the other two sides. From jetties, rafts and great piles of lumber were poled out into the stream to drift to the-gods-knew-what market – probably Nuln eventually, Felix thought.

As they approached, they had seen dozens of the square wooden blockhouses within the thick wooden walls, each built like a miniature fort, with their stout log walls and their flat turf ceilings. The place spoke of the functional; he imagined some of the buildings were storehouses and trading posts. One had a crude hammer shape made from two logs stuck onto the roof – a temple to Sigmar.

Once through the heavy fortified gate, he had seen that the people of Flensburg were like their town: dour, spare, functional. Most of the men were garbed in fur; they were sullen, hard-faced and hard-eyed. They looked at the strangers warily. Their watchfulness seemed inbred. Most carried heavy woodsman's axes. Some, the ones garbed in functional ranger's clothing, carried bows. The women wore gayer colours, thick multi-layered skirts, padded jerkins; their hair was wrapped in red spotted scarves. Matrons marched down the muddy streets carrying baskets of produce, trailed by processions of children like mother ducks leading a line of young.

The people here near the southern border of the woods were shorter than the citizens of the Empire's cities. Their hair was predominantly sandy-brown and their complexions darker and more tanned. Felix knew that they had a reputation as a gloomy, god-fearing folk, superstitious, poor and ill-educated. Looking at these people he could believe it, but he knew that his city-bred prejudices told only half the story.

He had not been prepared for their pride and fearlessness. He had expected something like the downtrodden serfs of a noble's estate. He had found people who looked him fearlessly in the eye and stood tall and straight in the frightening shadows of the great forest. He had thought Messner exceptional but he could see he was typical of his folk. Felix had expected serfs and found freemen, and for some reason that pleased him.

Gotrek looked at the walls and the blockhouses, and turned to Messner. 'Best call your people and tell them what to expect. It won't be good.'

Felix stared out from the watchtower across the cleared area surrounding the village towards the woods beyond. Now that he was out of their shadow, the trees seemed threatening again: giant, alien, alive, their gloom giving shelter to something inimical. He watched the last stragglers of the day filter in through the gates. Beside him, Messner kept watch with his cold grey eyes.

'Things look bad an' that's for sure,' he said.

'I would have thought you often had to deal with the beasts, living in these woods.'

'Right enough we fight them and the outcasts and other things every now and again. But it's always been skirmishes. They steal a child, we kill a few. They raid for pigs, we hunt them down. Sometimes we have to send to the old Duke for troops an' mount an expedition when the raids get too fierce. Ain't seen nothin' like this before though. Somethin's got them stirred up bad an' that's for sure.'

'Could it be this woman, this champion?'

'Seems more than likely. You hear about them in the old stories – the Dark Ones, the champions of Chaos – but you never expect to come across them.'

'There have been times when I've thought that those old stories contain much truth,' Felix said. 'I've seen a few strange things in my travels. I'm not so quick to doubt these days.'

'That's right true, Herr Jaeger. An' I'm glad to hear an educated man like yourself admit as such. I've seen a few strange things myself in these woods. An' there's many an old tale of me da's I don't doubt either. They say there's a Black Altar in those woods somewhere. A thing dedicated to the Dark Ones where humans are sacrificed. They say beastmen and other... things... worship there.'

They lapsed into uneasy silence. Felix felt gloom settle over him. All this talk of the Dark Ones had unsettled him and left him deeply uneasy. He glanced out once more into the clearing.

The women and children had stopped working in the fields and were returning to the safety of the walls, their baskets full of potatoes and turnips. Felix knew that they would take them to the storehouses. The village was preparing itself for a siege. The other women, who had been gathering nuts and herbs in the wood, had returned hours ago when the great warning horn was blown.

The foresters and woodsmen were within, checking the water barrels were full, whittling stakes and attaching the metal heads to spears. From behind him he could hear the continuous whizz and thunk of arrows impacting on targets as the archery practice continued.

Felix wondered whether it made more sense for him to stay or slip off into the woods. Maybe he could take a raft and drift away downriver. He did not know which was worse – the thought of being alone in the forest or of being trapped here with the forces of Chaos closing in. He tried to dismiss these thoughts as unworthy, to remember Gotrek's words about mastering fear, but the terror of being trapped in the maze of trees nagged constantly at the back of his mind.

As he looked out, a group of rangers hurried across the fields; Felix could see that they were carrying someone wounded. One kept glancing back over his shoulder as if expecting pursuit. Two of the remaining women moved to help him.

'That's Mikal and Dani,' Messner said. 'Looks like there's been trouble. Better go and find out what's happened. Stay here, keep your eyes peeled; if anything happens, blow the horn.'

He thrust the great instrument into Felix's hand, and before he could raise any objections Messner had swung himself down through the trapdoor and was halfway down the ladder. Felix shrugged and stroked the smooth metal of the horn with his fingers. The cool weight was reassuring even if he was uncertain as to his ability to sound it. He glanced down at the top of the hunter's head, noticing for the first time the bald spot on the top of his skull. He gave his attention back to the fields.

The men reeled forward bearing their companion. The gates creaked open and villagers rushed forward to help them, Messner in the lead. Felix saw the way they all jumped to obey the duke's man's orders. That Messner was something of a leader in the community had become obvious at the great public meeting held in the village square that afternoon. Burly lumberjacks and old men, stout housewives and slim girls alike had listened to his soft jovial voice as he outlined the danger approaching.

No one had argued with him or doubted him. With Messner to vouch for them, there had been no questioning of Gotrek or Felix's story. They had even listened respectfully to Kat, though she was just a child. He could remember all that had been said and done even now, after they had stopped speaking. The silence, the grim fatalistic expressions on the folk's faces, the warm afternoon sun on the back of his neck. He remembered the way the women with babies had turned and taken them to the central blockhouse, the Temple of Sigmar. The crowd had parted wordlessly to let them pass.

Equally wordlessly, the men had divided into squads of archers and axe-men. It was obvious to Felix that he was watching a well-practiced routine devised for just this eventuality. Messner had given orders in his usual calm voice. There was no shouting here, nor any need for it. These people had the discipline of those for whom discipline represented the only means of survival in a harsh land.

In a way, he had envied them their sense of community; they relied on each other implicitly. As far as he could tell, no one doubted the ability or loyalty of anyone else. It must be the flip side of the coin of living in an isolated community, he realised. Everyone here had known each other for most of their lives. The bonds of trust must be hard and strong.

For a time it had seemed to Felix that he was the only one out of place here, but then he noticed Kat. She too stood slightly apart from the crowd, marked among the children present as much by her strange hair as by her grubby clothing. He had felt a strong sense of sympathy for her then and wondered what would become of her. From what she and Messner had discussed en route, he had gathered she was an orphan. Felix's own mother had died when he was still a child and this had strengthened his feeling of sympathy for her.

Was she important to the Dark Warrior, he wondered? Had the beastmen he had fought been simple scouts or had they been seeking Kat? Not for the first time in his life he found himself wishing he knew more of the ways of Darkness. Knowing that to be a sinful thought, he pushed it aside.

He heard the wounded man groaning below as they brought him through the gate.

* * *

Kat hurried to the base of the watchtower, feeling a need for solitude. She had grown tired of sitting near the big central fire. Even the presence of Gotrek did not reassure her. She felt very lonely here amidst all the busy adults. There was no one, really, to talk to and for the first time it was coming home to her that she knew no one in this world now and had no place in it. The flames reminded her too much of the burning of Kleindorf. The ladder creaked slightly under her bare feet. She ascended, nimble as a monkey, to the watchpost.

Felix was sitting alone, staring out into the darkness. The sun had long ago set, like a bloody smear on the horizon. The greater moon had drifted skyward. Silver light washed down. A slight breeze chilled Kat's cheeks and made the forest whisper and rustle menacingly. Felix watched it as if hypnotised, lost in his own dark thoughts. She scuttled swiftly over and sat cross-legged beside him.

'Felix, I'm scared,' she said. He looked down at her and smiled.

'Me too, little one.'

'Stop doing that!'

'Doing what?'

'Calling me "little one". The same as Gotrek does. He never calls anyone by their proper names, does he? My name is Kat. You should call me that.'

Felix smiled at her. 'All right, Kat. Could you do something for me? It might be important for us all.'

'If I can.'

'Tell me about your parents.'

'I don't have any.'

'Everyone has a mother and father, Kat.'

'Not me. I was found by Heidi, Karl's wife, in a basket where she always picked berries.'

Felix laughed. 'You were found under a berry bush?'

'It's not funny, Felix. They say there was a she-monster nearby. The villagers killed it. They wanted to kill me too but Heidi wouldn't let them.' Felix struggled to keep his face straight. His mirth vanished when he saw how serious her expression was.

'No, you're right. It wasn't funny.'

'They took me in and looked after me. Now they're dead.'

'Did Karl and Heidi have any idea who your parents were? Any idea at all?'

'Why are you asking this, Felix? Is it really important?'

'It could be.'

Kat thought back, to that night when old Karl had got drunk. He and Heidi had thought she was asleep. She had slipped down to the kitchen to get a drink of water and overheard them talking. When she had realised that they were talking about her, she had frozen in place on the other side of the door. The memory of that evening came flooding back. She had wanted to ask them more, ask them what they had meant but she had been too scared to. Now she realised she would never get the chance.

'I once heard them talk about a young girl at the castle who had hair like mine,' she said quietly, struggling to remember it all. 'Her name was Justine. She was a distant cousin of Lord Klein or something, a poor relation who had come to live with the family. She vanished the year before I was born. No one ever found out what happened to her.'

'I think I know,' Felix said softly.

Footsteps approached the bottom of the tower. The ladder trembled and Messner's head poked through the trapdoor.

'There you are, Herr Jaeger. I've come to relieve you. Go below and get something to eat. You too, child. No sign of Rolf? He's still missing.'

'I haven't seen anything,' Felix said.

'I wonder what could have happened to him.'

'What is your name?' Justine asked. The bearded man whom her scouts had captured spat at her. She nodded to Malor. The beastman brought his fist forward. There was a crack as ribs broke. The man slumped. If it had not been for the two beasts supporting him he would have fallen.

'What is your name?'

The man opened his mouth. Blood trickled down his chin and onto his leather jerkin. Justine reached out and took some on her fingertip. When she tasted it, it felt warm and salty and strength flowed through her.

'Rolf,' he said eventually. Justine knew then that he would tell her whatever she asked. She knew that it had not been the foresters who had killed Tryell's band. The tracker who had survived the assault on the camp had told her about the girl's guardians.

'There is a dwarf and a blond-haired man travelling with a young girl. Tell me about them.'

'Go to the hell that spawned you.'

'That I will… eventually,' Justine said. 'But you will be there to greet me.'

He shrieked as one of the beastmen dislocated his shoulder. His entire body stiffened with pain. The muscles in his neck stood out like taut wires. Eventually the tale of how he had met with the dwarf, the man and the girl in the forest came tumbling from his cracked lips. At last the man stopped speaking and stood before her, drained by his own confession.

'Take him to the altar!' Justine commanded.

The man tried to struggle as they carried him towards Kazakital's cairn. His efforts to escape were futile. The beasts were too strong and too many. He wept with terror when he saw what awaited him. He was more daunted by the sight of that great cairn and the black altar atop it than he had been when he was taken captive by the beasts. He must know what's coming, Justine thought. The sight of the heads of Lord Klein and Hugo seemed to scare him most of all.

'No! Not that!' he shrieked.

She saw to his binding herself and carried him to the altar easily. The army gathered in anticipation of what was coming. As the moon broke through the clouds she gestured for the drummers to begin. Soon the great drum sounded rhythmic and slow as a heartbeat.

She stood atop the cairn and sensed the slow gathering of forces. She looked out and down at a sea of animal faces. They were upturned, eyes bright with anticipation. She drew her sword and brandished it above her head.

'Blood for the Blood God!' she shouted.

'Skulls for the skull throne!' The answering cry was torn from a hundred throats.

'Blood for the Blood God!'

'Skulls for the skull throne!' The response was even louder this time. It rumbled like thunder in the woods.

'Blood for the Blood God!'

'Skulls for the skull throne!'

The blade came down and parted Rolf's ribs. She reached forward and stuck her gauntleted hand into the sticky mass of the man's innards. There was a hideous sucking noise as she tore the heart free and held it high over her head.

Somewhere, in a space beyond space, in a time beyond time, something stirred and came in answer to her call. It flowed inwards, spiralling from beyond. In the space over the altar a red pulsing darkness gathered. It flowed into the heart she held above her and it began to beat once again. She reached out and placed the heart back within the sacrifice's chest.

For a moment, nothing happened and all was silence, then a great scream emerged from the throat of the thing that had once been Rolf. The flesh of the corpse's chest flowed together and began to smoke. The corpse sat upright on the altar. It eyes opened and Justine recognised the intelligence which peered out from within. The body was temporarily possessed by the mind of her daemonic patron, Kazakital.

Smoke rose from the corpses as flesh flowed beneath skin. A smell of rot and burning flesh combined filled her nostrils. The mind and the power contained within the deathless frame was moulding it into a new shape, a shape that bore some resemblance to the Daemon Prince's inhumanly beautiful form. Justine knew that the body would be burned out within minutes, unable to contain the power which pulsed within it, but that did not matter. She needed only a few minutes to commune with her lord and seek his council.

Swiftly she outlined what Rolf had told her. 'I will go to this place and kill everyone there.'

'Do that, beloved,' the Daemon Prince's lovely voice tolled like a bell from within its corrupting form. Once again she felt the sense of certainty and of worship that she always did in his presence.

'I will kill the girl. I will give you the hearts of the dwarf and the man if they try to protect her.'

'Best kill them quickly. They are a fell pair, ruthless and deadly. The dwarf carries a weapon forged in ancient days to be the bane of gods. They are both killers without mercy.'

'They are both as good as dead. I stand armoured in your prophecy. No warrior will ever overcome me in battle. If what you have spoken is the truth.'

'Search your heart, beloved. You know I have never spoken anything but the truth to you. And know you this also – if you do this thing, immortality and a place among the Chosen will most certainly be yours.'

'It will be done.'

'Go then with my blessing. Spread chaos and terror and leave none of your chosen prey among the living.'

The sense of presence ended. The corpse fell headlong into the dirt, already starting to crumble to dust. Justine turned to her troops and gave them the signal to move out.

Felix looked up at the ornate golden hammer. The sun's rays fell on it through the open door of the temple, making it shimmer in the early morning light. The runes that encrusted the hammerhead reminded him of those which adorned his own blade. He was not too surprised.

His sword had been the prized possession of the Order of the Fiery Heart, a group of Sigmarite Templars. It seemed only natural that the blade should have holy markings.

There were few other people present; just some old women who sat cross-legged on the floor and prayed. Babes and their mothers were outside taking in the fresh air while they could. Felix imagined that it could get very stuffy in here with the door barred.

The temple was a simple shrine. The altar was bare save for the hammer used to sanctify weddings and contracts. Sigmar was not so popular a deity here. Most woodsmen looked to Taal, Lord of the Forests, for protection, but he imagined that the Cult of the Hammer would find some favour. Few wanted to willingly offend the gods. The shrine would also provide a link with the distant capital. It was a sign that there was an Empire, with laws and those who would enforce them. The state cult was the link which bound the disparate, distant peoples of the Empire together.

The walls bore none of the friezes and tapestries so popular in richer areas. The altar itself was carved from a block of wood, not stone. He was tempted to touch the hammer, to find out if it were gilded or simply painted. The carving of the altar was of no ordinary quality, however. He admired the coiling around the edges and a representation of the First Emperor's head that would not have been out of place among the icons in Altdorf cathedral. He wondered who was responsible for the woodwork. He also wondered whether it would burn when the beasts came.

Felix bowed his head and made the Sign of the Hammer and prayed. He prayed that the town would be delivered, and that his life and the lives of his friends would be spared. He touched his hand to the hammer and then to his forehead for good luck and then rose to depart. He stretched, feeling his joints click. He had spent last night in the blockhouse of Fritz Messner and his family. The floor had been marginally preferable to a cold pile of leaves. He had to admit there were times when he missed his down-mattressed bed in Altdorf; there were times when being the son of a wealthy merchant had been not altogether bad. Right now, for instance, he could be sleeping off a hangover in his chambers rather than awaiting the attack of Chaos in some village no one had ever heard of.

'Felix…' It was the girl, pale and unsmiling. 'Herr Messner told me I would find you here.'

'He was right, Kat. What can I do for you?'

'I had a nightmare last night, Felix. I dreamt that something came out of the forest and dragged me away. I dreamt I was lost in the dark and things were chasing me...'

Felix could sympathise with that. Many times he had endured similar bad dreams.

'Hush, little one. They're not real. Dreams can't hurt you.'

'I don't think that's true, Felix. I had the same dream the night before the beasts attacked my home.'

Felix suddenly felt chilled to the bone. In his mind's eye, he could picture the forces of Chaos marching ever closer, bringing their inevitable doom.

Justine sat high in the saddle on the back of her immense, midnight-black charger. Overhead the storm clouds gathered, huge dark thunderheads that seemed to echo the mood of violent rage that boiled within her. This trail, part of the Imperial Highway, was clear. It had been constructed over the years to allow the Emperor's messengers to pass quickly.

She thought it ironic that such paths would speed the Empire's inevitable destruction by Chaos. Invaders from the wastes could use them to move quickly westward. She likened this process to the way diseases used the body's own bloodstream to spread. Yes, she thought, the Empire was dying and Chaos was the disease which would kill it. Secret cabals of cultists spreading corruption in the cities; bands of beastmen and mutants bringing terror in the forests; champions of the Ruinous Powers crossing the border from Kislev and the wastes beyond. She knew these were not unrelated occurrences but symptoms of the same blight. First the Empire and then all the kingdoms of men would fall prey to it. No – she mustn't think of it as a disease, she told herself. It was a crusade to scourge the earth.

She looked back on the small army that followed her. First the squads of beastmen; huge, deformed and mighty, each led by its own champion. After them rumbled the great black bulk of her secret weapon, the Thunderer, the long-snouted daemonic cannon which had destroyed the gates of Castle Klein and would make it possible for her to take other fortified towns. It was pulled by teams of captured slaves driven by the black-armoured artificers who would man it. Bringing up the rear were the scavengers, the ill-organised rabble who followed like jackals following a pride of lions. Mutants, malformed and demented, driven from their villages and homes by the hatred of their normal kin. They were driven by hate and ready to revenge themselves on humanity.

All the elements of her own life were there, she thought. This road, the route to death and destruction, was simply an extension of the path she had followed all her days. That thought saddened her. Today more than ever she felt riven. It was as if she were two souls inhabiting the same body. One was dark, driven, fed on slaughter and carnage; it gloried in its strength and despised others their weaknesses. It despised her own weakness. She knew this was the side of her Kazaki-tal cultivated as carefully as the gardeners of Parravon nurtured their hellflowers. It possessed the seeds of daemonhood and of immortality. It was a pure hateful being, driven, determined, strong.

The other soul was weak and she hated it. It was sickened by the unending violence of her life and just wanted it to stop. It was the side of her that felt pain, and the urge to give in to pain and not allow pain to befall others. It had been long submerged and twisted almost out of all recognition by the events of her life. Up until the death of Hugo, she had not even allowed herself to know that it still existed. The thought was too horrible, her need for revenge too strong and urgent. She had made her pact with the daemon seven long years ago; and she had needed to keep it in order to gain vengeance. Now her purpose had been fulfilled and once again she knew doubt.

The doubt centred upon the child. She could remember carrying it within her. She could remember feeling it grow and kick. She had borne it during the long, sick period of wandering in the wild, when she had scrabbled for roots and grubs, drunk from streams and slept in the hollows beneath trees. It had been her only companion in the wild days after she had run off in fear and horror. It had been a growing presence within her as hunger, hardship and horror had driven her slowly mad.

She doubted that she or it would have survived if she had not encountered the beastwomen in the forest; if they had not taken her in and guarded her and fed her. She remembered them as being oddly shy and gentle compared to the gors and ungors. They had acted on the instruction of their daemonic patron, that was now clear, but she was no less grateful to them for that. They had taken the child away from her on the day of its birth and she had not seen it from that day to this. She knew now, had earned the right to know through long years of tests and battle, that this had all been part of her patron's plan, a daemonic strategy designed to allow her to transcend her mere humanity and join the ranks of the Elect. She knew it was her last tie with frail humanity and she despised it – and wondered at it too.

She recalled how it had all begun. The beasts had dragged her before that great black altar in the forest. They had brought her to bow before the black stone inscribed with dreadful runes. They had laid her down on the rock and Grind had slashed her throat and wrists with his razor-edged obsidian blade while his acolytes chanted the praises of the Blood God.

She had expected to die then, and she would have welcomed it as an end to her suffering. Instead she had found the darkest of new lives. Her blood had burst forth, to be caught in the depression on the altar's surface. She had somehow pushed herself upright, kept on her feet by rage and defiance and a strangely serene hatred that blossomed within her. That was when she had sensed the presence. That was when she had seen the face.

In the pool of her own blood she had seen the daemon's form take shape. Crimson lips had emerged from the red liquid and mouthed questions and answers and promises. It had asked her whether she wanted revenge on those who had brought her to this. It had told her that the world was as corrupt and evil as she thought. It promised her power and eternal life. It had spoken its prophecy. Somehow she had stood, swaying and filled with pain, throughout the ordeal. Afterwards she seemed to remember that her own blood, blackened and smoking, had somehow flowed back from the altar and returned to her veins. The wounds slurped shut, while poison and power blazed through her.

For days she had lain in burning dreams while her body changed, touched by the daemonic essence carried within her own tainted blood. Darkness twisted her and made her strong. Her fangs grew in her mouth. Her eyes changed so that they could see in the dark. Her muscles grew far stronger than a mortal man's. She had emerged from her trance knowing that it was not chance which had brought her to this concealed altar in the forest's depths, it was a dark destiny and the malign whim of a daemon's will.

From somewhere the beastmen produced a suit of black armour, covered in runes. At the following full Morrslieb they had repeated the ritual. Once more her wrists had been cut, once more the daemonic presence appeared. This time the armour was fixed to her body. The blood had flowed and congealed between its plates, forming a network of muscles, veins and fleshy pads which made the armour a second metal skin. The process had left her weak. Once more she had dreamed, and in that dream she had seen what she must do.

She had left the beasts for long years of wandering. Her trek took her ever northwards, through Kislev, through the Troll Country, to the

Chaos Wastes and the long eternal war fought between the followers of Darkness. She had battled and fought for the favour of her Dark Gods and in every combat Kazakital's prophecy had proven true. She had overcome Helmar Ironfist, the bull-horned champion of Khorne. She'd sacrificed Marlane Marassa, the flame-hearted priestess of Tzeentch, on her own altar. She had torn Zakariah Kaen, the grossly obese champion of Slaanesh, limb from perfumed limb. She had fought in minor battles and great sieges. She had stalked her human-oid prey in the ruined mines beneath the lost dwarf citadel of Karag Dum. There she had recruited the servants of the Thunderer.

Each skirmish had brought her new gifts and powers. She had acquired her steed, Shadow, by challenging its owner, Sethram Sch-reiber, to single combat and tearing out his heart as an offering to Khorne. She had taken her hellblade from the mangled corpse of Leander Kjan, the leader of the Company of Nine, after the great battle at Hellmouth. She had overcome mutated beasts and monsters, and grown in skill and power until her patron had told her the time was right to return and take vengeance. And during all that time, as she felt the thrill of triumph and the exultation of victory and the sheer joy of battle sing in her tainted blood, she had sometimes wondered what became of the child, and whether the beasts had spared it.

It was nothing to her now, she knew. There was no connection. It was just another piece of flesh cast loose to live and die hopelessly amid the flotsam of this terrible world. It was the final pawn to be sacrificed in the game which would win her immortality. That was all.

So she told herself. But she knew that Kazakital did nothing with-out reason, and that the child had been spared for a reason. Perhaps this was the final test. Perhaps the daemon hoped to reveal some ultimate flaw within her for its own perverse reasons. In that case, it was doomed to disappointment. She would prove in the end that she was harder than stone. And let the Dark Gods take any who thought to stand in her way.

Felix watched the clouds overhead. They bolted across the sky, a tum-bling billowing mass driven by the fierce wind. The hue of the forest changed from light green to a darker, more ominous shade. It seemed that the trees, like everything else, were waiting.

He stood on the parapet atop the wooden barricade. He stared out over the fields, straining to catch any sight of movement in the undergrowth. He guessed that it was late afternoon. Beside him stood Gotrek, studying his axe disinterestedly. Every ten paces along the walls edge stood an archer – one of the foresters, men who could hit a bullseye at two hundred paces. Beside each were three quivers full of arrows. Measuring the distance to the edge of the trees, Felix realised that the space was a killing ground. Any attackers would get bogged down in the ploughed fields and be easy prey for the archers.

He tried to let the thought reassure him; it did not. Night in the forest was not like the night in the well-lit thoroughfares of Altdorf. When darkness came it was absolute. A man six paces away was a blurred outline. After dark, only the moons provided any light to see by and the clouds would block them out.

Earlier that day the foresters had lined the forest's edge with traps: sharpened branches bent back and tied that would snap forward when a tripwire was triggered; pits to trap the ankles of the unwary, some filled with sharpened stakes and covered with patches of turf; bear traps and mantraps, spring-driven steel jaws ready to bite any interlopers were there too. If the villagers survived the attack they would have their work cut out disarming their own devices. Perhaps the thoroughness with which they had saturated the wood reflected a belief that they would not survive, he thought.

Felix drummed his fingers on the top of the wall, feeling the rough touch of the lichen-covered wood against his fingers. Gotrek hummed tunelessly to himself, ignoring the irritated stares of the woodsmen. The waiting was always the worst of it. No fight he had ever faced had been as bad as the premonitions he had before it. Once action began he would be fine. He would be scared but the simple business of keeping alive would occupy his mind. For now he had nothing to do but stand and wait, and face the spectres his imagination conjured.

He pictured himself wounded, a great beastman standing over him. He imagined himself facing the woman in black and shuddered. He remembered the slaughter at Kleindorf and his terror strained against its leash of self-control. To comfort himself he tried to remember how he had felt after surviving the battle with the beastmen; the memory was pallid. He tried to envisage a scene after the battle with himself and the Slayer as the heroes who had rallied the troops and driven off the beasts. It seemed unconvincing.

'They'll be here soon enough, manling,' Gotrek said. He sounded almost happy.

'That's what I'm worried about.'

Nightmare shapes drifted to the edge of the wood. In the pale light, Felix thought he could see a great horn-headed figure among the trees.

An arrow rushed out from the parapet and fell short. Yes, they were there. More beast silhouettes became visible. Something disturbed the undergrowth. It rustled and moved like water displaced by great behemoths beneath its surface. The clouds parted and the moons leered down. Their glow illuminated a hellish scene.

'Grungni's bones!' Gotrek cursed. 'Look at that!'

'What?'

'There, manling! Look! They've got a siege machine. No wonder Kleindorf fell.'

Felix saw the black-armoured figures. They surrounded a great long-snouted machine, like a many-barrelled siege cannon. With whips they drove back a crowd of snarling mutants. As he watched he saw their twisted leader climb up into a seat at the engine's back. Other dark warriors hurried round the machine's base, pulling out metal legs to secure the thing in place. As the leader turned a great crank the weapon swivelled to bear on the village. Its barrel was moulded in the shape of a dragon's head. Even at this distance Felix could hear the creaks from its mounting. More arrows hurtled towards it but again they fell short. Jeering cries echoed from the woods.

'What is it, Gotrek? What will it do?'

'Damn them – it's a cannon of some sort! Now we know what did for the fortifications at Kleindorf.'

'What can we do?'

'Nothing! After full dark they'll breach the walls and then charge us. The beasts can see in the dark. The villagers cannot.'

'That sounds too sophisticated for beasts.'

'It's not just beasts we fight, manling. It's a Chaos Champion and her entire retinue. They do not lack intelligence. Believe me, I have fought their kind before.'

Felix tried to estimate the number of beastmen in the forest but could not. They kept too well out of sight, knowing that lack of knowledge of their numbers would frighten the defenders even more. Fear of the unknown was another weapon in their armoury. Felix felt his heart sink.

'Maybe we should sally forth and spike the cannon,' Felix suggested.

'That's just what they're waiting for. The killing ground out there will work just as well for them as it would for us.'

'Do they have bows, though – they're beasts.'

'Doesn't matter. There's too many traps out there for comfort. Someone would be bound to blunder into them.'

'I thought you wanted a heroic doom?'

'Manling, if I just stand here and wait it will come to me. Look!'

Felix glanced in the direction indicated by the dwarf's stubby out-stretched finger. He saw the black-armoured Chaos Warrior ride up beside the huge cannon. He could see now that a horde of bestial faces glared out from under the edges of the trees. As he watched, a veritable tide of horned figures flowed out from under the eaves of the forest, and began to form up in units, just out of bow-shot. Somewhere deep in the forest a huge drum began to beat. It was answered by the blast of a horn and the beating of another drum somewhere off to the south. A chorus of screams and bellows filled the night. Somehow, within the rhythmic cadences of the strange words he began to sense a meaning. It was as if the understanding had been bred into his ancestors in ancient times, and it had taken only this event to waken it. Blood for the Blood God. Skulls for the skull throne. He shook his head to clear the hallucination but it did not matter. Whatever he did, it seemed like the thread of understanding would come back.

The noise reached a crescendo, fell silent for a moment and then started again. It grated on the nerves and set the butterflies fluttering in Felix's stomach. Looking out, Felix could see that the chanting served a dual purpose. It worked to undermine the morale of the beastmen's enemies and it helped work the followers of Chaos up into a frenzy. He could see them clashing their weapons against their shields, gnawing the edges of their blades, slashing themselves. They danced insanely, raising their legs and then stomping the earth as if they were crushing the skulls of an enemy beneath their hooves.

'I wish they would just come on and get it over with,' Felix muttered.

'You're about to get your wish,' Gotrek said.

The Chaos Warrior raised her sword. The horde fell suddenly silent. She turned and spoke to them in their own bestial tongue and they answered her with cheers and growls. She turned to the armoured fig-ures atop the siege engine and gestured with her blade. One of them capered for a moment, then lit a fuse. After five long, silent heartbeats the mighty war engine spoke with a voice of thunder. There was a loud whistling sound and then a section of the wall near to Felix exploded, sending fragments of wood, torrents of earth and gobbets of flesh erupting into the air. The beastmen cheered and howled like the hordes of hell unleashed from torment.

Felix flinched as the cannon's barrel began to traverse on its mount. He could see that there was no way these wooden walls could with-stand the sorcerous power of that awful weapon. They had just not been built to stand up to anything like this sort of punishment.

Perhaps the best thing to do would simply be to leap down from the wall and take cover deeper within the township.

Gotrek seemed to sense his thoughts. 'Stay where you are, manling. They will hit the watchtower next.'

'How can you be so sure?'

'I have worked with cannons in my time, and this one is no different from any other. I can tell the trajectory they are shooting at.'

Felix forced himself to stand where he was, despite the way the flesh crawled down his back. He felt certain that he was virtually looking down the muzzle of the weapon. It spoke once more. Flame and smoke gouted from the barrel. Once more the whistling noise sounded. One of the legs of the great wooden watchtower was blasted away as the shot smashed a hole in the palisade in front of it. The tower teetered backwards and fell. One of the sentries fell from his post, arms wheeling, to crash to the ground below. His long wailing cry, audible even above the noise of the beasts, was cut off by his sudden impact on the earth below.

Felix smelled smoke and heard the crackle of burning from behind. He cast a glimpse over his shoulder and saw that one of the buildings and the remains of the tower had started to blaze. He could not tell whether it was as a result of the blast or not. Somewhere in the distance someone started shouting to others to bring water. He cast a glance along the wall where what seemed like a pitifully few defenders waited with their bows clutched near at hand. He exchanged glances with the nearest, a lad of not much more than sixteen years, his face white with dread.

Felix stared out desperately in the gloom, wondering how much longer this could go on, before either the morale of the defenders was broken or the town was reduced to a flattened ruin.

Justine watched as the great cannon smashed a third gap in the town's wall. It was enough, she judged. They needed to save powder for the next fortress they came to. The gaps were large enough for her force to flow through. The defenders were tired and rattled. It was time. She gestured to her trumpeter. He sounded the call to advance. Marching in step to the beat of their human-skinned drums, the beastmen started forward.

Justine felt the bloodlust grow within her, and her desire to offer souls to the Blood God along with it. Tonight she would make him a mighty offering.

Felix watched as the tide of beastmen advanced across the open ground. From the walls, the archers began to fire. Calmly, methodically and efficiently they chose their targets, and let fly. Arrows flashed through the gloom and found homes in bestial breasts and throats and eyes. The blood-crazed Chaos worshippers came on relentlessly, their infernal drums beating. They chanted their call to their foul god in time to the music. Once again, he thought he could pick out the words: Blood for the Blood God. Skulls for the skull throne!

His grip felt slick on the hilt of his sword. Felix felt useless crouched here behind the parapet while others did the fighting and killed their advancing foes. His heart beat faster in his chest. His breath came in short gasps as if he had already run a mile. He fought down a sense of panic. He knew that soon enough it would be time to descend into combat. For now he had a bird's eye view of the struggle. In the distance he saw the black-armoured she-devil urging them on. She looked like a daemonic goddess from the dawn of time come to exact tribute in blood and souls.

He saw one goat-headed beastman fall, his legs caught in the steel jaws of a bear-trap. His companions did not even slow down. They marched on, crushing him to bloody pulp beneath their iron-shod hooves. Casualties did not seem to affect them. They showed no sign of fear. Perhaps it was true. They were soulless daemons immune to all normal emotion. Or perhaps, he told himself, they simply knew that their chance for revenge would soon come.

The beasts were almost upon them now. Felix could see the gleam of firelight reflected in their eyes. He could see the bloody froth on their lips where they appeared to have bitten their own cheeks and tongues in their frenzy. He could smell the musty, furry stench they emitted. He could almost make out the crude runes etched into individual weapons.

All around the archers were letting fly with their last shafts and seizing up their swords and axes. Some had already taken to the ladders and moved to join the units of axe-men on the ground between the buildings. Some were lowering themselves down from the platform on which they stood, dangling at arm's length before dropping the last few strides to the earth below.

'Come, manling,' Gotrek said. 'It's time for bloodletting.'

Felix forced his locked limbs to move. It seemed to take some time to get them to obey him.

Justine smiled as the beastmen picked up their pace and surged through the gaps the great cannon had blown the walls in. She heard the sound of weapon on weapon, steel on steel as they encountered the defenders within. She touched her knees to her steed's flanks. It responded at once with its more than animal intelligence and bore her towards the fray.

Felix blocked the sweep of a beastman's axe. The shock felt like it would dislocate his arm. He dropped to one knee and stabbed upwards, taking the surprised beastman under the ribs and putting the ancient Templar's blade through his victim's heart. Ripping the weapon free, he jumped back just in time to avoid being knocked over by a ranger and a beastman locked in a deadly wrestling match. The two of them fell to the ground in front of him, grunting with effort.

It was obvious to Felix that, given time, the beastman's superior strength would prevail. For a moment he watched appalled ,unsure of what he should do. He did not want to simply flail into the combat with his sword. Instead, he came to an instant decision. He ripped his dagger left-handed from the scabbard, dropped down and stabbed it into the beastman's broad back. It rose from the fight, howling its agony, and as it did so Felix slashed its head from its shoulders with his blade.

Its former opponent rose to his feet, nodding his thanks to Felix. It was the pale-faced boy Felix had seen on the battlements. He had just time to shrug before another wave of beastmen raced towards them. Somewhere in the distance he thought he heard the sound of thunderous hoofbeats.

Justine charged into the mass of bodies around the middle entrance, lashing about her with her hell-blade, killing a man with every stroke. Her horse trampled the wounded beneath its hooves, and whinnied triumphantly as the smell of blood filled its nostrils. She held herself easily in the saddle, knowing that nothing could stand against her.

'To me!' she shouted, and the beasts rallied about her, forming a wedge and driving their human opponents back into the streets of their town. Behind her, reinforcements poured through and began to flood through the lanes and alleys. She felt triumphant. Many souls would be offered screaming to the Lord of Battles this evening.

The sense of triumph diminished slightly as her horse vented a bestial scream. She looked down to see an arrow protruding from its eye. Even dying, with uncanny discipline the animal did not rear and try to throw her; instead it sank down on its haunches, allowing her time to vault clear from her saddle.

Blazing rage filled her. Shadow had carried her all the way from the Chaos wastes and finding another steed would not be easy. She swore that whoever killed it would pay with his life, even if she had to slay every living thing in this pitiful dungheap. Then she smiled, revealing her long sharp teeth. Mad laughter bubbled from her throat. She was merely swearing to do what she had already decided upon, long before the battle.

Felix paused in the shadow of a building and glared around desperately. His breath came in ragged gasps. His clothing was soaked with blood and sweat. His sword arm felt numb. Where was Gotrek? They had become separated earlier in the battle without him realising it, when the fury of the action had prevented him from noticing anything except the movements of his current foe.

Now, he had a breathing space and the Slayer was nowhere to be seen. Felix knew that it was important that he find the dwarf, that his chances of surviving would be greatly increased in the presence of the Slayer's mighty axe. And if all else failed, he felt called upon to be present when the dwarf made his last stand, to perform his sworn task to witness it, even if he himself died shortly thereafter.

All around, the buildings were alight, and the flames added a hellish illumination to the scene. Amid billowing, reeking clouds of smoke the battle raged on. Felix saw shadowy beastmen fighting with the wraiths of human warriors in the mist. He could hear the bellow of the monsters, the screams of the dying and the clash of weapon upon weapon. All semblance of formations had been lost in the vast melee. It was kill or be killed, in a brutal struggle to the death.

Somewhere off in the distance, he thought he heard the Slayer's warcry. He gathered his strength and courage and forced his legs to move in the direction from which he thought it had come. He offered up a brief, hopeless prayer to Sigmar, asking the Lord of the Hammer to protect himself, the Slayer, Kat and all the others. For a moment, he wondered where the girl was.

Lost in the howling madness of the battle, Kat could see no escape. She had not wanted to remain within the Temple, knowing as she did that it was doomed. She needed a place to hide from the beasts. She still had not found it.

She ducked to one side and crouched behind a rain barrel. Nearby, two young men wrestled with a beast. One held it round the legs while the other dashed its brains out with a large boulder. Kat had never witnessed anything like this; the sheer insensate ferocity was appalling. All of the participants seemed possessed by a kind of madness that drove them to acts of hideous cruelty and lunatic bravery.

No quarter was given. No quarter was asked.

A great tide of warriors swept down the main street, carried along by their own fury and bloodlust. Screams of dying men and beasts filled the air. The clash of steel on steel rang out through the burning night. The muddy earth, churned by the feet and hooves of the mob, became slippery with blood.

A beast howled with triumph as it spitted a man on its spear. Its cry turned to a bellow of rage and fear as the man's friends chopped it to pieces. A circle of men surrounded a bull-headed giant. As it reached for one, another would leap in from its blind side and stab it. Soon it bled from a dozen small cuts; with a fierce bellow, it charged at the nearest warrior and by sheer weight bowled him off his feet, breaking out of the circle and into the mob.

Kat nearly screamed when the black-armoured woman strode through the throng. She feared that the Chaos Champion had come for her. Then Gotrek stepped from the shadows to issue his challenge. The woman snarled, revealing bloodstained fangs, and lashed out at the Slayer. The blow was a blur, nearly too fast for the eye to follow. She did not know how the Slayer got his axe in the way but he did. Black steel clashed with blue starmetal. Red sparks flew amidst the smoke.

The Slayer returned the woman's blow with one of his own. The axe flashed towards her with the irresistible force of a thunderbolt. The woman ducked beneath the stroke and thrust forward. Somehow the Slayer's axe was there, blocking the blow. They stood straining against each other, blade pressed against blade, inhuman strength measured against daemonic power. Neither gave. Great ropes of muscle bulged in Gotrek's arms and shoulders. Sweat ran down his face, great veins standing out in his neck and forehead. The woman stood as immobile as an ebon statue. Her armour seemed locked in place. Her pale face was a bone-white mask, a frozen image of bloodlust. The whites of her eyes had vanished; her eye sockets shone with red balefire.

Seconds raced by as the two of them stood locked in titanic conflict, each unable to budge the other. From the corner of her eye Kat spied a host of beastmen approach. They raced towards the battle, clearly intent on butchering the Slayer. Without thinking, Kat screamed a warning.

Gotrek glanced to one side as the beastmen reached him. At the last moment he stepped back and parried a swing which would have split him in two. Kat feared that the woman would take the opportunity to stab him but she need not have worried. The tide of battle swirled around the combatants and the Champion of Khorne and the Slayer were dragged apart in the melee. Kat breathed a sigh of relief.

Then she noticed that the woman was staring at her. She met the red gaze straight on and her heart nearly stopped. She wanted to scream, but when she opened her mouth no sound came out. The dark-clad warrior-woman marched closer.

The killing lust thundered in Justine's brain. The darkness rooted in her soul threatened to take over completely. Madness bubbled through her veins. The bloodlust filled her like a drug; she took ecstatic pleasure in the carnage. She wanted to find the dwarf and kill him. Of all the foes she had ever faced he had been the mightiest. A worthy offering to the Blood God indeed. At the last second, as she had been going to push aside his axe and slaughter him, fate, in the shape of her own idiotic followers, had intervened and torn them apart. She wanted to find him again and end the struggle.

Then she saw the girl. As if against her will, she saw the small scared face peeking out from its hiding place. She knew what she had to do. It was time to end this thing once and for all, to set her foot on the path that would end in eternal life, to seize her chance at a glorious destiny in the sight of Khorne. The dark thing that had been growing within her howled in triumph, knowing that its moment had come at long last.

Forgetting all about the dwarf, she marched towards her destiny.

Felix tore around the corner. He was instantly thrown into battle once more. The heat of the burning buildings warmed him. The acrid smell of smoke filled his nostrils. The clamour of battle rang in his ears. He could hear Gotrek's shouts as he hewed his foes down but his eyes were drawn with instinctive, unthinking horror to the Chaos Warrior – and the child who cowered in the darkness before her.

He could see the resemblance as plain as day now. It went beyond the white stripe in the hair. They had similar features: the same wide eyes, the same narrow jawline. Seeing the warrior raise her blade to strike, he ran forward, bellowing, knowing in his heart that he was going to be too late.

* * *

Justine watched her shadow fall on the child in front of her. She saw the look of fear in its eyes. The pallor of the face. She saw the resemblance to herself and wondered how it was that after all these years she truly felt nothing.

'What is your name, girl?' she asked quietly.

'Kat. Katerina.'

Justine nodded, surprised that she felt nothing whatsoever at this information.

In a flash of insight, she finally understood the ways of daemons. She saw all the tests, all the rituals, all the sacrifices for what they were, preparations for this one crucial moment. She knew now that all of this killings, and all of the bloodletting had been for a purpose. It had been a process which had changed her into something other than the human she had once been. She had been tempered by the process the way a blade is tempered by a master smith. She finally understood, after all the violence and all the massacres, that a human being could get used to anything, even to the destiny that made them a Chaos Warrior. She knew that at this moment, she could turn away from the child, that it would make no difference, she had finally and truthfully confirmed to herself that she was on the path of damnation. Killing the girl would make no difference now. She could do it if she wanted to, but it was meaningless – a piece of book-keeping, nothing more. She had passed the point of no return when she had decided to kill her a few moments ago. Still, she thought, it was always best to leave things tidy. With no more feeling now than if she was about to chop a log of wood, she raised her blade high.

And there was a flash of pain in her side as something crashed into her.

Felix leaped, crossing the distance between himself and the Chaos Warrior in one bound. He smashed into the woman just as she raised her blade, overbalancing her and sending them both toppling to the ground. Knowing that he would never get another opportunity he lashed out with his blade, piercing the woman's side. She gave no sign of pain beyond a small grunt.

As they rolled over on the trampled earth, locked in a deadly embrace, Felix knew at once that he was overmatched. The woman reached up with mailed hands and grasped him by the throat. He reached up to try to dislodge them, grateful at least that she had dropped her blade, and at once knew that he had made a mistake. The Chaos Warrior was far stronger than he, possessed of a supernatural strength which was as superior to his own as his was to that of a child. He fought to slacken her grip but it was like trying to pry loose the fingers of a troll.

She was on top of him now, and the weight of her armour knocked all the breath from him. He rolled, trying to raise his shoulders from the earth, to throw her off, but it was useless. She seemed to anticipate his every move with ease. In that moment, he knew he was going to die. He was faced with an opponent who was simply too strong for him, and Gotrek was not there to save him.

Darkness pressed on him, sparks flashing before his eyes. Somewhere in the distance he heard Gotrek's battle-cry and part of him, infinitely remote and infinitely detached, thought it ironic that the Slayer would witness his doom, and not the other way around.

'Now, mortal, you die,' the woman said calmly, and her hands began to twist his neck.

Felix strained as hard as he could, as the terrible pressure mounted, knowing that if he gave way his neck would snap like a twig, and death would come to him instantaneously. He felt the veins bulge and muscles began to tear as he tried to resist, knowing that it was futile and that in a moment it would all be over. The darkness deepened. He saw everything as a shadow. It was quiet save for the thunder of his breath within his chest and the distant tolling of his heartbeat. He knew he was beaten, that he could take no more, and his muscles started to relax in surrender.

Kat looked out on the terrible battle. She knew the Chaos Warrior had been about to kill her. She knew that Felix had tried to save her. She knew that the black-armoured woman was going to kill him. She knew she must do something.

Something glittered on the ground nearby. She saw it was the black sword which the Chaos Warrior had dropped. Its edge glittered brightly in the firelight. Perhaps there was something she could do. She reached out and tried to pick it up but it was too heavy. Maybe if she used both hands. Slowly, the blade started to rise. It twisted in her hands. The runes on its blade glowed bright red and she sensed the terrible power within it.

Now if only she could–

Suddenly Felix felt the terrible pressure cease. The Chaos Warrior looked down at him and then further, at her own chest. Felix followed her burning gaze and saw the blade of black metal which protruded there. The red runes glowed. Smouldering blood dripped from the wound and evaporated into poisonous smoke as it hit the ground. The Chaos Warrior stood upright, reeling to her feet, and turned to look in the direction the blow had come from.

Frantically Felix forced himself to move. Leadenly his limbs responded. He looked around seeking his blade, and reached out to grab it. His fingers folded round the hilt and he tried to raise it. It felt like he was trying to lift the weight of that great cannon outside the gate, but somehow he forced himself to do it. He pushed himself upright and saw that there was no one else around, only the Chaos Warrior, himself and Kat. The woman's eyes were locked on the girl's, her lips twisted into a terrible ironic smile. Mad laughter bubbled from her lips. She took a step forward, the blade still protruding from her chest and Kat took a step backwards, eyes wide with horror and fear.

Slowly it filtered into Felix's brain what must have happened. Kat had lifted the heavy blade and driven it into the warrior's back while they fought. She had saved his life. Now it was up to him to save hers. Slowly he forced his battered body to move. He dragged himself along the ground after the Chaos Warrior.

The woman's step faltered. Slowly she began to topple forwards.

Justine laughed inside even as the pain ate away at her consciousness. It was the final terrible joke. She had been killed by the one she had come to kill. A little girl had succeeded where mighty warriors had failed.

It was true, as the daemon had always said. A warrior had not killed her. Her own child had done it instead. She stumbled forward and fell into the waiting darkness.

Felix watched as the vile Chaos Warrior fell. Flesh melted, decomposing with horrid rapidity to leave only a reeking skeleton within the black armour. Somehow, without being told, Felix knew that he looked upon the body of someone who had died a long time ago. The sight of it made him want to vomit.

Something wet hit his face. The storm had broken at last and rain was starting to fall. Sizzling sounds from nearby told him that the raindrops were at war with the blaze. Good; perhaps the town would not burn to the ground after all.

Suddenly Kat was there, huddling beside him. 'Is it over now?' she asked.

Felix listened to the sounds of carnage all around him and nodded. 'It soon will be,' he said softly. 'One way or another.'

Felix slumped on a tree-stump looking back towards the town. Messner and Kat sat nearby, watching him reproachfully. Both of them thought he should not be up and about. His throat was still bruised and he had trouble speaking and eating, but it looked like he was going to be all right. He was just grateful to still be alive.

So were the two hundred or so villagers who had survived the great battle and its aftermath. He could still hear them chanting prayers of thanksgiving for their deliverance in the Temple of Sigmar.

A knight rode by, one of the mighty force despatched by the Duke in answer to Messner's message. He had the head of a beastman spiked on his lance. Felix and Messner watched him pass, and Felix could tell that the man was thinking the same as he was. There was a faint look of contempt on the woodsman's face. It was all very well for the knight to pose with his trophy now – but where were they when the real fighting was being done? The conquering heroes had arrived the morning after the battle.

'So you found the cannon?' he asked. His voice came out in a croaking whisper.

'Yes,' Messner said. 'It's an eerie thing. They say it feels as warm to the touch as flesh. Dark sorcery involved, for sure. We've sent for a priest to exorcise it. If that doesn't work, the old duke will send a wizard.'

'But the beasts are all dead.'

'Yes, we've hunted down every one of them. Gotrek just got back at dawn. He says that's the last.'

The two of them were just talking to keep Kat quiet and they both knew it. Neither wanted to let her get a word in. Still, this news gladdened Felix. It seemed that the beasts had lost heart and fled when word of their foul leader's death had got out. The rout had turned into a massacre as the foresters had pursued them. Now it looked like Kat had saved the whole town by her actions. She was a heroine and everybody told her that. Right now, she didn't sound much like one.

'I still want to go with you,' the girl said. Even after two days of argument she hadn't given up.

'You can't, Kat. Gotrek and I are bound for dangerous places; we can't take you. Stay with Messner.' He didn't want to tell her there was a price on his and Gotrek's heads. Not with a ranger present.

'You do that, girl,' Messner added. 'There's a place for you here with me and Magda and the kids. And you'll have friends among the other little ones, for sure.'

Kat looked at Felix imploringly. He shook his head and forced his features to remain stern and calm. He was not sure how much longer he could manage it when he heard the Slayer clump up. Gotrek grinned evilly. From his look Felix guessed he had added to the huge tally of deaths he had inflicted in the battle.

'Time's a-wasting, manling. We'd best be off.'

Felix got up slowly. Messner advanced and shook hands. Kat hugged first Felix and then the Slayer. Messner had to pull her away in the end.

'Goodbye,' she said tearfully. 'I'll always remember you.'

'You do that, little one,' Gotrek said softly.

They turned and walked away from Flensburg. The path was steep and the road rocky. Ahead lay Nuln and an uncertain future. At the top of the slope Felix turned and looked back. Below them Messner and Kat were two small figures, waving.

THE MUTANT MASTER

'It must sometimes occur to the readers of these pages that my companion and I were under some sort of curse. Without any effort on our part, and without any great desire on my part, we somehow managed to encounter all manner of worshippers of the Dark Ones. I myself have often suspected that we were somehow doomed to oppose their schemes without ever really understanding why. This sort of speculation never seemed to trouble the Slayer. He took all such events in his stride with a grunt and a fatalistic shrug, and dismissed any speculation along these lines as vain and useless philosophising. But I have thought long and hard on this matter, and it seems to me that if there is a power in this world which opposes the servants of Chaos, then perhaps it sometimes guided our steps, and even shielded us. Certainly, we often stumbled across the most outrageous and wicked schemes perpetrated by the most unlikely of evildoers...'

— From *My Travels with Gotrek, Vol. II*, by Herr Felix Jaeger
(Altdorf Press, 2505)

When he heard the snap of the twig, Felix Jaeger froze on the spot. His hand groped instinctively for the hilt of his sword, as his keen eyes searched his surroundings and spotted nothing. It was useless, Felix knew – the light of the fading sun barely penetrated the thick canopy of leaves overhead and the forest's dense undergrowth could have hidden the approach of a small army. He grimaced and ran his fingers nervously through his long blond hair. All of the peddler's warnings came back to him in a flash.

The old man had claimed there were mutants on the road ahead, packs of them, preying on all who travelled this route between Nuln and Fredericksburg. At the time, Felix had paid no attention to him, for the peddler had been attempting to sell him a shoddy amulet supposedly blessed by the Grand Theogonist himself, a sure protection for pilgrims and wanderers – or so the merchant had claimed. He had already bought a small throwing dagger in a concealable wrist sheath from the peddler, and he had not felt inclined to part with more money. Felix rubbed his forearm where the sheath chafed, making sure the knife was still secure.

Felix wished he had the amulet now. It had most likely been a fake but at times like this any weary traveller on the dark roads of the Empire would feel the need for a little extra protection.

'Hurry up, manling,' Gotrek Gurnisson said. 'There's an inn in Blutdorf and my throat is as dry as the deserts of Araby.'

Felix regarded his companion. No matter how many times he looked upon the dwarf, the Trollslayer's squat ugliness never ceased to astonish him. There was no single element that made Gotrek so outstandingly repulsive, Felix decided. It wasn't the missing teeth, the missing eye or the long beard filled with particles of food. It wasn't the cauliflower ear or the quiltwork of old scars. It wasn't even the smell. No, it was the combination of them all that did it.

For all that, there was no denying that the Trollslayer presented

215

a formidable appearance. Although Gotrek only came up to Felix's
chest, and a great deal of that height was made up of the huge dyed
crest of red hair atop his shaved and tattooed skull, he was broader
at the shoulders than a blacksmith. In one massive paw, he held a
rune-covered axe that most men would have struggled to lift with
both hands. When he shifted his massive head, the gold chain that
ran from his nose to his ear jingled.

'I thought I heard something,' Felix said.

'These woods are full of noises, manling. Birds chirp. Trees creak
and animals scuttle everywhere.' Gotrek spat a huge gob of phlegm
onto the ground. 'I hate woods. Always have. Remind me of elves.'

'I thought I heard mutants. Just like the peddler told us about.'

'That so?' Gotrek showed his blackened teeth in what could have
been a snarl or a smile, then he reached up and scratched under his
eye-patch, rubbing the socket of his ruined left eye with his thumb. It
was a deeply disturbing sight. Felix looked away.

'Yes,' he said softly.

Gotrek turned to face the woods.

'Any mutants there?' he bellowed. 'Come out and face my axe.'

Felix cringed. It was just like the Trollslayer to tempt fate like this.
He was sworn to seek death in battle with deadly monsters in order
to atone for some unmentionable dwarfish sin, and he wasted no
opportunity to complete that quest. Felix cursed the drunken night he
had sworn his oath to follow the Trollslayer and record his doom in
an epic poem.

Almost in answer to Gotrek's shout there was a further rustling in
the undergrowth, as if a strong wind had disturbed the bushes – only
there was no breeze. Felix kept his hand clasped on his sword hilt.
There was definitely something there and it was getting closer.

'I think you might be right, manling,' Gotrek smiled nastily. It
occurred to Felix that he had known there was something there all
along.

A horde of mutants erupted from the undergrowth, screaming oaths
and curses and the vilest of obscenities. The sheer horror of their
appearance threatened to overwhelm Felix's mind. He saw a repulsive
slimy-skinned creature that hopped along like a toad. Something
vaguely female scuttled along on eight spidery legs. A creature with
the head of a crow and greyish feathers screeched a challenge. Some
of the mutants had transparent skin through which pulsing organs
were visible. They brandished spears and daggers and what looked
like rusty kitchen implements. One of them launched itself towards

Felix, swinging a notched, blunt-edged cleaver.

Felix reached up and caught the creature's wrist, stopping the blade a moment before it crunched into his skull. He jabbed a knee into the monster's groin. As it bent double, he kicked it in the head, knocking it over. Its greenish vomit spewed all over Felix's boots before it rolled back into the undergrowth.

In the brief respite, Felix ripped his blade from its scabbard, ready to lay about him. He need not have bothered.

Gotrek's mighty axe had already cleaved a path of red ruin through their attackers. With one blow he cut down three more. Bones splintered under the impact. Flesh parted before the razor-sharp edge. The Trollslayer's axe flashed again. Two halves of a severed torso flopped down, and, briefly unaware that it was already dead, tried to crawl away from each other. Gotrek's axe completed its upswing, severing the head of another mutant.

Appalled by the sudden carnage, the mutants fled. Some of them rushed past Felix into the woods on the far side, others turned and ran back into the dark undergrowth from which they had come.

Felix looked at Gotrek speculatively, waiting to see what the Trollslayer did. The last thing he wanted was for them to separate and pursue the creatures into the darkening forest. Their victory had been too easy. It all smacked of a trap.

'Must've sent the runts of this litter after us,' Gotrek observed, spitting on a mutant corpse. Felix looked down to see the Trollslayer was right. Very few of the dead looked as if they would have come up to Gotrek's chest, and none of them looked taller than the Trollslayer.

'Let's get out of here,' Felix said. 'These things smell awful.'

'Hardly worth the killing,' Gotrek grumbled back. He sounded deeply disappointed.

The Hanged Man was one of the most dispiriting inns Felix had ever visited. A tiny cheerless blaze flickered in the fireplace. The taproom smelled of damp. Mangy dogs gnawed at bones that looked as if they had been lost for generations in the carpet of filthy straw. The landlord was a villainous-looking individual, his face tracked with old scars, a massive hook protruding from the stump of his right hand. The potboy was a wall-eyed hunchback with an unfortunate habit of drooling into the beer as he poured it. The locals looked thoroughly miserable. Every one of them glanced at Felix as if he wanted to plunge a knife into the youth's back but were just too depressed to summon up the energy.

Felix had to admit that the inn was appropriate for the village it served. Blutdorf was as gloomy a place as he had ever seen. The mud huts looked ill-tended and about to collapse. The streets seemed somehow empty and menacing. When they had finally intimidated the drunken gatekeeper into letting them enter, weeping crones had watched them from every doorway. It was as if the whole place had been overcome with grief and lethargy.

Even the castle brooding on the crags above the village appeared neglected and ill-cared for. Its walls were crumbling. It looked as if it could be stormed by a group of snotlings armed with pointed sticks, which was unusual for a town which appeared to be surrounded by a horde of menacing mutants. On the other hand, Felix thought, even the mutants about here seemed a particularly unfearsome bunch, judging by the attack they had attempted earlier.

He took another sip of his ale. It was the worst beer he had ever tasted, as thoroughly disgusting a brew as had ever passed his lips. Gotrek threw back his head and tipped the entire contents of the stein into his mouth. It vanished as fast as a gold purse dropped in a street of beggars.

'Another flagon of Old Dog Puke!' Gotrek called out. He turned and glared at the locals. 'Try not to deafen me with the sound of your mirth,' he bellowed.

The customers refused to meet his eye. They stared down into their beers as if they could discover the secret of transmuting lead into gold there, if they only studied it hard enough.

'Why all the happy faces?' Gotrek enquired sarcastically. The landlord placed another flagon on the counter before him. Gotrek quaffed some more. Felix was gratified to note that even the Trollslayer made a sour face when he finished. It was a rare tribute to the nastiness of the ale. Felix had never seen the dwarf show the slightest discomfort or hesitation in drinking anything before.

'It's the sorcerer,' the landlord said suddenly. 'He's a right nasty piece of work. Things have never been the same since he came an' took over the old castle. Since then we've 'ad nothin' but bother, what with the mutants on the road and all. Trade's dried up. No one comes here anymore. Nobody can sleep safe in their beds at night.'

Gotrek perked up at once. A nasty grin revealed the blackened stumps of his teeth. This was more to his liking, Felix saw.

'A sorcerer, you say?'

'Aye, sir, that he is – a right evil wizard.'

Felix saw that the customers were all glaring at the landlord strangely, as if he was speaking out of line, or saying something they had never expected to hear him say. Felix dismissed the thought. Maybe they were just frightened. Who wouldn't be, with a servant of the Dark Powers of Chaos in residence over their village?

'Mean as a dragon with toothache, he is. Ain't that right, Helmut?'

The peasant who the landlord addressed stood frozen to the spot, like a rat petrified by the gaze of a snake.

'Ain't that right, Helmut?' The landlord repeated.

'He's not so bad,' the peasant said. 'As evil sorcerers go.'

'Why don't you just storm the castle?' Gotrek asked. Felix thought that if the dwarf couldn't guess the answer to that from the whipped-dog look of these poor clods, he was stupider than he looked.

'There's the monster, sir,' the peasant said, shuffling his feet and staring down at the floor once more.

'The monster?' Gotrek asked, more than a hint of professional interest showing in his one good eye. 'A big monster, I suppose.'

'Huge, sir. Twice as big as a man and covered in all sorts of nasty mut... mut... mut...'

'Mutations?' Felix suggested helpfully.

'Aye, sir, those things.'

'Why not send to Nuln for help?' Felix suggested. 'The Templars of the White Wolf would be interested in dealing with such a follower of Chaos.'

The peasants looked at him blankly. 'Dunno where Nuln is, sir. None of us ever been more than half a league from Blutdorf. Who'd look after our wives if we left the village?'

'An' then there's the mutants,' another villager chipped in. 'Woods is full of them and they all serve the magician.'

'Mutants as well?' Gotrek sounded almost cheerful. 'I think we'll be visiting the castle, manling.'

'I feared as much,' Felix sighed.

'You can't mean to attack the sorcerer and his monster,' one of the villagers said.

'With your help, we will soon rid Blutdorf of this scourge,' Felix said shakily, ignoring the nasty look Gotrek threw him. The Trollslayer wanted no assistance in his quest for glorious death.

'No, sir, we can't help you.'

'Why not? Are you unmanly cowards?' It was a stupid question, but Felix felt he had to ask. It wasn't that he blamed the villagers. Under normal circumstances he would have been no more keen than they were to confront a Chaos sorcerer and his pet monster.

'No, sir,' the villager said. 'It's just that he has our children up there – he's keeping them as hostages!'

'Your children?'

'Aye, sir, every last one of them. He and his monster came down and rounded them all up. There was no resisting either. When Big Norri tried, the creature tore his arms off and made him eat them. Nasty, it was.'

Felix did not like the glint that had entered the Trollslayer's eye. Gotrek's enthusiasm for getting to the castle and fighting the monster radiated across the room like heat from a large bonfire. Felix wasn't so certain. He found that he shared the villagers' lack of enthusiasm for the direct approach.

'Surely, you must want to free your children?' Felix asked.

'Aye, but we don't want to kill them. The magician will feed them to his monster if we give him any lip.'

Felix looked over at Gotrek. The Trollslayer jerked his thumb meaningfully in the direction of the castle. Felix could see he was keen to be off, hostages or no hostages. With a sinking feeling, Felix realised that there would be no getting out of this. Sooner or later, he and the dwarf were going to end up paying Blutdorf Keep a visit.

Desperately, he searched for a way of staving off the inevitable. 'This calls for a plan,' he said. 'Landlord, some more of your fine ale.'

The landlord smiled and fussed about at the bar pouring some more ale. Felix noticed that Gotrek was eyeing him suspiciously. He realised that he wasn't really showing the proper enthusiasm for their quest. The landlord came back and thumped down two more steins with an enthusiastic smile.

'One for the road,' Felix said, raising his ale jack. He swigged away at the beer, which tasted even fouler than it had previously. Because of the taste, he wasn't quite sure, but he thought there was a faint chemical tang to the beer. Whatever it was, a few more sips left him feeling dizzy and nauseous. He noticed that Gotrek had finished his ale and was calling for another. The landlord obliged and the dwarf swigged it back in one gulp. His eyes widened, he clutched his throat and then he fell back as if pole-axed.

It took Felix a moment to register what had happened and he stumbled forward to examine his companion. His feet felt like lead. His head swam. Nausea threatened to overwhelm him. There was something wrong here, he knew, but he couldn't quite put his finger on it. It was something to do with the ale. He had never seen the Trollslayer fall over before, no matter how much beer he drank. He had never felt so bad himself, not after so few beers. He turned and looked at the landlord. The man's outline wavered, as if Felix was seeing him through a thick fog. He pointed an accusing finger.

'You drudged... I mean drunk... no, I mean you drinked our drugs,' Felix said and fell to his knees.

The landlord said, 'Thank Tzeentch for that. I thought they would never go down. I gave that dwarf enough skavenroot to knock out a horse.'

Felix fumbled for his sword but his fingers felt numb and he fell forward into the darkness.

'Cost me a crown a pinch, as well,' the landlord muttered. His peevish voice was the last thing Felix remembered before unconsciousness took him. 'Still, Herr Kruger will pay me well for two such fine specimens.'

Wake up, manling!' The deep voice rumbled somewhere close to Felix's ear. He tried to ignore it, hoping that it would go away and let him return to his slumber.

'Wake up, manling, or I swear I will come over there and strangle you with these very chains.' There was a threatening note to the voice now that convinced Felix he'd better pay attention to it. He opened his eyes – and wished that he hadn't.

Even the dim light of the single guttering torch illuminating their cell was too bright. Its feeble glow hurt Felix's eyes. In a way, that was alright, because it made them match the rest of his body. His heartbeat thumped in his temples like a gong struck with a warhammer. His head felt like someone had used it for kickball practice. His mouth was desert dry and his tongue felt like someone had sandpapered it.

'Worst hangover I ever had,' Felix muttered, licking his lips nervously.

'It's not a hangover. We were dru–'

'Drugged. I know.'

Felix realised that he was standing up. His hands were above his head and there were heavy weights attached to his ankles. He tried to bend forward to see what they were, but found that he could not move. He looked up to see that he dangled from manacles. The chains were attached to a great loop of iron set in the wall above him. He confirmed this by peering across the chamber and seeing that Gotrek was held the same way.

The Trollslayer dangled from his chains like a side of beef in a butcher's shop. His legs were not chained, though. His frame was too short to reach the ground. Felix could see that there were leg irons set in the wall at ankle height but the dwarf's legs did not stretch that far.

Felix looked around. They were in a large chamber, paved with heavy flagstones. There were a dozen sets of chains and manacles set in the walls. An oddly distorted skeleton dangled from the farthest set. In the wall to the far left was a huge bench covered in alembics and charcoal burners, and other tools of the alchemist's trade. A huge chalk pentagram surrounded by peculiar hieroglyphics was inscribed in the centre of the room. At each junction of the pentacle was set a beastman skull holding an extinguished candle made from black wax.

At the far right of the room, a flight of stone steps led up to a heavy door. There was a barred window in the door, through which a few shafts of light penetrated down into the gloom. Near the foot of the stairs Felix could see his sword and Gotrek's axe. He felt a brief surge of hope. Whoever had taken their weapons had not been very thorough. Felix could still feel the weight of the throwing dagger in the hidden sheath on his forearm. Of course, there was no way he could use it with his arms manacled, but it was somehow comforting to know it was there.

The air was thick and fetid. From the distance Felix thought he heard screams and chants and bestial roars. It was like listening to a combination of a lunatic asylum and a zoo. Nothing about their situation reassured Felix.

'Why did the landlord drug us?' Felix asked.

'He was in league with this sorcerer. Obviously.'

'Or he was afraid of him.' If he could have, Felix would have shrugged. 'No matter, I wonder why we're still alive?'

A high-pitched tittering laugh answered that question. The heavy door creaked open and two figures blocked out the light. There was a brief flare as a lucifer was struck, then a lantern was lit and Felix could see the source of the mocking laughter.

'A good question, Jaeger, and one I will be only too pleased to answer.'

There was something very familiar about this voice, Felix thought. It was high-pitched and nasal and deeply unpleasant. He had heard it before.

Felix squinted across the chamber and made out the voice's owner. He was just as unpleasant as his voice. A tall, gaunt man, he wore faded and tattered grey robes, patched at the sleeves and elbows. Around his scrawny neck hung an iron chain bearing a huge amulet. His long thin fingers were covered in rune-encrusted rings and tipped with long blackened nails. His pale, sweating face was framed by a huge turned-up collar. He wore a skull-cap trimmed with silver.

Behind the man stood an enormous creature. It was huge, half again as tall as a man, and maybe four times as heavy. Perhaps once it had been human, but now it was the size of an ogre. Its hair had fallen out in great clumps, and massive pustules erupted from its scalp and flesh. Its features were twisted and hideous. Its teeth were like millstones. Its arms were even more muscular than Gotrek's, thicker around than Felix's thighs. Its hands were the size of dinner plates. Its callused, sausage-sized fingers looked like they could crush stone. It glared at Felix with eyes full of insane hatred. Felix found he could not meet the thing's gaze and he turned his attention back to the human.

The man's features were gaunt and lined. His eyes were the palest blue and bright with madness. They were hidden only slightly by his steel-framed pince-nez glasses. His nose was long and thin and tipped with an enormous wart. A drip of mucus hung from his nose. He tittered again, sniffed to draw the drip back into his nostrils and then wiped his nose on his sleeve. Then, recovering his dignity, he threw his head back and strode purposefully down the stairs.

The effect of impressive sorcerous dignity was spoiled a little when he almost tripped on the hem of his robe and fell headlong.

It was this last touch which stirred Felix's memory. It brought everything else into focus. 'Albericht?' He said. 'Albericht Kruger?'

'Don't call me that!' The robed man's voice approached a scream. 'Address me as "Master"!'

'You know this idiot, manling?' Gotrek asked.

Felix nodded. Albericht Kruger had been in a few of his philosophy classes at Altdorf University before he had been expelled for duelling. He had been a quiet youth, very studious, and was always to be found in the libraries. Felix had probably never exchanged more than a dozen words with him in the whole two years that they had studied together. He remembered also that Kruger had vanished. There had been a bit of a scandal about it – something to do with books missing from the library. Felix could remember that a few witch hunters from the Temple of Sigmar had shown interest.

'We were students together back in Altdorf.'

'That's enough!' Kruger screeched in his thin and annoying voice. 'You are my prisoners and you will do as I say for what remains of your pitiful lives.'

'We will do as you say for what remains of our pitiful lives?' Felix stared back at Kruger in astonishment. 'You've been reading too many Detlef

Sierck melodramas, Albericht. Nobody speaks like that in real life.'

'Be quiet, Jaeger! That's enough. You were always too clever for your own good, you know. Now we'll see who's the clever one – oh yes!'

'Come on, Albericht, a joke's a joke. Let us out of here. Quick, before your master comes.'

'My master?' Kruger seemed puzzled.

'The sorcerer who owns this tower.'

'You idiot, Jaeger! I am the sorcerer.'

Felix stared in disbelief. 'You?'

'Yes, me! I have probed the mysteries of the Dark Gods and learned the source of all magical power. I have plumbed the secrets of Life and Death. I wield the mighty energies of Chaos and soon I will have total domination over the lands of the Empire.'

'I find that a little hard to believe,' Felix admitted honestly. The Kruger he had known back then had been virtually a non-entity, ignored by all the other students. Who would have guessed at the depths of megalomania that lurked in his head?

'Think what you will, Herr-clever-clogs-Jaeger with your la-di-da accent and your my-father-is-a-rich-merchant-and-I'm-too-good-for-your-sort manners. I have mastered the secrets of life itself. I control the alchemical secrets of warpstone and understand the innermost secrets of the Art of Transmutation!'

Out of the corner of his eye, Felix could see Gotrek's huge muscles beginning to bulge as he strained against the chains that held him. His face was red and his beard bristled. His body was contorted, arched to brace his feet against the wall. Felix did not know what the dwarf hoped to achieve. Anyone could see that these huge chains were beyond the strength of man or dwarf to break.

'You've been using warpstone?' That explained a lot, Felix thought. He did not know much about warpstone, but what he did know was disturbing enough. It was the raw essence of Chaos, the final and ultimate source of all mutations. Just a pinch of it was enough to drive a normal man mad. By his tone, it sounded like Kruger had consumed a barrel of it. 'You're insane!'

'That's what they told me back in Altdorf, back at their university!' Spittle dripped from Kruger's mouth. Felix could see that his eyes glowed an eerie green, as if there were tiny marshlights behind the pupils. Vampire-like fangs protruded from his gums. 'But I showed them. I found their forbidden books, all wrapped up in the vault. They said that they were not meant for the eyes of mortal man but I've read them, and they've done me no harm!'

'Yes, I can see that,' Felix muttered ironically.

'You think you're so clever, don't you, Jaeger? You're just like all the rest, all of them who laughed at me when I said I would be the greatest sorcerer since Teclis. Well, I'll prove you wrong. We'll see how smart you act once I have transformed you, the way I transformed Oleg here!'

He tapped the monster on the shoulder with paternal pride. It grinned like a dog whose stomach has been scratched by its master. Felix found the sight very disturbing. Behind them Gotrek was practically standing against the wall. His arms were at full stretch, the chains holding firm, leaving him parallel to the floor. The Trollslayer was blue in the face. His features were contorted in a grimace of rage and fury. Felix felt that something would have to give soon. Either the chains would break or the Trollslayer would burst a blood vessel. That might prove to be a mercy, Felix thought. He did not see how Gotrek could overcome the monster without his axe. The Slayer was strong, but this creature made him look like a scrawny child.

Kruger raised his arm, brandishing his staff. At the tip, Felix could see that a sphere of greenish warpstone was held in a lead claw. Felix could not help but notice that the hand that held the staff was scaly, and that its fingernails resembled the talons of a wild beast.

'It took me years to perfect the Spell of Transmutation, years,' Kruger hissed. 'You have no idea how many experiments I did. Hundreds! I laboured like a man possessed but at last I have the secret. Soon you will know it too.' The sorcerer tittered. 'Alas, it will do you no good, for you will not be clever enough to speak. Still, you'll provide fine company for Oleg.'

The glowing tip of the man's staff came ever closer to Felix's face. He could see strange lights in its depth. Its surface seemed to shimmer and swirl like oil dropped on water. He could sense the terrible mutating power emerging from it. It radiated out of the warpstone like heat from a glowing coal.

'I don't suppose begging for mercy would help?' Felix asked breezily. He was proud that he managed to keep his voice even.

Kruger shook his head. 'It's too late for that. Soon you will be even more of a witless dullard than you are now.'

'In that case, I have to tell you something.'

Gotrek's muscles bulged as he made one last superhuman effort, throwing himself forward like a swimmer diving headlong off a cliff.

'What's that, Jaeger?' Kruger leaned close to Felix's mouth.

'I never liked you either, you madman!'

Kruger looked like he was going to strike Felix with the staff, but instead he just smiled, revealing his feral teeth.

'Soon, Jaeger, you will learn the true meaning of madness. Every time you look in the mirror.'

Kruger began to chant in a strange, liquid-sounding tongue. It was not elvish but something even older and considerably more sinister sounding. Felix had heard it before, at other times when he and Gotrek had interfered with rites being performed by the followers of Chaos. Well, it looked as though this time the forces of Darkness were going to have the last laugh. He and the Trollslayer would soon be joining their ranks, however unwillingly.

With every word Kruger chanted, the warpstone glowed ever brighter. Its greenish glow drove back the gloom of the chamber and washed everything in its eerie light. Ectoplasmic tendrils emerged from the warpstone. At first they resembled glowing mist, then congealed into something more solid. There was about them the suggestion of something loathsome and diseased. As Kruger brandished his staff, its ectoplasmic emissions trailed behind it like the tail of a comet. He waved it around with grand sweeping gestures, as if with every wave the evil device gathered power.

His chanting now resembled insane shrieking. Sweat beaded the Chaos sorcerer's forehead and dripped down his glasses. Oleg, the mutated monster, howled in unison with his master's chanting, his bass rumbling providing an eerie counterpoint to the spell.

Felix felt his hair begin to stand on end, when the chanting stopped and an eerie silence blanketed the dungeon.

For a moment, everything was still. Felix could hardly see, so dazzled was he by the light of the Chaos staff. He could hear his own heartbeat and Kruger's frantic breathing as he gasped for breath after completing his invocation. There was a strange metallic creaking, and a grinding of metal on stone. He opened his eyes to see one of Gotrek's chains whip free from the wall, then the Trollslayer tumbled forward with a curse, ending up dangling above the flagstones.

Kruger turned at the sound. The monster opened his mouth and let out an enormous bellow.

Felix groaned. He had hoped the Slayer would be able to make a run for his axe. With his weapon in his hand, Felix would have backed the Trollslayer against any monster. However, Gotrek still hung from one of the chains. All he could do was dangle there, while the monster ripped him limb from limb.

Kruger seemed to realise this at the same time as Felix. 'Get him!' he yelled to his monster.

Oleg surged forward and Gotrek lashed out with his chain. The heavy metal links whipped towards the huge mutant's eyes. Oleg howled with pain as the chain hit his face, then reeled backwards, crashing into Kruger. There was a snapping sound as Gotrek used his moment's grace to break his other chain free from the wall. Kruger's face went white. He lurched to his feet and scuttled for the stairs. The last Felix saw of him was his departing backside.

'Now there will be a reckoning!' Gotrek pronounced, his flinty voice guttural with rage.

The monster surged forward to meet the Trollslayer, reaching out with one ham-sized hand. Gotrek brought the chain flashing forward and down, hammering the metal into the creature's hand. Once more it backed off. Gotrek's one good eye squinted sideways as though measuring the distance between himself and his axe. Felix could almost read his mind. The distance was too far. If he turned his back and ran for his weapon, the monster's longer stride would enable it to overhaul him.

Perhaps he could back towards it. As always, Felix misread the strength of the dwarf's lust for combat. Instead of backing off, he ran forward, swinging his chain in an eye-blurring arc. It smashed into the monster's chest, then a moment later Gotrek caught Oleg across the face with the second chain.

This time Oleg expected the pain. Instead of retreating, he advanced on towards the Trollslayer, scooping him up in a bear hug. Felix winced as he watched the giant mutant's arms constrict. Oleg's flexed biceps looked the size of ale-barrels. Felix feared that the Trollslayer's ribs would snap like rotten twigs.

Gotrek brought his head forward, butting Oleg in the face. There was a sickening crunch as Oleg's nose broke. Red blood spurted over Gotrek. Oleg howled with pain and cast the dwarf across the room with one thrust of his huge arms. Gotrek smacked into the wall and fell to the ground with a clattering of chains. After a few seconds, the Trollslayer staggered unsteadily to his feet.

'Get your axe!' Felix shouted.

The dazed dwarf was in no condition to take his advice. Besides, Gotrek was out for blood. He staggered towards Oleg. The giant stood there, howling and clutching his nose. Then, hearing the dwarf's reeling footsteps, he looked up and gave a mighty bellow of rage and pain. He rushed forward, hunkered down, arms outstretched, once more intending to catch the Trollslayer in his death grip. Gotrek stood on swaying legs as the monster thundered towards him, irresistible as an runaway wagon. Felix did not want to look – the mutant was big enough to crush the Slayer beneath his elephantine feet. Horror compelled him to watch.

Oleg reached for Gotrek, his enormous arms closing, but at the last second the Slayer ducked and dived between his legs, turned and lashed out with the chain. It wound around the monster's ankle. Gotrek heaved. Oleg tripped and sprawled, and the chain unwound like a serpent.

Gotrek looped a length of chain around the mutant's throat. Oleg pushed himself to his feet, pulling Gotrek with him. The Trollslayer's weight tightened the grip of the chain around his neck. Using it to hold himself in place, Gotrek pulled himself up to behind Oleg's neck and continued to tighten the chain. The flesh turned white around the mutant's windpipe as the metal links bit into flesh. Felix could see that Gotrek intended to strangle the monster.

Slowly the thought percolated into the mutant's dim mind, and he reached up with both hands to try and loosen the grip of the metal noose that was killing him. He grasped at the chain and tried to work his fingers into the links but they were too big and the chain was gripped too tight. Then he tried to reach behind his head to grasp Gotrek. The Trollslayer ducked his head and pulled himself in tight. He pulled the chain backwards and forward like a saw now. Felix could see droplets of blood emerging where the links had bit.

Now Oleg's hand fastened in Gotrek's crest of hair. It held fast for a moment as Oleg tugged, then his fingers slipped loose on the bear fat ointment that held the crest together. Felix could see fear and frustration begin to appear in the monster's eyes. He could tell that the mutant was weakening. Now Oleg panicked, throwing himself backward at the wall, slamming Gotrek into the stone with sickening force. Nothing could loosen the Slayer's grip. Felix doubted that death itself would make the dwarf loose his hold now. He could see that a fixed glazed look had entered Gotrek's eyes, and his mouth was half-open in a terrifying snarl.

Slowly Oleg weakened as his strength drained from him. He tumbled forward onto his hands and knees. A ghastly rattle emerged from his throat and he sank to the ground and was still. Gotrek tightened the noose one last time to make sure of his prey and then stood up, gasping and panting.

'Easy,' he muttered. 'Hardly worth the killing.'

'Get me down from here,' Felix complained.

Gotrek fetched his weapon. In four strokes of the axe, Felix was free. He raced over and retrieved his sword. From up above, he heard the sound of windlasses turning, great metal doors being raised, and the howling of a bloodthirsty horde. Felix and Gotrek had just time to brace themselves before the door to the laboratory was thrown open and a tide of frenzied mutants swept down the stairs. Felix thought he recognised some of the creatures from the earlier battle. This was the place where the mutants came from.

One dived from the landing, its reptilian eyes glazed with blood-lust. Felix used a stop-thrust to take it through the chest, and then let his arm slump forward under the weight so that its corpse slid free from his blade. The tide of mutants flowed on, inexorably, pressed forward by their own bloodlust and the weight of those behind them. Felix found himself at the centre of a howling maelstrom of violence, where he and the Trollslayer fought back to back against the chaos-spawn.

Gotrek frothed at the mouth and lashed out in a great figure-of-eight with his blood-stained axe. Nothing could stand in his way. With the chains still hanging from his wrists, he carved a path of red ruin through the howling mob. Felix waded along in his wake, dispatching the fallen with single thrusts, stabbing the few mutants who got past the flailing axe.

On the landing above, Felix could see Kruger. The sorcerer had caught up his staff once more. A greenish glow played around his face, and illuminated the whole scene with an infernal light. Kruger chanted a spell and suddenly viridian lightning lashed out. It arced downwards and narrowly missed Felix.

The mutant standing in front of Felix was not so lucky. Its fur singed and eyeballs popped. For a moment it danced on stilts of pure sorcerous power and then fell to earth, a twisted, blackened corpse. Felix dived to one side, not wanting to be the target of another such bolt. Gotrek surged forwards, cleaving a mutant in two as he hacked his way to the foot of the stairs.

The lightning lashed out, aiming for Gotrek this time. He was not so lucky as Felix had been. The green bolt hit him head-on. Felix expected to see the Trollslayer meet his long-threatened doom at last. Gotrek's hair stood even more on end than usual. The runes on his axe blade glowed crimson. He howled what might have been a final curse at his gods, then something strange happened. The green glow passed right through his body and along the length of the iron chain still attached to his wrist. It hit the ground in a shower of green sparks and dissipated harmlessly.

Felix almost laughed out loud. He had heard of such a thing before in his natural philosophy classes. It was called earthing: the same thing that let a metal lightning rod conduct the force of a thunderbolt harmlessly into the ground had saved Gotrek. He gave himself a moment to consider this, then flipped his hidden dagger from its sheath and cast it at Kruger.

It was a good throw. It aimed straight and true and buried itself in the foul sorcerer's chest. It hung there for a moment, quivering, and Kruger stopped his chanting to peer down at it. Kruger dropped his staff and clutched the wound. Greenish blood oozed from the gash and stained the wizard's fingers. He glared down at Felix in hatred – then turned and fled.

Felix gave his attention back to the melee but it was all over. The small mutants had again proved no match for the Slayer's axe. Gotrek stood triumphant, his muscular form covered in blood and ichor. A faint glow faded from his axe. Bear fat sizzled and spluttered on his hair.

Felix raced past him up the stairs and out into the corridor. A trail of greenish blood led off down the passage. It wound past a mass of open, empty cages. Felix guessed that it was from these that the mutants had come. They had been the products of Kruger's foul experiments.

'Let's free the children and get out of here.' Felix said.

'I want that sorcerer's skull for my drinking cup!' Gotrek spat.

Felix winced. 'You don't mean that.'

'It's just an expression, manling.'

From the look on Gotrek's face, Felix wasn't so sure about that.

They advanced down the corridor towards their goal. The thought of saving the children gave Felix some comfort. At least he and the Slayer would be able to do some good here, and return the young ones to their parents. For once, they would actually manage to act like real heroes. Felix could already picture the tear-stained faces of the relieved villagers as they were reunited with their offspring.

The rattling of the chain on Gotrek's wrist began to get on Felix's nerves. They turned the corner and came to a door. A single sweep of Gotrek's axe reduced it to so much kindling. They entered a chamber which had obviously once been Kruger's study.

The massive silver moon shone in through its single huge window.

The Chaos-corrupted sorcerer lay slumped over his desk, his greenish blood staining the open pages of a massive leather-bound grimoire. His hands still moved feebly as if he were trying to cast a spell that might save him.

Felix grabbed his hair from behind and pulled Kruger upright. He looked down into eyes from which the greenish glow was fading. Felix felt a surge of triumph. 'Where are the hostages?'

'What hostages?'

'The villagers' children!' Felix spat.

'You mean my experimental subjects?'

Cold horror filled Felix. He could see where this was leading. His lips almost refused to frame his next question. 'You experimented on children?'

Kruger gave Felix a twisted smile. 'Yes, they're easier to transmute than adults and they soon grow to full size. They were going to be my conquering army – but you killed them all.'

'We killed... them all.' Felix stood stunned. His visions of being feted by joyful villagers evaporated. He looked down at the blood that stained his hands and his tunic.

Suddenly blind rage, hot as the fires of hell, overwhelmed Felix. This maniac had transformed the village children into mutants, and he, Felix Jaeger, had taken a hand in slaughtering them. In a way that made him as guilty as Kruger. He considered this for a moment, then dragged Kruger over to the window. It looked down onto the sleeping village, a drop of several hundred feet down a sheer cliff face.

He gave Kruger a moment to consider what was about to happen and then gave him a good hard shove. The glass shattered as the sorcerer tumbled out into the chill night air. His arms flailed. His shriek echoed out through the darkness and took a long time to fade.

The Trollslayer looked up at Felix. There was a malevolent glitter in his one good eye. 'That was well done, manling. Now we'll have a few words with the innkeeper. I have a score to settle with him.'

'First, let's torch the castle,' Felix said grimly. He stalked off to turn the accursed place into a giant funeral pyre.

ULRIC'S CHILDREN

'In spite of all our efforts, yet somehow
unsurprisingly, we failed to reach Nuln before winter
set in. Worse yet, lacking a compass, or any other
means of navigating in the deep forest, we were soon
lost once more. I can think of few circumstances
more frightening or hazardous to the traveller
than to be lost in the woods in the winter snows.
Unfortunately, by some quirk of the dark destiny
that dogged our steps, it seemed we were just about
to encounter one of those "few circumstances"...'

— From *My Travels with Gotrek, Vol. II*, by Herr Felix Jaeger
(Altdorf Press, 2505)

The howling of the wolves echoed through the forest like the wailing of damned souls in torment. Felix Jaeger pulled his threadbare red Sudenland wool cloak tight and trudged on through the snow.

Over the past two days he had seen their pursuers twice, catching glimpses of them in the shadows beneath the endless pines. They were long, lean shapes, tongues lolling, eyes blazing with ravenous hunger. Twice the wolves had come almost within striking distance and twice they had withdrawn, as if summoned, by the howling of some distant leader, a creature so frightful that it had to be obeyed.

When he thought of that long wailing call, Felix shuddered. There had been a note of horror and intelligence in its cry that brought to mind the old tales of the darkened woods with which his nurse had frightened him as a child.

He tried to dismiss his evil thoughts.

He told himself he had merely heard the howling of the pack leader, a creature larger and more fearsome than the others. And, by Sigmar, the howling of wolves was a dismal enough sound without letting his mind populate the forest with monsters.

The snow crunched below his feet. Chilly wetness seeped through his cracked leather boots and into the thick woollen socks he wore beneath them. This was another bad sign. He had heard of woodsmen whose feet had been frozen solid within their boots who had to have their toes pared off with knives before gangrene set in.

He was not really surprised at finding himself lost deep in the heart of the Reikwald just as winter was setting in.

Not for the first time, Felix cursed the day he ever encountered the dwarf, Gotrek Gurnisson, and sworn to follow him and record his doom in an epic poem.

They had been following the tracks of a large monster that Gotrek swore was a troll when the snow had started to fall. They had lost the trail in the whiteout and were now completely lost.

Felix fought down a surge of panic. It was all too possible that they would trudge around in circles until they died of exhaustion or starvation. It had happened to other travellers lost in the woods in winter.

Or until the wolves picked them off, he reminded himself.

The dwarf looked just as miserable as Felix. He trudged along using the haft of his huge axe like a walking stick to test the depth of the snow ahead of him. The great ridge of red dyed hair that normally towered above his shaved and tattooed head drooped like the crest of some bedraggled bird. The sullen madness that glittered in his one good eye seemed subdued by their dismal surroundings. A great blob of snot dripped from his broken nose.

'Trees!' Gotrek grumbled. 'The only things I hate more than trees are elves.'

Another piercing howl broke Felix out of his reverie. It was like those earlier howls, full of malign intelligence and hunger, and it filled Felix with blind primordial fear. Instinctively he flicked his cloak over his shoulder to free his sword arm and reached for the hilt of his blade.

'No need for that, manling.' Malicious amusement was evident in the dwarf's harsh flinty voice. 'Whatever it is, it's calling our furry little friends away from us. It seems like they've found other prey.'

'The Children of Ulric...' Felix said fearfully, remembering his nurse's old tales.

'What has the wolf-god of Middenheim got to do with it, manling?'

'They say that, when the world was young, Ulric walked among men and begat children on mortal women. That those of his bloodline could shift shapes between that of man and wolf. They withdrew to the wild places of the world long ago. Some say their blood grew tainted when Chaos came and now they feast on human flesh.'

'Well, if any of them should come within reach of my axe I will spill some of that tainted blood.'

Suddenly Gotrek raised his hand, gesturing for silence. After a moment he nodded and spat on the ground.

Felix paused fearfully, watching and listening. Nowhere could he make out any sign of pursuit. The wolves had vanished. For a moment all he could hear was his own pounding heart and the sound of his rasping breath then he heard what had caused the Trollslayer to stop: the sounds of a struggle, battle-cries and the distant howling of wolves drifted on the wind.

'Sounds like a fight,' he said.

'Let's go kill some wolves,' Gotrek said. 'Maybe whoever they are attacking knows the way out of this hell-spawned, tree-infested place.'

* * *

Panting from the run through the thick snowdrifts, face stinging from where branches and briars had torn at him, Felix bounded into the clearing. A dozen crossbows swung to cover him. The smell of ozone filled the air. The corpses of men and wolves lay everywhere.

Slowly Felix raised his hands high. His gasping breath clouded the air in front of him. Sweat ran down his face despite the cold. He would have to remember that it was not a good idea to run through the winter woods in heavy clothing. That was if he was still alive to remember anything after this. The heavily armed strangers looked anything but friendly.

There were at least twenty of them. Several were garbed in the rich furs of nobles. They held swords and gave orders to the others: tough-looking, watchful men at arms. For all their obvious competence there was an air of deep unease about all these men. Fear was in their eyes. Felix knew that he was instants away from being pin-cushioned by crossbow bolts.

'Don't shoot!' he said. 'I'm here to help.'

He wondered where Gotrek was. He had run for quite a distance. In the heat of the moment he had let his excitement and his longer legs carry him in front of the dwarf. Right now that might prove to be a fatal mistake, although he was not sure what even the Trollslayer could do faced with this glittering array of missile weapons.

'Oh you are, are you?' said a sarcastic voice. 'Just out for a walk in the woods, were you? Heard the sounds of a scuffle. Come to investigate this little disturbance, did you?'

The speaker was a tall nobleman. Felix had never cared much for the Empire's nobility, and this man seemed like a prime example of the worst of that pox-ridden breed. A trim black beard framed his narrow face. Startling dark eyes glared out of his pale features. A great eagle beak of a nose gave his face a predatory air.

'My friend and I were lost in the forest. We heard the wolves and the sounds of battle. We came to help, if we could.'

'Your friend?' the nobleman asked ironically. He jerked a thumb towards a tall, beautiful young woman who stood chained nearby. 'Do you mean this witch?'

'I have no idea what you're talking about, sir,' Felix said. 'I've never seen that young lady before in my life.'

He glanced around him. The dwarf was nowhere to be seen. Perhaps it was just as well, Felix thought. The Trollslayer was not known for his tact. Doubtless right now, he would be saying something that would get them both killed.

'I was travelling with a companion…' It dawned on Felix that it might not be such a good idea to mention Gotrek right now. The Trollslayer was a conspicuous figure and an outlaw, and perhaps these men might want to claim the bounty, if they recognised him.

'He appears to have got lost,' Felix finished off weakly.

'Put down your sword,' the noble said. Felix complied. 'Sven! Heinrich! Bind his hands!'

Two of the men-at-arms raced forward to obey. Felix found himself kicked to the ground. He fell face first into the snow, and felt the cold wetness of it begin to seep into his tunic.

He opened his eyes and found he was lying in front of the corpse of a wolf. As he gazed into the creature's death-clouded eyes, the soldiers swiftly and efficiently bound his hands behind his back. Felix felt cold metal bite into his wrists and was surprised to find that they were using more than mere rope to hold him.

Then someone tugged down the hood of his cloak and pulled his head up by the hair. Foul breath assaulted his nostrils. Coldly crazy eyes gazed deep into his own. He looked up into a lined face framed by a greyish beard. A gnarled hand made a gesture in front of his face. As it swept through the air it left behind a trail of glittering sparks. Quite obviously this old man was a magician.

'He seems untouched by the taint of Darkness,' the sorcerer said in a surprisingly mellow and cultured voice. 'It may be that he tells the truth. I'll know more when we get him back to the lodge.'

Felix was allowed to slump forward into the snow once more. He recognised the voice of the noble speaking.

'Even so, take no chances with him, Voorman. If he is a spy for our enemies, I want him dead.'

'I'll find out the truth once I have my instruments. If he's a spy for enemies of the Order, we'll know!'

The noble shrugged and turned away, obviously dismissing the matter as beneath his concern. A boot hit Felix in the ribs again and knocked all the air out of his lungs.

'Get up and get on the sledge,' a burly sergeant said. 'If you fall off, I'll kill you.'

Felix drew his legs underneath himself and reeled to his feet. He glared at the sergeant, trying to memorise every line of the man's face. If he got out of this alive, he would have vengeance. Seeing his look, one of the men-at-arms drew back the butt of his crossbow as if to brain Felix. The magician shook his head mildly.

'None of that. I want him undamaged.'

Felix shivered. There was something more frightening in the magician's calm detachment than there was in the soldier's unthinking brutality. He climbed on to the back of the sledge.

As far as Felix could tell, the party consisted of the nobleman, some of his toadies, the men-at-arms, and the mage. The nobles rode in horse-drawn sledges. The soldiers clung to the running boards or sat up front driving.

Beside him sat the young woman. Her hair was pure silver in colour and her eyes were golden. She had a sleek predatory beauty and a naturally haughty bearing that was in no way diminished by the collar and chain that attached her to the back railing of the sledge or the strange rune-encrusted metal shackles that bound her hands behind her back.

'Felix Jaeger,' he murmured by way of introduction. She said nothing, merely smiled coldly and then seemed to withdraw within herself. She gave no further acknowledgement of his presence.

'Be silent,' the magician sitting opposite them said, and there was more menace in his calm, quiet tone than there was in all the angry glares of the guardsmen combined.

Felix decided there was nothing to be gained by defying the old man. He cast another look around the forest, hoping to see some sign of Gotrek, but the Trollslayer was nowhere in evidence. Felix lapsed into morose silence. He doubted that the dwarf could overtake them now, but he could at least follow the tracks of the sleds – providing it didn't snow too heavily.

And then what? Felix did not know. He had every respect for Gotrek's formidable powers of slaughter and destruction but he doubted that even the Trollslayer could overcome this small army.

Occasionally he risked a glance at the woman beside him, noting that she too was casting anxious glances towards the trees. He could not decide whether she was hoping that friends would come to her rescue or was simply measuring the distance of a dash for freedom.

A wolf howled in the distance. A strange inhuman smile twisted the woman's lips. Felix shuddered and looked away.

Felix was almost glad when the manor house loomed out of the gathering storm. The low, massive outline of the lodge was partially obscured by the drifting snowflakes. Felix could see that it was built from stone and logs in the style they called half-timbered.

He felt weary beyond belief. Hunger, cold and the long trudge through the snow had brought him almost to the end of his strength. It occurred to him that this was their destination and that here he would be prey for whatever foul schemes the wizard had in mind, but he simply could not muster the energy to care. All he wanted was to lie down somewhere warm and to sleep.

Someone sounded a horn and the gates were swung open. The sleds and the accompanying men-at-arms passed through into a courtyard, and then the gates were closed behind them.

Felix had a chance to glance around the courtyard. It was flanked on all four sides by the walls of the fortified manor house. He revised his earlier opinion. It was not so much a hunting lodge as a fortress, built to withstand a siege if need be. He cursed: his chances of escape seemed slimmer than ever.

All around, the party climbed down from the sledges. The nobles called for hot mulled wine. Someone ordered the drivers to see that the horses were stabled. All was bustling disorder. The breath of men and beasts emerged from their mouths like smoke.

The guards pushed Felix into the building. Inside it was cold and damp. It smelled of earth and pine and old woodsmoke. A massive stone fireplace filled the centre of the entrance chamber. The warriors and nobles stamped about inside, windmilling their arms and hugging themselves against the chill. Servants rushed forward bearing goblets of hot spicy wine. The scent of it made Felix's mouth water.

One of the warriors hastily laid kindling in the fire and then set to work, striking sparks from a flint. The damp wood refused to catch.

The wizard watched with growing impatience, then shrugged, gestured and spoke a word in the ancient tongue. A small burst of flame leapt from the end of his pointed index finger to the wood in the fireplace. The wood hissed, then roared. Ozone stink filled the air. Blue flames flickered around the wood, then the logs all caught fire at once. Shadows danced away from the fireplace.

The nobles and the wizard passed through one of the doors into another chamber, leaving the warriors and the prisoners alone. Tense silence reigned for a moment, then all the men began to speak at once. All the words that they had held in during the long trek to the lodge tumbled from the soldiers' mouths.

'By Sigmar's hammer, what a fight that was. I thought those wolves were going to have our nuts for sure!'

'I have never been so frightened as when I saw the hairy beasts loping out of the trees. Those teeth looked plenty sharp.'

'Yeah but they died quick enough when you put a crossbow bolt through their eyes or twelve inches of good Imperial steel through their mangy hides!'

'It wasn't natural though. I've never even heard of wolves attacking such a large party! I've never seen wolves fight so hard or long either.'

'I think we can blame the witch for that!'

The girl returned their stares impassively until none of them could meet her gaze. Felix noticed that her eyes were odd. In the gathering gloom, they reflected the light of the fire the way the eyes of a hound would.

'Yeah, just as well we had the wizard with us. Old Voorman showed them what real magic is and no mistake!'

'I wonder why the count wants her?'

At this a chill smile passed over the girl's face. Her teeth were small and white and very, very sharp. When she spoke her voice was low and thrilling and strangely musical.

'Your Count Hrothgar is a fool if he thinks he can hold me here, or kill me without my death being avenged. You are fools if you think you will ever leave this place alive.'

The sergeant drew back his hand and struck her with his gauntleted fist. The outline of his palm stood out stark and pink on her cheek where the blow fell. Anger blazed in the girl's eyes so hot and hellish and fierce that the sergeant shrank back as if he himself had been the one struck. The girl spoke again and her words were cold and measured.

'Hear me! I have the gift of the Sight. The veils of the future do not blind me. Every one of you, every single miserable lackey of Count Hrothgar, will die. You will not leave this place alive!'

Such was the compelling certainty in her voice that every man present froze. Faces went white with fear. Men glanced at each other in horror. Felix himself did not doubt her words. The burly sergeant was first to rouse himself. He slid his dagger from its sheath and walked over to the girl. He held the blade before her eyes.

'Then you will be the first to die, witch,' he said. The girl looked at him, unafraid. He drew back his blade to strike. Filled with sudden anger, Felix threw himself forward. Weighed down with chains he cannoned into the man and knocked him from his feet. He heard a low gurgle come from the man he had hit and felt a stab of savage exultation at taking some small revenge on the man who had struck him.

The other soldiers dragged him to his feet. Blows slammed into his body. Stars danced before his eyes. He fell to the ground, curling himself into a ball as heavy booted feet crunched into him. He pulled

his head against his chest and drew his knees up to his stomach as the
pain threatened to overwhelm him. A kick caught him under the chin,
throwing his head back. Darkness took him momentarily.

Now he was really scared. The angry soldiers were likely to keep up
this punishment until he was dead and there was nothing he could
do about it.

'Stop!' bellowed a voice he recognised as belonging to the sorcerer.
'Those two are my property. Do not damage either of them!'

The kicking stopped. Felix was manhandled to his feet. He looked
around him wildly, then he noticed the spreading pool of red liquid
on the floor that surrounded the recumbent form of the sergeant.

One of the soldiers turned the man over and Felix noticed the knife
protruding from the sergeant's chest. The sergeant's eyes were wide
and staring. His face was white. His chest did not rise and fall. He
must have fallen on the blade when Felix had knocked him over.

'Throw them in the cellar,' the sorcerer said. 'I will have words with
them both later.'

'The dying has begun!' the girl said with a note of triumph in her
voice. She looked at the spreading pool of blood and licked her lips.

The cellar was damp. It smelled of wood and metal and stuff contained in barrels. Felix caught the scent of smoked meat and cheeses
as well. It just made him hungrier than he already was, and he remembered that he had not eaten in two days.

A clink of chains reminded him of the girl. He sensed her presence in
the dark. He heard her shallow breathing. She was somewhere close by.

'What is your name, lady?' he asked. For a long time there was
silence, and he wondered if she was going to answer.

'Magdalena.'

'What are you doing here? Why are you in chains?'

Another long silence.

'The soldiers believe you are a witch. Are you?'

More silence, then: 'No.'

'But you have the second sight and the wolves fought for you.'

'Yes.'

'You're not very communicative, are you?'

'Why should I be?'

'Because we both appear to be in the same boat and perhaps
together we can escape.'

'There is no escape. There is only death here. Soon it will be night.
Then my father will come.'

She made the statement as if she was convinced that it was a complete answer. There was the same mad certainty in her voice, as convincing as it had been when she predicted death for all those armed men upstairs.

In spite of himself, Felix shuddered. It was not pleasant to think that he was alone in a dark basement with a madwoman. It was less pleasant to consider the alternative to her being mad.

'What do they want with you?'

'I am bait in a snare for my father.'

'Why does the Count want you dead?'

'I do not know. For generations my people have lived at peace with the Count's. But Hrothgar is not like his forefathers. He has changed. There is a taint about him, and his pet wizard.'

'How did they capture you?'

'Voorman is a sorcerer. He tracked me with spells. His magic was too strong for me. But soon my father will come for me.'

'Your father must be a mighty man indeed if he can overcome all the occupants of this castle.'

There was no answer except soft, panting laughter. Felix knew that the sooner he got out of here the better.

The door leading into the cellar was thrown open. A shaft of light illuminated the darkness. Heavy footsteps marked the approach of the wizard, Voorman. He held a lantern in his hand and leaned on a heavy staff. He twisted his head up to look Felix in the face.

'Having an interesting chat with the monster, were you, boy?'

Something in the man's tone rankled. 'She's not a monster. She is only a sad, deluded young woman.'

'You would not say that if you knew the truth, boy. If I were to remove those shackles binding her, your sanity would be blasted in an instant.'

'Really,' Felix said with some irony. The magician tittered.

'So sure of yourself, eh? So ignorant of the way the world really is. What would you say, boy, if I told you that cults devoted to the worship of Chaos riddle our land, that soon we will overthrow all that exists of order here in the Empire.'

The wizard sounded almost boastful.

'I would say that you are, perhaps, correct.' He could see that his reply surprised the sorcerer, that Voorman had expected the usual casual denial of such things one expected from the educated classes of the Empire.

'You interest me, boy. Why do you say that?'

Felix wondered why he had said that himself. He was admitting to knowledge that could get him burned at the stake if a witch-hunter overheard him. Still, right now, he was cold and tired and hungry and he did not like being patronised by this irritating and supercilious mage.

'Because I have seen the evidence of it with my own eyes.'

He heard a sharp intake of breath from the wizard, and sensed now that perhaps for the first time he had got his full attention.

'Really? The Time of Changes is coming, eh? Arakkkai Nidlek Zarug Tzeentch?' Voorman paused as if expecting a reply. His head tilted to one side. He rubbed his nose with one long bony finger. His foul breath filled Felix's nostrils.

Felix wondered what was going on. The words were spoken in a language he had heard before, during the rituals of depraved cultists that he and Gotrek had interrupted one Geheimnisnacht. The name 'Tzeentch' was all too familiar and frightening. It belonged to one of the darkest of dark powers. Slowly the air of expectancy passed from Voorman.

'No, you are not one of the Chosen. And yet you know the words of our Litany, or some of them. I can see that in your eyes. I don't think you are part of the Order. How can this be?'

It was obvious that the sorcerer did not expect an answer, that the last question was asked more of himself than of Felix. Suddenly there came the sound of the baying of many wolves outside the keep. The wizard flinched and then smiled. 'That will be my other guest arriving. I must go soon. He slipped through the net earlier but I knew he would come back for the girl.'

The wizard checked the chains that held Magdalena. He inspected the runes on them closely and then, apparently satisfied with what he saw, he smirked and turned and limped away. As he passed he looked at Felix. The younger man felt his flesh crawl. He knew that the wizard was deciding whether or not to kill him. Then the sorcerer smiled.

'No – there's time enough later. I would talk more with you before you die, boy!'

As the wizard shut the door behind him, the light died. Felix felt horror mount within his soul.

Felix was not aware of how long he lay there with despair growing in his heart. He was trapped in the dark with no weapons and only a madwoman for company. The wizard intended to murder him. He had no idea where the Trollslayer was or if he had any hope of rescue. It was possible that Gotrek was lost in the woods somewhere. Slowly it dawned on him that if he was going to get out of this, he was going to have to do it for himself.

It did not look good. His hands were chained behind his back. He was hungry and tired and ill with cold and weariness. The bruises from the beating earlier pained him. The key to his chains was on the belt of the wizard. He had no weapon.

Well, one thing at a time, he told himself. Let's see what I can do about the chains. He hunkered into a squat, drawing his knees up to his chest. The chains pooled around his ankles, then by dint of wriggling and squirming, he drew his arms underneath him so that they were in front of his body. The effort left him breathing hard and he felt like he had pulled his arms from his sockets, but at least now he could move more freely and the length of heavy coiled chain he held in his hands could be used as a weapon. Experimentally he swung it before him. There was a swishing noise as it cut through the air.

The girl laughed as if she understood what he was doing. Now he moved forward cautiously, placing one foot ahead of him gently testing the ground like a man might who was on the edge of a cliff. He did not know what he might stumble over in the darkness, but he felt it was wisest to be careful. This would be a bad time to fall and dislocate an ankle.

His caution was rewarded when he felt a stairway under his foot. Slowly, carefully, he worked his way up the steps. As far as he remembered they had not curved in any way. Eventually his outstretched hands struck wood. The chains clinked together softly as they swung. Felix froze and listened. It seemed to him that somewhere far off he could hear sounds of men fighting and wolves howling.

Wonderful, he thought sourly. The wolves had somehow got inside the manor. He pictured the long, lean shapes racing through the hunting lodge, and a desperate battle between man and beast taking place mere paces from where he stood. It was not a reassuring thought.

For long moments he stood undecided and then he pushed against the door. It did not move. He cursed himself and fumbled for a handle. His fingers clutched a cool metal ring. He twisted and pulled towards himself and the door opened. He was looking up a long flight of stairs dimly illuminated by a guttering lantern. He reached out for the lantern, then thought about the girl.

However strange she was, she was also a prisoner here. He was not going to abandon her to the tender mercies of Voorman. He edged back down the stairs and gestured for her to follow him. He caught sight of her face. It was pale and strained and feral. Her eyes definitely did catch the light like those of some animal. There was a ferocious inhuman aspect to her whole appearance that did not reassure Felix in the slightest. He moved towards the head of the stairs but the girl pushed past him into the lead.

Felix was glad not to have those fierce eyes burning into his back.

The sounds of fighting became clearer. Wolves bayed. War-cries rang out. Magdalena opened the door at the head of the stairs. They found themselves once more amid the mansion's corridors. The place was deserted. All the guards appeared to have been drawn toward the sounds of battle. A line of doorways edged the corridor. At one end a flight of stairs moved upwards. At the other there was a doorway beyond which was the sound of battle. Felix's nostrils twitched. He thought he smelled burning. Somewhere in the distance horses whinnied with terror.

Discretion told him to head for the stairs, to get away from the sounds of fighting. He was not part of either faction here, and discovery might prove fatal for him. The longer the others fought, the more the odds against him were whittled down, and the more chance he had of escaping.

Magdalena, however, felt differently. She moved towards the doorway at the end of the corridor. The one that led towards the battle. Felix grabbed her chains and tugged. She did not stop. Although he was taller and heavier, she was surprisingly strong, stronger perhaps than he was.

'Where are you going?'

'Where do you think?'

'Don't be stupid. There's nothing you can do there.'

'What do you know?'

'Let us look around. Perhaps upstairs we can find a way to remove these chains.'

For a moment, she stood undecided but the last point appeared to sway her. Together they moved up the stairs. Behind them the sounds of howling and war-cries reached a crescendo and then abruptly ceased.

For a moment, Felix wondered what had happened. Had the wolves overcome the defenders?

Then he heard men-at-arms begin to shout at each other once more. He heard noble voices tell the men to take the wounded inside and he realised that the men had won – for a while.

* * *

At the top of the stairs a window looked down into the courtyard of the lodge. He could see that there were dozens of dead wolves down there and maybe five dead men. Blood reddened the snow.

'How the hell did that gate get open?' he heard Count Hrothgar ask. Felix wondered the same himself, for he could see that the wooden gate lay wide open. The wolves had come right through it. Then he saw the thing, and he wondered no more.

On the roof of the stables lay a grey shape, half man and half wolf. The hairs on the back of Felix's neck prickled. The man-wolf rose and dropped back out of sight, leaving Felix wondering if he had imagined the whole thing. He offered a prayer to Sigmar that he had done so but somehow, in his heart of hearts, he doubted it. It looked like Ulric's Children were here.

'Let us go on,' he muttered and turned and headed down the corridor.

They entered a library. Bookcases so high that one would need a ladder to reach the highest volumes lined the walls. Felix was surprised by the size of it. Count Hrothgar had not seemed to him to be a scholar, but this was worthy of the chambers of one of Felix's former professors at the University of Altdorf. His guess was that this was the wizard's place.

Felix ran his eyes over the titles. Most seemed to be written in High Classical, the tongue of scholars across the Old World. The ones he could see mostly concerned voyages of exploration, ancient myths and legends and lorebooks compiled from dwarfish.

On the desk ahead of him was an open book. Felix walked over and picked it up. The tome was leather bound and no title was embossed on its spine. The parchment pages were thick and coarse and obviously ancient. For the thickness of the book there were surprisingly few pages.

It was not a printed volume set in the movable typefaces perfected by the Guild of Printers. It was done in the old style, hand-copied and illuminated around the borders. Felix picked it up and began to read and soon wished he had not.

Magdalena obviously noticed the look on his face. 'What is it? What is wrong? What does it say?'

'It's a grimoire of sorts… it deals with magic of a certain type.'

Indeed it did. Felix laboriously translated the Classical and a thrill of horror made him shiver. As far as he could tell it appeared to be a spell of soul transmutation, an invocation designed to let a man switch his very essence with that of another, to steal their shape and form. If the claims of the book were true, it would allow the wizard to take possession of another's body.

In another time, at another place, Felix would have found the whole thing ludicrous. In this out-of-the-way place, it all seemed rather likely. The madness of it did not seem out of place here.

None of this reassured Felix. He was trapped in an isolated keep by a group of mad cultists and their men-at-arms. The keep was surrounded by hungry wolves and cut off by a winter blizzard. As if that weren't bad enough, if his suspicions were true, there were not one but two werewolves within the walls of the fortress. And one of them was behind him.

Felix's flesh crawled.

They moved on through the second floor of the castle, down corridors lit by flickering torches and echoing with the howling of wolves. A faint unpleasant odour, as of wet fur and blood, reached Felix's nostrils just before they turned a corner. He poked his head round cautiously and saw the corpse of a man-at-arms lying there. The soldier's eyes were wide open. Great talon gouges ripped his chest. His face was white as that of a vampire. Blood poured from where huge jaws had ripped out his jugular.

A sword lay near the dead man's hand. There was a dagger at his belt. Felix turned to look at the girl. She was smiling evilly. Felix felt like taking up the sword and striking her but he did not. The thought occurred to him that maybe he could use her as a hostage and strike a deal with the man-wolf. He turned it over in his mind and then dismissed it as being at once impractical and dishonourable.

Instead he bent over the man and fumbled for his dagger. It was a long, needle-sharp blade almost as thin as a stiletto. He considered the lock of his chains. It was large and cumbersome and crudely made. He picked the blade up with his right hand and thrust it down into the lock of the manacle on his left wrist. He felt mechanisms move as the point went home. For long tense moments, he twisted and prodded. There was a click and the manacle opened. A weight fell from Felix's shoulders as the chain slid from his wrist. He tried repeating the process for the right hand chain but his left hand was clumsier and it took him longer.

Seconds stretched into minutes and he kept imagining that awful wolf-headed shape creeping up on him as he did so. Eventually there was a click and his other hand was free. Smiling triumphantly he turned and the smile faded from his lips.

The girl was gone.

* * *

Felix moved cautiously through the manor house. The wolves were quiet once more. The sword felt heavy as death in his hands. He had come across two more dead guards in his wanderings through the hall. Both their throats were torn out. Both had died with looks of horror on their face. The strange musk smell filled the air.

Felix considered his options. He could make a run for it out through the courtyard. That did not seem sensible. Outside snow covered the ground and wolves filled the woods. Even without their malevolent presence he doubted he would get very far without food or winter gear.

Inside the mansion was a sorcerer who wanted to kill him and the Children of Ulric. Plus a whole crew of scared men-at-arms to whom he was a stranger. That did not look too promising either.

Common sense dictated that he find some place to hide and wait for one side to slaughter the other. Maybe upstairs he could find an attic in which to hide, or maybe there was some quiet room where–

Voices approached. The door at the end of the corridor started to open. Swiftly Felix pushed the door beside him open and ducked through, pulling it closed behind him. He realised he must be in Count Hrothgar's study. A massive desk sat under the window. Family portraits glared down from the walls. A burnished suit of armour stood sentry in an alcove. Curtained drapes covered the windows.

Some instinct prodded Felix to race across the room and dive behind the drapes. He was just in time. The door to the chamber swung open. Two men talked loudly. Felix recognised their voices. One was the count. The other was the sorcerer.

'Damn! Voorman, I thought you said your chains held them fast as the clutches of daemons. How could they have disappeared?'

'The spells were not broken. I would have sensed it. I suspect some more mundane means. Perhaps one of your people...'

'Are you suggesting that one of my men could be in league with those things?'

'Or one of your servants. They stay here all year round. Who knows? The Children of Ulric have lived in this area longer than you. They say the folk about here used to worship them or at least sacrifice to them.'

'Maybe. Maybe. But can you find the prisoners? They can't just have disappeared into thin air. And what about my men? Over half are dead and the other half are frightened out of their wits, jumping at shadows. You'd best do something soon, wizard, or you will have some explaining to do to the Magister Magistorum. Things are not going as you promised the Order they would.'

'Don't panic, excellency. My magic will prevail and the cause will be stronger for it. The Time of Changes is coming, and you and I will have worked some of blessed Tzeentch's strongest magic. We will be immortal and unkillable.'

'Perhaps. But right now, at least one of the beasts is loose within these walls. Maybe two if you were wrong about the youth.'

'No matter. The spell of Transmutation is ready. Soon final victory will be ours. I go to find our vessel.'

'You go to find our vessel, do you, wizard? You plan treachery, more like. Be careful! The Magister gave me the means to deal with you, should you prove unfaithful to the Order!'

There was a ringing of steel as a weapon was drawn.

'Put it away, count.' The wizard sounded nervous now. 'You do not know the power of such a thing. There will be no need for its use.'

'Make sure that is so, Voorman. Make sure that is so.'

The door opened, then closed. Felix heard the nobleman slump down into his chair. Briefly he wondered about this Order. Who was this mysterious Magister? Mostly likely the head of some unspeakable cult. Felix dismissed the thought. He had other things to worry about.

He pulled the curtain to one side and saw the bald spot at the back of the count's head. A dagger lay on the desk in front of him. It was covered in strange glowing runes. Trying to follow their lines hurt Felix's eyes. Still, he thought, the dagger might be useful.

The nobleman rubbed his neck, feeling the cold draft from the window behind him. He began to reach for the dagger. Felix leapt from his place of concealment and brought the pommel of his sword down on Count Hrothgar's skull. The nobleman fell like a pole-axed ox.

Gingerly Felix reached out for the dagger. His skin prickled as he brought his hand near the blade. A dangerous energy radiated from the thing. He picked it up by the hilt and noticed that the handle was wrapped with dull metal: lead. He realised that he had seen a glow like the one from the blade before. It looked like warpstone had been used in the creation of this dagger. This was a weapon that could be as dangerous to its user as to its victim. He reached down and found the sheath the count had drawn the weapon from. It was lined with lead. Felix felt a bit better after he had returned the weapon to its sheath.

Briefly he considered discarding the dagger, but only briefly. In this hellish place, it might prove the only protection he might find. He buckled the sheath around his waist and got ready to move on.

* * *

There were three dead servants in the kitchen. They too had their throats torn out. It looked like the man-wolf intended to slay everyone in the mansion. Felix did not doubt that he would be included in that reckoning.

Looking at the dead bodies was almost enough to put Felix off his food. Almost. He had found fresh made bread on the table and cheese and beef in the larder. He gulped them down hungrily. They seemed like the best food he had ever tasted.

The door opened and two wild-eyed men-at-arms entered. They looked at the corpses and then looked at him. Fear filled their eyes. Felix reached for the naked sword on the table.

'You killed them,' one of the men said, pointing an accusing finger.

'Don't be stupid,' Felix said, his words muffled by the bread and cheese filling his mouth. He swallowed. 'Their throats were ripped out. It was the beast.'

The men paused, undecided. They seemed too afraid to attack and yet filled with fear-fuelled rage.

'You've seen it?' one asked eventually. Felix nodded.

'What was it like?'

'Big! Head like a wolf. Body of a man.'

An eerie howl echoed through the halls. It sounded close. The men turned and bolted for the door into the courtyard. As they did so, lean grey shapes sprang on them and pulled them down. Wolves had been waiting silently outside.

Felix raced forward but was too late to help the men. Looking out, he saw that the main gate was once again open. What looked like the girl stood near it. Her head was thrown back. She appeared to be laughing.

Hastily Felix closed the door shut and threw the bolts. He was trapped, but at least whatever had howled had not come any closer. He sat back down at the table, determined to finish what might be his last meal.

Felix crept through the corridors once more, sword in one hand, glittering dagger in the other. He had sat in the kitchen as long as he dared while fear made a home in his gut. Eventually it seemed like a better idea to go meet his doom head on than to sit there like a frightened rabbit.

He entered a great hall. The ceiling was high. Banners with the crest of Count Hrothgar hung from the ceilings. The heads of many animals, taken as hunting trophies, covered the walls. Two figures were present. One was the sorcerer, Voorman. The other was the man-wolf. It was monstrous, half again as tall as Felix, its chest rounder than a barrel. Great claws flexed at the end of its long arms. Undying hatred glittered in its red-wolf eyes.

'You came, as I knew you would,' the wizard said. At first Felix wondered how the sorcerer had known he was there, but then he realised that Voorman was talking to the man-wolf.

'And now you will die.' Lips never meant for human speech mangled the words. The sorcerer stepped back. His cloak billowed and light flared around his staff. The wolf stood frozen to the spot for a moment, then reached out and tore Voorman's head off with one massive claw. The sorcerer's body stumbled forward. Blood gouted from his severed neck and sprayed the beast-thing.

From outside came the sound of wolves howling, and combat. Doubtless, the last survivors were being mown down, Felix thought. He eyed the beast warily.

The sorcerer's blood steamed. A cloud of vapour rose over his corpse, taking on the outline of the mage. It stretched its arms triumphantly and flowed towards the Child of Ulric. The mist entered the creature's mouth and nostrils and it stood there for a moment, clutching its throat and seemingly unable to breath. The light vanished from its eyes and then a hellish green glow flickered there.

When the creature spoke again, its voice was Voorman's.

'At last,' it said. 'The spell of Transmutation is a success. Immortality and power are mine. The beast's strength is mine. I will live until Lord Tzeentch comes to claim this world. All things are indeed mutable.'

Felix stood aghast. A horrified understanding of what he had witnessed filled his brain. Voorman's plan had come to fruition. The trap was sprung. The corrupt soul of the wizard had taken possession of the man-wolf's body. His malign intelligence and sorcerous power would live on in its monstrous shape. Voorman now possessed the strength and invulnerability of the Children of Ulric as well as his own evil powers.

Slowly the terrible green gaze came to rest on Felix. He felt the strength leech off him under that baleful glare. Outside he heard the wolves whimper in fear and the bellow of a warcry that sounded strangely familiar. The man-wolf gestured and, hypnotised, Felix stepped closer until he was within striking distance of its massive blood-spattered claws. Voorman reached out, his massive talons closing...

Throwing off his fear, Felix ducked and lashed out with his sword. He might as well have struck a stone statue. The keen edge of the blade bounced. The man-wolf's return slash tore Felix's jerkin. Pain seared his side where the razor-edged claws bit deep. Felix sprang away. Only the fact that his reflexes were on a knife-edge had saved him from being gutted.

Things seemed to happen in slow motion. The man-wolf wheeled to face him. Felix circled. The beast sprang. Its rush was as irresistible as a thunderbolt. It bore Felix over, its enormous arms encircling him in a hug that threatened to snap his ribs like twigs. Frantically Felix stabbed downwards with the dagger in his left hand. To his surprise it pierced fur. There was a smell like rotting meat and the man-wolf threw back its head and howled.

Felix kept stabbing. Where he stabbed, the flesh became soft. The wolf's grip was weak now. Felix pulled himself clear and kept stabbing. Pockets of blackness appeared in the man-wolf's fur like spots of rot in overripe fruit. He kept stabbing. The man-wolf fell and the rot spread across its body, consuming it completely. The mighty form simply withered, overcome by the baneful runes on the dagger. Then the hellish glow left the weapon. It felt inert in Felix's grasp. He opened numb fingers and let it fall to the floor.

It was a long time before he pulled himself to his feet to look around the hall. The girl stood sullenly in the doorway. Gotrek stood behind her like an executioner. The blade of his massive axe lay against her neck.

'Thought I'd never get to the end of those damn tracks. Had to kill about fifty wolves to get in, too,' the Trollslayer said, inspecting the scene of carnage with a professional air.

'Well, manling, it looks like you've had a busy night. I hope you've left me something to kill.'

SKAVENSLAYER

SKAVEN'S CLAW

'I would like to forget the long, hard trudge through the winter woods which followed our encounter with the children of Ulric. And it pains me to this day to think of the punishment we meted out to the girl, Magdalena, but my companion was unrelenting, and no evil we encountered was ever spared if that could be avoided. In this case it could not be. With a heavy hearts, we entered the forest once more and set off northwards.

'At long last we found ourselves in the great Elector city of Nuln, a place of refinement, sophistication, wealth and great learning – and a city in which my family had long had business dealings. At that time, the Countess Emmanuelle was at the height of her fame, power and beauty and her city attracted the wealthy, the aristocratic and the famous like a candle flame attracts moths. Nuln was one of the most beautiful cities in all the Empire.

'Of course, our own entry into the life of the city was made at a level far lower on the social scale. Short of cash, hungry and weary from our long journey, we were forced to take employment in what was possibly the very worst occupation we were to pursue in our long wanderings. And during that period we encountered a fiend who was to bedevil our paths for long years to come.'

— From *My Travels With Gotrek, Vol. III*, by Herr Felix Jaeger
(Altdorf Press, 2505)

'Stuck in a sewer, hunting goblins. What a life,' Felix Jaeger muttered with feeling. He cursed all the gods roundly. In his time he had come to consider himself something of an expert on unprepossessing surroundings but this must surely take the prize. Twenty feet overhead, the population of the city of Nuln went about its lawful daily business. And here he was, in the dark, creeping along narrow walkways where a single slip could put him over his head in reeking foulness. His back ached from stooping for hours on end. Truly, in all of his long association with the Trollslayer, Gotrek Gurnisson, he had never before plumbed such depths.

'Stop moaning, manling. It's a job, isn't it?' Gotrek said cheerfully, paying not the slightest heed to the smell or the narrowness of the ledge or the closeness of the bubbling broth of excrement the sewerjacks called 'the stew'.

The Slayer looked right at home in the endless maze of brickwork and channels. Gotrek's squat muscular form was far better adapted to the work than Felix's own. The dwarf picked his way along the ledges as sure-footed as a cat. In the two weeks they had been part of the sewer watch, Gotrek had become far more adroit at the job than ten-year veterans of the service. But then he was a dwarf; his people were reared in the lightless places far beneath the Old World.

It probably helped that he could see in the dark, Felix thought, and did not have to depend on the flickering light of the watchmen's lanterns. That still did not explain how he endured the stink, though. Felix doubted whether even the dwarfholds smelled quite so bad. The stench down here was exquisitely vile. His head swam from the fumes.

The Trollslayer looked peculiar without his usual weapon. Felix had come to think of the battle-axe as being grafted to his hand. Now the dwarf had his huge starmetal axe strapped across his back. There was not enough space to swing it in most areas of the sewer. Felix had tried to get Gotrek to leave the weapon in the watch armoury alongside his own magical sword but had failed. Not even the prospect of its weight dragging him below the sewage if he fell in could cause the Slayer to part with his beloved heirloom. So Gotrek carried a throwing hatchet in his right hand and a huge military pick in the other. Felix shuddered when he imagined the latter being used. It resembled a large hammer with a cruel hooked spike on one side. Driven by the dwarf's awesome strength he did not doubt that it could shatter bone and tear through muscle with ease.

Felix tightened his grip on his own short stabbing sword and wished that he still carried the Templar Aldred's dragon-hilted mageblade. The prospect of facing goblins in the dark made him long for the reassurance of using his familiar weapon. Perhaps Gotrek was right to keep his axe so close.

In the gloom of the lantern light, his fellow sewerjacks were ominous shadowy figures. They wore no uniform save the ubiquitous scarves wrapped round their heads like Araby turbans, with a long fold obscuring their mouths. Over the last two weeks, though, Felix had become familiar enough with them to recognise their silhouettes.

There was tall, spare Gant whose scarf concealed a face turned into a moonscape by pockmarks and whose neck was a volcanic archipelago of erupting boils. If ever there was a good advertisement for not staying a sewerjack for twenty years Gant was it. The thought of his toothless smile, bad breath and worse jokes made Felix want to cringe. Not that he had ever pointed this out to Gant's face. The sergeant had hinted that he had killed many a man for it.

There was the squat, ape-like giant Rudi, with his massive barrel chest and hands almost as big as Gotrek's. He and the Trollslayer often arm-wrestled in the tavern after work. Despite straining until the sweat ran down his bald pate, Rudi had never beaten the dwarf, although he had come closer than any man Felix had ever seen.

Then there were Hef and Spider, the new boys as Gant liked to call them, because they had only been with the sewer watch for seven years. They were identical twins who lived with the same woman on the surface and who had the habit of finishing each other's sentences. So strange were their long, lantern-jawed faces and their fish-like staring eyes, that Felix suspected that in-breeding or mutation was part of their heritage. He did not doubt their deadliness in hand-to-hand combat, though, or their dedication to each other and their girl, Gilda. He had seen them do terrible things with their long hook-bladed knives to a pimp who had insulted her one night.

Along with the burly, one-eyed dwarf, these were the men he

worked with, as desperate a crew as he had ever known. They were vicious men who couldn't find work that suited them anywhere else and who had finally found an employer who asked no questions.

There were times when Felix felt like going along to the office of his father's company and begging for money so he could leave this place. He knew they would give it to him. He was still the son of Gustav Jaeger, one of the Empire's wealthiest merchants. But he also knew that word of his capitulation would get back to his family. They would know that he had come crawling back to them, after all his fine boasts. They would know he had taken the money he had affected to so despise. Of course, it had been easy to despise money on the day he had stormed from their house, because he had never known the lack of it. His father's threat to disown him was meaningless because he simply had not understood it. He had grown up rich. The poor were a different species: sad, sickly things that begged on street corners and obstructed the path of one's coach. He had learned since that day. He had endured hardship and he thought he could take it.

But this was very nearly the last straw: being forced to become a sewerjack, the lowest of the low amongst the hired bravoes of Nuln. But there had simply been nothing else for it. Since their arrival no one else would hire two such down-at-heel rogues as himself and Gotrek. It pained Felix to think of how he must have looked, seeking work in his tattered britches and patched cloak. He had always been such a fine dresser.

Now they needed the money, any money. Their long trek through the land of the Border Princes had yielded no reward. They had found the lost treasure of Karak Eight Peaks but they had left it to the ghosts of its owners. It had been a case of find work, steal or starve – and both he and the Trollslayer were too proud to steal or beg. So here they were in the sewers below the Empire's second greatest city, crawling beneath a seat of learning that Felix had once dreamed of attending, haunting slimy tunnels below the home of the Elector Countess Emmanuelle, the most famous beauty of the nation.

It was not to be borne. Felix wondered constantly what ill-omened star had marked his birth. He consoled himself with the thought that at least things were quiet. It might be dirty work but so far it had not proved dangerous.

'Tracks!' he heard Gant shout. 'Ha! Ha! We've found some of the little buggers. Prepare for action, lads.'

'Good,' Gotrek rumbled.

'Damn!' Felix muttered. Even as inexperienced a sewerjack as Felix could spot these tracks.

'Skaven,' Gotrek hawked and spat a huge gob of phlegm out into the main channel of the sewer. It glistened atop a patch of phosphorescent algae. 'Rat-men, spawn of Chaos.'

Felix cursed. On the job only two weeks and already he was about to meet some of the creatures of the depths. He had almost been able to dismiss Gant's stories as simply the imaginings of a man who had nothing better with which to fill his long tedious hours.

Felix had long wondered if there really could be a whole demented subworld beneath the city as Gant had hinted. Were there colonies of outcast mutants who sought refuge in the warm darkness and crept out at night to raid the market for scraps? Could there actually be cellars where forbidden cults held ghastly rituals and offered up human sacrifices to the Ruinous Powers?

Was it possible that immense rats which mocked the form of man really scuttled through the depths? Looking at those tracks it suddenly seemed all too possible.

Felix stood frozen in thought, remembering Gotrek's tales of the skaven and their continent-spanning webwork of tunnels. Gant tugged his sleeve.

'Well, let's get on with it,' the sergeant said. 'We ain't got all day.'

'Never been here before,' Hef whispered, his voice echoing away down the long stretch of corridor.

'Never want to come here again,' Spider added, rubbing the blue arachnid tattoo on his cheek. For once Felix was forced to agree with them. Even by the standards of Nuln sewers, this was a dismal place. The walls had a crumbled, rotten look to them. The little gargoyles on the support arches had been blurred by age until their features were no longer visible. The stew bubbled and tiny wisps of vapour rose when the bubbles burst. The air was close, foetid and hot.

And there was something else – the place had an even more oppressive atmosphere than usual. The hair on the back of Felix's neck prickled, as it sometimes did when he sensed the undercurrents of sorcery nearby.

'Doesn't look safe,' Rudi said, looking at a support arch dubiously. Gotrek's face twisted as if this were a personal insult.

'Nonsense,' he said. 'These tunnels were dwarf-built a thousand years ago. This is Khazalid workmanship. It'll last an eternity.'

To prove his point he banged the arch with his fist. Perhaps it was just bad luck, but the gargoyle chose that moment to fall forward from its perch. The Slayer had to leap to one side to avoid being hit on the head and narrowly avoided skidding into the stew.

'Of course,' Gotrek added, 'Some of the labour was done by human artisans. That gargoyle, for instance – typical shoddy manling workmanship.'

No one laughed. Only Felix dared even smile. Gant stared up at the ceiling. The lamp set down at his feet underlit his face, making him look eerie and daemonic.

'We must be below the Old Quarter,' he said wistfully. Felix could see he was contemplating the district of palaces. A strange melancholy expression transfigured his gaunt, bony features. Felix wondered whether he was pondering the difference between his life and the gilded existence of those above, contemplating the splendours he would never know and the opportunities he would never have. Momentarily he felt a certain sympathy for the man.

'There must be a fortune up there,' Gant said. 'Wish I could climb up and get it. Well, no sense in wasting time. Let's get on with it.'

'What was that?' Gotrek asked suddenly. The others looked around, startled.

'What was what?' Hef asked.

'And where was what?' added Spider.

'I heard something. Down that way.' All their gazes followed the direction indicated by the Trollslayer's pointing finger.

'You're imagining things,' Rudi said.

'Dwarfs don't imagine things.'

'Aw sarge, do we have to look into this?' Rudi whined. 'I want to get home.'

Gant rubbed his left eye with the knuckles of his right fist. He seemed to be concentrating. Felix could see he was wavering. He wanted to leave and be off to the tavern just as quickly as the rest of them, but this was his responsibility. If something was wrong beneath the palaces and anyone found out they had been there and done nothing about it, then it was his neck for the block.

'We'd better look into it.' he said eventually, ignoring the groans of his fellow sewerjacks.

'It shouldn't take long. I'll lay odds it's nothing anyway.'

Knowing his luck, Felix decided, that was a bet he wouldn't take.

Water dripped down from the arch of the tunnel. Gant had narrowed the aperture of his lantern so that only the faintest glimmering of light was visible. From ahead came the sound of voices. Even Felix could hear them now.

One of the voices was human, with an aristocratic accent. It was impossible to believe the other belonged to a man. It was high-pitched, eerie and chittering. If a rat had been given the voice of a human being it would have sounded like this.

Gant stopped and turned to look back at his men, his face pale and worried. He obviously didn't want to go on. Glancing round the faces of his fellow sewerjacks, Felix knew they all felt the same. It was the end of the day. They were all tired and scared and up ahead was something they didn't want to meet. But they were sewerjacks; men whose only virtue was courage and the willingness to face what others would not, in a place where others would not go. They had a certain pride.

Gotrek tossed the hatchet into the air. It spun upward, blade catching a little of the light. With no apparent effort the Trollslayer caught it by the haft as it fell. Spider pulled his long-bladed knife from its sheath and shrugged. Hef gave a feral smile. Rudi looked down at his shortsword and nodded. Gant grinned. The Trollslayer looked pleased. He was in the company of the sort of maniacs he could understand.

Gant gestured softly and they shuffled forward, picking their way carefully and quietly along the slimy ledge. As they turned the bend he opened up his lantern to illuminate their prey.

'Your payment, a token of my esteem. Something for your own personal use,' Felix heard the aristocratic voice say. Two figures stood frozen like trolls in a fairy tale, petrified by the sudden bright light. One was a tall man, garbed in a long black robe like a monk's. His face was patrician: fine-boned, cold and aloof. His black hair was cut short, ending in a widow's peak above his forehead. He was reaching forward to hand the other figure something that glowed eerily.

Felix recognised it. He had seen the substance before, in the abandoned dwarf fortress of Karak Eight Peaks. It was a ball of warpstone. The recipient was short and inhuman. Its fur was grey, its eyes pink; its long hairless tail reminded Felix of a great worm. As the thing turned to squint at the light, the tail lashed. It reached inside its long, patchwork robes and clutched something in its taloned paws. From its belt hung an unscabbarded rusty, saw-toothed blade.

'Skaven!' Gotrek roared. 'Prepare to die!'

'Fool-fool, you said you were not followed,' the thing chittered at its human companion. 'You said no one knew.'

'Stay where you are!' Gant said. 'Whoever you are, you're under arrest on suspicion of witchcraft, treason and unnatural practices with animals.'

The sergeant's confidence had been restored by the fact there were only two of them. Even the fact that one of the perpetrators was a monster seemed to leave him undaunted.

'Hef, Spider, take them and bind them.' The rat-thing suddenly threw the sphere it had withdrawn from its clothing.

'Die-die, foolish manthings.'

'Hold your breath!' Gotrek shouted. His hatchet hurtled forward simultaneously.

The skaven's sphere tinkled and shattered like glass and an unhealthy looking green cloud billowed outward. As he shoved Felix back down the corridor, Gotrek grabbed Rudi and pulled him with them. From inside the gas-cloud came the sound of gurgling and choking. Felix felt his eyes begin to water.

Everything went dark as the lantern went out. It was like being caught in a nightmare. He couldn't see, he was afraid to take a breath, he was stuck in a narrow corridor underground and somewhere out there was a monster armed with deadly, incomprehensible weapons.

Felix felt the slick slime of the stone under his hands. As he fumbled he suddenly felt nothing. His hand was over the stew. He felt unbalanced and afraid to move, as if he could suddenly topple in any direction and plunge into the sewage. He closed his eyes to keep them from stinging and forced himself to move on. His heart pounded. His lungs felt as if they were about to burst. The flesh between his shoulder blades crawled.

He expected a saw-toothed blade to be plunged into his back at any moment. He could hear someone trying to scream behind him and failing. They gurgled and gasped and their breathing sounded terribly laboured as if their lungs had filled with fluid.

It was the gas, Felix realised. Gotrek had told him of the foul weapons which the skaven used, the products of a Chaos-inspired alchemy allied to a warped and inhuman imagination. He knew that to take one breath of that foul-smelling air was to die. He also knew that he could not keep from breathing indefinitely.

Think, he told himself. Find a place where the air is clear. Keep moving. Get away from the killing cloud. Don't panic. Don't think about the huge rat-like shape creeping ever closer in the dark with its blade bared. As long as you keep calm you'll be safe. Slowly, inch by torturous inch, his lungs screaming for air, he forced himself to crawl towards safety.

Then the weight fell on him. Silver stars flickered before his eyes and all the air was driven from his lungs. Before he could stop himself he took in a mouthful of the foul air. He lay in the dark gasping and slowly it dawned on him that he wasn't dead. He wasn't choking. No knife had been driven into his back. He forced himself to try and move. He couldn't. It was as if a great weight lay across him. Terror flashed through his mind. Maybe his back was broken. Maybe he was a cripple.

'Is that you, Felix?' he heard Rudi whisper. Felix almost laughed with relief. His burden was his huge fellow sewerjack.

'Yes... where are the others?'

'I'm all right,' he heard Hef say.

'Me too, brother.' That was Spider.

'Gotrek, where are you?' No answer. Had the gas got him? It seemed impossible. The Trollslayer couldn't be dead. Nothing as insidious as gas could have killed him. It wouldn't be fair.

'Where's the sarge?'

'Anybody got some light?'

Flint sparked. A lantern flickered to life. Felix saw that something large was shuffling towards them along the shadows of the ledge. Instinctively his hand reached for his sword. It wasn't there. He had dropped it when he fell. The others stood poised and waiting.

'It's me,' said the Trollslayer. 'Bloody human got away. His legs were longer.'

'Where's Gant?' Felix asked.

'Look for yourself, manling.'

Felix squeezed past and went to do so. The gas had vanished as quickly as it appeared. But it had done its work on Sergeant Gant. He lay in a pool of blood. His eyes were wide and staring. Trickles of red emerged from his nostrils and mouth.

Felix checked the body. It was already cooling and there was no pulse. There was no wound on the corpse.

'How did he die, Gotrek?' Felix knew about magic but the fact that a man could be killed and have no mark left on him made his mind reel.

'He drowned, manling. He drowned in his own blood.' The Slayer's voice was cold and furious.

Was that how he dealt with fear, Felix wondered? By turning it into anger. Only after the dwarf went over and started kicking the corpse did he notice the dead skaven. Its skull had been split by the thrown hatchet.

* * *

Wearily Felix lay on his pallet of straw and stared at the cracked ceiling, too tired even to sleep. From below came the sound of shouting as Lisabette argued with one of her seemingly interminable stream of customers.

Felix felt like banging on the floor and telling them to either shut up or get out, but he knew that it would only cause more trouble than it would solve. As he did every night, he resolved that he would begin looking for another rooming house tomorrow. He knew that tomorrow night he would be too tired to start.

Ideas chased each other like frolicking rats inside the cavern of his brain. He was at that stage where weariness made his thoughts strange even to himself. Odd conjunctions of images and maze-like chains of reasoning came from nowhere and went nowhere in his mind. He was too tired even to be angry about the fate of Sergeant Gant, killed in the line of duty and destined for a pauper's grave on the fringes of the Gardens of Morr. A watch captain too bored to pay much attention to reports of monsters in the sewers. No family to mourn him, no friends save his fellow sewerjacks, who were even now toasting his memory in the Drunken Guardsman.

Gant was a cold corpse now. And the same thing could so easily have happened to me, Felix thought. If he had been in the wrong place when the globe exploded. If Gotrek had not told us to hold our breath. If the Slayer had not pushed him away from the gas. If. If. If. So many ifs.

What was he doing, anyway? Was this how he intended to spend the rest of his days; chasing monsters in the dark? His life seemed to have no reason to it any more. It merely moved from one violent episode to the next.

He thought of the alternatives. Where would he have been now if he had not killed Wolfgang Krassner in that duel, if he had not been expelled from university, if he had not been disinherited by his father? Would he be, like his brothers, working in the family business: married, secure, settled? Or would something else have gone wrong? Who could tell?

A small black rat scuttled across the rafters of the room. When he had first viewed this attic with its one small window, he had imagined that it would at least be free from the rats which infested all of the buildings in the New Quarter. He had deluded himself with the thought that the rodents would have heart attacks from the effort of climbing all those stairs. He had been wrong. The rats of the New Quarter were bold and adventurous and looked better fed than many of the humans. He had seen some of the larger ones chasing a cat.

Felix shuddered. Now he wished he had not started thinking about rats – it made him think of the mysterious aristocrat and the skaven in the sewers. What had been the purpose of that clandestine meeting? What profit could any man find in dealing with such alien monstrosities? And how could it be that folk could roister and whore through the teeming streets of Nuln and be unaware of the fact that evil things burrowed and crawled and nested not six yards beneath their feet? Perhaps they just didn't want to know. Perhaps it was true, as some philosophers claimed, that the end of the world was coming and it was best to simply lose oneself in whatever pleasures one could find.

Footsteps approached on the stairs. He could hear the old rickety boards creak under the weight. He had been going to complain that the whole place was a firetrap but Frau Zorin had always seemed too pitiful and poor to bother.

The footsteps did not stop on the landing below but continued to come closer.

Felix reached beneath his pillow for his knife. He could think of no one who would be visiting him at this time of night and Frau Zorin's was right in the roughest part of the New Quarter.

Noiselessly he rose and padded on bare feet to the door. He stifled a curse as a splinter embedded itself in the sole of his foot. There was a knock on the door.

'Who is it?' Felix asked, although he already knew the answer. He recognised the old widow woman's wheezing breath even through the thin wood.

'It's me,' Frau Zorin shrieked. 'You have visitors, Herr Jaeger.'

Cautiously Felix opened the door. Outside stood two huge burly men. They carried clubs in their hands and looked as if they knew how to use them. It was the man they flanked that interested Felix. He was handing the landlady a gold coin, which she took with an ingratiating smile. As the man turned to look at the door Felix recognised him. It was his brother, Otto.

'Come in,' Felix said, holding the door open. Otto stood staring at him for a long time, as if he couldn't quite recognise his younger brother. Then he strode into the room.

'Franz, Karl, remain outside,' he said quietly. His voice carried an authority that Felix had not heard in it before, an echo of their father's calm, curt manner.

Felix was suddenly acutely aware of the poverty of his surroundings: the uncarpeted floor, the straw pallet, the bare walls, the hole in the sloping roof. He saw the whole scene through his brother's eyes and wasn't at all impressed.

'What do you want, Otto?' he asked brusquely.

'Your taste in accommodation hasn't changed much, has it? Still slumming.'

'You haven't come all the way from Altdorf to discuss my domestic arrangements. What do you want?'

'Do you have to hold that knife so ready? I'm not going to rob you. If I was, I would have brought Karl and Franz in.'

Felix slid the knife back into its scabbard. 'Maybe I would surprise Karl and Franz.'

Otto tilted his head to one side and studied Felix's face. 'Maybe you would at that. You've changed, little brother.'

'So have you.' It was true. Otto was still the same height as Felix but he was far broader. He had put on weight. His chest had thickened and his hips broadened. His large soft belly strained against his broad leather belt. Felix guessed that his thick blond beard hid several chins. His cheeks were fatter and seemed padded. His hair was thinner and there were bags under his eyes. His head jutted forward aggressively. He had grown to resemble the old man. 'You look more like father.'

Otto smiled wryly. 'Sad but true. Too much good living, I'm afraid. You look like you could use some yourself. You've become very skinny.'

'How did you find me?'

'Come on, Felix. How do you think I found you? We have our agents and we wanted to find you. How many tall blond men travelling in the company of dwarf Slayers do you think there are in the Empire? When the report came into my office about two mercenaries answering the description I thought I'd better investigate.'

'Your office?'

'I run the business in Nuln now.'

'What happened to Schaffer?'

'Vanished.'

'With money?'

'Apparently not. We think he was deemed politically undesirable. The Countess has a very efficient secret police. Things happen in Nuln these days.'

'Not Schaffer! There was never a more loyal citizen in the Empire. He thought the sun shone out of the Emperor's fundament.'

'Nuln is only just part of the Empire, brother. Countess Emmanuelle rules here.'

'But she's the most flighty woman in the Empire, or so they say.'

'Von Halstadt, her Chief Magistrate, is very efficient. He's the real ruler of Nuln. He hates mutants. And rumour has it that Schaffer had begun to show stigmata.'

'Never.'

'That's what I said. But believe this, little brother: Nuln is no place to come under suspicion of being a mutant. Such people vanish.'

'But it's the most liberal city of the Empire.'

'Not any more.' Otto looked around fearfully as if realising that he had said too much. Felix shook his head ruefully. 'Don't worry, brother. No spies here.'

'Don't be too sure about that, Felix,' he said quietly. 'In these days, in this city, walls have ears.' When he spoke again his voice was loud and held a note of false heartiness. 'Anyway I came around to ask if you'd like to dine with me tomorrow. We can eat out if you'd like.'

Felix half wanted to refuse and half wanted to talk to his brother some more. There was much family news to catch up on and perhaps the possibility of returning to the fold. That thought alone frightened him as well as intrigued him.

'Yes, I'd like that.'

'Good. I'll have my coach collect you from here.'

'After I've finished work.' Otto shook his head slowly. 'Of course, Felix. Of course.'

They said their goodbyes. It was only after his brother had left that Felix began to wonder what could so frighten a man of Otto's power and influence that he would worry about eavesdroppers in a place like Frau Zorin's.

Fritz von Halstadt, head of the secret police of Nuln, sat among his files and brooded. That damned dwarf had come within an inch of catching him. He had actually tried to lay his filthy hands on him. He had come so near to undoing all his good work. One blow would have been enough. It would have brought Chaos and darkness to the city von Halstadt was sworn to protect.

Von Halstadt reached out and raised his cut glass pitcher. The water was still warm. Good, the servant had boiled it for exactly eleven minutes as he commanded. He was to be commended. Von Halstadt poured some into a glass and inspected it. He raised the glass to the light and checked it for sediment, for stuff floating in it. There was none. No contamination. Good.

Chaos could come so easily. It was everywhere. The wise knew that and used it to their advantage. Chaos could take many forms; some were worse than others. There were relatively benign forms, like the skaven – and there was the festering evil of mutation.

Von Halstadt knew that the rat-men just wanted to be left alone, to rule their underground kingdom and pursue their own form of civilisation. They were intelligent and sophisticated and they could be dealt with. If you had what they wanted, they would make and keep bargains. Certainly they had their own plans, but that made them comprehensible, controllable. They were not like mutants: vile, insidious, evil things that lurked everywhere, that hid in secret and manipulated the world.

We could all so easily be puppets on the end of the mutant's foul strings, he thought. That is why we must be vigilant. The enemy are everywhere, and more and more are spawned all the time.

The commoners were the worst for it, spawning an endless string of slovenly, lazy, good-for-nothings. Most mutants were born among the herd. It made a sick kind of sense. There were more of them and they were notoriously immoral and lewd and licentious.

The thought made him rigid with horror. He knew that the mutants took advantage of the commoners' stupidity. They were so clever. They used the ill-educated, lazy oafs: filled their heads with seditious nonsense, fed their envious anger of their betters; whipped them up to riot and loot and destroy. Look at how they had ruined his poor father, burned the estate to the ground in one of their brutish uprisings. And his father had been the kindest and gentlest man who had ever lived.

Well, Fritz von Halstadt would not make that mistake. He was too clever and too strong. He knew how to deal with revolutionaries and upstarts. He would stand guard and protect mankind from the menace of the mutant. He would fight them with their own weapons; terror, cunning and ruthless violence.

That was why he kept his files, even though his beloved ruler Emmanuelle laughed at them, calling them his secret pornography. Within these lovingly detailed and carefully cross-indexed records was a kind of power. Information was power. He knew who all the potential revolutionaries were. His web of spies and agents kept him informed. He knew which nobles secretly belonged to the Dark Cults and had them watched at all times. He had sources that could penetrate any meeting place, and who no one ever suspected.

That was part of his bargain with the skaven. They knew many things and could find out many more. Their little spies were everywhere, unsuspected. He used their dark wisdom and dealt with the lesser of two evils to keep the greater anarchy at bay.

He picked up the small framed portrait Emmanuelle had given him and licked his thin lips. He thought about her choice of words for his files: 'pornography'. He was shocked that she had used such a word, even knew what it meant. It must be that brother of hers! Leos was a bad influence. Emmanuelle was too good, too pure, too unsullied to have learned such a word herself. Perhaps he should put his spies on her, just to watch out for–

No, she was his ruler! He did this all for her. Though the countess could not see its worth now, one day she would. Spying on her would be crossing a line he had set for himself. Besides, sometimes he suspected that the lies which he heard about her might just conceivably contain a kernel of truth, and finding out that would be too painful.

He put the picture back down on his desk. He had been allowing himself to drift from the main problem. The dwarf and the sewerjacks. Could they have recognised him? And what would he do about it if they had? They were simple men doing their simple job. Like him, they were struggling to keep Chaos at bay. But would they understand the necessity of what he did? If they did not, perhaps they would understand that it was necessary to ensure their silence forever.

Slowly the hungover sewerjacks lowered themselves into the depths. One by one they clambered down the ladders lowered through the access ports. Rudi, now acting sergeant, lit the lantern and illuminated the tunnel.

The stink hit Felix like a hammer even as he carefully stepped from the ladder onto the ledge. This was the trickiest part of the operation. There was only about one foot clearance between the ladder and the edge of the walkway. A misstep had carried many a still-drunk sewerjack into the stew.

'You missed yourself last night, young Felix,' Hef said.

'We gave the sarge a fine send-off,' Spider added.

'Gotrek downed seven jacks of ale one after the other and wasn't even sick. We took a week's wages off the first watch.'

'I'm very pleased for you,' Felix said. Gotrek looked none the worse for his exploits. Of all the sewerjacks he was the only one who didn't appear ill. The rest were ghastly, pale, and walked with the shuffling gait of old men.

'Ah, there's nothing like the smell of the stew to clear your head in the morning,' Hef said, proceeding to stick his head out over the edge of the walkway and be violently sick.

'Fair clears the head it does,' Rudi added, with no trace of irony.

'I can see that,' Felix said.

'We're going to sweep through the area where the sarge got taken,' Rudi said. ' We decided it last night. We want to see if we can find the scumbag who deals with the skaven. And maybe if we can't find him we'll find some of his pink-tailed little friends.'

'And what if they've got more of those gas bombs?' Felix asked.

'Not to worry. Gotrek's an old tunnel fighter. He explained how to deal with it.'

'Oh, did he? '

'Yes. We soak our scarves in piss and breathe through them. That cuts out the gas.'

'I knew it would be something like that,' Felix said, glaring at the Trollslayer, wondering if the others were really convinced by Gotrek's claims or whether they were simply humouring him. One look at their haggard, determined faces convinced him that it was the former.

'It's true, manling. My ancestors fought the skaven at Karak Eight Peaks and it worked for them.'

'If you say so,' Felix said. He could tell it was going to be a long day.

They followed the route of the previous day towards the area beneath the Old Quarter. As they went, Felix had time to reflect on how strange his life was. His brother's house was somewhere above his head and he had not known it. He had not even known Otto was in the city. The fact that his brother had found him was certainly a testimony to the efficiency of his spy network.

Felix suspected that such things were necessary to anyone who wanted to do business in Nuln nowadays. What Otto had said about Schaffer and the countess's secret police was worrying too. Felix was sorry for the old man but he was more worried about himself. Both he and the Trollslayer were wanted by the law for their part in the great Window Tax riots in Altdorf. If the secret police were so efficient here, and he and Gotrek were really so recognisable, then they too might vanish. He consoled himself with the thought that the capital was a long way away and that the local authorities would probably not be interested in what happened outside their jurisdiction.

In a way it was even more reassuring that they were part of the sewer watch. It was tacitly understood that the watch did not look too closely into the backgrounds of those who volunteered for it. Indeed it was said to be a sure way of having them ignore your previous crimes. All of the others had been involved in acts of criminal violence at some point in their lives, or so they claimed. No, there wasn't too much to worry about. He hoped.

More immediately worrying was the prospect that they might actually come across some skaven. He did not fancy facing such vicious foes in their own environment. Frantically he tried to recall what Gotrek had told him of the rat-men, hoping to remember something that would give him an edge if it came to a fight. He knew that they were a race of vicious mutant rats, products of warpstone in ancient times. They were said to inhabit a great, polluted city called Skavenblight, the location of which nobody knew. Rumour had it that they were divided up into clans, each of which had their own function: the practice of sorcery, the making of war, the breeding of monsters and so forth. They were lighter than a man but faster and more vicious, and possessed of a feral intelligence which made them deadly enemies.

He could recall one book he had read about the battles of the ancients that described their few interventions on surface battlefields: their terrifying charges in great, chittering hordes, their twisted evil and their penchant for torturing their prisoners. It had been a skaven horde which had undermined the walls of Castle Siegfried and broke the siege after two years of trying. Legend said that Prince Karsten had paid a terrible price for the service of his allies. Sigmar himself destroyed an army of them before his ascension to the heavens. It had been one of his less well-known exploits.

Felix himself had seen some evidence of the skaven's handiwork in Karak Eight Peaks. The thought of the warpstone-polluted wells and the great mutated troll gave him the chills even after all this time. He hoped that he would not have to face any more of their monstrous creations in his lifetime. Looking at the others he could tell that they did not share his hope.

Until yesterday, Felix had never given a second thought to the number of rats in the sewers. Now he saw that they were everywhere. They scuttled away from the lights as the watchmen approached and he could hear the pitter-patter of their feet behind them after they had gone. Their eyes caught the reflection of the lantern and glittered like tiny stars far off in the darkness of the undercity.

He found himself wondering now if there was any connection between the rats and the skaven. He started to imagine the little ones as spies for their larger brethren. It was a madman's fantasy, he knew, one straight out of the tales of sorcery he had read as a boy, but the more he thought of it the more terrifying the prospect became. Rats were everywhere in the great cities of man, living amid the garbage and refuse of civilisation. They could see much and overhear much and go, if not unnoticed, at least unsuspected.

He began to feel their cold eyes staring malevolently at him even as he walked. The walls of the sewer seemed to close in about him threateningly and he imagined himself caught in a vast warren. Thinking of the skaven out there, it suddenly seemed possible to him that he was in a vast burrow, that he and the others had been shrunk to the size of mice and that the skaven were ordinary rats, walking upright and dressed in a fashion that aped man.

The fantasy became so vivid and compelling that he began to wonder whether the fumes of the stew were going to his head or whether the scent-deadening narcotics prescribed by the city alchemists had hallucinatory side-effects.

'Steady, manling,' he heard Gotrek say. 'You're looking very pale there.'

'I was just thinking about the rats.'

'In the tunnels your mind creates its own foes. It's the first thing a tunnel fighter learns to guard against.'

'You've done this sort of thing before then,' Felix said, half sarcastically.

'Yes, manling. I was fighting in the depths before ever your father was born. The ways around the Everpeak are never free of foes and all the citizens of the King's Council do their share of military service in the depths. More young dwarfs die that way than any other.'

Gotrek was being unusually forthright, as he sometimes was before moments of great peril. Danger made him garrulous, as if he wanted to communicate with others only when he realised he might never get another chance. Or perhaps he was simply still drunk from the night before. Felix realised he would never know. Fathoming the dwarf's alien mind was nearly as far beyond him as was understanding a skaven.

'I can remember my first time in the tunnels. Everything seemed cramped. Every sound was the tread of some secret enemy. If you listen with fearful ears you are soon surrounded by foes. When the true foe comes you have no idea from which quarter. Stay calm, manling. You'll live longer.'

'Easy for you to say,' Felix muttered as the hefty Slayer shoved past. All the same, he was reassured by Gotrek's presence.

* * *

With some trepidation they approached the place where Gant had been killed. Mist rose from the surface of the stew and in places a slow current was evident in the sludge. The area of the fight looked very much the same as Felix remembered it, except that the body was gone. The area where the corpse had lain was disturbed.

There was a trail in the slime that suddenly ended at the ledgeside, as if the body had been dragged a short way, then dumped. He knew they should have shifted it yesterday, when they had the chance, but they had been too shaken, disturbed and excited by what had happened to do so. No one had wanted to carry the mangy, rat-man body. Now it wasn't there.

'Someone took it,' Hef said.

'Wonder who?' Spider said.

Gotrek scanned the ledge where the body had been. He bent down and peered closely at the tracks, then rubbed his eye-patch with his right fist. The hatchet which had killed the skaven came dangerously close to his tattooed scalp.

'Wasn't a man, anyway. That's for sure.'

'All sorts of scavengers in the sewers,' Rudi said. He voiced the common belief of all sewerjacks. 'There are things you wouldn't believe living in the stew.'

'I don't think it was any scavenging animal,' Gotrek said.

'Skaven,' Felix said, voicing their unspoken thoughts.

'Too big. One of them was anyway. The other tracks might be skaven.' Felix peered out into the gloom; it suddenly appeared even more menacing.

'How big?' He cursed himself for taking on the same monosyllabic way of speaking as the others. 'How large exactly was this creature you referred to, Gotrek?'

'Perhaps taller than you, manling. Perhaps heavier than Rudi.'

'Could it be one of the mutants you say the skaven breed? A hybrid of some sort?'

'Yes.'

'But how can all those prints simply vanish?' Felix asked. 'They can't all have thrown themselves in the stew, can they?'

'Sorcery,' Hef said.

'Of the blackest sort,' Spider added.

Gotrek looked down at the ledge and cursed in his native tongue. He was angry and his beard bristled. The light of mad violence shone in his one good eye. 'They can't just disappear,' he said. 'It's not possible.'

'Could they have used a boat?' Felix asked. The idea had just struck him. The others looked at him incredulously.

'Use a boat?' Hef said.

'In the stew?' Spider said.

'Don't be stupid,' Rudi said. Felix flushed.

'I'm not being stupid. Look, the tracks end here. It would be quite simple for someone to step down from the ledge into a small skiff.'

'That's the daftest thing I've ever heard,' Rudi said. 'You've got some imagination, young Felix. Who'd ever have thought of using a boat down here?'

'There's a lot of things you'd never think of,' Felix snapped. 'But then thinking's not your strong suit, is it?' He looked at the other sewerjacks and shook his head. 'You're right – a boat doesn't make sense. Much better to believe they vanished by magic. Maybe a cloud of pixies wafted in and carried them away.'

'That's right, a cloud of pixies. That's more like it,' Rudi said.

'He's being sarcastic, Rudi,' Spider said.

'A very sarcastic fellow, young Felix,' added Hef.

'Probably right though,' Gotrek said. 'A boat wouldn't be too hard to come by. The sewers flow into the Reik, don't they? Easy to steal a small boat.'

'But the outflows into the river all have bars,' Rudi said. 'To stop vagrants getting in.'

'And what's our job, if not hunting down those self-same vagrants when they file through the bars?' Felix asked. He could see the idea was starting to filter into even Rudi's thick skull.

'But why, manling? Why use boats?' Felix felt briefly elated. It wasn't often that Gotrek admitted that Felix might know more than him. He considered the matter rapidly.

'Well for a start, they don't leave tracks. And they might be connected with a smuggling operation. Suppose someone was bringing warpstone in by river, for instance. Our noble skulker yesterday seemed to be paying the rat-man off with it.'

'Boats make me sick. The only thing I hate more than boats is elves,' Gotrek said as they set off again.

They searched for the rest of the day and found no trace of any skaven, although they did find that the bars had been sawn away on one of the outflows to the Reik.

Felix stepped out of the street and into the Golden Hammer. He stepped from reality into a dream. The doorman held the great oak door for him. Servile waiters ushered him away from the squalor of the streets into a vast dining hall.

Richly clad people sat at well-filled tables, and dined and talked by the light that sparkled from huge crystal chandeliers. Portraits of great Imperial heroes watched the diners sternly from the walls. Felix recognised Sigmar and Magnus and Frederick the Bold. The style of the brushwork was Vespasian's, the most famous Nulner painter of the past three centuries. The far wall was dominated by a portrait of the Elector Emmanuelle, a ravishing raven-haired beauty garbed in a less than modest ball gown.

Felix wished his borrowed clothing fitted him better. He was wearing some of his brother's old garments. Once, he and Otto had been of the same size and build, but in the years of his wandering Felix had grown thinner and Otto more stout. The linen shirt felt baggy and the velvet vest felt loose. The trousers had been cinched with a leather belt tightened to its last notch. The boots were a comfortable fit, though, as was the cap. He had tilted it to a rakish angle to show off the peacock feather in the band. He let his hand toy idly with the golden pomander that dangled from a chain round his neck. The smell of fine Bretonnian perfume wafted up from it. It was nice to smell something other than the sewers.

The servant led him to a booth in the corner in which Otto sat. He had a leather-bound accounts book in front of him and was ticking entries off in it with a quill pen. As Felix approached he looked up and smiled. 'Welcome, little brother. You're looking much better for a bath and a change of clothes.'

Having studied himself in the great silvered mirror in Otto's townhouse earlier, Felix was forced to agree. A warm bath, scented oil and a change of clothing had made him feel like a new man. In the looking glass he had seen the foppish young dandy he once had been, albeit with more lines round the eyes and a firmer, narrower set to the mouth.

'This is a very charming establishment,' he said.

'You could dine here every evening if you wished.'

'What do you mean, brother?'

'Simply that there is a place for you in the family business.'

Felix looked around to see if they were being overheard. 'You know I'm still a wanted man in Altdorf because of the Window Tax business?'

'You exaggerate your notoriety, little brother. No one knows who the leaders of that riot were. Altdorf isn't Nuln, you know.'

'You've said yourself Gotrek is a very easily recognisable figure.'

'We're not offering the Trollslayer employment. We're offering you your birthright.' And there it was; what Felix had half hoped for and half feared. His family would take him back. He could give up the restless uncomfortable life of the adventurer and return once more to Altdorf and his books. It would mean a life chained to the ledgers and the warehouses, but it would be safe. And one day he would be rich.

It was a tempting prospect. No more crawling around in sewers. No more beatings at the hands of thugs. No more catching strange illnesses in terrible, out-of-the-way places. No more muscle-searing treks through wild, savage lands. No more descents into darkness. No more confrontations with the Chaos-worshipping minions of obscure cults. No more adventures.

He wouldn't have to put up with Gotrek's sullenness or his whims any more. He could forget his oath to follow the Trollslayer and record his doom in an epic poem. The promise had been made when he was drunk; surely it didn't count? He would be his own master. And yet, something held him back.

'I'll have to think about it,' he said.

'What is there to think about, man? You can't actually tell me that you prefer being a sewerjack to being a merchant, can you? Most people would kill to be given this opportunity.'

'I said, I'll think about it.'

They ate on in uncomfortable silence. After some minutes, the door to the great room opened and a tall man was led in by the servant. He was clad in black and his monkish robes made him seem out of place in his opulent setting. His face was thin and ascetic, and his black hair ended above his forehead in a widow's peak.

As he crossed the room, silence spread in his wake. Felix saw that the wealthy diners were afraid of him. As he passed close to the table Felix was shocked to recognise him: it was unquestionably the man he had seen in the sewers with the skaven. His mind reeled. He had assumed that the man was some kind of sorcerer or renegade. He pictured a cultist or a desperado. He had not expected to see him here in the haunts of Nuln's wealthiest and most respectable citizens.

'What's the matter, brother? You look like you've seen a ghost.'

'Who– who is that man?'

Otto let out a long sigh. 'You don't want to know. He's not a man that you ask questions about. He asks them about you.'

'Who is he, Otto? Do I have to go over and ask him?' Felix saw a look of alarm and admiration pass across his brother's face.

'I do believe you would, too, Felix,' he whispered. 'Very well. That is Chief Magistrate Fritz von Halstadt, the head of Countess Emmanuelle's secret police.'

'Tell me about him.'

'There are those who see him as the enemy of corruption everywhere. He is hard-working and no one doubts his sincerity. He sincerely hates mutants and for that reason he has the backing of the Temple of Ulric. His home is guarded by their Templars.'

'I thought the Temple of Ulric had no power here, that the countess disliked it.'

'That was before von Halstadt's rise to power. He came from being a minor court functionary to the most powerful man in the city-state very quickly. Some say it was by blackmail; some say his enemies have a habit of being found dead under mysterious circumstances. He's risen far for a man whose father was a minor nobleman in an out-of-the-way province. A callous cunning old swine, by all accounts.

'Von Halstadt is cold, cruel and dangerous, not just because of his influence. He has a deadly blade. He's killed several people because they've insulted the honour of the countess.'

'I would have thought her brother, Leos, did enough of that without him having to.'

'Leos is not always about and rumour has it that our chief magistrate would be prepared to fight him over the countess. Apparently he's got it hard for her.'

'Then he's mad. Leos is the deadliest blade in the Empire and Emmanuelle's not worth fighting over.'

Otto shrugged. Felix stared at von Halstadt, wondering what the connection between the skaven and the head of the countess's secret police could be. And hoping against hope that the man did not recognise him.

Von Halstadt was tired. Not even his usual excellent supper could cheer him. His mind was filled with worry and the cares of high office. He looked around at his fellow diners and returned their smiles, but in his heart of hearts he despised them. Shallow, indolent cattle. Garbed like nobles but with the hearts of shopkeepers. He knew that they needed him. They needed him to keep Chaos at bay. They needed him to do the work they were too soft to do themselves. They were barely worth his contempt.

It had been a trying day. Young Helmut Slazinger had failed to confess, despite von Halstadt himself supervising the torture implements.

It was strange how some of them maintained their innocence even unto the grave. Even when they knew that he knew they were guilty. His secret sources had told him that Slazinger belonged to a clandestine cell of Slaanesh-worshipping cultists. The jailers had been unable to find any of the usual tattoos that marked coven members, but that meant nothing. His most trusted informants, the skaven, had let him in on the secret. That in fear of his ruthless crusade, his hidden enemies had taken to using sorcerous tattoos visible only to fellow coven members.

Gods, how insidious the mutant fiends were! Now they could be everywhere; they could be sitting right in this very room, their initiation tattoos plain to each other on their faces and he would not know. They could be sitting there right now mocking him and there was nothing he could do about it. That lanky young fellow in the ill-fitting clothes could be one. He was certainly studying von Halstadt intently enough. And come to think of it, there was something quite sinister about him. Perhaps he should be the next subject of an official investigation.

No, get a grip on yourself, von Halstadt told himself. They cannot hide forever. The blinding light of logic can pierce the deepest darkness of falsity. So his father had always told him before yet another beating for his sins, real or imagined. No, his father had been correct. Von Halstadt had done wrong. Even if he could not work out exactly what. The beatings had been for his own good, to drive out sin. His father had been a good man, doing the work of the righteous. That was why he smiled as he punished him. He didn't enjoy it. He told him that often and often. It was for his own good. In a way it had been a great lesson. He had learned that it was often necessary to do painful, bad things for the greater good.

It had made him hard. It enabled him to do what he had to today, free from the weakness of lesser men. It enabled him to stand up for right. It had made him into a man his father could be proud of and he should be grateful. He was strong without being malicious. He was like his father.

He had taken no pleasure in the torture of young Slazinger. He had taken no pleasure in the skaven report that the nobleman was a Slaaneshi cultist. Although he had to admit that it was a fortunate coincidence, given the rumours concerning Slazinger and Emmanuelle. More malicious lies: someone as pure as the countess would not, could not, have anything to do with the likes of Slazinger. The worm was a notorious rake, the sort of handsome young dandy who thought it witty to speak out against the lawful servants of the state, to criticise the harsh measures needed to maintain law and order in this festering sink of iniquity and sin.

He pushed Slazinger from his mind and gave his thoughts over to other matters. His agent in the watch house had brought him the report on the Gant incident. No action was being taken. It would cost too much to make a full sweep through the sewers beneath the Old Quarter and that would cut into the take the watch captain got from his station's financial allocation. Well, even corruption sometimes has its uses, thought von Halstadt.

His spy had brought him word that Gant's patrol had been nosing around in the area of his death, though, which was more worrying. They might accidentally come across some more skaven going about their business. They might even discover the skiffs that ran from the docks to van Niek's Emporium. He doubted, though, that they could ever discover that the shop was simply a government front which channelled warpstone from outside the city to the skaven in payment for their services. He smiled.

It was an arrangement with a certain pleasing symmetry. He paid the skaven in the currency they wanted. They did not seem to realise it was both useless and dangerous. Warpstone actually caused mutation. The skaven claimed to use it as food. Well, it was a relatively harmless way of disposing of an incredibly dangerous substance and it provided him with a fine source of information at the same time.

Yes, a pleasing symmetry indeed. In a way, it was a pity that he could not make known the service he was doing the Empire by disposing of the evil stuff in a safe way. It had been a lucky day for all mankind when von Halstadt had got lost in the sewers and stumbled across the skaven. It was fortunate they had recognised him as a man with whom they could do business.

He must get some more. This very evening he must contact another skaven agent and see to it that the watchmen met with an accident. He was sorry to have to do that to men who were only doing their duty, but his security must come first.

He was the only man who understood the real dangers threatening Nuln and he was the only man who could save the city. He knew this wasn't simply vanity; it was the truth. Tonight he would contact the new skaven leader, Grey Seer Thanquol, and order him to eliminate his enemies. The thought of this secret use of his power made him shiver. He told himself it was not with pleasure.

* * *

'I'm telling you I saw him last night,' Felix insisted. The other sewer-jacks stared at him out of the gloom. Overhead he heard the thunder of wheels as a cart passed over a manhole cover. 'At the Golden Hammer. He was standing not twenty feet away from me. His name is Fritz von Halstadt and he's the man we saw dealing with the skaven.'

'Sure,' Rudi said, glancing back worriedly. 'And he was having dinner with the Countess Emmanuelle and the enchanter Drachenfels. What were you doing in the Golden Hammer anyway? It's where nobs go. They wouldn't let a sewerjack in if his clothes were made of spun gold. You don't expect us to believe you were there.'

'My brother took me. He's a merchant. And I'm telling you that's where I saw our man, von Halstadt.'

'You're not from Nuln, are you, young Felix?' Hef spoke calmly and helpfully, as if he were genuinely concerned with clearing up any misapprehension the young sewerjack might have. 'Do you know who Fritz von Halstadt is?'

'The head of the Nuln secret police, is who he is. The scourge of mutant scum in this city,' Spider said. A tic moved somewhere far back in the twin's jaw. Felix had not realised the twins were such great admirers of von Halstadt's. 'And the head of the secret police don't go about consorting with rat-men.'

'Why not?'

'Because he's the head of the secret police and the head of the secret police wouldn't do that sort of thing. It stands to reason, don't it.'

'Well, that is irrefutable logic, Rudi. But I'm telling you I saw him with my own eyes. It was the man from the sewers.'

'Are you sure you're not mistaken, manling? It was very dark down there and human eyesight is not good in the dark.'

'I'm certain,' said Felix. 'I've never been more certain of anything in my life.'

'Well, young Felix, even if you're right, and I'm not saying that you are, mind, what can we do about it? We can hardly go marching up to the Countess Emmanuelle and say "By the way your majesty, did you know your most trusted advisor has been sneaking around the sewers below your palace in the company of giant talking rats?"' Hef didn't even smile as he said this.

'She'd ask you how much weirdroot you'd been chewing and order her Kislevite lover to throw you in the cells,' Spider said.

Felix could see their point. What could they do? They were just ordinary watchmen and the man he was talking about was the most powerful person in the city. Perhaps it would be best just to forget the whole thing. He was seeing Otto again this evening, was going to have a fine meal in his townhouse. Soon he could be far from here and it wasn't his problem.

But the thought nagged at him. What was the terrible and feared master of the countess's secret police doing in the company of skaven? What hold could they possibly have over him?

'Right, lads, enough of this,' Rudi said. 'Back to work.'

Hostleader Tzarkual Skab looked back at his stormvermin. They filled this tunnel chamber and the smell of their musk was sweet. His heart swelled with something akin to pride. These were big, burly skaven and their black fur was sleek and well groomed. It matched their fine lacquered black armour and their rune-encrusted helms of black iron. They were elite: well fed, well turned out, disciplined, as far above the lowly clanrats and slaves as he was above them. He commanded two dozen of the finest warriors his clan could field. In the coming war this would be swelled to two hundred or more.

He did not need the full force for this mission; this was simple. The elimination of some pink flesh manthings. Easy. Grey Seer Thanquol had made it plain it would be so. Even though he didn't like Skrequal's replacement, he agreed. He doubted he would even need four claws of stormvermin to deal with some lowly manthing warriors. Behind him Thanquol gave a discreet little bark of impatience. The rat-ogre which accompanied the sorcerer rumbled angrily.

A little shimmer of fear passed through Tzarkual when he contemplated the giant hybrid's formidable muscles and claws. He would not want to face it in battle. It must have cost the grey seer a fair stash of warpstone to purchase from the packmasters of Clan Moulder, and from what Tzarkual had heard it would prove worth every ounce.

Yet he would not let himself be hurried. There were certain proprieties to be observed. He must keep face in front of his troops. He allowed none of his anxiety to show in his bearing and he controlled the urge to squirt the musk of fear.

He twitched his nose authoritatively and then lashed his tail to get their attention. Two dozen pairs of alert pink eyes turned to look at him. 'We go to the bigstink below the mancity,' he told them. 'We go to kill five manthings who guard the tunnels. They are enemies of our clanlord and have killed-dead a clanbrother, yes. Vengeance and manblood will be ours. Fight well and more breeders and more warptokens will be yours. Fight badly and I will chew your guts with my own fangs.'

'We hear, hostleader,' they squeaked thunderously. 'Glory to the clan. Vengeance for our clanbrother!'

'Yes-yes, blood-vengeance for our clanbrother!' Tzarkual smiled, revealing row on row of sharp serrated teeth. In skaven it was a gesture of menace and his followers fell silent. He was pleased by the fear he had imposed on them.

Yes, he wanted vengeance for Skrequal. They had belonged to the same birthing, had fought their way to the top of their clan together. Had connived and killed and assassinated their way to power. He understood his brother's ambitions and insofar as he trusted anybody he had trusted Skrequal. He wanted the blood of his killers. It would in some way make up for the inconvenience of having to find another ally in the great game of clan politics.

Perhaps Thanquol might do, if the grey seer didn't attempt to slip a saw-knife into his back first. Well, only the future would tell.

He covered his teeth once more and the stormvermin relaxed. He was looking forward to visiting the undercity once more. He liked slinking through the vast stinking maze that reminded him of Skavenblight. It made a change from this hideously barren outpost of the Underway he had been forced to occupy since Warlord Skab dispatched him here. He was glad the stupid manthing had enough sense to contact them about his problem. The guards were potentially a threat to the great plan. Nothing must menace their pawn before they took over the city.

He wasn't sure what the great plan was but that didn't matter. He was a simple and vicious soldier. It was not his place to philosophise on the ways the Thirteen Lords of Decay chose to order the Universe. It was his task simply to kill the enemies of Clan Skab. That was what he intended to do.

Felix was worried. It wasn't just the number of rats he had seen, it was the way they followed him that was worrying. He told himself not to be stupid. The rats weren't following him. They were just there, like they always were in the sewers. His imagination was playing tricks on him, as it always did.

He gazed round what the other sewerjacks called 'the cathedral'. It was a major confluence of several of the city's greatest sewerways. It had been designed in a style he thought he recognised from the halls of Karak Eight Peaks. He called it Dwarf Imperial. The dwarfs who had built these sewers were refugees, he knew. They had fled from the Worlds Edge Mountains when their lands had become too dangerous.

They had come to the human lands bringing a great store of engineering knowledge and a tremendous nostalgia for their ancestral homes under the mountains.

The then-Elector of Nuln had been an enlightened man. He put their knowledge and skills to good use, improving the sanitation of his fast-growing city. They had responded to the challenge by creating places that resembled great temples rather than sewers. Mighty arches supported masonry that had lasted nearly a thousand years. Intricate carved stonework adorned the arches, revealing the traditional dwarf hammer and shield designs. The work had been made beautiful in its way, as well as functional. Of course, time had eroded much of it. Coarse patchworks of plaster and brick filled gaps where human repair teams less skilled than the original builders had been at work. But this place almost directly below the elector's palace was a sewer fit for an emperor.

Then suddenly Felix saw it. He saw how vulnerable those ancient master builders had made the city. He remembered Gotrek's tale of how the skaven had attacked Karak Eight Peaks from the direction least expected: from below.

The sewers provided a means of access to below any place of importance in the city. Teams of assassins or shock troops could be moved through them by a foe adapted to the darkness. They were a perfect highway for a skaven invasion. The great walls of Nuln would prove no barrier to them. The watchers on the roof of the temple of Myrmidia would notice nothing.

The peril to the city was even greater if its own chief magistrate were in league with the rat-men! The pieces clicked. He knew how von Halstadt's foes disappeared. They were dragged down into the depths by the skaven. He would bet anything that a web of access tunnels existed which gave access to the palaces and walled houses above. If nothing else, a small enough assassin could gain access through the sewage channels, gross as that thought was.

The question now was why? Why was von Halstadt doing it? What did he stand to gain? The demise of his enemies? Perhaps he was a mutant in league with the forces of darkness. Perhaps he was mad. Felix asked himself whether he could walk away now, knowing what he did. Could he take the offer of a safe job alongside his brothers and leave the second greatest city of the Empire in the hands of its enemies?

It was infuriating; there was nothing he could do. No one would believe him if he accused the chief magistrate. The word of a sewerjack against that of the most influential man in the city? And if he revealed who he really was, that would only get him into deeper trouble. He was a known revolutionary and an associate of the dwarf who had slaughtered ten of the Emperor's own elite household cavalry. No one would be too bothered if the pair of them disappeared. Perhaps it would be best to let things be. It was only then, as he came to his decision, that he noticed that the rats had vanished and the sound of soft padding could be heard behind him.

'We're being followed, manling,' Gotrek said quietly. 'Several groups. One behind. Two taking tunnels parallel to us. There's more up ahead.'

'Followed? By what?' Felix had to force his words out. His throat felt constricted and his voice was barely louder than a whisper. 'Skaven?'

'Yes. We're going to be ambushed. Our scuttling little friends should be quieter. Dwarf ears are keen.'

'What can we do?'

'Fight bravely and, if need be, die heroically, manling.'

'That's all very well for you – you're a Slayer. The rest of us aren't quite so keen to get ourselves killed.'

Gotrek glared at him contemptuously. Felix felt the need to find an excuse for his fear. 'What if it's an invasion? Someone has to warn the city. It's our duty. Remember the oath we swore when we joined the watch.'

He could see this made an impression on the Trollslayer. Dwarfs were always impressed by talk of duty and of oaths.

'You have a point, manling. At least one of us should get away and warn the city. Best talk with the others and make up a plan.'

Tzarkual saw that his prey had stopped. They were huddling together in the passage and talking in low tones. He knew they were afraid. It had finally dawned on even their dim manbrains that they were being followed. He knew the righteous fear that the true skaven warrior inspired in most humans. He had seen the look of cringing horror in many a human eye. The terrifying majesty and dignity of the skaven form filled the manthings with awe.

He stood taller and preened his fur with his tongue. At times, looking in the polished mirror of his shield, he almost understood their feelings. There was no denying he cut an impressive figure even among the regal forms of his fellow high-ranking skaven. It was only proper that manthings should be suitably impressed by the master race.

He gestured for his stormvermin to halt. He would allow his victims

William King

a minute's grace to fully savour their fear. He wanted them to understand the hopelessness of their position. Perhaps he might even allow
them to beg for their lives. Some victims did. He knew it was a tribute
to the impressive bearing he mustered.

'Hostleader. Should we not attack now? Maimslay the manthings
while they are in confusion?' Clawleader Gazat asked.

Tzarkual shook his head. Gazat had showed his true lack of understanding of the finer points of strategy. He thought it better to simply
attack rather than wait for the correct moment when their foes were
paralysed with fear.

The hostleader twitched his tail indulgently. 'No-no. Let them know
fear. When they spray musk and know hopelessness then we shall
charge-charge.'

Tzarkual could see that Gazat was dubious. Well, let him be. Soon
he would see the superiority of his leader's tactical knowledge for
himself.

'Hostleader! They come back to our path.'

'Doubtless they flee in panicked terror. Prepare to meet them with
fixed weapons.' The ledge here was wide enough for two skaven
abreast. The stormvermin took up position, their pole-arms braced to
meet the charge. Tzarkual waited expectantly.

Triumph filled his heart as the terror-struck manthings confronted
his elite warriors. So full of fear were they that they did not even stop
their headlong rush. Blind panic drove them to throw themselves
onto the blades.

Surely it was only luck that allowed the sweep of the dwarf's hatchet
to chop though both weapons. Yes, he could see more clearly now.
The dwarf was so scared that he frothed at the mouth like a clanrat
with rabies. He howled fearful prayers to whatever gods he worshipped. He knew he was doomed.

Still, in his terror he was doing terrible damage, as panic-stricken
brutes often did. One blind swing clove the head of a trooper. The
frantic thrashing of his axe knocked two trusty stormvermin into the
channel of the sewer.

If Tzarkual had not known better he would have sworn that the
skaven had leapt into the filth to avoid the blade. Surely not! A tall
blond-tufted manthing had joined the dwarf. He fought with a certain
precision. A thrust from his shortsword took another skaven in the
throat.

No! This wasn't happening. Four of his best warriors had gone
down and the manthings had not even taken a casualty. The furless

288

ones had been lucky. He was filled with pride as more brave storm-vermin leapt into the fray.

Now, he felt certain that victory would be his. The manthings just didn't know it. They kept coming. More worthless vermin fell before their weapons. Tzarkual knew that he had been betrayed! Instead of elite stormvermin, he had been sent useless clanrats. Some cunning enemy back in Skavenblight must have arranged it to discredit him.

It was the only explanation of how two puny surface-dwellers could chop through half a dozen skaven so-called warriors without taking a cut. Tzarkual steeled himself to face the foe. He, at least, was not afraid to face the dwarf's hatchet or the man's sword. He was a hostleader. He knew no fear.

It was simply excitement that made his tail twitch and his musk-glands swell as the dwarf painted the sewer wall with blood with a flick of the small axe. Tzarkual knew he could take any manthing, but he decided to hang back as Clawleader Gazat tackled the dwarf. He wanted to study his foe's fighting style to best advantage.

It was certainly impressive the way that the dwarf caught the flying skaven by the throat and dashed his brains out against the ledge floor.

It definitely wasn't terror that made Tzarkual fling himself into the sewage when he confronted the foaming-mouthed berserker. It was just that he knew that this was not the correct time to fight. It would be more elegant to take the foe off guard, by surprise, say, when they were asleep. Less wasteful of skaven lives too. He would tell Thanquol this as soon as he had finished his swim.

'They were after us, weren't they?' Felix said, glancing around worriedly. He dabbed at some of the blood on his face and inspected the tips of his fingers distastefully. He was not surprised to learn that skaven blood was black.

'Don't be foolish, manling. Why would they be after us?'

Felix was getting annoyed at people telling him not to be foolish. 'Well, doesn't it seem odd that we managed to go for two weeks without meeting a single thing down here, then barely two days after you kill that skaven we're ambushed? Come to think of it, it's only one day after I saw von Halstadt at the Golden Hammer. Perhaps he recognised me.'

Gotrek flicked his hatchet forward. Black blood speckled the ledge where the droplets fell. 'Manling, he couldn't recognise you. For a start you were dressed differently. And you were behind the lantern that Gant shone on him – all he could make out would be your outline.

That's if he saw anything at all. Most likely he was too busy running.'

It slowly sank in what Gotrek had said. Or rather what he hadn't said. He hadn't questioned the fact that Felix had seen von Halstadt at the Golden Hammer.

The other sewerjacks back from inspecting the bodies. 'Good work, you two,' said Hef. 'You can certainly fight.'

'Might have left us some, though? I thought there was some coming up behind us but they seemed to stop when you two got stuck in.'

'Probably scared them away.'

'Well, let's take a body and show it to the watch captain. Maybe they'll believe us this time.'

'Right-o, young Felix. You going to carry it?'

Felix kept his mouth shut as he bent to lift the smelly, furry carcass. Even amid the stink of the sewers the smell of the corpse was offensive. Felix was quite pleased when, halfway back to the watch station exit, Hef offered to take a turn carrying it.

'And you say that there are rat-men below the city, brother? In the sewers even?'

Looking around the dining chamber of Otto's house, Felix found it easy to understand his brother's incredulity. Everything here seemed solid and safe and unthreatening. The expensive brocade curtains shut out the night just as effectively as the high walls enclosing the garden shut out the city. The solid teak furniture spoke of wealth based on a firm foundation of prosperity. The silver cutlery, different for each course, reflected an ordered world where everything had its place. Here in his brother's stone-walled house it was hard to recall details of the nightmare battle he had fought that morning.

'Oh yes.' As he said it he saw again the snarling feral rat-face of the skaven he had killed. He remembered the bubbles of bloody froth blowing from its lips. He felt its stinking weight press against his body as it fell. He forced the memory back and concentrated on the goblet of fine Parravonian wine his brother had placed before him.

'It seems almost impossible to believe. Even though you do hear rumours.'

'Rumours, Otto?'

The merchant looked around. He got up and walked around the chamber, making sure each of the doors was securely closed. His Bretonnian wife, Annabella, had retired to her chambers, leaving the two men to talk business in private. Otto returned to his seat. His face was flushed from the wine. Candlelight flickered off little beads of sweat on his face.

'They say that there are mutants in the sewers and goblins and other monsters.' Felix smiled at his brother's seriousness. Otto was telling this to a sewerjack as if it were a great secret. 'You may smile, Felix, but I've talked to folk who swear it's true.'

'Really?' It was hard to keep a note of irony from his voice. Otto didn't notice it.

'Oh yes, the same folk who swear that there's a great mutant undertown called the Night Market. They say it's on the edge of the city. In an abandoned graveyard. It's frequented by followers of certain depraved cults.'

'Slaanesh worshippers, you mean?'

Otto pursed his lips primly. 'Don't use that word in my home. It's cursed unlucky and I don't want to attract the attention of the Dark Powers. Or their followers.'

'Unlucky or not, these things exist.'

'Enough, brother.'

At first Felix found it hard to believe his brother was serious. He wondered what Otto would say if he told him that he had once witnessed a Slaaneshi orgy on Geheimnisnacht. Best not to, he decided. Seeing his brother's serious, fear-filled face he realised quite how large the gap between them had grown.

Could he really once have been as sheltered as his elder brother, shivering and fearful at the mention of a dark power about which he knew not the slightest thing? He had to admit that it was perhaps possible. He began to understand how the cultists got away with it. There was a veil of secrecy drawn over the whole subject in polite society; it wasn't mentioned or discussed. People preferred to believe, or pretend to believe, that such things as Chaos cults couldn't exist. If they were mentioned, they didn't want to talk about them. Everyone abhorred mutants and talked about them widely.

That was fine. It was easy to pick on visible targets, they provided a focus on which to vent deep seated unease. But bring up the fact that normal, supposedly sane folk might be interested in the worship of the dark ones and a door was slammed in your face.

The playwright Detlef Sierck had been right when he wrote: 'Ours is a land chained by silence; ours is a time when the truth goes unspoken.' People just didn't want to know.

Why? Felix did not understand. Did they honestly think that pretending a problem did not exist would make it go away? The watch captain today had looked at the body and could not deny its existence, even though he had obviously wanted to. He was forced to report the matter to a higher authority.

A sudden chill ran through Felix when he recalled who had come to collect the corpse for examination. They were men from the office of Chief Magistrate von Halstadt. Felix wondered if the body of the dead skaven would ever be seen again.

'Tell me more about von Halstadt,' Felix asked. 'Where does he live?'

Otto seemed glad to change the subject. 'His father was a minor noble, killed in one of the peasant uprisings in the early seventies. He studied for the Sigmarite priesthood, but was never ordained. There were hints of a scandal, something to do with spying on the nunnery. He is efficient. He's said to keep files on everyone. And his enemies disappear mysteriously.'

Felix fell silent. A pattern had emerged. He believed he understood what had happened. It would take a little checking though. He would make a start early tomorrow. 'You say he lives nearby.'

'Two streets away. Near the palace, on Emmanuelleplatz.'

'Well, well.' Felix leant back in his chair and yawned expansively. 'Well, brother, it's late and I really must go. I have work tomorrow.'

'Very well.' Otto rang the small bell that sat beside his plate. 'I'll have Franz bring your cloak.'

'I told your predecessor never to come here,' von Halstadt said, staring at the skaven with barely concealed distaste. He hated it when anyone else but him entered his filing chamber. 'The servants might see you.'

The rat-man met his gaze levelly. There was something about this one that made von Halstadt nervous. Perhaps it was the greyish fur or perhaps it was the strange, blind-seeming eyes, but there was something different about this one. Something scary, almost.

'This one is not as the other, manthing. Grey seer this one is. Magelord in the service of the Thirteen. Contracted to the clan but not of it. Important I see you. Things went badly with the guards. Many skaven dead.'

'But my servants–'

'Worry not, foolish manthing – they snoresleep. A simple spell.'

Von Halstadt laid down his file. He marked the place with a uninked quill and closed it gently. He let his hand fall near the hilt of his blade. The touch of it reassured him somewhat. He met the skaven's stare and dared it to look away. 'I'm unused to being called "foolish". Do not do so again.'

The skaven smiled. It was not calming. For a second the magistrate felt as if it might leap forward and bite him. He kept his hand on his weapon. With an almost imperceptible shake of its head the skaven stopped smiling. It twitched its tail.

'Of course. So-sorry. Many apologies, yes. Grieve for the loss of kin. Cost many warptokens to replace.'

'I accept your apology.' Von Halstadt was reassured. It was obscurely pleasing that even so monstrous seeming a creature as the rat-man felt a sense of loss at the death of its relatives. Still, he found himself longing for the day when he would no longer have to deal with the skaven and could have them destroyed. He picked up the file and returned it to its precise place in the proper cabinet.

'The manthings are dangerous to our association. Know your appearance and can pickchoose you from others. They must not be allowed to threaten you or us.'

'True.' The thought was worrying. Von Halstadt's enemies were legion and the slightest hint of scandal would be used against him. The treacherous sewerjacks would sell that information to the highest bidder, he felt sure. Their lack of loyalty to the cause of humanity sickened him. They deserved to die. And to think he had once felt sorry for them. 'They must die.'

'Yes-yes, and you must show us where to find them.'

'That is straightforward enough. I had their watch captain interviewed today.' he opened a new cabinet and pulled out a slim dossier. 'Here is my file on them.'

'Good-good. Soon they will all die-die.'

Once safely back in the sewer, Grey Seer Thanquol cursed to himself. He was tired of dealing with morons like Tzarkual and the manthing von Halstadt. He would have preferred to have been back home in his warm burrow in Skavenblight, surrounded by his breeders and with a few captive humans to run through his maze. He missed the beautiful rotting aroma of the swamps and he was worried about the intrigues which might be taking place against him in his absence. He hated working with the idiot Tzarkual, who could not even carry out the simple assassination of five manthings properly.

The thought of the hostleader's chittering excuses made Thanquol want to bite his own tail with anger. By the Thirteen, it was true! If you wanted a bone gnawed properly you had to gnaw it yourself. No sense entrusting vital tasks to the likes of the useless hostleader.

Still, his masters had assigned him to Tzarkual's clan and he was obliged by the binding oaths of his order to implement and expedite their plans. And this one was sound. It resounded to Clan Skab's credit in the Great Game being played back in Skavenblight. He could see that, foolish though he was, von Halstadt represented a valuable agent to have in place. Of all the humans he had ever met, the spymaster thought most like a skaven – a very stupid skaven, admittedly, but still a skaven. He was easy to manipulate due to his strange jealousy of, and attraction to, the breeder Emmanuelle, prepared to believe anything so long as it was connected to her. Imagine thinking that the skaven use the city's rats as spies, foolish manthing!

However, von Halstadt had proven useful in removing those who might prove to be a threat to the long-term plans of the Thirteen and he was an adroit and effective collector of the warpstone so necessary for the continued research plans of the seers.

Yes-yes, it would be wise to resist the urge to slay the manthing. He was more useful alive than dead, at least until the Great Day came and humanity writhed beneath the talons of the skaven once more.

Thanquol easily deciphered the strange scratchmarks humans called writing. He had trained all his life for this. The study of mankind and its arts were his particular forte. Von Halstadt had thoughtfully attached the maps showing the closest sewers to the victim's dwellings. The manthing was not entirely incompetent. How convenient! Two of the manthings dwelled together in an easily accessible place. He would start with them.

'Come-come, Boneripper. I have work for you this night,' Thanquol squeaked.

The rat-ogre growled its assent from the shadows. Enormous claws slid smoothly from their sheaths at the prospect of food.

Hef was lurching drunkenly down the muddy side-street when he heard the sounds of a struggle coming from the hovel which he shared with Gilda and his brother. He knew he shouldn't have stayed in the tavern for that last pint with Gotrek. If Big Jax and his men had returned for vengeance while he was away, he would never forgive himself.

The hook knife felt cool and reassuring in his hand. He wished he were more sober, but that was not to be helped. He broke into a trot and almost immediately tripped over a pile of rotting garbage in the path. At night, without street lighting the New Quarter was a death-trap.

He picked himself up and set off more carefully along the lane. As he recalled there was an open sewer near here and it wouldn't do to fall in. He heard Gilda scream and all thought of caution vanished when the scream ended in a moan of pain. He ran, scrabbling over the garbage, knocking over a pile of muck. He knew that no one else but him would answer a scream for help in Cheap Street. It was that sort of area.

Flames started to leap skyward over the hovel. Someone must have knocked over a lamp in the struggle. He heard a feral snarl from within the hut. Maybe Jax had brought his tame war-dogs, as he had threatened. Hef covered the open ground near the entrance in one final spurt. By the light of the flames flickering within he could see that the door had been ripped off its hinges.

Something moved within. His brother met him at the door. Spider opened his mouth and tried to speak. Blood gushed forth. Hef caught him as he fell forward. As his arms met round his brother's back, he felt the hole and the great soft mass of the lungs pumping though it. Spider moaned and was still.

It was a nightmare. He had returned home and his home was in flames. His brother was dead. No, that could not be. He and Spider had been inseparable since they could walk. They had served on the same fishing boat, stolen the same money, ran off together to the same city, lived with the same girl. They had the same life. If Spider was dead, then...

Hef stood absolutely still. Tears streamed down his face as the monstrous shape emerged from the ruins of the burning hut and loomed over him. The last thing he heard was the sound of chittering from behind him.

Felix was up bright and early. He made his way down the muddy streets of the New Quarter, ignoring the pall of smoke that rose from the shantytown near Cheap Street. Another fire, he supposed. Well, he had been lucky, the wind had not fanned the flames in the direction of Frau Zorin's tenement. If they had, he might have died in his sleep. And he couldn't afford to die just now. He still had things to do.

He turned left down Rotten Row and hit the cobbled streets of Commercial Way. Coaches clattered past as merchants made their way to the coffee houses before starting business for the day. He found his way to the Hall of Archives and made his way to the division of the planning office with responsibility for sewers.

He knew he would find what he needed there. Three quarters of an hour, much browsing through ancient, dust-covered files and plans, two threats and one bribe later, he had proven himself to be correct. Pleased with himself, Felix made his way to the watch house.

* * *

They were instantly assigned to help out the rest of the watch in the area that had burned: burying the dead, searching the rubble for the living. They marched up to the shantytown to take a look. The fire had ripped through many hovels, the burned and the disfigured dead were everywhere. A little boy, his face blackened by soot, sat near an old woman who whimpered quietly to herself.

'What happened here, son?' Felix asked.

'It was the rat-daemon what did it,' the boy said. 'I saw it myself. It killed the men who lived there and carried them below to feast. Ma says it'll come for me next if I don't behave.'

Felix exchanged looks with Gotrek. Savage interest was evident in the Trollslayer's one good eye.

'There's no such thing as rat-daemons, lad. Don't lie to us – we're with the watch.'

'There is too. I saw it with my own eyes. It was taller than you and heavier than that big one-eyed dwarf. It was led by a smaller rat-man with grey skin and horns on its head.'

'Did anyone else see it?'

'Don't know. I hid. I thought they might take me too.'

Felix shook his head and went to check the ruins of Hef and Spider's hut. There was little left of the pitiful building save the burned-out remains and the charred corpse of a woman.

'No sign of Hef or Spider?'

Gotrek shook his head and pointed with his toe to something grey and sharp lying in the ashes. 'That's Hef's knife.'

Felix bent and picked it up. The metal was still warm from lying in the embers. Felix looked at the corpse. The smell of burnt meat filled his nostrils.

'Gilda?' said Felix.

Felix shook his head. Sorrow and rage filled him. He had liked the brothers. They had been good men. Now he wanted vengeance.

'You were an engineer once, Gotrek. Tell me what these mean.'

Felix ignored the Trollslayer's incredulous look. He cleared a space on the table in the watchroom and spread out the charts. Rudi watched curiously as he smoothed the cracked old parchment flat and weighed down each corner with an empty tea mug.

The Slayer gave his attention back to the papers. 'These are charts of the sewers, manling. Dwarf-made plans of the Old Quarter.'

'That's correct. They show the area beneath Chief Magistrate von Halstadt's mansion. If you look closely, you'll discover that it's not too far from the place where Gant was killed. I'd also bet if we looked we'd find a way up from the sewers to his house.'

A frown creased Rudi's low brow. 'You're suggesting that we break into Fritz von Halstadt's house! We'll be hung if we're caught. We might even lose our jobs!'

'That would be a pity. What do you say, are you in? Rudi?'

'I don't know…'

'Gotrek?'

'Yes, manling – with one provision.'

'What's that?'

'If von Halstadt is the Chaos worshipping, skaven-loving, snotling-fondler we saw in the sewer then we kill him.'

An appalled silence hung over the chamber. The import of the Trollslayer's words sunk into their brains. Felix felt his mouth go dry. What the dwarf was suggesting was murder, pure and simple.

No, he decided, thinking of Gant, and the dead in the New Quarter, it wasn't murder, it was justice. He'd go along with that. 'Fine.'

'There's no backing out then. Rudi?' The bald-headed man looked shocked. His face was pale and fear was in his eyes.

'You don't know what you're suggesting.'

'Are you coming with us or not?' Rudi didn't answer for a second. 'Yes,' he said at last. 'I'll come. I just hope you're wrong, that's all.'

'I'm not,' Felix said.

'That's what I'm afraid of.'

The sewers had never seemed so ominous to Felix. Shadows danced away from the lantern light. Every time he heard Rudi's heavy tread behind him, he had to fight the urge to look around. The sound of the Slayer continually tapping the walls with his hatchet blade was getting on his nerves. He knew that Gotrek was only doing it to see if he could find a hollow area but that did not make it any easier to take.

Something was out there. He knew that now. Something had killed Hef and Spider, and their girl too, and it would surely kill the rest of them if they let it. It was the not knowing that was so terrifying. Not knowing what it was that hunted them. Not really knowing why. Not knowing how many skaven might appear, nor what daemonic henchmen they might have. The brothers had been formidable fighters and they were gone.

Worse, half of the Cheap Street shantytown had gone with them. Whatever dark thing sought them had no qualms about killing a lot of people to get the ones it wanted. He asked himself why he had not simply fled the city-state.

He could be on the road even now, not creeping about in this dark, smelly stinkhole. Why did he have to be cursed with this urge to interfere in what was really none of his business?

He already knew the answer. He had to take a stand somewhere, for something. Because if he did not, he would be exactly like his brother, Otto, and all the others like him, pretending that he did not know what was going on; making deals with the Darkness so that it would leave him alone; pretending all was right with the world when he knew that it wasn't.

Knowing that something was wrong meant that he had to do something about it, even if the only reason for doing it was to keep his self-image intact and allow him to feel superior to those he despised. And if that made him feel a little more like the heroes he used to read about when he was young, well, so much the better.

Thinking about his reasons kept his mind occupied and allowed him to forget his fears. He made himself concentrate on what he knew. The only real lead he had was that he knew that the head of the city's secret police was in league with the skaven. He had seen it with his own eyes. He did not know why such a thing should be; he only knew that it was so. And that it should be stopped.

'Stop daydreaming, manling. We've been down here for hours and we still haven't found this secret entrance of yours. It'll soon be dark up above and we're still no further forward.' Felix gave his attention back to scanning the walls. From up ahead the sound of Gotrek tapping the brickwork with the blade of his hatchet continued.

Thanquol stared around the darkened room. He felt exposed here in the surface world, so high above the ground. He gazed out through the single window and then looked at the straw pallet. Boneripper stood hunched near the doorway, flexing his great claws.

They had stood here in the dark for nearly two hours and still there was no sign of their prey. He lashed his tail in frustration. Where was the stupid manthing? Why wasn't he home in bed where he should be? They were all the same, frittering away their time in drunkenness and debauchery. They deserved to be replaced by the Master Race. He swore that he would make this particular manthing pay for wasting a grey seer's valuable time.

He didn't have any more time to waste. He had to meet with von Halstadt and check on the arrangements that had been made for the countess's homecoming ball. Soon it would be time to reveal to him that Emmanuelle's guest, the Emperor's own brother-in-law, was secretly a mutant and worse yet, the countess's latest lover.

The fact that neither of these things were true was not in the slightest bit important. What was important was that when von Halstadt had the graf kidnapped and tortured, word of it would be released. War would come between Nuln and the rest of the Empire. The Emperor could not stand for the insult of his own brother-in-law being tortured by the Elector's secret police. Civil war would erupt. The greatest kingdom of mankind would be thrown into anarchy. The power of the skaven would grow.

The thought so excited Thanquol that he had to take some powdered warpstone snuff to calm his nerves. The drug bubbled into his brain and filled him with delightful visions of torture, bloodshed and agony.

The sound of footsteps coming up the stairs brought him out of his reverie. He nodded to Boneripper. There was a tentative knock on the door. 'Herr Jaeger, it's me, Frau Zorin. Rent time!'

Before Thanquol could countermand him, Boneripper threw open the door and dragged the old woman inside.

'Herr Jaeger, there's no need to be so rough!' They were Frau Zorin's last words before Boneripper tore her throat out.

Well, at least he wouldn't have to feed the rat-ogre for another three hours, thought the grey seer. He waited for Boneripper to finish his meal.

'Come-come, we have business elsewhere,' he told him. They headed for the sewers and their meeting with von Halstadt.

'Success, manling!' Gotrek exclaimed, and tapped again to make sure. He nodded his head smugly. 'I've found the passage or my mother was a troll!'

I wouldn't bet against that, thought Felix, but kept the thought to himself. He watched as the Slayer set down his hatchet and began to run his fingers around the brickwork.

'Nice bit of work this. Well concealed. Probably dwarf, I'd say. No wonder I missed it the other day. The git must have paid a dwarf crew to dig his bolt-tunnel and then sworn them to secrecy. Now if I'm right there should be–'

His stubby powerful fingers pushed against a single brick. It sank into the wall. There came a quiet grinding sound, as of perfectly balanced counterweights shifting. A section of the wall slid back. Felix saw a small vestibule and a metal ladder leading up. Gotrek turned and smiled, revealing his missing teeth. He looked genuinely pleased. 'Very nice work indeed. Bugger must have outdistanced me, turned that corner and ducked in. No wonder I couldn't find him. My eyes were still stinging from the gas, too.'

'There's no need to make excuses, Gotrek,' Felix said.

'No excuse, manling. I just want–'

'Are we going to stand here all night, young Felix, or are you going to go up and take a look around?' Rudi interrupted.

'Me?'

'Well, all this was your idea.' Felix saw the unease written on Rudi's face. The big man was scared by the prospect of burgling so important a citizen's home. Not surprisingly, thought Felix. He's a watchman. He's spent the last ten years catching criminals, not being one.

'Are you going to do it, manling, or should I?' The thought of the Trollslayer clumping around upstairs galvanised Felix into action. He remembered Otto's words about there being Templars of the White Wolf on guard above. He didn't relish the prospect of being discovered by them.

'I'll take a look first,' he said, 'and I'll let you know if it's safe.'

Felix held his breath and glanced around. The ladder emerged in another small chamber with a single door. This led out into a large wine cellar.

Looking back, Felix saw that the door was attached to a wine rack, so that when it was closed it was virtually invisible. Felix checked a label on one of the bottles. He blew away dust to reveal the emblem of one of the best Parravonian vineyards, Desghulles.

'Someone has expensive tastes,' he told himself. He turned swiftly reaching for his sword when he heard the ladder creak behind him. Gotrek's head poked round the edge of the doorway.

'Don't wet yourself, manling, it's me,' he said. Rudi emerged from behind him. 'Right, let's check the house and see if we can find our friend, the chief magistrate.'

'Not much noise above. The place sounds empty.'

'Let's hope so.'

'I'll stay here,' Rudi said. 'And make sure your line of retreat is covered.'

Felix shrugged. It was probably better than having the big man blundering about up above. 'You do that.'

* * *

Felix made his way cautiously to the foot of the stairs, keeping his lantern to the narrowest aperture so that only the faintest glimmer of light showed.

'I told you so: the house is empty,' Gotrek said.

Felix had to admit it looked like the dwarf was right. Where were the White Wolf guards? Where were the servants?

'Guards are most likely at the gatehouse. But where are the servants? A place this size should have some.'

'You'd know about that, I suppose.'

'Yes.'

Felix gently put his foot on the stairs. A shiver ran down his spine as it creaked under his weight. He paused and held his breath. No one came to investigate.

'Why are you being so quiet, manling? There's no one here.'

'I don't know. Maybe it's just because it's not my house. I feel like a criminal. Why are you whispering?'

'You are being a criminal. So am I. Let's search this place and see what we can find. You take upstairs. I'll take below.'

It was only after he padded off near silently that Felix noticed that Gotrek was moving stealthily too. Felix moved on up the stairs, hoping that they would not creak.

In the bedroom, Felix closed the aperture of his lantern completely before sliding aside a curtain and looking outside. He glanced down into a large walled courtyard and he could see over the high walls into the street beyond. A large gate opened into the courtyard. On the left of the square was a stable and coach-house; on the right was a small barracks and a privy for the servants. Old oak trees lined the square. There were sentries: tall blond men in full armour, white wolf pelts draped round their shoulders. One paced from the gatehouse across the courtyard.

For a moment Felix feared that the man might be coming inside, but he soon turned off and headed towards a small barracks next to the stables. Slowly Felix let the curtain slide back into place and then he allowed himself to exhale.

No, it wouldn't do to get caught here. The White Wolves had a reputation for ferocity that equalled that of a Slayer, and there were at least half a dozen of them out there.

The most appropriate thing to do when he found the locked door was to force it. He jimmied it open with the blade of his shortsword and went in. He found himself in a place that reminded him of the ledger hall in his father's warehouse back in Altdorf.

It was a big room dominated by an oak desk large enough to hold a party on. The walls were lined with filing boxes, hundreds and hundreds of them. He opened one at random and pulled out a thick sheaf of papers written in a precise hand. Glancing through it, he came upon the name of the countess and notes referring to several of her better-known lovers. There was an extensive section dealing with suspected mutation in her family. Many sources were quoted.

What drew Felix's attention were the references to 'our most special source' and 'our friends down below'. He picked up another file and went through it. There were similar notes. One referred to the need for a certain Slazinger to disappear. The files were sorted alphabetically. He couldn't resist it. He sought out the one on the Jaeger family. After finding one concerning a family of bakers on Cake Street who shared the same name, he got his own family file on the second try.

Felix felt his stomach lurch when he came across references to the merchant house of Jaeger and Sons. The file remarked on how amenable his brother Otto was and noted that he was a sound man who gave generously to the elector's fund for the maintenance of civil order. As he flipped the page he saw his own name mentioned. He read on.

Thanquol noticed that the secret entrance to von Halstadt's had been disturbed almost as soon as he entered. There was a strange manscent in the air of the chamber at the foot of the ladder. Several manscents in fact, and something that smelled like dwarf.

Fool-fool! he cursed inside, gnawing at the tip of his tail. The spymaster had been discovered. It didn't take the application of a mind as clever as Thanquol's to work out by whom. He had two manthings and a dwarf left to kill.

Well, the manthings had saved him the bother of tracking them down. Their desire to meddle in business that was not theirs would prove to be their undoing.

He nodded to Boneripper and chittered his instructions. The ladder groaned under the weight of the rat-ogre. It swarmed up the rungs, as agile as an ape.

Felix shook his head. He was referred to as a spendthrift younger son who had vanished under mysterious circumstances. There was a line devoted to his duel with Krassner and a hastily scribbled memo in pencil to the effect that a further investigation should be conducted.

Well, perhaps there were worse things to be than the black sheep of the Jaeger family. Perhaps he should show Gotrek. Maybe there was something in the files about the Slayer too. He was just about to look when he heard the door open down below.

Damn, he thought, closing the chamber door. He'd have to wait.

Von Halstadt knew he was running late. He hoped the skaven was too. He deplored giving the wrong impression even to a brute like the skaven. But Emmanuelle was due back tomorrow and he wanted every little detail of her household to be perfect.

He imagined the smile with which she would reward his diligence and knew that all his care had been worthwhile. Even if he had been forced to waste fifteen minutes punishing that young footman for his clumsiness in setting the paintings. The flogging had left the magistrate tired and sweaty, and in need of a bath.

He picked up a house lantern and lit it. The gloom rushed away from him. Von Halstadt was going to call a servant to draw some water when he recalled that he had given them all the night off because the skaven was coming. He would have to forego the pleasure of a wash until later. The skaven's tidings were more important.

Before departing last night he had intimated that his agents were about to ferret out a particularly important mutant plot. Von Halstadt had to admit he was far more concerned with the assassination attempt on the sewerjacks. He knew that Hef and Spider were dead. His agents had reported on the fire in Cheap Street.

That had been a neat bit of work, disposing of two traitors and half a hundred riffraff at the same time. Come to think of it, perhaps the ratman had inadvertently provided a solution to another problem. Perhaps he could have fires set across the New Quarter. That would certainly cut down on the numbers of mutant-worshipping scum who dwelled there.

The thought of burning the dregs of society out of their festering sinkhole of vice warmed the cockles of his heart. He took the stairs two at a time and rushed down the corridor to his filing room. But his heart sank when he saw the door had been forced. Anger filled him. Someone had desecrated his sanctum. After Emmanuelle, his beloved files were the most important thing in his life. If someone had harmed a page of them...

He drew his sword and pushed the door open with his foot. A lantern shone in his face.

'Good evening, von Halstadt,' a cultured voice said. 'I think you and I have some business.'

As the chief magistrate's eyes grew accustomed to the illumination he recognised the face of the young man he had seen with Otto Jaeger the other night. 'Who are you, whelp?' he asked.

'My name is Felix Jaeger. I am the man who is going to kill you.'

Rudi had never seen so much wine before. It was everywhere in the cellar: old bottles covered in a thick layer of dust and cobwebs, newer ones with only the slightest gilding of dirt. There was so much of it he wondered how any one man could drink it all. Maybe if he had plenty of guests, he supposed.

What was that noise? Probably nothing. It would be best to pretend there was nothing there.

Ever since they had found the rat-man in the sewers, nothing had gone right. Perhaps he could hide. But there was no place into which he could squeeze his large frame.

He should go back to the top of the ladder and take a look. He was sure he had heard the rungs of the metal ladder creak. Yes, he should.

He swallowed and tried to make himself move back to the hidden niche. His limbs responded slowly. It was as if all strength had been drained out of them. His heartbeat sounded loud in his ears. It raced like he had just run a mile.

He realised that he had been holding his breath, and let it out in a long sigh. The sound seemed unnaturally loud in the silence. He wished Gotrek or even that cocky young snob Felix would come back. He didn't like being here on his own, in the basement of a powerful noble whose wealth and influence he could hardly imagine.

It was ridiculous, he told himself. He'd spent nearly fifteen years, man and boy, in the sewers, hunting mutants and monsters in the dark. He shouldn't be frightened. Ah, but it had been different then. He had been younger and he'd been with friends and comrades, Gant and the brothers and the others now dead or gone.

The last few days had truly shaken him. The solid foundations of his life had vanished. He was alone: no wife, no children. His last friends had vanished or died. And if young Felix was right, the order that he had sworn to protect, the city's rulers who he was pledged to defend against all enemies, were the enemy. Life didn't make sense any more.

Wait! There was definitely something moving inside the niche. Something heavy had stealthily pulled itself over the lip of the sink-hole. It was here in the cellar.

'Who's there?' Rudi asked. His voice sounded weak and strange to him. It was the voice of a stranger. The soft padding footfalls came closer.

His lantern revealed the shape as it emerged into the wine cellar. It was huge, a head taller than him and perhaps twice as heavy. Great muscles bulged under its ruddy fur; long claws slid from the sheaths in its fingertips. Its face was a mixture of rat and wolf. A chilling, malign intelligence burned in its pink, beady little eyes.

Rudi raised his club to defend himself, but it was on him with one leap, startlingly swift for so large a creature. Pain flared through Rudi's weapon arm as its great claws bit into the flesh of his wrist. He opened his mouth to scream. He looked up into the pink eyes of death. He felt the breath of the monster on him. It smelled of blood and fresh meat.

'Don't be foolish, young man,' Fritz von Halstadt said. As he spoke, he put his hand on the hilt of his longsword. He was confident. He was a formidable swordsman and his opponent had only a short stabbing blade. 'One shout and I'll have six Knights of the White Wolf in here. They'll hand me your head.'

'Perhaps they'll be interested in the fact that you consort with skaven and keep a ledger of your dealings with them.'

Felix's words chilled von Halstadt to the bone. He didn't know whether the grey seer was in the house already or about to arrive. He couldn't risk summoning the knights if that was the case. They were reassuringly anti-mutant but their zeal also extended to dealing with the likes of the skaven.

'You don't know what you're talking about, boy!' the magistrate spat. His blade rung as he pulled it from the scabbard.

'I'm afraid I do. You see, I saw you in the sewers the other day. I saw you with my own eyes. I nearly didn't believe them when I saw you again in the Golden Hammer.'

The young man seemed certain. There would be no reasoning with him, he would have to die. Von Halstadt let his blade point to the floor as he moved closer. He let his shoulders slump in defeat.

'How did you know?'

'I'm a sewerjack.'

'You can't be. Sewerjacks don't eat at the Golden Hammer. Not in the company of Otto Jaeg...' As he spoke the words, realisation dawned on von Halstadt. Felix Jaeger, Otto Jaeger. The family black sheep. He knew that had been worth looking into.

'What do you want, boy? Money? Preferment? I can arrange for either but it will take time.' He edged ever closer. The young man had relaxed a little, seeing how cowed he had become. Soon it would be time to strike.

'No, I think I want your head.'

Even as Felix spoke, von Halstadt struck, serpent-swift. To his surprise the young man parried his blow. Steel sparked where the blades met. Felix lashed out with his foot catching von Halstadt on the shin. Pain flared in his leg. He only just managed to leap back out of the way as the younger man thrust. He knew he had to keep his distance, to use his longer blade to advantage.

They circled and wheeled, moving with the precision of masters as they sought out openings. Blades wheeled and glittered in the shadows of the two lanterns. They moved too fast for the eye to follow, danced with a life of their own, seeking holes in the other's defences. Von Halstadt allowed himself a snarl of satisfaction as he pinked Jaeger's arm. It turned into a smile as he cut open a nasty gash above the young man's eye.

Soon blood would drip down, blinding him. Both breathed hard now. But Fritz von Halstadt knew that he would win this duel. He could sense it. He would fight defensively for the moment. It was simply a matter of waiting.

Thanquol heard the noise upstairs. It sounded like a dance was taking place. Heavy boots slammed into the stone floor. Well-well, he thought, it was fortunate that he had arrived when he did. It would seem that von Halstadt's enemies had tracked him to his lair and were even now in the process of assassinating him.

Assassination had a long and honourable history in skaven politics, and Thanquol was tempted to let things run their course. It would gratify his sense of petty malice to let the manthing die. Pleasing though the thought was, he couldn't allow himself the pleasure. It would interfere too much with the great plan.

He kicked Boneripper. The rat-ogre raised its bloody muzzle from the remnants of its meal. It growled at him. Thanquol glared at it, letting his slave feel his will. Slowly the rat-ogre rose. They climbed the stairs out of the cellar towards the battle above.

Felix was forced to admit that perhaps this had not been such a good idea after all. He blamed too much watching the plays of Detlef Sierck as a youth. He had always wanted to play out one of those melodramatic scenes where the hero confronts the scheming villain.

Unfortunately things weren't quite going according to script. It was the story of his life. His arms burned with fatigue and the pain of the wound von Halstadt had inflicted. He jerked his head quickly to one side to shake off the blood running down his forehead, a risky move against a swordsman as skilled as his opponent.

Red droplets splattered onto the desktop. Felix was relieved that von Halstadt hadn't been quite swift enough to take advantage of the opening. His breathing was coming swift and laboured. It sounded like a bellows. Pain interfered with the smooth flow of his movements.

Von Halstadt's long blade seemed to be everywhere. It was the sword that made the difference. Felix believed that had the blades been of equal length he would just have been the nobleman's superior. But they were not and it was killing him.

'Hurry-hurry!' Thanquol ordered Boneripper as they ran towards the bottom of the stairs. The fight above was still going on but now that he had decided to save his pawn he didn't want to take the chance of fate intervening.

An accident at this stage would be most annoying. Boneripper let out a little moan and stopped so suddenly that Thanquol ran into the solid wall of his back and bounced. The pain in his snout was considerable. The grey seer glanced around his pet. He saw why Boneripper had halted.

A dwarf stood there, blocking the way to the stairs. He was massive and his fur was strangely crested. In one hand he held an enormous battle-axe. He, too, looked as if he had been racing to get up the steps and intervene in the ongoing fight. He, too, looked astonished to discover there was another in the house.

'Bloody palaces!' he grumbled. 'You never know who you'll meet in them.'

'Die-die, foolish dwarfthing,' chittered Thanquol. 'Bonerip-per! Kill! Kill!'

Boneripper surged forward, claws extended. He loomed up over the dwarf, a terrifying daemonic apparition, a living tribute to the fearsome imaginations of the sorcerer-scientists of Clan Moulder. It would not have surprised Thanquol if the dwarf, too, was paralysed with fear by the very sight of him, as the others had been.

'Chew on this,' the dwarf said.

Brains splattered everywhere as the axe clove Boneripper's head in two. Thanquol found himself confronting an irate Trollslayer.

The musk of fear sprayed as he reached into his pouch for a weapon. Then, deciding discretion was the better part of valour, he turned and scuttled off. To his relief the dwarf did not follow, but raced up the staircase. Thanquol headed for the sewers, swearing that if it took him a lifetime, he'd make that dwarf pay.

Both men heard the noise from below. It sounded like an immense tree had crashed to the ground. Felix saw von Halstadt's eyes flicker to the window. He knew this would be his only chance. Throwing caution to the wind he dived straight at the nobleman, all defences down. Momentarily he expected to feel von Halstadt's blade bite into his chest. The split-second of distraction proved almost enough. Too late, his opponent tried to bring his blade around. Felix was already within the sweep. It bit into his side as his own shortsword tore up through von Halstadt's stomach, under his ribs and into the heart. With a gurgle, the chief magistrate died. Agony seared Felix's brain and he fell.

'Wake up, manling. This is no time to be lying around.'

Felix felt water splash over his face. He coughed and spluttered and shook his head.

'What the–'

'We'd better get out of here before the White Wolves arrive.'

'Leave me alone.' Felix just wanted to lie there. 'You go and fight them. You always wanted to die heroically.' Gotrek shuffled his feet and looked embarrassed. 'I can't, manling. I'm a Slayer. I'm supposed to die honourably. If we're caught now folk might think we were committing a burglary.'

'So?'

'Theft brings disgrace. I'm trying to atone for my disgrace.'

'I can imagine some worse crimes, like drowning a dying man, for instance.'

'You're not dying, manling. That's barely a scratch.'

'Well, if we must.' Felix pulled himself to his feet. He looked around at the files. It occurred to him that the information here would be worth a fortune to the right person. Even a small selection of what was here would be invaluable. The possibilities for blackmail and extortion were endless.

He looked at the Slayer and remembered what he had said of theft. Gotrek wouldn't condone him taking the papers. Even if he would, Felix decided he could not take them. It was corrupt, the life work of a maniac like von Halstadt. Contained in those papers were things that could ruin men's lives. There were too many secrets already in Nuln. These represented too much power to fall into anybody's hands. He took the lanterns and poured their oil over the filing cases. Then he set them alight.

Running downstairs with the smell of burning paper filling his nostrils, Felix felt oddly free. He realised that he would not be going to work with Otto after all, and that pleased him tremendously.

GUTTER RUNNERS

'Needless to say, we could not tell the authorities
the whole truth of our encounter with the skaven,
for in doing so we would implicate ourselves in the
murder of a high official of the court of the Countess
Emmanuelle. And murder, no matter how deserving
the victim, is a capital crime.

'We were dismissed from service and forced to
seek alternate employment. As luck would have it,
during a drunken spree in one of the less salubrious
quarters of the city, we happened upon a tavern,
the owner of which had been a companion of the
Slayer's in his mercenary days. We were employed
to eject undesirables from the bar, and believe
me when I tell you that people had to be very
undesirable indeed to warrant being thrown out of
the Blind Pig.

'The work was hard, violent and unrewarding but
at least I thought we were safe from the skaven. Of
course, as was so often the case, I was wrong. For it
seemed that one of them at least had not forgotten
us and was plotting revenge...'

— From *My Travels With Gotrek, Vol. III*, by Herr Felix Jaeger
(Altdorf Press, 2505)

Felix Jaeger ducked the drunken mercenary's punch. The brass-knuckled fist hurtled by his ear and hit the doorjamb, sending splinters of wood flying. Felix jabbed forward with his knee, catching the mercenary in the groin. The man moaned in pain and bent over. Felix caught him around the neck and tugged him towards the swing doors. The drunk barely resisted. He was too busy throwing up stale wine. Felix booted the door open, then pushed the mercenary out, propelling him on his way with a hard kick to the backside. The mercenary rolled in the dirt of Commerce Street, clutching his groin, tears dribbling from his eyes, his mouth open in a rictus of pain.

Felix rubbed his hands together ostentatiously before turning to go back into the bar. He was all too aware of the eyes watching him from beyond every pool of torchlight. At this time of night, Commerce Street was full of bravos, street-girls and hired muscle. Keeping up his reputation for toughness was plain common sense. It reduced his chances of taking a knife in the back when he wandered the streets at night.

What a life, he thought. If anybody had told him a year ago that he would be working as a bouncer in the roughest bar in Nuln, he would have laughed at them. He would have said he was a scholar, a poet and a gentleman, not some barroom brawler. He would have almost preferred being back in the sewer watch to this.

Things change, he told himself, pushing his way back into the crowded bar. Things certainly change.

The stink of stale sweat and cheap perfume slapped him in the face. He squinted as his vision adjusted to the gloomy, lantern-lit interior of the Blind Pig. For a moment he was aware that all the eyes in the place were on him. He scowled, in what he hoped was a fearsome manner, glaring around in exactly the fashion Gotrek did. From behind the bar, big Heinz, the tavern owner, gave a wink of approval for the way in which Felix had dealt with the drunk, then returned to working the pumps.

313

Felix liked Heinz. He was grateful to him as well. The big man was a former comrade from Gotrek's mercenary days. He was the only man in Nuln who had offered them a job after they had been dishonourably discharged from the sewer watch.

Now that was a new low, Felix thought. He and Gotrek were the only two warriors ever to be kicked out of the sewer watch in all its long and sordid history. In fact they had been lucky to escape a stretch in the Iron Tower, Countess Emmanuelle's infamous prison. Gotrek had called the watch captain a corrupt, incompetent snotling fondler when the man had refused to take their report of skaven in the sewers seriously. To make matters worse, the dwarf had broken the man's jaw when he had ordered the pair of them horsewhipped.

Felix winced. He still had some half-faded bruises from the ensuing brawl. They had fought against half of the watch station before being bludgeoned unconscious. He remembered waking up in the squalid cell the morning after. It was just as well his brother Otto had got them out, wishing to hush up any possible scandal that might blacken the Jaeger family name.

Otto had wanted the pair of them to leave town, but Gotrek insisted that they stay. He was not going to be run out of town like some common criminal, particularly not when a skaven wizard was still at large and doubtless plotting some terrible crime. The Trollslayer sensed an opportunity to confront the forces of darkness in all their evil splendour and he was not going to be robbed of his chance of a mighty death in battle against them. And bound by his old oath, Felix had to remain with the dwarf and record that doom for posterity.

Some mighty death, Felix thought sourly. He could see Gotrek now, huddled in a corner with a group of dwarfish warriors, waiting to start his shift. His enormous crest of dyed orange hair rose over the crowd. His hugely muscular figure hunched forward over the table. The dwarfs slugged back their beer from huge tankards, growling and tugging at their beards, and muttering something in their harsh, flinty tongue. Doubtless they were remembering some old slight to their people or working through the long list of the grudges they had to avenge. Or maybe they were just remembering the good old days when beer was a copper piece a flagon, and men showed the Elder Races proper respect.

Felix shook his head. Whatever the conversation was about, the Trollslayer was thoroughly engrossed. He had not even noticed the fight. That in itself was unusual, for the dwarf lived to fight as other folk lived to eat or sleep.

Felix continued his circuit of the tavern, taking in every table with a casual sidelong glance. The long, low hall was packed. Every beer-stained table was crowded. On one, a semi-naked Estalian dancing girl whirled and pranced while a group of drunken halberdiers threw silver and encouraged her to remove the rest of her clothes. Street-girls led staggering soldiers to dark alcoves in the far wall. The commotion from the bar drowned out the gasps and moans and the clink of gold changing hands.

One whole long table was taken up by a group of Kislevite horse archers, guards for some incoming caravan from the north. They roared out drinking songs concerning nothing but horses and women, and sometimes an obscene combination of both, while downing huge quantities of Heinz's home-distilled potato vodka.

There was something about them that made Felix uneasy. The Kislevites were men apart, bred under a colder sun in a harsher land, born only to ride and fight. When one of them rose from the table to go to the privy, his rolling, bow-legged walk told Felix that here was a horseman born. The warrior kept his hand near his long-bladed knife – for at no time was a man more vulnerable than when standing outside in the dim moonlight, relieving himself of half a pint of potato vodka.

Felix grimaced. Half of the thieves, bravos and muscle boys in Nuln congregated in the Blind Pig. They came to mingle with newly arrived caravan guards and mercenaries. He knew more than half of them by name; Heinz had pointed them out to him on his first night here.

At the corner table sat Murdo Mac Laghlan, the Burglar King who claimed to be an exiled prince of Albion. He wore the tartan britches and long moustaches of one of that distant, almost mythical island's hill-warriors. His muscular arms were tattooed in wood elf patterns. He sat surrounded by a bevy of adoring women, regaling them with tales of his beautiful mountainous homeland. Felix knew that Murdo's real name was Heinrik Schmidt and he had never left Nuln in all his life.

Two tall hook-nosed men of Araby, Tarik and Hakim, sat at their permanently reserved table. Gold rings glittered on their fingers. Gold earrings shone in their earlobes. Their black leather jerkins glistened in the torchlight. Long curved swords hung over the back of their chairs. Every now and again, strangers – sometimes street urchins, sometimes nobles – would come in and take a seat. Haggling would start, money would change hands and just as suddenly and mysteriously the visitors would up and leave. A day later someone would be found floating face down in the Reik. Rumour had it that the two were the best assassins in Nuln.

Over by the roaring fire at a table all by himself sat Franz Beckenhof, who some said was a necromancer and who others claimed was a charlatan. No one had ever found the courage to sit next to the skull-faced man and ask, despite the fact that there were always seats free at his table. He sat there every night, with a leather bound book in front of him, husbanding his single glass of wine. Old Heinz never asked him to move along either, even though he took up space that other, more free-spending customers might use. It never pays to upset a magician, was Heinz's motto.

Here and there, as out of place as peacocks in a rookery, sat gilded, slumming nobles, their laughter loud and uneasy. They were easy to spot by their beautiful clothing and their firm, soft flesh; upper-class fops out to see their city's dark underbelly. Their bodyguards – generally large, quiet, watchful men with well-used weapons – were there to see that their masters came to no harm during their nocturnal adventures. As Heinz always said, no sense in antagonising the nobs. They could have his tavern shut and his staff inside the Iron Tower with a whisper in the right ear. Best to toady to them, look out for them and to put up with their obnoxious ways.

By the fire, near to the supposed necromancer, was the decadent Bretonnian poet, Armand le Fevre, son of the famous admiral and heir to the le Fevre fortune. He sat alone, drinking absinthe, his eyes fixed at some point in the mid-distance, a slight trickle of drool leaking from the corner of his mouth. Every night, at midnight, he would lurch to his feet and announce that the end of the world was coming, then two hooded and cloaked servants would enter and carry him to his waiting palanquin and then home to compose one of his blasphemous poems. Felix shuddered, for there was something about the young man which reminded him of Manfred von Diehl, another sinister writer of Felix's acquaintance, and one which he would rather forget.

As well as the exotic and the debauched, there were the usual raucous youths from the student fraternities, who had come here to the roughest part of town to prove their manhood to themselves and to their friends. They were always the worst troublemakers; spoiled, rich young men who had to show how tough they were for all to see. They hunted in packs and were as capable of drunken viciousness as the lowest dockside cut-throat. Maybe they were worse, for they considered themselves above the law and their victims less than vermin.

From where he stood, Felix could see a bunch of jaded young dandies tugging at the dress of a struggling serving-wench. They were demanding a kiss. The girl, a pretty newcomer called Elissa, fresh from the country and unused to this sort of behaviour, was resisting hard. Her struggles just seemed to encourage the rowdies. Two of them had got to their feet and began to drag the struggling girl towards the alcoves. One had clamped a hand over her mouth so that her shrieks would not be heard. Another brandished a huge blutwurst sausage obscenely.

Felix moved to interpose himself between the young men and the alcoves.

'No need for that,' he said quietly.

The older of the two youths grinned nastily. Before speaking he took a huge bite of the blutwurst and swallowed it. His face was flushed and sweat glistened on his brow and cheeks. 'She's a feisty wench – maybe she'd enjoy a taste of a prime Nuln sausage.'

The dandies laughed uproariously at this fine jest. Encouraged, he waved the sausage in the air like a general rallying his troops.

'I don't think so,' Felix said, trying hard to keep his temper. He hated these spoiled young aristocrats with a passion, had done ever since his time at the University of Altdorf where he had been surrounded by their sort.

'Our friend here thinks he's tough, Dieter,' said the younger of the two, a crop-headed giant larger than Felix. He sported the scarred face of a student duellist, one who fought to gain scars and so enhance his prestige.

Felix looked around for some help. The other bouncers were trying to calm down a brawl between the Kislevites and the halberdiers. Felix could see Gotrek's crest of dyed hair rising above the scrum. No help from that quarter, then.

Felix shrugged. Better make the best of a bad situation, he thought. He looked straight into the duellist's eye.

'Just let the girl be,' he said with exaggerated mildness – then some devil lurking at the back of his mind prompted him to add, 'and I promise not to hurt you.'

'You promise not to hurt us?' The duellist seemed a little confused. Felix could see that he was trying to work out whether this lowly bouncer could possibly be mocking him. The student's friends were starting to gather around, keen to start some trouble.

'I think we should teach this scumbag a lesson, Rupert,' Dieter said. 'I think we should show him he's not as tough as he thinks he is.'

Elissa chose this moment to bite Dieter's hand. He shrieked with pain and cuffed the girl almost casually. Elissa dropped as if pole-axed. 'Bitch took a chunk out of my hand!'

Suddenly Felix had just plain had enough. He had travelled hundreds of leagues, fought against beasts, monsters and men. He had seen the dead rise from their graves and slain evil cultists on Geheimnisnacht. He had killed the city of Nuln's own chief of secret police for being in league with the wretched skaven. He didn't have to take cheek from these spoiled whelps, and he certainly didn't need to watch them beat up an innocent girl.

Felix grabbed Rupert by the lapels and swung his forehead forward, butting the duellist on the nose. There was a sickening crunch and the big youth toppled backward, clutching his face. Felix grabbed Dieter by the throat and slapped him a couple of times just for show, then slammed the student's face into the heavy tabletop. There was another crunch. Steins toppled.

The spectators pushed their chairs backwards to avoid being soaked. Felix kicked Dieter's legs out from under him and then, after he hit the ground, kicked him in the head a couple of times. There was nothing pretty or elegant about it, but Felix was not in the mood to put up with these people any more. Suddenly they sickened him and he was glad of the chance to vent his anger.

As Dieter's friends surged forward, Felix ripped his sword from its scabbard. The razor-sharp blade glittered in the torchlight. The angry students froze as if they had heard the hissing of a deadly serpent.

Suddenly it was all deathly quiet. Felix put the blade down against the side of Dieter's head. 'One more step and I'll take his ear off. Then I'll make the rest of you eat it.'

'He means it,' one of the students muttered, Suddenly they did not look so very threatening any more, just a scared and drunken bunch of young idiots who had bought into much more trouble than they had bargained for. Felix twisted the blade so that it bit into Dieter's ear, drawing blood. The young man groaned and squirmed under Felix's boot.

Rupert whimpered and clutched his nose with one meaty hand. A river of red streamed over his fingers. 'You broke my node,' he said in a tone of piteous accusation. He sounded like he couldn't believe anyone would do anything so horribly cruel.

'One more word out of you and I'll break your fingers too,' Felix said. He hoped nobody tried to work out how he was going to do that. He wasn't quite sure himself, but he needn't have worried. Everybody took him absolutely seriously. 'The rest of you pick your friends up and get out of here, before I really lose my temper.'

He stepped away from Dieter's recumbent form, keeping his blade between himself and the students. They hurried forward, helped their injured friends to their feet, and hurried towards the door. A few kept terrified eyes on Felix as they went.

He walked over to Elissa and helped her to her feet.

'You all right?' he asked.

'Fine enough. Thanks,' she said. She looked up at him gratefully. Not for the first time, Felix noticed how pretty she was. She smiled up at him. Her tight black ringlets framed her round face. Her lips pouted. He reached down and tucked one of her jet-black curls behind her ear.

'Best go and have a word with Heinz. Tell him what happened.'

The girl hurried off.

'You're learning, manling,' the Trollslayer's voice said from behind him.

Felix looked around and was surprised to see Gotrek grinning malevolently up at him. 'I suppose so,' he said, although right at this moment he felt a little shaky. It was time for a drink.

Grey Seer Thanquol perched on the three-legged bone stool in front of the farsqueaker and bit his tail. He was angry, as angry as he could ever remember being. He doubted he had been so angry even on the day he had made his first kill, and then he had been very, very angry indeed. He dug his canines into his tail until the sensation made his pink eyes water. Then he let go. He was sick of inflicting pain on himself. He felt like making someone else suffer.

'Hurry-fast! Scuttle-quick or I will the flesh flay from your most unworthy bones,' he shrieked, lashing out with the whip he carried for just such occasions as this.

The skaven slaves squeaked in dismay and scuttled faster on the lurching treadmill attached to the huge mechanisms of the far-squeaker. As they did so, the powerglobes began to glow slightly. Their flickering light illuminated the long musty chamber. The shadows of the warp engineers of Clan Skryre danced across the walls as they made adjustments to the delicate machine by banging it lightly with sledgehammers. A faint tang of warpstone and ozone became perceptible in the air.

'Quick! Quick! Or I will feed you to the rat-ogres.'

A chance would be a fine thing, Thanquol thought. If only he had a rat-ogre to feed these slaves too. What a disappointment Boneripper had proved to be – that cursed dwarf had slain him as easily as Thanquol would slaughter a blind puppy. Just the thought of that hairless dwarf upstart made Thanquol want to squirt the musk of fear. At the same time, hatred bit at Thanquol's bowels and stayed there, gnawing as fiercely as a newly born runt chomping on a bone.

By the Horned Rat's foetid breath, he wanted revenge on the Trollslayer and his henchman! Not only had they slain Boneripper and cost Thanquol a lot of precious warptokens, they had also killed von Halstadt and thus disrupted the grey seer's master plan for throwing Nuln and the Empire into chaos.

True, Thanquol had other agents on the surface, but none so highly placed or so malleable as the former head of Nuln's secret police. Thanquol wasn't looking forward to reporting the failure of this part of the scheme to his masters back in Skavenblight. In fact, he had put off making his report for as long as he decently could. Now he had no option but to talk to the Seerlord and report how things stood. Warily he looked up at the huge mirror on top of the farsqueaker, as he waited for a vision of his master to take form.

The skaven slaves scuttled faster now. The light in the warpglobes became brighter. Thanquol felt his fur lift and a shiver run down his spine to the tip of his tail as sparks leapt from the globes at either end of the treadmill, flickering upwards towards the huge mirror at the top of the apparatus. One of the warp engineers rushed over to the control panel and wrenched down two massive copper switches. Forked lightning flickered between the warpglobes. The viewing mirror began to glow with a greenish light. Little flywheels began to buzz. Huge pistons rose and fell impressively.

Briefly Thanquol felt a surge of pride at this awesome triumph of skaven engineering, a device which made communication over all the long leagues between Nuln and Skavenblight not only possible but instantaneous.

Truly, no other race could match the inventive genius of the skaven. This machine was just one more proof, if any was needed, of skaven superiority to all other so-called sentient races. The skaven deserved to rule the world – which was doubtless why the Horned Rat had given it into their keeping.

A picture took shape in the mirror. A towering figure glared down at him. Thanquol shivered again, this time with uncontrollable fear. He knew he was looking on the features of one of the Council of Thirteen in distant Skavenblight. In truth, he could not tell which, since the picture was a little fuzzy. Maybe it was not even Seerlord Tisqueek.

Swirls and patterns of interference danced across the mirror's shimmering surface. Perhaps, Thanquol should suggest that the engineers of Clan Skryre make a few adjustments to their device. Now, however, hardly seemed the time.

'What have... to... report... Seer Thanq...' The majestic voice of the council member emerged from the machine's squeaking trumpet as a high-pitched buzzing. Thanquol had to strain to make out the words. With his outstretched paw he snatched up the mouthpiece, carved from human thighbone and connected to the machine by a cable of purest copper. He struggled hard to avoid gabbling his words.

'Great triumphs, lordly one, and some minor setbacks,' Thanquol squeaked. His musk glands felt tight. He fought to keep from baring his teeth nervously.

'Spea... up... Grey... I... hardly hear you... and...'

Thanquol decided there were definitely a few problems with the farsqueaking machine. Many of the Seerlord's words were being lost, and doubtless his superior was only catching a few of Thanquol's own words in return. Perhaps, thought the grey seer, this could be made to work to his advantage. He must consider his options.

'Many triumphs, lordly one, and a few minor setbacks!' Thanquol bellowed as loud as he could. His roaring startled the slaves and they stopped running. As the treadmill slowed, the picture started to flicker and fade. The long tongues of lightning dimmed. 'Faster, you fools! Don't stop!'

Thanquol encouraged the slaves with a flick of his lash. Slowly the picture returned until the dim outline of the gigantic skaven lord was visible once more. A cloud of foul-smelling smoke was starting to emerge from the farsqueaker. It smelled like something within the machine was burning. Two warp engineers stood by with buckets of foul water drawn directly from the nearby sewers.

'...setbacks, Grey ...eer Thanquol?'

If ever there was time for the machine's slight irregularities to prove useful, now was that time, thought Thanquol. 'Yes, master. Many triumphs! Even as we speak our warriors scout beneath the man-city. Soon we will have all information we need for our inevitable triumph!'

'I said... setbacks... Seer Thanquol.'

'It would not wise be to send them back, great one. We need every able-bodied skaven warrior to map the city.'

The councillor leaned forward and fiddled with a knob. The picture flickered and became slightly clearer. Thanquol could now see that the speaker's head was obscured by a great cowl which hid his features. The members of the Council of Thirteen often did that. It made them seem more mysterious and threatening. Thanquol could see that he was turning and saying something to someone just out of sight. The grey seer assumed his superior was berating one of the engineers of Clan Skryre.

'...and how is... agent von Halstadt...'

'Indisposed,' Thanquol replied, a little too hastily for his own liking. Somehow it sounded better than saying he was dead. He decided to change the subject quickly. He knew that he had better do something to save the situation and fast.

No matter how cunningly he stalled his masters on the farsqueaker, he knew that word of Fritz von Halstadt's death would get back to them eventually. Every skaven force was full of spies and snitches. It was only a matter of time before the news of his scheme's failure reached Skavenblight. By then Thanquol knew he had better have some concrete successes to report.

'We have news... change of plans... we send army to Nuln... when ready... ttack city...' The Seerlord's words made Thanquol's ears rise with pleasure. If an army was being dispatched to Nuln, he would command it. Taking the city would increase his status immeasurably.

'Warlord Vermek Skab will command... render him all... sible assistance...'

Thanquol bared his teeth with disappointment. He was being replaced in command of this army. He sniffed as he considered the matter. Maybe not. Vermek Skab might have an accident. Then Grey Seer Thanquol could rise majestically to claim his full and rightful share of the glory!

Thanquol's nose twitched. The billowing cloud of smoke from the machine almost filled the chamber now, and Thanquol was pretty sure that the device was not supposed to be emitting great showers of sparks like that. The fact that two of the warp engineers were running for the door wasn't a good sign either. He considered following them.

'I have foreseen the presence... ill-omened elements in your future, Than... I predict disaster for you unless... do something about them.'

Suddenly Thanquol was rooted to the spot, torn between his desire to flee and his desire to hear more. He almost squirted the musk of fear. If the seerlord prophesied something then it had almost as good as happened. Unless, of course, his superior was lying to him for purposes of his own. That happened all too often, as Thanquol knew only too well.

'Disaster, lordly one?'

'Yes... see a dwarf and a human... destinies are intertwined with yours... you do not slay them then...'

There was a very loud and final bang. Thanquol threw himself off his stool and cowered on the floor. An acrid taste filled his mouth. Slowly the smoke cleared and he saw the fused and melted remains of the farsqueaking machine. Several dead skavenslaves lay in its midst, their fur all charred and their whiskers burned away. In one corner a warp engineer lay curled up in a ball, mewling and writhing in a state of shock. Thanquol was unconcerned about their fate. The Seerlord's words filled him with a great fear. He wished he had been able to speak with his superior a little longer, but alas, he had not that option. He raised his little bronze bell and tinkled it.

Slowly members of his bodyguard entered the chamber. Clawleader Gazat looked almost disappointed to see him alive, Thanquol thought. Briefly the idea that the warrior might have sabotaged the farsqueaker crossed Thanquol's mind. He dismissed it – Gazat did not have the imagination. Anyway, the Grey Seer had more important things to worry about.

'Summon the gutter runners!' Thanquol squeaked in his most authoritative tone. 'I have work for them.'

For a moment silence fell over the chamber. A foul smell made Thanquol's whiskers twitch. Just the mere mention of the dreaded assassins of Clan Eshin had caused Clawleader Gazat to squirt the musk of fear.

'Quick! Quick!' Thanquol added.

'Instantly, master,' Gazat said sadly and scuttled off into the labyrinth of sewers.

Thanquol rubbed his paws in glee. The gutter runners would not fail, of that he was assured.

Felix unlocked the door of his chamber and entered his room. He yawned widely. He wanted for nothing more than to lie down on his pallet and sleep. He had been working for more than twelve hours. He put the lantern down beside the straw-filled mattress and unlaced his jerkin. He tried to give his surroundings as little attention as was possible, but it was difficult to ignore the loud moans of passion coming from the next room and the singing of the drinkers downstairs.

The chamber wasn't good enough for paying guests, but it suited him well enough. He had occupied better, but this one had the great virtue of being free. It came with the job. Like a minority of old Heinz's staff, Felix chose to live on the premises.

Felix's little pile of possessions stood in one corner, under the barred window. There was his chainmail jerkin and a little rucksack which contained a few odds and ends such as his fire-making kit.

Felix threw himself down on the bed and pulled his old, tattered woollen cloak over himself. He made sure his sword was within easy reach. His hard life on the road had made him wary even in seemingly safe places, and the thought that the skaven they had recently encountered might still be about filled him with dread.

He recalled only too well the huge corpse of the slain rat-ogre lying at the foot of the stairs in von Halstadt's mansion. It had not been a reassuring sight. Somehow he was unsurprised that he had heard nothing at all about the fire at von Halstadt's mansion. Perhaps the authorities had not found the skaven bodies, or perhaps there was a cover-up. Right now, Felix didn't even want to consider it.

Felix wondered how men could ignore the tales of the skaven. Even as a student he had come across scholarly tomes proving that they didn't exist, or that if they had ever existed they were now extinct. He had come across a few references to them in connection with the Great Plague of 1111 and of course the Emperor of that period was known as Mandred Skavenslayer. Yet that was all. There were innumerable books written about elves and dwarfs and orcs, yet knowledge of the rat-men was rare. He could almost have suspected an organised conspiracy to cloak them in secrecy but that thought was too disturbing, so he pushed it aside.

There was a soft knock at the door. Felix lay still and tried to ignore it. Probably just one of the drunken patrons lost and looking for his room again, he told himself.

The knock came again, more urgently and insistently this time. Felix rose from the bed and snatched up his sword.

A man could never be too careful in these dark times. Perhaps some bravo lurked out there, and thought a sleep-fuddled Felix would prove easy prey. Only two months ago Heinz had found a murdered couple lying on bloodstained sheets a mere three doors away. The man had been a prominent wine merchant, the girl his teenage mistress. Heinz suspected that the merchant had been slain by assassins on order of his harridan of a wife, but claimed also that it was none of his business. Felix had got his new tunic all covered in blood when he dumped the bodies in the river. He hadn't been too thrilled about having to use the secret route through the sewers either.

The knocking came a third time, and he heard a woman's voice whisper, 'Felix.'

Felix eased his blade from its scabbard. Just because he heard a girl's voice didn't mean that there was only a girl waiting for him out there. She might have brought a few burly friends who would set about him as soon as he opened the door.

Briefly he considered not opening the door at all, of simply waiting until the girl and her friends tried to batter the door down then he realised quite how paranoid he had become. He shrugged. Since the deaths of Hef and Spider and the rest of the sewer watch he had every reason to be paranoid. Still, was he going to wait here all night? He slipped the bolts and opened the door. Elissa was waiting there.

She looked up at him nervously, brushing a curl from her forehead. She was very short but really very pretty indeed, Felix decided.

'I... I wanted to thank you for helping me earlier,' she said eventually.

Felix thought that it was a bit late for that. Couldn't she have waited until the morning? Slowly, though, realisation dawned on him. 'It was nothing,' he muttered, feeling his face flush.

Elissa glanced quickly left and right down the corridor. 'Aren't you going to invite me in, I wanted to thank you properly.'

She had to stand on her tiptoes to kiss his lips. He stood there dumbfounded for a second then pulled her into the room and slammed the door, slipping the lock into place.

As his henchling Queg reached twelve in his muttered count, Chang Squik of Clan Eshin twitched his nose and sampled the smells of the night.

Strange, he thought; so like the stinks of the man-cities of Far Cathay and yet so unlike. Here he could smell beef and turnip and roast pig. In the east it would have been pickled cabbage and rice and chicken. The food smelled different but everything else was the same. There was the same scent of overflowing sewers, of many humans living in close proximity, of incense and perfume.

He opened his ears as his master had trained him as well. He heard temple bells tolling and the rattle of carriage wheels on cobbles. He heard the singing of drunks and the call of the night watchmen as they shouted the hour. It did not trouble him. He could not be distracted. He could, if he so wished, tune out all extraneous sound and pick out one voice in a crowd.

The skaven squinted out into the darkness. His night-vision was keen. Down there were the shadowy shapes of men and women leaving the taverns arm in arm, heading for brief liaisons in back alleys and squalid rooming houses. Chang did not care about them at all. His two targets were in the building that humans called a tavern.

He did not know why the honourable grey seer had selected these two, out of all the inferior souls in this city, for inevitable death. He merely knew it was his task to ease the passing of their souls into the maw of the Horned Rat. He had already offered up two sticks of narcotic incense and pledged their immortal essence for his Dark God's feast. He could almost, but not quite, feel sorry for the doomed ones.

They were there in that tavern, under the sign of the Blind Pig, and they did not know that certain doom approached. Nor would they, for Chang Squik had trained for years in the delivery of silent death. Long before he had left the warm jungles of his eastern homeland to serve the Council of Thirteen in these cold western climes, he had been schooled to perfection in his clan's ancient art of stealthy assassination. While still a runt, he had been made to run bare-pawed through beds of white hot coals, and snatch coins from the bowls of blind beggars in human cities. Even at that early age he had learned that the beggars were often far from blind, and often viciously proficient in the martial arts.

By the time of his initiation he had become proficient in all forms of unarmed combat. He was a third degree adept in the way of the Crimson Talon and held a black belt in the Path of the Deadly Paw. He had spent twelve long months being trained in silent infiltration in the jungles, and a month in fasting and meditation high atop Mount Yellowfang with only his own droppings for food.

Since that time he had killed and killed again in the name of the Council of Thirteen. He had slain Lord Khijaw of Clan Gulcher when that mighty warlord had plotted the downfall of Throt the Unclean. He had served as personal assistant to Snikch when the great assassin had killed Frederick Hasselhoffen and his entire household, and he had been rewarded with one-on-one instruction by the Deathmaster himself.

Chang Quik's list of triumphs was long, and tonight he would add another to it. It was his task to slay the dwarf, Gotrek Gurnisson, and his human henchling, Felix Jaeger. He did not see how he could fail.

What chance had a one-eyed dwarf and his stupid human friend against a mighty skaven trained in every art of death-dealing? Chang Squik felt confident that he could take the pair himself. He had been almost insulted by Grey Seer Thanquol's insistence that he take his full pack of gutter runners.

Surely the dire rumours of this dwarf were exaggerated. The Trollslayer could not possibly have slaughtered a unit of stormvermin single-handed. And it seemed well nigh unbelievable that he could have slain the rat-ogre, Boneripper, without the aid of an entire company of mercenaries. And, of course, it was impossible that this could be the same dwarf who five years ago had slain Warlord Makrik of Clan Gowjyer at the Battle of the Third Door.

Chang exhaled in one long controlled breath. Perhaps the grey seer was right. He had often proved to be so in the past. It was simple prudence to assign the task of slaying the dwarf to Slitha. Chang would slay the human, and if there were any difficulties he would race to the assistance of his henchling's squad. Not that there would be any difficulties.

Queg stopped counting at one hundred and tapped his superior on the arm. Chang lashed his tail once to show that he understood. Slitha and his team, with the clockwork precision which characterised all skaven operations, would be in position at the secret entrance to the tavern by now. It was time to proceed.

He loosened his swords in their scabbards, checked to make sure that his blowpipe and throwing stars were ready at paw, and whistled the signal to advance.

Like a dark wave, the pack of gutter runners surged forward over the rooftop. Their blackened weapons were visible only as shadowy outlines in the moons' light. Not a weapon clinked. Not an outline was visible. Well, almost.

Heinz made his last rounds of the night, checking the doors and windows of the lower floor to make sure they were securely barred. It was amazing how often thieves tried to break in to the Blind Pig and steal from its cellars. Not even the reputation for ferocity of Heinz's bouncers could keep the desperately poor and alcoholic denizens of the New Quarter from making the attempt. It was quite pathetic really.

He made his way down into the cellars, shining his light into the dark corners between the great ale barrels, and wine racks. He could have sworn he heard a strange scuttling noise down here.

Just his imagination, he told himself.

He was getting old, starting to hear things. Even so, he went over and checked the secret door that led down into the sewers. It was hard to tell in this light but it looked undisturbed. He doubted anybody had used it since he and Felix had dumped those bodies two months back and saved everybody quite a scandal. Yes, he was just getting old, that was all.

He turned and limped back to the stairwell. His bad leg was playing up tonight. It always did when there was going to be rain. Heinz smiled grimly, remembering how he'd got the old war wound. It had been stamped on by a Bretonnian charger at the Battle of Red Orc Pass. Clean break. He remembered lying there in the bloody dirt and thinking it was probably a just payback for spiking the horse's owner on his halberd. That had been a bad time, one of the worst he had faced in all his years of soldiering. He'd learned a lot about pain that day. Still there had been good times as well as bad during his career as a mercenary, he was forced to admit that.

There were occasions when Heinz wondered whether he had made the right decision, giving up the free-spirited life of the mercenary companies for the life of a tavern keeper. On nights like this he missed the camaraderie of his old unit, the drinking round the campfires, the swapping of stories and recounting of tales of heroism.

Heinz had spent ten years as a halberdier, and had seen service on half the battlefields of the Empire, first as a lowly trooper and later as a sergeant. He had risen to captain during Emperor Karl Franz's campaigns against the orc hordes in the east. During the last Bretonnian scrap he had made enough in plunder to buy the Blind Pig. He had finally given in to old Lotte's promptings to settle down and make a life for the two of them. His old comrades had laughed when he had actually married a camp follower. They had insisted she would run off with all his money. Instead the two of them had been blissfully happy for five years before old Lotte had to spoil it all by going and dying of the Wasting Sickness. He still missed her. He wondered if there was anything to stay here in Nuln for now. His family were all dead. Lotte was gone.

As he reached the head of the stair, Heinz thought he heard the scuttling sound again. There was definitely something moving down there.

Briefly he considered calling Gotrek or some of the other lads, and getting them to investigate, then he spread his huge hands wide in a gesture of disgust. He really was getting old if he would let the noise of some rats scrabbling round in his cellar upset him. He could just imagine what the others would say if he told them he was scared to go down there himself. They would laugh like drains.

He drew the thick cosh from his waistband and turned to go back down. Now he really was uneasy. He would never have drawn the weapon normally. He was too calm and easy tempered. Something definitely did have him spooked.

His old soldier's instincts were aroused, and they had saved him on more than one occasion.

He could still remember that night along the Kislevite border when he had somehow been unable to get to sleep, filled with a terrible sense of foreboding. He had risen from his bed and gone to replace the sentry, only to find the man dead at his post. He had only just roused the camp before the foul beastmen attacked. He had a similar feeling in the pit of his stomach now. He hesitated at the top of the stair.

Best go get Gotrek, he thought. Only the real hardcore drinkers were still in the tavern by now. The rest were asleep, under the tables, in the alcoves, in the private rooms, or else gone home.

There it was again, that skittering sound, like the soft scrabble of padded claws on the stone stairs. Heinz was definitely worried now. He pulled the door closed and turned, almost running down the corridor until he came out in the main bar area. A handful of the bouncers chattered idly with a few of the barmaids.

'Where's Gotrek?' Heinz asked. A burly lad, Helmut, jerked his thumb in the direction of the privies.

Slitha reached the head of the staircase and flung the door open. So far, so good. All was going like a typically well-oiled Clan Skryre machine. Everything according to plan. They had entered the tavern undetected; now it was simply a case of searching the place until they came upon the dwarf and killed him. And furthermore killed anything else that got in their way, of course.

Slitha felt a little irritated. It was typical of his superior to take the easy task. They had already found out where the human Jaeger slept, and their leader had taken the task of killing him for himself. Surely that was the only explanation. It could not be that the great Chang Squik was afraid of an encounter with the Trollslayer. Not that Slitha cared. When he dispatched the feared dwarf it would simply reflect all the more to his credit. He gestured for his fellows to go in first.

'Quick! Quick!' he chittered. 'All night we haven't got!' The gutter runners moved quickly into the corridor.

Felix and Elissa lay on his palette, kissing deeply, when suddenly Felix shifted uneasily. He thought he heard the faintest of scrabbling sounds from outside the window.

He gently untangled Elissa's arms from around him, and was suddenly aware of the area of heat and sweat where their bodies met. He looked down on the serving girl's face. Her face was a little puffed on the left side from where the student had hit her but she really was very pretty.

'What is it?' she asked, looking up at him with wide, trusting eyes. He listened for a moment and heard nothing.

'Nothing,' he said, and began kissing her again.

Slitha bounded down the corridor. He smelled dwarf. He followed the scent, whistling commands to his fellows in the fore. Surprised by skaven stealth, speed and savagery, their weak foe would swiftly be dragged down. What chance would a mere dwarf have against the deadliest warriors of the master race? Slitha almost felt sorry that he was in the rear, the traditional position of honour any skaven leader adopted whenever possible. He would have liked a chance to be the first to sink his blade into the dwarf and offer up his soul to the Horned Rat.

They reached the end of the corridor. The stench of dwarf intensified. He must be very close now. Slitha's heart rate accelerated dramatically. Blood raced through his veins. His tail stiffened and lashed. The claws in his feet extruded instinctively. As he made ready for combat, he bared his fangs in a snarl. The scent was very strong: they must be almost on top of the Trollslayer. His warriors lashed their tails proudly, ready to overwhelm their opponent with their numbers and savagery.

Suddenly a red mist filled Slitha's eyes. It looked as if a huge axe had cut Klisqueek in half, but that could not be. They could not have been detected. It was impossible that a mere dwarf would have the cunning to ambush a pack of skaven gutter runners.

Yet suddenly Hrishak was squeaking in pain and terror. A huge fist had caught him by the throat. The butt of a monstrous axe cracked his skull. The thick, cloying scent of the musk of fear filled the air now. Klisqueek's body had already started to dissolve into a puddle of black slime, as the Clan Eshin decomposition spells took effect.

Slitha looked out into a swirling melee where half a dozen of his finest gutter runners were attempting to swarm over a massive dwarfish form. His pale hairless flesh was emphasised by the black of the skaven's cloaks. Slitha saw the huge axe swing around in a deadly arc. He heard bones crunch and brains splatter.

'Try and sneak up on me, would you,' muttered the dwarf in

Reikspiel. He added a guttural curse in Dwarfish as he clove a path of red ruin through the skaven assassins. The dwarf bellowed and chanted a strange war-cry as he fought.

Slitha shuddered. The noise was enough to awaken the dead, or at least any sleeping human guards. He felt the advantage of stealth and surprise slipping away. His eyes widened with terror as he watched the dwarf complete his bloody work, cutting down Snikkit and Blodge with one stroke. Suddenly Slitha realised that he was alone, facing one very angry and very dangerous dwarf.

It was impossible to believe, but the dwarf had killed most of his brethren in a matter of seconds. Nothing in all the world, not even an assassin of Clan Eshin, could conceivably be so deadly. Slitha turned to flee but a hob-nailed boot descended on his tail, pinning him in place. Tears of pain filled Slitha's eyes. The musk of fear voided from his glands.

The last thing he heard was the whoosh of a huge axe coming closer.

Despite himself, Felix untangled himself from Elissa again and looked around. What was that noise? It sounded like fighting downstairs. He was sure he could recognise Gotrek's deep-throated battle-cry. The girl was looking up at him, puzzled, wondering why he had stopped kissing her. She opened her mouth to speak. Felix placed a hand gently over her lips. He leaned forward until his mouth was over her ear.

'Be very quiet,' he whispered. A cold trickle of fear ran through him. He could definitely hear a strange scrabbling sound coming from over by the window. Felix lifted himself off the recumbent girl and reached for his dragon-hilted sword. He slipped backwards off the straw pallet and fell into a half crouch.

Placing one finger against his lips to indicate she should be quiet, he gestured for the woman to get up off the bed. She stared at him uncertainly, then followed his gaze over to the window.

That was when she screamed.

Chang Squik watched as Noi swung down on the rope. He felt almost proud of his pupil. Noi had fixed the grapnel in the guttering perfectly, then abseiled down the side of the tavern like a great spider. He had sprayed the metal bars covering the window with acid, then filed through the weakened iron like a master burglar. He reached up and gestured to the rest of the squad on the tavern roof. They fixed their ropes in position and made ready to follow Noi. Chang would be last in, as befitted the glorious strike leader. Noi kicked himself back from the wall, swinging out into space, gaining momentum to crash through the window.

The window caved in and a black-clad skaven crashed through it. It hit the floor rolling and emerged into a fighting crouch, tail lashing, a long curved blade glinting evilly in each claw. Felix didn't wait for it to get time to orientate itself. He lashed forward with his own blade, almost catching the thing by surprise. Sparks flashed as the creature parried, deflecting Felix's blade so that it only seared along its cheek.

'Run, Elissa!' Felix shouted. 'Get out!'

For a moment, he thought the girl was too shocked to move. She lay on the straw pallet, her eyes wide with horror, then suddenly she sprang up. The distraction almost killed Felix. The moment he took to look at her was a moment he did not look at his opponent. Only the deadly whine of the skaven's blade as it darted towards his skull warned him. He ducked his head, and the sword passed over him, coming close enough to shave a lock off his hair. Felix lashed back instinctively. The skaven sprang away.

'Felix!' Elissa shouted.

'Run! Get help!' Over the skaven's shoulder, he could see other feral forms crowding round the window. They seemed to be struggling to force a way in, each getting in the other's way. The window was packed with mangy, scarred skaven faces. Things did not look good.

'Die! Die! Foolish man-thing,' the skaven chittered, bounding forward. It feinted a stroke with its right blade, then lashed out with its left. Felix caught its hand just above the wrist and immobilised it. The thing's tail snaked obscenely round his leg and tried to trip him. Felix brought the pommel of his sword down behind the skaven's ear. It fell forward, but even as it did so it struck with its blade, forcing Felix to jump away. He bounded back across the room and skewered the skaven as it started to rise. Blood frothed from the foul thing's lips as it died. A strange reeking stink filled the air. The skaven's flesh started to bubble and rot.

Felix heard Elissa throw the door bolts. He risked a glance at her. She had turned and was looking at him in a mixture of horror and confusion, as if she did not know whether to leave him or to stay.

'Go!' he shouted. 'Get help. There's nothing you can do here.'

She vanished through the doorway, leaving Felix feeling obscurely relieved. At least now he wasn't responsible for her safety. As he turned to look back he saw that the skaven he had killed was gone.

It had left behind only a pool of black slime and its rotting clothing. Felix wondered what deadly sorcery was at work.

A hiss of displaced air warned him of another threat. From the corner of his eye, he caught sight of several glittering objects hurtling towards him. He dived forward, aiming for the bed, hoping it would break his fall. His mouth filled with straw from the mattress as he landed. He fumbled with his left hand for his old red cloak and pulled its wadded mass up in his left fist. He was just in time. More shining objects spun through the air towards him. He brought the cloak up and they impacted in the roll of thick wool. Something sharp penetrated the cloth just between his fingers. Felix looked down. He saw a throwing star, smeared with some foul reddish substance, doubtless poison.

Two more skaven had extricated themselves from the mass outside the window and dropped into the room. They scuttled towards him with eye-blinding speed, evil shadows of man-sized rats, their yellow fangs glistening in the lantern-light. He knew better now than to even glance at the doorway. There was no way he could reach it without taking a blade in his back.

Why me, he asked himself? Why am I standing here half-naked and alone, facing a pack of skaven assassins? Why do these things always happen to me? This sort of thing never happened to Sigmar in the legends!

He threw the cloak over the head of the oncoming skaven. It writhed in the tangle of woollen folds. Felix ran his blade through it. His razor-sharp sword cut through flesh like butter. Black blood soiled the garment. Felix struggled to pull the blade free. The second rat-thing took advantage of his preoccupation and sprang forward, both blades held high, swinging downwards like butcher's cleavers. Felix threw himself backwards; the blade came free with an awful sucking sound. He landed flat on his back, his sword clutched in his hand. He raised its point and the flying skaven impaled itself on it. As it fell, its weight pulled the blade free from Felix's grasp.

Damn, he thought, rising to his feet. Weaponless. The point of his blade was visible, protruding from the skaven's back. He was reluctant to touch the foul beast with his naked flesh but he had no choice if he wanted the blade. His cloak was already starting to flatten as the skaven decomposed with terrifying rapidity.

Too late! More skaven leapt in through the window. There was no time for any qualms. He picked up the skaven sword and charged. The sheer fury of his rush took the skaven by surprise. He cleaved one's skull before it could react and disembowelled another with his return stroke. It fell, trying to hold in its ropy guts with one claw, even as it attempted to strike Felix with the other.

Felix hacked at it again, severing the limb. He cut around him in blind fury, feeling the terrible shock of impact run up his arm from every blow. Slowly, though, more and more skaven pressed into the room, and remorselessly, defending himself as best he could every step of the way, he was pressed back towards the wall.

Heinz looked up in surprise as Gotrek stomped into the bar. In one hand he held his blood-smeared axe. His other huge fist clutched a dead skaven by the scruff of the neck. The thing was decomposing at a frightening rate, seemingly undergoing weeks of decomposition in moments. Gotrek glared around at the surprised bouncers with his one good eye and dropped the body. It squelched and formed a puddle at his feet.

'Bloody skaven,' he muttered. 'Whole bunch of them lurking just outside the privy. Too stupid to know dwarfs have good ears.'

Heinz moved over to stand by the Trollslayer. He looked down at the pool of rot with a peculiar mixture of fascination and distaste written on his features.

'That's a skaven alright.'

Gotrek looked up at him in surprise. 'Of course it was a bloody skaven! I've killed enough of them in my time to know what they look like by now.'

Heinz shrugged apologetically. Then he swivelled on his heels as a scream emerged from the top of the stairwell. Heinz looked up in surprise at the partially clad form of Elissa appearing at the head of the stairs. The girl looked pale with terror.

'Felix!' she shouted.

'What has Felix done, girl?' he asked soothingly. She threw herself at him. He enfolded her shivering form with his brawny arms.

'No. They're trying to kill him. Monsters are trying to kill Felix. They're in his room!'

'Has that girl been taking weirdroot?' a bouncer asked placidly.

Heinz looked over at Gotrek and the rest of the bouncers. All his earlier forebodings returned. He remembered the scrabbling in the cellars. He could see that the dwarf was having the same thought as he was.

'What are we doing standing here?' Heinz roared. 'Follow me, lads!'

This was better. This was more like the old days.

* * *

Felix knew that he was doomed. There was no way he could fight all these skaven. There were too many of them and they were too fast. If he had been wearing his chainmail shirt perhaps he would have some chance of surviving all those stabbing blades. But he wasn't.

His foes sensed victory and advanced. Felix danced in the centre of a whirlwind of stabbing blades. Somehow he managed to survive with only a few nicks and scratches. He found himself standing beside his bed. Thinking quickly, he kicked the lantern over. Oil spilled out onto the straw and lit it. In an instant, a wall of flame separated him from the rat-men. He reached out and grabbed the nearest one, hurling it into the flames. The skaven shrieked in agony as its fur caught fire. It began to roll around on the floor, howling and squeaking. Its fellows leapt back to avoid its blazing form.

Felix knew he had bought himself only a moment's breathing space. He knew now there was only one chance. Doing what the skaven least expected, he dived directly through the flames. Heat scorched his flesh. He smelled the stink of his own singed hair. He saw a gap in the skaven line near the door and dived through it, almost slamming into the corridor wall. Heart pounding, breath rasping in his lungs, blood pouring from a dozen nicks, he raced for the head of the stairs, as if all the hounds of Chaos were at his heels.

A head poked out from the room next door. He recognised the bald pate and lambchop whiskers of Baron Josef Mann, one of the Blind Pig's most dedicated customers.

'What the hell is going on out there?' the old nobleman shouted. 'Sounds like you're performing unnatural acts with animals.'

'Something like that,' Felix retorted as he sprinted past. The old man saw what was following him. His eyes went wide. He clutched his chest and fell.

Chang Squik glanced out round the doorway and gnawed the tip of his tail in frustration. It was all going wrong. It had all started going wrong from the moment that fool Noi had swung in through the window. In their enthusiasm to be part of the kill, the rest of the pack had all tried to get in behind him at once, all eager to claim their share of the glory. Of course their lines had become entangled, and they had all ended up clutching the window sill and each other and frantically trying to scuttle into the room. Several of the idiots had fallen to their deaths on the hard ground below. Serves the fools right too.

It was ever the fate of great skaven captains to be let down by incompetent underlings, he thought philosophically. Not even the most brilliant plan could survive being executed by witless cretins. It was starting to look like his entire command consisted of those. They could not even kill a single feeble manling, even with all the advantages of surprise, numbers and superior skaven armament. It made him want to spit with frustration. Personally he suspected treachery. Perhaps rivals in the clan had sent him a bunch of ill-trained louts in order to discredit him. All in all, that seemed the most likely explanation.

Briefly Chang considered taking a hand in the fray himself, but only briefly. It was glaringly obvious to his superior intellect what was going to happen next. The entire tavern would be roused and his underlings would soon encounter stiff, and very likely fatal, resistance.

Let them get on with it, Chang thought. They deserve whatever fate befalls them.

He slid back into the room, petulantly threw some of the manling's clothing on the fire to add to the blaze, and then leapt out the window. He caught the climbing line easily in one hand and swarmed up the side of the building to safety.

Already he was considering what would be the best way to report this minor setback to Grey Seer Thanquol.

Heinz grunted as something slammed into him. He almost toppled backwards as the weight hit him.

'Sorry,' said a polite voice that Heinz recognised as belonging to Felix Jaeger. 'I was having a little trouble back there.'

Throwing stars whizzed past Heinz's ear. The smell of burning filled his nostrils. He looked down a corridor crowded with scurrying rat-men. A cold fury filled him. Those cursed skaven were trying to burn down the Blind Pig and rob him of his livelihood! He pulled out his cosh and made to rush forward. He need not have bothered. Gotrek pushed him to one side and charged headlong into the throng. The rest of the bouncers advanced cautiously behind him. From the far end of the corridor, various nobles and their bodyguards emerged and slammed into the skaven from the rear. Terrible carnage began.

It was all over very soon.

Felix sat in front of the fire, wrapped in a blanket and shivering. He looked across at Elissa. The girl smiled back at him wanly. All around, the bouncers hurried upstairs with buckets of water, making sure that the fire did not spread from Felix's room.

'I thought you were very brave,' Elissa said. There was a look of complete doting admiration in her eye. 'Just like a hero in one of those Detlef Sierck dramas.'

Felix shrugged. He was tired. He was riddled with dozens of cuts and bruises. And he knew now that the skaven were definitely trying to kill him. He didn't feel very heroic. Still, he thought, things could be worse. He reached out and put an arm around Elissa's shoulder and drew her to him. She snuggled in close.

'Thank you,' he said, and for a moment the girl's smile made everything feel more worthwhile.

NIGHT RAID

'It is a frightening thing to be sought by enemies
unknown, invisible and untraceable, who can strike
at you when they will without fear of vengeance
or punishment. At least, I found it to be so. If my
companion shared these feelings, he never gave any
sign of it to me. Indeed he seemed rather to enjoy
the situation – which I suppose was natural enough,
given that his avowed purpose in life was to seek a
violent death. Yet I was worried. The attack on the
alehouse had left me shaken, and the knowledge
that somewhere out in the night an implacable foe
was lurking did nothing to calm my fraught nerves.
But it seemed that we had allies as well, who were
determined to aid us for their own unfathomable
purposes.'

— From *My Travels With Gotrek, Vol. III,* by Herr Felix Jaeger
(Altdorf Press, 2505)

'What are you doing there, young Felix?' A shadow fell on Felix Jaeger. Startled, he reached for the hilt of his sword. The book fell from his lap, almost landing in the fire, as he started to rise from the overstuffed leather armchair. Looking up he saw that it was only old Heinz, the owner of the Blind Pig tavern, standing over him, polishing a tankard that he held in one huge, meaty fist. Felix let out a long sigh, suddenly all too aware of how tightly wound he was. He sank back into the chair, forcing his hand to release its tight grip on the weapon hilt.

'You're a little tense this evening,' Heinz said plainly.

'A little,' Felix agreed. A quick glance around told him that the old ex-mercenary wasn't going to hassle him to start working. His services as a bouncer were not needed just yet. It was early evening and few patrons were about. Normally the tavern didn't really start jumping until well after dark. On the other hand, for the first time, Felix noticed that the Pig was much quieter than usual. Custom had definitely dropped off since last week's skaven attack, an event which had not improved the Blind Pig's already dire reputation.

Felix reached down and picked up his book, a cheap printed manuscript of one of Detlef Sierck's more melodramatic plays. It had served the purpose of distracting his thoughts from the fact that the rat-men were apparently out to get him.

'It will be a quiet night tonight, Felix,' Heinz said.

'You think?'

'I know.' Heinz held the tankard up to the light, making sure he had removed every last speck of dust from the thing. He set it down on the mantelpiece. Felix noticed the way the light gleamed on the old mercenary's bald head. Felix sighed and laid his book down on the chair arm. Heinz was a sociable sort and he just naturally liked to chat. Besides, maybe Heinz was just as nervous as himself. The tavern keeper had every reason to be. He had almost lost his livelihood to ferocious Chaos-worshipping monsters. It was only in the last few days that all the damage the rat-men had done had been repaired.

'Business has been bad since the skaven attack,' Felix said.

'Business will pick up again. Same thing happened after that murder a couple of months back. The nobs will stay away for a bit but then they'll come back. They like a sense of danger when they drink. It's what they come here for. But we'll see nobody this evening, if I'm not mistaken.'

'Why's that?'

'The Feast of Verena. It's a special night here in Nuln. Most folk will be at home, praying and fasting, making sure everything's spic and span. She's the patron of this city, as well as of you bookish folk, and this is her special night.'

'There has to be someone wanting a drink.'

'The only folk that will be having any fun are the Guild of Mechanics and their apprentices. Verena's their patron too. The countess has a big feast for them tonight in her palace. Nothing but the best for them.'

'Why does the countess feel compelled to give a feast for commoners?' Felix was curious. Countess Emmanuelle was not famed for her generosity. 'She's not normally so fond of us.'

Heinz laughed. 'Aye, but these are special commoners. They run her new College of Engineering for her. They're making steam tanks and organ guns and all sorts of other special weapons for her forces, same as the Imperial College does for the Emperor. She can afford to give them a nice dinner once a year if it keeps them happy.'

'I'll wager she can.'

'I thought maybe you might like to take the night off and be with Elissa. I know it's her day off. I did notice you've been seeing a lot of each other recently.'

Felix looked up. 'You disapprove?'

'Nothing wrong with a man and a maid being together, I always say. Just making an observation.'

'She's gone back to her village for the day. One of her relatives is sick. She should be back tomorrow.'

'Sorry to hear that. There's a lot of sickness about. Folk are starting to mutter about the plague. Well, I'll let you get back to your book then.'

Felix opened the book once more but didn't turn the page. He was amazed that Heinz could be so sanguine just a few days after the attack. Felix was jumping at shadows, but he was happily polishing his tankards. Maybe all those years of being a mercenary had given the old warrior nerves of steel. Felix wished he had them too. Right now he could not help but wonder what the skaven were up to. He was sure it was nothing good.

Grey Seer Thanquol leaned against the huge bulk of the Screaming Bell. He gazed malevolently around the vast chamber and out at the teeming sea of ratty skaven faces. All around him Thanquol sensed the surge of activity, smelled the packed mass of the assembling skaven troops in the surrounding tunnels. All the warriors of Clan Skab were here, reinforced by contingents from all the great and powerful factions in skavendom. It was good to be away from the sewers, to be back here in the Underways, the subterranean highways linking all the cities of the Under-Empire. It was good – but right now he could take no pleasure from it. He was too angry.

He fought the feeling, reminding himself that somewhere, far over-head, the humans went about their business, ploughing their fields, chopping their forests, unsuspecting, not knowing their days of dominance were nearly done, that soon their city and then their Empire would fall beneath the iron paw of skaven military genius. Not even these thoughts cheered him up or helped dispel his rage.

He ran a talon over the bell, drawing forth a slight ringing tone, still seeking to control his anger. The bell swung slightly at the grey seer's touch, and the carriage on which the ancient artefact sat groaned as it moved. The seething magical energies within the bell comforted Thanquol a little. Soon, he told himself, he would unleash these enormous forces against his enemies. Very soon, he hoped, but right now he was filled with a terrible, all-consuming rage and he needed to find someone to vent it upon.

Chang Squik grovelled in the dirt before him, waiting for the grey seer to decide his fate. It had taken nearly a week for Thanquol to locate him. The would-be assassin sprawled face down in the shadow of the great bell. His tail lay flat. His whiskers drooped despondently. The leader of the gutter runners continued to mutter pathetic excuses about how he had been betrayed, about how the targets had been warned of his otherwise irresistible attack, of how they had used vile sorcery to slay his warriors – above all, about how it had not been his fault. Near the assassin stood Thanquol's lieutenants, hiding their mouths with their paws to cover the sound of their mirth.

Thousands of faces peered up at Thanquol, eager to know what he would do next. It was not often that they got to see one of the mighty abase himself. Thanquol let his glance rest on each of the warleaders. They squirmed under his inspection. Their tittering stopped. None of them wanted to be the focus of his anger – which was unfortunate for them, because one of them was going to be.

The grey seer looked at the representatives of Clan Moulder, Clan Eshin, Clan Skryre and Clan Pestilens. All of them were his to order about, at least until his replacement, Warlord Vermek Skab, arrived. And that was not going to happen. Thanquol had prepared a little surprise for the warlord. Skab would never reach this place alive. The thought made his tail rigid. And yet...

Yet, despite all this power under his control, he could not get this one dwarf killed.

Anger and fear bit at the base of his stomach. Gotrek Gurnisson and his worthless human henchman were still alive. It beggared belief! How could this be?

It was almost as if he, the great Thanquol, was under a curse. He shuddered at the very thought. Surely the Horned Rat would not withdraw his favour from one of his chosen? No, he told himself sternly, that was not the real reason why the dwarf was still alive. The real reason was the worthlessness of his underlings.

Thanquol bared his fangs and allowed his rage to show. The accursed gutter runners had failed him. By their sheer incompetence, they had let the dwarf and the manling escape. Thanquol had a good mind to have Chang Squik hung up by his tail and flayed alive. Only his fear of possible reprisals by Clan Eshin kept him from ordering his bodyguards to seize the gutter runner.

Rumour had it that Squik was a favoured pupil of Deathmaster Snikch himself. That being the case, such straightforward vengeance was out of the question. But, Thanquol thought, there was more than one way to skin a rat. Someday he would make Chang Squik pay for this monstrous failure. Thanquol's problem right now, however, was to find a way to safely vent the killing rage that was on him, without making powerful enemies in the process. He lashed his tail in frustration.

Thanquol glared at Izak Grottle. The monstrously obese skaven lounged on a palanquin born by rat-ogres. The Clan Moulder packmaster had arrived this very morning, keen to take part in the triumph that was sure to follow this great offensive. He and his retinue had scuttled along the Underways from the skaven secret base at Night Crag in the Grey Mountains.

Grottle tried to hold Thanquol's burning gaze but could not. He looked away and ran a paw over the largest of his bodyguard of rat-ogres, a creature so massive that it made the late and unlamented

Boneripper look small. The creature bellowed its pleasure as Grottle fed it a tasty titbit of human fingers. Behind Grottle, other packmasters and their beasts stood waiting. Thanquol decided that he would spare Grottle. He did not doubt he could destroy the fat one. He was not so sure that he could survive an attack by the outraged beasts if they got out of control. Anyway he could not blame the recently arrived packmaster for the failure of last week's attack.

He turned his attention to the rotting form of Vilebroth Null, low abbot of the plague monks of Clan Pestilens, who stood alone, well apart from any other skaven. From within the abbot's cowl, pus-filled, fearless green eyes met his own. Thanquol instantly dismissed the idea of venting his rage on the diseased one. Like every skaven, he knew that the plague monks were quite mad. It was useless to antagonise them. Thanquol let his gaze slide slowly aside. The plague monk triumphantly blew his nose on the sleeve of his mouldering robe. A huge bubble of foul green snot swelled on his wrist and then burst.

Next in line was the armoured form of Heskit One Eye, master warp engineer of Clan Skryre. One Eye was small by skaven standards, dwarfed by his retinue of jezzail-armed bodyguards. Thanquol was still angry with him for the explosion of the farsqueaker. He suspected some sort of assassination attempt there, though, in truth, it seemed unlikely that Clan Skryre would be behind it. Intentionally blowing up one of their own precious devices to kill an enemy was not their style. Thanquol decided to spare Heskit. He was not in the slightest bit influenced by the fact that the bodyguard's long-barrelled rifles could shoot the wings off a fly at this range. No, not in the slightest.

He knew he couldn't punish these ones. They were too powerful. Their clans were too influential and he needed them to spearhead the attack on the mancity. Still, he had to kill someone, both to re-establish his own authority and for his own pleasure. It wouldn't do just to let them all off. It was not the skaven way.

An example had to be made.

One by one he turned his gaze on the Clan Skab warleaders. They were all present now, save for Warlord Vermek Skab himself. All wore the red and black livery of their clan. Each also had the single scar running from their left ear to their left cheek which was the badge of their clan. Each of them was as proud as a skaven could be, the unchallenged master of a host of vicious warriors, yet each of them hurriedly looked away when the grey seer met their eyes. They knew of his foul temper by reputation. Even Tzarkual, the gigantic leader of the stormvermin, would not face his wrath. He studied his feet like a small runt facing discipline from his elders.

Good, thought Thanquol. They were cowed. He took a pinch of warpstone snuff and watched them quake. Bright, mad visions of horror and carnage skittered through his brain. He puffed with self-confidence, convinced that at this moment he could face one of the Council of Thirteen and triumph. As always, the drug-induced confidence receded after a heart-stopping moment, leaving the afterglow of pure, Chaos-induced power searing through his veins. Quickly, before the heat could fade, he selected a victim. He stabbed out a pointing talon at Lurk Snitchtongue, the weakest of the warleaders and, not coincidentally, the one with least allies both here and back in Skavenblight.

'You find something amusing, Snitchtongue?' Thanquol demanded in his most intimidating high-pitched chitter. 'You think something is very funny, perhaps?'

Snitchtongue licked his snout nervously. He bobbed his head ingratiatingly and held up his empty paws. 'No! No, great one.'

'Don't lie. If humour there is in the abject failure of the mighty gutter runners, please share it. Your insight may prove most useful. Come! Speak! Speak!'

The skaven on either side of Lurk backed away, cautiously putting as much distance as they could between themselves and their doomed fellow. In moments Lurk found himself standing in an open space twenty feet across. He glanced over his shoulder, seeking some way to escape, but there was none. Not even his personal bodyguard would stand near him with the grey seer staring angrily down. Lurk shrugged, lashed his tail and put his hand on the hilt of his blade. He had obviously decided to brazen it out.

'If gutter runners failed it was because they were too subtle,' Lurk said. 'They should have attacked head-on, in a massed rush, blades bared. That is the skaven way. That is the Clan Skab way.'

Chang Squik glared across at the skaven warrior. If looks could kill, Lurk would have left the chamber in a casket. Thanquol was suddenly intrigued by the situation. Here was an opportunity to twist the assassin's tail with no possibility of reprisals against himself. The grey seer decided that he would let Lurk live for a few moments longer.

'You are saying that you could have handled the situation better than your brothers of Clan Eshin? You are saying you could succeed where trained gutter runners of mighty Eshin failed?'

Lurk's jaws snapped shut. He stood for a moment, considering the implications of that last statement, seeing the trap that the grey seer had prepared for him. If he openly criticised Squik, he would make an enemy of the powerful gutter runner, and doubtless take a knife in his belly as he slept. On the other paw, he also obviously realised that he had been singled out to face the grey seer's wrath no matter what. He knew it was a choice between immediate and inevitable death – or possible doom in the future. He rose to the occasion like a true skaven warrior.

'Maybe,' he said.

Thanquol giggled. The after effects of the warpsnuff still dizzied him. The rest of the skaven present echoed their leader's amusement with great roars of false chittering laughter.

'Then perhaps you should take your warriors to the mancity above and prove it, yes.'

'Indeed, great one,' the warleader replied. His voice sounded relieved. He had a slim chance of living after all. 'Your enemies are as good as dead.'

Somehow Thanquol doubted it, but he did not say so. Then he cursed himself for his leniency. He had allowed Snitchtongue to wriggle out from under his paw and not blasted him into a thousand pieces as an example.

At that moment, a runner entered, puffing breathlessly. In the traditional cleft thighbone of a human he carried, he held a message. Seeing Thanquol he immediately abased himself before the grey seer and prodded the bone forward.

Thanquol was tempted to blast him for his insolence. There was a fine old skaven tradition of killing the messenger who brought bad news to be kept up, but at this moment Thanquol did not even know that the news was bad. Curiosity got the better of him and he pulled the parchment from the stick. He noted that the corners were creased and it had obviously been well-pawed.

No surprises there, then. Doubtless every spy between here and Skavenblight had bribed the messenger so that he could look at what he carried. That, too, was the skaven way. Thanquol did not care. He had established his own codes, cunningly concealed within deceptively innocuous messages, in order to keep his communications secret.

He looked down at the blocky runes scrawled in a strong skaven paw. The message read simply: The package has been delivered. A sense of triumph filled Thanquol and dispelled his earlier anger. He fought to control his sense of exultation and keep his pleasure from his face. He looked down at the messenger and sneered, knowing above all that appearances must be kept up and an example must be made.

'This message has been opened, traitor-thing!' he snarled and raised his paw. A sphere of greenish light sprang into being around Thanquol's clenched fist. The messenger cringed and tried to beg for mercy but it was too late. Tentacles of hideous dark magical energy leapt downwards from Thanquol's paw to encircle the doomed skaven's body. The bands separated themselves and flowed around the messenger, swimming through the air in the way that eels swim through water, with a horrible sinuous wriggling. After a few moments, the bands of energy lunged inwards, stabbing through the skaven's body, boring through the flesh and emerging darker on the other side.

Again and again they stabbed inwards, stripping away flesh and muscle and sinew. Again and again the messenger let out high-pitched, agonising screams. The smell of the musk of fear mingled with the scent of blood and the ozone taint of the spell. In a matter of seconds only a stripped skeleton stood before Thanquol. After a heartbeat it collapsed into a pile of bone. The ribbons of magical energy flowed together, somehow consuming each other as they did so, until there was nothing left of them. The whole assembled skaven host let out a great sigh of wonder and disbelief at seeing their grey seer demonstrating his power in this satisfying manner.

Thanquol raised his paw and gestured for silence. In a moment all was calm, save for a few coughs from the back rows.

'Lament, skaven! Tragic news!' Thanquol said, and even the coughing stopped. 'Mighty Warlord Vermek Skab is dead, killed in a terrible accident involving a loaded crossbow and an exploding donkey. We will have the traditional ten heartbeats of silence to mark the return of his soul to the Horned Rat.'

Immediately all the skaven started to talk among themselves. The chitter of conversation only fell silent when Thanquol raised his paw again and let the warning glow reappear around his talons. All of them sensed the menace in the gesture and went quiet. None of them wanted to be the next to be consumed by those terrible wiggling bands of energy.

'Now we will prepare for the next phase of the master plan,' Thanquol said. 'In the sad absence of Lord Skab, I must reassume control of the army of conquest.'

'With great respectfulness, Grey Seer Thanquol, such is not the case. As senior skaven here, my duty it is to assume command.' The booming voice of Izak Grottle filled the chamber. 'Clan Moulder had provided many warptokens to finance this expedition and I must see that they are spent wisely.'

'What nonsense is this?' Vilebroth Null inquired. The words bubbled phlegmishly from his ruined throat. 'If any is to command here, it should be me. To Clan Pestilens will go the honour of overthrowing the mancity. We have great plans! Great plans! It is our secret weapon that will destroy the human city!'

'No! No! I disagree,' chittered the reedy, high-pitched voice of Heskit One Eye. 'The siege machines of Skryre will make victory possible and so to Skryre should fall the leadership. Naturally, as the ranking representative of Clan Skryre I will now assume my duties as supreme commander.'

'This is a vile usurpation of Clan Moulder's privileges,' Izak Grottle roared. The rat-ogres, hearing the anger in his voice, bellowed with barely suppressed fury. The sound of their wrath echoed around the cavern. 'Mutinous behaviour cannot be tolerated! No! For the good of the force, warn you I must that one more word of such treachery and my warriors will execute you instantaneously.'

The jezzail teams around Heskit swiftly brought their weapons to bear on Izak Grottle. 'Your warriors? Your warriors? There speaks a mad skaven. By what right do you name the warriors of my command your troops?'

'Both of you are trying my patience,' Vilebroth Null burbled. 'Seeing my two senior lackeys bickering in such a runtish manner cannot help but demoralise my army. Cease such treacherous behaviour at once or face the hideous and inevitably fatal consequences.'

Null flexed his paws menacingly and suddenly there was a package of filthy stuff in his hands. No one present could doubt that it was dangerous. The plagues of Clan Pestilens were famously deadly.

Grey Seer Thanquol looked on in baffled rage and barely concealed glee. He half hoped that the various leaders would come to blows, that violence would erupt and that these upstarts would slaughter each other. Unfortunately, until circumstances proved otherwise, he had to assume that he needed all of their help to overthrow the mancity. So it was time to put a stop to this nonsense.

'Brother skaven,' he said in his most diplomatic voice. 'Consider this. Until the coming of Vermek Skab, the Council of Thirteen placed me in command of this army. Since Vermek Skab is sadly no longer with us, the leader's place in the rear must still fall to me by edict of the council. Of course, if any of you wishes to challenge the council's ruling I will notify them of this at once.'

That quietened them, as Thanquol had known that it would. No skaven in his right mind would even hint at the possibility of disobeying a direct edict from the council. The dread rulers of the skaven race had a long reach and their punishments were swift and certain. By invoking the council's authority, Thanquol knew that he would ensure the obedience of all present until such a time as they could check back with their clan's rulers and representatives on the council. Hopefully in that time Thanquol would have brought the mancity to its knees.

'Of course, you are correct, Grey Seer Thanquol,' Heskit chittered. 'It is only that, as your second-in-command, I felt that these others were overstepping the bounds of their authority.'

'I know not how Heskit can claim to be your second-in-command, grey seer, when all know my respect for you is boundless, and my devotion to your cause without limit,' Izak Grottle said.

Vilebroth Null merely coughed enigmatically and said: 'It pains me to see these overbearing oafs challenging your rightful authority, grey seer. Surely the power of my clan and my proven dedication to your person must mean that I rank second here.'

'I have yet to decide who the Underleader will be. I must retire to my burrow to contemplate strategy.' So saying, he descended from the bell carriage and the seething sea of skaven parted before him. Thanquol felt satisfied for the moment that he had the challenge to his leadership under control.

This was more like it, thought Thanquol. Let them bicker over who gets the scraps. The glory will belong to me.

As was only right.

Lurk Snitchtongue crouched down in his favourite hiding place, a small cave above a long narrow gallery far from the main Underways. He was worried as only a skaven of a naturally nervous disposition could be. He knew that he had only days to make good on his claim to be able to destroy the dwarf and the human who had humiliated Chang Squik, or else he would suffer the same fate as the messenger from Skavenblight.

He shuddered when he thought of that demonstration of the grey seer's awesome power. Truly, the warpstone magic that Thanquol wielded was to be feared. He knew that hiding would not help him, that the grey seer would find him no matter how deep he burrowed, but old instincts were hard to overcome. Even as a small runt, in times of trouble Lurk had always sought out the hidden places where he could spy on the bigger skaven and plan his revenge.

Somewhere in the back of his mind, rage skittered around on small, padded claws. He knew that Thanquol had picked on him and the instinctive need for vengeance made him want to bury his fangs in the grey seer's throat. The fact that he understood why he was Thanquol's chosen victim did not make it any easier to take. Basic skaven instinct told him the reason for Thanquol's decision. From an early age, every young rat-man learned to sense who it was unwise to antagonise and who it was possible to bully with impunity. Those who did not, died in all manner of horrific ways and were usually eaten by those who killed them. On one level, he understood that Thanquol had victimised him for good, sound political reasons because he was the youngest of the skaven leaders, and the least secure in his position.

Lurk had risen to his current position as a junior warlord in Clan Skab by being the favourite of Vermek Skab, and by informing on those who had plotted against his distant cousin. He had a nose for ferreting out information that might be useful, a talent that was more than useful in a society so full of intrigue as that of a skaven clan. But now Vermek Skab himself was dead, and Lurk doubted that even his powerful kinrat would have been able to protect him against the wrath of a grey seer. No, he decided more realistically, Vermek would not have found him useful enough to be even bothered to try.

It was looking like his promising career was about to come to an end. He would either die at the axe of a maniacal dwarf whom, rumour had it, even Grey Seer Thanquol feared – or he would be blasted by the seer's mind-bogglingly potent sorcery. Neither prospect was particularly appealing to an ambitious young skaven. Still, at the moment, there didn't seem to be anything he could do about it.

Lurk heard voices coming from below him. He froze in place, realising that others had sought out this lonely place for their own purposes. He knew it was best to be quiet, for he was on his own and packs of skaven had been known to fall upon and devour solitary rat-men they found in remote tunnels. If truth be told, Lurk had done it himself. He listened carefully, his keen ears twitching, hoping to find out more about the approaching skaven.

'Curse Grey Seer Thanquol!' he heard a voice that he recognised as belonging to Heskit One Eye. 'He has denied me my rightful place at the head of this army, yes. Credit for victory over the humans should rightfully belong to me and, of course, to Clan Skryre.'

Lurk's whiskers twitched. This was treasonous talk and he was sure that Grey Seer Thanquol would like to hear about it. He listened now as if his life depended on it, thinking that he might have found a way out of his predicament, a path on which to creep back into the grey seer's good graces.

'Yes-yes, greatest of lords. A fool Thanquol is. Perhaps he too could have an accident like Vermek Skab!' Lurk recognised the fawning voice as belonging to Heskit's henchling, Squiksquik.

'Hush-hush! Speak not of such things. It has been tried before but somehow accidents always seem to happen to someone else, not to Grey Seer Thanquol. Perhaps it is true. Perhaps he does enjoy the favour of the Horned Rat!'

So even the mighty Heskit feared the grey seer. This did nothing to reassure Lurk about his own position. But still – what a patron the grey seer would make if Lurk could ingratiate himself. By clinging to Thanquol's tail, Lurk could rise very far indeed. The next thing he heard made his tail stand on end.

'The farsqueaker explosion should have worked but Thanquol has the luck of a daemon, most far-sighted of plotters.'

'Never, never refer to that again. The farsqueaker malfunctioned – that is all. Nothing more. If Grey Seer Thanquol was even to suspect that it was anything else, the consequences would be very bad, very bad. How goes the... other plan?'

'Well, greatest of warp engineers! We have located a hidden route into the manplace. Our warriors stand ready to grab the devices the moment you command it. Tonight is auspicious. The humans have all been summoned to a feast by their ruling breeder.'

Lurk felt the soles of his paws tingle. Here was something else to report back to Thanquol. A secret Clan Skryre scheme to acquire human treasures. Surely Grey Seer Thanquol would reward anyone who would report such a thing to him. He leaned forward stealthily so that so he could see what was going on below him. The movement dislodged some pebbles and sent them skittering to the floor. The noise disturbed the Clan Skryre skaven, he saw them jump into defensive stances and whip out their blades.

'What was that sound-noise?' Heskit demanded.

'I do not know, bravest of leaders,' Squiksquik said. 'Quick! Quick! Go! Investigate.'

'A leader's place is in the rear. You go!'

Lurk cursed his bad luck. The noise had interrupted the Skryre's plotting and now he might never know what they were up to.

'Most likely it is nothing, wisest of warleaders. Subsidence merely. Tunnels are old.'

The two of them stood immobile in postures of listening. Lurk hoped they did not look up. He dared not even pull himself back into the shadows lest the movement attract the attention of their keen skaven senses. He felt sure that they would be able to hear the pounding of his heart. It was all he could do to keep from squirting the musk of fear.

Slowly the two nervous Clan Skryre rat-men relaxed, letting their breath come out slowly and easily. After a few more heartbeats, they returned to their plotting.

'What are your orders, most cunning of commanders?'

'We will attack the man-things' steamworks tonight during the dark of the moon. Their gun machines must be ours so that we can improve on them. Their steam-chariots must be examined to see how we may increase their effectiveness ten-thousand fold.'

'It will be as you wish, most superlative of technicians.'

'See that it is so!' Heskit barked and turned his back on Squiksquik to stalk away. Lurk could not help but notice that as soon as Heskit's back was turned, his lackey flicked his thumb against his protruding incisors in the traditional skaven gesture of disrespect. Heskit turned. By the time his leader's eye was upon him, Squiksquik had once again adopted a posture of fawning adoration.

'Do not stand there all day. Come! Come! Quick! Quick! There is much work to be done.'

In the darkness, Lurk smiled. He had learned many useful things here, and it was time to visit the grey seer.

'What do you want?' Grey Seer Thanquol inquired, looking up from the scroll which he had been reading. 'I thought you went to the surface. To kill the dwarf!'

'No, most potent of sorcerers,' Lurk replied, adopting the form of address that worked so well for Squiksquik. He understood now its power. Thanquol seemed to swell visibly at the flattery and began to preen his fur. 'While rushing to obey your most clever command, I stumbled upon evidence of plotting and knew that only the great Thanquol himself would have the intelligence to know how to deal with it.'

'Plotting? Explain yourself! Hurry-hurry!'

Quickly, and leaving out only the details of how he came to be there, Lurk outlined what he had overheard. Thanquol tilted his head to one side and bared his fangs at the news. As he listened his tail began to lash backwards and forwards, a sure sign that a skaven was agitated. When Lurk was finished, Thanquol glared at him for so long and with such an expression of piercing intelligence that Lurk feared his time had come and that he was about to be blasted. But the grey seer merely licked his lips, stroked his imposing horned head with one paw, and said: 'You have done well, Lurk Snitchtongue. I must consider what you have told me. Hold yourself ready to instantly obey my commands.'

'Yes, most shrewd of supreme commanders.'

'And Snitchtongue–'

'Yes, mightiest of sorcerers?'

'Say nothing of what you have told me, to anyone. On pain of instant and most painful annihilation.'

'Yes! Yes! To hear is to obey, most merciful of potentates.'

Thanquol lolled back on the throne he had installed in this makeshift command cave. He scratched his itching back against the wood of the throne's back, then leaned his horned head forward on his paw. That fawning sluggard Lurk had given him something to consider indeed. So, as he had suspected, the farsqueaker explosion had been no accident. When he thought how close he had come to death on that day, rage and fear warred in the pit of Thanquol's stomach. Had Heskit stood before him at this moment, Thanquol would have blasted him into a thousand fragments, and let the Horned Rat take the consequences.

And this news of Heskit's treachery gnawed at his bowels. He fought to bring himself under control, knowing that such thinking was dangerous, that to give way to his rage would lead to eventual certain destruction. He had not reached his high position in skavendom by giving way to such impulses. He told himself that he would find other, more subtle ways of gratifying his thirst for righteous revenge. He would find other ways to pay back the treacherous filth for his attempt on Thanquol's life. And this new scheme of Heskit's – it was exactly the sort of thing he would have expected from those machine-obsessed traitors at Clan Skryre. Always lusting after new technologies and new machines. Always willing to betray the skaven cause for their own advancement. Always looking for ways to cheat their rightful leader out of his well-deserved share of the credit.

But wait! Was it possible that Lurk Snitchtongue had concocted this whole thing simply to ingratiate himself with Thanquol? The grey seer immediately discounted this possibility. Lurk was simply too stupid and unimaginative to come up with such a tale. Furthermore, it fitted with reports which Thanquol's other spies had brought him, of secret massing of elite Clan Skryre troops, of secretive comings and goings in the burrows that Heskit had commandeered for his forces.

Thanquol considered the possible outcomes. The warp engineers were planning on attacking the new College of Engineering, that was obvious. They wanted to acquire steam tanks and organ guns for themselves. The grey seer did not doubt that Heskit could make good on his boast of improving these human weapons a million-fold. He knew that no other race could match skaven genius when it came to constructing machines, and unfortunately, Clan Skryre were the most brilliant mechanics of a brilliant race.

These new weapons would doubtless increase Clan Skryre's power, and with that power would come increased influence on the Council. Just the news that Heskit had succeeded in acquiring the human weapons would bring a consequent increase in Clan Skryre's prestige, perhaps even enough to have Thanquol called back to Skavenblight and Heskit awarded the supreme leadership of this army. Such an outcome was unthinkable. A clod like Heskit could only lead this mighty force to disaster. It needed the titanic intellect of Thanquol to ensure crushing victory over the human scum. It was Thanquol's duty to his people to ensure that he stayed in charge.

But what were his options? He had already decided that Heskit was too powerful and too useful to be destroyed out of hand. So what could he do? He could confront Heskit with the knowledge of his treachery. Not good enough. The warp engineer could simply deny it and it would be Lurk's word against his. And doubtless he would simply find another way forward with his plans to steal the human machines when Thanquol's back was turned and his mind occupied with more pressing affairs.

Thanquol cursed Heskit and all his treacherous, ill-natured brood! Why did this have to happen now? He should be using his towering intellect to deal with more pressing matters than treacherous underlings. He should be planning the inevitable conquest of the mancity of Nuln and the destruction of Gotrek Gurnisson and Felix Jaeger.

But wait! Perhaps this was the key. Perhaps the Horned Rat had sent him the means to kill two babies with one bludgeon. A brilliant idea started to percolate into Thanquol's mind. What if he used his two enemies as a weapon against Heskit? What if he simply informed them of where and when the warp engineer's attack was to take place? Doubtless they would take steps to thwart the attack.

Yes! Yes! The Slayer's foolish quest for glory, and the fact that the pair were already discredited, would keep them from informing the stupid human authorities. Doubtless they would be moved to interfere in their usual blundering fashion, and would seek to stop Heskit's plan. They were too stupid ever to work out that they were Thanquol's pawns, and even if they suspected a trap it would not matter. The Slayer's own pride and his desire for a heroic death would ensure his interest even in the face of overwhelming odds. No! No! Particularly in the face of overwhelming odds.

And this way, if anything went wrong, Thanquol's hands were clean. No one would ever trace the Slayer's intervention back to him, he could ensure that. The idea of using the pair to thwart his other enemies' schemes was too good to resist.

He turned the scheme over from all sides, examining the possible outcomes and finding it foolproof. Either the dwarf and the manling would foil the plot in their usual, brutally inept manner or they would be killed trying to do so. Either outcome suited Thanquol. If they foiled Heskit's plan, the warp engineer would be discredited. If they died, Thanquol would have lost two potent enemies and could still organise some nasty surprises for the Clan Skryre warlocks on their return. In the best of all possible worlds, the two sides would eliminate each other. Thanquol helped himself to some warpstone snuff and consumed it with glee. What a scheme! So intricate! So cunning! So truly skaven! Here once more was proof of his own incredible genius.

Now all he had to do was think of a way of letting the dwarf and his henchman know about Heskit's plan. It would have to be complex, subtle and ingenuous. Those half-witted fools would never suspect that they were aiding their mightiest enemy.

'Message for you, sir,' said the small, grubby faced boy, holding out his hand for payment. In his other hand, he clutched a piece of coarse parchment.

Felix looked down at him and wondered if this was some sort of trick. The beggar lads of Nuln were particularly known for their ingenuity in parting fools from their money. Still, he might as well pay attention. The lanterns had just been lit. It was early yet and the Blind Pig had not even started to look like it would fill up this evening.

'What's this? You do not look like a courier.'

'I dunno, sir. This funny-looking gentleman handed me this scrap of paper and a copper penny and told I would get the same again if I delivered it to the tall blond-furred bouncer at the Blind Pig.'

'Blond-furred?'

'He spoke kind of funny, sir. Looked kind of funny, too. To tell the truth, he smelled kind of funny an' all.'

'What do you mean?'

'Well, his voice wasn't exactly normal. It was kind of high pitched and squeaky. And he was wearing a monk's robe with a cowl that covered his face. I thought his robes hadn't been washed for a long time. They smelled like a dog or some furry animal had been sleeping in them. I know, 'cause my dog, Uffie, used to–'

'Never mind Uffie right now. Was there anything else you noticed about him?'

'Well, sir, he walked funny, all hunched forward...'

'Like an old man?'

'No, sir, he moved too quick for an old man. More like one of the crippled beggars you see down on Cheap Street 'cept he moved too quick to be crippled and... well, there's one more thing but I was scared to tell you in case you thought I had been at the weirdroot.'

'And what was that?'

'Well, as he was moving away, I thought he had a snake under his robes. I could see something long and snaky moving around.'

'Could it have been a tail? Like the tail of a rat?'

'It could have been, sir. It could have been. Do you think it could have been a mutant, sir? One of the changed?' A note of wonder and horror had entered the child's voice. He was obviously thinking that he might just have had a close call.

'Perhaps. Now, where did you see this beggar?'

'Down Blind Alley. Not five minutes ago. I rushed over here thinking I'd get myself a nice bit of pie with the copper piece you was going to give me.'

Felix tossed the kid a copper and snatched the piece of paper from his hand. He glanced across the bar to see if Gotrek was about. The Slayer sat at a side table, his massive shoulders hunched, clutching an ale in one brawny fist and his monstrous axe in the other. Felix beckoned him over.

'What is it, manling?'

'I'll tell you on the way.'

* * *

'No sign of anything here now, manling,' Gotrek said, peering down the alley. He shook his head and ran a brawny hand through his huge dyed crest of hair. 'No scent either.'

Felix could not tell how the Slayer could smell anything over the stench of the trash that filled Blind Alley, but he did not doubt that Gotrek was telling the truth. He had seen too much evidence of the keenness of the dwarf's senses in the past to doubt him now. Felix kept his hand on the hilt of his sword and was ready to shout for the watch at a moment's notice. Since the child had brought the note, he had suspected an ambush. But there was no sign of one. The skaven, if skaven it had been, had timed things well. It had given itself plenty of time to get away.

Felix took another glance down the alley. There was not much to see. Some light filtered in from the shop lanterns and tavern windows of Cheap Street but not enough for him to make out more than the outlines of rubbish, and the cracked and weather-eroded walls of the buildings on either side of the alley.

'This leads down into the Maze,' Gotrek said. 'There's a dozen entries to the sewers down there. Our scuttling little friend has got clean away by now.'

Felix considered the winding labyrinth of alleys which comprised the Maze. It was a haunt of the city's poorest and most desperate wretches. He did not relish the prospect of visiting during broad daylight, let alone trying to find a skaven there in the darkness of this overcast and moonless evening. Gotrek was probably right anyway: if it was a skaven, it was in the sewers by now.

Felix backed out into the street and moved under the lantern that illuminated an all-night pawnbroker's sign. He unfolded the coarse paper and inspected the note.

The handwriting was odd. The letters were formed with jagged edges, more like dwarf runes than the Imperial alphabet, but the language was definitely Reikspiel, although poorly composed and spelled. It read:

> *Frends – be warned! Evil ratmen of the trecherus skaven klan*
> *Skryre – may they be poxed forever, espeshully that wicked feend*
> *Heskit Wan Eye – plan to attak the Colledge of Ingineering this*
> *nite during the dark of the moon. They wish to steel your secrets*
> *for their own nefare-i-us porpoises. You must stop them or they*
> *will be wan step closer to conquering the surface world,*
>
> *Yoor frend.*

Felix handed the letter to Gotrek. The Trollslayer read it and crumpled it up in one brawny fist. He snorted derisively. 'A trap, manling!'

'Maybe – but if so, why not simply lure us here and attack us?'

'Who can tell how the rats' minds work?'

'Maybe not all skaven are hostile. Maybe some of them want to help us.'

'Maybe my grandmother was an elf.'

'All right. Maybe one faction has a grudge against another faction and want us to settle it for them?'

'Why not settle it themselves?'

'I don't know. I'm just thinking aloud. Tonight is the Feast of Verena. There will only be a few people in the college. All the others will be at the Countess Emmanuelle's Feast for the Guild. Perhaps we should warn the watch.'

'And tell them what, manling? That a skaven sent us a note warning us his brother was going to burgle the Elector Countess's special arsenal. Perhaps you've forgotten what happened the last time we tried to warn anybody about the skaven.'

'So you're saying we should do nothing?'

'I'm not saying anything of the sort. I'm saying that we should look into this ourselves and not count on getting any help from anyone else.'

'What if it's a trap?'

'If it is, it is. A lot of skaven will die.'

'So might we.'

'Then it will be a heroic death.'

'We'd best get back to the Blind Pig first. Heinz will be wondering where we've got to.'

'You delivered the note as instructed?' Grey Seer Thanquol asked.

'Yes! Yes, most ingenuous of masters,' Lurk said.

'Good. You are dismissed. Hold yourself ready for further instructions. If anyone asks you what you were doing on the surface, tell them you were spying on the dwarf in preparation for killing him. In a way, it will be the truth.'

'Yes, yes, cleverest of councillors.'

Thanquol rubbed his paws together with glee. He did not doubt that the stupid dwarf and the hairless ape would fall into his cunningly woven trap. His beautifully composed and lovingly crafted message would see to that. Now all he had to do was wait and make sure that, whatever happened, Heskit's warriors failed in their task. And he knew just the way to do that.

Heskit surveyed his corps of warp engineers with pride. He watched a team of warpfire throwers check their bulky and dangerous weapon, showing all the care of well-trained skaven engineers. The smaller of the two lovingly banged the firebarrel with a spanner to make sure it was full, while the other kept the dangerous nozzle pointed at the ceiling most of the time, in case of accidents.

Bands of sweating slaves rested for a moment, their breath coming in gasps, their tongues lolling out after long exertion. They had laboured long and lovingly to prepare the way for this night's work. They had spent many hours luring the sewer watch away from this place, and days working with muffled picks to finish these structures. Now the ramps were all in place, and they were ready to breach the surface and swarm out through the manburrow.

Heskit inspected their work with a well-trained professional eye. During his apprenticeships, he had overseen the construction of scaffolding around the great skaven warships. Scaffolding that almost never collapsed killing those upon it, Heskit thought with pride. It had been the wonder of his burrow. Well, after tonight, his fellow engineers would have even more to wonder about. He would surpass Mekrit's invention of the farsqueaker, and do more to advance the skaven cause than Ik had done with his invention of the portable tormenting machine. After tonight he would possess all the proudest secrets of the race of man. And then he would improve them in a thousand ways.

Heskit knew that he had picked his time well. Today was the Feast of Verena. The human guards were but a skeleton watch compared to their usual numbers, and doubtless were all drunk. Even now Clan Eshin assassins were moving above, picking off the few sentries which remained on duty. Soon it would be time to go forward with the plan.

A Poison Wind globadier hurried past, his face obscured by his metallic gas-mask. Only the globadier's nervous darting eyes were visible through the quartz lenses. He clasped his glass sphere of chemical death to his chest, protecting it against accidents the way a mother bird might protect a precious egg.

Heskit's chronometer chimed thirteen times. He tugged its chain and pulled the ornate brass device out of his fob pocket. He held it to his ear, and was rewarded by the sound of loud ticking from the lovingly crafted mechanism within. He flicked the chronometer open and glanced at the face. It showed a little running skaven. Its feet moved back and forth every heartbeat. Its long tail pointed to the thirteenth hour, and so did the short stabbing sword it clutched. It was exactly thirteen o' clock, to the hour, to the minute. Heskit turned and gave the sign for the operation to begin.

Felix looked at the outside of the new College of Engineering. It was a most impressive building, more like a fortress than any University College he had ever been in. The tall, broad towers at each corner would have been more at home on a castle than on a place of study. All the windows at ground level were barred. There was only one way in, through a massive archway, large enough for a horse-drawn carriage.

A soft thud behind him told him that Gotrek had arrived and most likely fallen into one of the flower beds. He heard the dwarf curse in his harsh, guttural tongue.

'Best be quiet!' Felix whispered. 'We really should not be here.'

It was true. Only authorised members of the Guild of Engineers and Mechanics, their apprentices and members of the Imperial military were allowed into this highly secret place, on pain of death or at least a long stay in the dungeons of the Countess Emmanuelle's infamous prison.

'The sentries are all too drunk to notice anything, manling. It's a disgrace but it's what you expect from humans.'

Felix reached up and tugged his new cloak off the low wall. It was ripped where the broken glass and nails set on top of the wall had pierced it. Still, Felix thought sourly, better a ripped cloak than a ripped hand. He glanced over at the sentry boxes beside the locked iron gates and was forced to agree with Gotrek. It was a disgrace.

One of the sentries was so drunk that he was simply lying asleep beside his post. Then Felix saw that there was something odd in the man's posture and he stepped over cautiously to have a look. As he did so, he saw more recumbent figures. Was it possible that all of the sentries were drunk and asleep? He crept up for a closer look, then ripped his sword from its scabbard.

The sentries were not drunk. They were dead. Each lay in a pool of blood. One of them still had a knife sticking from his back. Felix bent and examined it and immediately recognised the workmanship from his own encounter with the skaven assassins at the Blind Pig.

'It looks like our friend was telling the truth,' he said to Gotrek, who had joined him.

'Then let us go take a look inside.'

'I was afraid you were going to say that.'

Heskit stalked the corridors of the college, surrounded by his bodyguards. In a way this was a comforting place for him. He was surrounded by familiar things: forges and benches and lathes and braces, and all the tools familiar to engineers the world over, whatever their race. The smell of charcoal and metal wafted through the place on the night breeze. Skaven seethed through the corridors like an invading army, ransacking the place as they went. He hoped that his lackey, Squiksquik, had managed to get into position in the central armouries, otherwise all the choicest of loot would have vanished.

To his right, he could see a rack of long muskets of a novel design. He immediately rushed over and pulled one down. It had the half-complete look of a new prototype. Its barrel was bound with copper wire, and a small telescope had been mounted above it. Nothing to get excited about, Heskit thought, simply an inferior attempt at the jezzails his own bodyguard already carried. Without access to warpstone for their powder mixes, the humans would never be able to get the same range and hitting power. He hoped that the other stuff here was more worthy of his consideration, or it was going to be a wasted night.

'Most perspicuous of lords, this way,' he heard Squiksquik call. Heskit strode down the long hall and found himself in another machine shop. This was more like it, he thought, when he saw the round stubby mass of the organ gun. This was worth having. He strode over and ran his paws over the cold metal of one of the barrels. Yes, indeed, this was worth having.

He looked down and saw the mechanism that would cause the barrels to rotate and the striker which ignited the fuses at the same time. Very clever! He wondered whether the tolerances of the metal could withstand the use of warpstone powder. Most likely not but then again, some of those new lead-warpstone alloys he had been experimenting with might just do the trick. He had not had any accidents with them since the last automated cannon had exploded and killed ten of his assistants.

'Quick! Quick! Take it!' he instructed Squiksquik. His lackey chittered a few commands and a party of Skryre slaves rushed forward. There was a slight squeaking as they wheeled the gun away. This did not bother Heskit. In fact, he found it quite relaxing.

He pushed on deeper into the halls, wondering what new toys he would find in this strange and exciting place.

* * *

Felix fumbled with the door handle. He had been half hoping to find it locked but it was already open, and he suspected he knew why. There was a very familiar smell in the air, a combined scent of musk and wet fur and sewer reek. No doubt about it, the skaven were here.

'Perhaps we should go and inform the watch,' he whispered to Gotrek.

'And tell them what? We just broke into your armoury and discovered some skaven there. We weren't trying to steal anything, honestly. We just wanted to look. Being hung as a thief is not my idea of a mighty doom, manling.'

'Then maybe we shouldn't have come here,' Felix muttered. He was already regretting that he had agreed to this hare-brained scheme. In the heat of the moment, carried along by the momentum of events, it had seemed to possess a certain logic, but now he could see that it was nothing but pure madness. They were in a place where they had no business being, and most likely surrounded by fierce skaven warriors. By the time any help could get to them, they would in all probability be dead, and even in the unlikely event they survived until help came, their rescuers would, as Gotrek had suggested, most likely hang them as spies. How did he get himself into these situations, Felix wondered?

'Are you going to stand there all night – or are you going to open that door?'

Half expecting to feel a blade being thrust into his face, Felix slowly and cautiously pushed the door open. Ahead of him a long corridor loomed. It was dark save for the light that filtered in from outside. Felix wished that he had a lantern with him. There must be lights here, he thought – then realised that all they would do was draw unwelcome attention.

Gotrek pushed past and stomped off down the corridor, massive axe held ready to deal death. There was nothing for it but to follow him. Felix did not relish the prospect of being left in this vast and echoing building on his own.

'There is a problem, most decisive and responsible of leaders,' Squiksquik said quietly. Heskit turned and glared at his lieutenant petulantly.

'Problem? What problem could there be, Squiksquik? Explain! Quick! Quick!'

'Overseer Quee thinks that, now he has seen the steam tank, there might be some problems. He thinks that the supports might not be strong enough to take the weight. It might be unwise to take it down into the sewers.'

'Tell Overseer Quee to solve this problem quickly, otherwise he will have to be replaced by someone more competent. We must have this steam tank! We must study the engines! We must see how it works! Clan Skryre must possess this weapon.'

Heskit clambered up on top of the steam tank. His followers had lit the place with the green glow of warpstone lamps, the better to see what they were doing. Just being on top of this mighty machine made Heskit's tail stiffen. He put his paws on his hips, struck a commanding posture and looked down on the chamber.

He looked around at this, the largest of halls, the place where steam tanks were built. It was impressive. All the parts, lovingly hand-crafted, lay on workbenches nearby. Huge schematics had been pinned to a board on the wall for the guidance of apprentices. Overhead were all manner of pulleys, and wires and guy ropes for lowering all the pieces into place. It was a tangled and intricate enough web to cheer the heart of any skaven.

Nearby sat a partially assembled steam tank, looking for all the world like the half-devoured carcass of some Leviathan. Above him were the galleries from where the masters could survey the work of their labourers and see that everything was done properly. Yes, there were definitely some ideas here which could be adapted to the skaven cause.

Heskit turned back and was soon lost in contemplation of the huge mechanical monster, overwhelmed by the possibilities hinted at in its design. Truly, the steam tank was a most awesome concept. He ran a paw over the riveted metal and felt his heartbeat quicken. He could just see himself driving around in one of these, only his would be bigger and better, with a warpstone-powered engine and a warpfire thrower instead of a cannon. Bullets would ping off the armour of the hull. Arrows would be turned aside by the thickness of the walls. His foes would be crushed to bloody pulp under him. He would have a periscope to look out through so he wouldn't have to expose his head to enemy fire, and he would have tracks instead of these silly wheels so that he could pass over the roughest of terrain with ease.

It was a design with which the skaven could conquer the world, and he, Heskit One Eye, would be responsible for it.

Ahead Felix could see a huge open courtyard. In the centre of the courtyard was a massive gaping pit, from which emerged the familiar stench of the sewers. The courtyard was lit by eerie flickering green lights. In their glow, Felix could see a horde of rat-men scampering backwards and forwards between the pit and the building proper. Each had a chest or a piece of machinery over his shoulder. It looked like they were looting the whole building. Felix wasn't sure what they were going to do. There were simply too many of the skaven for them to overcome.

Heskit clambered down into the steam tank and looked at the controls. There was a small seat moulded to fit a human driver, but the bulk of the chamber was taken up by a monstrous cannon and a huge boiler. Doubtless the boiler provided power.

The controls were simplicity itself for a skaven of Heskit's intelligence to figure out. This lever was forward; that lever was reverse. The whistle could be used to make terrifying noises and to relieve pressure on the boiler. This small wheel would let you guide the steam tank right and left, and this one would aim the cannon. It was all too easy.

Suddenly Heskit knew exactly what he wanted to do, and since he was a master warp engineer there was no one here who could stop him. He was going to take this vehicle for a test drive, just to make sure it worked. It would also save all the effort of carrying it to the pit mouth and down into the sewers. He barked instructions to summon two slaves and he soon had them loading up the boiler with wood. Within minutes he had the engine under pressure and was ready to go.

Heskit pulled the lever and the steam tank lurched forward.

In the distance Felix heard a rumble like a dragon clearing its throat. 'Sounds like a monster,' he whispered to Gotrek.

'Sounds like a steam engine more like, manling. We'd better investigate.'

They hurried up the stairs and around the gallery above the courtyard. Here and there lay the bodies of sentries, killed by the same skaven blades as they had encountered earlier. Felix flinched and kept his sword ready. At any moment, he expected to run into a pack of fierce killers like those which had attacked him and Elissa in his room the other night.

The sensation of speed and power was awesome. Heskit had never experienced anything like it. He felt like he could crush anything that got in his way, smash through any obstacle. With this one tank, he could overcome any foe. Visions of huge armies, spearheaded by warpstone-powered steam tanks danced through his head. With such a force manned by fierce skaven warriors, Clan Skryre could conquer the world. And, of course, he, Heskit One Eye, would be suitably rewarded for his genius in coming up with the plan. He would see to that.

Heskit looked up to see where he was going. What was that foolish Poison Wind globadier doing standing in front of him with a look of panic on his face, Heskit wondered?

Felix emerged onto a gallery above a huge hall which seethed with skaven. In the middle of the hall stood a gleaming new steam tank. Smoke billowed from its chimneys and even as he watched, Felix saw that the vehicle was starting to move. It picked up speed fast and ran over a small skaven who stood clutching something in front of it. The skaven fell and something like a glass sphere rolled from its hands. The sphere fell and shattered into a million pieces. As it did so, a horrible cloud of greenish gas emerged. All of the rat-men down below who were caught in the cloud clutched their throats and fell, coughing blood. They lay on the floor, tails lashing, feet kicking the ground. In a way they looked as if they were drowning.

He remembered Gotrek's tales of skaven gas weapons. He remembered that awful moment during his fight with the skaven in the sewers when he thought he had been gassed. He also remembered that the Slayer had suggested the solution was a handkerchief soaked in piss and placed over your mouth. He currently didn't have the time or the inclination to test that theory. Felix noticed gratefully that the gas appeared to be heavier than the surrounding air, and did not rise far. Indeed, it was already starting to disperse.

Was he dying, Heskit wondered? Or had he managed to hold his breath in time? He did not know. His eyes watered from the gas which had seeped in through the open hatch. The two skaven slaves lay gurgling and gasping in front of him. Heskit knew he did not feel any pain. Perhaps the heartbeat of warning he had got when he saw the globadier had been enough. He had just enough time to snatch a lungful of air and hold his breath. He had certainly not wasted it on shouting a warning to the others. As a consequence of his own quick thinking, he had managed to save himself.

Heskit peered out through the green murk with watering eyes, and tried to guide the tank into the clear. Something bumped and squished under the wheels and he thought he heard a howl of agony.

He ignored it and concentrated on staying alive. That was the most important thing.

His lungs felt like they were bursting. His heart beat at three times its usual rate. He had already squirted the musk of fear and soiled his fine armour. He did not care. All that mattered now was that he did not breathe until he saw clear air, and that he kept himself alive, in spite of the treacherous attack of the foolish globadier.

All around him he heard sounds of confusion, of skaven shouting orders, of barked commands, and weapons being brought to bear.

'We're under attack!' he heard Squiksquik shout. It wasn't until the jezzail shots started thumping of the side of the tank that he realised that the idiots thought that he was attacking them.

Felix watched in mounting confusion at the scene of carnage. The gas had killed dozens of the skaven. The rest of the rat-men had turned on the steam tank. Several teams of skaven equipped with long rifles had started taking pot-shots at the tank. Two weirdly equipped skaven were manhandling a huge and very unwieldy-looking weapon into a position where it could fire at the tank.

Was there still a human alive down there, and had he somehow managed to get the war-engine to work? Was he even now fighting for his life and in desperate need of help? Felix turned to consult with the Slayer – and only then realised that Gotrek had gone. Felix could guess where.

The skaven had manoeuvred their odd-looking weapon into position. One of them crouched down with a barrel braced on its back, the other wielding the connected gun. Suddenly a jet of greenish flame gouted forth and sprayed towards the tank. It clung to the metallic side panels, burning intensely, the flare illuminating the whole chamber and making Felix stand out in stark relief on the balcony. He knew this because a whole group of skaven were suddenly pointing at him and chittering.

He had a terrible feeling that he knew what was going to happen next.

Heskit closed his eyes and hoped that he would still be able to see when he opened them. The heat was intense and the warpflames of the fire thrower licked through the viewing slit of the steam tank. Heskit screamed and squirted the musk of fear again, soiling the seat below him.

'Stop! Stop! Fools!' he shrieked. 'It is I, Heskit, your leader!'

If anyone heard him over the roar of the steam tank, they gave no sign. All was confusion and madness. It was possible that his ratkin had lost sight of him in the confusion and thought he was a human attacker. It was equally possible that some vilely ambitious underling knew full well that he was in here and was taking this opportunity to try and assassinate his superior.

In fact, the more Heskit thought of this second option, the more likely it seemed to him. Those firethrower bearers, for example, were not stopping their assault, despite his express command. They might claim they could not hear him over the roar of the engine but Heskit knew better. He could see it all so clearly now. It was all part of a devilish plot to remove him from his rightful office. He would not be in the least bit surprised if Grey Seer Thanquol was behind the whole thing.

Filled with righteous vindictive anger, Heskit bared his fangs in rage and steered the steam tank directly at the warpfire throwers. Too late, the treacherous vermin realised their peril and attempted to scuttle aside. Heskit was rewarded by the crunch of their bones under his wheels. Then there was a hideous crump as the barrel of phosphorescent chemicals exploded.

Felix was trapped. Skaven were flowing out onto the balcony on which he stood in a grim furry tide. There were dozens of them, far more than he could fight. He did not doubt that he could take out one or two of them on the narrow walkway but while he was doing so others would come rushing up behind him and drive their nasty little blades into his back. Damn Gotrek! Where was the Slayer when he was needed?

As if in answer to his unspoken query, he heard a thunderous bellow from below him. Risking a quick glance, Felix saw that the Slayer had emerged into the room below, leaving a trail of dead and dying rat-men behind him. A dripping wet rag was wrapped round his face. Evidently the Slayer was taking no chances of being gassed before he achieved his heroic death.

Also below him, Felix could see the steam tank as it careened onward. Blazing green flames raged around its wheels and along its belly. It bumped and bounced through the workspace leaving a comet trail behind it, crushing everything that got in its way. Then it slewed around, coming almost to a stop, its front end facing in the direction of the Slayer. Gotrek stood his ground, confronting the massive machine, for all the world like an Estalian matador facing a bull. All around the dwarf, panicked skaven scuttled for cover.

That was all that Felix had time to see, as the seething mass of skaven bore down on him. He knew that if he stayed where he was, he was dead. Seeing nothing else for it, he scabbarded his sword, leapt up onto the banister and reached up to grab one of the overhead lines. Swiftly he swung himself hand over hand until he was out over the middle of the courtyard. Felix hung there for a moment, getting his breath back.

Suddenly he felt the line begin to falter under his weight. He risked a glance backwards and saw an evilly grinning skaven sawing at the rope with his blade.

Oh no, thought Felix, as the line gave way with a snap.

Heskit could not believe his eyes. Was that a dwarf standing in front of him brandishing a huge axe? How could there be a dwarf here, in the middle of this manburrow? Had he accidentally taken a whiff of the globadier's gas? Was he hallucinating? The whole tank was getting warm, and not just from the boiler. Heskit was certain he could smell warpfire burning somewhere. And where had all his lackeys gone? Surely the dwarf and the gas could not have killed them all. Well, one thing was certain: no dwarf could survive a face-to-face encounter with this steam tank. Heskit upped the acceleration and raced directly at Gotrek.

The line parted and Felix arced down towards the ground. He saw that Gotrek was almost directly below him and that the steam tank was almost upon him. It looked like the Slayer was about to be crushed to a bloody pulp beneath the wheels of the blazing steam tank. But at the last second, he stepped to one side and his axe struck the side of the vehicle with a deep, resonant clang like the tolling of a great bell.

Felix braced himself for a painful impact with the ground. Then at the last second he realised that the arc of his trajectory was taking him directly into the path of the steam tank. It seemed all too likely that he was going to end up beneath its wheels.

Heskit's head ached from the fumes and from the great ringing echo inside the tank. And what had that second bump been against the tank's side? He was beginning to regret that he had ever allowed his lackeys to persuade him to get into this accursed death-trap. Heads would roll once he brought the thing to a stop, that was certain!

He tugged hard on the braking lever and it came away in his hands. Ahead of him, the wall of the building loomed. It approached with appalling speed.

* * *

All the breath was knocked out of Felix's lungs as he slammed into the top of the steam tank. He felt himself start to slip. He could feel the heat beginning to scorch the soles of his boots. He reached out and grabbed for something to hold onto. His fingers caught the edge of the open hatch. Using the leverage this gave him, he pulled himself up and crouched on top of the speeding tank. He could see the wall approaching quickly. He tried to throw himself clear but it was too late. The force of the impact sent him tumbling headfirst through the hatch and down into the interior of the burning steam tank.

There was a huge roar and a grinding sound as the steam tank went right through the brick wall. The whole tank shook and the smell of burning intensified. Suddenly a heavy weight dropped on Heskit and he found human hands scrabbling against his fur.

Felix flinched as the skaven bared huge jaws full of needle-sharp teeth and snapped at him. This was a nightmare, thought Felix. He was trapped, hanging upside down, in a tiny enclosed space, aboard a speeding vehicle, with a hideous mutant monster trying to tear out his throat. He pulled his head aside and lashed out with a fist, catching the skaven on the snout. All around he noticed that steam had started to billow and sparks had started to fly from the boiler.

The skaven lashed out at him. Razor-sharp claws tore his cheek. Felix had a moment to be glad that the space was too confined for the skaven to use its weapons. He let himself drop the whole way into the cabin and landed with his full weight on the rat-man. The two of them grappled and rolled around the cabin, hitting the control levers and sending the steam tank skidding uncontrollably first left and then right. Through the viewing slit, Felix caught sight of terrified skaven running for cover. The steam engine was making weird snorting sounds. The heat and humidity were appalling.

It was a ferocious brawl. Felix was much bigger and heavier but the skaven had a horrible wiry strength and the advantage of possessing long sharp teeth.

Pain flared through Felix as it sank them into his shoulder. He felt hot blood as it spurted through his shirt. With the pain and fear came a terrible anger.

'Right, that's it!' Felix spat, getting his hands around the skaven's throat and starting to squeeze. At the same time, he shoved the skaven's head away from him and started to smash it into the side of the steam tank.

* * *

This was not a good night, Heskit One Eye thought, as the maniacal human bashed his head against the steel wall for the third time. The skaven could feel the strength draining out of him. There was no air in his lungs and no way to breathe with those iron-strong human hands around his throat. It was like being stuck in the gas once more, only a hundred times worse. If only he hadn't been betrayed by his worthless underlings, this would never have happened.

Over his attacker's shoulder, through the viewing slit, Heskit could see the open mouth of the pit leading down into the sewers. A mass of skaven were diving into it, fleeing from the scene of the battle. The steam tank, too, was heading right for it.

Felix had an awful sinking sensation in the pit of his stomach as the steam tank lurched and tumbled. They must have hit an obstruction or fallen into a pit, he thought, as he was thrown about the cabin. This is it, he thought, I'm going to die. Suddenly the steam tank came to rest with a horrid gurgling splash, and the familiar stink of the sewers filled Felix's nostrils.

His grip on the skaven's throat loosened and the thing took the opportunity to break free. It scampered up and out of the hatch like a ferret up a drainpipe. Judging by the flames coming from the boiler, Felix thought he'd better do the same. Painfully he reached up and pulled his battered frame up through the open hatch. He stood perched on top of the steam tank for a moment, glaring at the skaven he had just fought.

As he had thought, the vehicle had fallen through the pit the skaven had dug in the courtyard and was now sinking into the sewers. Smoke and steam and flames flickered through the hatch below him, scorching his boots and setting his trousers to smouldering. The whole steam tank bucked and shuddered in the mire. All around him, Felix could see a host of red eyes glittering in the dark. He was surrounded by skaven.

Out of the frying pan, into the fire, he thought.

Where had all these warriors come from, Heskit wondered dazedly? They should be up above fighting with the dwarf and his human ally, not cowering down here away from the fight. Not that it mattered right at this very moment. As a highly skilled warp engineer, Heskit recognised all the signs of a very serious malfunction in the steam tank. He did not doubt that he had mere moments to get clear before it exploded.

Fear lent his feet wings. He sprang out into the tightly packed mass of skaven. Before they could react, he skittered across their shoulders, trampling on their heads as he went. Even so, he knew that he was not going to get clear in time. There was only one thing for it.

Holding his snout, Heskit dived headlong into the sewer.

Judging by the speed with which the terrified skaven took off over the heads of its fellows, Felix knew that something terrible was about to happen. He had to act, right now. He sprang upwards, grabbed the lip of the pit and pulled himself clear, just as the mass of skaven swarmed forward over the steam tank.

He felt claws rip the leg of his britches as one of the pack leaders made a grab for him. Frantically he kicked out with his other foot, and felt something break as his boot connected with teeth.

Looking out into the greenly lit courtyard, he saw the Slayer jogging towards him.

Felix pulled himself upright and raced for the dwarf, shouting: 'Get down! It's going to ex–'

Behind him there was an enormous thunderous roar and a mighty flash like a lightning strike. A huge cloud of stinking smoke billowed forth. The shockwave threw Felix onto the ground hard. He was vaguely aware of a number of skaven forms tumbling headlong through the gloom around him. Then his head smacked into the ground and consciousness left him.

When Felix pulled himself upright, Gotrek was standing nearby, peering down into the mouth of the pit. All around them were hideously mangled skaven corpses. Felix could not guess whether they were the products of the explosion or Gotrek's efforts. Not that it mattered. The result was the same in the end.

Behind him there was a sudden, mighty crash. Felix looked back to see that the whole wall of the college had collapsed. Indeed, peculiar greenish flames were lapping through the entire building. Something told him that no amount of effort by fire-fighters was going to extinguish that blaze until its sorcerous fury was spent.

He turned to look back at the Slayer, noticing for the first time the huge splashes of blood which painted the dwarf's body and dripped from his axe. Gotrek grinned and showed his missing teeth.

'Got most of them. The rest ran away,' he said in disgust. 'They seemed to lose heart after I killed the first fifty.'

'Yes, but at what a price! We've burned the college to the ground! Think of all that knowledge lost.'

'Colleges can be rebuilt, manling.' The Slayer tapped his head with one brawny finger. 'Knowledge is in here. The masters and apprentices survived. Things will go on.'

'We'd better go on and get out of here. The guard will be coming soon.'

Wearily, they made their departure. Somewhere in the distance the alarm bells were already tolling.

Heskit raised his head above the brown sludgy mass and spat out a mouthful of rank sewer water. That had been too close for comfort, he thought. Only the fact that the jelly-like consistency of this part of the flow had absorbed the shock of the blast had enabled him to survive, he was sure. It looked like all the others were dead.

Still, he was alive, that was the main thing, he thought as he padded along through the water with strokes of his paws and lashes of his tail. Now all he had to do was find an explanation for this fiasco which the cursed grey seer would accept. Because somehow he was sure that Thanquol would know all about this night's work.

PLAGUE MONKS OF PESTILENS

'Having shed some light on the disaster which befell the College of Engineering in that accursed year, I feel that I can move on to cover another topic. It was during this period of my life that I acquired more knowledge of the foul breed of rat-men known as skaven than I ever wished or deemed advisable. Even the possession of such knowledge as I had would have been considered cause enough for burning at the stake by our more fanatically dedicated witch hunters. I have often thought that if such people showed half the zeal in persecuting the real enemies of our society as they do in pursuing innocent scholars, our world would be a safer and happier place. Of course, the real enemies of our society are a far more dangerous breed than innocent scholars and have allies in far higher places. I leave my readers to draw their own conclusions from that.'

— From *My Travels With Gotrek, Vol. III*, by Herr Felix Jaeger
(Altdorf Press, 2505)

The man clutched his throat, gave a gurgling moan and keeled over, froth pouring from his lips, vile green stuff oozing from his nostrils. He lay on his back in a midden heap and frantically beat the muddy pavement with his fists, then all the strength seemed to leave him. His limbs twitched feebly in a final spasm of motion, then he gave a last long groan and lay still.

The people in the street all around looked at each other in fright, then raced away from the body as fast as they could. Beggars crawled away from their resting places. The one-legged man hopped away, almost dropping his crutch in his haste. Peddlers abandoned their stalls; goodwives ducked back into their buildings and locked their doors. Rich merchants urged their palanquin bearers to greater speed. Within moments, the street was all but deserted. Throughout the hubbub of the departing crowd ran one word – plague!

Felix Jaeger glanced around the suddenly empty street. It didn't look like anyone else was going to help the poor devil, so it seemed the job fell to him. He covered his mouth with his tattered cloak and knelt beside the body. He laid a hand on the man's chest, searching for a heartbeat.

It was too late. The man was beyond any help: he was dead. Felix had enough experience of death to know.

'Felix, come away. I'm frightened.'

Felix looked up. Elissa stood nearby, her face pale and her eyes wide. She ran a hand through her curly black hair, then brought it back to her mouth.

'Nothing to be frightened of,' Felix said. 'The man is dead.'

'It's what killed him that scares me. It looks like he died of the new plague.'

Felix stood up, superstitious fear filling his mind. For the first time he was forced to consider the death he had just witnessed and the reason why everyone else had fled.

Plagues were terrible things. They could strike anywhere, kill anyone, rich or poor. No one knew what caused them. Some said the dark influence of Chaos. Some said they were the wrath of the gods on sinful humanity. The only certainty with plague was that there was very little that you could do to save yourself once you caught it, save pray. Such virulent diseases could baffle the best of physicians and the most potent of mages. Felix stepped away from the body quickly and moved to put his arm around Elissa reassuringly. She shied away, as if he carried the contagion.

'I don't have the plague,' he said, hurt.

'You never know.'

Felix glanced down at the body and shivered.

'It certainly wasn't that poor soul's lucky day,' Elissa said.

'What do you mean?'

'Take a look. There's a black rose on his tunic. He'd just been to a funeral.'

'Well, now he's going to his own,' Felix said softly.

'That's the fourth death today from the plague that I've heard of,' Heinz said when Felix told him the news. 'The lads in the bar are talking about nothing else. They've a sweepstake going on how many it will be by nightfall.'

In a way, Felix was glad of this news. For the past few days, the citizens had talked of nothing but the burning down of the College of Engineering. Most claimed it was sabotage perpetrated by Chaos worshippers or the Bretonnians. Felix continually felt spasms of guilt as he was reminded of his own participation in the event.

'What do you think?' Felix asked, looking around at how many people were present. The bar was packed to capacity, and the inevitable jostling was already causing friction. Felix felt certain there would be trouble this evening.

'I put my money on it being ten. Last year, when the Red Pox came, there were twenty people gone by noon. But then the Red Pox was a nasty one. Worst in twenty years. Still, you never know – this one might be worse before it's done.'

'I meant, what do you think caused it?' Felix said. 'How do you think it spreads?'

'I'm not a physician, Felix, I'm a bartender. I guess that it's spread by tinkers and witches. That's what my old wife Lotte used to say.'

'Do you think I could have caught it from that poor man?'

'Maybe. I wouldn't worry. When Old Man Morr pulls your name out of his big black hat, there's nothing you can do about it, that's what I think. One thing's for sure, though.'

'What's that?'

'It's good for business. Soon as plague comes, people hit the taverns. They want to forget about it as quick as they can.'

'Maybe they want to die drunk.'

'There's worse ways to die, young Felix.'

'That there is.'

'Well, you'd better get over there and stop those Tileans drawing knives on each other, or we'll soon have a graphic demonstration of just that.'

'I'll deal with it.'

Felix moved to hastily intervene in the dispute. In a few seconds he had far more immediate dangers to worry about than catching the plague.

'So you're not worried about the plague?' Felix said, ducking a swing from a drunken mercenary.

'Never catch the things, manling,' Gotrek Gurnisson replied, grabbing the mercenary's ear, pulling his head down level with the dwarf's own and then dropping the man with a headbutt which sent blood from the man's bleeding nose spraying outwards to add a new and brighter tint to the Slayer's great crest of red-dyed hair. 'Been right through a dozen sieges. Humans dropped like flies; I was fine. Dwarfs don't usually get the plague. We leave that to less hardy races like elves and men.'

Felix caught two of the mercenary's squabbling comrades by the scruffs of their necks and hauled them upright. Gotrek grabbed one, Felix grabbed the other and they ran them out through the swinging doors into the muddy streets.

'Worst thing I've ever had was a bad hangover,' Gotrek said. 'And don't come back!' he bellowed out into the street.

Felix turned to survey the bar. As Heinz had predicted, it was full. Slumming nobles mingled with half the cut-throats and rakehells of the city. A big gang of mercenaries fresh in from the Middenheim caravan route were spending their money like there was going to be no tomorrow.

Maybe they were right, Felix thought; maybe there wouldn't be a tomorrow. Maybe all the streetcorner seers were right. Maybe the end of the world was coming. Certainly the world had ended today, as far as that man who had died in the street was concerned.

In the far corner, he could see that Elissa was talking to a brawny young man garbed in the rough tunic and leggings of a peasant. Their conversation became animated for a moment, then Elissa turned to leave. As she did so, the youth reached out and grabbed her wrist. Felix began to move over to intervene. Being pawed was an occupational hazard for the serving wenches but he didn't like it happening to Elissa. She turned and said something to the youth. His hand opened and he let go immediately, a look of something like shock on his face. Elissa left him there, his mouth hanging open and a pained look in his eyes.

Elissa hurried past, chin up, carrying a tray full of empty tankards. Felix caught her by the arm, turned her around, kissed her cheek.

'I don't have the plague,' he said, but she still wriggled away.

Felix could hear the word 'plague' being discussed at every table. It was as if there were no other topic of conversation in the whole blasted city.

'Really, I don't,' Felix added softly. He turned around and noticed that the youth who had been talking to Elissa was staring at him with a look of anger in his eyes. Felix was tempted to go over and talk to him but before he could, the young peasant got up and stalked none too steadily to the door.

'I know you don't have the plague,' Elissa said, snuggling closer to Felix on the pallet they shared. She picked up a piece of straw which had burst out of the hole in the mattress and began to tickle him under the nose with it. 'You don't have to keep telling me. Really, I wish you'd just shut up about it.'

'Maybe I'm trying to reassure myself,' he said, grabbing her wrist and immobilising her hand. He reached over with his other hand and began to tickle her. 'Who was that you were talking to earlier?' he asked.

'When?'

'Down in the bar. A young man. Looked straight off the farm.'

'Oh, you saw him, then?' she asked, her voice all feigned innocence.

'Apparently so.'

'That was Hans.'

'And who is Hans?' Felix said levelly.

'He's just a friend.'

'He didn't seem to think so, judging by the look he gave me.'

'We used to go out together back in my village but he was very jealous and he had a terrible temper.'

'He hit you?'

'No, he hit any man who looked at me in what he thought was the wrong way. The village elders got fed up with it and put him in the stocks. After that he ran away to the city, to look for his fortune, he said.'

'Is that why you came here, to find him?'

'Maybe. It was a long time ago and Nuln's a big place. I never saw him again, until tonight, when he came into the Pig. He hasn't changed much.'

'You were close?'

'Once.'

'Not now?'

'No.' Elissa looked at him seriously. 'You ask a lot of questions, Felix Jaeger.'

'Then stop me asking,' he said and began to kiss her hungrily. But in his mind, he was still wondering about Elissa and Hans and what had gone on between them.

Grey Seer Thanquol helped himself to another pinch of warpstone snuff. The brain-blastingly potent drug sent a charge of pure energy through his body, and his tail stiffened in ecstatic joy. He basked in the warm glow of triumph.

His intricately woven scheme had succeeded and his rival Heskit One Eye's plan to seize all of the technological secrets of the human College of Engineering had been thwarted. Thanquol bared his fangs in a death's head grin when he considered Heskit's discomfiture. He had made the proud warp engineer grovel in the dirt before his whole army while he explained what he had been doing. He had berated Heskit for almost jeopardising the whole glorious campaign to assault Nuln by his ill-considered actions, and sent him slinking off with his tail between his legs.

Now Heskit had retired to his chambers to sulk, while he waited for reinforcements to arrive from Skavenblight to replace the warriors he had lost on the surface. With any luck no new warriors would come. Heskit might even be recalled to Skavenblight to explain his actions to his superiors. Perhaps, Thanquol thought, with a word in the right ear this course of action could be encouraged.

The curtain which separated Thanquol's private burrow from the rest of the Underways was wrenched open and a small skaven entered the chamber.

Reflexively Thanquol sprang back behind his throne. The eerie glow of dark magic surrounded his paw as he summoned the energy to blast the interloper to atoms, but then he saw that it was only Lurk Snitchtongue, and he stayed his spell for a moment.

'Grave news, most potent of potentates!' Lurk chittered, then fell silent as he noticed the aura of magic which surrounded the grey seer. 'No! No! Most merciful of masters, don't kill me! Don't! Don't!'

'Never, on pain of death most excruciating, ever burst into my chambers unannounced again,' Thanquol said, not relaxing his vigilance for a moment. After all, you could never tell when an assassination attempt might happen. Jealous rivals were everywhere.

'Yes! Yes, most perceptive of seers. Never again shall it happen. Only...'

'Only what?'

'Only I bring most important tidings, great one.'

'What would those be?'

'I have heard rumours–'

'Rumours? Do not barge into my sacred chambers and talk to me about rumours!'

'Rumours from a usually reliable source, greatest of authorities.'

Thanquol nodded. That was different. Over the past few days Thanquol had come to have a certain respect for Lurk's host of informants. The little skaven had a talent for ferreting out information that rivalled even Thanquol's... almost. 'Go on. Speak! Speak! Waste not my precious time!'

'Yes! Yes! I have heard rumours that Vilebroth Null and his chief acolytes have left the Underways and went surfacewards to the mancity of Nuln, there to establish a secret burrow.'

What could the Clan Pestilens abbot be up to, thought Thanquol, his mind reeling? What did this signify? It inevitably meant some sort of treachery to the sacred skaven cause, some scheme to grab the glory that was rightfully Thanquol's. 'Go on!'

'It may be that they took with them the Cauldron of a Thousand Poxes!'

Oh no, thought Thanquol. The cauldron was one of the most hideously powerful artefacts that Clan Pestilens was thought to possess. Since early runthood, Thanquol had heard dire tales of its powers. It was said to be the means of infallibly brewing terrible diseases, an artefact stolen from a temple of the Plague God, Nurgle, back when the world was young, and reconsecrated to the service of the Horned Rat.

If the cauldron was on the surface somewhere, that could only mean

Vilebroth Null meant to start a plague among the humans. Under normal circumstances, Thanquol would have been only too pleased by such an eventuality – just as long as he was a thousand leagues away! Clan Pestilens plagues had a habit of running out of control, of afflicting skaven as well as their intended victims. Only the plague monks themselves seemed immune. Many seemingly assured skaven triumphs had been undermined by just this occurrence. Now Clan Pestilens were only supposed to unleash their creations by special authorisation of the Council of Thirteen.

The last thing Thanquol wanted at this moment was his army destroyed by a runaway plague. He considered the implications still more. Of course, the council did not argue with success. Perhaps the plague might succeed in weakening the humans without afflicting the skaven horde. But if it succeeded, the Council of Thirteen might extend its favour to Vilebroth Null, and withdraw its patronage from Thanquol. Null might even be rewarded with the leadership of the invasion force.

Thanquol considered. What else could be going on here? If the scheme was an honest effort to help the invasion, why had Thanquol not been informed? He, after all, was supreme commander. No – this had to be some sinister scheme of Null's to seize power. Something would have to be done about this treachery and this blatant defiance of the Council of Thirteen's edicts.

Then another thought struck Thanquol. His agents on the surface had already reported tales of some new and dreadful disease spreading among the human burrows. Undoubtedly Vilebroth Null had already begun to implement his wicked plan. There was no time to waste!

'Quick! Quick! Where did those treacherous vermin go?'

'I know not, most lordly of lords. My agents could not say!'

'Run! Quick! Quick! Scuttle off and find out.'

'At once, most decisive of leaders!'

'Wait! Wait! Before you go, bring me parchment and pen. I have an idea.'

'You sneezed!' Elissa said.

'Did not!' Felix said, well aware that he was lying. His eyes felt puffy and his nose was dripping. He was sweating a little too. And was that the first faint tickle of a sore throat he felt?

Elissa began to cough hackingly. She covered her mouth with one hand but her whole body shook.

'You coughed,' Felix said, and wished that he had not. Tears had started to appear in the corner of the girl's eyes.

'Oh Felix,' she said. 'Do you think we have the plague?'

'No. Absolutely not,' Felix replied, but in his heart of hearts he was far from certain. Cold dread clutched at him. 'Get dressed,' he said. 'We'll go and see a physician.'

The doctor was a busy man today; that much was obvious, thought Felix. There had been a queue stretching halfway around the block from his small and dingy office. It seemed like half the city was there, coughing and wheezing and hawking and spitting into the street. There was an air of barely suppressed panic. Once or twice Felix had seen people come to blows.

This was useless, Felix decided. They would never see a physician today under these conditions, and the aisles of the Temple of Shallya were full of supplicants. There had to be a better way.

'Come on. I have an idea,' he said, grabbing Elissa by her hand and pulling her from the queue.

'No, Felix, I want to see the doctor.'

'You will – don't worry.'

'Felix! What are you doing here?' Otto did not look pleased. In fact, he had not looked pleased since Felix had refused his offer of returning to the family business and, instead, started work in the Blind Pig. Felix looked at his brother keenly. Otto was dressed particularly richly today in a gown of purple brocade trimmed with ermine, and Felix felt his own ragged appearance keenly. It had taken him nearly ten minutes to convince the clerks to let him in and see his brother.

'I thought you might be able to help me.' Felix sniffed. There was a strange scent in the room, of spices and the sort of flowers that one usually only smelled at funerals. Felix wondered where it had come from.

'I'll do what I can, of course.' Otto regarded him warily.

Ever the merchant, thought Felix, waiting to see what price was going to be asked.

'I need to see a doctor.'

Otto's eyes darted from Felix to Elissa and back to Felix again. Felix could almost see the thoughts forming behind his brow.

'You haven't… got this girl into trouble, have you?'

Felix laughed for the first time that day. 'No.'

'Then what's the problem?'

Quickly Felix told his brother about the man who had died in the streets, about his own symptoms and the huge queues at the doctor's and the Temple of Shallya. Otto steepled his fingers and listened attentively, occasionally fumbling with a brass pomander which he lifted to his nose and breathed deeply from. At once Felix identified the source of the smell in the chamber.

'What's that?' he asked.

'A pomander of wildroot and silverspice from Far Cathay. The vapours are a sovereign remedy for all airborne fluxes and evil humours, or so Doctor Drexler assures me. Perhaps you'd like to try it?'

He unhooked the chain from around his neck and extended the small perforated sphere to Felix. The smell was very strong. He politely handed it to Elissa. She placed it beneath her nostrils inhaled deeply and began to cough.

'It certainly clears the nostrils,' she gasped, eyes watering.

Felix took the pomander and breathed deeply. He immediately understood what Elissa had meant. The vapours cut through the air like a knife. They had a sharp, minty tang and almost at once a feeling of warmth spread through his head and chest. His nose felt clearer and his breathing came easier.

'Very good,' he gasped, returning the device. 'But can you help us see a physician?'

Otto pursed his lips primly. 'Of course, Felix. You are my brother.'

'And Elissa?'

'Her too.'

It's amazing how money smoothes all paths, Felix thought, looking around Doctor Drexler's chambers. Without the use of Otto's name, he doubted the servant would have let him through the doors of the doctor's luxuriously appointed townhouse. Felix had to admit that it was quite a place.

On the oak-panelled walls were framed certificates from the Universities of Nuln, Altdorf and Marienberg, as well as hand-written testimonials from maybe half the crowned heads of the Empire. A massive portrait of the good doctor painted by the famous Kleinmann beamed down impressively from the middle of them all. Of course, for the fees that he charged, Drexler could certainly afford the services of the great portrait artist.

Felix glanced over the doorway. The doctor and Elissa were in his consulting room. Felix had been left outside for the moment. He rose from the comfortable leather armchair and looked around.

Along one wall was a collection of large glass jars which would not have been out of place in an alchemist's shop. The bookshelves were lined with musty leather-bound tomes. Felix picked one up. It was Johannes Voorman's *Der Natur Malorum*. A first edition, no less. The pages had been cut, which meant that someone around here had read it. It wasn't just window-dressing, straight from the bookbinders. Felix examined the other titles and was surprised to discover that only half of them were medical or alchemical in nature. The rest dealt with a variety of subjects, from natural history to the motion of the Spheres. It seemed that the doctor was indeed a well-read man.

'You are a scholar, Herr Jaeger?'

Felix turned to find that Drexler had emerged from the consulting room. He was a short, slender man with a narrow, friendly face and a short, well-trimmed beard. He looked more like a successful merchant than a doctor. His robes were as rich as Otto's and there was not a sign of blood stains anywhere. Felix could not even see the traditional pot of leeches.

'I've read a little,' he admitted.

'That is good. A man should always improve his mind whenever there is an opportunity.'

'How is Elissa?'

Drexler took off his glasses and breathed on them, then polished them on the hem of his robe. He beamed reassuringly. 'She is fine. She has a summer cold. That is all.'

Felix understood why the rich were so willing to pay for the services of this man. There was something hugely reassuring about his quiet soft-spoken voice and his calm, certain smile. 'Not... not the plague then?'

'No. Not the plague. No buboes. No lesions. No suppurating ulcers of the skin. None of the usual symptoms of any of the greater plagues. Of that I am sure.'

Elissa emerged from the consulting room. She smiled at Felix. He forced himself to smile back. 'I understand that you were exposed to a plague bearer yesterday, Herr Jaeger,' the doctor said, suddenly all seriousness.

'Yes.'

'Best have a look at you then. Let me see your arm.'

For the next few minutes the doctor performed all manner of arcane rituals the like of which Felix had never seen. He touched his wrist and counted, while keeping track of a chronometer on the wall. He tapped Felix's chest painfully. He looked into Felix's eyes with a magnifying glass.

This was not what Felix had expected. Where were the scalpels, and unguents, and leeches? Was this man some sort of charlatan? He was certainly most unlike any doctor or barber Felix had ever encountered. His robes were not filthy and crusted with dried blood, for one thing. And the man was tanned, unusually so for a man who spent most of his life indoors. Felix mentioned this fact and Drexler looked at him sharply.

'I have spent time in Araby,' Drexler said. 'I studied medicine at the great School at Kah Sabar.'

Felix looked at the wall. There was no diploma there from any Arabyan university. Drexler obviously understood his train of thought, for he laughed. 'They do not give degrees in Kah Sabar! By the time you leave you are either a healer or you are not. If you are not, no piece of paper will make you one.'

'A fair point. But what did you learn there that you could not learn here in the Empire?'

Like all of its citizens Felix considered the Empire to be the most advanced and enlightened human nation on the face of the planet. He could not conceive that there was anything the Arabyans had to teach one of its people. The elves and dwarfs, certainly – but not the Arabyans.

'Many things, my friend. Including the fact that we have no monopoly on wisdom and that much of what our doctors teach is simply wrong.'

'For example?'

'Well… I do not bleed my patients. It does more harm than good.'

Felix was at once relieved and shocked. Relieved because like most people he dreaded the physician's scalpel. Shocked because the man was obviously a charlatan! Everybody knew that bleeding was essential to release the foul humours in the blood and speed the patient's recovery. And yet, Otto had claimed that this man was the best doctor in Nuln and had cured more people than all the other surgeon-barbers put together. Furthermore, Drexler did seem like a profoundly civilised and educated man.

'Do you think I have the plague?' Felix asked suddenly, surprised at the fear and anticipation that filled him as he waited for Drexler's reply.

'No, Herr Jaeger, I do not. I think you have a slight cold, nothing more. I think most of the people in this city who think they have the plague probably have the same, and I think that the panic such beliefs cause will be more harmful than the plague itself.'

'You don't think the plague is real, then?'

'Oh I certainly believe it's real. I think many people will die from it, as the summer heat comes on, and more people come in from the country. But I know you do not have it, nor do any of the wealthy people who come to see me. If you did, you would already be dead or dying.'

'That would make it easy to diagnose,' Felix said dryly. Drexler laughed again.

'I will give you and Fraulein Elissa the same herbal pomanders as I gave your brother and his family. The herbs are a protection against plague emanations, and I have cast a few spells on them as well.'

'You are a magician as well as a doctor, then?'

'I am a healer, Herr Jaeger, and I use whatever means best help my patients. I dabble in enchantments of a protective sort. I cannot utterly guarantee their effectiveness, you understand, but they should help if you are exposed to the plague.'

'I thank you for that.'

'Don't thank me, Herr Jaeger. Thank your brother, after all he is paying my bill.'

Just as Felix turned to go, he noticed that Drexler was staring at him hard. His face had turned pale and his eyes hard.

'What is it?' Felix asked.

'The... the sword you carry. Would you mind telling me where you got it?'

'Not at all. It belonged to a friend, a Templar of the Fiery Heart named Aldred. He died and I took it, hoping one day to return it to his order. Why do you ask?'

'You were a friend of Aldred's?'

'We travelled together in the Border Princes. He was on a quest when he died.'

'I knew Aldred. We were friends for a long time. We studied in the Sigmarite Seminary together. I had not heard word of him in a long time.'

'Then I am sorry to be the bearer of such bad news to you.'

'He died well?'

'He died like a hero.'

'It is what he would have wanted. I'm sorry to have bothered you with this, Herr Jaeger.'

'No, I am sorry to be the bearer of such bad tidings.'

'He seemed like a very nice man,' Elissa said. 'And so wise. Very reassuring.'

'What did you say?'

Felix looked up at her. He was disturbed by the coincidence that Drexler had known the dead Templar, and he felt vaguely guilty about not having made a greater effort to return the blade. Still, it was a very fine weapon, and it had saved his life on more than one occasion.

'I said, he was very reassuring.'

'Very.' Felix looked at her sourly. She had been singing the doctor's praises all the way back to the Blind Pig and her hand had never strayed very far from the herbal pomander. Felix wondered if it was possible that he was jealous. He actually agreed with the woman but admitting it was difficult for some reason. Elissa seemed to sense this. She looked up at him and smiled teasingly.

'Why Felix, are you jealous?'

Why did women seem to have such an uncanny instinct for these things, he wondered – even as he muttered his denials.

Gotrek looked up as they entered the tavern. He held a rolled tube in one massive fist. He tossed it straight at Felix.

'Catch,' he said.

Felix snatched the tube out of the air and recognised it at once for what it was. The parchment was of the same crude weave as the earlier message they had received, the one which had warned them of the skaven attack on the College of Engineering. He hastily unrolled it, and was not at all surprised to find that it had been written in the same semi-literate scrawl:

> *Frends – be warned!! The evil trechrus ratmen of Klan Pestilens do plot to spred playgue in yoor city, may the Horned Rat gnaw there entrails for it. I do not no wher or how they plan to do this. I kan only tell yoo to be ware of the Kaldrun of a thousand poxes.*
> *Yoor frend.*

'It was delivered when you were out,' Gotrek said.

'Same messenger?'

'No, another beggar. Claims it was given to him by a monk.'

'You believe him?'

'I saw no reason not to, manling. I got him to show me the place where he had met this monk. It was close to spot where the last message was delivered.'

'You think we should check out the sewers in that area?'

'What are you talking about, Felix?' Elissa asked.

'Skaven,' Gotrek said ferociously, and the girl's face went pale.

'Not those creatures which attacked the inn the other night?'

'The same.'

'What do they have to do with you and Felix?'

'I do not know, girl. I wish I did. It seems like we have become involved in some feud among them.'

'I wish you had not told me that.'

'I wish you had not told her that,' Felix said.

'Do you think they will attack the Pig again?' Elissa asked, glancing at the doors and windows as if she expected an attack at any second.

'I doubt it,' Gotrek said. 'And if they do, we'll just slaughter them again.'

Elissa sat down in a chair near to the Slayer. He cocked his head to one side and smiled, showing several missing teeth. 'Do not worry, girl. Nothing will harm you.'

Gotrek was not normally what Felix would consider a reassuring sight, but his words seemed to calm Elissa.

'Do you think the skaven could have anything to do with this new plague?' Felix whispered, hoping that no one could overhear him.

'Our ratty friend would like us to believe this.'

'Then why hasn't he told us any more?'

'Perhaps he does not know any more himself, manling.'

Thanquol stared into his divining crystal. It was no use. He had no luck locating the plague monks and their accursed cauldron, and that in itself was not reassuring. A seer of his prowess, having invoked the proper rituals and made obeisance in the correct way to the Horned Rat, should have been able to detect an artefact of its power easily. Instead he had found no trace of it or its bearers anywhere. It suggested to Thanquol's keen mind that they were using magic of their own to cover their tracks. He knew that Vilebroth Null was a powerful sorcerer in his own right, and must have invoked spells of bafflement. Further proof of his treachery – as if any were needed!

Of course the traitor would claim that he had used the magic to escape detection by the human authorities, but Thanquol could see through such transparent ruses. He had not been born yesterday. The plague monks were simply trying to keep themselves hidden from their rightful leader until they could implement their plan and claim unwarranted glory.

Thanquol knew he must prevent this eventuality at all costs – as well as enforcing the Council of Thirteen's edict, of course. He would simply have to find another way of locating his prey. He wondered if the dwarf and his human ally had taken any action yet. Or were they too stupid to do anything without prompting from Thanquol?

* * *

Felix hurried through the darkness, his cloak wrapped around him. He stopped to cast a glance over his shoulder and to fumble at the pomander full of herbs at his throat. The smell of some fresh night soil which had been cast from the windows high above assaulted his nostrils. He dreaded putting his foot in it as much as he dreaded stumbling into one of the heaps of rubbish that lay decomposing in the street.

Why were all the houses not connected to the sewers, he wondered? Why did people still insist on dropping their rubbish and filth into the streets? He realised that his long trek through the wilderness with Gotrek had changed him. Until then he had been a lifelong city dweller and would never even have noticed the trash which packed the city streets. He paused for a moment to listen.

Was that the distant echo of footsteps? Was he being followed? He strained his ears for any noise but heard nothing.

He was not reassured by the silence. This was the wealthiest quarter of Nuln, but not even the rich went abroad in the darkness without a full quota of bodyguards. Robbers and footpads were everywhere. It was not just the prospect of normal everyday robbery that bothered Felix. Ever since the night of the skaven attack he had dreaded another ambush by the rat-men assassins. He felt certain that he had survived their last assault by pure luck alone, and he was all too aware how quickly someone's luck could change.

Still, he felt the potential gravity of the situation warranted risking these benighted streets. He needed help and he knew of only one source that might be able to provide the sort of aid he required. The door he sought was directly ahead of him. Drexler was an expert on diseases and he might be able to tell Felix something useful, if the skaven really were behind the current outbreak of plague. He knew that the man would most likely think him mad, but he was prepared to take that chance. He was out of his depth, dealing with an enemy that could wield noxious plagues the way a man might wield a sword. What he needed was knowledge, and Drexler impressed him as the man who might have it.

He reached up and pulled the handle of the doorbell. He noticed that it was moulded in the shape of a grinning gargoyle's head. In and of itself this was not unusual, but the appearance was disturbing here and now amid the night and fog. He heard footsteps from within the building and a peephole within the door rattled open. A faint glimmer of light appeared, level with Felix's eye.

'Who is it?' asked a voice. Felix recognised it as belonging to Drexler's servant.

'Felix Jaeger. I need to see Doctor Drexler.'

'Is it an emergency?'

Felix considered for a moment before replying, 'Yes!'

'Stand away from the door and be warned. We have firearms within.'

Felix did as he was told. He heard huge bolts being thrown and the barking of very large dogs. It was apparent that the physician took no chances with his own safety, and Felix in no way blamed him for this. Such precautions were only sensible in the great cities of the Empire.

'Throw back your cowl and stand where I can see you.'

Felix did as he was told and the beam of a lantern was shone full on his face. He saw that the old man had recognised him.

'Sorry, Herr Jaeger,' the manservant said. 'You can't be too careful these days.'

'I quite agree,' Felix said. 'Now please take me to your master. I have urgent business with him.'

Drexler sat by the fire in a huge study. The flicker of the flames underlit his face and made it look vaguely daemonic. He leaned forward with a poker and prodded the glowing coals until they collapsed, then added more from the bucket beside the fireplace. When he looked up, the flames were reflected in his glasses. The effect was eerie.

'Now, how can I help you, Herr Jaeger?' he said calmly, then smiled. 'You do not appear to be ill. Is it the girl?'

Felix glanced around the room. The servant had already retreated, the thick Arabyan rugs absorbing his footsteps. It was an impressive chamber, even larger than his father's library in Altdorf and with a far greater selection of books. Felix's keen eyes sought out dark corners as if he half expected to find enemies there, then he turned and looked directly at Drexler.

'What do you know of the skaven?' he asked bluntly.

Drexler stiffened for a moment and then carefully placed his poker back in the stand. He took off his glasses, polished them on the cuff of his robe and gave every appearance of serious consideration to Felix's question.

'They are a race of rat-men, considered to be extinct by many scholars. Spengler thinks they were a sub-breed of human mutant. Leiber theorised that they might be the product of ancient sorcery. It is said that in ancient times they warred with the dwarfs but...'

'I know they are not extinct.'

Drexler looked at Felix sharply. 'You know?'

'Yes. I have fought with them. They are here. In Nuln.'

Drexler sat back in his chair, placed his spectacles on the bridge of his nose and gripped an arm of the chair with each hand. 'Please be seated. You interest me.'

Felix allowed himself to slump down in the chair facing Drexler's. The heat from the fire had warmed one arm of it and made him uncomfortable. He pushed it away from the hearth slightly, before he started to speak. He told Drexler of his time in the sewer watch and their encounter with the rat-men in the tunnels beneath the city. He omitted only the fact that they had broken into the house of Fritz von Halstadt and killed him. He spoke of the skaven attack on the Blind Pig which he presumed was some sort of revenge attempt by the rat-men. He left out any mention that he and Gotrek had also fought with the rat-men within the College of Engineering on the night it had been burned to the ground. Drexler watched him with increasing astonishment. When Felix had finished, he spoke.

'Herr Jaeger, if all this is true, why have I not heard more of it. Why haven't the authorities acted?'

'I do not know. Perhaps the skaven have allies in high places.' He was thinking of von Halstadt now. How many more like him occupied positions of power in Nuln and the rest of the Empire? 'I sometimes think that there is a conspiracy within our society to cover up the effects of Chaos and all its works.'

He noticed that Drexler flinched slightly at the word 'conspiracy', but that the mention of Chaos did not seem to disturb him at all.

'If you were not so obviously sane, I would suspect you of being a lunatic,' Drexler added. 'Certainly, some of what you are saying sounds like the ravings of a madman.'

'I know it,' Felix said. 'Unfortunately, it is all true.'

'That is certainly a possibility. In Araby they do not consider the rat-men legendary and I have spoken with several dwarfs who have claimed to have encountered them. The elf seafarers also tell tales of the rat-men's power. But I fail to see why you have come to me other than to confide your tale.'

Felix handed over the letter that Gotrek had received. Drexler unrolled it and read it calmly.

'Clan Pestilens,' he said eventually. 'Yes, I have read of them.'

'What?'

'Clan Pestilens. Certain of the old tomes, most notably Leiber's *The Loathsome Ratmen And All Their Vile Kin*, claim that the skaven are divided into many different clans, each with its own role in skaven society, and its own unique brand of sorcery. Leiber claims that Clan

Pestilens were plague makers. He goes so far as to state that they were responsible for the Great Plague of the year 1111. If whoever sent you this letter is a hoaxer, he is certainly an erudite one. I doubt that there are more than twenty people in the Empire who now own a copy of Leiber's book.'

'Do you?'

'Yes. I came across references to Leiber's theory about the Great Plague in Moravec's work and sought it out. I have what you might call a professional interest in these things.'

'May I see it?'

'Of course. But first, you must answer a few of my questions.'

'Certainly. Ask away!'

'Do you really 'seriously' believe that the skaven may be behind this new outbreak of plague in the city?'

'Yes. From what I've seen of them it would suit their method of warfare. I believe that perhaps they are undergoing a resurgence and that soon our world will no longer doubt their existence.'

'Such would accord with Leiber's own theories.'

'What do you mean?' Felix looked up.

'Leiber claims that the skaven have a very high birth-rate and that when the conditions are right their population grows explosively. At such times they devour all the food in their own realms and must seek food and resources elsewhere. At such times, they explode onto the surface world in huge, hungry hordes. And they keep fighting until either they conquer, or so many of them are killed that they can once more subsist in their own realm.'

'I must read this book.'

'Yes. It is very interesting. He makes other claims that are difficult to verify.'

'Such as?'

'He claims these eruptions usually correlate with strange disturbances and erratic behaviour from Morrslieb, the lesser moon.'

'Such as the one which preceded the Great Plague in 1111?'

'You are a learned man, Herr Jaeger. Yes, such as that occurrence and the one which preceded the great Chaos Incursion two hundred years ago. I believe that another may be due to occur in our own time.'

'So all the soothsayers and astrologers claim.'

'There may be truth in it.'

'Do you have any other questions?'

'Yes, but they can wait. I can see you are anxious to get at Leiber's work and far be it from me to stand between a fellow scholar and his books.'

Drexler brought a small set of steps and a lantern and they proceeded through the rows of bookcases to the furthest corner of the room. From the highest shelf Drexler dragged down a musty leather-bound tome, handling it reverently with both hands. He blew the fine patina of dust off its cover and handed it to Felix.

'There is a table and a reading lamp over there. I will leave you for a few minutes. I have some tasks to perform.' Felix nodded, now totally wrapped up in his excitement over finding this volume.

It was heavy. The title and author's name embossed in gold leaf on the spine had been almost rubbed away. Two massive hinges of brass held the covers in place and helped them swing outwards. Felix sat down at the table and lit the reading lamp from a candle, turning the tiny handle at the base to extend the wick to its fullest length then placing the shade back over the flame. The pungent smell of aromatic oil filled the air as he began to read.

The book's title page said it had been printed by Altdorf Press over one hundred and eighty years ago. That meant that Leiber had most likely been around during the last great incursion of Chaos, or had at least known people who had been. It was possible that he might even have had first-hand experience of the rat-men.

As he read, Felix discovered that this was exactly what the author claimed. In the introduction he stated that he had encountered a horde of rat-men during the Great Chaos War. Unlike his fellows, Leiber had been convinced that they were not simply a new form of beastman but a completely separate race, and he had devoted the next ten years of his life to uncovering all manner of information about them. He referred to various scholarly sources, such as Schtutt, van Hal and Krueger, which Felix made a mental note to consult later.

His book was divided into short chapters, each dealing with an aspect of the structure of skaven society and its various clans. Felix read, horrified, as Leiber dwelled on Clan Moulder's vile experiments with living creatures, changing them into all manner of foul mutant monsters. He recognised the artificers of Clan Skryre as the creatures he and Gotrek had encountered at the College of Engineering. The thing which had set the monster on them in Fritz von Halstadt's mansion was a grey seer, some sort of verminous priest. Leiber may have written like a ranting maniac but everything he wrote tallied with Felix's own hard-won experience. Even if the scholar was discredited, he was also correct.

Felix paid particular attention to the section on Clan Pestilens, and about how they created diseases and used all manner of foul devices to spread their filthy plagues. The descriptions of the Boil Lurgy and the Flea Buboes made his skin crawl. There were horrors here that went beyond any he had previously imagined.

A shadow fell on him and he looked up to see Drexler standing over him. He realised that he must have been reading for hours in the gloom, and that his eyes hurt from the strain.

'Have you found what you were looking for?' Drexler asked.

'More than I ever wanted to know.'

'Good. Come and see me tomorrow and I may be able to help you. You may take the book with you if you wish. '

'Help me. How?'

'We will visit the city morgue.'

'How will that help?'

'You will see tomorrow, Herr Jaeger. Now go home and sleep.'

Gotrek looked up from his plate as Felix entered the Blind Pig. 'Look what the cat dragged in,' he said, and stuffed a hunk of black bread into his mouth.

Elissa looked up from her place beside him. 'Oh, Felix, I was so worried. You said you'd be back in a couple of hours and it's almost dawn. I thought the rat-men might have got you.'

Felix laid the book down on the table and hugged her tight. 'I'm fine. I just had to find out a few things.'

'*The Loathsome Ratmen And All Their Vile Kin*,' Gotrek read, tilting his head and reading the spine of the book.

Elissa looked at him in astonishment. 'I didn't know you could read,' she said.

Gotrek grinned, showing the blackened stumps of his teeth. He flicked the book open with one greasy finger and began turning pages until he found the one bookmarked at Clan Pestilens. 'He knows his stuff, this Leiber. Must have consulted dwarfish sources.'

'Yes, yes,' Felix said tetchily. 'Must have.'

'Where did you get this, manling?'

'Doctor Drexler.'

'He's a man of many interests, your friend Drexler, if he owns books like this one.'

'You'll get a chance to find out for yourself.'

'Will I indeed? How so?'

'Because we're going with him to the morgue.'

* * *

Grey Seer Thanquol scurried backwards and forwards, pacing the floor of his lair like one of the captured humans he kept working the tread-mills back in Skavenblight. His mind raced faster under the pressure of all the warpstone snuff he had consumed.

Still those verminous Clan Pestilens traitors had conspired to elude him. Their sorcery had proved effective, even against his most subtle and potent divinations. His spies had not been able to uncover another word about their location no matter how deep they dug. It was all very frustrating.

Somewhere deep in his bowels, Thanquol could sense with omi-nous certainty that the hour when the plague monks' plan would be implemented was drawing very close. He knew that he must be correct in this, for in the past such premonitions had never been wrong. He was a grey seer, after all.

A terrible sense of impending doom filled Thanquol's mind. He wanted to run for cover, to scurry to a hiding place, but right at this moment he could think of nowhere to go.

Plague, he kept thinking. Plague was coming.

'Good morning, Doctor Drexler,' the priest of Morr said, and coughed. He looked up from his table set in an alcove at the entrance to the city morgue. His black cowl hid his face, making him seem as sinister as the god he served. The air was filled with the smell of black roses, fresh-plucked from the Gardens of Morr. 'What is it you require?'

'I would like to see the corpses of the latest plague victims.'

Felix was astonished at the calm manner in which the doctor made his request. Most of the people in the city would rather run a thou-sand miles than do what the doctor wanted to do. The priest obviously thought so too. He threw back the cowl of his robes to reveal a pallid, bony face framed by a stringy black beard.

'That is a most unusual request,' he said. 'I will have to consult with my superiors.'

'As you wish,' Drexler said. 'Tell them I simply want to ascertain whether all the victims died of the same disease or whether we're going to have a variety of plagues to deal with this summer.'

The priest nodded and retreated within the shadowy depths of the temple. Somewhere off in the distance a great bell tolled gloomily. Somewhere, Felix knew, another funeral service was about to begin.

The priest returned presently. 'The arch-lector says you may pro-ceed,' he said. 'However, he also asked me to tell you that most of the bodies have already been sent to the Gardens of Morr for internment. We only have the four who came in last night.'

'That should be sufficient,' Drexler said. 'I hope.'

Felix, Gotrek and Doctor Drexler all paid the ceremonial copper piece and donned the black robes and headpieces of Morr. This was sacred ground, the priest told them, and it was needful that they do so. The robes had obviously been made for humans and the hems of Gotrek's dragged along the floor. Without another word they set off into the gloomy interior of the mortuary.

It was cool and it was dark. The floors were clean, washed with some sacred unguents. The smell of attar of black roses was everywhere. It was not what Felix had expected. He had expected rot and the smell of spoiled meat. He had expected the scent of death.

The central chamber of the Death God's house was arrayed with marble slabs. Upon each slab lay a corpse. Felix averted his eyes. The bodies belonged to people who had died under unusual circumstances and who needed special rites said over them to ensure their soul's easy passage into the afterlife. Many of them were not pretty. On one slab lay the blue and bloated corpse of a fisherman which had obviously recently been dragged from the Reik. On another lay the body of a woman who had been hideously cut up and mutilated by some madman. They passed the body of a child which, Felix saw when he looked closer, had had its head separated from the body. He looked away swiftly.

Here the smell overcame the scent of incense and unguents. Felix understood with a start why their cowls had a special flap of cloth which could be drawn over the mouth and nostrils. He adjusted his to cut down on the stink and moved on to the section where the plague victims lay. Nearby stood two priests, eyes closed, censers held in their hands. They muttered prayers for the dead and showed no fear of what had killed them.

Perhaps they were simply inured to fear by their long exposure to death, Felix thought. Or perhaps they simply did not fear to die? They were, after all, priests of the Death God and were assured of preferential treatment in the hereafter. He decided that if he ever encountered one of the priests later he would ask him about this. He was curious how they had become so hardened.

Drexler advanced cautiously to the slabs and exchanged words and coins with the priests. They nodded, ceased their muttering, and withdrew. Without fuss, Drexler drew back a sheet from the nearest body.

It was the body of a short man, a trader, dressed in his best. A black rose was set in the lapel of his tunic. He looked oddly exposed and defenceless in death. He had been cleaned up since he died.

'Some bruising on the hands and knees as well as on the forehead,' Drexler pointed out. 'Most likely from where the man fell over in the last extremities of his anguish.'

Felix thought of the spasming of the man he had seen in the street and understood how this could have happened.

'Notice the swollen areas on the chest and throat and the slight crust of greenish stuff on the upper lip and nostrils.'

Drexler pushed the eyelids back with his fingers and there were faint traces of green around the eye rims as well. 'I am sure that if I performed a dissection, something which our priestly friends here would object to, we would find the lungs filled with a green viscous fluid. It is this which eventually kills the victim. They literally drown in it.'

'A horrible way to die,' Felix said.

'In my experience few diseases kill pleasantly, Herr Jaeger,' Drexler said. He moved on to the next body and drew back the sheet. This was the corpse of a middle-aged woman, dressed in black. Her eyes were open and stared at the ceiling in horror. There was trace of rouge on her cheeks and of kohl around her eyes. Felix found that there was something rather pathetic about this attempt to improve the appearance of one who was now dead.

'At least she's dressed in the right colours,' Gotrek said – somewhat tactlessly, Felix thought.

Drexler shrugged. 'Widow's robes. Her husband must have died within the last year or so. She'll be joining him now.'

He moved along to the next slab and studied the body of a small child. There was a family resemblance to the dead widow. Drexler looked at the piece of parchment that was around her neck. 'Daughter. An unlucky family, it seems.'

He turned and looked at Felix. 'Nothing unusual, unfortunately. It is quite common for plagues and other diseases to spread among families and those who live together generally. It seems this plague can shift like a summer cold.'

Felix sniffed. 'What exactly are we looking for here, Herr Drexler?'

'A pattern. Something out of the ordinary. Something that would tell us whether there was any common factor that all of these poor victims shared.'

'How would that help us?' asked Gotrek.

Felix already knew the answer. 'If we could find that, we might find out how the disease is spreading. We might be able to take steps to isolate it. Or if it's really coming from the skaven we might be able to trace it back to its source.'

'Very good, Herr Jaeger. In a way, it's like solving a murder or a mystery. You need to be able to see the clues, that way you'll find the culprit.'

'And have you seen any clues?' Gotrek asked.

Drexler removed the last sheet from the last body. It was a young man, barely out of his twenties. Felix felt a sudden shocking sense of his own mortality. The plague's victims could not be much older than he.

'Anything?' Felix asked, his mouth suddenly dry.

'Unfortunately not,' Drexler said, and turned to leave.

After the gloom of the mortuary, the daylight seemed impossibly bright. After the quiet of the halls of the dead, the cacophony of the street seemed impossibly loud. After the perfumed smell of the vaults, the stench of the city was nearly overwhelming. Felix's nose was runny and there was a slight pain in his joints. Not the plague, he told himself, fingering the pomander, just a summer cold. His earlier unanswered question returned to him.

'Why don't the priests of Morr get all the plagues and diseases that kill their... clients? Does their lord extend them some special protection?'

'I do not know. Their mausoleum is clean and well washed, and in my experience that helps stop the spread of disease. They are priests and thus well fed and well rested; that helps too.'

'Really?'

'Oh yes. Grief, stress, poor living conditions, dirt, bad food – all contribute to the spread of disease, and sometimes help decide who will survive it.'

'Why's that?'

'I do not know. I can only say I have observed it to be true.'

'So you think these things help make the priests of Morr immune to disease?'

'I never said they were immune, Herr Jaeger. Every now and again, one of them falls ill.'

'What then?'

'He goes to his god, with no doubt a special dispensation in the afterlife due to the strength of his faith.'

'That's not very reassuring,' Felix said.

'If you want reassurance, Herr Jaeger, talk to a priest. I am a physician, and unfortunately, I must now return to making my living. I am sorry I could not have been of more help.'

Felix bowed to him. 'You've already been a great help, Herr Doctor. Thank you for your time.'

Drexler bowed back and turned to go. At the last moment, he turned and spoke. 'Let me know of there are any new developments,' he said. 'Look for a pattern.'

'I will,' Felix said.

'I'm going to look for a beer,' Gotrek said.

'I think that might be a good idea,' Felix said, suddenly wanting desperately to get the taste of the mortuary out of his mouth.

Felix stared down into his third beer and considered what they had seen. His head ached a little from what he kept having to tell himself was a summer cold, but the beer was helping to take away that pain. Gotrek sat slumped beside the fire staring into the flames. Heinz was standing by the bar, getting things ready for the evening rush. The other bouncers nursed their drinks and played hook-knife at the next table.

Felix was troubled. He felt baffled and stupid. He knew that there must be a pattern here but he just could not see it. It looked like something invisible and deadly was killing the people of Nuln and there was nothing he could do to stop it. It was frustrating. He almost wished for another raid by the gutter runners, or another attack by skaven warriors. What he could see, he could fight. Or to be absolutely specific, what he could see, the Slayer could fight and most likely beat. Thinking, Felix realised, was not their strong suit.

Once he had prided himself on being a clever and well-educated man, a scholar and a poet. But things had changed in his wanderings. He could not remember the last time he had put pen to paper, and last night was the first night in a long, long time when he had opened a book with any pretensions to scholarship. He had fallen right into the role of wandering mercenary adventurer, and his brain appeared to have fallen dormant.

He was out of his depth, he knew. He was not a razor-witted investigator of the sort which featured in the plays of Detlef Sierck. And to be honest, he did not believe that in real life things worked quite the way they did in the theatre, with clues arranged in neat chains of logic, pointing towards an inevitable solution. Life was messier than that. Things were rarely simple, and if there were really clues, doubtless they could be given far more than one neat and logical interpretation.

He thought about Drexler. So far the doctor had done nothing but help them, but it would be easy to put a sinister interpretation on his work and his motives. He possessed too much knowledge of the sort that was frowned on in the Empire, and that in itself was suspicious. In the more superstitious parts of the human realms, just the possession of the books that Drexler owned would be cause for burning at the stake. The reading of them would cause a witch hunter to execute him without trial.

And yet Felix himself had read one of those books, and he knew he was no friend to Chaos. Could not Drexler be in the same boat? Could he simply be what he appeared to be, a man who was concerned with acquiring any knowledge that would help him in his vocation of curing people, no matter what the source? It was all too difficult, Felix thought. The beer was starting to make his head spin.

Ultimately he knew in his heart of hearts that there had to be a link between the deaths of all the people. He was certain, in fact, that he had already seen evidence of it but was just too foolish to know what it was. So far the only link he could think of was that they had all ended up in the Halls of the Dead, in the temple of Morr, and that was no link at all. Eventually every man and every woman would end up there en route to burial in the Gardens of Morr. Every citizen of Nuln would end up in that huge cemetery one day.

He wanted to laugh bitterly at that, but then a thought struck him. Wait! There was a link between most of the people he knew had died of the plague. The man he had seen in the street two days ago had worn a black rose. Another victim, the one in the mortuary, had also worn a black rose, the traditional symbol of mourning. The woman and her child had been widow and orphan. Only the last one had not shown any connection, but perhaps if he dug deeply enough he would find one.

What could it mean? Was the Temple of Morr itself involved in the spread of the plague? Did the corruption run so deep? Somehow Felix doubted it. The first man he had seen had just been to a funeral. Had any of the others? The one wearing the rose was virtually a certainty. The mother and child? He did not know, but he knew a way to find out. He pulled himself up out of the chair and tapped Gotrek on the shoulder.

'We need to go back to the Temple of Morr,' he said.

'Are you developing a morbid attachment to the place?'

'No. I think it may hold the key to this plague.'

* * *

It was dark when they arrived at the temple. It did not matter. The gates were open. Lanterns were lit. As the priests never tired of pointing out, the gates to Morr's kingdom were always open, and a man could never tell when he might pass through them.

Felix asked to talk with the priest who he had spoken to earlier. He was in luck. The man was still on duty. The offer of some silver procured the information that he was always willing to talk. Felix and the Slayer were shown into a small, spartan antechamber. The walls were lined with books. They reminded him of the ledgers which lined the walls of his father's office. In a way, that was what they were. They contained the names and descriptions of the dead. Felix did not doubt they contained records of donations for funeral services and prayers to be offered in the temple. He had had dealings with the priests of Morr before.

'So you are Doctor Drexler's assistants?' the priest asked.

'Yes. In a manner of speaking.'

'In a manner of speaking?'

'We are helping with his researches into the plagues. We're trying to find a way to stop them.'

The priest showed a slow, sad smile. 'Then I don't know if I should help you.'

'Why?'

'They're good for business.'

Seeing Felix's shocked look, he gave a small, polite cough. 'Just a small attempt at humour,' he said eventually.

'You look tired,' Felix said to break the silence. The priest gave a long hacking cough. 'And ill.'

'In truth, I do not feel so well and it's been a long day. The brother who should have replaced me has himself fallen sick and is cloistered in his cell. He's not been well since he presided over the inhumations yesterday.'

Felix and Gotrek exchanged looks.

Felix nodded politely. Gotrek growled.

'Your, errm, associate does not look much like a physician, Herr Jaeger,' the priest said.

'He helps with the heavy work.'

'Of course. Well, how can I help you?'

'I need to know more about those people Doctor Drexler looked at this morning.'

'Not a problem.' He tapped the leather bound book in front of him. 'All the appropriate details will be in the current libram. What exactly do you need to know?'

'Had any of the deceased attended any funeral services just recently?'

'Frau Koch and her daughter had. I officiated at the inhumation of Herr Koch myself last week at the Gardens.'

'And the other gentleman?'

'No, I do not think so. He is not a man who we would allow to attend any of our services. Except his own inhumation, of course.'

'What do you mean? I thought anyone could enter the Gardens of Morr.'

'Not quite. Herr Gruenwald belonged to that noxious class of criminals who make their living by robbing family crypts and stealing corpses to sell to dissectionists and necromancers. He was under interdict. He would never be allowed within the gates of the garden on pain of supreme chastisement.'

'Death, you mean.'

'Precisely.'

'And the man wearing the black rose?'

'I will check the records. I suspect that given the nature of his adornment we will find that he too had attended an inhumation recently. You are not from Nuln, are you, Herr Jaeger? I can tell from your accent.'

'You are correct. I come from Altdorf originally.'

'Then perhaps you did not know it is a local custom to pick one of the black roses from the Death God's Garden when you attend a ceremony there.'

'I thought people bought them from the flower sellers.'

'No. The roses grow only in the Gardens and it is forbidden to sell them for profit.'

There was silence for a few minutes as the priest studied the records. 'Ah, yes. His sister passed away last week. Inhumed in the Gardens of Morr. Is there anything else I can do for you?' he asked brightly.

'No. I think you've told us enough.'

'Can you tell me what all this is about?'

'Not at the moment. I'm sure Doctor Drexler will inform you when he has completely formulated his theory.'

'Please ask him to do so, Herr Jaeger.' As they left, the priest was bent almost double in a fit of coughing.

'Tell me what all of this is about, manling,' Gotrek said as they entered the street. Felix glanced around to make sure that there was no one close enough to overhear them.

'All of the people who we know have died of the new plague have visited the Gardens of Morr recently. The tomb robber as well, most likely.'

'So?'

'That's the only connection I've been able to see and Drexler told us to look for connections.'

'It seems unlikely, manling.'

'Do you have any better ideas?' Felix asked allowing a measure of his frustration to show in his voice. The Slayer considered for a moment then shook his head.

'You think we'll find our little scuttling friends brewing plagues up in the city cemetery?'

'Possibly.'

'There's only one way to find out.'

'I know.'

'When?'

'Tonight. After work. It will be quiet then and we can take a look around.'

Felix shuddered. He could think of many places he would rather be than crawling around the city's main cemetery after midnight with a bunch of skaven in attendance, but what else was he going to do? If they took their tale to the authorities they would most likely not be believed. Perhaps the skaven would get wind of their presence and move their operation. At least he felt sure that there could not be too many of the rat-men up there. A small army camped in the grave-yard would be noticed. Hopefully they would be few enough for the Slayer's axe to take care of.

Felix certainly hoped so.

The gates of the Gardens of Morr were not open. Steel bars filled the archway, padlocked by heavy chains. A small postern gate was occupied by a night-watchman who sat warming his hands at a brazier. Spikes covered the high wall which surrounded the city graveyard. Felix wondered at that. In some ways the cemetery resembled a fortress but he was unsure as to whether the walls were intended to keep grave robbers out or the dead in. There had been times in history, he reflected, when the dead had not slept easily in their graves.

There was a basic primal fear at work here, he thought. Something intended to separate the dead from the living. In its way, the physical barrier was reassuring. Except, of course, when you intended to broach it, as he and the Slayer did tonight.

What was he doing here, Felix wondered? He should be at home, back in the inn, sharing his pallet with Elissa now that the night's work was done. Not skulking around in the shadows, preparing to break into the city graveyard, a crime for which the penalty was several years imprisonment, and interdiction by the Temple of Morr.

Surely there had to be an easier way than this. Surely somebody else could deal with the problem. But he knew this was not true. If he and Gotrek did not hunt down the skaven, who else was interested? They were the only people crazy enough to involve themselves in these affairs. If they did not do it, no one else would.

The authorities seemed to want to turn a blind eye to the evil which was happening in their midst. The best possible interpretation Felix could put on it was that they were ignorant or afraid. The worst possible interpretation was that they were in collusion with the Powers of Darkness.

How many more Fritz von Halstadts occupied positions of trust throughout the Empire? Most likely he would never know. All he could really do was act out his part. Perform the share of the actions which seemed to be allocated to himself and the Slayer, and hope things turned out for the best.

What else could he do? If he left the city, it was possible the plague would spread, and that it would wipe out Heinz and Otto and Elissa and the others that he knew and cared about here. It was possible that thousands might die, if he and the Slayer failed to solve this riddle.

And, if he was honest with himself, he had to admit that the thought of the responsibility thrilled as well as frightened him. In a way it was like being the hero of one of the stories he had read when he was a child. He was involved in intrigue and danger and the stakes were high.

Unfortunately, unlike the stories he had read when he was a child, the stakes were also all too real. It was easily possible that he and the Slayer might fail, and that death would be their reward. It was that thought, not the cold night air, which made him shiver.

They made their way round the walls of the cemetery until they found a conveniently dark place. Felix made sure the lantern he carried was securely attached to the clip on his sword belt, then vaulted up, caught one of the metal spikes and used it for leverage to pull himself to the top of the wall. Perhaps the spikes were mere ornaments after all, he told himself, and served no other purpose.

The moon broke through the cloud and he found himself looking out over the graveyard. It was an eerie sight in the silvered light. Mist was rising. Gravestones loomed out of it, like islands rising from some dismal sea. Trees leaned like enormous ogres, raising branched arms in worship to the Dark Gods. Somewhere in the distance, the lantern of a night-watchman flickered and then vanished, whether because its bearer had returned to the watch-house or for some other, darker, reason, Felix hoped never to find out. It was still. He was not sure whether it was sweat or mist that beaded his forehead.

The thought that this excursion would do nothing to help his cold struck him, and the incongruity made him want to laugh. He flinched as the beak of Gotrek's great axe curved over the stone beside him, and the Slayer used it to pull himself up the wall. The dwarf was swift and surprisingly nimble when he wanted to be – and when he was reasonably sober, Felix thought.

'Let's get on with it,' he muttered, and they dropped down into the silent graveyard.

All around them loomed the gravestones. Some were tumbled. Others were overgrown with weeds and black rose bushes. Here and there an engraved inscription was almost visible in the moonlight. The graves were laid out in long rows, like streets of the dead. Old gnarled trees overshadowed them in places. Everywhere the mist drifted spectrally, sometimes becoming so thickly cloudy that vision was obscured. The smell of black roses filled the air. During the day it was possible that the Gardens of Morr was a pleasant place but at night, Felix found his mind turning all too quickly to thoughts of ghosts.

It was easy to envision the countless bodies decomposing under the ground, worms burrowing through rotting flesh and the empty eye sockets of corpses. From there it was but a short leap of the imagination to picture those corpses emerging from beneath the ground, skeletal hands reaching upward through the soil, like the fingers of drowning swimmers emerging from beneath the sea.

He tried to push the thoughts from his mind, but it was hard. He had seen stranger things happen, had encountered the walking dead before, in the hills of the Border Princes on his cursed trip across those empty lands with the exiled von Diehl family. He knew that old dark magic was capable of stirring the dead into an unholy semblance of life, and filling them with a terrible hunger for the flesh and the blood of the living.

He tried telling himself that this was holy ground, consecrated to Morr, and that the Death God protected his charges from such awful happenings. But these were strange times, and he had heard dire rumours that the powers of the Old Gods were waning as the power of Chaos increased. He tried telling himself that perhaps such things happened in far-off lands like Kislev which bordered the Chaos Wastes, but this was Nuln, the heart of the Empire, the core of human civilisation. But part of him whispered that Chaos was here too, that all of the human lands were rotten to the core.

To reassure himself he glanced down at Gotrek. The Slayer seemed unafraid. A look of grim determination was engraved on his face. His axe was held ready to strike and he stood immobile, nose twitching, head cocked, listening to the night.

'Many strange scents tonight,' the dwarf said. 'Many strange noises. This is a busy place for a boneyard.'

'What do you mean?'

'Things moving. A bad feeling in the air. A lot of rats in the undergrowth. You were right about this place, manling.'

'Wonderful,' Felix said, wondering why he was usually right when he least wanted to be. 'Let's get moving. We want to find the area where there are fresh graves. That's where the funerals will take place. And that's where the plagues are coming from, I think.'

They moved along the thoroughfares between the graves, and Felix slowly realised that the Gardens of Morr were truly a necropolis, a city of the dead. It had its districts and its palaces just like the city outside. Here was the poor quarter, the area where paupers were thrown into unmarked communal graves. There were the neatly tended gravestones where the prosperous middle classes were buried. They competed with each other in the ornateness of their headstones, the way jealous neighbours might compete in life. Winged saints armed with stone swords held aloft books inscribed with the names and occupations of the dead. Stone dragons hunched over the last resting places of merchants like dogs protecting bones. Cowled, scythe-wielding figures of Morr stood guard over stones of black marble. In the distance Felix could see the large marble mausoleums of the rich nobles. They occupied palaces in death as they had in life.

Here and there black roses had been placed in bowers. Their sickly sweet perfume assaulted Felix's nostrils. Sometimes there were letters, or gifts or other mementoes from the living to the dead. An overwhelming feeling of sadness started to mingle with Felix's earlier feelings of fear. These things were some indicators of the futility of human life. It did not matter how rich or successful the men who lay in those graves had been. They were gone now. Just as one day Felix would be. He could understand in some ways the Slayer's desire to be remembered.

Life is written on sand, he thought, and the wind is blowing the grains away.

They chose a place near the open graves and concealed themselves behind some toppled tombstones. The smell of fresh turned earth filled Felix's nostrils. The chill of the mist bit through his clothing. He felt patches of dampness on his britches where they touched dew-bedecked plants. He pulled his cloak tight against the cold, and then they settled down to wait.

Felix glanced up at the sky. The moon had more than half completed its passage and still nothing had happened. All that he had heard in that time was the scrabbling of ordinary rats. All they had seen were some vicious, mad-eyed vermin. There was no sign of the skaven.

Perhaps, he thought, half disappointed and half relieved, he had been wrong. Maybe they had best consider going home. Now would be a good time to leave. The streets would be deserted. Most every honest person would be safely asleep. He wiped his nose with the edge of his cloak. It was running and he knew this night outside would do nothing for his cold. He stretched his legs, trying to work the stiffness and numbness out of them when he felt Gotrek's hand on his shoulder.

'Be still,' the Slayer whispered. 'Something comes.'

Felix froze and glared out into the darkness, wishing that he possessed the dwarf's keen senses and penetrating night vision. He heard his heart beat loudly within his chest. His muscles, locked in their unnatural position, began to protest against the strain, but still he held himself immobile, hardly daring to breathe, hoping that whatever was coming would not notice him before he saw it.

Suddenly he scented a foul and loathsome taint in the air. It smelled of rotting flesh and weeping sores, like the body of a sick man left unwashed in a hospice for weeks or years. If disease had a smell, it would be like this, Felix thought. He knew in an instant that his suspicions had been correct. In order to keep from gagging, he held the pomander close to his nose, and prayed that its spells would make him proof against whatever was coming.

A hideous figure limped into view. It resembled a skaven, but it was like no rat-man Felix had ever seen before. Here and there great boils erupted from its mangy fur, and something hideous dripped from its weeping skin. Most of its body was wrapped round with soiled bandages encrusted with pus and filth. It was emaciated and its eyes glowed with a mad, feverish light. Its movements were almost drunken; it reeled as if in the grip of a disease which interfered with its sense of balance. And yet, when it moved it sometimes did so with bursts of obscene speed, with the unholy energy of a sick man mustering the last of his strength for some hideous task.

It tittered loathsomely as it moved and talked to itself in its strange tongue. As it did all this, Felix noticed it held a cage in one palsied hand, and in that cage seethed rats. It stopped for a moment, hopped on one stringy leg. Then it opened the cage and took out a rat. Others burst free of the open door and dropped to the ground into the graves. As they fell, they leaked urine and foul excrement. When it touched the earth, for a brief moment there was a hideous, overwhelming stink that threatened to make Felix gag, and which only slowly subsided. The rats pulled themselves from the graves and dragged themselves feebly into cover. Felix could see that they left a trail of noxious slime in their wake, and it was obvious they were dying. What foul thing was going on here, Felix wondered?

The skaven capered past. Felix was surprised and appalled when the Slayer did not immediately strike it down, but instead gestured for Felix to follow and then set off on its track. It took Felix but a few moments to understand Gotrek's plan. They were going to follow the plague monk of Clan Pestilens – for such Felix guessed it to be – back to its lair. They were seeking a path into the very heart of corruption in the Gardens of Morr.

As they followed the capering plague monk through the mist-enshrouded cemetery, Felix noticed that there were other skaven present. Judging by the empty cages they carried they had all been on the same evil errand and were now returning to their lair. Some limped along, borne down by the weight of rotting corpses – recently exhumed, judging by the earth which still clung to their grave clothes.

He and the Slayer were forced to move cautiously, lurking behind tombstones, taking refuge in the shadows beneath the trees, moving from patch of cover to patch of cover. In some ways, Felix thought it was unnecessary. The plague monks did not seem as alert as normal skaven. They seemed quite mad, and often oblivious to their surroundings. Maybe their brains were as rotted as their bodies by the diseases they carried.

Sometimes they would stop for minutes and scratch themselves until they bled, or their festering scabs broke and then they would taste the pus which stained their claws. Sometimes they would pause and stare into space for no reason. At times foul excrement would belch forth from beneath their tails and they would lie down and writhe in it, tittering insanely. Felix felt his flesh crawl. These creatures were not sane even by the crazed standards of skaven.

Now at last they were making their way towards a vast mausoleum deep in the noble quarter of the Gardens. They were walking along paved pathways, between well-tended gardens. Here and there statues loomed over sundials that were useless at this hour. More and more plague monks were becoming visible, and more than once Felix and the Slayer hid themselves within the arched entrances to the tomb of some noble clan. Only when the skaven had passed did they rejoin the nightmare procession making its way deeper into the old part of the cemetery, where the largest and most tumbledown of the tombs were.

They paused at a corner and Felix noticed the skaven disappearing into the mouth of the largest and most ancient of the mausoleums. The building was built almost like a temple, in the old Tilean style with pillars supporting the roof of the entrance hall and statues of what Felix assumed were the builder's families held in niches between the columns. Only after the last skaven had disappeared did he and Gotrek advance to the stairs leading up to the entrance.

In the moonlight Felix could see that the mausoleum was in a state of great disrepair. The stonework had crumbled, the friezes had been eaten away by the effects of centuries of wind and rain, the faces had crumbled off the statues to be replaced by lichen. It looked like the stone itself was suffering from some terrible disease. The gardens around it were wild and overgrown. Felix could not be sure but he guessed that the family who had built this place had died out. The place had an uncared-for look, as if no one had visited the place in years. By day this would be a forbidding enough place. On this night, Felix felt no great urge to look within.

Gotrek, however, bounded up the stairs as fast as his short legs could carry him. The runes on his axe gleamed in the moonlight. He grinned at the prospect of confronting the skaven in their lair. Briefly it struck Felix that the dwarf was just as mad in his own way as the skaven were in theirs – and perhaps the best thing he could do was scuttle off and leave them all to their own devices. Felix fought to bring this urge under control as they reached the doorway. He was surprised to find that there was no way in, only a blank stone wall. Gotrek stood before it, puzzled for a minute, scratched his tattooed head with one blunt finger and then reached out to touch one of the stone faces on the side of the arch. As he did so, the wall in front of them slowly and silently rotated to reveal an entranceway.

'Shoddy work,' Gotrek muttered. 'Dwarf work would not be so easy to detect.'

'Yes, yes,' Felix mumbled uneasily and then followed Gotrek through the open entrance of the tomb.

The door slid silently closed behind them.

The stench was worse within. The walls were thoroughly caked with filth. Felix could feel it squelch under his hands as he fumbled his way forward through the darkness. Remembering the foul acts he had witnessed the plague monks perform made him want to vomit. Instead, though, he forced himself to follow the faint glow of the runes on the Slayer's axe ahead of him.

Gotrek moved quickly and surely, as if he had no difficulty seeing even in the absence of light. Felix suspected that this might be the case, and that the Slayer's vision might be as good in the gloom as it was in the daylight. He had followed the dwarf through dark places before and was certain that the Slayer knew what he was doing. All the same, he wished that he could light the lantern he carried.

From somewhere off in the distance, he heard a faint scratching sound, and he revised that thought. Perhaps a lantern would not be such a good idea after all. It would certainly warn the skaven of their presence, and Felix felt sure that their one chance of survival in the face of the rat-men's greater numbers was to attack swiftly with the advantage of surprise. Still, if he was going to fight he was going to need light at some point, he thought. He prayed he had a chance to light his lamp before moving into battle.

He almost lost his balance as he put his weight forward and there was nothing there. Recovering himself, he realised that he was on a stair heading down. This was indeed a large mausoleum. Whoever had built this place had certainly spent a lot of money, he thought. And why not? They were going to spend eternity here, or so they had thought.

Ahead of them now he could hear a loud chittering. It sounded like the skaven were involved in some obscene ritual. A faint glow of greenish, sickly light illuminated the corridor ahead. It looked like they were about to confront the rat-men in their lair.

Vilebroth Null cackled as one of his leprous fingers broke off and fell into the bubbling cauldron. It was a good sign. His own plague-eaten flesh would help feed the spirit which lurked there and strengthen the brew that would soon bring death to his enemies. The Cauldron of a Thousand Poxes was at once a sacred relic and a weapon for Clan Pestilens, and he intended that it would fulfil both purposes at once.

From his pouch he took out a thick handful of warpstone dust and threw it into the great vat. His remaining fingers tingled from the warpstone's touch and he licked them clean, feeling the tingling transfer itself to his tongue as he did so. He licked his gums so that some of the dust would contaminate the abscesses and ulcers there and perhaps make their contents even more contagious.

Null hawked a huge gob of phlegm into his mouth and then spat it into the thick soupy mixture for good measure, all the while stirring with the great ladle carved from the thigh bone of a dragon. He could sense the pestilential power rising from the cauldron the way an ordinary skaven might feel the heat from a fire. It was as if he stood in front of a mighty conflagration of toxic energies.

He breathed deeply, pulling the heady vapours that rose from the mixture into his lungs, and instantly was rewarded with a thick, treacly cough. He could almost feel his lungs clogging with fluid as the corruption brewed there. It was a just reward, he thought. His plans were going well. The tests were almost complete.

The new plague was as virulent as could be hoped, but most importantly it was his. He had used an old recipe but had added the new secret ingredient himself. Forever afterwards among the faithful of Clan Pestilens it would be known as Null's Pox. His name would be inscribed in the great *Liber Bubonicus*. He would be long remembered as the originator of a new disease, one that would ravage the furless ones like a ferocious beast of prey.

With every night, the brew grew thicker. With every new plague corpse added to the mix, the disease grew stronger. Soon, he judged, it would be ready. Already bodies suffering from the symptoms of the plague had been returned to the cemetery. He gave humble thanks to the Horned Rat for the inspiration which had made him seek out a hiding place where he could observe the results of his handiwork. And where else could he find such a rich source of contaminated bodies to drop into the brew!

Tomorrow night, he would dispatch his agents to drop contaminated rats into the wells, and through the roofs of the great abattoirs where the humans slaughtered their meat. After that, the plague would spread most swiftly.

He added more of the corpse roses to the mixture. These were his final secret ingredients to the brew. There were no finer and no stronger ones to be found. They grew on plants whose roots dug through the flesh of corpses. They were ripe and strong with accumulated death energies.

He breathed deeply of the scent of corruption and peered out with his filmed eyes at his followers. They lay sprawled across the ancient human death-chamber, twitching and scratching, coughing and hawking like the true members of Clan Pestilens they were. He knew that each and every one of them was united in their sincere dedication to the cause of the clan. They were filled with the sort of brotherhood which few other skaven could understand. Not for them the endless intrigues and the constant scrabble for advantage. They had sought and found abnegation of self in true worship of the Horned Rat in his most concrete form: the Bringer of Disease, the Spreader of Plague.

For each and every member of the clan knew that their body was a temple which harboured the countless blessings of their god. Their rotted nerve endings no longer felt the pain, save occasionally when they felt ghostly echoes of their suffering, like someone hearing the tolling of a distant bell while drowning in deep water. He knew that other skaven thought them mad and avoided them, but that was because other skaven lacked their purity of purpose, their total commitment to serving their god. Each and every plague monk present was prepared to pay any price, make any sacrifice to reach the goals of clan and deity. It was this commitment that made them the most worthy of all the Horned Rat's servants, and the most suitable leaders of the entire skaven people.

Soon all the other clans would realise this. Soon this new plague would bring the human city of Nuln to its knees, even before the mighty verminous hordes entered its precincts. Soon all would bear witness that the triumph belonged to Clan Pestilens, to the Horned Rat, and to Vilebroth Null, the humblest of the great horned lord's chosen servants. Soon he would be established as the only vessel suitable to bear the Horned Rat's word. It would be fitting, for although he was but the humblest of the Horned Rat's servants, he knew where his duty lay, and that was not true of all skaven in this devolved age.

He knew that many of his fellow rat-men had lost sight of their race's great goals, and had lost themselves in the pursuit of self-aggrandisement. Grey Seer Thanquol was an example of just such a tendency. He cared more for himself and his status than he did for the overthrowing of the Horned Rat's enemies. It was disgusting behaviour for one who should have been among the most dedicated of the great god's servants, and Vilebroth Null humbly prayed that he would never fall into similar error.

He felt sure that, had Thanquol known about this experiment, he would have forbidden it, simply out of envy of one who possessed knowledge of powers beyond his limited imagination. That was why they had to scurry to the surface in secret and perform their rituals without the grey seer's knowledge. The great work must progress despite the machinations of those who would prevent it. After the success of this plague, the foolish edicts of the Council of Thirteen would be repealed, and Clan Pestilens could show its true power to the world. And those like Grey Seer Thanquol who would seek to prevent this most sacred of the Horned Rat's works would be made to grovel in the dust.

Perhaps it was true, as some whispered, that Thanquol was a traitor to the great skaven cause, and should be replaced by one more humbly dedicated to the advancement of his people. It was an idea that certainly deserved the scrutiny of lowly but devoted minds.

Null opened the cage which lay close at hand, reached in and pulled out one of the large grey rats. It bit him viciously, drawing some of his black blood, but Vilebroth Null hardly felt the sharp teeth cleave his flesh. Pain was a near-meaningless concept to him. He closed the cage and left the other rats scrabbling within.

Taking the subject by the tail and ignoring its frantic struggling, he lowered it into the brew. The creature struggled as its head entered the foul liquid. Its eyes gleamed madly and it scrabbled frantically with its claws to try to keep itself above the surface. The abbot of plague monks took his other hand and pushed it down until its squeals were drowned out by the liquid entering its open mouth. He held it under for so long that its struggles almost ceased and then he drew it up again, still dripping, and set it down on the floor of the vault.

The rat sat there for a moment, blinking in the light, as if unable to believe that it had been reprieved. Null scooped it up and threw it into the second cage, where the newly treated rats were. It sniffed and vomited. Vilebroth Null scooped up some of the warm sickness and tossed it back into the cauldron. Soon the cage would be full and he would dispatch one of the brothers to release them in the cemetery, there to begin the spread of the new plague. And tomorrow, they would be sent far and wide through the city.

From somewhere Vilebroth Null heard coughing. In itself that was not unusual. His followers were all blessed with the symptoms of many diseases. No, there was something about the tone of the coughing. It was different from that of a skaven. Deeper, slower, almost human-like...

Felix cursed and tried to stop coughing, but it was no use. His lungs were rebelling against the foul stench from within the vault. Tears streamed from his eyes. He had never smelled anything quite so foul in all his life. It was as if the combined essences of all stinks in all the sickrooms he had ever smelled were assaulting his nostrils. He felt ill just breathing it, and he had to fight down the urge simply to run off and vomit.

The sight of what was going on in the burial vault had not helped settle his stomach either. He had glanced into a chamber illuminated by the eerie glow of warpstone lanterns. In one long chamber, a dozen or so of the foulest and most leprous-looking skaven he had ever seen lolled amidst the opened sarcophagi of long-dead nobles. Great stone coffins lay flat on the chamber's floor. Their lids had been removed and their contents scattered. Skulls and bones lay everywhere. Among them lay skaven, enervated and ill-looking, sprawled in pools of their own pus and vomit and excrement, gnawing at the bones of the dead. At the far end of the room, the sickest and most evil-looking skaven Felix had ever seen stirred a vast cauldron which rested upon a blazing fire, pausing now and again only to spit in it or add some foul rotting meat torn from a worm-eaten corpse.

Even as Felix had watched, one of the thing's own fingers had dropped into the bubbling evil brew and the creature had not even blinked. It had paused only for a breath and added a glowing dust that could only be warpstone, and then continued to stir. Then he had witnessed the strange ritual by which a living rat had been lowered into the foul brew and then recovered. Even the Slayer stood rooted to the spot by horrified fascination, watching every move made by the skaven as if trying to fix it forever in his mind.

Felix knew that what he was witnessing had something to do with the spreading of the plague. He did not understand quite how or why, but he was certain that it was so. These vile degenerate rats and their hideous rune-inscribed cauldron had to be involved in the creation of the disease. One look at their vile appearance told him that it just had to be so. Then he had felt the uncontrollable urge to cough. He had tried to hold it in, but the more he did so, the more the inside of his lungs tickled and threatened to explode. Eventually, the cough had burst out of him. Unfortunately, it did so during one of the rare moments of silence in the burial chamber.

Now the chief skaven stood frozen, its nose twitching, almost as if it sensed Felix's presence – although how it could do so over the cacophony of coughs, fruity farts and rasping breathing that filled the chamber Felix could not deduce.

All doubts vanished, however, when it gestured in his direction with one rotting paw. Felix breathed a prayer to Sigmar for protection and brought his sword to the ready position. Beside him Gotrek stirred from his frozen horror, raised his axe and bellowed his war cry.

Interlopers, Vilebroth Null thought! Humans had found their way to this sacred place consecrated to the most holy manifestation of the Horned Rat by his most humble servants. Had some vile treachery brought them here, he wondered? Not that it mattered. The fools would soon pay for their folly with their lives, for the plague monks of Clan Pestilens were among the most deadly of all skaven warriors when roused to righteous frenzy. And if that failed, he could call on the mighty mystical powers loaned to him by his foul god.

As Felix watched, the plague priest raised its staff high above its head and threw back its head. It barked a series of incantations in the skaven's high-pitched chittering language. The words seemed to be wrenched from deep within it, forming into figures of fire on its tongue. As it spat them out they became flaming runes which burned on the retina, bending and flickering forth before leaping out and touching each of its followers in turn. As they did so, a great halo of sickly light surrounded the skavens' flesh and then seemed to be absorbed into their bodies. The skavens' mangy fur stood on end, their tails stiffened and an eerie glow entered their eyes. They leapt to their feet with an electric grace and energy. High keening cries of challenge were torn from their throats.

Gotrek charged into the warm, misty chamber, Felix following him. The rat-men scuttled to their feet, picking up their loathsome, crusted weapons. Gotrek struck right and left, killing as he went. Nothing could stand in the way of his axe. No one sane or sensible would have tried to resist it.

And yet these skaven did not turn and flee as other skaven might have. They did not even hold their ground. Instead they attacked with an insane frenzy which matched the Slayer's own. They sprang forward, foam pouring from their mouths, their eyes rolling and wild. For a moment, the Slayer was halted by the sheer force of their rush and then they swarmed all over him, biting and clawing and stabbing as they came.

Felix lashed out at the nearest and it turned, swift and sinuous as a serpent to face him, air hissing from between its teeth, madness evident in its eyes. He could see that yellow pus stained the bandages around the creature's chest. He poked the area with his sword and it sank in with a hideous slurping sound, almost as if Felix had struck into jelly.

The pain did not stop the rat-man. It came straight at him, pushing forward against Felix's blade, driving it deeper into its own chest. If it felt any pain, it gave no sign. Felix watched in horror as it opened its mouth to reveal yellowish fangs and a white, leprously furred tongue. He knew then that of all the bad things that might happen here, letting the creature bite him was the worst.

He lashed out with his left fist, catching the plague monk on the side of its snout, knocking its jaws to one side. The force of the blow sent several rotting teeth flying out of the creature's mouth to skitter across the dirty floor. It turned to glare at him with wide, evil eyes. Felix took the opportunity to shift his weight, hook his leg around the creature's own leg and send it toppling to the floor. He turned his blade in the plague monk's chest as he pulled it free but still the creature would not die. It beat at the stone flagstones around it with its fist, in a spasm of horrid nervous energy. Felix knew that evil sorcery was at work here, when creatures so weak and sickly could prove so hard to kill.

He brought his boot crashing down on the creature's throat, crushing its windpipe and pinning it in place while he hacked repeatedly at it, and still the creature took a long time to die.

Felix looked around to see how Gotrek was doing. The Slayer was holding his own against the crazed skaven, but no more. He held one at bay with his huge hand but others swarmed over him, immobilising his deadly axe arm. It was an enormous ruck, a wrestling match between the Slayer's mighty strength and the horde of sorcerously enhanced plague monks.

Felix glanced around desperately, knowing that if the Slayer fell he would have mere moments to live. The sound of padding footsteps behind him told him that more skaven were arriving, returning from whatever insidious mission they had been on. Runes of fire still leapt from the lips of the chanting priest. They rushed over his head and Felix turned to see the eerie glow settle on the fur of two more plague monks, and the awful transformation overcome them. Things were not looking good, Felix thought. Unless something was done about the priest, it was all over. Sick at heart, he knew he was the only one in a position to do anything.

Without giving himself time to think, he vaulted on top of the nearest sarcophagus. He leapt to the next one, passing over the melee between Gotrek and the skaven, and kept moving towards the chanting priest. More and more fiery runes sprang up between the priest and its supporters and Felix knew for certain that the chanting leader was the source of its follower's strength. His leaps brought him ever closer to the bubbling cauldron and its hideous master. He paused at the last, frozen for a moment by fear and indecision.

His next leap was going to have to carry him over the cauldron and into combat with the priest. It was an awful prospect. One slip, or a single misjudgement of the distance and he would find himself in that bubbling brew. He did not even want to consider the consequences of what would happen if he did that.

He heard Gotrek's war cry ring out and, turning, he saw the Slayer struggling with the new arrivals. It looked like he had mere moments in which to act. Offering up a silent prayer to Sigmar, Felix leapt. He felt heat below him, and the foul vapours of the cauldron caressed his face as he passed through them, then his feet connected with the plague priest's face and they both tumbled to the ground.

The skaven's chanting stopped but it reacted with surprising speed for one so decrepit, bounding to its feet as if on springs. Felix lashed out with his sword but the skaven leapt back and brought its bone staff down in a blurring arc which would have crushed Felix's skull had he not leapt aside.

Felix hastily pulled himself to his feet and circled warily, looking for an opening. From behind the cauldron, out of his sight, came the sounds of hideous carnage, which he could only hope was Gotrek piling into the plague monks. To his surprise, and unlike most solitary skaven Felix had ever fought, the one in front of him attacked swiftly and viciously. Felix parried another blow from the staff with his sword, and was surprised by its speed and power. The shock of the impact almost drove the sword from his hand. Another blow rapped his knuckles and this time he let go of his blade. A loathsome, oily tittering escaped from the skaven's lips as it saw the look of shock on his face.

'Die! Die! Stupid man-thing!' it screeched in badly accented Reikspiel. Once more the staff descended. This time Felix managed to move aside, and it thudded into the ground where he had stood mere moments before. Before the skaven could raise its staff again, Felix made a grab for it. In a heartbeat he found himself wrestling with the skaven for possession of the weapon. Its wiry strength was far greater than Felix would have guessed. Its foetid jaws snapped shut a hairs-breadth from his face. The sight of the diseased saliva drooling from those broken fangs made Felix quiver, but he continued to grapple with a strength born of terror.

Now he had the advantage of weight. He was taller and far heavier than the emaciated creature, and he used that advantage to spin around on the spot, all the while continuing to tug at the creature. When he had it facing in the right direction, he stopped pulling at the staff and pushed instead. The surprised skaven went tumbling backwards. It let out a shriek as its backside impacted on the hot metal sides of the cauldron. Felix ducked down, grabbed its feet and picked them up. With a mighty wrench he sent the skaven leader tumbling into its own cauldron.

It vanished from sight for a moment beneath the surface of the bubbling brew and then erupted from the surface, gasping for air, horrid liquid dribbling from its jaws. Desperately it tried to climb out of the cauldron. Felix picked up the staff and whacked it over the head, forcing it back under. Then, prodding down with the staff, he felt the struggling skaven move. Swiftly he pinned it firmly with the staff and leaned forward with all his weight. The writhing skaven tried to push back against him but Felix was too heavy to be moved.

Slowly its struggles ceased. Eventually Felix relaxed his weight and breathed easily. Looking down from the dais he saw the Slayer lash out with his axe and behead the last of the plague monks. The corpses of the others lay in various stages of dismemberment at his feet. He looked up at Felix and seemed almost disappointed to find out that he was still alive. Felix grinned and gave him the thumbs-up sign.

At that moment, something horrible emerged from the cauldron before him.

Vilebroth Null felt dreadful. He had swallowed so much of his own brew that he felt like he was going to explode. He had taken such a beating at the hands of that accursed human that even he could feel the pain. Worse yet, he had almost been drowned like a rat, yes, like a rat. It seemed like an eternity before that cruel human had taken his weight off Null's own staff and given him a chance to break the surface.

A quick glance around told him that all was lost. His acolytes lay dead on the flagstones and the ferocious-looking dwarf with the huge axe was racing towards him. Null felt that he had barely been able to hold his own with the human. Against the two of them he would have no chance whatsoever.

Now the surprised-looking human was recovering himself and stooping for his sword. Null knew he had only one chance to act. He threw up his arms, summoned all of his power and called up the Horned Rat to save him. For a moment, nothing happened, and Null knew that it was all over. The sword arced closer. He kept his eyes open and forced himself to watch his own death approach. Then he felt a faint tingling surround his body and knew that the Horned Rat had answered his prayer.

Felix slashed with his sword, determined that this time there would be no mistake. This time, the foul plague priest was going to die, and Felix was going to chop it into little pieces just to be certain. The skaven shrieked what Felix hoped was a plea for mercy – and something strange happened.

An eerie glow surrounded the skaven. Felix tried to stop his blow, fearing some more noxious sorcery, but it was too late. Even as he watched the blade connected but an odd thing happened. Space seemed to fold in around the priest, and it shimmered and vanished with a pop like a bubble bursting. Felix almost overbalanced as his sword passed through the empty air where the rat-man had been.

'Damn,' he muttered and spat in frustration.

'I hate it when that happens,' Gotrek muttered, looking woefully at the space where the skaven had stood. Felix cursed again and muttered venomously as if by sheer force of his imprecations he could make the skaven reappear for execution. He vaulted down from the dais and kicked the severed head of a plague monk just to relieve his frustrations. Then he glanced up at the Slayer. To his surprise, the dwarf was looking almost thoughtfully at the cauldron.

'Well, manling,' he said, 'what are we going to do about this?'

Felix studied their surroundings. The place was strewn with corpses. The tombs were broken open and the huge cauldron full of its foul and contagious brew continued to bubble. The cages which had held the rats had been broken at some point in the struggle and a few of the beasts lurked in the shadows of the room. Others had disappeared.

Felix himself was a mess. His clothes were covered in blood and pus and the foul substances that the rat-men had exuded as they died. His hair felt filthy and matted. The Trollslayer did not look any better. He was bleeding from a dozen small cuts and gore smeared his entire body. Some instinct told Felix that they needed to get clean as soon as possible and that all those bites and wounds should be treated by Drexler. Otherwise they might well go bad.

The main problem, though, was the great cauldron. If what Felix suspected was true, it represented as big a threat to the city as an army of skaven, perhaps more so, for at least an army could be fought against. Unfortunately, Felix was even less of an expert on dark sorcery than he was on loathsome diseases. It seemed obvious that the brew needed to be destroyed in some manner that rendered it harmless, but how?

Pouring it into the river might do more harm than good. Simply leaving it here would mean that the skaven might come back and collect it at their leisure. They obviously had their own secret ways into the Gardens of Morr and could come and go as they pleased. Not to mention that their sorcery apparently allowed them to vanish at will. There did not appear to be any way they could set fire to the tomb.

As Felix considered all this, he realised that the Slayer had his own ideas. While Felix thought, the dwarf was already busy levering the cauldron over with the blade of his axe. The contagious brew spilled off the dais and onto the floor, covering the festering corpses of the rat-men in a nasty viscous pool. Eventually, the cauldron tipped over and lay there upside down.

'What are you doing?' Felix asked.

'Destroying this foul thing!' Gotrek took his axe and brought the blade down on the cauldron. Sparks flashed and a hollow booming sound echoed round the mausoleum chamber as the starmetal blade connected with the sorcerously forged iron. The runes flared along the axe blade and across the side of the skaven artefact. Gotrek's blade smashed through the side of the cauldron. There was a huge spark, followed by a mighty explosion of mystical energy, as the cauldron shattered into a thousand pieces. Felix covered his eyes with his arm as bits of shrapnel flew everywhere, adding to his mass of cuts.

The swirling surge of power stormed through the chamber. Sparks flickered, corpses began to burn. Felix was surprised to see that the dwarf still stood seemingly shocked by the result of his actions. Felix saw felt something burning against his chest, and realised that it was the talisman given to him by Drexler, apparently overheated by its efforts to protect Felix from the force that had been unleashed.

'Let's get out of here!' Felix yelled, and they dived for the entrance through a blazing curtain of mystical energy.

Felix watched his old clothes burn. He had scrubbed himself clean with coarse lye soap a dozen times and still he wasn't sure he had removed the entire taint of the mortuary from himself. He clutched

the protective pomander tight and hoped that it would prove effica-
cious against the plague. At least it seemed to have cooled down. He
pushed the memory of the previous night's events aside. It had been a
long trudge back from the Gardens of Morr, helping the reeling Slayer
to Drexler's door.

Gotrek stomped into the courtyard. His scratches had been treated
with some sort of ointment. He too carried one of Drexler's amulets.

'Well, what did you expect?' he asked sourly. 'Dying of plague is no
death for a Slayer.'

Vilebroth Null looked around him. It was dark and gloomy, but
somehow he knew he was back in the Underways. The Horned Rat
had heard his prayer and his invocation of escape had worked. It
seemed obvious to Vilebroth Null that his lord had preserved his
most humble servant for a reason. And that reason was most likely
to uncover the vile traitor to the deity's cause who had betrayed the
abbot's scheme to that accursed meddling twosome.

On careful consideration, it seemed likely, even to an intellect as
lowly as his, that those two could never have found his carefully concealed lair without help. It had been carefully chosen, well concealed
and ringed round with spells to baffle all scrying. No, those two interfering fools must have had help from somewhere. It seemed unlikely
that they could have simply stumbled across the lair. Vilebroth Null
swore that he would uncover the traitor if it took him the rest of his
life, and that when he found him, the treacherous rat-man would
enjoy a slow and excruciating death.

And, thought Vilebroth Null as he began the long, limping trudge
back to the skaven army, he suspected that he had a good idea where
to start looking. As he hobbled back into the skaven camp, he paid no
attention to the number of warriors who started to cough and sneeze
as he passed.

BEASTS OF MOULDER

'The plague had come to Nuln. Fear stalked the streets. Not even the corrupt authorities could keep a lid on all the rumours that flew back and forth. On every street corner one began to hear tales of mutants and rat-men and huge wild-eyed rats which brought death and disease to all they encountered. I can now reveal some of the sinister truths behind those rumours...'

— From *My Travels With Gotrek, Vol. III*, by Herr Felix Jaeger
(Altdorf Press, 2505)

'You're moving in high society these days, Felix,' Heinz the landlord said, giving Felix Jaeger an uneasy grin.

'What do you mean?' the younger man asked.

'This came for you when you were out.' He handed Felix a sealed letter. ''Twas delivered by a footman in the tabard of Her Highness, the Countess Emmanuelle no less. He had a couple of the city guard to keep him company too.'

A sudden sick feeling grabbed Felix in the pit of his stomach. His eyes flickered towards the door, making sure he had a clear way out. It looked like his past had caught up with him at last. Quickly he reviewed all the things the authorities might want him for.

Well, there was a standing bounty on his and Gotrek's heads posted by the authorities in Altdorf for their involvement in the Window Tax riots. There was the fact that he had murdered the Countess's chief of secret police, Fritz von Halstadt. Not to mention the fact that they had been involved in burning her new College of Engineering to the ground.

How had they found him? Had they been recognised by one of the hundreds of informers who swarmed through the city? Or was it something else entirely? Where was Gotrek? Perhaps if they moved quickly enough they could still escape the jaws of the trap.

'Aren't you going to read it then?' Heinz asked, naked curiosity showing in his eyes. Felix shook his head, his reverie broken. He realised that his heart was pounding and his palms were sweating. Noting the way Heinz was looking at him, he realised that he must look guilty as sin. He forced a sickly grin onto his face.

'Read what?'

'The bloody letter, idiot. You must be able to tell we're all dying of curiosity here.'

Felix glanced around, and saw that Elissa, Heinz, and the rest of the staff were all staring at him quite openly, keen to know what business the ruler of their great city-state might have with him.

'Of course, of course,' Felix said, forcing himself to remain calm, to make his hands stop shaking. He walked over to his customary chair by the fire and sat down. The horde of curious onlookers followed him over and scrutinised his face intently. Felix glared at them meaningfully until they all backed off, then gave his consideration to the letter.

It was inscribed on the very finest vellum, and his name was written in good quality ink. There were no blots or smudges and whoever the scribe was possessed a fine hand indeed. The wax seal had not been broken and it showed the crest of the Elector Countess.

A measure of calm returned to Felix. You did not write letters to men you were going to arrest. If you were a stickler for formalities, you read them the warrant and then clapped them in irons. If you were the Elector Countess Emmanuelle, your thugs bashed them over the head with a club and they woke up in chains in the Iron Tower. Perhaps, he told himself, things were not going to be so bad after all. Still, he doubted this. In his experience, in this life whatever could go bad did go bad.

With nervous fingers he broke the seal and studied the message within. It was written in the same beautiful and courtly hand as the address, and was as simple as it was enigmatic:

> *Herr Jaeger,*
> *You are commanded to present yourself at the palace of Her*
> *Serene Highness, the Countess Emmanuelle, at the evening bell*
> *on this day.*
> *Yours in faith,*
> *Hieronymous Ostwald, Secretary to Her Serene Highness*

How very curious, thought Felix, turning the letter over and over in his hands, as if by doing so he would find some clue as to why he was being summoned. There was none. He was left to wonder what the ruler of one of the greatest fiefdoms of the Empire might want with a penniless mercenary wanderer, and no answers were forthcoming. He realised that everybody was still staring at him. He stood up and smiled.

'It's all right. I've just been invited to visit the countess,' he said eventually.

Elissa still looked impressed and a little shocked, as if she could not quite believe there wasn't some mistake.

'It's a great honour,' she told him as they sat together by the fire.

'I'm sure it's nothing. It's probably for my brother, Otto, and was sent here by mistake.' He reached out and took her hand. She pulled it away quickly. She had been doing that a lot recently.

'You will go, won't you?' she said, and smiled.

'Of course. I cannot refuse a command from the local ruler.'

'Then what will you wear?' He was going to say 'my own clothes, of course', but immediately saw her point. His tunic was stained and soiled in a hundred places from all the brawling and fights he had been in. His cloak was ragged and ripped at the hems where strips had been torn from it to make bandages. His boots were holed and cracked. His britches were patched and filthy. He looked more like a beggar than a warrior. He doubted that he would be able to get past the front gate of the palace looking like he did. They were more likely to throw him a bone and send him on his way with kicks.

'Don't worry,' he said. 'I'll think of something.'

'Best do it quickly then. You've only got eight hours till the evening bell.'

Felix looked across the desk at his brother. Newly bathed and with his tattered clothes hastily washed and dried in front of the fire, he felt self-conscious. His hands toyed idly with the silvered pomander which dangled from his neck. He wished he'd never come to the warehouse where Otto's office was located.

Otto got up from behind his heavy oaken desk and lumbered over to the window. He put his hands behind his back. Felix noticed that his right hand was clutching his left wrist. It was an old habit of Otto's. He had always done that when called upon to answer difficult questions by their tutors.

'Why do I only see you when you want something, Felix?' he asked eventually.

Felix felt a surge of guilt. Otto had a point. The only times he had been near his brother recently was when he had needed a favour. Like he did now. He considered the question. It wasn't that he disliked Otto. It was just that they had nothing much in common anymore. And perhaps, Felix feared that he would ask him to join the business again, and he would have to refuse again.

'I've been busy,' he said.

'Doing what?'

Crawling through graveyards, burning scholarly institutions to the ground, fighting monsters, killing things, Felix thought, wondering how much, if any, of this he would ever be able to tell his brother.

Fortunately Otto did not give him a chance to reply, as he had some suggestions of his own.

'Brawling, I suppose. Hanging about with tavern wenches and rakes. Frittering away that expensive education father paid for. When you should be here, helping run the business, following in the family tradition, helping to make…'

Felix could not tell whether Otto was angry or simply hurt. He fought to keep his own feelings under control. He stretched his legs out, pushing the chair back until it rested on its two rear legs. A huge portrait of his father glared down at him from behind Otto's desk. Even from up there, the old man managed to look somehow disapproving.

'Do you know the Countess Emmanuelle?' The question interrupted the flow of Otto's ranting, as Felix had intended it to. His brother stopped, turned around and looked sharply at his younger brother.

'I met her on the last high feast day of Verena, when I was presented at court. She seemed a spirited and somewhat flighty young woman.'

Otto paused and turned away from the window. He slumped back into his comfortable chair again and opened a huge ledger. He had marked his place with a quill pen. It was a gesture so reminiscent of his father that Felix smiled. For a moment Otto's brow furrowed in concentration. He dipped the pen in the inkwell and inscribed something in the ledger. Without looking at Felix, he said: 'I've heard some rumours about her.'

Felix leaned forward until he almost touched Otto's neatly arranged desk. The front legs of his chair clunked back onto the stone floor. 'Rumours?'

Otto cleared his throat and smiled in embarrassment. 'She's supposed to be somewhat wild. More than somewhat, actually. It's not uncommon at Emmanuelle's court. They are all, shall we say, a little less than moral.'

'Wild?' Felix enquired. His interest was piqued. 'In what way?'

'She's said to be the mistress of half the young nobles of the Empire. Has a particular fondness for rakes and duellists. There have been a number of scandals, apparently. Only rumours, of course, and I don't pay any attention to gossip,' he added hastily, like a man who fears that what he is saying might suddenly be overheard. 'Why do you ask?'

Felix placed the letter on top of the ledger which Otto had been studying. His brother picked it up and turned it over in his hands. He studied the broken seal then slid the parchment from out of the envelope and read it. Otto smiled the same cold and calculating smile that their father showed in the portrait above.

'So you're moving among the nobility now. I won't ask how this has come about.'

It had been their father's ambition to buy the family's way into the nobility for as long as he could remember. So far he had not succeeded, but Felix reckoned that it was only a matter of time. The old man was both wealthy and persistent. Otto continued to give him that long, measuring look. He ran his eyes over Felix's old and tattered clothing.

'Of course, you need money,' he said eventually. Felix looked back, considering his options. He didn't really want to take his family's money but under the circumstances it seemed advisable. He would certainly need better clothing for his visit to the court.

'Yes, brother,' he said.

Felix walked out through the warehouse door feeling slightly sick of himself. The pouch of gold jingling within his jerkin was like a badge of his betrayal of his own ideals. The letter from Otto instructing any of the Jaeger businesses to give him what he required seemed tainted with his own greed. After so much time spent shunning his family, the generosity seemed almost excessive.

Felix shook his head and strode across to the river wharves. He looked down into the grey, misty murk of the Reik and studied the great barges which had come all the way from Altdorf carrying their cargoes of Bretonnian wines and Estalian silks. They lay at rest along the piers, like whales momentarily surfaced, bobbing in the river flow. He watched the sweating dockhands lifting the casks from the holds with hooked knives, and saw them roll heavy barrels up long gangplanks towards the warehouse. And he heard loud coughs and saw men holding handkerchiefs over their mouths. The plague had claimed hundreds over the past few weeks.

It seemed that his and Gotrek's efforts in the Gardens of Morr had at best slowed its spread, and at worst had no effect at all. He wondered how it was spread, and in his mind, he pictured the rats that the plague monk had been dipping into that vile cauldron. Somehow he just knew they had something to with it.

One of the men, older than the rest, remembered Felix from his younger days. He raised his hand and waved at him. Felix waved back. He could not even remember the man's name, but he was shocked to find him still labouring away after all these years. The dock worker had not been young even then.

Here, Felix thought, was the difference between the nobility of the Empire and those they ruled. That docker would continue to work for the pittance which the Jaeger family paid him until he keeled over and died. The nobles would lounge in their palaces, collecting the revenues of their estates and never raise their hands in honest toil in all their lives. There were times when Felix found himself in agreement with the revolutionists who preached rebellion across the Empire.

He smiled ironically. Fine words, he told himself, for a man who had just taken a hefty handout from his own rich family. Well, he had not made this world, he just had to live in it. He turned and walked along the bank of the river, losing himself in the sounds and smells and sights of the dockside.

The smell of fish assaulted his nostrils. Felix gagged and held the pomander he had acquired from Doctor Drexler under his nose. Its perfumed scent was starting to fade, but it was still enough to sweeten the tainted air. Felix noticed that the smells of the street and other people seemed keener now that he'd had his first bath in weeks.

The rumble of huge drayage carts competed with the shouts of the dock workers. An armed guard in the black tabard of the city-state stopped to take a pear from the cart of a small trader. A child pickpocket made a daring rush for the purse of an old trader too poor to afford bodyguards. It was all very much as Felix remembered it from his childhood visits to Nuln with his father and brothers. He headed onwards, making for the better part of town.

He had a niggling feeling that someone was following him, but when he turned around to look no one was there.

Felix studied his reflection in the mirror. Very nice, he thought. He knew he cut a fine figure. At the best of times he was tall, athletic and quite good-looking, if he said so himself. Now he was dressed to make the most of it. He took a deep breath, revelling in the smell of luxury, of oak panelling and fine old leather. This discreet tailor's shop, catering only to the highest category of nobles, was one of the Jaeger family's less well-known businesses. It had not even existed when Felix had last been in Nuln. It had been set up by Otto, using introductions passed on by the late Fritz von Halstadt. For once Felix was glad of Otto's corrupt association with the man he had killed.

His fine new clothes felt strange. The high leather boots pinched. The tunic felt a little stiff, the padded lining felt too soft. The white linen shirt smelled too fresh. He realised how used he had become to the harsh life on the road, when he had not changed his clothes for months. Only the new cloak of red Sudenland wool felt familiar. It resembled his old one, ruined by skaven blood during the attack on the Blind Pig. The sword he had taken from the Templar, Aldred, was encased in a fine new sheath of plain black leather.

'Would sir like any alterations made?' the assistant asked obsequiously.

Felix studied the bald-headed, sour faced fellow. Only an hour ago, when Felix had entered the shop, the assistant had inspected him as if he were a particularly large and repulsive cockroach. In a way, Felix could not blame him. He had been dressed like a beggar. Of course, the assistant's attitude had changed within seconds of reading Otto's hastily scrawled note. When Otto Jaeger himself told his minions to give this client anything he wanted, fawning courtesy was thrown in as part of the bargain.

Felix gave the man his best condescending smile. 'No. I would like several copies of these garments delivered to my residence within the day. And have my old clothing packed and returned immediately.'

'Of course, sir. And where would sir's residence be?'

'At the sign of the Blind Pig, in the New Quarter. Have the clothes delivered to Felix Jaeger.'

Felix enjoyed looking at the man's face when he gave the address. He looked as if he had just swallowed that large and particularly nasty cockroach.

'The Blind Pig, sir? Isn't that a–'

'Where I stay is my own business, don't you think?'

'Of course, sir. It is simply that sir took one rather by surprise for a moment. A thousand apologies.'

'No need. Just make sure my clothes are delivered on time.'

'I will see to it personally, sir.'

Felix wondered if the man would have the nerve to come to the New Quarter himself. Maybe he would. He was obviously paid enough to make it worth his while to stay in Felix's favour.

'Will that be all, sir?'

'For the moment, yes.'

Felix emerged from the tailor's into the late afternoon gloom. He glanced around. No pursuers were visible. If there had actually been any, perhaps they had grown bored with waiting while Felix was in the tailor's. He hoped so at least.

He noticed he was standing taller and he felt more poised than he had before. He carried himself like a different man from the weary wanderer who had presented himself at Otto Jaeger's warehouse earlier. It was amazing the difference a bath and a change of clothes could make in a man.

A feeling of nervous anticipation had been gathering in his stomach all day. It was not quite fear. It was more like a vague uneasiness about what he would encounter within Elector Countess Emmanuelle's palace. He was forced to admit that he prayed he would not embarrass himself in front of the nobility.

He considered that thought for a moment, then forced a smile. His manners were good. He was well-spoken and well-dressed. There was nothing to be afraid of. Yet he knew this was not true. The nobility did not like upstart newcomers from the merchant class. During his time at university he had endured many snubs by young nobles who had taken pains to communicate this to him. At the same time, he had always resented being looked down on by people who were often stupider and less well-educated than he, whose only qualification was that they happened to be born into the right inbred bloodline. Now he could not help but laugh at himself. He was certainly not working himself into the correct frame of mind for this interview.

He thanked Sigmar for small mercies: at least Gotrek had not been summoned as well. He could just picture a confrontation between the local high-born and the sullen Trollslayer. It would be an encounter fated to end in disaster. Felix had never known the Slayer show deference to anything or anyone, and he doubted that the countess or her minions would appreciate his independence of spirit.

Suddenly a new problem presented itself, and one that he had not even bothered to consider earlier. The streets were muddy and full of rubbish. The gutters were overflowing. The crowds were unwashed and tightly pressed. He could not get to the palace without some of the dirt of the streets transferring itself to his superb new clothes. He knew it would never do to appear at the palace looking less than immaculate. He glanced around, hoping that a solution would present itself.

He gestured with his arm, summoning a passing palanquin. The litter's curtains were open, showing it was for hire. The two burly bearers approached him deferentially. Felix was startled for a moment. Normally two such bravoes would have cursed him or exchanged coarse jibes, but now they were all attentive respect. Of course, he realised, it was the clothes. They saw him as a rich noble and a potentially lucrative fare. It was an impression which was in no way diminished when he said: 'The palace, and swiftly.'

He clambered into the plushly upholstered seat and the bearers set off at a fast striding pace. Felix pulled open the curtains at the back of the palanquin, checking to see if he was being followed once more. Was it just his imagination or had someone just ducked back into the mouth of that alley?

The way to the palace was steep and winding. The townhouses of the nobility arrayed themselves around the highest hill in the city. From where Felix sat he could see a fine view of the roofs of the merchants below, and the great curve of the River Reik. He could see the spires of the temples and the great building site where workmen laboured to rebuild the College of Engineering.

Horses' hooves clattered on the cobbled streets. Coaches swept past. Servants in the liveries of a dozen famous families swarmed everywhere, carrying messages, leading beasts, holding great satchels full of provisions. The lowest of them were better dressed than some of the city's merchants, and the highest ranking wore uniforms scarcely less ornate than a mercenary captain's. Everyone looked cleaner and better fed than the commoners down below.

Here and there nobles garbed in splendid raiment walked with their retainers and bodyguards, the crowd parting as if under the influence of some mysterious force before them. Felix studied their haughtiness, thinking that he recognised a few of the younger ones who played at being poor in the Blind Pig of an evening. He doubted that any of them would recognise him now.

Ahead of them loomed the walls of the palace. It dwarfed the stately townhouses around it. Even now, with its walls replastered and ornate statuary lining the approach, it looked far more like a fortress than a palace. The great arch of the gateway was huge, and the heavy oaken gates were shod with bronze and looked like they could resist a hundred battering rams. Sentries barred the entrance and scrutinised all who attempted to pass. Some were recognised immediately and allowed to go in unhindered. Others were stopped and challenged, and Felix guessed he would be in the latter category.

He tapped on the canopy of the palanquin to indicate that they should stop, paid the footmen the two silver shillings and added another shilling for a tip, then watched them depart. He patted his tunic to make sure his summons was still there, then strode as confidently as he could manage in the direction of the gate.

When one of the guards asked him his business, he showed them the letter and the seal and was surprised when a tall, lean man garbed all in black emerged from within the gatehouse. He looked at Felix with cold, grey eyes.

'Herr Jaeger,' he said in a calm, emotionless voice. 'If you would be so good as to accompany me? I will explain the nature of this business on the way.'

Filled with sudden trepidation, Felix fell into step beside him. He could not help but notice that two armed guards dogged their steps. They moved down long corridors, passed through a series of galleries and an enormous ballroom, before going down some steps into the dungeons below. Somewhere in the distance, the evening bell tolled.

Felix studied the office warily. It was large and sumptuously furnished, not at all what he had expected. He had expected a torture chamber or a cell, but not this. Nevertheless, the two men-at-arms had followed them in and positioned themselves against the far wall where they stood, immobile. As Felix watched, a lamplighter in the livery of the palace entered, carrying a small ladder. Another bearing only a lit taper clambered up the ladder and lit the candles set in the massive chandelier. Its light dimmed the rays of the setting sun that filtered in through the narrow window.

The tall man gestured to the massive leather armchair which sat in front of his equally enormous desk. 'Please, Herr Jaeger, be seated.'

Felix allowed himself to sink into the chair. The tall man wandered over to the window and stared out for a moment, before pulling the heavy brocade drapes closed. He considered the window as if he were looking at it for the first time. It was narrow, obviously designed as an arrow slit.

'This place was a fortress before it was a palace,' he said.

His words hung in the air. Felix turned them over, wondering if there was some hidden meaning. He did not respond but waited for the man to continue, to amplify his statement if he was going to. The man considered this and smiled for the first time. His teeth were a brilliant white and made even his pale skin look sallow.

'Forgive me, Herr Jaeger; you are not quite what I expected.'

'And what did you expect, Herr...?'

The man bowed as one would to an opponent who had just scored a point in a fencing match. 'Forgive me, once more. It has been a long and harrowing day and I quite forget my manners. I am Heironymous Ostwald. I am the personal secretary to Her Serenity.'

Felix was not sure whether he should rise and bow back. He was not given the chance. Ostwald moved swiftly behind his desk and sat down. Felix noticed that even in that comfortable chair he sat with his back straight, like someone used to the iron discipline of a soldier.

'In answer to your question, from the description I had of you, I expected someone less... polished than yourself. Serves me right, I suppose.' He opened a small leather book in front of him. 'You are a member of the Jaeger family, I see. Good. Very good.'

'Why am I here?'

'Dieter! Johan! You may wait outside.' Ostwald gestured to the men-at-arms. They opened the door and quietly and discreetly vacated the room. Once they had gone, Ostwald steepled his fingers and started again.

'Tell me, Herr Jaeger, are you familiar with the skaven?'

Felix felt like his heart was about to stop. His mouth felt suddenly dry. He considered his words very carefully indeed. 'I know of them. I am not personally acquainted with any.'

Ostwald laughed again. It was a cold, mechanical laugh and there was no humour in it. 'Very good. I had understood that this was not the case.'

'What are you getting at?' Felix's nervousness made him sound snappish. He did not know the way this conversation was going but he could imagine several possible outcomes, none of them pleasant.

'Merely that you have served in the sewer watch and you claimed to your superiors there that you had encountered them. Is that not the case?'

'You know it is.'

'Yes. I do.' Again Ostwald smiled. 'You do not seem to me like a typical sewerjack, Herr Jaeger. The sons of rich merchants rarely leap at the chance to hunt goblins in our sewers.'

Felix was getting used to this now. He was not as surprised as he might have been by the unexpected nature of the statement. He could see that this was all part of Ostwald's technique. He liked to keep the people he was dealing with off-balance. It was like getting the measure of your opponent in a duel. Felix smiled back at him.

'I am the black sheep of my family.'

'Indeed. How interesting. You must explain to me how that came about some time.'

'I suspect you already know.'

'Perhaps. Perhaps. Let us return to the skaven, Herr Jaeger. How many times have you encountered them?'

'On several occasions.'

'How many precisely?'

Felix counted the number of times he was prepared to admit to. There was the encounter in the sewer. There was the attack on the Blind Pig. There was his fight in the Gardens of Morr. He decided that under the circumstances it might be undiplomatic to mention his meeting with the rat-ogre in von Halstadt's house and his battle with the warlocks of Skryre in the College of Engineering.

'Three.'

Ostwald consulted his book again. Another piece of the puzzle fitted into place, Felix thought to himself. He doesn't really know anything. He's just fishing. His style is to intimidate people and then see what they let slip. Of course, thought Felix, this knowledge will do you no good, if he orders you taken down into the dungeons and tortured. He decided to try a few questions himself.

'On whose authority are you doing this?' he asked.

'The Elector Countess Emmanuelle's,' Ostwald said with absolute certainty. 'Why do you ask?'

'I am just trying to work out what is going on here.'

Ostwald gave him a long cold chilling smile. 'I can explain that to you quite easily, Herr Jaeger. What do you know of Fritz von Halstadt?'

Once again, Felix felt his heart leap into his mouth. He fought to keep his guilt and his surprise off his face. A slight amused flicker in Ostwald's eyes told him that the man had noticed something.

'It's a familiar name,' he said. 'I think I saw him once at my brother's club.'

'Very good, Herr Jaeger. Allow me to share something with you – on the understanding on your word as a gentleman, that nothing I tell you goes beyond the confines of this room.'

The tone in which the words were said told Felix that Ostwald was not simply counting on his word as a gentleman. Felix did not doubt that there would be serious and violent reprisals if he betrayed the man's confidence.

'Please go ahead. You have my word I will tell no one.'

'Fritz von Halstadt was murdered.'

Felix thought he was going to be struck down on the spot. He felt sure that his guilt was written all over his face and that Ostwald was going to summon the guard to have him thrown into the dungeon.

'By the skaven.'

Felix let out a long, rushing sigh of relief.

'I can see you are appalled, Herr Jaeger.'

'Am I?' Felix collected his scattered wits. 'I mean – aren't I just?'

'Yes. It's a terrifying thought, isn't it? I will tell you something else.

Fritz von Halstadt was no ordinary servant of the crown. He was the chief of Her Serenity's secret police. We think he must have discovered some skaven plot and been murdered because of it.'

If you'd used the word 'joined' instead of 'discovered', I would have to agree with you, Felix thought. What he said instead was: 'What makes you think this?'

'In the burned-out remains of his home we found the skeleton of a creature that was not human. We suspect that it was some monster conjured by the skaven to assassinate Von Halstadt. He must have fought with it and killed it, then died of his wounds. The house was probably set on fire during their struggle.'

'Go on.'

'Interestingly enough, soon after that there was an attempt on your life. As far as I know, you and your associate, the dwarf Gurnisson, were the only people who had then claimed to have seen the skaven. Perhaps this was an effort to cover their tracks.'

'I think I see what you mean.'

'There are other things you may not know, Herr Jaeger, and I tell you them now only so you will realise the seriousness of the situation. You may have heard that there was a fire at the College of Engineering?'

'Yes.'

'What you may not be aware of is that the fire was the work of the skaven too. I assure you, Herr Jaeger, this is nothing to smile about. The gods were against those rat-man devils in one way. There seems to have been some sort of accident, for we found many skaven corpses at the scene.'

'Why have I not heard more of this?' Felix said.

'You would have, except that Her Serenity deemed it wise to avoid a panic, and panic there would surely be if the common herd were to find out that our city is under siege by the skaven!'

Felix was astonished. After many fruitless attempts by himself to get someone to take the skaven threat seriously, someone was now trying to convince him of it! He did not know whether to laugh or be angry. He decided to play the part allotted to him, for on consideration he realised that showing more knowledge than Ostwald believed him to have could easily prove dangerous.

'I am not joking, Herr Jaeger. Since you and Gurnisson reported the presence of skaven war parties in the sewers, there have been other sightings, skirmishes even. And bands of the rat-men have even raided our docks by night, stealing food and even a grain barge. I tell you, we are under siege.'

'Siege? Isn't that a little strong? Where are the armies, the war engines, the chittering hordes?'

'They are strong words, Herr Jaeger, and in truth the situation calls for them. The chief of secret police assassinated. Citizens assaulted. A great Imperial armoury destroyed – and now the threat of plague!'

'I–'

'Now, Herr Jaeger. I know you take this seriously. I know you have some knowledge of this. We have a mutual acquaintance and he has told me all about your actions in this matter.'

'Mutual acquaintance?'

Ostwald produced a pomander similar to the one that hung about Felix's neck. He held it beneath his nose and breathed deeply from it before setting it down upon the desk.

'I refer, of course, to Herr Doctor Drexler. He has told me about your visit to the Gardens of Morr and what you found there. He treated your henchman, after all.'

'How do you know Doctor Drexler?' Felix asked to buy some time. He fervently hoped Ostwald never referred to Gotrek as his henchman within the Slayer's hearing.

'As a patient and as a friend. He is the physician to many noble families.'

'But–'

'I see that you are aware of another and deeper connection. I suspected a man of your resources might.'

Felix had being going to ask 'But why did Drexler tell you all this?' but he decided to keep his mouth shut and see what coldly clever explanation this cold and clever man came up with.

'I tell you this only because the situation is truly desperate, Herr Jaeger, and we badly need your help.'

Things must be desperate indeed, thought Felix, if you need my help. Particularly when I haven't a clue about what you're talking about.

'Drexler and I are both initiates of the Order of the Hammer.' As he said this, he made a peculiar variation of the sign of the hammer over his heart, reversing the normal order, of left, right, centre, down. 'You have heard of us?'

'Some sort of Sigmarite secret society,' Felix guessed. It was not a difficult guess to make. The hammer was the sign of the Imperial Cult, and there were many strange hidden societies with their own signs and passwords.

'That is correct. An order of dedicated men sworn to protect our ancient civilisation from the threat of Chaos. We share many goals and much ancient knowledge. He tells me that Aldred himself chose you as his successor.'

'Successor?' Felix was bewildered.

'You bear his blade, Herr Jaeger. You knew the man.'

'Mmm…'

'I know Herr Aldred was a member of several secret orders as well as the one to which he nominally belonged. He was a devout and fearless man, Herr Jaeger. Much like yourself he dedicated himself to fighting the forces of Chaos wherever he found them.'

'I do not belong to his order.'

'I can understand that you would deny this, Herr Jaeger. Herr Aldred belonged to many orders with even stricter vows of secrecy than our own. I will not press you on this.'

Just as well, Felix thought wryly, otherwise you'd find out exactly the depth of my ignorance.

Ostwald paused for a moment and then spoke as if trying to change the subject: 'Drexler tells me that you possess a great deal of knowledge yourself.'

'I possess only a little.'

'It may be that the little you know is actually a great deal, Herr Jaeger. Tell me about this strange skaven who writes you the letters of warning. How did you meet it?'

So, Felix thought, this is where all this talk of secret societies and grave threats is leading. It is an attempt to get this information.

He realised that Drexler must have reported their entire conversation to Ostwald, so he saw no sense in hiding anything about the letter.

'I have never met it,' Felix said honestly. 'In truth I have no idea why it has selected me to communicate with. Perhaps it hasn't. Perhaps it has chosen Gotrek.'

'That seems unlikely, Herr Jaeger, given the dwarf's avocation. No, I am convinced that you are the chosen one. Why?'

'Perhaps because I can read.'

'You can read skaven runes?'

'No, but I can read Imperial script.'

'So the letter was written in Imperial script?' Ostwald looked astonished.

'Of course. How else could I read it?'

'You have these letters on you?'

'No, they vanished in a puff of smoke five heartbeats after I read them,' Felix said ironically. He was going to add that he did not normally carry the letters on his person but Ostwald interrupted him.

'Powerful sorcery indeed! Herr Jaeger, you must understand something. I have taken over Fritz von Halstadt's duties. The security of this great state of Nuln lies in my hands. Should this skaven contact you again, well, you must inform me at once.'

'Nothing would please me more,' Felix said sincerely.

'No, please take me seriously, Herr Jaeger. I sense that you know more than you are currently willing to tell me. That is fair. We must all have our little secrets. But I must insist that you let me know. I want no more midnight forays into the graveyards. I know you are a brave and resourceful man, but these things are best dealt with by the authorities.'

'I agree completely.'

'Good, Herr Jaeger. Do not attempt to deceive me in this. My reach is long.'

'I would not dream of it. You have my word.'

'Good. Then you are free to go. Just remember–'

'Do not worry, Herr Ostwald. Rest assured I will inform you as soon as I learn anything of the skaven's plans,' Felix said, fervently hoping against hope that he never ever came into the possession of such information again.

Izak Grottle pulled himself from his palanquin and lumbered over to the great barred window. His breathing was heavy and already he felt hungry. It had been a long trudge through the Underways to reach this secret burrow. Soon it would be time to eat once more. He congratulated himself. It was amazing from what simple sources the most brilliant of inspirations sprang. The entire enormous effort of this secret research warren had sprung from his own hunger. He doubted that any other skaven would ever have thought of something so simple and yet so inspired. Let others come up with intricate and complex schemes, thought Grottle! Soon he would demonstrate to all of them that the simplest plans were the best.

He looked down into the great warp vats and saw the monsters taking shape within their bubbling, glowing feeding fluids. He inspected the massive warpstone orbs which fed carefully measured jolts of mutating power into the vats when the watching vatmasters deemed the conditions perfect. The rank smell of ozone and strange chemicals wafted up and made his nostrils twitch. It was a reassuring smell to him, the smell of the warrens in which his clan had raised him, from where he had begun the long climb to the power that he wielded today.

He smiled, showing his great yellow fangs and felt the pangs of his dreadful hunger once more. All skaven suffered from it from time to time, usually after combat or some other violent activity. They called it the Black Hunger and for most of them it was a sign of triumph and indicator that they could devour prey. Izak Grottle suffered from it all the time. He had long suspected that continual exposure to warpstone dust and mutagenic chemicals had done something to him. He would not be the first Clan Moulder packmaster to acquire the stigmata of some mutation, nor would he be the last. In his case he also suspected that the change had done something to his brain – stimulated it, made him much cleverer and more cunning than other skaven, rewarded him with fantastic insight. That was why he needed to eat so much, of course, to fuel his incredible mind.

He stuffed his own tail into his mouth to try to control the terrible hunger pangs. Great gobs of saliva drooled down the bulbous flesh. He had already devoured every last scrap of the huge mound of dried meat he had intended to see him through his visit. He knew there was nothing much edible in this alchemical laboratory except his own bearers, and, in fairness, they had done nothing today to displease him. The jars all around contained mostly toxic chemicals; nothing there for him. He breathed deeply and fought to bring his appetite back under control.

Skitch looked up at him nervously. Grottle could tell that the little hunchbacked skaven was uneasy. Perhaps he was thinking of all the other lackeys which rumour claimed that the packmaster had devoured. Grottle licked his lips with his long pink tongue. As he liked to tell all of his research vermin, those rumours were utterly true. The light of warpstone lanterns illuminated the pebble-thick lenses that Skitch used to compensate for his bad eyesight. Grottle nodded his head and twitched his tail just for the pleasure of seeing Skitch leap back nervously.

Skitch was small and weak, and so near-sighted that he could hardly see one paw in front of his face without his glasses. In many other skaven clans, such weakness would soon have caused him to have been killed and eaten, but Clan Moulder had recognised his potential and kept him alive and for that, Grottle knew, the little runt was truly grateful. And he had proven useful to Clan Moulder. Skitch was quite possibly the best vatmaster in the long and glorious history of the clan. He was a genius when it came to breeding and moulding all manner of beasts. Now he held out the cage that contained what was most likely to be Clan Moulder's greatest triumph.

Izak Grottle took the cage and inspected its contents. It was a huge, sleek fat female rat, already pregnant by the looks of things. The untrained eye would detect very little different from an ordinary rat, Grottle thought. Perhaps they would think it a little larger, a bit more vicious. Perhaps they would even notice the wicked gleam of some abnormal emotion in its eye. But they would never suspect that they were looking at one of the most potent weapons the world had ever known.

'It doesn't look like much, does it?' Grottle said in his slow, deep rumbling voice. 'Does it?'

Grottle liked to repeat himself. He was proud of his voice, so powerful and so unlike a normal skaven voice. Skitch knew a cue when he heard one.

'Perhaps not, master – but then appearances are deceptive.' The vat-master's voice was unusually high for a skaven's, and his words had an odd insinuating quality. 'This beauty will lay waste to entire cities, will bring nations to their knees, will cause the world to bow before the genius of Clan Moulder!'

Grottle nodded in a slow, satisfied way. He knew this was true. He just liked to hear his lackey say it. 'You are sure there will be no problems, Skitch? Absolutely sure?'

'Yes, yes, master, I am certain. We have bred thousands of these creatures and we have tested many of them to destruction in the approved manner.'

'Good! Good! And what did you find?'

'They have a huge appetite for almost any material. They will eat wood and waste if nothing else is available, but mostly they seek out and devour grain, meat and other foodstuffs.'

'Excellent.'

'They can consume their own body weight in less than a hundred heartbeats and be ready to eat again in hours.'

'You have done splendidly, Skitch. Splendidly.'

The hunchback seemed almost to swell up with the effects of the praise. 'And they can breed in litters of up to a hundred.'

'They grow quickly, of course?'

'They reach full mature size within a day, providing they find enough to eat.'

'And the breeders?'

'Can bear a litter each and every day, as you specified, master.'

Grottle threw back his head and let his deep rumbling laughter pour forth. Such a simple idea, he thought. When these rats were released into the human city, they would consume all the food within days.

All the stored crops from the harvest would be devoured. All the food in shops would vanish underneath a furry avalanche of hunger. They would eat and breed and eat and breed unstoppably. And when no other food was available, they would eat the humans and their animals. And when all other foodstocks were exhausted they would consume each other. Or die.

Their lifespan was measured only in days. But before that happened, the humans would starve or flee from their city and the triumph would belong to Clan Moulder. Word would soon reach the Council of Thirteen and a suitable reward would be found for Izak Grottle.

'We are ready to begin?'

'Yes master, We have the captured grain barge almost ready. The conversion will be done in days. We will ship the specimens to where it is hidden. It can begin its journey any time you wish, after that.'

'Perfect. Perfect.' The human warehouses were near the docks. All they would have to do would be to take the boat into the harbour and open the cages. A few disposable house troops could see to that easily enough. Perhaps some rat-ogres just to be on the safe side. 'Do so as soon as preparations are complete.'

'Of course, master.'

'You say you have thousands more of these?' Grottle said, reaching into the cage to stroke the sleek fat rat.

'Yes, master. Why?'

'Because I'm feeling a little peckish.' With that, Izak Grottle grasped the somnolent rat and stuffed it, still living, into his salivating mouth. It was still struggling futilely as it went down his throat. It tasted good, thought Grottle.

Just like victory.

Felix walked through the swing doors of the Blind Pig and every head in the place turned to look at him. At first, he wondered what for, but when Katka, one of the serving girls, came to take his order, he realised it was because no one recognised him. He smiled at her, and was rewarded with a look of confusion until she saw who he was.

'Why, Felix, I would never have guessed it was you. Did the countess give you some new clothes?'

'Something like that,' he murmured as he raced up the stairs to get to his room and change clothes. He was grateful to discover that the package containing his old garments had come from the tailor's shop.

Thank Sigmar, he thought. It wouldn't do to go brawling in this fine suit. Then it dawned on him that simple possession of this new finery was changing him. This morning he would never even have given a thought to such matters. Probably because he didn't have to. And what was he going to do with the pouch full of gold that Otto had given him? To his brother, it probably seemed like little enough money, but it was more than Felix could earn in a whole season of working at the Blind Pig. Gently he pried up a loose floorboard and dropped it into place there.

As he changed for work, he considered his encounter with Herr Ostwald. It seemed that, at long last, the authorities were taking the skaven threat seriously. At the same time, Ostwald appeared to have made some very strange assumptions about Felix. He seemed to assume that Felix was far cleverer and more involved with all of this than he actually was. He guessed that Ostwald was simply projecting his own reasoning and perceptions onto what he knew of Felix. Well, as long as he asked no questions about the death of Fritz von Halstadt and the burning of the college, Felix was not going to disappoint him. The fact that Ostwald had deduced a vast and well-organised skaven conspiracy from several random acts that Felix and the Slayer had perpetrated themselves might have been amusing – except for one thing.

It was quite evident that there was indeed a vast and well-organised skaven conspiracy. Even though he himself had killed von Halstadt, there had been powerful rat-men present. Clan Eshin assassins had nearly burned down the Blind Pig, and monsters had been sighted just before the blaze which destroyed much of the Poor Quarter. Even though he and Gotrek had interrupted them, the warlocks of Skryre had been robbing the college. Even though they had stopped the plague monks' ritual, the skaven had managed to infiltrate the Gardens of Morr and the plague was still spreading through the city like wildfire.

Hastily Felix put the enchanted pomander around his neck and breathed deeply of the herbs. Ostwald had made no secret of the fact that rat-men patrols had been sighted in the sewers and other areas around the city; scouting parties, most likely.

Felix knew that one of the creatures Gotrek had seen in von Halstadt's house was a grey seer, one of the rarest and most powerful of all the rat-men magicians according to Leiber's book. A being, in fact, usually only sighted when the skaven had great plans afoot.

A chill struck Felix, and it was not just caused by his tattered clothes.

He was forced to concede that, wrong though many of his facts had been, Ostwald's basic conclusion was most likely correct. The skaven planned something big here in Nuln. But what?

Grey Seer Thanquol took another pinch of warpstone snuff and stroked his whiskers. Things were going well. He inspected the mass of papers that lay before him and revelled in the messages they contained. Almost ten thousand crack skaven troops would soon be in position in the Underways beneath and around the city of Nuln.

So large a host had not been mustered since the time of the Great Chaos Incursion. It was the largest force the Council of Thirteen had dispatched to assault a human city since the time of the Great Plague, when the entire human Empire had briefly lain under the iron paw of skaven rule. And it was his to command. When he gave the word, it would attack and in a frenzy of overwhelming ferocity would overwhelm the pitiful humans above.

For a brief instant the warpstone conjured up delightful visions of destruction and death before Thanquol's reddened eyes. He could picture the burning buildings, the humans hacked to pieces or led off in great slave trains. He saw himself striding through the ruins triumphant. The very thought made his tail stiffen.

Things were going very well indeed. Even Thanquol's enemies were aiding his plans. That vile twosome Gurnisson and Jaeger had, guided by Thanquol's brilliant insight, uncovered the lair of Vilebroth Null and stopped his plans in their tracks. The abbot had returned from the surface world alone, and no trace could be found of the Cauldron of a Thousand Poxes. Null had spent the last few days limping around the Underways muttering darkly about traitors. Thanquol tittered. There was a certain poetic justice in it all: it had been the abbot's intended treachery to the cause of Thanquol, and of course the entire skaven nation, which had been the cause of his undoing.

It even appeared that the abbot might have done the invasion force a favour, for Thanquol's agents on the surface reported some dire disease was dropping the humans in their tracks. Of course, potentially this meant that there would be less slaves once the conquest of Nuln had been effected, so perhaps then would be the time to have the abbot punished. He could trump up the charges for the council and let them deal with Null. Yes, it was true, Thanquol thought: every cess-pit has a warpstone dropping in it, if only you know how to look.

He studied the plans of the city before him. The various invasion routes were well marked in red, blue and green warpstone ink. They glowed in front of his eyes in a bright tangle and snarl of lines. Here and there circles indicated breakout points where the army would erupt onto the surface. The sheer labyrinthine complexity of it all filled Thanquol's brain with pleasure. But the most pleasure came from his contemplation of what would happen afterwards.

The city would be garrisoned against human attempts to retake it. He would set up labour camps and make the captured human slaves build a big ditch around the city. Then they could dam the river with a great waterwheel which would provide power for the skaven's machines and sweatshop factories. At some point they would erect a huge, one hundred tail-length high statue of their conquerors, and it seemed only fair to Thanquol that he should be the model for it, for truly he would personify the skaven spirit of conquest to them. It would be a glorious time, and the first of many victories that would end with all the human lands permanently and utterly under skaven rule.

He heard a not very discreet hacking cough outside the curtains of his sanctum. A hoarse voice said: 'Greatest of generals, it is I, Lurk Snitch-tongue, and I bring news most urgent.'

Disturbed from his reverie, Thanquol was inclined to be snappish but Lurk had proven to be an invaluable lackey just recently, and his sources of information had been excellent.

At this moment, he seemed a little ill, but Thanquol was sure that would pass.

'Enter! Enter! Quick! Quick!'

'Yes! Yes! Swiftest of thinkers!'

'What is this urgent news?'

Lurk twitched his tail. It seemed obvious to Thanquol that the little skaven had indeed come with interesting information, and intended to savour his moment of triumph.

'I once blasted a lackey who kept me waiting a moment too long. Stripped his flesh to the bones.'

'A moment, most patient of masters, while I gather my thoughts. Some explanation is needed.'

'Then explain!'

'My birthkin Ruzlik serves Clan Moulder.'

'Indeed. And you think this information is worthy of the consideration of a grey seer?'

'No! No, most perceptive of potentates! It's just that he has a habit of gossiping when he has consumed fungal winebroth.'

'I see. And you, of course, are often sharing a flask or two with him.'

'Yes! Yes! Only this morning, in fact. He has told me that his master, Izak Grottle, has a great plan afoot. One that will bring the human city to its knees, and I hesitate to mention this, most understanding of skaven…'

'Hesitate no more. Quick! Quick!'

'He claims that Grottle's plan will bring him great glory, will make him more famous even – his words, not mine, master – than Grey Seer Thanquol.'

News of this treacherous claim came as no surprise to Thanquol. It was ever the fate of great skaven to be undermined by jealous lackeys. Doubtless Grottle sought to win esteem in the eyes of the Council of Thirteen at the expense of Thanquol. Well, the grey seer knew ways of dealing with that.

'And what is this plan? Speak! Speak!'

'Alas, the fool could not say. He has merely heard the Moulders chitter among themselves. He knows it has something to do with a grain boat, for he himself led the raid to steal one from the humans. He has no other hard details.'

'Then go and find some. Now!'

'I may need to spend warptokens, most generous of masters.'

'What you need will be provided – within reason.'

'I go, master.' Lurk bowed and scraped as he retreated back through the drapes.

Thanquol slumped down in his throne. Certain things were starting to make sense. He had heard reports that one of the human grain barges had been stolen. He had merely put it down to some claw leaders exceeding their orders, and doing some private plundering. Now it seemed that there was another ulterior and sinister motive. Thanquol knew that his position would not be safe until he found out what that was.

'I don't like you,' the man said, slumping down in his chair. 'I really don't like you.'

'You're drunk,' Felix said. 'Go home!'

'This is a tavern! My copper's as good as anyone's. I'll go home when I please. I don't take orders from the likes of you.'

'Fair enough!' Felix said. 'Stay, then.'

'Don't try and smooth-talk me. I'll go if I like.'

Felix was getting tired of this. He had seen drunks like this before: belligerent, full of self-pity, just looking for trouble. Unfortunately, Felix was usually the candidate they chose for it. They always picked him for an easy mark. He supposed they were all too scared of Gotrek and the other bouncers. There was something familiar about this one though. His coarse features and squat muscular form looked familiar even in the shadowy gloom of this corner of the tavern. He had been in several times over the past few days since Felix had returned from his interview with Herr Ostwald.

'Elissa's my girl,' the drunk said. 'You just leave her alone.'

Oh, of course; it was the peasant lad who used to go out with Elissa. He'd come back.

'Elissa can make up her own mind about who she wants to see.'

'No she can't. She's too sweet. Too easily led. Any city slicker with a smooth tongue and a nice cloak can turn her head.'

Felix saw the part he was being cast for. He was the heartless seducer leading the poor peasant girl astray.

'You've seen too many Detlef Sierck plays,' he said.

'What? What did you call me?'

'I didn't call you anything!'

'Yes, you did. I heard you.'

Felix saw the punch coming a league away. The man was drunk and slow. He raised his hand to block it. His forearm stung from the force of the blow. The man was strong.

'Bastard!' Hans shouted. 'I'll show you.'

He lashed out with a kick that caught Felix in the shin. Sharp pain stabbed through Felix. By reflex, he lashed out with his right hand and caught Hans under the jaw. It was quite possibly the best punch he had ever thrown against a man who was in no state to do anything about it. Hans dropped like a pole-axed ox.

The surrounding crowd applauded. Felix turned around to bow ironically and he saw Elissa looking at him with a look of horror in her eyes.

'Felix, you brute!' she said, moving past him to nurse Hans's head in her lap.

'Oh Hans, what did that heathen do to you?'

Just looking at her, Felix could tell that any explanation of what had happened would be useless.

'You have found out more of the Moulder's schemes, I hope?' Thanquol allowed some of his anger and impatience to show in his voice. Over the past few days Lurk had spent considerable sums from the grey seer's treasure chest but still had not produced any results. The little skaven gave a wheezing cough.

'Yes, yes, most perspicacious of masters. I have.'

'Good! Good! Tell me – quick, quick!'

'It's not good, most forgiving of masters.'

'What? What?' Thanquol leaned forward to glare down at the little rat-man and watched him flinch. Few could endure the grey seer's red-eyed stare when it suited him to use it.

'Regretfully, the wicked Moulders may already have implemented their plan.'

Cold fury clutched Thanquol's heart. 'Go on!'

'My birthkin overheard the packmaster gloating. It seems a grainship bearing Clan Moulder's secret weapon will arrive in the man-city tonight. Once it arrives, the city will fall. He knows that it has something to do with the city's grain supply but he's not sure what. Clan Moulder are very technical and have their own words for many things.'

'May the Horned Rat gnaw your birthkin's entrails! Is he hearing any more?'

'Just that the barge has been painted black to conceal it from human eyes and that it will arrive this very night. It may even have done so already, most magnificent of masters.'

Thanquol's fur bristled. What could he do? He could mobilise his troops and interfere but that would mean moving openly against Clan Moulder and every instinct the grey seer possessed rebelled against that. What if he summoned his troops, and they failed to find the ship? Thanquol would be a laughing stock and could not endure that. There was no time to waste. He knew that this called for urgent and desperate measures.

Swiftly he reached for pen and parchment, and inscribed a hasty message. 'Take this to the burrow where the dwarf and the man Jaeger dwell. Make sure they get it – and quickly! Deliver it personally!'

'P-p-personally, most revered of rat-men?'

'Personally.' Thanquol made it clear from his tone that he would brook no argument. 'Go. Quick! Quick! Hurry-scurry! No time there is to waste!'

'At once, mightiest of masters!'

Vilebroth Null looked up with rheumy hate-filled eyes. He coughed, but the sound of his coughing was lost amid the hacking coughs of other skaven in the corridors. At last his patience had been rewarded. His long hours of lying in wait near Thanquol's lair had finally paid off. Somehow Vilebroth Null knew the grey seer had been behind the failure of his carefully contrived plan. So where was that little sneak Lurk Snitchtongue going at his hour? The abbot knew there was only one way to find out.

'He started it!' Felix said, all too aware that he sounded like he was whining. He looked around the room they shared, his eyes caught by the package of clothes the tailor had delivered. He had still not unwrapped them.

'So you say,' said Elissa inflexibly. 'I think you're just a bully. You like hitting people like poor Hans.'

'Poor Hans put a bruise the size of a steak on my shin!' Felix said angrily.

'Serves you right for hitting him,' Elissa said. Felix shook his head in frustration. He was just about to get himself in deeper water when suddenly the window crashed in. Felix threw himself over Elissa to cover her as broken glass rained down. Fortunately, not too much landed on them. Felix rolled to his feet and scanned the chamber in the lantern light. Something dark and bulky lay on the floor.

Swiftly he drew his sword and prodded it. Nothing happened.

'What is it?' Elissa said, getting to her feet fearfully and pulling her nightgown tight around herself.

'Don't know,' Felix said, bending over to inspect it more closely. As he did so he recognised the shape, and he thought he recognised the thing wrapped round it. 'It's a brick, and it's wrapped in paper.'

'What? It'll be young Count Sternhelm again. He and his cronies are always breaking windows when they get drunk!'

'I don't think so,' Felix said, gingerly unwrapping the paper. It was the same thick coarse parchment all the other skaven messages had come on. He unfolded it and read:

> *Frends – the Black Ship brings doom to yoor city! It comes*
> *tonite and carries certin deth! It is a grane barge loded wiv bad!*
> *Yoo must stop it! Go QUIK! QUIK! Yoo do not hav much time!*
> *They wil destroy yoor grane!*

Felix pulled himself to his feet and started to pull on his clothes.

'Run and get me some paper! I need to send a message to the palace. Move! Quickly!'

The urgency in his voice compelled Elissa from the room without asking any more questions.

* * *

Lurk rubbed his paws together and offered up a prayer of thanks to the Horned Rat. His message was delivered and somehow he had managed to avoid being chopped up by the dwarf's fearsome axe. Mere minutes after he had lobbed the brick through what he had ascertained was Jaeger's window he saw all the lights in the inn go on, and shortly thereafter, the human and the dwarf raced from the building bearing weapons and lighted lanterns.

A job well done, he told himself with satisfaction and rose to go. He sniffed heavily, trying to clear his nose. He was not feeling too well, and had been feeling less than well for days. He wondered if he was going down with the strange new disease that, rumour had it, was going around the skaven camp... the disease so strangely similar to the plague which was felling the humans. Lurk fervently hoped not. He was still young and had many things to accomplish. It would not be fair for him to pass away without achieving them.

He almost fainted when a heavy hand fell on his shoulder and a hideous bubbling voice whispered in his ear: 'You will tell me what you have been doing! All of it! Quick! Quick!'

Even through the thick wad of snot that filled his nostrils, Lurk recognised the oppressive stench of Vilebroth Null.

'What's the hurry, manling?' Gotrek rumbled. 'We don't even know where we're going.'

'The river,' Felix said, feeling a strange sense of urgency. The note had said they did not have much time, and their skaven informant had never lied to them before. 'A ship must arrive by river.'

'I know, manling, but it's a big river. We can't cover it all.'

'It's a barge! There are very few places where a barge can tie up, and it must follow navigable channels.'

Felix considered the possibilities. What certainty did he have that this 'Black Ship' was going to tie up, rather than say, explode? None, really; he was just hoping that this was the case. Then it came to him. The big grain warehouses were down by the wharves and the letter had mentioned grain. At least, he hoped it had.

'The granaries,' he muttered. 'The Northside docks are near the granaries.'

'The Northside docks would seem to be the best bet then,' Gotrek said, hefting his axe.

'Well, we need to start somewhere.' They jogged on. Felix hoped fervently that the tavern boy had managed to deliver his note to Count Ostwald.

* * *

Skitch cursed as the barge shifted off course again. It was not a vessel the skaven were used to handling and the helmsman had had a lot of trouble with the tricky currents on their way down-river. Skitch hoped that they would arrive soon, for if they did not reach the manbur-row during the hours of darkness the whole plan would be ruined. The barge painted black to be inconspicuous on this moonless night would stick out like a human baby in a litter of runts by day.

Well, he supposed the ship had been necessary. There was no other way such a huge number of specimens could have been carried through the Underways and released into the human city without arousing suspicion. He knew the last thing that his master wanted was for either Grey Seer Thanquol or the humans to have any ink-ling of what was going on. It was a well-known fact that the plans of Thanquol's rivals had a tendency to fail if he found out about them. Skitch shuddered at the thought of what would happen if the humans found out what was going on.

He shook his head and returned to inspecting his charges. They scrabbled at the bars of their cages, hungry and desperate to be free.

'Soon! Soon!' he told them, feeling a certain kinship for these short-lived vermin that his mighty intellect had created. He knew they were flawed, just like he was. They would live only days.

The ship moved on through the night, coming ever closer to the sleeping city.

The docks by night were not a reassuring place, Felix thought. Lights spilled from many seedy taverns, and many red lights illuminated the alleys. Armed patrols of watchmen moved between the warehouses, but were careful not to enter the areas where the sailors took their pleasure. They were more intent in protecting their employers' goods than stopping crime. Still, Felix was reassured to know that there were armed men within call if things went horribly wrong.

He stood on the edge of the wharf and stared out into the river. The Reik was wide at this point, perhaps a league across, and navigable by ocean-going ships. Not that many of them came this far. Most traders chose to drop their cargoes in Marienberg and have it shipped upriver on barges.

From here he could see the running lights of both barges and the small skiffs which carried folk across the river all hours. He assumed that there would be many more craft out there than lights. Not at all boats or their passengers wanted their businesses known. Felix assumed that the Black Ship would be among their number. Only instead of carrying a cargo of illegal goods it was carrying some awful skaven weapon. Felix shuddered to contemplate what it might be. The Cauldron of a Thousand Poxes and the weapons of Clan Skryre had been terrible enough for him.

The wind blew cold and he drew his old tattered cloak tight about his shoulders. What am I doing here, he wondered? I should be at home back in the Pig, trying to patch things up with Elissa.

Or maybe not. Maybe that was what he was doing here, avoiding Elissa.

He wondered where things were going with the girl, and he had no real idea. It was just something he had drifted into, not something he ever imagined would have a future. He knew he did not love Elissa the way he had loved Kirsten. Recently, he would not even say they were friendly. He thought that for her, too, it was just a passing thing, something that had happened. Maybe she would be better off with her peasant boy. He shrugged and continued to peer out into the darkness, and listen to the waves slopping gently against the wooden supports of the wharf.

'Our scuttling little friends have picked a good night for it,' Gotrek muttered, taking a swig from the flask of schnapps.

Felix studied the sky. He could see what the Slayer meant. The sky was cloudy and the greater moon was a sliver. The lesser moon was not visible at all.

'Smugglers' moon,' Felix said.

'What?'

'My father used to call moons like this "smugglers' moons". I can see why. Dark. The excisemen would find it hard to see you on a night like this.'

'River patrols too,' Gotrek said. 'Not that humans can see worth a snotling's fart at night anyway.'

'I suppose,' Felix said, wanting to contradict the Slayer, but knowing that he was right in this case.

'Aye, well just be glad a dwarf was here, manling. Even though he has only one good eye.'

'Why?'

'Because there is your black ship! Look!'

Felix followed the dwarf's pointing finger and saw nothing. 'You've had too much schnapps,' he said.

'Your people have yet to brew a draft that could get a dwarf drunk,' Gotrek said.

'Only legless…' Felix muttered.

'At least I'm not blind.'

'Just blind drunk.'

'I'm telling you there's a ship there.' Felix squinted into the gloom and began to think the dwarf might be right. There was something large out there, a shadowy presence moving erratically in the deep water.

'I do believe you're right,' Felix said. 'I apologise most sincerely.'

'Save your breath,' the Slayer said. 'There's killing to be done.'

'Faster!' Felix said, standing on the prow of the skiff and keeping his eyes fixed on the shadowy shape ahead.

'I'm going as fast as I can, master,' the boatman said, poling with all the energy of an arthritic hedgehog. He was a hefty man, slow-moving and ponderous.

'A one-armed man could pole faster,' Gotrek said. 'In fact, I'll bet if I chopped off one of your arms, you could move quicker.'

Suddenly the boatman found a surge of new strength from somewhere and they picked up speed. Felix wasn't sure whether to be glad or not. He was nervous about approaching the skaven ship in this small craft. He wished they had summoned the watch but the Slayer had become overcome with battle frenzy and insisted there was no time to waste. He assured Felix that the commotion they would soon be generating would attract the river patrols. Felix did not doubt that he was right.

As they came closer, he could see that it was a black ship all right, a huge grain barge painted all black and moving swiftly downriver. He wondered why the skaven had done this. Certainly black made the ship inconspicuous at night, but during the day the barge would be as noticeable as a hearse in a wedding parade. Maybe it had travelled downriver unpainted and they had disguised it this very evening. Maybe they had a concealed base somewhere within a night's sailing upriver. Such a base could be quite some distance away, for a barge could cover a lot of water in one night, moving with the current as this one was.

Felix dismissed all such speculation as pointless. He knew he was only doing it to keep his mind occupied and distracted from fear of the coming encounter.

What were they up to on the barge, he wondered? If they weren't skaven then they were the worst sailors he had ever seen. The barge now appeared to be drifting in a great half circle. He could hear a faint muffled drumbeat and the creaking and clashing of oars. It sounded like there was some difficulty in guiding the craft.

'It's them, all right,' Gotrek said. 'Skaven are even worse sailors than I'd heard.'

Felix could hear the distant squeaking calls of the skaven now, and knew the Slayer was correct. Unfortunately, the boatman had heard him too.

'Did you say "skaven"?' he asked, superstition and fear engraved across his fat, sweat-sheened face.

'No,' Felix said.

'Yes,' Gotrek said.

'I'm not going anywhere near a barge if there are Chaos-worshipping monsters on board!' the boatman declared.

'My friend was only joking,' Felix said.

'No I wasn't,' Gotrek said.

The boatman stopped poling. Gotrek glared at him.

'I hate boats almost as much as I hate trees,' he said. 'And I hate trees almost as much as I hate elves. And what I particularly hate are people who keep me on boats longer than I have to be on them, when there are monsters to slay and fighting to be done.'

The boatman had become very pale and very still, and Felix was almost sure that he could hear his teeth chatter.

Gotrek continued to rant: 'You will pole this boat till we reach that rat-man barge or I will rip off your leg and beat you to death with it. Do I make myself clear?'

Felix had to concede that the sheer amount of menace the Slayer managed to get into his voice was impressive. The boatmen certainly thought so.

'Perfectly,' he said, and began poling with redoubled speed.

As they approached the black barge, Felix saw a new problem. Their skiff was low in the water but the barge had high sides. On level ground, it would have been a simple climb, but on two moving vessels bobbing on water it was an entirely different proposition. He mentioned this to Gotrek. 'Don't worry,' the Slayer said. 'I have a plan.'

'Now I am worried,' Felix muttered.

'What was that, manling?' The Slayer looked close to berserk rage.

'Nothing,' Felix said.

'Just grab that lantern and be ready to move when I tell you.'

* * *

The skiff drifted into contact with the ship. As it did so, Gotrek smashed his axe into the barge's side. It bit deep and held there and the Slayer used it to pull himself up until he reached a porthole.

'Very stealthy,' Felix said sourly. 'Why not give a hearty shout of welcome while you're at it.'

Another smashing stroke saw Gotrek over the ship's side. He stood there for a moment and then lowered the axe, blade first.

'Grab hold,' he roared. Felix leapt up and grabbed hold of the axe shaft with his right hand, while holding the lantern in the other. Gotrek raised the axe one-handed, lifting it up, apparently effortlessly, despite Felix's weight and the uncomfortable angle. He swung the axe inwards over the ship's side and brought Felix with it. Felix dropped to the deck, amazed by the awesome strength the dwarf had just displayed.

'Looks like we're expected,' he said, nodding at the mass of skaven swarming up onto the deck.

'Good,' Gotrek said. 'I need a bit of exercise.'

What was that, Skitch wondered? He had heard an almighty crash and the sound of wood splintering. Had those buffoons managed to crash the barge onto a sandbar again? He would not have put it past them. They had claimed to be experienced sailors and that crewing a human ship would be no problem. So far that had not proved the case.

If they jeopardised this mission, Izak Grottle would tear them all limb from limb and devour their entrails before their dying eyes, but such thoughts brought Skitch no consolation. He knew he would be the first course at the packmaster's punishment feast.

When he heard the crew's squeaks of alarm, Skitch knew it was even worse than running aground. They had been discovered by a human patrol. He cursed the bad luck which had enabled the humans to discover them. It must have been a million-to-one chance. Now he wished he had brought some rat-ogres after all. He had not done so, for fear that their roars and bellows would give away the ship's position, but that did not seem to matter now.

Part of him wanted to squirt the musk of fear, but then again it was his responsibility to see to his charges. He raced from the cabin into the hold. All around him, massive rats thrashed in their cages, desperate to get free and to eat. Seeing the look of feral hunger in their eyes, Skitch was glad that he had doused himself in oil of swamptoad, a substance that he knew his creations found repellent.

Hearing the sounds of terrible carnage from above, Skitch swiftly began to throw open the cages. The rats swarmed hungrily up the gangplanks, moving towards their living, breathing food.

Felix lashed out with the lantern. Its flame flared bright as it rushed through the air. The dazzled skaven before him leapt back, momentarily blinded. Felix took advantage of its confusion to stab it through the throat with his sword.

The deck was already slippery underfoot with blood and brains. The Slayer had left an awful trail of destruction behind him. His axe had reduced a dozen skaven to limbless corpses. The others were fleeing backwards or jumping over the side of the barge to avoid him. Felix moved along behind, killing those who sought to outflank the dwarf and putting the dying out of their misery.

His heart beat loudly within his chest. His sword's hilt felt sweaty in his grip but he was not as afraid as he usually was in mortal combat. Compared to some of the fights he had been in, this one was relatively easy. Suspiciously so, in fact, considering there was supposed to be some terrible skaven weapon on board this vessel.

Not that the relative ease of the fight would make much difference, he told himself, springing aside to duck a knife cast by one of the skaven sailors, and lunging forward to take another rat-man through the heart. All it would take would be one lucky blow, and he would be just as dead as if a rat-ogre had torn him into little pieces.

Concentrate, he ordered himself – and then stopped in horror as the tide of furry forms started swarming up from the hold.

Skitch snuck up the stairway and peered out at a scene of terrible violence. A monstrous squat dwarf wielding a flailing great axe had killed half the crew and seemed intent on massacring the other half. In this he was assisted by a tall, blond-furred human who held a lantern in one hand and a wicked-looking blade in the other. All around, the killer rats gnawed at the bodies of dead and dying skaven.

Skitch froze on the spot and squirted the musk of fear. His paws locked on the last cage, in which frantic rats struggled to get away from the stink of the oil on his fur. Skitch recognised the pair who had invaded the ship. They had become something of a dark legend amongst the skaven besieging Nuln. This was the fearsome pair whom even the gutter runners had failed to slay, who had routed the warlocks of Skryre, whom it was said even Grey Seer Thanquol feared to meet again. They were formidable killers of skaven – and they were here, on this very barge!

Skitch was no warrior and he knew he could be of no aid to the skaven in the battle above. It was possible that even the killer rats would fail to overcome this seemingly invincible twosome. It was plainly his duty, then, to escape, carrying the last of the surviving rats, to preserve them for the future when they might be used again.

So thinking, he held the cage high above his head and leapt into the night-black waters.

Felix watched as more and more of the huge rats poured from the hold. There was a hunger and madness in their eyes which frightened him, and he wondered if these could be the skaven secret weapon. One large fierce brute threw itself at him. He felt the horrid scurry of its paws on his leg. He lashed out, sending the beast flying and stamped down, feeling the spine of another crack beneath the heel of his boot.

He looked around at Gotrek. The Slayer beheaded another of the skaven crew, sending a great fountain of black blood belching into the air. Before the skaven corpse hit the ground, more and more rats had swarmed over it.

Something dropped onto Felix from above. He felt paws scrabbling in his hair, and small sharp teeth nipping his ear. A foul animal stench filled his nostrils. He dropped the lantern and reached up, feeling muscles squirm beneath fur as he plucked the rat free. Fangs nipped at his fingers as he threw the thing over the side and into the river.

More and more rats dropped from above or pounced from the deck. He felt like he was in the centre of a swirling storm of fur. Gotrek stamped and hacked and kicked but he was in the same position. The rats were too numerous and too fierce to overcome. If they stayed they would die a horrible death by a thousand bites.

'Not a death for a Slayer, I would say!' Felix shouted.

'Torch this blasted floating rats' nest!'

'What?'

'Torch it and let's begone!'

Felix looked around and saw the lantern. He picked it up and threw it with all his force onto the deck. Burning oil spilled everywhere. Felix had often heard his father say what a danger fire was on a ship. They were, after all, built of wood and sealed with inflammable pitch. Felix had never thought he would be grateful for that fact, but he certainly was now. Flames started to flicker and dance all around him.

The smell of burning fur and flesh reached his nostrils. Squeaking rats scurried everywhere, their fur smouldering and blazing as they tried to escape the hot flames. Some leapt overboard and plummeted into the water like small living meteors. Others continued their attack with redoubled fury, as if determined to drag something else down in death with him.

Felix decided that this was their cue to depart.

'Time to go!' he shouted. A backwash of heat blazed towards him, singeing his hair and eyebrows.

'Aye, manling, I think you are right.'

Felix sheathed his sword, turned and vaulted over the side. He tumbled into the water, rats falling all around him. After the heat of the burning ship it was almost a relief to feel the shock of cold dark water closing over his head. He kicked out and up and his head broke the surface.

He could see that there were boats all around, come to look at the fire. Fighting the weight of his scabbard, he struck out for the nearest vessel.

Sopping wet, Felix sat glumly on the wharf and kept his eyes peeled. So far there was no sign of the Slayer. He had not seen Gotrek since he plunged into the water. He wondered if the dwarf could swim. Even if he could, was it not possible that he had drowned trying to hold on to his precious axe? It would not exactly have been the glorious death he craved.

His clothes were wet and his teeth were starting to chatter but still he sat, wishing that he had some of the schnapps Gotrek had been swigging earlier. Felix wondered about the skaven weapon that was meant to have been on board the black ship. He knew now that he would never find out what it was. The barge was a burned-out hulk resting on the bottom of the river. The boatmen who had picked him up had held their position in mid-river and watched it burn, before accepting a handful of silver in payment for carrying Felix to the shore.

There was a wet, slapping sound nearby Felix looked warily to his right. One of the huge, hungry rats had made it off the ship then. It clambered up the side of the ladder from the landing stage, shook its fur dry like it was a dog and trotted off up the wharf. Felix watched it go.

Briefly Felix considered finding the boatmen again and going out to search the river for the Slayer. He knew it would be a futile effort; the Reik was too wide and the current too strong. If the Slayer had drowned, doubtless his corpse would eventually be recovered and put on display at the Old Bridge, waiting with all the others the river had taken for someone to come and claim it. Felix could check there tomorrow.

He stood up wearily from the mooring post on which he sat and prepared for the long trudge home. As he did so, he caught sight of a familiar figure, berating an equally familiar boatman who was poling towards the landing stage. Felix waved a welcome.

'Current carried me down river,' Gotrek called, hauling himself up onto the wharf. 'Ran into our old friend here. Took most of the night to get back.'

'Going against the current,' the weary boatman said. He looked as tired as any man Felix had ever seen, and deeply scared too. Felix could guess the nature of the threats which Gotrek had used to motivate him.

'Well,' he said, 'let's get back to the Pig and have some beer. I think we've earned it.'

'Forgive me if I don't join you,' the boatman said. 'And… and there's the small matter of my fee.'

Cold, wet and bedraggled, Skitch finally scuttled into the Underways. It had been a truly dreadful night. He had swum through the chilly waters carrying the last cage of rats. After that, he had scuttled along the riverbanks until he found a sewer outflow, and then he had spent the rest of the night wandering through the tunnels until he had found the familiar scent of skaven. Dodging human patrols in the dark, the trail had finally led him here.

He was proud of himself. He had managed a long and difficult trek. He had lost his bifocals and could barely see but he had made it, and he had managed to preserve a cage full of his precious specimens. Better yet, in the cage were several pregnant females so he would easily be able to start all over again. The rats were healthy too. Even now they were showing signs of agitation. Skitch realised it was because they could smell food. He was close to the storage chambers where the supplies for the great invasion force were kept.

Now, he thought, all he needed was a cover story to tell the sentries to explain his business. Easy enough; he would just say that he was bringing food for Izak Grottle. Anybody who knew the packmaster would believe that.

The thought made him titter. He was still tittering when his near-blind eyes failed to pick out the stone in front of his feet and he tripped, sprawling clumsily into the dirt. The cage rolled free from his grip. The battered lock clicked and it sprang open. The killer rats bounded forth and raced off in the direction of the skaven stores.

Skitch groaned. He knew what the consequences of that were going to be. Soon it would not be just Izak Grottle who was hungry.

THE BATTLE FOR NULN

'The days grew darker. Fear and hunger were constant companions. The great skaven plot drew to its inevitable conclusion, and it seemed to be our lot to be drawn into it. And yet, along with terror and horror, there was hope and heroism. As well as loss there was honour. The hour of utmost danger arrived and I pride myself that my companion and I were not found wanting...'

— From *My Travels With Gotrek, Vol. III*, by Herr Felix Jaeger
(Altdorf Press, 2505)

Thanquol sat brooding on his great throne. Around him was marked a pentacle, inscribed with the head of the Horned Rat and surrounded by a double circle of the most potent protective symbols. He had invoked all of the great defensive spells he knew to shield him from the dire forces gnawing at his destiny. These were runes sovereign against curses, diseases, ill-luck and all manner of death-bringing spells. They numbered among the most powerful wards the grey seer had learned in a long career pursuing the Darker Mysteries. It was a measure of how bad the situation had become that Thanquol thought it necessary to expend so much of his carefully hoarded mystical power to invoke them all.

Thanquol lowered his great horned head into his hands and beat a tattoo on his temples with his claws. He was worried. Things were not going according to plan. Events were starting to slip beyond his control, he could sense it. His highly trained grey seer's intuition could feel forces at work here that were sending matters spiralling beyond the ability of any skaven, no matter how clever, to predict.

He was not quite sure how it had all happened. At first everything had gone so well. His agents reported the destruction of the Black Ship and he knew that once more his unwitting pawns, Jaeger and Gurnisson, had done his work for him. Mere days later, the Council of Thirteen had authorised an increase in size of his invasion force. It looked like utter crushing victory over the humans was within his grasp. But then…

But then the accursed plague had started to spread among his own forces. Soon the Underways were full to bursting with sick and dying skaven warriors. As fast as the bodies could be burned, dozens more followed. Even the skaven slaves manning the funeral ovens were falling sick. The symptoms – a hacking snuffling cough, an evil pus filling the lungs and finally a sudden onset of fatal spasms – were remarkably similar to the disease striking down the humans on the surface. Perhaps it was the same plague. It would not be the first time a contagion had made the leap between the two races.

As if the plague were not bad enough, another menace had arisen. The corridors now swarmed with large, fierce, hungry rats. They were everywhere, devouring the corpses, eating the food supplies, fighting over scraps, defecating and urinating everywhere, helping spread the cursed disease – and at the same time starving the army. Even now some of them lurked, beady-eyed, in the corner of his chamber, avoiding his pentagram but gnawing the furnishings. He could hear some of them moving beneath his throne. They must have been there when he cast his spells. Now they were trapped inside with him.

It would not have been nearly so bad if the offending creatures had not been rats. It was almost a sign that the Horned Rat had turned his snout away from the great invasion force, and withdrawn his blessing from the army. Certainly some of the more superstitious warriors were starting to mutter such things, and none of Thanquol's pointed speeches and sermons had reassured them.

It did no good for him to point out that the humans were suffering just as much, if not more, from these twin catastrophes: their granaries were empty, their food supplies consumed by the verminous host. The skaven warriors simply did not believe him. They did not have access to Thanquol's extensive spy network on the surface. They saw only that they themselves were starving and that their comrades were falling ill, and that there was a good chance that they in turn would be the next to be smitten by the plague. Morale had suffered, and no one knew better than Thanquol that morale was always a chancy thing at best for a skaven army.

He had done his utmost to hunt down those shirkers who muttered disloyal and treacherous remarks. He had assigned elite units of stormvermin to execute deserters on the spot. He had blasted several traitors himself with his most spectacular and destructive spells – but it had all been to no avail. The rot had set in. The army was slowly starting to fall to pieces. And there did not seem to be anything he could do about it.

Thanquol kicked one of the rats from under his feet, where it was gnawing at the bones of the last messenger who had brought him bad news. It flew through the air and impacted on the curtain of spells surrounding the pentagram. Sparks flickered, smoke belched and the rat gave an eerie keening cry as it died. The air was full of the smell of burned fur and scorched flesh as the creature fried in its own body fat. Thanquol's whiskers twitched in appreciation and he gave a brief savage smirk of satisfaction before returning to his brooding.

Since word of the armies' misfortune had filtered back to Skaven-blight, no more reinforcements had arrived. It was not quite the overwhelming mass of skaven warriors he had hoped for, but it would be enough, if Thanquol used all his resources of cunning and far-sighted planning. Something would have to be done to save the situation, and soon, while there was still an army left that was capable of fighting. He did not doubt that he still had enough troops at his command to overwhelm the human city if they attacked swiftly and savagely and with the advantage of surprise. Even if the army then dissolved, he would have achieved his goal. Nuln would be conquered and Thanquol could report success to the Council of Thirteen. It would then be up to his masters to rush garrison troops here to hold the city. If they did not get here in time that would not be Thanquol's fault.

The more Thanquol thought of it, the more this plan made sense. He could still achieve his assigned mission. He could still grasp his share of glory. He could then shift the blame for anything that happened afterwards to where it belonged – upon his incompetent underlings, and those traitors to the skaven cause who deserted the army just before its hour of triumph.

He reviewed the forces under his control. He still had close to five thousand almost-healthy warriors drawn mostly from Clan Skab. He still had several teams of gutter runners and a cadre of Clan Eshin assassins. The various foolish adventures undertaken by their treacherous leaders had left him with only a token force from Clan Skryre and Clan Pestilens. Izak Grottle and his force of rat-ogres, though, were still a formidable presence.

He knew that a simple frontal assault was not necessarily the best of plans under the circumstances. What he needed was a bold stroke that would lead to certain and overwhelming victory. And he believed he knew how that could be achieved.

Soon, his spies told him, the breeder the humans called the Elector Countess would be giving a masked ball, in a futile effort to distract her court from their troubles. If the palace could be taken with all the human nobles inside, then the human army in Nuln would be left leaderless and easy prey to the skaven assault. If the raid could be timed so that the two attacks were combined, so much the better. On the night the skaven took the palace, the city would also fall in blood and terror. Perhaps, with their chief breeder in Thanquol's clutches, the humans could even be induced to surrender.

It would have to be done soon, if he was to have any hope of success, but at least here was a chance that he could snatch victory from the slavering jaws of defeat.

Before that, though, he had another slight problem. He would have to negate the protective spells surrounding him so he could leave his chamber and begin giving orders. With a long-suffering sigh, Grey Seer Thanquol began the incantations that would let him out from inside his own pentagram.

Felix Jaeger kicked a huge fat rat from underfoot, sending it flying through the air to land in a midden heap. It turned and immediately began to devour the foulness in which it lay. Felix watched in hopeless disgust and despair.

The rats were everywhere, eating anything that was edible and a lot that was not. There were thousands of them, possibly millions. At times, whole streets seemed to be nothing but a seething sea of vermin. His employer, Heinz, had heard tales that they had taken to devouring babies in cribs and small children who got too close to them. Huge packs of the vile beasts flowed across the city streets, and the cats and dogs were too terrified to stop them.

The only good thing was that the rats appeared to be mysteriously short-lived. It looked like they aged months within a few days. But when they died, the rats' corpses lay strewn like some hideous furry carpet across the cobbles. It was not natural. In fact, the whole thing stank of skaven sorcery and Felix wondered if there was some evil purpose to it.

The city of Nuln appeared to be under a curse, Felix thought. The air smelled of sickness and disease, and human flesh burned on great pyres in the square outside the Temple of Morr. Whole tenement buildings had been boarded up, and turned into tombs. Felix shuddered when he thought of the mouldering corpses of the dead within them. Even worse, though, were the thoughts of those who had been entrapped there alive, victims of the plague who no one wanted to help. There were hideous rumours circulating of people recovering from the plague, only to die of starvation There were worse tales of cannibalism and folk feasting on flesh from the corpses of their family and friends. It was a horrifying thought. And it made Felix think that Sigmar and Ulric had turned their gaze from this city.

Ahead of him he heard the rumble of wheels and the tolling of a bell. He stepped aside to let the plague cart pass. The driver was garbed all in black and his face was hidden by a skull mask and a great peaked cowl. On the back of the cart, an acolyte of Morr swung a censer of incense, presumably to protect him from the plague. It was like watching Death himself ride through the doomed city, accompanied by his servants. Felix could see the rotting corpses piled high on the backboard of the vehicle. The bodies were naked, already stripped of their valuables by their families or bold scavengers. Rats gnawed at the bodies. As Felix watched he saw one tear out an eyeball, and devour it whole.

The plague carts moved constantly through the streets, bells tolling to announce their presence, summoning those still strong and healthy to dispose of the bodies of those who were not. But not even the plague carts were safe. If they stopped for a moment, the rats were upon them, fighting each other to feast upon the corpses.

Felix's belly grumbled, and he pulled his belt a notch tighter. He hoped the others were having more luck in their foraging for food than he was. He had found nothing to eat on sale that had not been contaminated by rat droppings, and even that was being sold for ten times its normal price. Some citizens were getting rich from the ruination of this mighty city. There were always those, he thought, who could find profit in even the most dire of situations.

He wished that Gotrek would give up his mad desire to remain in the city. He had already considered slipping away himself, joining those hosts of the poor and the lowly who had snatched up their few possessions and departed. He had not done so for several reasons. The first and best of them was that he would not desert his friends. The second was a desire to see this thing through to its end. He suspected that soon the dire events would reach their climax, and at least part of him wanted to find out what would happen.

The final reason was simple. He had heard tales that the local nobles had quarantined the city, and that archers were shooting those who tried to depart by the public highways. Many of the barges which had set sail from the docks in the past two desperate weeks had returned, reporting Imperial naval ships on the river sinking any vessel which tried to pass them.

Perhaps a small band moving by night could slip through, but Felix did not want to try it without Gotrek. The lawless lands around the city would be even more dangerous now with all the local soldiers and road wardens enforcing the quarantine and bands of armed men robbing any refugees.

Law and order had already broken down in parts of the city inside the walls. By night gangs of looters roamed the streets searching for food, helping themselves to anything that wasn't guarded by armed men. Only two nights ago a mob had broken into the city granary, despite the presence of several hundred soldiers. They had broken down the gates only to discover that the place was empty, filled only with the skeletons of the rats which had gorged themselves on the grain and then died.

A group of feral children was watching him with hungry eyes. One of them was roasting a dead rat on a spit. Normally he would have tossed them a coin out of pity but twice in the past few days he had almost been assaulted by such gangs. They had only turned back, discouraged, when he had drawn his sword and whipped it through the air menacingly.

He remembered the words of Count Ostwald. The city was indeed under siege, but it was a siege of a most horrifying type. There were no siege towers. No weapons had been brought to bear except hunger and disease. There was no enemy which could be sought out and battled. Despair was the foe here, and there was no sword with which it could be fought.

Ahead of him lay the Blind Pig. Outside it lolled several men-at-arms, mercenaries who had billeted themselves in the inn because they knew it and its owner, and stuck there now in a mass for their own protection. Felix knew them all and they knew him, but even so they watched him warily as he came closer. They were hard men who had decided that since they could not outrun the plague, they might as well be comfortable while they waited for it to strike them down. The Elector Countess was offering double pay to those who helped keep the peace by reinforcing her guards and the sadly depleted city watch. These men were earning their extra pay.

'Any news?' one of them asked, a burly Kislevite giant known as Big Boris. Felix shook his head.

'Any food?' asked the other, a sour-faced Bretonnian everyone called Hungry Stephan.

Felix shook his head again and stepped past them into the inn. Heinz sat at the table beside the fire, warming his hands. Gotrek sat with him, glugging back an enormous stein of ale.

'Looks like it will be rat pie for supper again,' Heinz said. Felix was not quite sure if he was making a joke. 'Young Felix has come back empty handed.'

'At least you still have beer,' Felix said.

'If it were dwarf ale we could live on it and nothing else,' Gotrek said. 'Many a campaign I've fought with nothing in my belly save half a barrel of Bugman's.'

'Unfortunately, it's not Bugman's,' Felix said dryly. Since the food shortages began, the dwarf had taken to reminiscing constantly and in a most annoying manner about the nutrient powers of dwarf ale.

'More skaven have been seen,' Heinz said. The city guard clashed with them in the Middenplatz last night. They seemed to be foraging for food as well, or so the guard claimed.'

'Most likely want to make sure we're starving,' Felix said sourly.

'Whatever's going to happen is going to happen soon,' Gotrek said. 'There's something in the air. I can smell it.'

'It's beer you smell,' Felix said.

'I hear Countess Emmanuelle is throwing a big fancy dress ball,' Heinz said with a grin. 'Maybe you'll be invited.'

'Somehow I doubt it,' Felix said. He had not heard from the palace since he had been summoned by Ostwald two weeks ago to explain the burning of the Black Ship. Of course, since then, all those mansions on the hill had become fortified camps, as the rich and the blue-blooded isolated themselves in an effort to escape the plague. Rumour had it that any commoner even setting foot on those cobbled streets was shot on sight.

'Typical of your bloody human nobles,' Gotrek said and belched. 'The city is going to the dogs and what do they do? Throw a bloody party!'

'Maybe we should do the same,' Heinz said. 'There are worse ways to go!'

'Anybody seen Elissa?' Felix asked, wanting to change the gloomy direction this conversation was taking.

'She left earlier, went for a walk with that peasant lad... Hans, is it?' Suddenly Felix wished he hadn't asked.

Lurk Snitchtongue glanced around the gloomy chamber and controlled the urge to squirt the musk of fear. It took a mighty effort for he could never in all his life recall being cornered by three such fearsome skaven. He stifled a cough and fought to hold back a sneeze in case either would draw attention to him, but it was no use. Those three sets of malevolent eyes were drawn to his shivering form like iron filings to a magnet. Vilebroth Null, Izak Grottle and Heskit One Eye all stared at him as if he were a tasty morsel. Particularly Izak Grottle.

Lurk wished his body would stop aching. He wished his paws would stop sweating. He wished the pain that threatened to split his skull would go away. He knew that they would not. He knew that he had the plague and he knew that he was going to die – unless Vilebroth

Null did as he had promised and interceded for him with the Horned Rat.

Truly, Lurk thought, he was caught with his tail between the cleaver and the chopping block. The only way he could save his life was by doing what the terrifying plague monk leader said. Unfortunately, Vilebroth Null wanted him to betray his master, Grey Seer Thanquol. Lurk shuddered to think of the consequences should that formidable sorcerer find out what had happened. The wrath of Thanquol was not something any sane skaven cared to face.

The three skaven put their heads together once more and started to whisper. Lurk would have given anything to know what they were talking about. On second thoughts, considering they were probably discussing his fate, he might conceivably be able to live without the knowledge. Lurk cursed his own weakness. He had known he was in trouble when he saw who had been waiting in the chamber that Null had led him to. He knew then, all too well, that the weeks of negotiations the abbot had alluded to had paid off, and two of the most powerful factions of skavendom were arrayed alongside Clan Pestilens.

In that secret chamber, far from eavesdroppers and shielded by Null's potent sorcery, Heskit One Eye and Izak Grottle had been waiting. As soon as he saw them, Lurk had known the game was up. Under Null's prodding he had told them everything. He had explained that Thanquol had somehow learned of their schemes (leaving out only his own part in their discovery) and he had told them, too, of the messages Thanquol had sent to their arch enemies, the human Jaeger and the dwarf Gurnisson. It went without saying that these lordly skaven were outraged by what they saw as the grey seer's despicable treachery.

He had sensed their murderous rage in the air and done everything in his power to avoid being the focus of it. He had heard all about the gory details of Clan Skryre's Excruciation Engines, and many times he had shuddered at the tale of how Grottle liked to consume his enemies' entrails before their very eyes while they still lived.

In order to avoid this fate, he had wracked his mind for every little detail he could remember, to convince them that he was co-operating thoroughly. The prospect of immediate painful death overcame any reluctance caused by the thought of what Grey Seer Thanquol might do to him in the future. And, in one small, cunning and deeply hidden part of Lurk's mind, it occurred to him that if these three could be made angry enough to take vengeance on Grey Seer Thanquol, then Thanquol would be too dead to take any revenge on him in turn.

He was pretty sure now that he had succeeded. Heskit One Eye had gnawed his own tail in rage as Lurk explained how the grey seer had sent explicit details to their enemies concerning Clan Skryre's plan to invade the College of Engineering. He had even fabricated a few convincing details of how the grey seer had laughed and gloated about how his stupid enemies would soon fall into his trap. Well, thought Lurk, Thanquol most likely had.

Izak Grottle had become so outraged he even spluttered out a mouthful of food when Lurk explained how Thanquol had told him that the fat fool would never suspect his idiotic plan to smuggle a secret weapon into the city on a converted barge would be betrayed by Thanquol's cunning.

Vilebroth Null called down the curse of the Horned Rat on his rival when Lurk told him how Thanquol, jealous of the favour their god had shown the abbot, decided to remove a dangerous rival by revealing the whereabouts of his secret lair in the human cemetery to his two most trusty agents on the surface, Gurnisson and Jaeger.

'Are you certain the grey seer is in league with those two?' Grottle demanded. 'Absolutely, definitely certain?'

'Of course, mightiest of Moulders. He forced me, on pain of hideous death, to deliver notes to them and they always responded to his instructions, did they not? I can only conclude that either they are in Grey Seer Thanquol's pay or–'

'Or what?' Vilebroth Null burbled.

'No. The thought is too hideous. No true skaven would stoop to–'

'Stoop to what? To what?'

'Or he is in their pay!' Lurk said, amazed by his own powers of invention. This set off another burst of outraged chittering.

'No! No! Impossible,' Heskit One Eye said. 'Thanquol is a grey seer. He would never submit to taking orders from any but another skaven. The thought is ludicrous.'

'And yet…' Vilebroth Null said.

'And yet? And yet?' Izak Grottle said.

'And yet it is indisputable that Grey Seer Thanquol had been in touch with the surface dwellers, and had betrayed our plans to them!' Null said. 'How else could they have got wind of our schemes? How else could such magnificently cunning plans have failed?'

'Are you seriously suggesting that Grey Seer Thanquol is a traitor to the skaven cause? Seriously?' Izak Grottle asked, showing his terrifyingly huge fangs in a great snarl.

'It's possible,' Lurk dared to add.

'All too possible, I fear,' Heskit One Eye said. 'It is the only explanation for why the grey seer would interfere with our mighty machinations, when all we were attempting to do was further the skaven cause.'

'And yet the human and the dwarf are his enemies too. By all accounts they almost killed him in the lair of the human, von Halstadt.'

'And he sent the gutter runners against them,' Vilebroth Null added. 'That was a true contract. Chang Squik still spits when he thinks of his failure.'

'What if Grey Seer Thanquol is cunning enough to use his enemies against us?' Heskit One Eye said excitedly. 'He pits them against us. He cannot lose! He thwarts a rival or we kill his sworn enemies for him.'

There was a moment of silence in the chamber, and Lurk knew that whatever else his enemies thought of the grey seer, they had suddenly gained enormous respect for his cunning. On consideration, he had to admit that he had too. Whatever flaws he might possess, it was hard to dispute that Grey Seer Thanquol was possessed of all the qualities of a truly great skaven.

'Even so, even allowing that Grey Seer Thanquol possesses devilish cunning, he has still betrayed us to the enemy! That is beyond dispute. He has revealed our hidden plans, and the hidden plans of our great clans to the enemy,' Izak Grottle said. 'Grey Seer Thanquol is a traitor and an enemy of all our peoples.'

'I agree,' Heskit said. 'A traitor he most certainly is. And more – he is our personal enemy. He has acted against us all once and almost caused our deaths. Perhaps he will be more successful with his next attempt.'

All three of them shivered when they thought of the daemonically clever intelligence which worked against them. Lurk could see the fear written on their faces, and in the nervous twitching of their whiskers.

'I humbly suggest,' Null said, 'that it might be the will of the Horned Rat that we remove Grey Seer Thanquol from his command of the army, and send him to make his explanations to the Council of Thirteen.'

'I heartily agree with your sentiments. Heartily!' Izak Grottle said. 'But how are we to accomplish this? The traitor remains in command of almost five thousand Clan Skab warriors while our own forces are but a shadow of what they once were.'

'Doubtless as the traitor planned,' Heskit said.

'Doubtless,' the other two agreed simultaneously.

'There is always assassination,' Heskit suggested.

'Possibly! Possibly!' Grottle said. 'But who would take the chance that the Eshin might be deluded enough to report the request for such a thing to the traitor himself?'

'We could do it ourselves,' Vilebroth Null said.

'Grey Seer Thanquol, despite his known treachery, is a lamentably powerful sorcerer,' Heskit One Eye said. 'We might fail and we might die!'

All three shuddered and then, as one, all three pairs of eyes turned on Lurk. He quivered to the soles of his paws, for he knew what they were thinking.

'No! No!' he said.

'No?' Heskit One Eye said menacingly, reaching for the butt of his pistol.

'No?' Izak Grottle rumbled hungrily, and licked his lips.

'No?' Vilebroth Null said, hawking a huge lump of green phlegm onto the floor beside Lurk's feet where it bubbled corruptly.

'No! No! Most merciful of masters, I am but a lowly skaven. I possess not your mighty intellects and awesome powers. Any of you might expect to best Grey Seer Thanquol in combat or cunning, but not I.'

'Then why should we preserve your life?' Izak Grottle said silkily. 'Why? Speak! Quick! Quick! I am hungry.'

'Because... because...' Lurk floundered around frantically seeking a path out of this hideous maze. He cursed the day he had ever encountered Grey Seer Thanquol or bore his messages to the human and the dwarf. Wait! That might be the answer. Perhaps in the grey seer's own great example was the solution to his problem. 'Because... because there is a better way!'

'Is there?'

'Yes. Yes. One that holds fewer risks and is more certain!'

'You interest me, Lurk Snitchtongue,' Izak Grottle said. 'What is there that you can see that we cannot?'

'Yes! Yes! Go on! Explain!' Vilebroth Null said in his hideous bubbling voice.

'You could use the grey seer's own methods against him!'

'What?'

'He has used Jaeger and Gurnisson against you. Why not use them against him?'

There was another pause while the three great skaven exchanged glances.

'They are certainly formidable,' Vilebroth Null said. 'For non-skaven.'

'Perhaps! Perhaps they could do it!' chittered Heskit One Eye.

'Do you think so? They are not skaven and Thanquol is a grey seer. A grey seer!' Izak Grottle said and banged his fist on the table for emphasis.

'With every humble respect,' Vilebroth Null said, 'you have not encountered this pair. Heskit of Skryre and I have. A more wicked and dangerous set of opponents it is hard to imagine. Even I, with all my magical powers, barely eluded them.'

'They slaughtered well over half of my company,' Heskit said, leaving out his own part in the massacre.

'I defer to your greater experience,' Grottle said. 'But the question remains: how will we get them to go after Grey Seer Thanquol?'

'A letter!' Lurk suggested, carried away by the sheer pleasure of plotting.

'Yes! Yes! A letter,' Vilebroth Null said.

'It is fitting that Grey Seer Thanquol should be undone by the device by which he sought to undo us.'

'But where and how will our two assassins get their chance at him?'

'We must wait for the opportunity to arise,' Null said.

'And how will we write this letter?' Grottle asked. 'I for one have no knowledge of these primitive human runes.'

'I have some knowledge of the human script,' Heskit One Eye said almost apologetically. 'I need it for reading human schematics.'

'We must use the exact paper and pen that the grey seer uses,' Grottle said.

'Our friend Lurk can acquire those,' Vilebroth Null said, smiling horribly to reveal rotting teeth.

'And he can deliver the message too, in his usual way,' Heskit said smugly.

'It appears that I won't be eating you today then, Lurk Snitchtongue,' Izak Grottle. said 'We need you alive. Of course, should you attempt to betray us...'

'That will change,' Heskit finished.

Lurk did not know whether to be glad or sorry. He appeared to have prolonged his life but only at the risk of incurring Grey Seer Thanquol's wrath. How did he get himself into these things?

'We're leaving the city,' Elissa said challengingly. She glared up at Felix as if expecting him to contradict her. 'Hans and I. We have decided to go.'

'I don't blame you,' Felix said. 'It's a bad place to be and it's going to get worse.'

'Is that all you have to say?'

Felix looked around at the room they had shared during their brief time together. It seemed small and empty, and soon it would seem emptier still, once she had gone. Was there anything more to say? He really could not blame her for wanting to leave and, to be honest, he could see no real future for them together. So why did it still hurt? Why did he have this feeling of hollowness within his chest? Why did he feel this urge to ask her to stay?

'You're going with Hans?' he asked, just to hear some words. She looked at him coldly and crossed her arms together under her breasts defensively.

'Yes,' she said. 'You're not going to try and stop us, are you?'

She seemed almost to want him to say yes, he thought. 'It's not very safe outside the city right now,' he said.

'We're only going back to our village. It's less than a morning's walk.'

'Will they take you? I hear that people from the city are being stoned and shot with arrows if they go near villages and farms. In case they have the plague.'

'We'll survive,' she said, but she sounded less sure of herself. 'Anyway, it can't be worse than it is here, with the plague and the gangs and the rats and all. At least back in the village they know us.'

'They certainly know Hans. I thought you said the elders hated him.'

'You would cast that up, wouldn't you? They'll take us back. I'll tell them we're going to be married. They'll understand.'

'Are you? Going to be married, I mean.'

'I suppose so.'

'You don't sound very enthusiastic.'

'Oh Felix, what else am I supposed to do? Spend the rest of my life being pawed by strangers in bars? Going about with footloose mercenaries? It's not what I want. I want to go home.'

'You need any money?' he asked.

Suddenly she looked a little shifty. 'No,' she said. 'I'd best be going. Hans is waiting.'

'Be careful,' he said, and meant it. 'It's not a safe city out there.'

'You should know,' she said. Suddenly she leaned forward and kissed him passionately on the mouth. Just as he was about to take her in his arms, she broke free and made for the door.

'You look after yourself now,' she said, and he thought he detected a glimmer of tears in the corner of her eyes. Then she was gone.

It was only afterwards, when he checked the loose floorboard, that he discovered the purse of money Otto had given him was gone. He lay on the bed, unsure whether to laugh or to cry. Well, he thought, let her have the money. The chances were he would not live long enough to spend it himself.

Grey Seer Thanquol glanced around the chamber at the assembled skaven captains. His burning gaze seemed to defy anyone to speak out. No one did.

Lurk counted the commanders present. All of the Clan Skab leaders were here, plus Izak Grottle, Vilebroth Null and Heskit One Eye. Chang Squik, the Clan Eshin assassin, skulked in one corner, glaring occasionally at Lurk with hate-filled eyes. He had not forgotten what Lurk had said about him on that long-ago day when the grey seer had humiliated them both in front of the whole army.

The grey seer threw his arms wide. Trails of fire followed his paws as he gathered magical power. That got everyone in the room's attention, Lurk thought. Suddenly all eyes were riveted on Thanquol as if, with a single gesture, he might choose to annihilate anyone who did not look at him. That was certainly a possibility, Lurk thought. If he recognised the signs correctly, the grey seer had consumed an awful lot of warpstone powder.

Lurk shivered and continued to chew on the foul herbs that Vilebroth Null had given him to abate the plague. He fought down the urge to check within his breastplate and make sure the parchment and quill he had stolen from Thanquol's private stock were not sliding into view. He knew that nothing would draw attention to him quicker. He reassured himself that they were there. He could feel the nib of the pen poking into the tender fur beneath his armpit.

'Tonight is the night you have all been waiting for!' Thanquol said.' Tonight we will smash-crush the humans once and for all. Tonight we will invade the city and enslave all the occupants. Tonight we will strike a blow for the Under Empire and the skaven nation that will long be remembered!'

Thanquol paused impressively and glanced around the room once more, as if waiting for an interruption. No one dared to speak, but Lurk saw Null, One Eye and Grottle exchange glances, before looking at him. He hoped for all their sakes that the grey seer had not noticed. He glanced nervously at Thanquol, but fortunately the grey seer seemed to be caught up in the flow of his own mad eloquence.

'We will grind the humans beneath the iron paw of our massed skaven army. We will carry them off into inevitable slavery. Their wealth will be ours. Their city will be ours. Their souls will be offered screaming to the Horned Rat.'

Thanquol paused once more and Izak Grottle found the courage to ask the question that Lurk could tell had been on everyone's mind.

'And how is this to be accomplished, great leader?'

'How? How indeed! By a plan at once simple and yet staggeringly cunning. By a use of force and sorcery which will be talked about down the ages. By overwhelming ferocity and superior skaven technology. By–'

'By what precise means, Grey Seer Thanquol?' Vilebroth Null interrupted. 'I humbly suggest that, like every skaven out of runthood, we are all familiar with the general methods of attack.'

For a moment Lurk could tell that Thanquol was weighing up the pros and cons of blasting the plague monk into his component atoms for his insolence. He was glad when prudent skaven caution won out and the grey seer continued to speak.

'I was just coming to that, as you would have discovered had you not interrupted me. We will attack through the sewers. Each of you will lead your assigned force to a point marked on the map.' With this, the grey seer indicated the complex mass of symbols inscribed on the large sheet of parchment hanging behind him. Many of the assembled leaders leaned forward to see where they would be sent.

'I do not see your rune on this plan,' Heskit One Eye said. 'What will you be doing, grey seer?'

Thanquol glared at him with burning red eyes. 'I will be where you would expect your leader to be, performing the most difficult and dangerous of tasks.'

Silence fell over the assembled skaven leaders. This was not in point of fact where they would have expected their leader to be at all. They would expect him to be safely in the rear directing operations. The warpstone Thanquol had consumed appeared to make him talkative. He spoke on, into the silence.

'I will be leading the crowning attack. I will lead the assault by our stormvermin which will seize the palace of the breeder, Emmanuelle, and capture all of the city's rulers. Tonight they are having a ball, one of their purposeless social events. I will fall on them by surprise and have them all in my paw. Leaderless, the humans will surely fall to our attack.'

There were more murmurings from the assembled skaven. It was a good plan, and a bold one. Lurk wondered if any of the others saw what he saw. The grey seer had chosen his place in the assault carefully. By managing this bold stroke, by capturing the human leaders, he would assure himself of the lion's share of the glory. Further, it would undoubtedly be a lot safer attacking a bunch of humans and their breeders dressed for a ball than fighting massed troops in the city.

'Such a position is too dangerous for a leader of your great cunning,' Heskit One Eye said. 'It would be a tragedy if the genius of Thanquol was to be lost to skavendom. To prevent such a tragedy, I will lead this assault. I will shoulder the terrible risks.'

Lurk covered his mouth with a paw to prevent a snigger escaping; at least one other skaven had realised what was going on.

'No! No!' Izak Grottle said. 'I and my rat-ogres are ideally suited for this task. We will overwhelm all–'

Grottle's words were drowned out by the shouts of all the other skaven volunteers. Thanquol let them call out for a few minutes before silencing them with a gesture.

'Unfortunately, it will require my potent sorcery to effect entrance to the palace. I must be present.'

'Then I will gladly lay down my life to guard you,' Izak Grottle said, obviously determined to be present to share in the triumph.

'And I,' Heskit One Eye said.

'And I,' shouted every other skaven present, save Lurk.

'No! No! I appreciate your concern, brother skaven, but your leadership will be required on other, no-less-critical parts of the battlefield.'

It was obvious that Thanquol intended to share his glorious triumph with no one. The assembled war leaders subsided into disappointed chittering.

'I have here a route map, and a schedule for each of you, inscribed with precise instructions. All of you, that is, except for Lurk Snitchtongue. I would have a word with Lurk in private.'

Lurk felt his heart start to race, and it was all he could do to prevent himself squirting the musk of fear. Had the grey seer found out about his plotting with the three clan representatives? Was he about to enact some terrible revenge? Was there any way Lurk could avoid this meeting?

He turned desperate eyes on his three co-conspirators and saw that they glared at him evilly. If looks could kill, Lurk knew, those three would have put him in a coffin. They feared he would betray them to save his own skin – and of course they were right.

As the war leaders trooped forward one by one to receive the grey seer's blessing and their final instructions, Lurk prayed to the Horned Rat to preserve him.

Felix wandered around until he arrived at his brother's townhouse. He was not surprised to see that it was locked and guarded. He was surprised to find that Otto and his wife had not fled the city, and furthermore that the guards recognised him and allowed him to pass.

Otto waited in his study to greet him. He was still working, inscribing things in his ledgers and writing dispatches that might never be received, intended for other branches of the Jaeger businesses. Felix was strangely proud of him at that moment. It took a great deal of courage to continue to work under these trying circumstances.

'What can I do for you, Felix?' Otto asked, without looking up.

'Nothing. I just came by to see how you were.'

'Fine!' Otto gave a wan smile. 'Business is booming.'

'Is it?'

'Of course not! Rats are eating the stock. The workers are stealing everything that isn't nailed down. The customers are dying of the plague.'

'Why haven't you left town?'

'Someone has to remain and look after our interests. This will all pass, you know. Disturbances always do. Then there'll be the business of rebuilding. Folk will need wool and timber and building materials. They'll need luxury goods to replace what's been looted. They'll need credit to buy it all. And when they do, Jaegers of Altdorf will still be here.'

'I'll bet you will.'

'And what about you?' Otto asked, looking up at last.

'I'm waiting to see the end of this all. I'm waiting for the skaven to show themselves.'

'You think they will?'

'I'm sure of it. I'm certain that this is all their doing somehow.'

'How can you be so sure?'

Felix looked at his brother long and hard. 'Can you keep secrets?'

'You know I can.'

Felix decided that it was true. In his business Otto would need a great deal of discretion.

'What I'm going to tell you could get me hanged or burned at the stake.'

'What you and the dwarf did in Altdorf could get you that already. You're a long way from the capital, Felix, and I'm not going to turn you in.'

Felix guessed that was true, and somehow he felt a need to tell someone exactly what had happened. So he told Otto the full tale of his encounters with the skaven, from the first day in the sewer to the last battle on the barge. He omitted nothing, including his duel with von Halstadt. Otto looked at him with an expression that went from incredulity to seriousness to, finally, belief.

'You're not making this up, are you?'

'No.'

'You always did take those hero tales you read too seriously, little brother.'

Felix smiled and Otto smiled back. 'I did, didn't I?'

'What is it like, living in one?'

'Not what I expected. Not what I expected at all.' Felix decided it was time to say what he had come to say.

'Otto – I think you and your wife should leave the city. I think the skaven are going to come soon, and that things will not be pleasant.'

Otto laughed. 'We have armed servants and this house is a fortress, Felix. We will be much safer here than in the country.'

Felix knew his brother well enough to understand that there would be no persuading him. 'You know your own business best,' he said.

Otto nodded. 'Now come eat, man. I can hear your stomach rumbling from here.'

'What is it, mightiest of mages? What do you require?'

Lurk Snitchtongue bowed and scraped before Grey Seer Thanquol, searching for the words that would save him. He felt sure that the grey seer's supernatural powers had enabled him to see Lurk's treachery and that now he was going to be punished. The terrible glow of warpstone still filled Thanquol's eyes, and Lurk could almost sense the dark energies that seethed within him.

'It concerns Vilebroth Null,' Grey Seer Thanquol said with an evil smile.

Lurk felt his musk glands contract. He would have spoken then but his tongue was tied. It felt like it had suddenly stuck to the roof of his mouth. All he could do was nod his head in a guilty fashion.

'And Heskit One Eye,' Thanquol said, his malevolent grin stretching still further.

A plea for mercy stuck in Lurk's throat. He tried to force it out but it just would not come.

'And Izak Grottle,' Thanquol added. His burning eyes held Lurk pinned to the spot.

The smaller skaven felt like a bird paralysed before the gaze of a serpent. He nodded again and fell to his knees, paws clutched before him in a gesture of abasement.

'Get up! Get up!' Thanquol said. 'They are not so fearsome. No! Not at all. Now is the time to be rid of them once and for all and you will help me do it!'

'Get rid of them, mightiest of masters?'

'Yes! Did you see the way they questioned me when I was giving orders to the army? Did you see the way they tried to steal the glory from my brilliant plan? My mind is made up! I will tolerate them no longer. This night they will die!'

'How? How, lord of seers? Will you blast them with magic?'

'No! No! Idiot! My hands must remain clean. No – we will use the tried and tested method. I will inform my two pawns of their whereabouts. This evening, when the battle comes, my enemies will meet with the dwarf's axe. Then, hopefully, the rest of their force will bring down that interfering twosome.'

'How will you engineer this, cleverest of conspirators?'

'I have assigned all three to one strike group. Its place of emergence is very close to the burrow where Jaeger and Gurnisson and a horde of mercenaries dwell. You are also assigned to that group. You will go through first, on pretext of scouting, and you will warn that horrid pair of what is about to occur!'

'Yes! Yes! Consider it done, most supreme of schemers!'

'Take this message and see that it is delivered. Then flee to my presence and I will see that you are… suitably rewarded for your loyalty!'

Lurk did not like the emphasis the grey seer put on that last phrase at all, but he took the letter and, still bowing, backed from Thanquol's presence.

Felix rang Drexler's doorbell more from hope than any real belief that the doctor would be there, so he was pleasantly surprised when the viewing slot was opened and a servant peered out.

'Oh, it's you, Herr Jaeger,' he said. 'Are you alone?'

'Yes, and I would speak with your master.'

'Best come in then.' Felix heard bolts being thrown and the door creak open. He glanced back over his shoulder to make sure that no bandits were poised to take advantage of the situation, then hurried through. The servant slammed the door behind him.

Felix strode through the corridors of the doctor's mansion. It felt like years since he had first come here with Elissa, though in fact it had only been weeks. How had things changed so quickly, he asked himself, suppressing a flash of loneliness and sadness at the thought the woman was gone. He shook his head and smiled sadly, knowing that her departure was one of the reasons why he was here. He was just moving around to keep himself busy and avoid thinking about things.

The servant showed him into Drexler's study. The doctor sat by his fire, looking drained and weary. Weeks of treating plague victims had obviously taken something out of him. There were lines on his face that had not been there when Felix had last seen him, and a hint of pallor beneath his tan.

'Herr Jaeger, what can I do for you?'

'I've brought back your book,' Felix said, producing the doctor's copy of Leiber's work. 'I would have returned it sooner, but I have been very busy.'

The doctor smiled wanly. 'So Herr Ostwald has told me. It seems Aldred chose a worthy successor for ownership of his blade.'

'I'm not so convinced,' Felix said, gesturing vaguely in the direction of the city. 'All of my and Gotrek's efforts seem to have come to naught.'

'Do not be sure of that, Herr Jaeger. What man can tell of all the consequences of his actions? It may be that things would be a lot worse without your intervention.'

'I wish I could believe that but I do not think it is so.'

'Only Sigmar can judge a man's actions, Herr Jaeger, and I believe that in some ways he smiles upon you and your friend. You are still here, aren't you? How many others would be able to say the same if they had undergone your adventures? I know I could not.'

Felix looked at him, struck by the fact that there was some truth in the man's words. 'You are a good doctor, Herr Drexler. I feel better just for talking to you.'

'Perhaps you should wait until you see my bill before you thank me,' Drexler said. His smile showed that he was joking. 'You found what you wanted in the book?'

Felix set it down on the table. 'More than I ever wanted. I'm not sure that it helps knowing how evil and depraved the rat-men are.'

'Again, Herr Jaeger, who knows what knowledge might prove useful? Have some food. I have managed to preserve something from the afflictions of our city.'

Felix thought guiltily of the meal which he had already eaten at Otto's. His stomach felt full but, well, on the other hand he had no idea when he might eat again. If Gotrek's theory about the skaven's imminent onslaught was going to be correct, he was going to need all his strength. 'Why not?' he said. 'It may be the last meal I get!'

'Why do you say that?' Drexler asked, and Felix decided that now was the time to deliver his warning.

'Because I believe that the skaven will attack the city soon. I also think that you should leave. I say this as a friend.'

'I thank you for the warning, Herr Jaeger, but I cannot go today. You see, tonight I am attending a ball at the palace, in the presence of Elector Countess Emmanuelle herself.'

Somehow the thought sent a shiver running down Felix's spine.

Lurk knew it was going to be bad when he felt the heavy hand of one of Izak Grottle's troops on his shoulder and he was hustled unceremoniously into the fat skaven's palanquin. He found himself looking up into the folds of flesh beneath the chin of the gigantic Moulder packmaster. Grottle's huge belly virtually pressed him back against the cushions of the palanquin with a life of its own.

'Now where are you going?' Izak Grottle asked. 'Where indeed?'

Lurk thought fast. He did not like the hungry gleam that had appeared in the packmaster's eye. He thought of the letter that he bore for the grey seer. He thought of the disease that threatened to fill his lungs with pus, unless the abbot continued to intervene on his behalf with the Horned Rat. 'I was just on my way to see you, most majestic of Moulders.'

'Then it is fortunate I have found you. Tell me, what is it that you are carrying?'

Lurk told him everything. He had expected Izak Grottle to reach out with one podgy hand and snap his neck but the packmaster merely laughed a rich booming laugh. 'It would appear the grey seer has been too clever for his own good. You will deliver your message, but it will be one I shall dictate and Heskit One Eye shall write down.'

'As you wish, most potent of all packmasters.'

Felix trudged back towards the Blind Pig, feeling almost too full to move. Over the past few weeks his stomach had shrunk and what once might have been a normal meal now left him feeling bloated. Two such meals in one day made him feel like he was going to explode.

He wore a new herbal talisman given to him by the doctor and he carried another within his pouch for Gotrek. It was a slight reassurance to him. So far, he had not caught the plague, but that might not signify anything. Nobody else he knew had either. Perhaps it was mere chance that had spared them, or perhaps it was the fact that Heinz insisted they kill every last rat they spotted around the Pig. Felix could not even begin to guess. He only knew that he was grateful to Drexler for the gift.

He looked around into the gathering gloom and shivered. The city looked like a mere ghost of the thriving metropolis it had been when he and Gotrek first arrived. Many buildings had burned down. More were empty. No lights shone in most of the tenements. The bustling life of the streets had been replaced by an aura of fear. The only ones likely to be abroad now were predators – and their victims.

He felt the flesh crawl between his shoulder blades, and was suddenly convinced that someone was watching him. He turned his head to look at the mouth of a nearby alley. The whoosh of air alerted him too late. Something hit him on the skull. He shook his head in response, half expecting a surge of pain. None came. He raised his fingers to his brow but felt no blood. He looked down to see what had hit him and saw that it was a rolled-up piece of parchment, similar to all the others which had borne a warning concerning the skaven. He bent down to pick it up and glanced round at the same time. He heard the sound of scuttling down a nearby alley, and realised that it was most likely whoever had thrown the paper.

Without thinking, Felix scooped up the parchment and raced off in pursuit. He stretched his long legs to the maximum as he ran down the alley. Ahead of him he thought he caught sight of a cowled figure. Was it possible that that was a long rodent-like tail protruding out from under that monkish robe? All too possible, he decided.

The figure had reached the end of the alley and turned hastily down another of the winding maze of streets. Felix raced past open doorways, scattering amazed-looking beggars and treading monstrous rats underfoot as he raced onwards. His heartbeat sounded loud in his chest and sweat poured down his face. He felt nauseous and wished that he had not eaten quite so much at Doctor Drexler's, particularly after the heavy meal at his brother's. He clutched the scroll tight in one hand and restrained the scabbard flapping on his belt with the other.

'Stop, skaven!' he shouted. His words had no effect on the fleeing rat-man. All the beggars leapt for cover within the nearest door. Felix raced on.

Why am I doing this, he asked himself? As far as he knew, the skaven ahead had done them nothing but favours by warning him of his brethren's plans. In that case, why was he fleeing, Felix asked himself – but he already had an answer. Who could tell why the rat-men did anything? Who could guess at the reasons of a creature that was not even human?

Felix's heart leapt as he saw the rat-man trip and fall. Perhaps he could overhaul it after all. Caught up in the fury of the chase, he desperately wanted to do so. He wanted to grab the rat-man and look into its eyes and question it. Not, he thought, that it would likely understand the human tongue. According to Leiber, the rat-men had their own languages, including a number of specialised dialects used by the various clans. Still, at least this one knew enough Reikspiel to write its notes, Felix thought, so perhaps it could be interrogated. He ran faster, hope blazing in his breast that at last he might be able to get some answers to his questions about the skaven.

Lurk glanced back over his shoulder and chittered a curse. It was no use. That foolish human was still following him! Why? What did it hope to achieve by persecuting him in this way? Why could it not leave him alone and read the message that Heskit One Eye had inscribed on the parchment? If it did that, it would surely realise that it had more urgent business this night – like heading to the palace and thwarting Grey Seer Thanquol's plan.

Life was so unfair, Lurk thought unhappily. Here he was, in poor health, brow-beaten by some of the most ferocious skaven who ever lived, about to make an enemy of one of the mightiest sorcerers of his race. His head hurt. His eyes burned with fever. His heart felt like it was going to give out from the strain of this race. His lungs felt like they were on fire. And where was he? Not in some comfortable burrow back in Skavenblight, but being pursued through the horribly open streets of this human city by a large and terrifying warrior. It was like some dreadful nightmare. The sheer unfairness of it all galled Lurk. What had he ever done to deserve this?

He shot another backward glance and saw that his pursuer was starting to narrow the distance that separated them. Lurk prayed that night would come, or that mist would arise. He felt certain that in darkness and shadow, he could lose the human. Or if he could just reach the hidden entrance to the sewers where the bulk of the invasion force waited, he would find safety. He risked another look back – and cursed as he felt his feet go out from beneath him.

He knew he should have looked where he was going!

* * *

Felix closed the gap quickly as he saw the skaven scrabble to its feet. He wondered briefly whether he should pause and draw his sword. He decided against it. He would lose ground again and the skaven did not appear to be armed. He could always produce his blade when he had the rat-man cornered. Breathing heavily, he ran on.

Praise the Horned Rat, thought Lurk! Ahead of him he could see the opening into the sewers. He knew that he merely had to leap down it and he would be safe in the comforting bosom of the skaven army. Down there waited Vilebroth Null, Izak Grottle, Heskit One Eye and all their soldiers. But as he gathered his legs beneath him in preparation for the mighty leap that would carry him to safety, he felt a powerful hand clamp onto his shoulder.

Felix felt the skaven stiffen as he grabbed it. He pulled hard, spinning it around – and almost let go as the wicked-looking creature glared up at him with hate-filled eyes. Of all the rat-men he had ever encountered this was the most sly and nasty looking. It was smaller and thinner than most but had a wiry strength that made it difficult to hold.

'Now,' Felix panted. 'Tell me what you're doing here!'

A sudden pain flared in his left wrist as the rat-man bit it. Overcome by shock, Felix let go.

Lurk broke free from his tormentor's grip and dropped gratefully into the sewer. Breaking the surface, he looked around and saw that the skaven assault force had already gathered. A horde of rat-men waited in attendance. He looked around and saw Izak Grottle and the others waiting in the leader's position at the rear. A stormvermin clawleader looked down at Lurk as he pulled himself out of the filth and shook his fur clean.

'What is it?' the clawleader asked.

'I am pursued...' Lurk gasped without thinking. Before he could expand on his statement the clawleader reacted, keen to grab some glory.

'Right!' the skaven shouted. 'Quick-quick! Charge!'

Felix inspected his bitten wrist. It did not look too bad, he thought. Then he glanced up in horror as he heard the first of the rat-men begin to swarm up the sewer access ladder. Only moments before he had debated whether to pursue the escaping skaven into the sewers.

Now he saw that it would have been suicidal. Already the leering face and snapping jaws of a burly, black-armoured rat-man had emerged into the gloom. Felix wasted no time. He launched a hefty kick that sent the furiously squeaking skaven tumbling back down among his fellows, and then turned and ran.

Moments later a mass of furiously chittering skaven warriors emerged into the alley. Somewhat ahead of schedule, the great invasion of Nuln had begun.

'No! No!' Lurk squeaked as the tightly packed mass of skaven warriors surged past him. The press of furry bodies pushed him back into the foul waters of the sewer. For a horrible moment he felt like he was going to drown, but then he broke the surface once more, just in time to see the last of the stormvermin clambering with unrestrained fury into the light. Above him, the mad face of Vilebroth Null leered down.

'Did you deliver the message?' burbled the low abbot of the plague monks.

'Yes! Yes!' Lurk chittered, thinking that now was possibly not the best time to tell Null that the skaven troops above were now doing their best to hunt down and kill the man to whom the message had been delivered.

Felix could hear the shouts of his foul pursuers behind him, and the screams of the unfortunates who got in their way. A quick glance over his shoulder revealed that the skaven were putting anyone in their path to the sword. The sight of it sickened Felix but in a way he was also glad. Every little pause and hesitation enabled him to increase his lead over them.

His wrist throbbed where the little skaven had bitten it. He noticed that the scroll it had thrown at him was crumpled in his hand. Briefly he toyed with throwing it away. Instead he thrust it inside his tunic and continued to sprint. At least he was not weighed down with heavy armour the way his pursuers were.

The thought trickled slowly into his mind that the skaven invasion must have started. The sight of so many heavily armed rat-men in the streets could only mean that they were ready to begin an all-out attack on the city and that they had no fear of the defenders. Right now, Felix guessed, their confidence was justified. He could not see a single member of the city guard. Of course, most of them were probably up in the Noble Quarter around the palace, making sure all the guests at the countess's party were safe.

Felix slammed into a wall and rebounded again, turning quickly to hurtle down a connecting alley. This area or narrow lanes and alleys was a veritable maze and he was not at all sure he was heading in the right direction. He could only move as quickly as possible and listen to the noise of his pursuers, praying that he did not blunder round in a complete circle and run right into them again.

He searched his brain for a plan, but all he could come up with was to get back to the Blind Pig as quickly as possible and warn Gotrek and the others. At least there was a strong force of mercenaries and a potential rallying point for any human warriors. Now all he had to do was find a way out. His heart filled with fear, he continued to run.

Lurk tried to keep himself right in the middle of the teeming mass of warriors. He had endured enough excitement for one evening and did not need any more. He focused his attention on keeping Izak Grottle in sight. The Moulder packmaster's bodyguard of huge rat-ogres represented his best hope of protection in the coming conflict. Lurk seriously doubted that anyone would want to attack the huge creatures.

So far, the assault appeared to be going well. The skaven force in this area had met with little resistance. He could smell burning and the distinctive oil-and-naphtha smell of warpfire throwers. From the backwash of light off to the south he realised that some of the Clan Skryre warpfire throwers were using their weapons on the buildings. Squinting through the shadows, Lurk could see jets of flame squirting out at the tenements. Fire licked and curled at the woodwork. Stone began to splinter and crack under the sheer heat generated by the awesome skaven weapons.

Lurk was not so certain that this was a good idea. He was not sure Grey Seer Thanquol would approve of such indiscriminate destruction of his future property. Of course, if the message Lurk had delivered achieved its goal, the grey seer would be in no position to voice his objections. He would be dead.

Lurk wondered whether the human, Jaeger, had managed to escape. Part of him hoped not. He could still remember the wretched human's hand clamped on his shoulder, and the pain where the iron fingers had bit into his fur. There was no sign that he had been taken prisoner, nor any sign of his corpse. Not that that meant anything, Lurk thought. In these winding alleys, already crammed with skaven victims, a body could be lying almost anywhere. Already the skaven force had started to break up and fan out. Some of the warriors, meeting little resistance, had already begin looting and eating.

Lurk was not sure that this was a good idea either. Surely things could not go so easily. Surely they would meet more resistance than this? Where were the accursed human warriors? His questions received no answers. All around, buildings were beginning to burn.

Chang Squik clambered up the sheer face of the cliff leading to the palace of the human breeder, Emmanuelle. The line attached to his grapnel held firm. The heavy weight of the rune-encrusted seeing stone entrusted to him by Grey Seer Thanquol personally rested securely in the knapsack on his back. Chang Squik braced himself and scrabbled with the claws of his feet for purchase on the smooth stone of the cliff face. Things were going well. In a few more minutes he would be in position with the stone placed within the halls of the palace, ready for whatever mighty magic the grey seer had planned. He would have played his part in the skaven victory today – and gone some way towards mitigating the disgrace of his failure to kill the dwarf and his human henchman. Hopefully that painful memory was something which could be laid to rest before this night was over too.

Suddenly below him, in the distance, he heard the faint but distinct chittering of skaven war cries, and the answering screams of their human victims. Twisting on the rope he glanced back and saw the eerie glow of what could only be warpfire throwers being used in the distance. Surely the attack had not begun already? The fools were supposed to wait until he was within the palace and Grey Seer Thanquol's plan had been implemented!

He cursed and redoubled his efforts to climb. The noise and the sight of the fire would draw human sentries and other spectators to the battlements above him. Chang Squik could ill afford to have his grapnel line discovered. All it would take would be one human with a knife to slice the black rope, and his long and honourable career would come to an end. Controlling his urge to squirt the musk of fear, the Clan Eshin assassin pulled himself upward.

The strange greenish light in the sky confirmed Felix's suspicions that the invasion had indeed begun. He recognised the colour of the flames as being the same as those produced by the strange weapons which had destroyed the College of Engineering. Looking back, he could see fire leaping from the rooftops of blazing tenements. The college had been a separate building isolated behind the walls of its own grounds. The buildings here in this part of the city, in contrast, were packed as tight together as drunks in a crowded tavern. Many of them leaned conspiratorially over alleyways. Some were linked by high bridges far above the ground, and by supporting arches in the alleys. Most had thatched roofs and wooden support beams. Felix shivered in spite of himself. The conflagration was going to spread quickly. The city was going to burn.

Still, at least for the moment he seemed to have lost his pursuers. There was not a rat-man in sight. Better yet, he recognised this street at last and knew that he was not too far from the Blind Pig. He paused, leaning forward with his hands braced on his knees, panting for breath and shaking his head to clear the sweat from his eyes. Once he reached the tavern he would be able to put together a plan with Gotrek and the others.

Suddenly, from the mouth of a nearby alley he heard a shrieked war cry. Looking up, he saw a large group of skaven erupt out into the cobbled street. Gathering all his energy, Felix ran for his life.

Grey Seer Thanquol led his elite force of stormvermin into position. His keen grey seer's intuition told him that directly above them was the palace. He could sense its presence. He trampled the corpse of the sewer watchman beneath his paw and allowed himself to gloat. So far the Clan Eshin assassins had done their work. Every human in the sewers who might have given away their presence was dead. By now, teams of gutter runners would be in position at the base of the cliff on which the castle rested. Hopefully, by now Chang Squik would be in position.

Thanquol produced the scrying stone from within his robes. He began to mutter the incantations which would link it to the twin carried by the leader of the Eshin forces. Now would be the time for a mighty feat of sorcery, one that would grant the skaven swift and inevitable victory. In order to perform it, Thanquol knew he would need vast amounts of power and therein lay the danger.

In order to acquire enough mystical energy to power the spells that he needed to perform, Thanquol would have to consume an enormous amount of warpstone, and that had its dangers. This was not the mild, refined stuff which made up his snuff. No, this was the pure product, the very essence of magic, concentrated and purified by skaven alchemists. It was a substance capable of providing its user with awesome power, but its use carried equally awesome dangers. Many grey seers had been driven over the edge into madness by the corrosive effects of the substance on their sanity. Others had been reduced to mindless Chaos-spawn by its mutating effects. Taken in large enough doses by those of insufficiently strong will, warpstone could devolve its user into a formless, amorphous thing.

But what was that to him, mightiest of grey seers? Thanquol was a practiced user of warpstone, was capable of consuming it in gigantic quantities without ill effect. The things that happened to all those others could not happen to him. Definitely, positively not...

For a moment, brief niggling doubt flared in Thanquol's mind. What if there was something wrong with the warpstone? What if it were not pure but contaminated with other stuff? Such things had happened. What if Thanquol were not as strong as he believed? Mistakes in dosage were always possible. But only for a second did the grey seer hesitate, before his natural confidence in his own mighty abilities returned. He was not one to flinch from the dangers of warpstone. In fact, he admitted to himself, he rather enjoyed it. He reminded himself of this as he reached into his pouch and put the first luminous piece of warpstone onto his tongue. It tingled even as he consumed it. Now memories of his long-gone youth came back to him. He recalled his initiation into the use of warpstone.

No, thought Thanquol, there was nothing to fear here. So thinking, he began preparing himself, making himself ready for when the correct time came to cast the spell which would grant his forces victory.

Ahead Felix could see the lights of the Blind Pig. A wave of relief passed through him. If the tavern did not quite represent safety, at least it had to be better than this nightmare chase through the darkened streets with a horde of shrieking rat-men on his trail. He could see Boris and Stephan and a host of their companions standing in the street, shielding their eyes as they studied the distant fires.

'Beware! Skaven!' Felix shouted and saw them all reach for their weapons. In moments, swords glittered in the half-light of the burning city. From inside the tavern a number of armoured figures spilled out into the gloom. Felix was relieved to see the massive squat figure of Gotrek among them. There was something enormously reassuring under these circumstances about the massive axe clutched in his hands.

Felix raced up to the warriors as they braced themselves for the skaven attack. Behind him the skaven, unwilling or unable to give up the heady rush of the chase, came on like an avalanche of fur and fury.

Felix made his way through the throng to stand beside Gotrek. The Slayer had the usual look of mad joy in his one good eye that he always got before combat.

'I see you found our scuttling little friends, manling,' he said, running his thumb along the blade of his axe until a bright red bead of blood appeared.

'Yes,' Felix gasped, struggling to get his breath back before the combat began.

'Good. Let's get killing then!'

Doctor Drexler looked around him. Something was very wrong. Many of the warriors had gone to the battlements to look at the fires and not come back. Ostwald had already herded the women back into the ballroom. Messengers had been rushing to and fro between Ostwald, Countess Emmanuelle and those outside. Something was very definitely happening and he needed to find out what it was. If he had not known better, he would have sworn that Ostwald had ordered the orchestra to play louder to drown out the sounds of the disturbance.

That must be it, Drexler thought, knowing that he had guessed the truth. Something was happening and in order to forestall a panic, Hieronymous was covering it up. He glanced around at the others present, and adjusted his mask. Most of the people in the ballroom consisted of ladies of rank, together with a sprinkling of hangers-on, toadies and those simply too drunk to leave the hall. Of course there were footmen present, and a few guards too, but the situation was not very reassuring. He glanced across at Ostwald, not wanting to divulge the connection between them but filled with curiosity about what was going on. The secretary was garbed as a wood elf warrior, complete with bow. Drexler walked up to him, still nibbling at a savoury.

'What has happened?' he asked.

'Some disturbance in the town, Herr Doctor. Arson and possibly worse. With Her Serenity's permission, I have ordered troops from the barracks to quell the problem.'

'Nothing wrong in the palace then?'

'Not as far as I know, but I have ordered the guards to double-check.'

'Let us pray to Sigmar that it is only some looters. Things have been dreadful recently.'

'I fear the worst,' Ostwald said, looking up as another courier approached. Drexler agreed. Somewhere nearby his sorcerously trained senses told him that powerful magic was gathering.

Chang Squik cursed and ducked for cover. The place smelled like a reeking midden. Looking around with his dark-accustomed eyes, he could tell this was, in truth, a human privy. Well, there were worse places to hide, he told himself, but this was not going to help his mission.

He knew it was no use. He was not going to make it to the great chamber above the ballroom that he and the grey seer had agreed on. All of the stolen maps of the palace he had studied and still carried in his head told him this. He just did not have the time to get there and, even with his supreme skills at sneaking and skulking, he doubted that he could find his way, unseen, through the mass of humans crowding the palace corridors and heading to the battlements in search of a view of what was going on below. This place was just going to have to do.

He took the knapsack from his back and reached within. The heat and the glow produced by the seeing stone told him that he was only just in time. Perhaps even a little late. He wondered how long the grey seer had already spent glaring out into the darkness of the inside of his pack. He shuddered when he thought of the wrath of Thanquol, as he squatted down, pressed his nose to the side of the stone, and gave the thumbs-up sign.

Felix ducked the swipe of a jagged scimitar and lashed out with his sword. His blow took the skaven beneath the ribs, and cleaved upwards in search of its heart. The skaven gave an eerie high-pitched shriek, clutched its chest, and died. It fell to the ground even as Felix withdrew his blade from its chest.

Felix glanced around at the swirling melee. To his right he saw Heinz dash out the brains of a skaven leader with the cosh he held in his left hand, while he fended off the attack of another skaven with the blade he held in his right. Boris and Stephan fought back-to-back in the teeth of the tide of rat-men. Somewhere in the distance he could hear Gotrek's bellowed war cry.

Right at this moment, it was difficult to tell how the fight was going. The mercenaries seemed to be holding their own against the skaven, and the battle seemed to have attracted the attention of others. Humans were pouring out of the nearby tenements. Some clutched bedpans and pokers and other improvised weapons. Others carried swords and blunderbusses and other, rather more useful-looking, instruments of destruction. It seemed that the citizens had decided that they would rather meet their end in battle with their foes than be burned to death in their homes. That was good, thought Felix, for the mercenaries needed all the help they could get as more and more skaven were being drawn through the blazing streets to the sound of battle.

Even as he stood there, a severed head came flying out of the gloom, spinning, spilling blood from disconnected arteries, spraying all those below it with a shower of black raindrops. It arced straight toward Felix and he batted it aside with his sword. Salty black fluid splattered his face and he fought the urge to lick his lips to clean them. Looking down he saw that the head belonged to a huge skaven warrior.

He wiped his face with his cloak quickly, worried that something might take advantage of his blindness and stab him. Shaking his head he moved forward cautiously to where he could hear Gotrek shouting. Ahead of him he could see an enormous ruck. The Slayer stood poised atop what first Felix took to be an enormous mound of bodies but swiftly realised was a plague cart. A wave of furious skaven scrabbled to reach him but were being hewn down by the awesome power of the Slayer's axe.

In the distance, looming over the great mass of lesser skaven, Felix could see a huge wedge of creatures he had come to think of as rat-ogres. Gotrek obviously saw them too, for he dived from the top of the plague cart into the seething sea of skaven. Within moments, his flickering axe had left a wall of broken and dying bodies all around him as he thrust his way towards the giant monsters that were his goal. Felix debated for only a moment whether to follow him and then pushed forward, shouting: 'Follow me, lads! Let's kill some bloody rat-men.'

As he hacked to left and right, he hoped the mercenaries were listening and following, otherwise he and Gotrek were in for a hard time when they closed with the rat-ogres.

Thanquol glared into his scrying crystal. His head swam. His brain felt aflame. The power of the warpstone flowed through his veins like a drug. It made him feel dizzy and wonderful at the same time. At this moment, he felt sure he could perceive the underlying pattern of mystical forces focused on the crystal. He concentrated harder on making the thing work.

At last the darkness had cleared. At last he could see the leering face of Chang Squik. It appeared that the Clan Eshin assassin had reached his objective. Good, Thanquol thought. About time. He could barely contain the enormous mass of warpstone-fuelled mystical energy which boiled within him. He felt so saturated with power that it seemed that at any minute he might explode. His head swam and his vision blurred; everything seemed to swim around him. Frantically he tried to remember the syllables of the spell he had memorised so long ago in that great black book in the Accursed Library.

For a long moment the words eluded him, squirming and sliding just out of reach of his thought processes. Thanquol bit the insides of his cheek until he tasted blood. The pain seemed to sharpen his wits, for eventually the words came to him. He opened his lips and the syllables of his ancient language seemed to vomit forth from his mouth, ejecting with them a roiling cloud of dark, magical energy.

Thanquol's heartbeat accelerated to levels he would not have believed were endurable. His heart thumped wildly in his chest and his breathing was ragged and choked. He knew he was losing control of his spell and fought to rein in the flow of power before it destroyed him. Brain-blasting visions danced through his mind, and he knew that his seer's gifts had been driven to incredible new heights by the unprecedented amounts of warpstone he had consumed. Briefly his consciousness seemed to leave his body and scenes flickered through his mind in swift succession.

For a moment his spirit hovered over the city and he had a panoramic view of all that was happening. Below him the streets blazed with fire and violence. A river of skaven raced through the city, killing all that were in their path. Here and there they had encountered pockets of armed resistance where human garrisons or just the mobs of citizens had taken to the streets in defence of their homes. He saw swift, savage scuffles and giant rats devouring the corpses of man and skaven alike. He saw burning buildings and broken bodies. He saw the whole of the great ancient mancity of Nuln in flames.

Thanquol's attention was drawn to one particular struggle which suddenly leapt into focus when he recognised two alarmingly familiar figures. The dwarf and the human, followed by a disciplined pack of human warriors, were hacking through the skaven warriors towards the hulking bodyguard of Izak Grottle. In his trance state, Thanquol could see the roaring rat-ogres – and the appalled look on the face of his henchling Lurk as he contemplated the prospect of imminent violence. He saw the mad eyes of Vilebroth Null glaring into space as if he sensed the presence of some disembodied watcher. It looked very much to the grey seer like his plan was working and the interfering twosome were about to destroy his bitterest rivals.

Good, he thought, let them! Thanquol would brook no others claiming an unfair portion of his glory.

He saw Heskit One Eye bark instructions to his jezzail-equipped bodyguards and saw the long-barrelled rifle swing to bear on the dwarf. No! No, Thanquol thought furiously. None of that! With an almost imperceptible flicker of his thoughts, he touched the sniper's mind. Its fingers curled on the trigger but its warpstone bullet went wild, smashing into the skull of a rat-ogre, almost killing the brainless beast. The thing roared and went wild, surging forward into the skaven troops from the rear, killing as it went.

Thanquol felt dizzy and realised that he was losing himself in his spell. His power was bleeding away and, if he intended to accomplish what he wanted, he had better do it soon. With a wrench he sent his spirit soaring back towards the castle. He funnelled it into the link with the scrying stone and looked out once more on Chang Squik. Suddenly, with a snap, he was back in his own body again and the words of the spell were tumbling from his mouth.

He concentrated with all his might, bringing to bear all the relentless discipline of his many years as a grey seer and the spell swiftly returned to his control. In the air before him, the dark cloud shimmered and parted, revealing a rift in space running from the point just in front of where Thanquol stood to the ground around Chang Squik's scrying crystal.

'Quick! Quick! Forward!' he shouted to his Stormvermin guard. They walked forward into the black cloud, shimmered and vanished to reappear – Thanquol most earnestly hoped! – in the very heart of the breeder Emmanuelle's palace.

Ahead of them, Felix could see the rat-ogres. They loomed head and shoulders above the crowd, monstrous creatures, man-shaped but with the heads of immense rabid rats. Vast boils erupted through their mangy fur. The stigmata of a variety of foul mutations marred their flesh. Each had paws the size of shovels which ended in claws like daggers. Huge tusk-like fangs dripping with saliva filled their mouths. Their bellows were audible even over the din of battle.

At the sight of them, Felix felt the urge to halt and flee. He could tell the mercenaries following him felt the same way. The momentum of their charge was dissipating as they contemplated the horrific appearance of their foes. Only Gotrek showed no fear. He ploughed onward, unwilling or unable to be bothered by the fearsome nature of his foes. The rat-ogres were no more troubled by the Trollslayer's arrival than he was by theirs. With an ear-shattering roar, they charged rabidly to meet him.

It seemed unlikely to Felix that anything could survive the mad rush of such huge creatures. It was like expecting someone to be able to withstand the charge of a herd of elephants. Nothing should have been able to withstand the onslaught of that huge mass of muscle and teeth and claws. For a moment, all heads turned and even the skaven stopped their relentless advance to watch.

Completely undaunted by the fact his opponents were twice his size, Gotrek came on. His axe flashed, glowing red in the lurid blaze of the burning buildings, and one of the rat-ogres tumbled backwards, its leg chopped off at the knee. As it fell the Slayer's axe slashed back again and severed its arm. Clutching at the bloody stump with its good paw, the creature rolled over on the ground, writhing and shrieking.

Another of the immense creatures reached out and made a grab for the dwarf. Its razor-like talons bit into his ruddy flesh. Bloody droplets appeared on Gotrek's shoulder as the mighty beast raised him high above its head. It opened its huge jaws to the fullest extension as if intending to drop the Slayer in and devour him in one bite. Gotrek brought his axe crashing down. Powered by all the awesome strength of the Slayer's mighty arm, it smashed the rat-ogre's head in two. Blood, brains and teeth exploded everywhere. The Slayer went flying backwards through the air, propelled skyward by the reflex action of the rat-ogre's death spasm.

Seeing the remaining rat-ogres begin their advance towards Gotrek's recumbent form, Felix mustered all his courage and shouted: 'Charge! Charge! Let's send these foul vermin back to the hell that spawned them.'

Not daring to look back over his shoulder to see if anyone was following him, he raced forward into the fray.

Chang Squik watched in amazement as the air in front of him shimmered. For a moment, it appeared like a small, bright hole had been punched in the very fabric of the world. Through that hole leaked a vile black gas which smelled of warpstone and dark magic. Even as the assassin watched, the cloud expanded and shimmered until it stood higher than any skaven. Then the cloud itself parted to reveal a gateway joining the privy in which Chang Squik stood to the place where the grey seer was.

Chang Squik heard a sudden noise behind him and span around to see an ornately garbed human enter the privy, fumbling with his codpiece as if he intended to make water. The human reeked of alcohol. He paused in amazement and looked at the skulking skaven, then shook his head as if to clear it.

'I say,' he said. 'That's a ruddy good costume!'

Then his eyes widened further as he noticed the ranks of storm vermin starting to pour through Thanquol's sorcerous gateway. He opened his mouth and had just time for one shriek of warning before Chang Squik's throwing knife buried itself in his heart.

More and more skaven warriors flowed into the chamber, bursting out from the privy and into the corridors of the palace.

Felix ducked, threw himself flat, and rolled under a blow that would have taken his head off, had it connected. Up close the rat-ogres were, if anything, even more frightening to behold. Their muscles were like the cables used to moor ships and they looked as if they could smash through a stone wall with little effort. The creature's massive tail lashed through the air with a crack like a whip. Worse yet was the smell, an awful combination of animal reek, wet fur, and warp-stone. It reminded Felix of old and very sour cheese but was infinitely stronger, and threatened to bring tears to his eyes.

He rolled to one side as a fist the size of his head smashed into the ground where he had been. He kicked out at the rat-ogre's leg, hoping to unbalance it, but he might as well have been kicking a tree trunk. Hot saliva dribbled from the thing's mouth and landed on his hand. Felix fought down the urge to flinch and kept moving, knowing that his life depended on it.

Mad triumph appeared in the monster's small beady eyes. It opened its jaws and bellowed so loudly that Felix thought he would go deaf.

The creature reached for him, and from his prone position Felix lashed out with his blade and caught it across the knuckles with the razor-sharp edge. The rat-ogre's eyes went wide in surprise at the pain. Whimpering like a child, it pulled its hand back to its mouth to lick the wound. Taking advantage of its distraction, Felix half rose and stabbed upwards, driving the point of the sword right into the rat-ogre's groin.

The creature gave a shriek like the whistle of a steam tank and reached down to touch its severed nether parts. Felix drove the point of his blade into the thing's opened jaws, pushing it right through the roof of the mouth and into its tiny malformed brain. The light went out of its eyes as it died instantly. Felix felt a momentary surge of tri-umph – which faded almost instantly as he realised that the rat-ogre's corpse was going to topple on him.

Felix sprang hastily to one side as the monstrous form crashed to the ground like a felled tree. Pausing to catch his breath a moment, he looked around. The last of the rat-ogres was going down, the mercenaries swarming over it like rats over a terrier, but the victory had been won at awful cost. Many human corpses covered the ground for every rat-ogre which had fallen. It looked like only he and Gotrek had bested one of the beasts in single combat.

Still, briefly and temporarily though it might turn out to be, it looked like the tide of battle had turned in their favour. The skaven leaders, including the grossly fat monster which had ordered the rat-ogres to attack, were fleeing backwards to regroup.

More and more people were massing in the streets to fight off the invaders. In the distance, Felix could hear the sound of horns and drums as the small army which surrounded the Noble Quarter began to advance down into the city. He wished he had some idea of how the battle was going. In the raging maelstrom of conflict it was difficult to say. They had won a victory here but it was all too possible that the skaven were triumphant in every other part of the city. Perhaps now would be a good time to make a run for it, he thought.

Then he saw the Trollslayer. Gotrek marched through the crowd towards him. A terrible grin revealed his missing teeth. Mad battle lust filled his one good eye.

'You brought a good fight with you, manling,' he said.

Felix nodded – and then remembered how this had all started. He fumbled within his tunic to retrieve the scrap of parchment, then slowly unrolled it to read its message.

Grey Seer Thanquol watched the last of his troops pass through the gateway and then stepped through himself. He felt a sense of relief as the mystic portal closed automatically behind him. Even for a grey seer of Thanquol's awesome powers, holding it open while hundreds of stormvermin poured through had been a terrible strain.

Now he could relax and watch his plan unfold before him. His tail lashed in anticipation of his triumph. Victory was within reach! Soon he would hold the human rulers hostage and command them to order their troops to surrender on pain of most hideous death. If they refused – which Thanquol rather hoped they would – he would make an example of some of them until they did agree. He was looking forward to some sport. Then the twitching of his nostrils warned him that something odd was happening, and he squinted around the chamber to confirm his suspicions.

Yes, it was true. Even Thanquol's warpstone addled senses could tell that this room was the wrong size, and it did not smell like a great hallway. It smelled like a midden. Thanquol stuck his head through the door. He looked into a corridor in which stormvermin milled in confusion. This was not the hallway they had been told to expect. He could see their clawleader studying his map with a look of puzzlement on his face. The awful truth dawned on Thanquol: that incompetent buffoon Chang Squik had placed his scrying crystal in the wrong place!

Thanquol bared his fangs in a ferocious snarl. It was just as well for the Clan Eshin assassin that he was not in sight, thought Thanquol. The grey seer swore that when he found Squik he would flay his flesh from his bones using the darkest magic that he could command.

Warpstone-driven euphoria and drugged rage warred in Thanquol's mind as he stalked out into the corridor to search for his goal.

Felix looked down at the parchment. It was hard to tell in the gloom but the writing looked somehow different, smaller, neater, more precise. Not that it mattered right now, as Felix read in horror what it had to say:

> *Hoomans! the traitur Grey Sere Thanquol will invade the palaz*
> *this nite and kapture the breeder Eeman-yoo-ell and all yore*
> *pack leeders! Yoo must stop him or yore city will fall.*
>
> *Also this Thanquol is a very powerful sorcerur and will yoose*
> *his eevil majik to stop yoo. He must die-die or no hooman in*
> *yore city wil be safe.*

Felix looked down at Gotrek then passed him the note. 'Well?' he said.

'Well what, manling?'

'Do we go to the palace and rescue our noble rulers from this skaven menace?'

'They're your rulers, manling, not mine!'

'I think this grey seer is the thing we encountered in von Halstadt's house. The rat-man which got away. I think it might be behind this whole invasion.'

'Then killing it would be a great deed – and dying in the attempt would be a mighty doom!' Gotrek rumbled.

'Only one problem, then: we're going to have to fight our way through the city to get there!'

'Where's the problem in that?'

'Who knows how many rat-men stand in our way?'

Felix wracked his brain for a way out of this dilemma. It would take an army to fight its way across the city.

In a flash of inspiration worthy of a Detlef Sierck hero, the answer came to him.

Lurk Snitchtongue cowered in the shadow of Izak Grottle. The huge Clan Moulder packmaster looked at him hungrily. He still seemed to be in a state of shock from watching the defeat of his prized rat-ogres.

'I thought you said the human and the dwarf had received the message and were on their way to... intercede with Grey Seer Thanquol.'

'The message was delivered, master of Moulders! I cannot be held responsible for what happens next. Maybe they were caught up in the fighting.'

'Maybe! Maybe! All of this has left us exposed, though. Very exposed. We must find another skaven force quickly or return to the safety of the sewers.'

'Yes, yes, most perceptive of planners.'

'Have you seen Heskit One Eye or Vilebroth Null?'

'Not since we were attacked, greatest of gorgers.'

'A pity. Well, let us be on our way!'

'At once.'

Filled with warpstone-fuelled rage, Thanquol stalked the corridors of the palace. The damnable place was huge and it was as much a maze as anything he made his pet humans run through. His carefully contrived plan had fallen apart because of the incompetence of Chang Squik. It had relied on speed, surprise and the fury of the skaven assault to overwhelm the defence. Now his stormvermin were reduced to racing through the corridors and fighting skirmishes with groups of sentries. It was only a matter of time before the humans realised what was going on, concentrated their forces, and began to fight back. Thanquol still expected a victory under those circumstances. His warriors were many and bold, but there was always the possibility that something might happen to tip the odds against them. Thanquol would have much preferred a sudden overwhelming victory, not this period of anger and doubt.

Heskit One Eye chittered in excitement. Once again he watched the warpfire throwers sweep through the buildings. These huge human structures burned well. Their wooden supports caught fire easily, and the soft stone and brick from which they were made melted in the fierce heat of the warpflames.

Heskit had thought it politic to separate from the others when his jezzail team had accidentally shot one of Izak Grottle's rat-ogres. It was an accident, Heskit knew, but the skaven of Clan Moulder were insanely suspicious. Heskit had no desire to have Izak Grottle 'accidentally' stab him in the back so he had led his troops away from the main battle to continue spreading destruction.

And how glad he was that he had done so. There was something truly enthralling about watching the machineries of destruction at work, of feeling the heat and flames his warriors had caused warm his face and watching these giant structures tumble down.

Heskit stared upwards for a long time, watching the tenement collapse. It was only at the very last moment that he realised that tons of brick and blazing wood were crashing down right on top of him. And by then, it was far too late for him to escape.

Felix leapt on to the back of the plague cart. Bodies squelched under his feet. The stink was appalling. He really would have preferred to stand somewhere else but this was the only way he could get the attention of the crowd.

'Citizens of Nuln!' he bellowed in the orator's voice he had not used since the Window Tax riots. 'Listen to me!'

A few heads turned in his direction. Most of the others were too busy hacking at skaven corpses or shouting gleefully at their neighbours.

'Citizens of Nuln! Skaven slayers!' he shouted. A few more people looked at him. They began to tug their neighbour's arms and point in his direction. Slowly but surely Felix felt the attention of the crowd turn on him. Slowly but surely, the crowd fell silent. These people had seen him and Gotrek slay rat-ogres. They had also seen them lead the charge into battle. These people were leaderless and in need of direction. Felix thought he could provide them with both.

'Citizens of Nuln! The skaven have attacked your great city. They have burned your homes. They have killed your loved ones. They have brought madness and plague to your streets.'

Felix saw that he had them now. All eyes in the crowd were riveted to him. He could sense the crowd's anger and hatred and fear, and he could sense that he had given it a focus. He felt a sudden thrill at the power he held. He wet his lips and continued to speak, knowing that he must sway them to the course he wanted now or he would lose them.

'You have killed many skaven. You have seen their monsters fall. You have seen their vile weapons fail. Victory is within your grasp. Are you ready to kill more skaven?'

'Yes!' cried a few of the crowd. Many still looked uncertain. For the most part they were not warriors, just ordinary people suddenly thrown into a situation they did not truly understand.

'Are you ready to drive the skaven from your city? For if you do not, they will return and carry you away as slaves! '

Felix had no idea whether this was true or not, but it was what they had done in the past and it sounded good. More to the point, it sounded frightening. More voices shouted: 'Yes.'

'Are you ready to slaughter these monsters without mercy? For rest assured, if you do not, they will slaughter you!'

'Yes!' roared the whole crowd in a frenzy of rage and fear.

'Then follow me! To the palace! Where the chief of all this foul breed even now threatens the life of your rightful ruler!'

Felix leapt down from the cart and landed on the cobbled street. Hands stretched out from the crowd to pat him on the back. More still shouted their support. He saw Heinz and the surviving mercenaries give him the thumbs up. He looked down at Gotrek; even the dwarf looked pleased. 'Let's go,' Felix said and they broke into a run.

As one, the crowd followed them through the burning streets of the city.

Chang Squik drew his long black cloak in front of his face and stalked forward, blade in hand. He kept to the shadows, moving quietly on the balls of his feet, ready to strike in any direction at the slightest provocation.

In the dim distance he could still hear the sound of fighting. From up ahead, he could hear the strange scraping noise that humans called 'music'. He emerged onto a balcony and blinked his eyes, momentarily dazzled.

He stood looking down upon a huge chamber. The vaulted ceiling above him was painted with an enormous picture of the human gods looking down benevolently. Enormous chandeliers, each holding hundreds of candles, provided dazzling illumination. Down below an orchestra played and many gowned breeders and a few costumed males stood at ease, drinking and eating happily. The smell of food made Squik's nostrils twitch and drew his attention to the tables below. They groaned beneath the weight of roasted fowl and pig. Platters of cheese and bread and all manner of savouries were there. So

much for starving the city, thought the Eshin assassin! Then he realised that maybe the ordinary people were starving, but the rulers had
preserved all these dainties for themselves. In this, then, the humans
were not too different from skaven, he decided – then started at the
sound of footsteps on the balcony behind him.

Two figures, a male and a breeder, had emerged onto the balcony
behind him. Their clothing was in a state of disarray and it looked
odd even for humans. The man was garbed as a shepherd in some
sort of tunic. He carried pan pipes, and a golden mask shaped to
have small horns like a goat's covered his face. The woman, too, was
masked but she was dressed in some sort of dancer's costume, with
diamond-patterned tights, a tricorned hat and a domino mask. They
stared at him and to his surprise emitted the strange wheezing sound
that humans called laughter. They stank of alcohol.

Chang Squik was so surprised that he paused in the middle of his
death stroke. He had intended to strike them down and withdraw into
the shadowy corridors. 'I say, what a super costume!' the man said.

'Absolutely wonderful,' the woman agreed. She bent over and
tugged at Squik's tail. 'So realistic.'

Squik had no idea what they were saying. He understood no words
of their odd rumbling language but it was starting to filter into his
brain that these people were wearing some sort of costume, like high
ranking skaven performing a religious rite. And they appeared to have
mistaken him for one of them.

Was it possible that these people were so drunk and so uncaring that
they did not realise that there was a skaven invasion going on outside?
To his astonishment Chang Squik realised that it must be so. Worse,
he could see that all eyes down below were on them. He considered
pushing the pair off the balcony and ducking back into the shadows
but that meant going back into corridors filled with fighting stormvermin and an angry Thanquol. Another plan struck him. Nodding
politely to the two revellers, he put away his blade, walked down the
stairs and into the crowds of masked and disguised humans.

He helped himself to a savoury from a tray carried by a passing
waiter, picked up a goblet of wine, and strolled through the hall,
nodding left and right to those he passed. Perhaps if he could find
the breeder, Emmanuelle, he might yet redeem himself in the eyes of
Grey Seer Thanquol.

Vilebroth Null looked up in astonishment at the onrushing horde of
humans. Where had they all come from? How had they mustered such

a huge force so suddenly? Had Grey Seer Thanquol underestimated their numbers? Certainly that was possible and, if so, just another example of the grey seer's incompetence. Not that it would make any difference if he did not get out of their way.

He had spent the night since the invasion force had erupted from the sewer wandering lost through the twisting maze of alleys and lanes, killing any humans he encountered, and trying to locate Izak Grottle and the others. He cursed the initial blind rush which had separated them all. Now he was left to face this horde of humans without any sort of bodyguard.

He looked up and realised that he recognised the leaders of the charge – and what was worse, they recognised him! It was the human and the dwarf who had interrupted his ritual and destroyed the Cauldron of a Thousand Poxes. For a moment, a vast righteous anger swept through Vilebroth Null. Almost without thinking, he summoned his powers and an eerie green light swept into being around his head and paws. He mumbled the chant that would summon destructive spirits of disease to smite his foes.

The humans did not even slow their headlong rush. Vilebroth Null realised that they could not. The ones at the back were pushing the ones at the front of the herd forward. If the leaders slowed they would be trampled. He kept chanting, desperate now to summon the powers which would protect him, knowing that most likely it was already too late. The humans were upon him.

The last thing Vilebroth Null saw was a huge axe descending towards his skull.

Felix shuddered. He had recognised the green-robed rat-man in the last seconds before the crowd had trampled it. It was the plague priest from the cemetery. And Felix was glad that it was dead.

He was warm now, sweating from exertion and the heat of the blazing buildings which surrounded them. He tried to ignore the screams of those trapped within and focus on taking vengeance on those responsible. Somewhere off in the distance he heard a crashing sound. A pillar of sparks rose skyward as a tenement collapsed. Felix knew that if anyone survived this, they would have their work cut out for them rebuilding the city. This was as bad as the Great Fire of Altdorf.

They hit the slopes around the palace, and Felix noticed that many of the buildings here were intact. They were like his brother's house, small fortresses as well as mansions. Ahead of them was a force clad in the black tabards of the Nuln city guard. They had their halberds raised to repel a charge but lowered them confused when they saw that the mob were human, rather than rat-men.

'Skaven!' he shouted. 'There are skaven in the palace!'

He did not know whether the captain of the guard believed him or not, but he did not have much choice. If his men stood there much longer they would either have to use their weapons on their fellow citizens or be trampled under foot. The captain made a snap decision: he barked an order and his men stood aside. Felix could see that the great gate of the palace was still open. It must have been left that way to allow the coaches of the guests to enter, Felix decided.

He rushed onwards, praying that they were in time to save Countess Emmanuelle.

Drexler turned to look in the direction of the scream. Suddenly the balcony seethed with huge, black armoured skaven. Those were not costumes, he could tell immediately. These were the real thing. Monstrous, man-sized, anthropomorphic rats armed with huge scimitars and bearing round shields inscribed with the sigil of their evil god.

He saw a few of the guards, elite troops, move to interpose themselves between the guests and the skaven. They were cut down swiftly by the disciplined phalanx as it poured down the stairs and into the room. Slowly the orchestra stopped playing. The notes faded out into discordant echoes. Screaming guests in fancy costumes were herded towards the great throne dais by massive snarling rat-men.

Drexler wondered if he should risk a spell, but decided against it. There were too many skaven for him to affect them all. Where were the guards, he wondered? Where were all the men who had gone to the battlements to look at the fire?

Then he sensed the presence of terrible magical energy. Looking up he saw a huge, horned, grey-furred rat-man descending the stairs. It looked like an evil god come to bring doom to all mankind.

Thanquol strode forward across the corpses of the dead humans. At last, from up ahead he could hear a gratifying number of screams. It seemed that his stormvermin had discovered the Great Hall at last, and that the human leaders were finally within his grasp. Filled with a tremendous sense of his inevitable righteous triumph, the grey seer advanced to victory!

Felix led the charge into the courtyard. Looking up, he saw a struggle taking place on the battlements.

'Quick!' he shouted to Heinz. 'Scour the battlements! Kill any skaven you find!'

'Right-o, young Felix,' Heinz said, rushing towards the steps with the mercenaries in tow. 'Follow me, lads!'

Felix glanced around at the mob pouring into the courtyard. They looked ferocious, ready to kill anything they saw. A number of them began to race after Heinz.

'Where to now, manling?' Gotrek asked. 'I want to get to grips with that rat-man wizard. My axe thirsts for more blood!'

Good question, thought Felix, wishing he had an answer. Think, he urged himself. Where is the logical place to go? The grey seer wanted to capture Emmanuelle. Tonight he knew from Drexler a great ball was taking place. The logical place for the countess to be was the ballroom that Ostwald and he had passed through the first time he had visited the palace. Now, if only he could remember the way there!

'Follow me!' he shouted, trying to make his voice as confident as possible.

Thanquol paused at the head of the stairs to survey the great ballroom. He wanted to give the pitiful humans the chance to appreciate the full awful majesty of their conquerors. He wanted to savour his moment of ultimate triumph.

All eyes turned to look at him. He could tell the humans were impressed by his dignity and his presence. They always were. The majestic form of a grey seer always inspired respect and admiration in equal parts from all who saw him. He glanced at the crowd and looked around to see if he could find his chosen prey.

In truth, he had expected to be able to tell her by the elaborate nature of her costume, and by the fact that she wore a crown, but he could see that all the humans present were garbed in strange disguises, almost as if they had intended to thwart him. Well, well, he thought, they would see that a grey seer was not so easily balked. He singled out one of the human males, a man garbed like some primitive tribesman.

'You, man-thing! Where is your chief breeder? Answer me! Quick! Quick! ' Thanquol asked in his best Reikspiel.

'I haven't the faintest idea what you're talking about, old man,' came the reply. Sweat dribbled down the man's face. Thanquol blasted him with a surge of pure magical power. Women's screams filled the air as the stripped and blackened skeleton of his victim fell to the floor. Thanquol selected another victim, a woman dressed like one of the humans' goddesses.

'You! Tell me where is the chief breeder? Answer! Now! Now!'

The woman looked at him blankly. 'What is a breeder?' she asked. Thanquol's answer was to blast her with magic as well. Another charred corpse tumbled to the floor. Thanquol selected a man very cunningly disguised as a Clan Eshin assassin.

'You! The chief breeder! Where?!' Thanquol bellowed. The disguised assassin turned, its tail twitching remarkably like a real skaven.

'No, master! Don't blast me!' it cried in fluent skaven. Remarkable, thought Thanquol. A human who speaks our language! Then he realised that this was no human. It was that damnable Chang Squik, hiding himself among the humans. Thanquol looked at the assassin and licked his lips, thinking of how the assassin's folly had almost cost Thanquol his triumph, remembering all the other failures Chang Squik had been responsible for.

This was perfect, thought Thanquol. If anybody ever asked, he could claim that it was all a terrible error. He summoned all of his powers. Chang Squik screamed most satisfactorily as dark magic consumed his body.

Thanquol gloated for a brief but joyous moment, then picked out another human. 'You! Where is the chief breeder? Answer! Quick-quick! Or your miserable life is forfeit!'

'But I don't know what a breeder is,' whimpered the fat man garbed as a huge pink rabbit. Thanquol shrugged and blasted him. Yet more bones clattered onto the marble floor.

It began to occur to Thanquol, even through the haze of warpstone clouding his mind, that there was something wrong with his strategy. The humans did not quite seem to understand what he was getting at. What could it be? Where were their feeble minds going astray? He had asked for their chief breeder, after all. Perhaps if he asked for her by name? He signalled out a cringing breeder, and pointed one talon at her.

'You! You! Are you the chief breeder Emmanuelle?'

The breeder was obviously too overwhelmed by the sheer majesty of Thanquol's presence to speak. He blasted her as a lesson to the others that they should reply when he asked a question. He selected another male next, hoping that it would be slightly less witless than the breeder.

'You – where is the chief breeder Emmanuelle?' The male shook its head defiantly.

'I will never tell you. I have sworn to serve the Elector Countess wi–'

Thanquol yawned and unleashed another blast of dark magic before the human could finish its speech. He so hated it when they became contrary. His specimens back home in Skavenblight could be the same way sometimes, particularly after he took their breeders and runts away to experiment on. An amazing race in some ways certainly, he thought, but so stupid.

Out of the corner of his eye, Thanquol caught sight of two human breeders muttering to each other. Slowly he swung his burning gaze towards them. As one the breeders straightened and one of them strode towards him. She pulled off her mask to reveal a pale but determined face.

'I believe you are looking for me,' she said defiantly. 'I am Elector Countess Emmanuelle!'

Thanquol was almost disappointed. The warpstone power still surged within him, and he had been enjoying using it. There was nothing quite like the thrill of blasting lesser beings to bits, unless it was the sense of power doing just that gave one.

'Good! Good!' Thanquol said. 'You will order your troops to surrender immediately and I will let you live. Fail to do so and...'

Drexler shuddered as he watched the monstrous horned skaven stride through the crowd. Just the sight of it filled him with fear. It wasn't the red, glowing eyes or the way its fur bristled that scared him. It was the power it so obviously carried within it.

Drexler's mystically attuned senses could see that the thing fairly bristled with dark magical energy. He was enough of a sorcerer himself to see that there was something deeply unnatural about it. No living creature should be able to wield or contain such power without suffering the consequences. At the very least, it should go mad. At most it might explode, blown apart by the vast energy roiling within its body.

Where could it have acquired such power, Drexler wondered? The only possible source of so much energy was said to be pure warpstone. Could the creature possibly be consuming the stuff? Such a supposition beggared belief.

Perhaps the creature had not escaped its use unscathed. Its slurred speech and stumbling, jerky movements certainly hinted that something was wrong with it. The way its whiskers quivered and its head twitched made it look as if it were in the terminal stage of some fatal addiction. Yes, the creature was mad. No doubt about it. The way it had so casually blasted apart anyone who did not answer its questions to its satisfaction stated that fact clearly. The question now was what was he, Drexler, going to do about it?

He was appalled by his own cowardice. Each time the creature had gathered its dark powers, he had sensed it. He could have at least tried to work a counter-spell but he had not. He had been too overcome by the horror of the thing's appearance and the thought of what might happen to him if he had intervened. He felt sure that he would lose any mystical duel with this rat-man and that attracting its attention would be fatal. Even if he could somehow hold the skaven mage in check, its black-armoured lackeys filled the room. At a word from it, they would surely cut him down with those cruel swords.

So he had done nothing and half a dozen people had died. He was proud of what Baron Blucher had done, the way the man had defied the skaven before he died. Why could he not summon such courage? The healer in him was appalled that he had done nothing to prevent such loss of life. Now the countess herself stood in peril, willing to give her own life to spare her subjects. Drexler vowed that this time, he would intervene, if the skaven attacked.

There would be no more magical killings if he could help it.

'I will do no such thing,' Countess Emmanuelle said shakily. 'I would rather die than order my troops to surrender to you foul vermin.'

'Foolish breeder – that is just what you will do, if you defy me!' Thanquol said. He raised his paw and dark magical energy played around it menacingly. The breeder flinched slightly, but did not move or open her mouth. Thanquol wondered if there was some way around this impasse. Perhaps if he ordered some of the humans tortured before her eyes she would weaken. Thanquol's experiments had led him to believe such a course would often work. Yes, that was it!

Then from somewhere around him in the ballroom, he sensed the slow build-up of magical energies. They were not skaven magical energies either. He heard footsteps rushing closer too, even as he turned his head to seek their source.

'Well, well, what have we here?' a harsh grating voice said like two great boulders rubbing together, cutting like a knife to the very core of Thanquol's being. 'It looks like we're just in time to kill some rats.'

Thanquol quelled the urge to squirt the musk of fear. He recognised that harsh, flinty growl! The grey seer jerked his head to one side just to confirm his worst fears, and he saw that they were true. Standing in the entrance to the chamber were the dwarf Gurnisson and the human Jaeger, and behind them was a teeming mass of human troops.

Thanquol howled in frustration and rage. He reached deep into his corrupt soul and hurled all his lethal power at his enemies in one mighty blast.

Felix prepared himself to spring to one side as he saw the midnight black thunderbolt gather around the grey seer's paw. The nimbus of evil mystical power around the rat-man's head was so bright that it was almost impossible to look at. Gotrek held his ground unflinchingly, seemingly totally unafraid, as the enormous blast of destructive power was suddenly unleashed directly at him.

There was a mighty flash and a crackling, booming noise as of thunder unleashed directly overhead. The air was filled with the burnt-metal reek of ozone. Felix was vaguely aware that two bolts of energy had leapt from the grey seer's paws. One was aimed at him. One was aimed at Gotrek. He closed his eyes, fully expecting to die.

Instead of the anticipated blast of incredible pain, he felt nothing except a mild tingling on his flesh and his hair starting to stand on end. He opened his eyes and saw that both he and the Trollslayer were enveloped in a golden field of energy. Long golden lines raced from the aura that surrounded them back to the hands of Doctor Drexler. Felix could see the look of strain on the doctor's face. Grateful as he was to the physician for saving them, he knew that the doctor could not long stand against the storm of magical power which surrounded them.

'Is that the best you can do?' Gotrek bellowed. 'Rat-man, your life is over!'

The Slayer charged through the corona of coruscating energy. Felix charged right beside him.

No! No! Grey Seer Thanquol thought in panic as he saw his two enemies racing towards him. This was not happening! How could this be? How could this abominable pair appear to thwart him in his hour of triumph? What evil deity protected them, and kept them alive to interfere in his plans time after time? He bared his lips in a snarl and continued to unleash his destructive energies against the swirling golden shield which stood between the pair and destruction. He could feel it start to give way under the relentless pressure of his magical energies.

Unfortunately it was not giving way quickly enough. At the rate the human and the dwarf were closing the distance between them, they would reach Thanquol before he could shred their flesh from their bones. He snarled a curse, and reined in his spell, knowing that something other than magic was needed now.

'Quick! Quick!' he ordered his stormvermin. 'Kill them! Now! Now!'

With visible reluctance, the stormvermin moved to the attack. They had heard of this pair. Tales of the destruction they had wreaked among skaven were legend among the army assaulting Nuln. Their very presence was demoralising to Thanquol's troops. The way the dwarf decapitated the experienced clawleader as if he were a mere puppy did nothing to reassure the skaven. Nor did the vast howling tide of angry humans flowing into the ballroom. Thanquol sensed that the morale of his force was mere moments from breaking.

Swiftly he weighed the odds of victory, and saw that his moment had passed, and that triumph had slipped through his talons. Now it was a case of measuring his chances of survival. If he left now, while his troops still slowed down the pursuit, Thanquol realised he might reach the privy. Once there he could use the scrying stone to create a gate back to the sewers. Of course, now with his power at a low ebb, he would not have the strength to hold it open for all his warriors. In fact, he doubted that more than one solitary skaven would escape through it.

Still, he knew the genius of Thanquol must be preserved. On another day, he would return and take his revenge.

'Forward, my brave stormvermin, to inevitable victory!' Thanquol shouted, before he turned tail and ran with all his might. He did not need his grey seer's intuition to tell him that the slaughter behind him was going to be one-sided and merciless.

EPILOGUE

'So it was that the skaven were driven forth from the city, although at great, terrible cost in lives and damage to property. I had thought to rest and catch my breath after our exertions but it was not to be. The hand of doom reached out for my companion. And so began a journey that was to end at the furthest and most gods-forsaken reaches of the world...'

— From *My Travels With Gotrek, Vol. III*, by Herr Felix Jaeger
(Altdorf Press, 2505)

Felix sat in his favourite chair in the Blind Pig and finished inscribing the notes in his journal. He would leave this book in storage with Otto until such a time as he returned to claim it. If ever he did get round to writing the tale of the Trollslayer's heroic doom, it might prove invaluable.

From outside he could hear the sound of hammers. The builders had been at work for weeks now, trying to restore the battle-scarred city to its former glory. Felix knew that it would be many years before Nuln recovered fully, if it ever did. Still, he was not hugely troubled. Things had ended well, more or less.

The countess had been grateful, but there was not much she could do to reward two criminals wanted by the authorities in Altdorf without antagonising the Emperor himself. There had been many protestations of gratitude and sweet smiles of thanks, but nothing more. Felix did not care. He was just glad to have avoided being thrown into prison, just as he was glad to have survived the night of conflict which had followed the storming of the palace.

He still shivered to think of the savage battles which had been fought in the streets between man and skaven. It had taken all night and most of the rest of the following day to clear the city, and even after it was done most people had remained awake the following night, not quite able to believe they were safe. It had taken many more days of hunting afterwards to winkle the skaven out of all their hiding places, and he was still not sure that the sewers were entirely free of them.

On the other hand, the plague had abated. Perhaps the great fire had cleansed the city – or maybe it had simply claimed all the lives it was capable of taking. Drexler claimed that this was often the way with plagues. It had vanished now. No more deaths were reported. No more people had been stricken.

And for a wonder, the great plague of rats had ended too. For days, more and more of them had appeared but they seemed weaker, and bore the stigma of mutations, as if something had gone wrong with them before even they were born. Many of the later generations had been still-born. It was as if they had been created with some deliberate flaw by the skaven. Perhaps they had been intended to scourge the city and then die out, leaving the skaven free to claim everything. It was an idea of such devilish cunning that it made Felix shiver. Were the rat-men really capable of such a thing? Or had it all been merely an accident?

Somewhere in the distance, temple bells rang. Of course, the priests were claiming that their particular gods had intervened to save Nuln. Such was their way. Felix had seen precious little evidence that the immortal ones had acted to preserve Nuln at all, but who was he to say? Perhaps they had been there, invisibly shielding the folk, as Drexler claimed. Certainly Felix thought that Gotrek and himself had been very lucky, and perhaps that was the favour of the gods.

The gods had spared others. Otto and his wife were safe, prospering even. As his brother had predicted, there was a great demand for all manner of stuff for use in the reconstruction and Jaegers of Altdorf were helping provide it.

Drexler had recovered almost fully from his sorcerous battle with the grey seer. Felix had been to see him several times since the fateful night, and the man looked as calm and cheerful as ever. One time, he had even encountered Ostwald at the doctor's townhouse. The spymaster had treated Felix with a deference close to hero worship, which Felix had found embarrassing.

Heinz and most of the mercenaries were well. The old innkeeper had taken a nasty knock on the head, and his head was swathed in so many bandages that he looked like an Arabyan, but he was still there behind the bar, pulling pints.

Felix had no idea where Elissa was. He had not seen her or Hans since the day before the battle, and no one he knew had any knowledge of her whereabouts. He sincerely hoped she was well and had escaped back to her home village. He still missed her.

They never found the skaven grey seer, despite searching the palace from top to bottom. All that the court magicians had found were some strange magical resonances in the privy. It was assumed that Thanquol had used magic to effect his escape.

For the most part, the citizens were happy. They had survived and were rebuilding. In any case life went on as usual and Felix was looking forward to a nice long rest.

Having avoided meeting his heroic doom yet again, Gotrek had stomped around like a bear with a sore head in the days after the fighting finished before consoling himself with a three day long binge of boozing and brawling. Now he sat in the corner of the Blind Pig, nursing his hangover and bellowing for ale.

The saloon doors swung open and another dwarf came in. He was shorter than Gotrek and lighter in build. A circlet of bright red cloth was wrapped round his head and his beard was clipped short. The tunic he wore was divided into red and yellow squares of ungodly brightness. The newcomer looked around and his eyes widened when he saw Gotrek. He strode across to the Slayer with a purposeful step. Felix closed his journal, put down his pen and watched with interest.

'You are Gotrek, son of Gurni, a Slayer?' the newcomer said, speaking in Reikspiel as dwarfs often did when humans were listening. Felix knew they liked no one to hear their secret tongue.

'What if I am?' Gotrek said in his most brutish and surly fashion. 'Want to make something of it?'

'I am Nor Norrison, a bonded messenger to the clans. I have a message for you of great importance. I have come a thousand leagues to deliver it.'

'Well, get on with it then! I don't have all day,' Gotrek grumbled impatiently.

'It is not a verbal message. It is written in runescript. You can read, can't you?'

'About as well as I can punch out the teeth of messengers who cheek me.'

The messenger produced a parchment envelope with a great flourish. Gotrek took it and tore it open. He started to read – and as he did so all the colour left his face. His beard bristled and his eyes went wide.

'What is it?' Felix asked.

'A mighty doom, manling. A mighty doom indeed.' He rose from his chair and reached for his axe. 'Get your gear. We're leaving.'

'For where?'

'The ends of the earth, most likely,' Gotrek said, and could be prevailed upon to say nothing more.

DAEMONSLAYER

'After the dire events in Nuln, we travelled northwards, for the most part following back roads, lest the Emperor's roadwardens come upon us. The arrival of the dwarf-borne letter had filled my companion with a strange anticipation. He seemed almost happy as we made our weary way to our goal. Neither all the long weeks of journeying, nor the threat of bandits or mutants or beastmen ever served to daunt him. He would barely stop for meat or, more unusually, drink, and would answer my questions only with muttered references to destiny, doom and old debts.

'For myself, I was filled with anxiety and recrimination. I wondered what had happened to Elissa and I was saddened by my parting with my brother. Little did I guess how long it would be before I would meet him again, and under what strange circumstances. And little, too, did I guess how far the journey which began in Nuln was to take us, and how dreadful our eventual destination was to be.'

— From *My Travels With Gotrek, Vol. III*, by Herr Felix Jaeger
(Altdorf Press, 2505)

ONE
THE MESSAGE

'You spilled my beer,' Gotrek Gurnisson said.

If the man who had just knocked over the flagon possessed any sense, Felix Jaeger thought, the menacing tone of the dwarf's flat gravelly voice would have caused him to back off immediately. But the mercenary was drunk, he had half a dozen rough-looking mates back at his table and a giggling tavern girl to impress. He was not going to back down from anybody who only came up to his shoulders, even if that person was nearly twice as broad as he.

'So? What are you going to do about it, stuntie?' the mercenary replied with a sneer.

The dwarf eyed the spreading puddle of ale on the table for a moment with a mixture of regret and annoyance. Then he turned in his seat to look at the mercenary and ran his hand through the huge crest of red-dyed hair which towered over his shaven and tattooed head. The gold chain that ran from his nose to his ear jingled. With the elaborate care of one very drunk, Gotrek rubbed the patch covering his left eye socket, interlocked his fingers, cracked his knuckles – then suddenly lashed out with his right hand.

It wasn't the best punch Felix had ever seen Gotrek throw. In truth, it was clumsy and unscientific. Still, the Trollslayer's fist was as large as a ham, and the arm that fist was attached to was as thick as a tree-trunk. Whatever it hit was going to suffer. There was a sickening crack as the man's nose broke. The mercenary went flying back towards his own table. He sprawled unconscious on the sawdust covered floor. Red blood gushed from his nostrils.

On considered reflection, Felix decided through his own drunken haze, as punches went it had certainly served its purpose. Given the amount of ale the Slayer had consumed it had been pretty good, in fact.

'Anybody else want a taste of fist?' Gotrek inquired, giving the mercenary's half-dozen comrades an evil glare. 'Or are you all as soft as you look?'

The soldier's comrades rose from their benches, spilling foaming ale onto the table and tavern wenches from their knees. Not waiting for them to come at him, the Slayer swayed to his feet and bounded towards them. He grabbed the nearest mercenary by the throat, pulled his head forward and head-butted him. The man went down like a pole-axed ox.

Felix took another sip of the inn's sour Tilean wine to aid his reflections. He was already several goblets south of sober, but so what? It had been a long, hard trek all the way here to Guntersbad. They had been moving constantly ever since Gotrek had received the mysterious letter summoning them to this tavern. For a moment, Felix considered reaching into the Slayer's pack and examining it again but he already knew that it would be a useless effort. The message had been penned in the strange runes favoured by dwarfs. By the standards of the Empire, Felix was a well-educated man but there was no way he could read that alien language. Foiled by his own ignorance, Felix stretched his long legs, yawned and gave his attention back to the brawl.

It had been brewing all night. Ever since they had entered the Dog and Donkey, the local hard boys had been staring at them. They had started by making nasty remarks about the Slayer's appearance. For once, Gotrek had paid not the slightest attention, which was very unusual. Usually he was as touchy as a penniless Tilean duke and as short-tempered as a wolverine with toothache. Since receiving the message, however, he had become withdrawn, oblivious to anything but his own excitement. All he had done all evening was watch the door as if expecting somebody he knew to arrive.

At first Felix had been quite worried by the prospect of a brawl but several flagons of the Tilean red had soon helped settle his nerves. He had doubted that anybody would be stupid enough to pick a fight with the Trollslayer. He had reckoned without the sheer native ignorance of the locals. After all, this was a small town on the road to

Talabheim. How could they be expected to know what Gotrek was?

Even Felix, who had studied at the University of Altdorf, had never heard of the dwarfs' Cult of Slayers until the long-ago night when Gotrek had pulled him from under the hooves of the Emperor's elite cavalry during the Window Tax riots back in Altdorf. On the mad drunken spree which followed, he had discovered that Gotrek was sworn to seek death in combat with the fiercest of monsters to atone for some past crime. Felix had been so impressed by the Slayer's tale – and to tell the truth, so drunk – that he had sworn to accompany the dwarf and record his doom in an epic poem. The fact that Gotrek had not yet found his doom, despite some heroic efforts, had done nothing to reduce Felix's respect for his toughness.

Gotrek slammed a fist into another man's stomach. His opponent doubled over as the air whooshed out of his lungs. Gotrek took him by the hair and slammed his jaw down hard onto the table edge. Noticing that the mercenary still moved, the Slayer repeatedly banged his groaning victim's head on the table edge until he lay still, looking strangely rested, in a pool of blood, spittle, beer and broken teeth.

Two big burly warriors threw themselves forward, grabbing the Slayer by an arm each. Gotrek braced himself, roaring defiance, and hurled one of them to the ground. While he was down there, the Slayer planted his heavy boot into the man's groin. A high-pitched wailing shriek filled the tavern. Felix winced.

Gotrek turned his attention to the other warrior and they grappled. Slowly, even though the man was more than half-again Gotrek's height, the dwarf's enormous strength began to tell. He pushed his opponent onto the ground, straddled his chest, and then slowly and methodically punched his head until he was unconscious. The last mercenary scuttled for the door – but as he did so he slammed into another dwarf. The newcomer took a step back, then dropped him with one well-aimed punch.

Felix did a double-take, at first convinced he was hallucinating. It seemed unlikely that there could be another Slayer in this part of the world. But Gotrek was now looking at the stranger as well.

The recent arrival was, if anything, bigger and more muscular than Gotrek. His head was shaved and his beard cropped short. He had no crest of hair; instead it looked for all the world like nails had been driven into his skull to make a crest and then painted in different colours. His nose had been broken so many times it was shapeless. One ear was cauliflowered; the other had actually been ripped clean away, leaving only a hole in the side of his head. A huge ring was set in his nose. Where his body was not criss-crossed with scars it was covered in tattoos. In one hand he held an enormous hammer and thrust in his belt was a short-hafted, broad-bladed axe.

Behind this new Slayer stood another dwarf, shorter, fatter and altogether more civilised looking. He was about half Felix's height, but very broad. His well-groomed beard reached almost to the ground. His wide eyes blinked owlishly from behind enormously thick glasses. In his ink-stained fingers he carried a large brass-bound book.

'Snorri Nosebiter, as I live and breathe!' Gotrek roared, his nasty smile revealing missing teeth. 'It's been awhile! What are you doing here?'

'Snorri's here for the same reason as you, Gotrek Gurnisson. Snorri got a letter from old Borek the Scholar, telling Snorri to come to the Lonely Tower.'

'Don't try and fool me. I know you can't read, Snorri. All the words were bashed out of your head when those nails were bashed in.'

'Hogan Longbeard translated it for Snorri,' Snorri said, looking as embarrassed as it was possible for such a hulking Trollslayer to look. He glanced around him, obviously wanting to change the subject.

'Snorri thinks he missed a good fight,' the dwarf said, eyeing the scene of terrible violence with the same sort of wistful regret that Gotrek had expended on his spilled ale. 'Snorri thinks he'd better have a beer then. Snorri has a bit of a thirst!'

'Ten beers for Snorri Nosebiter!' Gotrek roared. 'And better make that ten for me as well. Snorri hates to drink alone.'

An appalled silence filled the room. The other patrons looked at the scene of the battle then at the two dwarfs as if they were kegs of gunpowder with a burning fuse. Slowly, in ones and twos, they got up and left, until only Gotrek, Felix, Snorri and the other dwarf were left.

'First to ten?' Snorri enquired, knuckling his eye and looking up at Gotrek cunningly.

'First to ten,' Gotrek agreed.

The other dwarf waddled towards them and bowed, politely in the dwarfish fashion, raising his beard with one hand to keep it from dragging on the ground as he leaned forward.

'Varek Varigsson of the Clan Grimnar at your service,' he said in a mild, pleasant voice. 'I see you got my uncle's message.'

Snorri and Gotrek looked at him, seemingly astonished by his politeness, then began to laugh. Varek flushed with embarrassment.

'Better get this youth a beer as well!' Gotrek shouted. 'He looks like he could use being loosened up a little. Now stand aside, youngling, Snorri and I have a bet to settle.'

The landlord smiled ingratiatingly. A look of relief passed over his face. It looked like the dwarfs were set on more than making up for all the custom they had driven away.

The landlord lined the beers up along the low counter. Ten sat in front of Gotrek, ten in front of Snorri. The dwarfs inspected them the way a man might inspect an opponent before a wrestling match. Snorri looked over at Gotrek, then looked back at the beer again. A swift lunge brought him within range of his chosen target. He grabbed the flagon, lifted it to his lips, tilted back his head and swallowed. Gotrek was a fraction slower to the draw. His jack of ale reached his lips a second after Snorri's. There was a long silence, broken only by the sound of dwarfs glugging, then Snorri slammed his flagon back on the table a fraction of a second before Gotrek slammed his. Felix looked over in astonishment. Both flagons had been drained to the last drop.

'First one's easiest,' Gotrek said. Snorri seized another flagon, grabbed a second with his other hand and repeated the performance. Gotrek did the same. He snatched up one in each hand, raised one to his lips, drained it, then drained the other. This time it was Gotrek who put down his beers fractionally before Snorri. Felix was staggered, particularly when he considered how much beer Gotrek had already drunk before Snorri had arrived. It looked like the two Slayers were entering into a well practiced ritual. Felix wondered if they really intended to drink all that beer.

'I'm embarrassed to be seen drinking with you, Snorri. A girly elf could do three in time it took you to down those,' Gotrek said.

Snorri gave him a disgusted look, reached for another ale and tipped it back so fast that suds erupted from his mouth and frothed over his beard. He wiped his mouth with the back of one tattooed forearm. This time he finished before Gotrek.

'At least all my beer went in my mouth,' Gotrek said, nodding his head until his nose chain jingled.

'Are you talking or drinking?' Snorri challenged.

Five, six, seven beers went down in quick succession. Gotrek looked at the ceiling, smacked his lips and let out an enormous cavernous belch. Snorri swiftly echoed it. Felix exchanged glances with Varek. The scholarly young dwarf looked back at him and shrugged his shoulders. In less than a minute the two Slayers had put back more beer than Felix would normally drink in one night. Gotrek blinked and his eyes looked slightly glassy, but this was the only sign he gave of the enormous amount of alcohol he had just consumed. Snorri looked not the slightest worse for wear, but then he had not been drinking all night already.

Gotrek reached out and downed number eight, but by that time Snorri was already half way through number nine. As he set down the flagon, he said, 'Looks like you'll be paying for the beer.'

Gotrek didn't answer. He picked up two flagons at once, one in each hand, tilted back his head, opened his gullet and poured. There was no sound of gulping. He was not swallowing, just letting the beer run straight down his throat. Snorri was so impressed by the feat that he forgot to pick up his own last pint before Gotrek had finished.

Gotrek stood there swaying slightly. He belched, hiccuped and sat down on his stool.

'The day you can out-drink me, Snorri Nosebiter, is the day Hell freezes over.'

'That will be the day after the day you pay for a beer, Gotrek Gurnisson,' Snorri said, sitting down beside his fellow Trollslayer.

'Well, so much for starters,' he continued. 'Let's get down to some serious drinking then. Looks like Snorri has some catching up to do.'

'Is that proper Worlds Edge tabac you have there, Snorri?' Gotrek asked, looking hungrily at the stuff Snorri was tamping into his pipe. They had all settled down by the roaring fire in the best seats in the house.

'Aye, 'tis old Mouldy Leaf. Snorri picked it up in the mountains afore coming here.'

'Give some here!'

Snorri tossed the pouch over to Gotrek, who produced a pipe and started filling it. The Slayer glared over at the scholarly young dwarf with his one good eye.

'So, youth,' Gotrek growled 'What is the mighty doom your Uncle Borek has promised me? And why is old Snorri here?'

Felix leaned forward interestedly. He wanted to know more about this himself. He was intrigued by the thought of a summons which could excite even the normally morose and taciturn Slayer.

Varek looked at Felix warningly. Gotrek shook his head and took a sip of beer. He leaned forward, lighted a spill of wood in the fire then lit his pipe. Once the pipe was burning well, he leaned back in his chair and spoke earnestly.

'Anything you want to say to me, you can say in front of the manling. He is a Dwarf Friend and an Oathkeeper.'

Snorri looked up at Felix. Surprise and something like respect showed in his dull, brutish eyes. Varek's smile showed sincere interest and he turned to Felix and bowed once more, almost falling out of his chair.

'I'm sure there is a tale there,' he said. 'I'd be most interested in hearing it.'

'Don't try and change the subject,' Gotrek said. 'What is this doom your kinsman has promised me? His letter dragged me halfway across the Empire and I want to hear about it.'

'I wasn't trying to change the subject, Herr Gurnisson. I simply wanted to get the information for my book.'

'There will be time enough for that later. Now speak!'

Varek sighed, leaned back in his chair and steepled his fingers over his ample stomach. 'I can tell you little enough. My uncle has all the facts and will share them with you in his own time and fashion. What I can tell you is this is possibly the mightiest quest since the time of Sigmar Hammerbearer – and it concerns Karag Dum.'

'The Lost Dwarfhold of the North!' Gotrek roared drunkenly, then suddenly fell silent. He looked around, as if fearing that spies might have overheard him.

'The very same!'

'Then your uncle has found a way to get there! I thought he was mad when he claimed he would.' Felix had never heard such an undercurrent of excitement in the dwarf's voice. It was contagious. Gotrek looked over at Felix.

It was Snorri who interrupted. 'Call Snorri stupid if you like, but even Snorri knows Karag Dum was lost in the Chaos Wastes.' He looked directly at Gotrek and shivered. 'Remember the last time!'

'Be that as it may, my uncle has found a way of getting there.'

A sudden trepidation filled Felix. Finding the location of the place was one thing. Having a method of getting there was another. It meant that this wasn't simply a fascinating academic exercise but a possible journey. He had a terrible sinking feeling that he knew where all this was going to end up, and he knew that he wanted no part of it.

'There is no way across the Wastes,' Gotrek said. Something more than mere caution was in his voice. 'I have been there. So has Snorri. So has your uncle. It is insanity to attempt to cross them. Madness and mutation wait for those who would go there. Hell has touched the world in that accursed place.'

Felix looked at Gotrek with new respect. Few people had ever travelled so far and returned to tell the tale. To him, as to all folk of the Empire, the Chaos Wastes were but a dire rumour, a hellish land in the far north, from which the terrible armies of the four Ruinous Powers of Chaos emerged to reave and plunder and slay. He had never heard the dwarf speak of having been there, but then he knew little of the Slayer's adventures in the days before they had met. Gotrek did not speak of his past. He seemed ashamed of it. If anything, the dwarf's obvious fear made the place seem even more daunting. There was little enough in this world which dismayed the Slayer, as Felix well knew, so anything that did was to be feared indeed.

'Nonetheless, I believe that is where my uncle wants to go, and he wants you to with him. He has need of your axe.'

Gotrek fell silent for long moments. ''Tis certainly a deed worthy of a Slayer.'

It sounds like absolute madness, Felix thought. Somehow he managed to keep his mouth shut.

'Snorri thinks so too.'

Then Snorri is an even bigger idiot than he appears to be, thought Felix, and the words almost burst forth from his lips.

'Then you will accompany me to the Lonely Tower?' Varek asked.

'For the prospect of such a doom, I would follow you to the mouth of Hell,' Gotrek said.

That's good, Felix thought, because it sounds like that's exactly where you're going. Then he shook his head. The dwarf's madness was beginning to infect him. Was he actually taking all this talk of journeys to the Chaos Wastes seriously? Surely this was just tavern talk and the fit of madness would pass by morning…

'Excellent,' Varek said. 'I knew you'd come.'

TWO
MARK OF THE SKAVEN

The bouncing of the wagon did nothing for Felix's hangover. Every time a wheel hit one of the deep ruts in the road, his stomach gave a troubled lurch and threatened to send its contents arcing out onto the roadside hedges. The inside of his mouth felt furry. Pressure was building up inside his skull like steam within a kettle. Oddest of all, now he had a terrible craving for fried food. Visions of fried eggs and bacon sizzled through his mind. Now he regretted not having taken breakfast earlier with the Trollslayers, but at the time the sight of them throwing back piled plates of ham and egg and chomping on great hunks of black bread had been enough to turn his stomach. But now he was almost prepared to commit murder for the same food.

It was some consolation to him that the Slayers were more or less silent, save for grumbles in dwarfish which he assumed concerned the awfulness of their hangovers or just how plain dreadful human beer was. Only young Varek seemed cheerful and bright-eyed, but then he ought to. Much to the disgust of the other two, he had stopped drinking after three ales, claiming that he had had enough. Now he guided the mules with sure tugs of the reins and whistled a happy tune, oblivious to the dagger-like looks his companions aimed at his back. At that moment, Felix hated him with a passion which could be explained only by the intensity of his hangover.

To distract himself from that, and from thoughts of the awful adventure that was surely to come, Felix gave his attention to their surroundings. It was indeed a beautiful day. The sun was shining brightly. This part of the Empire looked particularly productive and cheerful. Huge half-timbered houses rose from the surrounding hill-tops. Thatch-roofed cottages, the homes of the peasant labourers, surrounded them. Big splotch-sided cows grazed in enclosures, bells tinkling cheerfully on their necks. Each bell had a different tone, which Felix deduced was to enable the herdsmen to track each individual cow by sound alone.

Alongside them a peasant drove a gaggle of geese along the dusty track for a while. Later, a pretty peasant girl looked up from the hay she was forking into a stack and gave Felix a dazzling smile. He tried to muster the energy to smile back but couldn't. He felt like he was a hundred years old. He kept his eyes on her until she disappeared around a bend in the road though.

The wagon hit another rut and bounced higher.

'Watch where you're going!' Gotrek growled. 'Can't you see Snorri Nosebiter has a hangover?'

'Snorri doesn't feel too good,' the other Slayer confirmed and gave an awful muffled gurgle. 'It must have been that goat and potato stew we had last night. Snorri thinks it tasted a bit off.'

More likely it was the thirty or so jacks of ale you threw back, Felix thought sourly. He almost said this out loud, but even through the misery of his hangover a certain prudent caution stopped him. He had no wish to be cured of his hangover by having his head chopped off. Well, maybe, he thought, as the wagon and his stomach gave another lurch.

Felix gave his attention back to the hard-packed stony earth of the road that jarred and juddered along beneath them, trying to focus his mind on anything except the awful churning in his stomach. He could see the individual rocks jutting out of the ground, any one of which looked like it could break the wagon's wooden wheels if hit at the wrong angle.

A fly landed softly, ticklingly, on the back of his hand and he swatted at it miserably. It eluded the blow with contemptuous ease and proceeded to buzz around Felix's head. His initial effort had exhausted him and Felix gave up the attempt to strike the insect, only shaking his head when it came too close to his eyes. He closed his eyes and focused his willpower on the creature, urging it to die, but it refused to oblige. There were occasionally times when Felix wished that he was a sorcerer and this was one of them. He bet that they didn't have to put up with hangovers and the disturbances created by fat-bodied buzzing flies.

Suddenly it got darker and slightly cooler on his face, and he looked up to see that they were passing through a copse of trees which had overgrown the road. He glanced around quickly – more from habit than fear – because these were the sort of woods that bandits liked to frequent, and bandits were not uncommon in the Empire. He wasn't sure what sort of fools would attack a wagon which contained two hungover Trollslayers, but you could never tell. Stranger things had happened to him on his travels. Maybe those mercenaries from the night before would come back seeking revenge. And there were always beastmen and mutants to be found in these dark times. In his time Felix had encountered enough of them to be something of an expert on that subject.

To tell the truth, Felix thought, he would almost welcome taking an axe blow from a beastman the way he felt right now. At least it would put him out of his misery. It was strange, though, how his eyes were playing tricks. He was almost sure he could see something small and pink-eyed skulking amongst the undergrowth a little way back from the track. It was only there for a second and then it was gone. Felix almost called Gotrek's attention to it but decided against doing so, because interrupting the Slayer's recovery from a hangover was never a good idea.

And it really probably was nothing after all, just some small furry animal scuttling for safety as travellers moved by on the road. Still, there was something familiar about the shape of the head that nagged at Felix's numb brain. He couldn't quite place it just yet but if he thought about it long enough he was sure it would come back to him. Another great lurch by the cart almost threw him off. He fought to keep last night's goat and potato stew within his stomach. It was a long fight and he only won it when the stew had battled halfway up his throat.

'Where are we heading?' he asked Varek to distract himself from his misery. Not for the first time he swore that he would never touch another drop of beer. It sometimes seemed that most of the troubles in his life had somehow begun in taverns. It was amazing, really, that he had not had the sense to realise this before.

'The Lonely Tower,' Varek said cheerfully. Felix fought down the urge to punch him, more because he couldn't summon the energy to do it, than from any other reason.

'Sounds… interesting,' Felix managed to say eventually. What it really sounded was ominous, like so many other places he had visited in his sorry career as the Slayer's henchman. Any place called the

Lonely Tower to be found anywhere in the Empire was most likely to be the sort of place no one in their right mind would visit. Fortifications in the middle of nowhere had a habit of being overwhelmed by orcs, goblins and other worse things.

'Oh, it's an interesting place all right. Built on top of an old coal mine. Uncle Borek took it over and renovated it. Good sound dwarfish workmanship. Looks like new. Better in fact, because the original work, human, – no offence – was a bit slipshod. It was abandoned for several hundred years till we came along, except for the skaven. Of course, we had to clear them out first, and there might still be a few lurking down in the mine.'

'Good,' Gotrek grunted. 'Can't beat a spot of skaven-slaughtering for sport. Clears up a hangover better than pint of Bugman's.'

Personally Felix could think of dozens more appealing ways of spending the time than hunting for vicious rat-like monsters in an abandoned and doubtless unsafe mine but he did not communicate this information to Gotrek.

Varek looked back over his shoulder to where his passengers huddled alongside their gear. They must have made a pitiful sight, for Snorri wasn't any better equipped than Gotrek or Felix. His pack was as empty as a sailor's purse after a spree in port. He didn't appear to own a cloak or even a blanket. Felix was glad that he had his red Sudenland wool cloak to huddle under. He did not doubt that the nights would get pretty cold. He did not look forward to the prospect of a night on cold ground.

'How long till we get there?' he asked.

'We're making good time. If we take the short path through the Bone Hills, we'll be there in two, three days at most.'

'I've heard bad things about the Bone Hills,' Felix said. It was true. Then again, there were few places beyond the cities and towns of the Empire that he had not heard bad things about. At once Gotrek and Snorri looked up, interest written all over their faces. It never ceased to amaze Felix that the worse things sounded, the happier a Slayer looked.

'The skaven from the mine used to haunt them, and attack travellers. They'd come down and raid the farms as well. Nothing to worry about now though. We've seen them off,' Varek said. 'Snorri and I came all the way down here in the cart by ourselves, never sniffed a hint of trouble.'

The two Slayers slumped back into apathetic contemplation of their hangovers. Somehow Felix was not reassured. In his experience, trips through the wilderness never went smoothly. And something about the mere mention of skaven caused that rat-like shape he had noticed back in the wood to begin niggling worryingly at the back of his mind.

'You came all the way here yourselves?' Felix asked.

'Snorri was with me.'

'Are you armed?' Felix asked, making sure that his own longsword was within easy reach.

'I have my knife.'

'You have your knife! Oh good! I'm sure that will be very useful if skaven attack you.'

'Never saw any skaven. Just heard a little scuttling some nights. Whatever it was, I think Snorri's snoring scared it away. Anyway, if something attacked I have my bombs.'

'Bombs?'

Varek fumbled inside his robe and produced a smooth black sphere. A strange metal device appeared to have been glued to the top. He handed it to Felix who inspected it closely. It looked like if you pulled the clip on top, it would come free.

'Be careful with that,' Varek said. 'It's a detonator. You pull that, it tugs the flint striker which lights the fuse which sets off the explosive. You've got about four heartbeats to throw it, then – boom!'

Felix looked at it warily, half-expecting the thing to explode in his hand.

'Boom?'

'It explodes. Shrapnel everywhere. That's assuming the fuse fires. It sometimes doesn't. About half the time, actually, but it's very ingenious. And of course, very, very occasionally they go off for no reason at all. Almost never happens. Mind you, Blorri lost a hand that way. Had to have it replaced with a hook.'

Felix swiftly handed the bomb back to Varek who tucked it back inside the pocket of his robes. He was beginning to think this mild-mannered young dwarf was crazier than he looked. Perhaps all dwarfs were.

'Makaisson made it, you know. He's good at that sort of thing.'

'Makaisson. Malakai Makaisson?' Gotrek asked. 'That maniac!'

Felix looked at the Slayer in open-mouthed astonishment. He wasn't sure he wanted to meet this Makaisson. Anyone who Gotrek could describe as a maniac must be crazed indeed. Could probably win prizes for their madness, in fact. Gotrek caught Felix's look.

'Makaisson believes in heavier-than-air flight. Thinks he can make things fly.'

'Gyrocopters fly,' Snorri piped in. 'Snorri been up in one. Fell out. Landed on head. No damage.'

'Not gyrocopters. Big things! And he builds ships! Ships! That's an unnatural interest for a dwarf. I hate ships almost as much as I hate elves!'

'He built the biggest steamship ever,' Varek said conversationally. 'The *Unsinkable*. Was two hundred paces long. Weighed five hundred tons. It had steam-powered gatling turrets. It had a crew of over three hundred dwarfs and thirty engineers. It could sail at three leagues an hour. Such an impressive sight it was, with its paddles churning the sea to foam and its pennons flying in the breeze.'

It certainly sounded impressive, Felix thought, suddenly realising how far the dwarfs had taken this strange magic they called 'engineering'. Like everybody else in the Empire, Felix knew about steam tanks, the armoured vehicles which were the spearhead of the realm's mighty armies. This thing sounded like it made the steam tank look like a child's toy. Still, if it was so impressive, he wondered, why had he never heard of it?

'What happened to the *Unsinkable*? Where is it now?'

There was a brief embarrassed silence from the dwarfs.

'Err… it sank,' Varek said eventually.

'Hit a rock on its first trip out,' Snorri added.

'Some people claim the boiler exploded,' Varek said.

'Lost with all hands,' Snorri added with the almost happy expression with which dwarfs always seemed to confront the worst news.

'Except Makaisson. He was picked up later by human ship. He was thrown clear by the explosion and clung to a wooden spar.'

'Then he built a flying ship,' Gotrek said, savage irony evident in his voice.

'That's right. Makaisson built a flying ship,' Snorri said.

'The *Indestructible*,' Varek said.

Felix tried to imagine a ship flying. In the abstract he could manage it. In his mind's eye, he saw something like the old river barges on the Reik, their sails filled, their sweeps tugging. It was powerful sorcery indeed that could do that.

'Amazing thing it was,' Varek said. 'Big as a sailing ship. Wrought iron cupola. Fuselage almost hundred paces long. It could fly at ten leagues an hour – with the wind behind it, of course.'

'What happened to it?' Felix asked, a sinking feeling hinting that he already knew the answer.

'It crashed,' Snorri said.

'Crosswinds and some liftgas leaks,' Varek said. 'Big explosion.'

'Killed everybody aboard.'

'Except Makaisson,' Varek said, as if this made a big difference. He seemed to think this was an important point. 'He was thrown clear and landed in some treetops. They broke his fall along with both his legs. Had to use crutches for the next two years. Anyway, the *Indestructible* had a few teething problems. What do you expect? It was the first of its kind. But Makaisson has sorted them now.'

'Teething problems?' Gotrek said. 'Twenty good dwarf engineers killed, including Under-Guildmaster Ulli and you call that "teething problems"? Makaisson should have shaved his head.'

'He did,' Varek said. 'After he was drummed out of the guild. He couldn't face the shame, you know. They did the Trouser Legs Ritual to him. Pity. My uncle says he's the best engineer who ever lived. He says Makaisson is a genius.'

'A genius at getting other dwarfs killed.'

Felix was thinking about what Gotrek had said about Makaisson shaving his head. 'Do you mean Makaisson became a Trollslayer?' he asked Varek.

'Yes. Of course. He still does engineering work though. Says he'll prove his theories work or die trying.'

'I'll bet he will,' Gotrek muttered darkly.

Felix wasn't listening. He was wrestling with another, far more troubling concept. Counting Gotrek and Snorri, that would make three Trollslayers in one place. What was Varek's uncle up to? A mission which required three Slayers didn't sound good. In fact, it sounded positively suicidal. Suddenly something that Varek had said earlier came sharply into focus in Felix's mind, cutting through even the awful fog of his hangover.

'You said earlier you heard scuttling,' Felix said, thinking of the small shape he had seen in the undergrowth. He was starting to have an awful suspicion about that. 'On your way to meet Gotrek and myself.'

Varek nodded. 'Only at night, when we made camp.'

'You've no idea what made the scuttling?'

'No. A fox, maybe.'

'Foxes don't scuttle.'

'A big rat.'

'A big rat...' Felix nodded his head. That was exactly what he hadn't wanted to hear. He looked over at Gotrek to see if the Slayer was thinking what he was thinking, but the dwarf had his head thrown back and was staring blankly into space. He appeared to be lost in his own thoughts and was paying not the slightest bit of attention to the conversation.

Rats made Felix think of only one thing, and that thing scared him. They made him think of skaven. Could it be possible that the foul rat-men had tracked him even here? It was not a comforting thought.

Felix sat beside the fire and listened to the tremulous whickering of the mules. The darkness and the occasional distant howls of the wolves made them nervous. Felix rose and ran his hand over the nearest one's flanks in an effort to calm it and then returned to the fire where the others were sleeping.

All day the track had risen into the Bone Hills, which had turned out to be as bleak and unprepossessing as their name suggested. There were no trees around them, only lichen covered rocks and sharp hills covered by short stunted grass. It was fortunate that Varek had thought to bring firewood with them or they would have spent an even more uncomfortable night camped out. It was cold in the hills, despite the summer heat of the day.

Supper had consisted of some bread bought at the inn back in Guntersbad and hunks of hard dwarf cheese. Afterwards, they had sat round the fire and all three dwarfs had lit their pipes. For entertainment they had the distant howling of the wolves. Felix found this marginally less depressing than dwarfish conversation which always seemed to rotate around ancient grudges, tales of misery long endured and epic drinking bouts. And horrifying as the howling was, it at least drowned out the sound of dwarfish snoring. Felix had drawn the short straw and won the dubious privilege of taking the first watch.

He tried not to stare into the fire and kept his eyes turned in the direction of the darkness so that he would not ruin his night vision. He was worried. He kept thinking about skaven and the thought of those ferocious Chaos-spawned rat-men appalled him. He remembered encountering them in the Battle of Nuln. It had been like a scene from a nightmare, battling in the dark with man-sized humanoid rats who walked upright and fought with weapons just as humans did. The memory of their hideous chittering language and the way their red eyes glittered in the darkness came back to him and made him shudder.

The most awful thing about the skaven was that they were organised in a hideous parody of human civilisation. They had their own culture, their own fiendish technologies. They had armies and sophisticated weapons that were in some ways more advanced than anything humanity had ever produced. Felix had seen them when they had erupted from the sewers to invade Nuln. He could still picture that monstrous horde rushing through the burning buildings, spearing anything that got in their way. Vividly he remembered the green flames of their warpfire throwers illuminating the night and the sizzle of human flesh as it was eaten away by the blazing jets.

The skaven were the implacable enemies of humanity, of all the civilised races, but there were those who sided with them for pay. Felix himself had killed their agent, Fritz von Halstadt, who had risen to become the chief of the Elector Countess Emmanuelle's secret police. He wondered how many other agents the rat-men had in high places. He did not want to think about it now in this lonely spot. He pushed thoughts of the skaven aside and tried to turn his mind to other things.

He let his thoughts drift back into the past. The howling reminded him of the terrible last nights of Fort von Diehl down in the Border Princes, where he watched his first great love Kirsten die, murdered by Manfred von Diehl, and seen most of the population slaughtered by goblin wolf riders let in by Manfred's treachery. It was strange, but he could still remember Kirsten's gaunt face and her soft voice. He wondered if there was anything he could have done to make things turn out differently. It was a thought that tormented him sometimes in the quiet watches of the night. It was an event that still caused him pain although of late he had felt it less often and knew that it was fading. He could even consider other women now. Back in Nuln, there had been the tavern girl, Elissa, but she had left in the end.

The picture of the smiling peasant girl in the field came back to him very vividly. He wondered what she was doing right now. He resigned himself to the fact that he would never even know her name, just as she would never know his. There were so many encounters in the world like that. Chances that never turned out right. Romances which died stillborn before ever they had a chance to live. He wondered whether he would ever meet another woman who touched him as much as Kirsten had.

So engrossed was he in these thoughts that it took some time for him to realise that he was hearing scuttling, the soft sounds of claws scrabbling on flinty rock. He kept himself low to the ground and then glanced around, carefully, suddenly fearing that at any moment he might feel the searing pain of a poisoned knife driven into his back. As he moved, however, the scuttling sounds stopped.

He kept still and held his breath for a long moment and it started again. There. The sound came from off to his right. As he watched, he could see the glitter of red eyes, and dark silhouettes creeping ever closer over the ridge top. He slid his sword from its scabbard. The magical blade which he had acquired from the dead Templar Aldred felt light in his hand. He was about to shout a warning to the others when an enormous howling battle-cry erupted. He recognised the voice as Gotrek's.

A strange musky scent that Felix had smelled before filled the air. The rat-like shapes turned and fled immediately. The Slayer dashed past into the darkness, the runes on his huge axe glowing in the night, swiftly followed by Snorri Nosebiter. Felix would have raced after them himself, but his human eyes could not see in the gloom like a dwarf's. He flinched as Varek moved up beside him, one of his sinister black bombs in his hands. The firelight reflected off the young dwarf's spectacles and turned his eyes into circles of fire.

They stood side by side for long tense moments, waiting to hear the sounds of battle, expecting to see the sudden rush of a horde of rat-men. The only sound they heard was the stomping of boots as Gotrek and Snorri returned.

'Skaven,' Gotrek spat contemptuously.

'They ran away,' Snorri said in a disappointed tone. Treating the event as if nothing untoward had happened, they returned to their places by the fire and cast themselves down to sleep. Felix envied them. He knew that even once his watch had ended, there would be no sleep for him this night.

Skaven, he thought, and shuddered.

THREE
THE LONELY TOWER

Felix looked down into the mouth of the long valley and was overcome with awe. From where he stood, he could see machines, hundreds of them. Enormous steam engines rose along the valley sides like monsters in riveted iron armour. The pistons of huge pumps went up and down with the regularity of a giant's heartbeat. Steam hissed from enormous rusting pipes which ran between massive red brick buildings. Huge chimneys belched vast clouds of sooty smoke into the air. The air echoed with the clanging of a hundred hammers. The infernal glow of forges illuminated the shadowy interior of workshops. Dozens of dwarfs moved backwards and forwards through the heat and noise and misty clouds.

For a second the fog cleared as the cold hill wind cut through the valley. Felix could see that one vast structure dominated the length of the dale. It was built from rusting, riveted metal with a corrugated iron roof. It was perhaps three hundred strides long and twenty high. At one end was a massive cast-iron tower, the like of which Felix had never seen before. It was constructed from metal girders, with an observation point and what looked like a monstrous lantern at its very tip.

High over the far end of the valley loomed a monstrous squat fortress. Moss clung to its eroded stonework. Felix could make out the gleaming muzzles of cannons high among the battlements. From the middle of the structure loomed a single stone tower. On the face nearest the roof was a massive clock, whose hands showed that it was almost the seventh hour after noon. On the roof, an equally gigantic telescope pointed towards the sky. Even as Felix watched, the hand reached seven o'clock and a bell tolled deafeningly, its echoes filling the valley with sound.

The eerie wail of what could only have been a steam whistle – Felix had heard something like it once at the College of Engineering in Nuln – filled the air. There was a chugging of pistons and the clatter of iron wheels on rails as a small steam-wagon emerged from the mine-head. It moved along iron tracks, carrying heaps and heaps of coal into some great central smelting works.

The noise was deafening. The smell was overwhelming. The sight was at once monstrous and fascinating, like looking at the innards of some vast and intricate clockwork toy. Felix felt like he was looking down upon a scene of strange sorcery of a kind which, if truly unleashed, might change the world. He had not realised what the dwarfs were capable of, what power their arcane knowledge gave them. He was filled with a wonder so strong that, for a moment, it overcame the fear which had been nagging at the back of his mind all day.

Then the thought came back to him, and he remembered the tracks he had seen this morning mingled with the hob-nailed boot prints of the Slayers. There could be no doubt that they belonged to skaven, quite a strong force at that. Felix knew that fearsome as the Slayers were, the rat-men had not fled out of terror. They had retreated because they had other things to do, and getting into a fight with his companions might have slowed them down in the performance of that mission. It was the only possible explanation for why so strong a party of skaven had fled from so few.

Looking at this place now, he understood what the probable objective of the skaven force was. Here was a thing which the followers of the Horned Rat would want to capture – or destroy. Felix had no idea what was taking place down in that valley but he was certain that it was important, because so much industry, energy and intelligence were being expended, and Felix knew that dwarfs did nothing without a purpose.

Once more, though, he felt his heart start to race. Here was industry on a scale that he had not imagined possible. It had a sordid magnificence and implied a terrifying understanding of things beyond the knowledge of human civilisation. In that moment Felix understood just how much his people had yet to learn from the dwarfs. From beside him he heard a sharp intake of breath.

'If the Engineers Guild ever finds out about this,' Gotrek rumbled, 'heads will roll!'

'We'd better get down there and tell them about the skaven.' Felix replied.

Gotrek looked at him with something like pride showing in his one mad eye. 'What could those people down there have to fear from a bunch of scabby ratlings?'

Tempted as he was to agree, Felix kept quiet. He was sure that he could think of something, given long enough. After all, the skaven had given him plenty of reasons for terror in the past.

Somewhere off to their right something glinted, like a mirror catching a beam of sunlight. Felix wondered briefly what it was and then dismissed it from his mind as being some part of the wondrous technology he saw being deployed all around him.

'Let's go tell them anyway,' he said, wondering why the dwarfs had put something that glittered so brightly amongst a clump of bushes.

Grey Seer Thanquol peered down at the scene through the periscope. The device was yet another magnificent skaven invention, combining the best features of a telescope and a series of mirrors, thus allowing him to watch those unsuspecting fools below unobserved from within the cover of this clump of bushes. Only the lens at the mechanism's tip was visible and he doubted that the dwarfs would notice even that. They were so slow-witted and stupid.

Still, even the grey seer had to admit that there was something magnificent about what the dwarfs had built down there. He wasn't sure what it was but even he, in his secret ratty heart, was impressed. It was fascinating to look at, like one of the mazes he kept for humans back home in Skavenblight. There was so much going on that the eye did not quite know where to look. There was so much activity that he just knew that something important was happening down there – something that might well redound to his credit with the Council of Thirteen once he had seized it.

Yet again he congratulated himself on his foresight and his intelligence. How many other grey seers would have responded to the reports of a bunch of skavenslaves who had been driven out of the old coal mines beneath the Lonely Tower?

None of his rivals had paused to consider that there must be something important going on when the dwarfs sent an army to reclaim an old coal mine in these desolate hills. Of course, he had to admit, none of them had had the chance because Thanquol had executed most of the survivors before they had an opportunity to tell anybody else. After all, secrecy was one of the greatest weapons in the skaven arsenal and none knew this better than he. Was he not pre-eminent among grey seers, the feared and potent skaven magicians who ranked just below the Council of Thirteen themselves? And given time even that would change as well. Thanquol knew that it was his destiny to take his rightful place on one of the Council's ancient thrones some day.

As soon as he was certain the report was true he had journeyed here with his bodyguards. And as soon as he had seen the size of the dwarf encampment, he had sent a summons to the nearest skaven garrison, invoking the name of the Horned Rat and enjoining the strictest secrecy of its commander, on pain of a long, protracted and incredibly agonising death. Now the valley was all but surrounded by a mighty skaven force, and whatever it was that the dwarfs sought to protect would soon be his. This very night he would give the command that would send his invincible furry legions surging forward to inevitable victory.

A flicker of movement attracted Thanquol's attention for a moment, a flutter of red in the breeze which reminded him vaguely of something ominous he had seen in the past. He ignored it and tracked the periscope along the side of the hill, inspecting the potent dwarf-built engines. Greed and a lust to possess them filled him; ignorance of their purpose did nothing to discourage him. He knew that they simply must be worth having. Anything which could make so much noise and create so much smoke was in and of itself a thing to make any skaven's heart beat faster.

Something about that fluttering scrap of red nagged at his mind but he dismissed it. He began to draw up a plan of attack, studying all the lines of approach along the valley edges. He wished he could summon a huge cloud of poison wind and send it blowing down the valley, killing the dwarfs and leaving their machine intact. The simple beauty of the idea struck him. Perhaps he should sell it to the warp engineers of Clan Skryre the next time he was negotiating with them. Certainly a device which could pump out gas the way those chimneys pumped out smoke would...

Wait a moment! The strange familiarity of that flapping scarlet cloak sunk into his forebrain. He suddenly remembered where he'd seen its like before. He remembered a hated human who wore something very similar. But surely... it couldn't be possible that *he* was here.

Hastily Thanquol twisted the periscope on its collapsible frame. He heard a grunt of pain from the skavenslave to whose back it was strapped, but what did he care? The pain of a slave meant less to him than the fur he shed each morning.

With a flick of his paws he brought the lenses into focus on the source of his unease. For a shocked instant he fought down an almost overwhelming urge to squirt the musk of fear. He stopped himself only by reminding himself that there was no way that the hairless ape could see him.

Thanquol flinched and ducked his horned head down, even though his mighty intelligence told him that he was already out of sight. He looked around to see if his two lackeys, Lurk and Grotz, had noticed his unease. Their blank faces looked up at him placidly and he was reassured that he had not lost face in front of his underlings. He took a pinch of warpstone snuff to calm his shaking nerves, then offered up something which could have been a prayer, or might conceivably have been construed as a curse to the Horned Rat.

He could not believe it. He simply could not believe it! As plain as the snout on his face, he had seen the human, Felix Jaeger, when he looked through the periscope. He leaned forward and snatched another glance just to be sure. No – there was no mistake. There he stood, as plain as day. Felix Jaeger, the hated human who had done so much to thwart Thanquol's mighty plans, and who mere months before had almost succeeded, beyond all reason, in disgracing him before the Council of Thirteen!

Justifiable hatred warred with the rational instinct of self-preservation which dominated Thanquol's soul. His first thought was that somehow Jaeger had sought him out and had come all this way to thwart his schemes of glory again. The cold light of logic told him that this could not be the case. Nothing so simple could possibly be true. There was no way that Jaeger could know where to find him. Not even Thanquol's masters on the Council of Thirteen knew his current location. He had cloaked his departure from Skavenblight in the utmost secrecy.

Then the terrifying thought struck Thanquol that perhaps one of his many enemies far away, back in the City of the Horned Rat, had by some arcane means located him, and was feeding the information to the human. It would not be the first time that wicked rat-men had betrayed the righteous skaven cause for their own gain or revenge on those they envied.

The more he thought of it, the more likely this explanation seemed to Thanquol. Rage bubbled through his veins along with the powdered warpstone. He would find this traitor and crush him like the treacherous worm he was! Already he could think of half a dozen culprits who would be deserving of his inevitable vengeance.

Then another thought struck the grey seer, one which very nearly sent the musk of fear squirting despite all of his efforts at self-control. If Jaeger was present it meant that the other one was most likely there as well. Yes, it meant that most likely the only other being on the planet who Thanquol hated and feared more than Felix Jaeger was there too. He did not doubt, and nor was he mistaken, that when he next looked through the periscope, that he would see the Trollslayer, Gotrek Gurnisson.

It was all he could do to suppress the mighty squeak of rage and terror that threatened to burst from his lips. He knew he was going to have to think about this.

The bustling activity of the place became even more evident to Felix as the wagon descended into the valley. All around them groups of dwarfs moved purposefully. Leather aprons protected their burly chests. Sweat ran down their soot-smudged faces. Dozens of odd-looking implements – which reminded Felix of instruments of torture – hung from loops on their belts. Some of the dwarfs wore strange-looking armoured suits; others were mounted in small steam-wagons with forked lifting tines on the front. These machines carried heavy crates and packages along the iron rails between the workshops and the central metal structure.

All around the factory complex a shanty town had sprung up where the dwarfs apparently lived. The buildings were of wood and dry-stone, with sloping roofs of corrugated metal. They seemed empty, all their occupants were out at work.

Felix looked at Gotrek. 'What is going on here?'

There was silence for a long moment as Gotrek appeared to consider whether he should even answer at all. Eventually he spoke in a slow, solemn voice.

'Manling, you are looking on something I had never thought to see, that perhaps only you of all your people will ever see the like of. It reminds me of the great shipyards of Barak Varr but... So many forbidden Guild secrets are being used here that I cannot begin to number them.'

'All of this is forbidden, you say?'

'Dwarfs are a very conservative people. We do not care much for new ideas,' Varek said suddenly. 'Our engineers are more conservative than most. If you try something and it fails, like poor Makaisson did, then you are ridiculed and there is nothing worse than that to a dwarf. Few are even willing to risk it. And of course some things have been tested and because the tests failed so… spectacularly… they were forbidden to be used, by the guild. There are things here which we have known of in theory for centuries, but which only here have we dared put into practice. I know that what my uncle wants to do is considered so important that many talented young dwarfs were prepared to take the risk, to work here in secret on our great project. They think it is worth the attempt.'

'And the expense,' Gotrek said, with something like awe in his voice. 'Somebody spent a pretty penny here, and no mistake.'

'Well, and that too,' Varek said, flushing red to the roots of his beard for no reason that Felix could understand.

Gotrek glanced around with a critical eye. 'Not very well fortified, is it?'

Varek gave an apologetic shrug. 'Things were built so fast, we didn't have time. We've only been here just over a year. And anyway, who would possibly think to attack such an out of the way place as this?'

Grey Seer Thanquol scuttled back down the slopes to where his army had mustered in the gathering gloom. Clawleaders Grotz and Snitchtongue were already in position at the heads of their respective forces. Both looked at him with the expression of brute submissiveness which he had come to expect from lackeys. The communication amulets he had hammered into their foreheads glittered with the fire of trapped warpstone.

He looked down on a seething sea of shadowy, rat-like faces, each one set with fierce determination to conquer or die. He felt his tail stiffen with pride as he looked upon this mighty horde of chittering warriors. He could see black armoured stormvermin where they loomed over the lesser clanrat warriors, the masked and heavily muffled warpfire thrower teams, and his own mighty bodyguard, Boneripper, the second rat-ogre to bear that name.

It was not the most formidable force he had ever commanded. In truth, it was a mere fraction of the size of the force he had led to attack the human city of Nuln. There were no plague monks present, none of the mighty war engines that were the pride of his race. He would have liked a doomwheel or a screaming bell, but there had not been time to drag them here through the tunnels or over the rugged hills to this remote place. Still, he was certain that the hundreds of fine troops standing before him would be enough for his purposes. Particularly attacking at night, and with the benefit of surprise.

And yet... A spasm of doubt shuddered through him and made his fur bristle. The dwarf and Jaeger were present down there and that was a bad omen. Their presence never seemed to augur well for Thanquol's plans. Had they not managed to somehow thwart his invasion of Nuln, and in some not-as-yet-understood way destroyed an entire skaven army? Had they not forced the grey seer himself to beat a hasty but prudent tactical withdrawal through the sewers, while the streets above ran black with skaven blood?

Thanquol dribbled some more warpstone snuff onto the back of his paw from the manskin pouch he always carried. He stuck his snout into it and sniffed, and felt anger and confidence surge back into his brain. Visions of death, mutilation and other wonderful things flooded through his soaring mind. Now he felt sure that victory would be his. How could anything resist his mighty powers? Nothing could stand in the way of the supreme skaven sorcery he commanded!

His hidden enemies back in Skavenblight had overreached themselves when they sent Jaeger and Gurnisson here. They thought to strike a blow against Thanquol by using his bitterest enemies to smite him! Well, he would show them that what they believed was cunning was merely sorely misguided folly! All they had succeeded in doing was placing the two fools he most wanted to humble within the grasp of his mighty paw. They had provided him with the opportunity to take a most terrible vengeance on his two most hated foes, while at the same time covering himself with glory by seizing the machinery the dwarfs had built in this place!

Surely, he thought as the foul stuff bubbled like molten Chaos through his veins, this would be his greatest triumph, his finest hour! For a millennium, skaven would speak in hushed whispers about Grey Seer Thanquol's cunning, ruthlessness and awesome intelligence. He could almost taste victory already.

He raised his paw and gave the signal for silence. As one, the entire horde laid off its chittering. Hundreds of red eyes looked at him expectantly. Whiskers twitched in anticipation of his words.

'Now we will smashcrush the dwarfs like beetle-bugs!' he squeaked in his most impressive, oratorical tones. 'We will roll over the valley from both sides and nothing will stop us. Forward, brave skaven, to inevitable victory!'

The horde's squeaking rose in volume until it filled his ears. He knew that tonight victory would certainly be his.

Felix shivered as he walked. A sense of foreboding filled his mind. Instinctively, he threw his cloak back over his right shoulder to free his sword arm. His hand strayed to the hilt of his sword, and he felt a sudden urge to pull it free and be ready to fight.

The castle loomed high above them, and he could see from this close that it was not quite as formidable as it looked from a distance. The walls were cracked and weakened; in some places the stone had crumbled away entirely. Despite what Varek had claimed, the work of the dwarfs did not in any way appear to have increased the defensibility of the place. Although Felix was no expert, he could see that Gotrek's claim that the place was not particularly well fortified was true. If they were to be attacked, this whole valley would turn out to be one big death-trap.

They were almost at the castle now. Their road had led all the way to the foot of the cliffs on top of which the castle sat. Despite the gathering gloom, Felix could spy an old dwarf with an enormously long beard who had emerged onto a turreted balcony above the castle portcullis. The ancient waved. Felix was about to wave back when he realised that the dwarf was greeting Gotrek. The Slayer looked up, gave a sullen grunt and raised his ham-like fist up a few inches in greeting.

'Gotrek Gurnisson,' the old dwarf called. 'I never thought I would see you again!'

'Nor did I,' Gotrek muttered. He sounded almost embarrassed.

Lurk Snitchtongue felt his heart beat faster with pride, excitement – and a certain justifiable caution. Grey Seer Thanquol had chosen him to lead the attack, while the skaven mage observed the battle site from the slopes to the rear. It was the proudest moment of Lurk's life and he felt an emotion which could almost have been described as gratitude to Thanquol, had gratitude not been a weak, foolish, un-skaven emotion. He had not been so happy since he had recovered from the plague which had threatened his life back in Nuln. It appeared he had been forgiven for his part in the failure in that great human warren. Once again he was Grey Seer Thanquol's favoured emissary. Of course, if Grey Seer Thanquol ever found out how Lurk had conspired with his enemies during the Nuln fiasco...

Lurk pushed that thought aside. He knew that if this attack succeeded he would be well rewarded with breeders, warptokens and promotion within the ranks of his clan. More than that, he would gain a great deal of prestige, which to a skaven like him was worth more than any of the other things. Those siblings who had sneered at him, mocked and ridiculed him behind his back would be silenced. They would know that Lurk had led his mighty horde to victory over the dwarfs.

The thought sidled sideways into his mind that it might even be possible to eliminate Thanquol and claim credit for this operation himself. He dismissed the idea as absurd immediately, fearing that the mage even now might be reading his thoughts through the amulet on his brow, but somehow the wicked notion stayed put, leaping into his consciousness despite all his attempts to suppress it.

He cast around for something to distract himself, and felt his heart race with anxiety. They had almost reached the crest of the hill and still they had not been spotted. Soon would come the moment of truth. As they broached the hilltop they would become visible to the dwarfs below unless their advance was concealed by the night and smoke. He raised his claw in the sign for silence. All around him, his stormvermin stalked near-silently forward, save only for the occasional clanking of sheath against armour that most likely would not be noticed by their dull-witted opponents.

It was not the slight noises of the stormvermin which worried Lurk. It was the racket that those stupid clan rat warriors and skaven slaves were making! Lacking the imperial discipline of the stormvermin, and the long hours of training, they were making a great deal of noise. Some of them were even chittering among themselves, trying to keep their morale up in the traditional skaven way – by boasting to each other about what torments they would inflict on their prisoners.

Much as Lurk sympathised with their sentiments, he swore that he would have those chatterers' lips sewn shut after his inevitable victory. Since he could not see who was talking at this distance, he decided that he would just have to pull out a few clanrats at random and make an example of them.

By now he knew that Clawleader Grotz was most likely in position on the other side of the valley. With typical skaven precision, they would be in place ready to sweep down on both sides of the valley, taking the surprised stunties from two sides and drowning them under a furry wave of unstoppable skaven might!

He looked around him and offered a silent prayer in hope that the warriors remembered his last feverish instructions – no burning of buildings, no taking of loot. Grey Seer Thanquol wanted everything left in one piece so that they could sell it to the warp engineers. He froze for a moment, almost hesitant to give the order to attack. Then the thought that Grotz might already be sweeping down on the valley and seizing all the glory took hold of him and swept away what remained of his caution. He crawled up the slope and looked down into the valley, driven on by the comforting smell of the mass of skaven around him.

The dwarfish settlement stretched out below him. By night it was even more impressive than by day. The flames of the foundries and the fires within the smokestacks illuminated the place with an eerie glow which was reminiscent of the great city of Skavenblight. The buildings bulked vast and shadowy in the gloom.

Lurk hoped there were no unpleasant surprises waiting down there, but then realised that it was impossible for there to be. Had not the great Grey Seer Thanquol himself planned this attack?

Volgar Volgarsson stared out into the gathering darkness and tugged his beard distractedly. He was getting mightily hungry, and the thought of the ale and stew which the others would be tucking into down in the Great Hall made his mouth water. He patted his belly just to make sure it was still there. After all, he hadn't eaten a morsel in over four hours. Except, of course, for that loaf of bread and hunk of cheese, but that hardly counted at all, not by Volgar's standards.

By Grungni, he hoped that Morkin would hurry up and relieve him. It was cold and uncomfortable up here in this sentry post and Volgar was a dwarf who valued his comforts. Of course, he was proud in his way to be part of the great work going on here, but there was a limit. He knew he wasn't smart enough to be an engineer and he was too clumsy to help in the manufacturing, so he did what he could, acting as a guard and sentry, spending long lonely hours with nary a morsel of food in this chill, damp place, keeping a look-out for anyone or anything creeping up on the valley.

He knew his position was a good one. The sentry's pillbox was set in the ground, with only an observation slot looking out on the far side of the valley. There were similar such posts on the other side and looking down on the road. All he had to do was keep an eye open for trouble and if he spotted anything nasty sound the horn. Simple really.

And in a way it was actually a good posting. What trouble could there possibly be in this gods-forsaken spot? Ever since they had kicked the skaven out, there had not been the slightest hint of a problem. Now there had been a good fight, Volgar told himself, taking a long pull from his hip flask, just to keep the chill away, of course. They'd helped settle the score for a few grudges against the rat-men there. Over a hundred of the furry little buggers killed and barely a dwarf scratched. He belched loudly to show his appreciation.

It had been so quiet that Volgar had even managed a quick nap this afternoon. He was sure he had missed nothing. That was the one good thing about the settlement being so undermanned. There was no troublesome fellow sentry to keep you awake with their talk about ale and the grudges they would settle when they got back to Karaz-a-Karak. Volgar liked a good natter about score-settling as much as the next dwarf but he preferred his kip more. Couldn't beat a good snooze right after luncheon. It helped set you up proper for the rest of the day.

And now, well, his dwarfish eyes were good at night, and his dwarf-ish ears, attuned to listening to the warning hints concealed within the sounds of subsidence in the depths of the earth, were more than capable of alerting him to any trouble. If there was anything out of the ordinary – like that faint scuttling sound – or even something which sounded like the clink of weapon on weapon – like the noise he had just heard, in fact – he would notice it in an instant, and be ready to respond.

Volgar shook his head. Was he hearing things? No, there it was again, and there was a faint high-pitched chittering as well. It sounded just like skaven. He rubbed his eyes to clear them of any obscuring film and peered out through the observation slot into the darkness. His eyes were not deceiving him. A tide of shadowy rat-like shapes were flowing up the hill all around him. Their beady red eyes glittered in the darkness.

His hand almost shook as he grasped the sentry horn. He knew that if he kept quiet, the skaven would most likely pass him by. They obviously hadn't spotted his concealed outpost. If instead he gave the signal, then he was going to die. He would give away his position to the horde which surrounded him and they would swarm over it like flies on carrion. The door behind him was strongly barred but it would not hold them forever, and then there was the poison gas and the flame-throwers, and all the other strange skaven weapons he had heard of. One poison globe through the observation slot and that would be the end for old Volgar.

On the other hand, if he did not give the signal, his companions would be overwhelmed by the rat-men, and would most likely die in his stead. The great work they were embarked on would fail and it would all be his fault. If he lived, he would have to live with the shame that he had brought on not only himself but on his ancestors.

Volgar was a dwarf, and for all his flaws he had a dwarf's pride. He took a last long pull from his flask, wasted a second on a final regretful thought of the dinner he was never going to have, took a deep breath, put the horn to his lips and blew.

The lonely bellow of the horn filled the valley. It seemed to come from below the earth itself. Felix looked around wildly.

'What was that?' he asked.

'Trouble,' Gotrek responded cheerfully, pointing at the vast horde of skaven swarming over the brow of the hill and into the valley.

THE SLAVE'S ATTACK

FOUR
THE SKAVEN ATTACK

Felix watched in abject horror as the dark tide of skaven flowed down the hill towards him. He was unsure how many there were but it looked like hundreds, maybe thousands – it was hard to tell in the darkness. He whirled to investigate as a great clamour arose behind him. Looking up he saw yet more skaven entering the valley from the other side. The jaws of a huge trap were closing.

Felix fought down a surge of panic. Somehow, no matter how many times he had been in situations like this – and he had been in many – it never got any easier. He felt a sick feeling spread in the pit of his stomach, a tenseness in his muscles, and somehow a strange light-headedness too. His mouth was dry and his own heartbeat sounded loud in his ears. Just for once he would have liked to have been calm and relaxed in the face of danger, or filled with furious berserker rage like all those heroes in the storybooks. As always, it didn't happen.

All around him, dwarfs were downing tools and snatching up weapons. Horns sounded, each one with a different tone, their long notes like the wails of souls in torment, adding to the cacophony all around. Felix turned again and was about to make a sprint for the portal of the castle when he realised that no one else was doing that. All around him dwarfs raced through the gloom towards the enemy.

Were they all mad, Felix wondered? Why did they not make a dash for the safety of the castle? Unsound as its walls appeared, they would doubtless have a better chance within them. It would almost certainly be safer inside the keep but these crazy dwarfs paid no attention.

He froze momentarily, overcome with curiosity and apprehension. The thought struck him that perhaps there was some good reason why they weren't going into the keep... and perhaps finding out that reason for himself was not such a good idea.

Slowly it percolated into Felix's panicking brain that the dwarfs were not going to leave their machines in the hands of the skaven. They were prepared to fight and, if need be, die in defence of these monstrous smoke-belching mechanisms. It showed a determination that was either truly impressive or monumentally stupid, Felix could not decide which.

While he was still making up his mind, an ominous clanking sound started up from behind him, followed by the ring of metal on stone. He turned just in time to see the keep's portcullis slam down. From inside he heard the grinding of gears and the whistling of a steam engine's boiler, then the enormous chains which held the drawbridge in place tightened and begin to raise the wooden structure. Suddenly there was a deep ditch between him and the castle. At least someone inside was showing some sense, Felix thought, even if they had trapped him outside in what promised to be a mad melee.

A thunderous roar erupted from the castle above. A huge cloud of smoke belched above his head and the acrid smell of ignited gunpowder filled the air. Felix realised that someone above had wit enough to bring one of the cannons to bear. There was a whistling sound and then an explosion ripped through the darkness. A dozen of the charging skaven were thrown into the air. Limbs flew in one direction, torsos in another. The dwarfs let out a loud cheer; the skaven emitted what sounded like a long hiss of hatred.

All around him dwarfs raced into battle positions. Deep voices bawled out harsh guttural words in the ancient dwarf language. Felix felt lost and alone in the midst of this maelstrom of furious and yet somehow ordered activity. He could see that from the mad whirl of shouting and running dwarfs a coherent pattern was starting to emerge. The engineers and warriors were taking up their places beside their brethren in the line. Felix felt that he was the only one here who did not seem to have some idea where he was supposed to go.

They were all rallying around the horns, Felix suddenly realised, and now the different notes made sense. They were like those individual bells he had seen on the cattle a few days before. They identified their owners, gave his comrades a point to rally to, a nucleus around which a hard armoured shell could form.

Felix could see now that this was a tactic which had long been drilled into the dwarfs, until they had it down perfectly. Where a few moments ago there had been a mass of disorganised souls just begging to be massacred, now there were well-disciplined ranks of dwarf warriors, wheeling to face their foes, marching with a discipline that would have shamed imperial pike-men. Perhaps whoever was in charge here knew what he was doing, Felix thought. Perhaps this was not going to be the utter bloody slaughter he had feared only a few moments ago.

He wasn't sure it would be enough, judging by the size of the skaven force tearing down the hill, picking up speed like a juggernaut, gathering what looked like irresistible momentum for its charge. The seething furry horde was so close now that he could see individual skaven, make out their foam-covered lips, the rabid fanaticism in their eyes. Some of them were larger, more muscular, and better armoured than others. He had fought such beasts in the past and knew that they would be the toughest. He kept his eyes peeled for any of those clumsy, awkward and yet oh-so-deadly field weapons the skaven loved, but mercifully could see none present.

Suddenly Felix felt very alone. He was not part of any of those hastily assembled dwarfish units. There was no one beside him to watch his back. Perhaps in the darkness the dwarfs might even take him for a foe. There was only one place for him here. He looked around for Gotrek but overcome with battle-lust, he and Snorri had raced off to get closer to the foe.

Felix spat out a curse and clambered hastily onto the wagon, to get a better view of his surroundings. He noticed that Varek was sitting there, peering interestedly out into the gloom, occasionally laying the bomb he held in his hand down on the seat beside him, and scratching a note in the book before him with what looked like some strange mechanical pen. His eyes glittered feverishly behind his glasses.

'Isn't this exciting, Felix?' he asked. 'A real battle! This is the first one I've ever been in.'

'Pray it isn't your last...' Felix muttered, taking a few practice sweeps with his sword, hoping to loosen his tense muscles before the horde smashed into the dwarf line. He took a quick glance around hoping that he would be able to pick out Gotrek.

The Slayer was nowhere in sight.

* * *

From his perch on the hill high above the battle, Grey Seer Thanquol peered down at his seeing stone. It lay blank and dormant before him. Within its depths there was perhaps a tiny flicker of warpfire, undetectable save to an eye as keen and all-seeing as Thanquol's.

Indeed, to the untrained skaven eye it looked merely like a large multi-faceted piece of coloured glass inscribed with the Thirteen Most Sacred Symbols. Thanquol knew enough about the race of man to know that, to a human eye, it would look like some tawdry gewgaw used by a sideshow fakir. He was also wise enough to know that the human eye would be mightily deceived, for this was a most potent artefact indeed.

At least, he hoped so. The raw moon-crystal had cost Thanquol many warptokens. The carving of those runes, each one inscribed on a different moonless night, had cost Thanquol much lost sleep. The embedding of potent spells within the crystal had been paid for in blood and pain, some of it the grey seer's.

Now was the moment to find out whether it had all been worth it. It was time, thought Thanquol, to begin to use his new toy. Hastily he scratched runes in the hard earth around him, making the Thirteen Sacred Signs of the Horned Rat with practised ease. Next he put his thumb into his muzzle and bit hard. His sharp teeth drew blood, though he hardly felt a thing through the haze of powdered warpstone snuff and the seething sorcerous energies which filled his brain.

Black blood dripped from the wound. He held his thumb out over the first rune. A droplet impacted in the centre of the symbol and as it did so Thanquol spoke a word of power, a secret name of the Horned Rat. Immediately the fluid vaporised into a puff of acrid smoke, forming a small skull-like mushroom cloud over the rune. The symbol flared to life, lines of green fire illuminating its outline brilliantly before fading down into a less lurid yet still visible glow.

Quickly and expertly Thanquol repeated the procedure with every rune and, once that was completed, he carefully dribbled three final droplets of his own precious blood onto the seeing stone itself. Instantly a dim picture flickered into life. He could make out the scene of chaos and imminent carnage in the valley below as if looking down on it from a great height, then the picture flickered and a cloud of static filled the stone. Thanquol administered an irritated thump to the side of the crystal and the picture cleared and settled. The sight of the battle came into view as clear as day. Well almost – there was a faint greenish tinge to the picture that would not go away, no matter how many gentle taps and thumps of adjustment Thanquol administered.

No matter! Thanquol felt like the master of some vast and secret game. All those skaven below were now but pieces for him to command. Pawns to be moved by his mighty paw. Tokens to be placed on the board and guided by his titanic intelligence. He took another pinch of warpstone snuff and almost howled with glee. He felt his power to be infinite. There was nothing like it, this sensation of control, of mastery. Best of all, he could exercise his power from well out of sight and personal danger. Not that he feared danger, of course, it was merely sensible to keep himself out of the way of unnecessary risks. It was every grey seer's greatest dream come true!

Thanquol allowed himself to gloat for a long moment, then gave his attention to the battle, trying to decide in exactly which spectacular way he would seize victory and immortal fame among skavenkind.

Felix splayed his feet wider, trying to find his balance on the back of the wagon. The vehicle rocked slightly on its suspension and he wondered whether it was wise to stand here. On the one hand, the footing was unsure and he was a conspicuous target standing upright on the wagon's back. On the other hand, at least up here he had the advantage of being on somewhat higher ground and having partial cover from the wagon's sides. He decided to remain where he was for the moment – and to jump to the ground at the first sign of missile fire. That was the logical thing to do. Besides, it looked like someone would have to stay here and look after Varek.

The unworldly young dwarf was scribbling away for all he was worth in his book. Felix was amazed that he could see to write. He knew from his long association with Gotrek that dwarfs could see in the dark better than humans, but here was astonishing proof of the fact. By the flickering furnace light, which showed Felix only the barest of outlines of objects, the young dwarf was writing for all the world like a scribe copying a manuscript by candlelight. If nothing else, it was an amazing feat of concentration.

To tell the truth Felix would have been happier if Varek paid more attention to the mules. The animals were showing distinct signs of distress as the skaven raced ever closer.

Felix glanced nervously about them, wondering if any of those nasty skaven assassins with poison blades were skulking around. It was unlike the rat-men to go for a simple frontal assault without springing some nasty, sneaky surprises. He knew from bitter experience what they were capable of. He nudged Varek gently with the tip of his boot.

'Best pay attention to the mules,' he said. 'They look restless.'

Varek nodded amiably, put his pen back in his capacious pockets, snapped his book shut and picked up his bomb.

Somehow Felix was not reassured.

Thanquol glared into the seeing stone with furious concentration. He placed a paw on either side of it and chittered frantic invocations, trying to keep control of his point of view. It was not nearly as easy to control as he would have liked.

He raised his right claw and the point of view swung up and to the right. He clenched his paw into a fist and punched it forward, and the viewpoint shifted until he had a panoramic view of the battlefield. He saw the skaven loping down the hillside towards the hastily marshalling dwarfs. He saw the great furry spearheads of stormvermin aimed directly at the centre of the assembling dwarf host. He saw the flanking forces of clanrats and skavenslaves running somewhat less enthusiastically by their sides. He saw his bodyguard, Boneripper, running along beside Lurk Snitchtongue.

The keep above the valley looked like a ratchild's toy when viewed from this height, and the whole vast intricate structure of the dwarf camp looked suspiciously ordered and patterned, almost as if every building, pipe and chimney were the component of one vast machine. It was all very fascinating and he had to fight to keep his attention on the upcoming conflict. One of the side-effects of warpstone snuff was that the user could become enthralled by the most trivial things, losing himself in contemplation of the majesty of his toenails while all around cities burned. Thanquol was an experienced enough sorcerer to be aware of this, but sometimes even he forgot for a moment. And it was such a tantalising scene, so...
He wrenched his thoughts back to the battle and willed his point of view to shift, zooming in like the eyes of a bird on the centre of the dwarf lines, to the wagon on which Felix Jaeger stood, sword in hand, looking tense and justifiably afraid.

A simple but brilliant plan struck the grey seer. He had some doubts as to whether this Boneripper could handle the Slayer any better than his predecessor had, but he had no doubts whatsoever that the monster could slaughter that Jaeger. He had some special instructions for the rat-ogre concerning the human and he knew that the fierce, loyal and stupid brute would obey them to the death. In a glorious rush, he knew that Felix Jaeger's painful death was assured.

Having located his intended victim, Thanquol sent his sorcerous gaze questing back in search of Boneripper. When he found the monstrous hybrid of rat and ogre, he muttered another spell which would allow his thoughts to communicate with those of his henchling.

He felt a sudden dizziness and the blast furnace of hunger, rage and brute stupidity that was the rat-ogre's consciousness. Swiftly he placed the image of Jaeger's position in the monster's mind and gave his instructions: *Go, Boneripper, kill!! Kill! Kill!*

Felix shivered. He knew someone was watching him. He could almost feel the burning eyes boring into his back. He glanced around, certain that he would see some malevolent skaven ready to plunge a knife between his shoulder blades, but when he did so, no one was there.

Slowly the eerie feeling passed from him, to be replaced by a more immediate worry. The skaven were almost upon them! He could hear their chittering, and their crude weapons clashing terrifyingly on their shields. With a great rushing hiss, a flight of bolts flashed overhead from the castle battlements. Dwarf crossbowmen were at work firing into the nearest and largest skaven. A few of them fell, but not enough to slow the skaven advance. Their fellows simply ran on, trampling their fallen comrades into the dirt, in their frantic haste to enter combat.

An enormous roar filled Felix's ears, the deep basso rumbling of a creature far larger than a human. The mules whinnied and reared in terror, fear foam frothing from their lips. Felix shifted his weight to keep his balance as the wagon shifted. He turned his head, gripped his sword tightly and turned to look at the monster he knew was behind him.

This time his premonition was correct.

Lurk fought the fear which filled him, threatening to overwhelm his ratty frame. It was a sensation that he was used to. It nagged at his mind and told him to scamper from the fray, chittering with fright. With the mass of his fellows around him, he knew he could not do that without being trampled so instead, as he knew it would, the fear turned inward and like a dammed river flowed in a new direction.

Suddenly he wanted desperately to get into combat, to face the source of his terror – to rend it with his weapons, stamp on its recumbent corpse, to bury his muzzle in its dead flesh and tear out its still warm entrails. Only by doing this could he slow his racing heart, fight down the urge to void his musk glands, and end this anxiety which was almost too terrible to be borne.

'Quick-quick! Follow me!' he chittered and, racing forward, hurled himself at a burly leather-aproned dwarf armed with an axe.

Felix doubted that he had ever come face to face with a humanoid creature quite so big. Even the monsters he had fought in the streets of Nuln were small by comparison. This thing was huge, immense. Its monstrous head, a distorted parody of that of a rat, was level with his own, despite the fact that he was standing high atop the back of a wagon. Its shoulders were almost as broad as the wagon itself, and its long muscular arms reached almost to the ground. Its vast hands ended in wicked curving claws that looked capable of shredding mailed armour. Enormous pus-filled boils erupted through its thin and mangy fur. A long hairless tail lashed the air angrily. Red eyes, filled with insane bestial hatred, glared into his own.

Felix's heart sank. The beast had come for him, he just knew it. There was a look of feral recognition in its malevolent eyes, and something oddly familiar in the way that it tilted its head to one side. A pink tongue flickered over its lips, suggesting an obscene and all-consuming hunger for human flesh. Sharp rending teeth, each as long as a dagger, showed themselves in its mouth. The creature let out another triumphant bellow – and reached for him.

It was all too much for the mules. Frenzied with fear, they reared and fled. The wagon lurched forward, almost tipping as the terrified beasts turned just in time to avoid the ditch around the keep. The wagon hit a rock and bounced, sending Felix sprawling in the back. He had just enough presence of mind to hold on to his sword.

The rat-ogre behind them gaped at him in stupid astonishment and then lurched forward in pursuit.

'No!' Thanquol shrieked, seeing Jaeger slip from Boneripper's grasp. The power of the seeing stone let him view the scene from close up. He had gloated in delight at the look of horror and apprehension on the man's face, felt a thrill of anticipation as Boneripper prepared to reach out, pull off his arm and eat it in front of Jaeger's horror-struck eyes – and been appalled when the mules had pulled the wagon into motion.

It was all so unfair.

And yet somehow it was typical of the human's luck that, just as he was about to receive his well-merited doom, those dumb brute creatures should save him. It was galling that the man should still be alive and unharmed, instead of writhing in agony. Briefly and bitterly

Thanquol wondered whether Jaeger had been born simply to thwart him, and then pushed the notion aside. He sent another thought arcing towards Boneripper: *What are you waiting for, idiotfool beast? Get after him! Follow quick-quick! Kill! Kill! Kill!*

Felix rolled about in the back of the wagon, instinctively trying to get his footing. He could hear Varek calling to the mules, trying to calm them and bring them under control. Briefly Felix wondered whether this was wise. At the speed they were currently moving they were at least keeping ahead of the rat-ogre... weren't they?

He managed to get his hands underneath him at last, and pushed himself up onto his knees. As he stuck his head above the level of the wagon's tailboard, he saw that the monster was pursuing them and closing the distance with appalling speed. Its long stride was covering the ground as fast as any charger. Its yellow fangs gleamed in the light of the furnaces. Its long tongue lolled out. It brandished its claws furiously. Felix knew beyond a shadow of a doubt that if ever he got within range of those talons he was going to die.

He heard something metallic rolling about on the floor of the wagon, then felt something cold and hard brush against his leg. He reached down and found that it was one of Varek's bombs. It must have rolled off the wagon seat when the animals shied. He almost dropped the thing in fright. He felt like at any moment it might explode; in truth, he was surprised that it hadn't done so already. He was tempted simply to lob it from him as fast and as far as he dared, when the thought struck him that that was exactly what he should do.

He fumbled the orb up in front of his face, fighting to hold onto it as the wagon lurched again, throwing him painfully against the wooden side wall. In the half-light, he could see the firing pin in the top and the complex cumbersome mechanism below. He frantically tried to remember how it worked. Let's see: you pull the pin, then you've got five – no! – four heartbeats in which to throw it. Yes, that was it.

He dared to glance up again. The rat-ogre was closer. It seemed like it was almost on top of them. In mere moments it was going to leap into the back of the wagon and shred his flesh with those awful claws and fangs. Felix decided he could wait no longer. He pulled the pin.

He felt resistance as the pin came free, and something long and soft whipped into his hand. As he did so he noticed sparks coming from the top of the bomb. It seemed that there was a string attached to the pin, and the string was attached to some sort of mechanical flint-striker. When you pulled the pin, the flint struck, lighting the fuse. All of these thoughts flickered idly through his head as he rapidly counted up to three.

One. The rat-ogre was only a few strides away, moving impossibly fast, a look of awful hunger distorting its face. From behind him, he could hear Varek beginning to shout 'Whoa–'

Two. The monster was so close now that Felix could almost count its monstrous tusk-sized teeth. He was uncomfortably aware of the huge claws reaching out to grasp him. He knew that he wasn't going to make it. Perhaps he should just throw the bomb now. Varek called '–oa–'

Three. Felix lobbed the bomb. It arced towards the creature, its fizzling fuse leaving a trail of sparks spraying behind it. The rat-ogre opened its mouth to bellow in triumph – and the bomb went in. Another lurch of the wagon threw Felix flat, slamming painfully on to the wooden boards. Varek finished shrieking '–aaaa!'

Time seemed to stretch out for a hour. Felix lay on the floor gasping hard, remembering what Varek said about these bombs often not working, expecting at any second to feel the great razor-like claws burying themselves in his neck and to be hefted from the back of the wagon. Then he heard a dull *crump*, and something horribly moist and jelly-like splattered onto his hair and face. It took a few moments for Felix to realise that he was covered in blood and brains.

Thanquol watched Boneripper's head explode and cursed the stupid brute long and loudly. It was true, he thought: if you want a bone gnawed properly, you had to gnaw it yourself. The foul and unreliable monster had been so close. Jaeger had been almost within his grasp. If the dumb brute had not swallowed the bomb, the human would now be writhing in pain. It was almost as if Boneripper had done it deliberately just to frustrate him. Perhaps the creature had been in league with his hidden enemies. Perhaps its idiot brain had been tampered with during its creation. Stranger things had happened.

Thanquol chewed his tail with frustration for a moment and expended a hundred furious curses on Boneripper, Felix Jaeger and every rival in skavendom he could think of. If pure malevolent wishes had been enough, their bones would have been filled with molten lead, their heads would have exploded and their guts turned to rotting pus in that singular moment. Unfortunately, such fine things were beyond even Thanquol's sorcerous powers at this range. Eventually he calmed, and contented himself with the thought that there was more than one way to skin a baby. He sent his point of view soaring over the larger battlefield once more.

Fortunately here things were going better. At a glance Thanquol saw that most of the dwarfish units had formed up in squares ready to resist the two-pronged skaven attack. The initial skaven rush has reached the dwarfish line. It had broken against it like the sea crashing down on a rock but the stormvermin, at least, were still fighting. As more clanrats and slaves poured into the melee, slowly the weight of numbers was starting to tell. Even as he watched, one closely packed dwarf unit started to break up and the melee became close and general. Under such circumstances, the greater number of skaven was a considerable advantage.

Thanquol saw one dwarf warrior bludgeon a stormvermin with his hammer, only to be leapt on from behind by a skavenslave. While the dwarf frantically tried to dislodge his clinging foe, he was dragged down like a deer surrounded by hounds by the rat-man's fellows. As he disappeared under the pile of skaven bodies, he managed a last blow with his hammer, smashing a clanrat's skull and sending blood and fragments of brain and bone everywhere. Thanquol felt no pity for the dead skaven. He would gladly make such a trade for a dwarf life with every heartbeat. There were always plenty more stupid warriors where those had come from. Thanquol knew that out of all skaven, only he was truly irreplaceable.

Thanquol watched happily as the green blaze flung from a warpfire thrower incinerated a clutch of dwarfs, melting their armour, causing their beards to ignite, reducing them first to skeletons and then to wind-blown dust within mere heartbeats. He was considering rewarding the weapon team when they themselves vanished in an enormous green fireball, killed by their own malfunctioning weapon. Still, thought Thanquol, at least they served the greater purpose... his purpose.

Slowly but surely, across the whole battlefield the tide was turning in favour of the skaven. The dwarfs were well-disciplined and brave in their foolish way, but they had been caught unprepared. Many of them were unarmoured and equipped only with the hammers they had been using to work with. They were inflicting incredible casualties on the skaven but these were meaningless. Thanquol did not care if they slaughtered his entire force, just so long as the dwarfs were all dead by the end of the evening. So far, he congratulated himself heartily, things were going just exactly as he planned – except on one corner of the battlefield.

Swift as thought, he sent his view arcing towards the disturbance.

Somehow he was not surprised to find two burly shaven-headed figures hewing a path of bloody carnage through his troops. One of them he recognised instantly as the hated figure of Gotrek Gurnisson. The other was new to Thanquol, but just as fearsome in his own way. Where Gurnisson fought armed only with that appallingly powerful axe, the second Slayer fought with a smaller axe in one hand and large hammer in the other.

The slaughter the pair wreaked was immense. With every blow at least one skaven fell. Sometimes Gurnisson would drive his axe through several bodies at once, hewing through skaven flesh and bone as if it were matchwood. At that moment Thanquol would have given anything for the presence of some jezzail teams. He would have ordered those cunning skaven snipers to pick off the gruesome pair from a distance. Still, there was no point in wishing for what you could not have. He would just have to do something about the pair himself.

His initial gambit was to send tendrils of his thought out to the leaders of two of his units, drawing them away from the main melee and into combat with the Slayers. It was regrettable that this would relieve pressure on the embattled dwarfs, but also necessary. Thanquol knew that he could not take the chance of leaving those two free to slaughter at will. It was sound good sense, as well as gratifying to his personal desire that Gotrek Gurnisson and his comrade should die.

Lurk looked up in disbelief as the voice spoke within his head. *Take your squad to your left and slaughter those two Slayers.*

He recognised the voice at once as belonging to Grey Seer Thanquol. A vivid picture of his route through the melee towards the tattooed dwarfs appeared in his mind. For a moment he considered the fact that he might be hallucinating but the voice spoke again in the familiar imperious chittering style which Lurk knew so well. *What are you waiting for, fool-scum? Go now-now or I will eat your heart!*

Lurk decided that it would be best to obey. 'At once, most superlative of sorcerers,' he muttered. He shrieked for his troops to follow him and raced off in the direction he had been ordered.

Drawn by the panicked mules, the wagon raced through the melee out of control. Hastily dwarfs and skaven threw themselves aside to avoid the creatures' flailing hooves. Felix rolled about in the back, trying frantically to regain his balance. He could hear Varek alternately shouting at the mules to stop and laughing maniacally as he tossed bombs into onrushing groups of skaven. It did not seem to have occurred to him that every time the tired mules appeared about to slow down, he spooked them some more by lobbing another of his explosive devices. It did not surprise Felix in the least that the poor mules were terrified. The bombs had that effect on him too. Every moment he half-feared that one of the devices would explode in Varek's hand, destroying the wagon and sending the dwarf and Felix straight to the grave.

Every so often he managed to pull himself above the level of the wagon's sides and he caught glimpses of sights that he knew would be burned into his memory forever. Some of the buildings had caught fire and the blaze was spreading. Clouds of sparks and soot floated on the wind. Perhaps other dwarfs had used bombs like Varek, perhaps it was the effect of some dread skaven weapon or sorcery, but Felix did not doubt that the conflagration would consume the entire complex. Already flames gouted from the great chimneys, fitfully illuminating the battle to produce a selection of scenes from some lunatic vision of hell.

He saw a skaven burst out from one the foundry buildings, its entire body in flames, burning hair trailing from its body like a comet's tail. The horrible but tantalising smell of scorched flesh filled the air. The creature's agonised squeaks were shrill and audible even above the roar of the battle. As he watched, the dying rat-man threw itself on a dwarf warrior and held on like grim death. The flames from its body lapped around its victim and the dwarf's clothing began to smoulder, even as he put the creature out of its death agony with a swift blow of his axe.

The wagon shuddered and bounced over the ground. Something cracked and there was hideous sensation of snapping and grinding. Looking backwards Felix could see they had run over the corpse of a dwarf. The wheel had squashed its chest, and blood and pulped flesh oozed from its mouth and beard.

Steam blinded him, and his skin felt momentarily scorched. Condensation gathered on his blade and brow, and he had a horrible feeling that this must be what it would be like to be boiled alive. After a brief, agonising moment they emerged from the cloud of steam. He saw then that one of the great pipes was broken, steam spraying freely across the battlefield. As he watched, a dwarf and two skaven rolled free of the cloud, hands still locked around each other's throats. The dwarf's face was lobster red and great patches of skin had blistered and come away from the heat. The skaven's fur looked horribly wet and sticky.

The wagon thundered into the centre of a great melee. Bodies were packed so close that there was no chance of anyone avoiding the mules' hooves. Skulls cracked and bones splintered as the wagon rolled through the ruck like a war-chariot. Those who fell were crushed beneath the iron-shod wheels. As the vehicle slowed, Felix managed to sway to his feet, and take a look around. Varek had stopped tossing his bombs. To do so now would be to cause indiscriminate carnage. The dwarfs and skaven were now too intermingled to provide any easy targets.

The mules reared and struck out with their hooves. As they did so the wagon started to unbalance. There were tides and currents in this vast ruck just like those in the sea. The press of bodies from one side began to tip the overbalancing wagon. Felix grabbed Varek by the shoulder and indicated that they should jump. Varek looked up at him and smiled. He paused only to snatch up his book, then leapt out into the throng.

From the corner of his eye, Felix thought that he saw two squat, tattooed figures hacking their way through a horde of skaven. From his high vantage point he could see a new force of rat-men emerging from the gap between two buildings and bearing down on the Slayers. Pausing only to fix the direction in his mind, Felix leapt down from the wagon, sword swinging. Even before he hit the ground, his blade was cleaving skaven flesh.

Lurk halted for a moment and let his warriors sweep past him. He pointed to the two dwarfs he had been sent to kill and barked an order: 'Quick-quick! Slay-slay!'

Heartened by the fact that they outnumbered their foes twenty-to-one, his brave stormvermin swept forward, frothing with eagerness to be in at the kill, to claim the credit and the glory. Lurk was tempted to join them but just the look of these two dwarfs made the fur near the base of his tail stand on end, and sent shivers of justifiable caution running up his spine.

He was not quite sure what it was about them. Certainly they were big for dwarfs, and certainly they looked fierce with their bristling beards, outlandish tattoos and their gore-caked weapons, but that was not it. There was something about the way they stood, their complete lack of fear, the suggestion that they might even be enjoying the fact that they faced hopeless odds which gave him pause. It seemed certain that they were quite insane, and that in itself was cause to give them a wide berth. Then he recognised one of them from the battle of Nuln, and he wanted no part in fighting that one. Was it possible that Gotrek Gurnisson was really here, of all places?

His forebodings became certainties as the first stormvermin reached the two. He knew the skaven: it was Underleader Vrishat, a pushy, fierce foolish skaven who all too obviously wanted to challenge Lurk for the position of clawleader. A fool, but a fierce warrior and one who would doubtless make short work of their stunted foes – although the dwarfs gave no sign of any concern. The familiar one, the one with a huge crest of dyed hair rising above his furless scalp, lashed out with his monstrously large axe, and parted Vrishat's head from his shoulders. He didn't wait for the following skaven to come to him either, but charged forward, axe swinging, roaring and bellowing outlandish challenges in his own brutish and uncivilised tongue.

Lurk fully expected to see the dwarf go down, overwhelmed by a tidal wave of skaven but no – he wasn't even slowed. He came on like a ship of steel crashing through a storm-tossed sea, massive axe whirling, ham-like fist lashing out, breaking bones, severing limbs, killing anything that got in his path.

The other one was no better. His mad laughter roared out over the battlefield as he struck out with a weapon in each hand, killing just as dextrously with either, his appalling strength displayed by the way his hammer reduced helmeted skulls to jelly, and his axe buried itself happily within thickly armoured stormvermin breasts.

As Lurk watched, one smaller, more cunning skaven managed to circle behind the Slayer and leapt at his back, fangs bared, bright blade gleaming in the light of the blazing buildings. Without pause, somehow aware of the skaven presence without even seeing him, the dwarf whirled and chopped down his foe with his axe, then for good measure broke his neck with the hammer – all the while laughing out loud like a maniac and calling: 'Snorri kill loads!'

Was the dwarf's hearing so good that he could not be snuck up on? Had he felt the merest presence of the skaven's shadow fall across his own in the half-light? Lurk could not guess but the lightning quickness with which he had turned and lashed out told Lurk that he himself wanted to get nowhere near those weapons, at least until their owners were tired and severely wounded. This was not a thought he decided to share with his followers. He booted the nearest towards the fray.

'Hurry quick. Weakening they are! The kill is yours.'

The warrior looked back at him somewhat dubiously. Lurk revealed his fangs and lashed his tail menacingly and was gratified to see the skaven charge, somehow more afraid of his clawleader than of the foe.

Lurk pushed another two forward, shrieking: 'Swift swift. Outnumber them you do. Good their hearts will taste.'

This reminder of superior numbers was all it took to encourage the rest of the claw to advance into the fray. Such a sign of superiority always heartened bold skaven warriors. Lurk only hoped he didn't run out of minions before the dwarfs tired.

Thanquol cursed once more. What fool had set light to the buildings? Thanquol swore that if it was one of his incompetent lackeys he would eat the fool's raw heart before his very eyes. If those buildings were destroyed, this great victory would count for almost naught. He wanted them taken whole and intact so that they could be inspected by the warp engineers, their secrets snatched and improved on by superior skaven technology. He did not want the whole complex burned to the ground before then. Right at this moment he could see nothing that he could do except order all of his clawleaders to take more care.

At least he would see the accursed Trollslayer destroyed, he consoled himself.

The agonised screams of the dying. The night pierced by the flickering light of burning buildings, the light dimmed further by the thick clouds of scalding steam. The press of hairy bodies. The shock of blade on bone. The sticky feel of warm black blood flowing over his hand. The look of sick hatred in the dimming eyes of the dying skaven. All of it, the whole infernal scene, seared itself into Felix Jaeger's memory. For a brief breathless moment time seemed to stop and he was alone and calm in the centre of this howling, turbulent maelstrom. His mind cleared of fear and horror. He was aware of his surroundings in a way that a man can only be when he knows each breath he draws may be his last.

Close by him, two burly dwarfs fought back to back against a pack of howling skaven. The dwarfs' beards bristled. Their hammers were caked with gore. Their leather aprons were soaked with glistening black blood. The rat-men were thin, stringy, underfed, with the gaunt feral look of winter wolves. Bloody froth foamed from their lips where they had bitten their tongues and the inside of their cheeks in their battle-frenzy. Their swords were nicked and rusty. Filthy rags covered their scabby hides. Their eyes glittered with reflected firelight. One of them bounded forward, clambering over his fellows in a hasty rush to get at his prey. It reminded Felix of the seething advance of a pack of rats he had once witnessed in the streets of Nuln. Despite their humanoid forms, at that moment there was nothing human whatsoever about the skaven. They were unmistakably beasts in man's image and their resemblance to humanity only made them all the more horrifying.

A terrible shriek from his right grabbed Felix's attention and he looked around to see a wounded dwarf warrior being dragged down by a pack of rat-men. There was a look of stoic endurance in the dwarf's eyes.

'Avenge me,' he croaked with his dying breath.

Something about the way the skaven fell to fighting over scraps of the still-warm corpse sickened Felix. He leapt over to where it lay and plunged his sword into the back of a skaven slave. The glowing blade passed right through the scrawny body and into the neck of a skaven below. A kick sent another skaven flying backwards. Felix ripped his weapon free and brought it down again, driving it with full force into the bodies below him. The shock of the impact flexed the blade until he feared it would break. Driven by his hatred, Felix rotated the hilt, opening the wound with a hideous sucking sound, then he stepped back with barely enough time to parry the stroke of the huge skaven who leapt at him.

He had passed beyond fear now. He was driven only by the instinct to kill. Knowing there was no way to avoid fighting, he was driven to do so as best he could. It made him an awful opponent. He lashed out with his foot, catching the skaven a crunching blow to the knee. As it hopped backward shrieking in agony, he drove the point of his sword into its throat, turning his head to avoid the blood which sprayed from the severed artery. Now was no time to be blinded.

In the distance he heard a familiar bull-like voice bellowing a battle-cry. He recognised it instantly as Gotrek's and began to move towards it, hewing to left and right as he went, not caring whether he killed his foes, merely intending to clear them from his path. The skaven gave way before his furious rush and in ten heartbeats he came upon a scene of the most appalling carnage. Snorri and Gotrek stood atop a great heap of skaven bodies, hewing all around them with their terrible weapons. Gotrek's axe rose and fell with the monotonous regularity of a butcher's cleaver, and every time it descended more skaven lives ended. Snorri moved like a dervish, whirling this way and that, the foam of berserker rage bubbling from his lips as he lashed out with axe and hammer, pausing occasionally only to headbutt any rat-men which had got within his guard.

All around the pair flowed a tidal wave of huge black-armoured rat warriors better armed than most. The hideous emblem of the Horned Rat was emblazoned upon their shields. There must have been two score of these elite skaven warriors and it seemed all but impossible that anything could survive their furious charge. Even as Felix watched, the press of bodies obscured Snorri and Gotrek from view. It seemed like they must surely be dragged down by sheer weight of numbers.

Felix stood frozen for a moment, unable to decide whether he was too late to be of assistance, then he saw Gotrek's axe pass through a skaven body, chopping the armoured figure in two despite its mail. In an instant the area around the Trollslayers was cleared. It seemed like nothing could live within the circle of that unstoppable axe. The skaven backed off and regrouped, trying to gather enough courage for a second rush.

Felix charged down into the fray, striking right and left, shouting at the top of his lungs, trying to make it sound like there was more than just the one of him. Gotrek and Snorri moved to meet him, killing as they came. It was all too much for the skaven, who turned tail and tried to flee into the night.

Felix found himself face to face with the Slayer, who paused for a moment to inspect the mound of dead and dying he had left in his wake. Blood caked the Slayer's entire form, and he himself bled from dozens of nicks and scratches.

'Good killing,' he said. 'Reckon I got about fifty of them.'

'Snorri reckons he got fifty-two,' Snorri said.

'Don't give me that,' grumbled Gotrek. 'I know you can't count above five.'

'Can too,' Snorri muttered. 'One. Two. Three. Four. Five. Er, seven. Twelve.'

Felix looked on in astonishment. The two maniacs looked almost happy in the midst of this scene of incredible destruction.

'Well, best get going. Plenty more to slaughter before this night is over.'

Thanquol bit his tail with a raging fury. He could not believe it. Those incompetent fools had failed to kill the Slayers despite their overwhelming advantage in numbers and superior skaven ferocity. Not for the first time, he suspected some hidden enemy was sabotaging his efforts by sending him inferior pawns. Doubtless it was the same wicked conspirators who had dispatched Jaeger and Gurnisson to this distant location in the first place. Well, there would be a reckoning, he would see to that!

Right now, though, he did not have time to worry about it. This was the moment to inspect the battlefield and see how his forces were doing. He pulled both hands backwards and upwards away from the seeing stone, and his point of view retracted until it seemed that he hovered over the battlefield like some enormous bat. Below him he could see the burning buildings – curse those incompetent fools! – and the signs of the savage struggle.

Here and there, huge clumps of warriors still battled it out. Weapon clashed with weapon. Sparks flew where skaven sword hit dwarf-forged axe blade. Blood gouted from fresh wounds. Headless corpses writhed in the dust, still spending the last of their life blood in a spasm of furious energy. Sparks rose, driven skywards by the night wind.

On the walls of the keep, a group of sweating dwarfs struggled to push a multi-barrelled organ gun into position.

It was obvious that this was the moment of crisis. Everything hung in the balance. It was equally obvious to the grey seer that his skaven were going to win. They had overwhelmed the dwarfs from both sides and the sheer weight of their numbers had ground down their ill-equipped opponents. Thanquol's frustration at the escape of his two deadliest enemies started to be replaced with the warm glow of imminent triumph.

Felix knew that he was going to die. Wearily he parried the blow of a skaven scimitar. His aching muscles turned his arms and sent a counter-blow arcing towards his foe. The huge black-furred thing sprang backwards, lithely avoiding the stroke. Its tail lashed out, entangling Felix's legs, trying to trip the human by tugging him off his feet. A spark of exhausted triumph flickered feebly in Felix's mind. He had seen this trick before and knew how to respond instantly. He lashed out with his sword, severing the tail near its root, but only just managed to get his blade back into guard position in time to block the downward sweep of the rusting scimitar.

The shock of the impact almost numbed his hand, and reflexively he clutched tighter on the hilt of his sword to prevent it from slithering from his sweaty grasp. The skaven shrieked in horror and swished the stump of its tail. It made the mistake of looking down to inspect the flow of blood. As its eyes left him, Felix took advantage of its distraction to launch his sorcerous blade into its stomach. Warm entrails tumbled over his hand. He fought down a feeling of disgust as he stepped back. Clutching its stomach with both paws, an almost human look of disbelief on its face, the skaven tumbled forward. Felix drove his blade through the back of its neck, severing the vertebrae just to make sure that it was dead. He had seen many warriors dragged down to death by foes they thought they had killed, and he was determined never to make that mistake himself.

For an instant all was calm. He looked around and saw Gotrek and Snorri and a whole group of battered and fierce looking dwarfs. They all looked bone-tired, even the Slayers. It seemed like they had been killing for hours, yet for every foe that fell another two strode forward to take its place. The skaven came on in seemingly inexhaustible waves. In the distance Felix could hear the clamour of weapon on weapon, so he knew somewhere others still fought on but even as they listened an ominous silence fell, and then there was a roar that seemed to have been torn simultaneously from a hundred bestial throats. The dwarfs exchanged glances that told Felix that they were all thinking the same thing as him. Perhaps they were the very last dwarfs left alive outside the keep.

That wasn't going to last. Looking around them, Felix could see that they were ringed by fierce skaven warriors. Hundreds of reddish eyes glittered in the darkness. The light of the burning buildings reflected off a similar number of glistening blades. The skaven had pulled back momentarily to regroup for what he knew would be their final rush. They moved with a strange precision as if being organised by some swift, evil and unseen intelligence. In that moment Felix knew that he was definitely going to die, right here.

He took advantage of the momentarily lull to wipe the sweat from his brow. His breath came raggedly from his lungs. He gulped in air as greedily as a drowning man. All his muscles were on fire. His blade weighed a ton or more. He felt sure that he could not raise it again, even to save his life, but was thankful that he had enough experience to know how false that feeling was. When the time came, there was always a little more strength with which to fight. Not that it made much difference now, looking out onto those rows and rows of silent rat-like faces.

'Form up there,' he thought he heard someone say behind him. 'Get ready to repel the charge. Let's give those verminous scum a taste of true dwarf steel!'

Felix wondered at the sheer stubborn courage of the dwarfs. The sergeant who spoke must know it was thoroughly hopeless, yet he was heartening his troops to sell their lives dearly. Felix prepared to do the same but only because he had no choice in the matter. If he could have seen a way out of here to live to fight another day, he would have taken it.

Somewhere in the distance he thought he heard a droning as of some monstrous insect – or an engine. What was going on? Was this some new infernal device that the skaven were launching at their foes. Oddly enough, it seemed to be coming from the direction of the castle. A faint hope stirred in Felix's breast. Perhaps the dwarfs had a surprise waiting for their attackers. Although it seemed unlikely they could do anything before the skaven overwhelmed their current position, perhaps they might be avenged.

The skaven leaders seemed to be grunting orders to their teeming followers. Slowly, almost reluctantly, as if they feared to be first to spend their lives against the living wall of their grim foes, the skaven began to advance. As they took their first faltering steps they seemed to gain in confidence and their advance picked up speed and momentum at a terrifying rate. The strange thrumming noise grew much louder. It seemed to be coming from overhead. Felix wanted to look up but couldn't tear his eyes from the rush of the rat-men.

'Come on and die!' Gotrek roared and the skaven looked prepared to take him at his word as they charged forward ever faster, brandishing their weapons, chittering their evil sounding war-cries, swishing their tails in fury. Felix braced himself for the impact and then fought the urge to throw himself flat as some outlandish shape roared close overhead. This time he did look up, and he saw a great flight of bizarre machines passing above them. Trails of fire leaked from their boilers as they blazed across the night. Enormous rotor blades whirled near-invisibly over their hulls.

'Gyrocopters!' he heard somebody roar and realised that he was witnessing the night flight of some of the legendary dwarfish aircraft.

Blazing sparkles of light descended from the machines and landed in the middle of the oncoming skaven. It was only when they began to explode in the rat-men's midst that Felix realised that they must have been the fizzling fuses of dwarf bombs.

The skaven rush slowed as the bombs tore their targets limb from limb. Their apoplectic leaders tried frantically to rally them, but as they did so one of the copters descended almost to head height and sent a wide jet of scalding, super-heated steam into their midst. Yelping with unutterable terror a huge group of the rat-men turned tail and fled. The panic was contagious. Within moments the charge had become a rout. The dwarfs around Felix watched with almost numbed disbelief, too weary even to chase after the fleeing foe.

FIVE
THE GREAT PLAN

Felix slumped down against the broken wreckage of the wagon and inspected the blade of his sword. It had seen a lot of use in this battle but somehow it wasn't notched. The edge was still as keen as ever, even after all the hacking and chopping he had done. The ancient enchantment on the weapon obviously still held good.

Somewhere off to his right, the wall of a burned-out shed, unable to support its own weight any more, came down with a crash. Overhead a gyrocopter moved with the sinister grace of an enormous insect, pausing for a moment to hover over a blazing building. Its nose swivelled downwards and with a hiss like an angry serpent a jet of steam emerged. Felix wondered what the pilot hoped to achieve.

The steam met the fire and the flickering flames changed colour, becoming a duller yellow with perhaps a hint of blue. As the jet continued to spray, the fire slowly died down, smothered by the vapour and condensation like a small rainstorm. Even as Felix watched, the gyrocopter swung around on the spot and moved towards the next nearest blaze.

He suddenly felt enormously tired, drained of all energy by the conflict. He was bruised and battered, bleeding from dozens of small nicks and cuts which he had not noticed during the frenzy of combat. His right shoulder, the shoulder of his sword arm, ached horribly. He was almost convinced that the repeated swinging of the sword had dislocated it. It was an illusion he was familiar with, having survived many other battles. He wanted to lie down and sleep for a hundred years.

Looking around him, he wondered where the dwarfs got their energy. Already they were starting to clear up the debris of the battle. Bodies of fallen dwarfs were being gathered for burial in the sacred earth. Skaven corpses, meanwhile, were being lugged into a huge pile for burning. Fully armoured sentinels had descended from the keep and kept watch, just in case the skaven should return.

Felix doubted that they would tonight. In his experience it took the skaven longer than a human army to recover and reassemble after a defeat. They did not seem to like to return so swiftly to the scene of a defeat, and for this he was profoundly glad. At this moment he doubted he could move a muscle, even if the rat-ogre was to rise from the dead and come looking for him. He pushed that evil thought from his mind and searched for a happier topic.

He found one: at least he was still alive. He was beginning to believe again that he just might live. Sometimes before and during a battle, when fear threatened to overwhelm his reason, he had this terrible sensation that he was certain to die. It settled on him like a curse, this certainty of his own mortality. Now it amazed him that he was still here, that his heart still beat, that breath still moved in and out of his lungs. Looking around he could see plenty of evidence that this could easily not have been the case.

Blood-covered corpses were everywhere, being pulled like sacks of dead meat through the thoroughfares by bone-weary, grumbling dwarfs. The sightless eyes of the dead stared at the sky. Despite his earlier imaginings, he knew they would not get up again. They would never laugh or cry or sing or eat or breathe. The thought filled him with a profound melancholy. Yet at the same time, he knew with certainty that he still lived, that he could do all those things, and for that he should therefore rejoice. Life is all too brief and fragile, he told himself, so enjoy it while you can.

He began to laugh softly, filled with a quiet joy which felt strangely like sorrow. After a moment he limped painfully off into the night to see if he could find Gotrek or Snorri or anybody else he might know amidst this vast shambles.

Thanquol could not believe it. How could it all have gone so wrong so quickly? One moment, victory was within his grasp. His brilliance seemed to have assured triumph. In the next, it had vanished as quick as a skavenslave turning tail in battle. It was a sickening, dizzying sensation. It took long, bitter moments of reflection to convince the grey seer that even the most brilliant of schemes could be foiled by the incompetence of underlings. Through no fault of his own, his lazy, cowardly and stupid minions had let him down once more.

Reassured by this brilliant insight, he considered his options. Fortunately he had a contingency plan, devised for just such an unlikely eventuality as this. Lurk was still alive and still reachable though his speaking stone. With any luck, he could be left in place, ready to report on the secrets the unscrupulous dwarfs had tried to conceal here.

Thanquol looked into the seeing stone once more and sent his mind questing for contact.

Felix felt a tug on his sleeve. Looking down he saw Varek. The young dwarf's blue robes were soiled with mud and blood. The sleeve of his robe had come away, ripped at the seams to reveal a torn and tattered white linen shirtsleeve. His glasses were broken; a crazy web of cracks marked their lenses. In one hand he clutched a small warhammer. The other held his leather-bound book tightly against his chest. Felix was surprised by how large Varek's hands were, how white the knuckles seemed. There was a mad feverish gleam in the youth's eyes.

'That was the most amazing experience of my life, Felix,' he said. 'I have never seen anything so exciting, have you?'

'It's the type of excitement I could cheerfully live without,' Felix said sourly.

'You don't mean that. I saw you fighting back there. It was like watching a hero from the days of Sigmar. I never knew humans could fight so well!'

Varek blushed, seeming to realise just what he had said. It was a dwarfish fault, being blunt about what they considered to be the inferior abilities of the younger races.

Felix laughed softly. 'I was only trying to stay alive.'

'And I hate skaven,' he added as an afterthought. He considered that fact and felt slightly appalled. He did not consider himself to be a particularly violent or vengeful man, but the skaven made his flesh crawl. He was slightly shocked by the idea that he took pleasure in killing them but inspecting his feelings now he was honest enough to admit that it was true.

'Everybody hates the skaven,' Varek agreed. 'Even other skaven, most likely.'

* * *

Lurk Snitchtongue moved stealthily through the burned-out ruins. Fear filled his heart and warred with his hatred of Thanquol. His musk glands felt tight and he fought down the urge to squirt the fear scent, for it might give away his presence to the dwarfs all around him.

Right now, away from the comforting scent and furry mass of his brethren, he felt terribly alone and exposed. He wanted to run swiftly into the night and find the other survivors of the battle. The thought goaded him intolerably.

Still, fear of the grey seer was uppermost in his mind. Staying here most probably meant death, but defying one of the Chosen of the Horned Rat meant an inevitable, agonising doom. There were worse things than a swift blow from a dwarf axe, as Lurk well knew. Not that he wanted one of those either.

Turn right, the nagging voice said inside his head.

'Yes, most magnificent of masters,' Lurk whispered. He followed orders, moving down a long, quiet alley towards the monstrous structure which dominated the centre of the dwarf settlement. He flinched, wondering whether Thanquol could read his thoughts. He certainly hoped not, after some of the things he had been ruminating on.

His paw toyed idly with the amulet and briefly he considered what would happen if he tore it from his flesh and threw it away. Something nasty, he was sure. It would be just like a grey seer to have some intricate curse woven into the device. He did not doubt that digging it from his skull would most likely kill him, or cause him severe pain at the very least, and Lurk was no keener on pain than most skaven.

Again he flinched, hoping that thought had not gone over the link to Thanquol. He hoped not; he was only supposed to be able to send when he touched the stone and concentrated. He supposed it would take a lot of effort to drive his thoughts through the ether. He didn't know that for sure, not having tried it, but right at this moment he actually hoped it was the case.

Stop! came the imperious command. He did so at once, automatically and instinctively. A moment after he did so, he heard the sound of booted dwarfish feet ahead of him. A moment after that, a small squad of dwarfs stomped past the alley mouth. Lurk shivered instinctively when he saw that they were dragging skaven corpses off to be burned. His whiskers twitched. He had already recognised the foul scent of scorching skaven flesh earlier.

Now – run quickly across the street. Hurry-scurry while the way is clear.

He steeled himself and leapt forward into the wide exposed space between the buildings, risking a quick glance right and left as he did so, and seeing that the way was indeed clear save for the backs of the departing dwarfs. He had to admit that, whatever else he might be, Thanquol was a mighty sorcerer. He had no idea how the grey seer was able to guide him so well, but so far he had made no mistakes.

Lurk dove into the cover of the alleyway opposite and hurried on. Directly in front of him now was the huge dwarfish building. Its metal roof gleamed in the moonlight. He saw that vast and powerful steam engines were attached to its side. His skaven curiosity was piqued. He wondered what could possibly be stored within so huge a structure.

Quick-quick – head right till you find the entrance or swift death will be yours.

Lurk hastened to obey. He slid through the entrance arch and halted – and stared upwards in wide-eyed wonder. A gasp of pure amazement was torn from his uncomprehending lips.

Felix wandered through the burning night, Varek by his side. Things look worse than they are, he told himself, hoping against hope that it was true. It was evident that both sides had taken enormous casualties. Many dwarfs had fallen in the conflict and each and every one of them seemed to have taken at least two skaven with him. The stink of burning rat-man flesh was well-nigh unbearable. Felix pulled his cloak across the lower half of his face to keep out the smell. No one else seemed at all bothered.

It looked like the vast complex had taken a lot of damage. Felix wondered whether it would be enough to set back whatever project the dwarfs had been working on, and realised that he was in no position to hazard a guess. He simply did not have enough knowledge of what was going on here.

'What is this all in aid of?' he asked Varek suddenly. The young dwarf stopped polishing his broken glasses on the hem of his tunic and looked up at him. He breathed on the lenses as if wanting time to gather his thoughts, then started to polish again, not noticing that a shard of glass had broken free.

'What is what in aid of, exactly?'

'All this machinery,' Felix said.

'Er – perhaps I should leave that for my uncle to explain. He is in charge here.'

'That's very discreet of you. Where can I find your uncle?'

'In the keep, along with the others.'

Before he could ask another question, a gyrocopter whizzed low overhead. Standing on the strut of the landing gear was a burly figure with a shaven head. He held a monstrous multi-barrelled musket. Something about the way he stood set Felix's senses to prickling. The dwarf turned a crank on the side of the musket and a hail of shot churned up the earth at Felix's feet. Felix pushed Varek to one side and threw himself flat, turning to track the gyrocopter, wondering what madness had possessed the demented dwarf. Surely he had not mistaken Felix for a skaven? Then from behind him Felix heard a chorus of agonised squeaks.

It was only as he turned his head that Felix saw the group of skaven who had been advancing noiselessly behind him, blades bared. Felix recognised them as gutter runners, the dread skaven assassins he had fought in the Blind Pig tavern back in Nuln. The dwarf on the gyrocopter had cut the things down with his strange weapon. He had most likely saved their lives, even if his lack of accuracy had almost killed them both.

The gyrocopter swept backwards and slewed down to a not-quite perfect landing. The musket-toting figure leapt down from its side, and hurried away from the flying machine in a low crouch designed to stop the swiftly rotating blades separating his head from his shoulders. The downdraft from the machine flattened the enormous crest of red dyed hair which rose above his head.

The gale sent Felix's cloak flapping in the wind and the dust the machine stirred up brought tears to his eyes. Varek was forced to squint through the lenses of his broken glasses. He had covered his mouth with his book to prevent himself from breathing in the dust. The strange chemical smell of the vehicle's exhaust reached Felix's nostrils even through the wool of his cloak.

The newcomer was short and incredibly broad. His chest was bare, revealing amazing muscular definition. Twin bandoleers of what must have been ammunition were looped over his shoulders. A red scarf was tied round his forehead. He wore high leather boots with a large dagger scabbarded on the right boot. A monstrous silver skull buckled the belt which held up his green britches. His white beard was cut short almost to his jaw. A two-headed Empire eagle was tattooed on his right shoulder.

Strange thick optical lenses covered his eyes. Felix could see that they were engraved with some sort of cross hairs. Judging from his appearance, Felix decided that this had to be another Trollslayer. The stranger clumped over to him and looked him up and down, then he spat on the corpse of one of the skaven.

'Nasty, evil wee creatures, skaven!' he said by way of a greeting.

'Never liked them. Never liked their machinery.'

He turned to Felix and executed a formal dwarfish bow. 'Malakai Makaisson, at your service and your clan's.'

Felix returned the bow with that of an Imperial courtier. He used the movement to cover up his expression of astonishment. So this was the famous mad engineer of which Gotrek and Varek had talked. He did not look that crazed. 'Felix Jaeger, at your service.'

The dwarf turned the crank on his musket again. The barrels spun. Shot tore into the skaven corpses. Black blood spurted as fur and flesh tore.

'Ye cannae be too careful with these beasties. They're awfae sleekit, ye ken.'

'He means they are very cunning,' Varek translated.

'Ach, awae wi' ye! Ah'm sure Herr Jaeger kens exactly what ah mean, don't ye, Herr Jaeger?'

'I think I follow you,' Felix said non-committally.

'Well, there ye go then. Best be gettin' up tae the castle. Auld Borek will be wantin' tae talk tae ye and the others. I suppose ye'll be wantin' tae ken what this is ah aboot.'

'That would be excellent,' Felix said.

'Well, just wait till they lower the brig then – unless ye want a wee lift back the noo. Ah think the copter will tek an extra body.'

It took Felix a few moments to work out that this maniac was offering him a ride on the landing gear of the gyrocopter. He tried to force a pleasant smile onto his face as he said, 'I think I'll just wait for the gate to open, if it's all the same to you.'

'Fine by me. See ye later then.'

Makaisson clambered back on to the landing gear of the gyrocopter and shouted something to the helmeted and goggled pilot. The engine roared and the machine lurched skyward – leaving Felix wondering whether the meeting had ever actually happened at all.

'Do all your engineers talk like that?' Felix asked Varek. The young dwarf shook his head.

'Makaisson's clan comes from the Dwimmerdim Vale, way up north. It's an isolated place. Even other dwarfs find their manner of speech strange.'

Felix shrugged. He could hear the creaking of huge chains as the drawbridge into the keep was lowered. He paced rapidly in the direction of the gate, suddenly aware of exactly how tired he was and hoping to find a place to lie down for the night.

* * *

Felix woke from a nightmare of insane violence, in which a great rat-ogre chased him round a burning town while the gigantic figure of an enormous pale-skinned skaven leered down from the sky. Sometimes the city was the dwarfish community around the Lonely Tower; sometimes he ran through the cobbled streets of Nuln; sometimes he was in his home city of Altdorf, the Imperial capital. It was one of those dreams where his foes' blades were bright and terribly sharp and his own blade simply bounced off unarmoured flesh. He ran and ran while mangy, flea-infested skaven-things clutched at his arms and legs, slowing him, and all the time his monstrous pursuer came ever closer.

His eyes snapped open and he found himself staring at the ceiling of an unfamiliar room, an awakening which always disoriented him, even after many years of wandering.

He found that he was lying in a bed designed for a much shorter and broader person, and that even though he was lying diagonally his feet still protruded over the bottom. He was sweating from the heavy blankets entangling his limbs and he began to see where the feeling of being dragged down in his dream might have stemmed from. He had vague memories of entering the castle the night before, being introduced to various dwarfs and being shown to this chamber. He could remember casting himself on the bed, and after that nothing – except his fast-fading bad dreams.

He had not even taken off his clothes. Blotches of blood and dirt stained the sheets. He sat upright and shook his head wearily, aware of all the aches in his muscles left behind by his participation in last night's battle. Still he felt a sense of exhilaration. He had survived to see a new dawn, and that was the main thing. There was no feeling quite like it, knowing that you were one of the lucky ones after a battle. He pulled himself off the bed and stood up, half-expecting to need to duck his head and therefore rather surprised to find that the castle had been built on a human scale.

He moved to one of the narrow arrowslit windows and gazed out into the valley. Clouds of smoke rose from below and with them came the stench of burning skaven flesh. He wondered how much of the obscuring vapours came from the machines down there and how much from the funeral pyres, and then he realised that he didn't care.

He was suddenly very hungry. There was a knock on the door and he realised the sounds of his awakening had been noticed.

'Come in!' he shouted.

Varek entered. 'Glad to see you're up. Uncle Borek wants to see you.

You're to come to breakfast in his study. Hungry?'

'I could eat a horse.'

'I don't think it will come to that,' Varek said.

Felix laughed – then from the expression on the dwarf's face he realised that Varek wasn't joking.

It was a comfortable room, which reminded Felix of his father's study. Books lined three walls, embossed spines showing Reikspiel script and dwarfish runes. Scroll racks filled some shelves. A huge map of the northern Old World, covered in pins and small flags, draped all of the fourth wall. The northernmost parts of the world showed symbols for cities and mountains and rivers in an area that Felix had never seen shown on any human map, and which he realised must have been long swallowed by the Chaos Wastes. A massive desk in the centre of the study was drowning beneath a sea of letters and scrolls and maps and paperweights.

Behind the desk sat the oldest dwarf Felix had ever seen. His huge, long beard was forked and reached all the way to the floor before being looped back up into his belt. The crown of his head was bald. Wings of snowy white hair framed his face, which was lined with deep furrows of age in the tough leathery skin. The eyes that peered out from behind the thick pince nez glasses twinkled like those of a youth, and at once Felix discerned a family resemblance to Varek.

'Borek Forkbeard, of the line of Grimnar, at your service and your clan's,' the dwarf said, advancing from behind the desk. Felix saw that he was so bowed as to be almost hunch-backed and walked only with the aid of a stout, iron-shod staff. 'Excuse me if I don't bow. I am not as flexible as I once was.'

Felix bowed and introduced himself.

'I must thank you for your aid in the battle last night,' Borek said, 'and for saving my nephew.'

Felix was going to say that he had only fought to save himself, but somehow that did not seem very appropriate.

'I only did what any man would under the circumstances,' he managed to force himself to say.

Borek laughed. 'I think not, my young friend. Few of Sigmar's people remember the old debts and the old bonds these days. And few indeed can fight like you do, if my nephew is to be believed.'

'Perhaps he exaggerates.'

'Few dwarfs speak anything but the truth, Herr Jaeger. You are making a serious accusation when you say such a thing.'

'I… I did not mean to say…' Felix stammered, then realised from the look in the old dwarf's eye that he was teasing him. 'I simply meant that…'

'Do not worry. I will not mention this to my nephew. Now you must be hungry. Why do you not join the others to eat? After that there are serious matters to be discussed. Very serious matters indeed.'

Breakfast lay spread across the table in the adjoining chamber. Huge ham hocks lay on plates of wrought steel. Monstrous slabs of cheese formed monuments to gluttony. Massive loaves of dwarf waybread, dark and yeasty, made mountain ranges across the middle of the spread. The smell of beer filled the air from the barrel that had already been broached. It came as no surprise to Felix, to see Gotrek and Snorri squatting down by the massive fire, swilling ale and cramming food into their mouths like they had just heard news of an imminent famine.

Varek watched them as if they were about to perform new prodigies of valour at any moment. His leather-bound book lay close at hand just in case he needed to record them. He wore new glasses of a style Felix now realised had been copied from his uncle's.

Another dwarf was also present, one whom Felix did not recognise and who did not immediately move forward to make his introductions in the dwarfish fashion. He glared at Felix suspiciously, as if expecting him to steal the cutlery. Ignoring his glares, Felix walked up to the table and helped himself to food. It was among the best he had ever tasted, and he wasted no time in saying so.

'Best wash it down with some ale, young Felix,' Snorri suggested. 'It tastes even better then.'

'It's a bit early in the day for that,' Felix said.

'It's after noon,' Gotrek corrected.

'You've slept through two watches, young Felix,' Snorri said.

'A minute wasted is like a copper spent,' grumbled the dwarf Felix did not recognise. He turned to regard him. He saw a dwarf shorter than most, and broader than most too. His beard was long and black; his hair was close cut and parted in the middle. His eyes were keen and piercing. His severe black tunic and britches while obviously well made were old and threadbare. His high boots looked old but well-polished. Metal segs protected the heels from wear and tear. He was portly and there was a fleshiness about his face which reminded Felix of his father and other rich merchants he had known. There was a suggestion to it of large meals eaten in well-appointed guildhalls where serious business was discussed. The dwarf's hands flexed at his belt as if constantly checking to see whether his rather flat purse was still there.

Felix bowed to him. 'Felix Jaeger at your service, and your clan's,' he said.

'Olger Olgersson at yours,' the dwarf said before bowing back. 'You wouldn't be connected with the Jaegers of Altdorf, by any chance would you, young man?'

Felix felt momentarily embarrassed. He was the black sheep of the family after all, and had left the family home under a cloud after killing a man in a duel. He forced himself to meet Olgersson's gaze calmly and said, 'My father owns the house.'

'I have done good business with them in the past. Your father has a good head for business – for a human.'

The near contempt in the dwarf's tone made Felix bristle but he kept calm, reminding himself that he was a stranger here. It would not do simply to take offence in a keep full of touchy dwarfs who may all be this stranger's kin.

'He'd have to be, if he made any money dealing with you, Olger Goldgrabber,' Gotrek said unexpectedly.

'Olger is a famous miser,' Snorri said cheerfully. 'Snorri knows that when he takes a coin from his purse the king's head blinks.'

The two Slayers cackled uproariously at this ancient joke. Felix wondered how much they had already drunk. Olgersson's face went red. He looked as if he would like to take offence but did not dare.

Obviously neither Gotrek or Snorri cared about his wealth, his influence or his kin.

'No one ever got rich by spending money,' he said huffily and turned and stalked back into the other room.

'You should be kinder to Herr Olgersson,' Varek said. 'He is the one funding this expedition.'

Gotrek sputtered out a mouthful of beer in astonishment. His head swivelled to inspect the young scholar as if he had just claimed that gold grew on trees. 'The greatest tightfist in the dwarf kingdom is giving you gold. Tell me more about this!'

'My uncle will, in just a few moments.'

Felix felt a mixture of trepidation and curiosity as they filed into Borek Forkbeard's study. He was curious to hear what had drawn all these disparate dwarfs to this out-of-the-way place. He was worried by the prospect of where this whole thing might lead. Looking out the window at those mighty industrial structures, recalling the ferocity of the skaven's attempt to take possession of them, and seeing the huge assemblage of craftsmanship and skill which had been put into place here made it difficult for him to imagine that the dwarfs were not serious about their mysterious purpose. It was all too easy to imagine how Gotrek and himself might be drawn into it.

Borek looked up at him with twinkling eyes. Olger stood in the far corner, swivelling a globe of the world with his hands, his back ostentatiously turned to the party. The old scholar grinned at them, and bade them all take a seat. Since the dwarf armchairs were too close to the ground for Felix he remained standing.

There was a moment's silence while Borek consulted some of the papers on his desk and made an annotation in runic with a quill pen. Then he coughed to clear his throat just like Felix's lecturers used to back at the University of Altdorf and began to speak.

'I am going to find the lost citadel of Karag Dum,' he said without preamble. There was a challenging look in his eye when he glanced over at Gotrek.

'You cannot,' Gotrek said flintily. There was a hint of bitterness in his voice. 'We tried all those years ago. We failed. The Wastes are impassable. Nothing can survive there sane and unchanged. You know that as well as I do. '

'I believe we have found a way.'

Gotrek snorted then shook his head in disbelief. 'There is no way. We tried to force a passage with the best armed and equipped expedition ever assembled for the purpose. You know how many of us survived. You, me, Snorri, maybe a handful of others. Mostly dead now or mad. I tell you it cannot be done. And you know how many died in the expeditions before ours.'

'You did not always think that way, Gotrek, son of Gurni.'

'I had not then seen the Chaos Wastes.'

'Then you will not even listen to what I have to say?'

'No, no. I will listen, old one. Go ahead, tell me what crazy scheme you have in mind. Perhaps it will give me a good laugh.'

There was a shocked silence in the room. Felix suspected that dwarfs were not used to hearing venerable loremasters spoken to in that way. To break the tension, he dared to ask, 'Why do you want to go to this place? What's so special about it?'

All eyes in the room turned to him. Eventually Borek spoke: 'Karag Dum was one of the greatest cities of our people, the mightiest in all the northern lands. It was lost over two centuries ago during the last great incursion of Chaos, just before the reign of the one you call Magnus the Pious. In the great Book of Grudges, on page three thousand, five hundred and forty-two of volume four hundred and sixty-nine, you will find a record of the debt of blood we owe to the foul followers of the Dark Powers. In the ancillary codicils, we find records of all the names of those who fell, of all the clans which were wiped out. The last message we had was that Thangrim Firebeard had led his brave hosts in a doomed defence of the citadel against a mighty host which came from the north as the Chaos Wastes advanced. Since then, there has been no word from Karag Dum, nor has any dwarf from our lands been able to reach the place.'

'Why?' Felix asked.

'For the Chaos Wastes advanced and swallowed all the lands between Karag Dum and the Blackblood Pass.'

'How can you know where to find it then?'

'It was I who brought the last message from Karag Dum,' Borek said, bowing his head sadly. 'The city was once my home, Herr Jaeger. I am kin to King Thangrim himself. During those last dreadful days, our foes had summoned a mighty daemon, and our need for aid was great. We drew lots to see who would carry the word of our need to our kinfolk. I and my brothers were chosen. We left the citadel by secret routes, known to but a few. Only myself and my brother, Varig, Varek's father, made it through the Wastes. It was a hard trek and not one I wish to recall at this moment. When we reached the south, we found that war raged there too and no aid was to be had. Then we found there was no way back.'

Was it possible that this dwarf was so old, Felix thought? He certainly looked ancient and Felix knew that dwarfs lived longer than men. Even so, it was an astonishing idea that this dwarf was at least ten times his age, perhaps more. Then another thought struck him.

'If the Wastes are so deadly, how could you make it through and then not get back?' Felix asked.

'I see you are a sceptic, Herr Jaeger. I must convince you. Well, let me just say that in the days of our escape, the Wastes had only just advanced and the influence of Chaos was not so strong. By the time we tried to return, the fell power of Chaos had grown great indeed and the land was impassable. Now, if I have your permission to continue...'

Felix realised that he was interrupting the old dwarf, and making him go over ground that everybody else present seemed familiar with. He suddenly felt embarrassed. 'Of course. Forgive me,' he said.

'Tell us of the treasure that was lost,' Olgersson cut in.

Borek looked less than pleased by the second interruption. He cast a quick glare at the merchant. Felix caught the glint which had appeared in the miser's eye. It was something akin to madness and Felix knew enough about dwarfs now to recognise it for what it was: gold fever. Suddenly it was no mystery why Olger was putting up money to fund this quest. He was in the throes of the near-insane thirst for gold which sometimes overtook even the sanest of dwarfs.

'Yes, the huge hoard of Karag Dum was lost when the city fell, and all the treasure was lost. And of all the treasures that were lost, the most precious were the Hammer of Fate, the mighty weapon born by King Thangrim himself, and the Axe of the Runemasters.'

At this point, Borek turned and looked at Felix. 'We are talking of such things that it is moot only for a dwarf or a Dwarf Friend to know, Felix Jaeger. Gotrek, son of Gurni, has spoken for you, but now I must ask you for your word that you will speak of nothing discussed here with any but a dwarf of the true blood or with another Dwarf Friend. If you feel that you cannot give your word on this, we will understand, but we must ask you to leave this gathering.'

As if a light had been shone upon him, Felix suddenly felt that he had reached a boundary, one which if he crossed would significantly change his life. He felt that if he agreed to stay he was in some way, tacitly committing himself to whatever mad scheme these dwarfs were undertaking. At the same time, he had to admit to a fascination with what was being discussed, with this tale of lost cities, ancient battles, old grudges and vast treasures. He certainly was curious – and surely there could be no harm in simply listening.

'You have my word,' he said, almost before he realised he had spoken.

'Very good. Then I will continue.' Somehow Felix had expected something more. He had expected to be asked to swear an oath or maybe seal the bond in blood as he had done with Gotrek during that epic drinking bout. This simple taking of his word at face value seemed altogether too casual for one about to be initiated into the lost secrets of an Elder Race. Something of his astonishment must have shown in his face, for Borek smiled at him.

'Your given word is enough for us, Felix Jaeger. Among our people, a warrior's word is a sacred thing, stronger than stone, more enduring than mountains. We ask for nothing more. If you will not hold to it, what use are written contracts, oaths sworn before altars or anything else?'

Felix realised that disagreement would only reflect badly on him, so he kept quiet while the old scholar continued to speak.

'Yes, the Hammer of Fate and the Runemaster's Axe, perhaps the most potent of the artefacts bequeathed to us by the Ancestor-Gods were lost to us, and with them a mighty portion of our ancient power and heritage. When Karag Dum fell, we believed it lost forever. The howling Chaos Wastes flowed over the ancient lands like a sea of corruption and buried the ancient peaks, and we wailed and gnashed our teeth in dismay and resigned ourselves to our loss. We thought them lost forever, and so it seemed for these two centuries.'

'And they remain lost,' Gotrek said grimly. 'And always will be. I repeat that there is no way through the Wastes.'

'Perhaps. Perhaps not. After we failed in our last attempt, Gotrek, I renewed my search through the lorehalls and libraries. In the master lorehall of Karaz-a-Karak I searched through the oldest galleries, pulled dust-encrusted tomes from shelves where they had lain mouldering for millennia. I recorded every tale and mention of survivors who claimed to have visited the Wastes. I gained access to the forbidden vaults of the Temple of Sigmar in Altdorf. In their records, taken from the confessions of wracked heretics across the centuries, I found references to runes, spells and talismans that would protect against the influence of Chaos. I was determined to succeed this time. And I believe I have found the man who can make them.'

'And who would that be?' The note of mockery had diminished somewhat in the Slayer's voice.

'The man you will meet soon enough, Gotrek. He has convinced me that his enchantments work. I give you my sworn word that I believe they will shield us.'

'For how long can you protect those who travel in the Chaos Wastes from madness and mutation?'

'Weeks, maybe. Certainly days.'

'Not long enough. It would take months to cross those wastelands to Karag Dum.'

'Aye, Gotrek – on foot, or in armoured wagons as we tried to use last time. But there is another way. Makaisson's way.'

'By airship?'

'Yes, by airship.'

'You are mad!'

'No – not at all. Listen to me. I have studied the phenomenon of the Chaos Wastes extensively. I know much more now than we did then. Most of the mutations are caused by warpstone dust contaminating the food and the water or being breathed into unprotected lungs. It is that which drives folk mad and twists their shapes and forms.'

'Aye, and it is present in the very sands of the Waste and in the clouds which rise from it. It is in the dust and the sandstorms and in the wells.'

'But what if we were to fly above the clouds?'

Gotrek paused for a moment and appeared to consider this. 'You would have to descend to take bearings, to check landmarks.'

'The airship will be sealed with screens of fine mesh. There will be portholes and filters of the type you see on the submersibles of our fleets.'

'The airship might be forced down by storms, or winds or mechanical failure.'

'The amulets would protect the crew until repairs could be effected or the storm cleared.'

'Perhaps repair would be impossible?'

'A risk, certainly, but an acceptable one. The amulets would allow survivors to at least attempt a march home.'

'No airship could carry enough coal for its engines to make the journey without stopping.'

'Makaisson has developed a new engine. It uses the black water instead of coal. It has the power to propel the airship and the fuel is light enough to make the journey.'

As quickly as his objections were overcome, the Slayer seemed to find new ones. He seemed to be frantic to find a hole in the loremaster's arguments.

'What about food and water?'

'The airship would carry enough of both to make the trip.'

'It would be impossible to build an airship large enough to do this.'

'On the contrary, we have already done so. It is what we have been building here.'

'It will never fly.'

'We've already made trial flights.'

Gotrek played his final card: 'Makaisson built it. It's bound to crash.'

'Maybe. Maybe not. But we're going to try it anyway. Will you come with us, Gotrek, son of Gurni?'

'You would have to kill me to stop me!'

'That is what I hoped you would say.'

'The airship – is that what the skaven were seeking?'

'Most likely.'

'Then you will need to move fast before they can amass another army.'

Felix paused for a moment, his mind reeling from what he had heard. It seemed that Gotrek was taking very seriously indeed all this lunatic talk of flying to the Chaos Wastes in an untried and highly dangerous machine, designed by a known maniac. And he did not doubt that he would be expected to come along for the ride. Then there was the fact that there was most likely some great foul daemon waiting for them at the end of the journey.

Worse yet, it appeared that the skaven knew all about this new machine and would stop at nothing to get their hands on it. What hellish sorcery had they used to find out about something so new and well concealed? Or had they secret traitorous agents in place even among these dwarfs? Felix's respect for the long reach and fiendish intelligence of the rat-men was raised another notch by this evidence of their foresight and planning ability.

As he heard the dwarfs approach, Lurk quickly scurried into cover. He had spent most of the night gnawing his way through the back of a packing crate and had finally broken through just in time. He wriggled into its innards just before it was picked up by one of the strange, steam-powered lifting machines. He seemed to going up some sort of ramp.

His mind was still reeling from what he had seen last night. Within the huge hangar a massive sleek thing like an enormous shark had hovered overhead, apparently unsupported by any girders. The thing had bobbed up and down like an angry beast. The resemblance had been increased by the fact that the dwarfs had seen fit to tether it with steel hawsers. The sight of the monster had caused Lurk to spurt the musk of fear, but he felt not the slightest sense of shame at having done so. He did not doubt that any other skaven would have done just the same under similar circumstances, even the great Grey Seer Thanquol.

It had taken him long moments of observation, during which he thought his pounding heart would fight its way out of his breast, before he had realised that the creature was not actually alive and was in fact a machine. Something very like wonder had filled his mind as he contemplated the scale of the thing. It was several hundred skaven tails long, larger and more impressive than any other piece of machinery Lurk had seen in Skavenblight or in this dwarf town.

He was amazed by the sorcery which could keep such a huge seeming thing airborne. The skaven warrior in him turned over the possibilities in his mind. With such a machine, a skaven army could fly over human cities and drop poison wind globes, plague sacks and all manner of other weapons, without ever being attacked by the defenders below. It was every skaven leader's dream come true: a means of attack against which there might be no sure defence! For surely such a large armoured vessel must be proof against anything, short of an attack by dragons. And even then, judging by the size of it, and were those – yes, they were! – weapons cupolas embedded in the thing's fuselage, the vessel would have a good chance of surviving. This vessel would provide an awesome weapon in the paws of any skaven intelligent enough to understand the possibilities it offered.

At that moment, he guessed that Grey Seer Thanquol had come to much the same conclusion, for a mighty voice had squeaked inside his head. *Yes-yes, this flymachine must be mine-mine!*

Perhaps, Lurk realised, he would soon have a chance to seize it, for the crate in which he was hiding was surely being raised on high into the very bowels of the mighty airship.

SIX
DEPARTURE

Felix stared out from the battlements of the keep. Below him the dwarf township filled the entire valley, but his eyes were glued to the huge central building, the one he now knew contained the airship. Beside him Gotrek leaned against the battlements. His massive head rested on his arms, which were folded atop the parapet. His axe lay near at hand.

Below them Felix could see long lines of dwarfs assembling in ranks before the great doors of the central hangar. Small but powerful steam-engines moved along the rails to the entrance. He picked up the telescope that Varek had lent him and placed it against his eye. A twist of his hands brought the scene into focus. He made out Snorri, Olger and Varek far below. They stood at the head of the line of dwarfs, almost like troops at attention.

Flags fluttered from the struts of the enormous steel tower which loomed over the hangar. It was an imposing structure, more like a spider web of girders than a fortification. At the very top of the tower was what appeared to be a small hut or an observation post with a balconied veranda running all the way around it.

Somewhere in the distance a steam whistle sounded its long lonely cry. By the side of the hangar one of the engineers pulled a huge lever. Pistons rose and fell mightily. Great cogwheels turned. Steam leaked from the monstrous pipes that had been hastily patched after the previous day's battle. Slowly, but surely, the top of the hangar opened. The roof itself slid apart, folding down the sides of the building. Eventually, an enormous structure rose into view, like a gigantic butterfly emerging from a monstrous chrysalis.

Felix knew at once that, as long as he lived, he would never forget his first sight of the airship. It was the most impressive thing he had ever seen. With painful slowness great hawsers were paid out and, like an enormous balloon, the airship rose into view. At first Felix saw only a tiny cupola raised on the top of the vehicle, and towards the rear an enormous fin-like tail. Then, like a whale of the northern seas breaking surface, the gleaming expanse of the airship rose from below.

It was like watching the birth of a new volcanic island in the midst of the trackless ocean. The vast body of the vehicle was almost as long as the hangar and it sloped smoothly downwards like the beaches of an island running down to the sea. As the great craft continued to rise, Felix saw that this first impression was wrong, for, having reached its widest point, the hull curled inwards again, a smoothly curved cylinder. At the stern of the vessel were four massive fins, like the flights of a crossbow bolt.

Dangling from below its belly was a smaller cylindrical structure constructed from riveted metal. In this smaller structure were portholes, and from it protruded cannons and rotors and other mechanical devices whose purpose Felix could only guess at. He focused the telescope on it and could see that this smaller structure resembled the hull of a ship. Right at the front of the airship was a huge glass window. Through this he could see Malakai Makaisson, standing at the controls. Around him were many engineers.

Slowly a strange thought occurred to Felix. Was it possible, he asked himself, that the real ship was the smaller vessel dangling beneath the mighty structure, that somehow the larger structure was something like the sail of a ship or the gasbag of a hot air balloon, huge and necessary for locomotion but not part of the living or working quarters below it? He did not know but he found himself at once repelled and fascinated by the idea, and he knew beyond a shadow of a doubt that, even if he only did so once in his life, he had to get aboard that craft. It was a thought which filled him with fear and curiosity. He glanced over at Gotrek, who was watching with equally rapt attention.

'Are you seriously considering going across the Chaos Wastes in this thing?' Felix asked.

'Yes, manling.'

'And you expect me to come with you?'

'No. That choice is yours alone.'

Felix looked over at the dwarf. Gotrek had not mentioned the oath that Felix had sworn, perhaps because he had felt that no reminder of it was needed – or perhaps because he was genuinely offering Felix the choice. Even after all this time Felix found it difficult to read the Slayer's moods.

'You have tried to cross the Wastes before, with Borek, and others.'

'Yes.'

Felix drummed his fingers on the cold stone of the battlements. For long moments there was silence and then, just when Felix thought the dwarf was not going to say any more, Gotrek spoke again.

'I was younger then, and foolish. There were many of us, young dwarfs, full of ourselves. We listened to Borek's tales of Karag Dum and the Lost Weapons and how it would make our people great again if we found them. Others warned us that the quest was madness, that no good would come of it, that it was impossible. We would not listen. We knew better than them.

'Even if we failed, we told ourselves, we would fail gloriously, seeking to restore the pride of our people. If we died, we would give our lives in a worthy cause, and not have to witness the long slow years of attrition which ate away at our kingdom and our kin. Like I said, we were fools, with the confidence only fools have. We had no idea of what we were letting ourselves in for. It was a mad quest but we were desperate for some of the glory that Borek promised.'

'The Hammer of Fate – what is it?'

'It is a great warhammer, about the length of your forearm but weighing much more. The head is made from smooth, impervious rock, inscribed deeply with runes that...'

'I meant, why is it so important to your people?' If Felix had not known better he would have suspected that Gotrek was trying to avoid the subject.

'It is a sacred object. The Ancestor Gods inscribed it with master runes when the world was young. Some think that it contains the luck of our people, that by losing it we brought a curse upon ourselves that we can only remove by recovering it. Certainly since the hammer was lost, things have not gone well for our race.'

'Do you really believe that bringing it back will change things?'

Gotrek shook his head slowly. 'Perhaps. Perhaps not. It may be that recovering the hammer will bring new heart to a people who have lost much over the past centuries. It may be that the weapon itself will unleash its magic to aid us once more. Or it may not. Even if not, the

Hammer of Fate is said to be an awesome weapon, able to unleash lightning bolts and slay the most powerful foes. I do not know, manling. I do know that it is a mighty quest, and a worthy doom to fall on such a quest. If we can find Karag Dum. If we can cross the Wastes.'

'And the axe?'

'Of that I know even less. It is as ancient as the hammer, but few have ever looked upon it. It was always kept in a secret holy place and brought forth only in times of greatest danger, wielded by the High Runemaster of Karag Dum. In three millennia it was carried into battle less than a dozen times. Some whisper that it was the lost Axe of Grimnir himself. Only the High Runemaster of Karag Dum would know the truth of that for certain and he is dead, lost when the Wastes swallowed that place.'

'Are the Wastes so bad?'

'More terrible than you can imagine. Much more terrible. Some claim they are the entrance to Hell. Some claim they are the place where Hell and Earth touch. I can believe it. In all my days I have never seen a more foul place.'

'And yet you would go back!'

'What choice have I, manling? I am sworn to seek my doom. How could I remain behind when old Borek and Snorri and even that young pup Varek will go? If I remain behind I will be remembered as the Slayer who refused to accompany Borek on his quest.'

It seemed strange to hear Gotrek express doubts or admit that he was considering accompanying the loremaster only because of the way others would remember him. He was usually so terrible and full of certainty that most of the time Felix had come to look upon him as something more than human, more like an elemental force. On the other hand, the Slayer was also a dwarf, and his good name meant far more to him that it could mean to even the proudest human. In this the Elder Race seemed truly alien to Felix.

'If we succeed, our names will live in legend for as long as dwarfs mine the under-mountains. If we fail…'

'You can but die,' Felix said ironically.

'Oh no, manling. Not in the Chaos Wastes. There, you really can find fates far worse than death.'

With this Gotrek fell silent and it was obvious that he would speak no more.

'Come on,' Felix said. 'If we're going we'd better get down there and join the others.'

* * *

The airship had emerged fully from the hangar now. It was moored, like a galleon at anchor, to the top of the great steel tower. It was only when he stood below it, and looked up at the tower's enormous metallic height that Felix truly appreciated the sheer size of the thing. It seemed as large as a cloudbank, big enough to block out the sun. It was larger than any ship Felix had ever seen, and he came from Altdorf, where ocean-going traders sometimes moored, sailing up the Reik all the way from Marienburg.

He had changed into clean clothes. His red woollen cloak flapped in the breeze. His pack was slung over his shoulder. He thought that he was packed and ready to go but now, for the first time, standing in the shadow of the immense metal tower with Gotrek and Snorri, he had some inkling of what he was really letting himself in for.

A metal cage descended from the heights, supported by great metal hawsers unwinding from a drum at the structure's base. The drum was powered by one of the dwarf's steam engines. As it moved it reeled the cable in and out and raised and lowered the cage as needed. It seemed like a mechanical marvel to Felix but Gotrek had remained unimpressed, insisting that such things existed in dwarf mines throughout the Worlds Edge Mountains.

The cage stopped next to them and its barred door was opened by one of the engineers. He bowed and gestured for them to enter. Felix felt a surge of trepidation, wondering whether the cable was strong enough to hold the combined weight of all three of them and the cage, wondering what would happen if it snapped, or something went wrong with the mechanism.

'Heh! Heh!' Snorri cackled. 'Snorri likes cages. Snorri's been going up and down in this one all day. Better than riding a steam-wagon it is. Goes much higher!'

He leapt in like a child given an unexpected treat. Gotrek followed him in showing no emotion whatsoever, his enormous axe slung lightly over his shoulder. Felix stepped tentatively inside and felt the metal floor flex under his feet. It was not a reassuring feeling.

The engineer slammed the cage door shut and suddenly Felix felt like a prisoner in a cell. Then another engineer pulled a lever and the engine's pistons started to rise and fall.

Felix's stomach gave a lurch as the cage began to move and the ground fell away beneath them. Instinctively he reached out to grab one of the bars and steady himself. He gulped in air as nervous as he had been before the battle with the skaven. He noticed that he could see the ground through the small holes in the floor beneath his feet.

'Whee!' went Snorri happily. The faces of the dwarfs on the ground shrank beneath him. Soon the machines were small as child's toys and the vast bulk of the airship swelled ever larger above them. Looking down gave Felix a very unsettling feeling. It wasn't as if they were really going that much higher than the topmost battlement of the castle, it just felt so much further.

Perhaps it was something to do with the motion, or the wind whistling past through the bars of the cage but Felix felt very much afraid. There seemed to be something unnatural about just standing there with all your muscles rigid and your knuckles white from gripping cold metal while the girders of the metal tower glided past. His heart almost stopped as the cage came to rest and all motion ceased save for the slight swaying of the cage on its hawsers.

'You can let go now, manling,' Gotrek said sarcastically. 'We've reached the top.'

Felix pried his grip loose to allow the engineer at the top to open the cage. He stepped through the opening and out onto a balcony. It was a structure of metal struts that ran around the top of the metal tower. The chill wind whipped his cloak and brought tears to his eyes. He felt suddenly frozen with fear when he saw how high he was above the ground. He could now no longer see all of the airship. It was too large for all of it to fit within his field of vision. A metal gangplank ran between the top of the tower and a door in the lower part of the airship's side. On the far side of it he could see Varek and Borek and the others waiting for him.

For a moment he could not make himself move. The ground was at least three hundred paces below him and that metal gangplank could not be that firmly attached to the airship or the tower. What if it gave way below him and he fell? There would be no chance of surviving a drop of this magnitude. The pounding of his heart sounded loud in his ears.

'What is Felix waiting for?' he heard Snorri ask.

'Move, manling,' he heard Gotrek say and then a powerful shove sent him stumbling forwards. 'Just don't look down.'

Felix felt the fragile metal bridge strain under his weight and for a moment thought that it was going to give way. He virtually bounded forward on to the deck of the airship.

'Welcome aboard the *Spirit of Grungni*,' he heard Borek say.

Varek grabbed him and pulled him further past. 'Makaisson wanted to call this ship the *Unstoppable*,' the dwarf whispered, 'but for some reason my uncle wouldn't let him.'

* * *

Felix slumped beside Makaisson at the helm of the airship. He had been forced to duck as he came below. The airship had been designed with dwarfs in mind and so the ceilings were lower and the doors wider than they would have been for humans.

The engineer was dressed differently today. He wore a short leather jerkin with a massive sheepskin collar raised against the cold. A leather cap with long earflaps covered his head. There was another flap cut in the top for Makaisson's crest of hair. Goggles covered the dwarf's eyes, presumably as some protection against the wind if the front window was to shatter. Heavy leather gauntlets enclosed the dwarf's large hands. Makaisson turned and looked up at Felix, beaming with all the pride a father might show when pointing out the achievements of a favourite child.

As far as Felix could tell, some of the controls resembled those of an ocean-going ship. There was an enormous steering wheel which looked rather like a cartwheel, except that it had handgrips around the rim at strategic intervals to allow the pilot a comfortable grip. Felix imagined that by swinging the wheel the pilot could alter the direction of the craft. Beside the wheel were set a group of levers and a square metal box bearing all manner of strange and alarming gauges. Unlike with a ship, the pilot stood at the bow of the craft behind a shield of glass so that he could see where he was going. Looking out the window over the prow Felix could see there was a figurehead, some bearded and roaring dwarf god, which Felix presumed was the dwarf god, Grungni.

'Ah can tell yer impressed,' Makaisson said, glancing over at Felix. 'An so ye should be – this is the biggest and best airship ever built. Actually, as far as ah ken it's only the second one ever built.'

'You're certain that this thing will fly?' Felix asked nervously.

'As certain as ah am that ah had ham fur breakfast. The balloon, that big thing above yer heed, is full of liftgas cells. There's enough o' the stuff up there to keep twice oor weight airborne.'

'Liftgas?'

'Och, ye ken, it's stuff that's lighter than air. It naturally wants to rise skyward, and as it does it taks us way it.'

'How did you manage to collect the stuff if it's lighter than air. Wouldn't it just float away?'

'A sensible enough question, laddie, an' one that shows ye hay the makin' o' an engineer. Aye, it's naturally rarer than hen's teeth but we make the stuff oorselves doon there in the toon. At least oor alchemist dae. Then we pipe it intae the balloon above us.'

'The balloon.' The thought worried Felix even more. It made him think of the tiny hot air balloons he had made of paper as a child. It seemed inconceivable that such a thing could lift a weight of solid metal, and he said so.

'Aye well, is a lot stronger than hot air and the balloon above yer heed is no made o' metal, nae metter what it looks like. It's made o' mare resilient stuff. Alchemists made that as weel.'

'What if the gas leaks out?'

'Och, it woudnae dae a thing like that! Ye see inside that big balloon are hunnerds o' wee balloons. We call them gasbags or cells. If yin bursts it disnae metter much, we'll still hae plenty o' lift. Ivver half they wee balloons would hae tae burst before we lost altitude and even then it would be gradual. It just woudnae be natural for them tae aw burst at yince.'

Felix could see the sense of this arrangement. If the balloon above held thousands of smaller balloons, it was indeed unlikely that they could all be burst at once – even if they were attacked with hundreds of arrows, only the gasbags on the outside would be punctured, if arrows could even penetrate the outer structure of the balloon. Clearly Makaisson had given considerable thought to the safety of his creation.

Somewhere at the rear of the ship a bell rang out. Felix looked around to see that the gangplank had been slid into place and a railing had been swung back round to cover the gap. He felt marginally safer.

'That's the sign that we're supposed to be awa',' Makaisson said. He pulled one of the smaller levers close to hand and a steam-whistle sounded. Suddenly engineers swarmed across the ship to take up positions all around. From the ground below Felix heard cheering.

'Brace yersel!' shouted Makaisson and tugged another lever. From somewhere below the ship came the sound of engines starting up. Their roar was almost deafening. At the sides of the ship the dwarfs were starting to reel in the hawsers on great drums, for all the world like a horde of sailors weighing anchor. Slowly Felix began to sense movement. Currents of air stroked his face. The airship began to rise and to move forward. Almost unwilling, he moved to the side of the ship and looked out through the porthole. The ground was starting to slip away below them, and the Lonely Tower complex fell away behind. The tiny figures of the dwarfs on the ground waved up at them and on impulse Felix waved back. Then he was overwhelmed by a sickening sense of vertigo and had to step back from the window.

For the first time it came home to him that he really was on a flying ship heading out for parts unknown. Then he started to wonder how they were ever going to land again. There were no hangars and no great steel towers that he knew of out in the Chaos Wastes.

Varek led him down a metal stepladder which had been welded into the structure of the airship. Felix was glad to be off the command deck, away from the mass of excited dwarfs. The drone of the engine was audible even through the thick steel of the vehicle's hull, and occasionally for no reason that Felix could detect the floor flexed beneath his feet.

Suddenly the whole vessel lurched to one side. Instinctively Felix reached out with his hand to steady himself against the wall. His heart leapt into his mouth and for a moment he was convinced that they were about to plummet to their doom. He realised that he was sweating, in spite of the chill.

'What was that?' he asked nervously.

'Probably just a crosswind,' Varek said cheerfully. Seeing Felix's confusion, he began to explain: 'The part of the ship we're in is called the gondola. Its not rigidly attached to the balloon above us. We're actually dangling from hawsers. Sometimes the wind catches us from one side and the whole gondola starts to swing in that direction. Nothing to worry about. Makaisson designed the airship so that it could fly through a gale if need be – or so he claims.'

'I hope he did,' Felix said, finding the nerve to put one foot in front of the other once more.

'Isn't this exciting, Felix?' Varek asked. 'Uncle says we're probably the first people ever to fly at this altitude in a machine!'

'That just means we have further to fall,' Felix muttered.

Felix lay on the short dwarfish bed and stared at the riveted steel ceiling of his stateroom. He found it difficult to relax with the thought of the long drop below him and the occasional motion of the vessel. He was pleased to discover that the cramped bunk had been bolted to the floor of the chamber to prevent it from moving about. The same was true of the metal storage chest in which he had thrown his gear. It was a good design and showed that the dwarfs had thought of things that he never would have. Which, he admitted, was typical; as a people, they were if nothing else thorough.

He turned on his stomach and pressed his face against the porthole, a small circle of very thick glass set in the airship's side. A chill communicated itself almost immediately to the tip of his nose and his breath misted the pane. He wiped it away and saw that they had risen still higher and that below them lay clouds in a near-endless rolling sea of white.

It was a view which Felix had imagined that only gods and sorcerers had ever seen before, and it sent a thrill of fear and excitement coursing through his whole body. Through a sudden gap in the clouds he could see a patchwork quilt of fields and woods spread out far below. They were so high that, for a moment, he could read the surface of the world like a map, glancing from peasant village to peasant village with a turn of his head. He could follow the course of streams and rivers as if they were the pen-strokes of some divine cartographer. Then the cloud closed again, to lie below him like a snow field. Above them the sky was an incomparable blue.

Felix felt privileged to be given even a glimpse from such heights. Perhaps this is what the Emperor himself felt like when he looked down from the saddle of his royal pegasus, he thought, and took in all the kingdoms of his domain, stretching off into the distance as far as his regal eyes could see.

The gondola of the *Spirit of Grungni* was very impressive, in a cramped, claustrophobic sort of way, Felix decided. It was as big as a river barge and certainly a lot more comfortable. En route to his state room they had passed many other chambers. There was a small but well stocked kitchen, complete with some sort of portable stove. There was a ship's mess with enough space for thirty dwarfs to dine at a sitting. There was a map room filled with charts and tables and a small library of volumes. There was even a huge cargo hold packed with wooden crates which Varek had assured him were full of all the food and gear they would require further north. The thought reminded Felix that when they next stopped – if they next stopped – he would have to pick up some winter clothing and equipment. He did not imagine that it was going to get any warmer the further north they got.

Felix wondered to himself whether this meant he was committing himself to going with the dwarfs. He wasn't certain. In its way, it was an exciting prospect, making such a journey in this mighty airship, to visit a place that no man had seen for three thousand years. If only they had been going any place other than the Chaos Wastes, Felix was certain that he would have chanced it in an instant.

He was not a particularly brave man but neither, he knew without false modesty, was he a coward. The thought of what this vessel was capable of excited him. Mountains and seas would prove no obstacle to a machine which could simply float over them, and this airship was capable of speeds far greater than the fastest ship. According to Varek it could average over two hundred leagues a day, a stupendous velocity.

By Felix's best reckoning it had taken him and the Slayer over a month to cover a similar distance on foot and cart. This vessel was capable of making passage to Araby or Far Cathay in under a week, journeys which took many months. Assuming the vehicle didn't crash or get blown from the sky by a storm or attacked by a dragon, it was capable of amazing feats of locomotion. The commercial possibilities were enormous. It could be used to move small precious perishable cargoes at speed between distant cities. It could do the work of a hundred couriers or stagecoaches. He was sure that there were those who would pay simply to be given a glimpse of the stupendous views he had witnessed through the gap in the clouds. Felix smiled ironically, realising that he was thinking as his father would under the circumstances.

But of course, having created this amazing vehicle, what did those crazed short-legged idiots propose to do with it? Nothing less than fly directly into the deadliest wilderness on the planet, a place which Felix had been brought up to believe was the haunt of daemons and monsters and those who had sold their souls to the Dark Powers – a belief that Gotrek had practically confirmed was true.

Felix wondered at that. Was there some strange compulsion lodged in the dwarfish mind to always seek destruction and defeat? Certainly they seemed to relish tales of disaster and woe the way humans relished epics of triumph and heroism. They seemed to enjoy brooding on their failures and recording their grudges against the world. Felix doubted that any such cult as the Slayer cult could attract worshippers in the Empire and then pulled himself up short. That was most likely not true. Even the incredibly evil Chaos Gods had found worshippers amongst his people, so there would probably be no shortage of human Slayers if they were offered the chance.

He dismissed this line of speculation as pointless, and realised that he did not have to come to any decisions right now about whether he would accompany the dwarfs. He could always decide when they stopped.

If they stopped, he corrected himself.

Lurk flexed muscles long cramped from inaction. He wondered where he was. He wondered what he was supposed to do. For many hours now, he had heard no communication from Grey Seer Thanquol. For many hours now, he had felt a sense of isolation that was quite new in his experience, and in a way terrifying.

He had been born in the great warrens of Skavenblight, eldest of an average sized litter of twenty. He reached full growth surrounded by his siblings and all the others in the cramped burrow. He had lived in a city filled to bursting point with his fellow skaven, hundreds of thousands of them. When he had left that city it had always been on military duties, as part of a mighty unit of skaven. Even in the smallest guard posts there had been hundreds. He had lived and ate, defecated and slept always within squeaking distance of his kind. There had never been an hour of his short life when he had not been surrounded by the scent of their musk and their droppings, or the sound of their constant stealthy movements.

For the first time in his life he felt that absence like a sharp pain, as a man newly blinded might feel the absence of light. Certainly, all his fellows had been his rivals for the favour of his superiors. Certainly, they would all have stabbed him in the back for a copper token, just as he would them. But always they had been there. There had been something reassuring about their massed presence, for it was a world full of danger, of lesser races who hated the mighty skaven breed and envied their superiority, and in numbers there was safety from any threat. Now he was isolated and hungry and filled with the urge to squirt the musk of fear although there were no fellow skaven around to heed its warning. Now it was all he could do to simply listen to his racing heart and not bury his head in his paws in paralysed terror. In that horrible moment, he realised that he even missed the presence of Grey Seer Thanquol in his mind. It came as a terrible revelation.

At that exact moment, the whole ship began to shake.

Felix opened his eyes in alarm. He realised that he must have dozed off. What was that banging sound? Why were the walls shaking. Why was his bed moving? Slowly it came to his puzzled mind that he was on the dwarf airship and it looked like something had gone terribly wrong. The floor was bucking and he could feel the vibration through his mattress. He rolled off the bed, sprang to his feet and banged his head painfully on the ceiling.

He fought down a feeling of claustrophobic terror as the whole airship thumped, creaked and vibrated round about him. In his mind's eye he pictured the ship breaking up and everyone in it plunging to their doom. Why had he ever allowed himself to set foot on this terrible machine, he asked himself as he opened the door. Why had he ever agreed to accompany these dwarf maniacs even this far?

Expecting something terrible to happen at any moment, he threw open his door and shuffled out into the corridor, praying frantically to Sigmar to get him out of this mess, and hoping against hope that he lived long enough to find out what was going on.

SEVEN
EN ROUTE

The rocking of the airship threw Felix headlong into the corridor. Stars flashed before his eyes and pain seared through his head as his skull struck one of the metal walls. He started to pull himself upright again, realised that he was simply begging to have his head cracked on the ceiling and instead stayed down and started to crawl along the corridor.

Of all the terrors he had ever faced, this was quite possibly the worst. Any second he expected the hull to shatter, the wind to snatch him up and then a long fall to his death. It occurred to him that, for all he knew, the gondola may already have parted from the balloon and be plunging to its doom. Impact with the solid earth might happen at any second.

It wasn't so much the fear that was appalling. It was the sense of helplessness. There was simply nothing he could do to alter his predicament. Even if he managed to get to the control room, he did not know how to steer the craft. Even if he found his way to an exit they were thousands of feet above the ground. Never before had he known a sensation quite like it. Even in the midst of battle, surrounded by enemies, he had always felt like he was in charge of his own destiny and could fight his way clear by virtue of his own skill and ferocity. On a tempest-tossed ship he might have been able to do something; if it sank, he could dive into the sea and swim for his life. His chances in either case might be slim but at least there was something that he could do. Here and now there was nothing to be done except crawl along this claustrophobic walkway, with the vibrating steel walls pressing in, and pray to Sigmar that he would be spared.

For a moment, something like blind panic threatened to overwhelm him, and he fought down an overwhelming urge to simply curl up in a ball and do nothing. He forced himself to breathe normally as he pushed these thoughts aside. He was not going to do anything to shame himself in front of these dwarfs. If death came he would face it standing, or at least crouching. He forced himself upright and slowly made for the control chamber.

Just as he was congratulating himself on his determination, the airship rose then fell mightily, like a ship breasting an enormous wave. For a long moment, he was convinced that the end had come and he stood there waiting to greet his gods. It took several heartbeats for him to realise that he was not dead, and several more before he could gather the nerve to put one foot in front of the other and continue.

On the command deck no one showed any signs of panic. Tense-looking engineers strode backwards and forwards, checking gauges and pulling levers. Makaisson stood straining at the wheel, his enormous muscles swollen under his leather tunic, his crest bristling through his helmet. All the dwarfs stood with their legs wide apart, maintaining perfect balance. Unlike Felix they were not having any trouble standing upright. Envy filled him. Maybe it was because they were smaller, broader and heavier, he thought. Lower centre of gravity. Whatever it was, he wished he had it.

The only one showing any discomfort was Varek, who had turned a nasty shade of green and had covered his mouth with his hand.

'What's going on?' Felix asked. He was proud that he managed to keep his voice level.

'Nithin tae worry aboot!' Makaisson bellowed. 'Joost a wee bit o' turbulence!'

'Turbulence?'

'Aye! The air beneath us is a wee bit disturbed. It's just like waves in water. Dinna worry! It'll settle itself doon in a minute. Ah've seen this before.'

'I'm not worried,' Felix lied.

'Guid! That's the spirit! This auld ship was built for far worse than this! Trust me! Ah should ken – I built the bloody thing!'

'That's what I'm worried about,' Felix muttered beneath his breath.

'Ah still wish they'd called her the *Unstoppable*! Cannae understand why they didnae.'

Lurk squirted the musk of fear again. The inside of the packing case stank of it. His fur was matted with fine droplets. He wished he could stop but he couldn't. The banging and shaking of the dwarf airship had him convinced that he was going to die. He knew he should stop, that the reek of the musk was only likely to draw attention to him but that thought just scared him more and kept him squirting the bitter acrid stench. It was only when his glands were empty and sore that he stopped. Bitterly he cursed Thanquol and the machinations that had placed him in this position of jeopardy. What was the grey seer doing now, he wondered?

Thanquol sat hunched in the desolate cave high in the mountains, pondering how he was going to get in touch with Lurk and find out the location of the airship. He had watched its departure, his heart filled with a lust to possess the thing such as he had never in all his life felt before. He finally understood what the dwarfs had been working on, and what it represented.

The military possibilities were endless. Judging by the speed with which the vehicle had gained height and flown off, it was capable of moving from one end of the Old World to the other in less than a week. The vision of a great fleet of such ships carrying the invincible skaven legions to inevitable victory filled his mind. The sky would be darkened by mighty vessels bearing the banner of the Horned Rat and Thanquol, his most favoured servant. Armies could be moved behind the lines of bewildered enemies before they realised what was happening. Cities could be brought to their knees by bombs, gas globes and plague spores dropped from above.

When he looked at that airship, Thanquol had known that he looked upon the very pinnacle of technological achievement in the Old World and that it was the destiny of the skaven race to possess it and improve on it in their own inimitable way. Refitted with superior skaven engines and weapons, the airship would become better, faster and more powerful than its creators could ever imagine. Thanquol knew that it was his duty to his people and to his own destiny as one of their leaders, to acquire that airship, whatever the cost, however long it took. Only a skaven of his brilliance could understand its true potential. He must have it!

But right now the first problem was to find out where the thing was.

He had lost contact with Lurk when his lieutenant had passed out of the range of the speaking stones. Thanquol knew he would have to extend himself to re-establish contact by sorcerous means. The link between his stone and his lackey's still existed but there was just not enough power in the spell. He believed he could compensate for that himself, given the opportunity.

He swiftly glanced round the cave. It was a propitious spot, one of the entrances to the great web of tunnels that linked the Under-Empire, the place where the survivors of his attack on the Lonely Tower had mustered beyond reach of dwarfish vengeance. It had been a long, tiring scuttle through the night to reach this place and Thanquol was weary as he had not been in many a year. Still, he was not about to let fatigue stop him from gaining possession of the airship.

He touched the amulet with the slender talon that tipped one of his long delicate fingers. He sensed the surge of warpstone energies trapped within the talisman. Patiently he sent his thoughts questing down the tenuous ectoplasmic link which streamed from the amulet. It was reassuring to know that it still existed in some form, even though it was stretched far beyond any distance he had ever envisioned. Slowly the grey seer gathered his power and sent his mind reaching out further. He closed his eyes to aid his concentration, feeling like one stretching further and further out over some abyss.

It was no use. He could not make contact over this distance, not unaided. He reached into his pouch and took a generous pinch of warpstone snuff, snorting it hungrily. The power aided him, bringing him the strength he required. Far, far off, at enormous range, he sensed the dim, frightened presence of the wretched Lurk. A smile of triumph revealed Thanquol's fangs. He knew instantly the distance and direction in which the airship flew. He could find it again when required. Now he needed more specific information.

Lurk, listen to me! Here are your orders!

Yes, mightiest of masters! the reply came back.

Felix looked out through the window of the command deck in astonishment. The turbulence had ended. Night had come. Below him he could see countless lights which marked the presence of taverns and villages spread across the hills and plains of the Empire. Some that moved marked the presence of coaches hastening through the darkness to inns or other refuges. Off to the left he caught the glitter of moonlight on a river and patches of denser shadow which marked a forest. It was a scene of strange and eerie beauty, and something that Felix knew few men had ever seen.

They had passed through the turbulence of the storm and everything seemed to be going smoothly. The droning of the engines was regular. None of the dwarfs showed the faintest signs of alarm. Even Varek had lost some of his greenness and headed off to his cabin to rest. All was peaceful in the control deck.

They had been aloft now for many hours and at last Felix was starting to believe that this ship really could fly. It had survived the shaking and bucking earlier. Aside from a bruise on his forehead there was no sign of any trouble. Incredible as it had seemed just a few hours ago, he was starting to enjoy the sensation of being airborne, of travelling at astonishing height at god-like speed.

He glanced around. By the soft lamplight he could see the skeleton crew on the command deck. Most of the dwarfs had gone off to rest. Makaisson was slumped in a padded command chair while another engineer took the wheel. His eyes were shut but a maniacal grin of justified triumph spread across his face. Behind him, with his back to Felix, Borek leaned on his staff and gazed out the window. Thighs burning from maintaining his unnatural crouch, Felix shuffled over to him.

'Where are we headed?' Felix asked quietly.

'Middenheim, Herr Jaeger. We're going to pick up some fuel and supplies and a few more passengers, then we'll be heading north-east to Kislev and the Troll Country. Makaisson says we lost some time against the head winds but we should reach the city on the spire by dawn tomorrow.'

'Dawn! But it must be scores of leagues from the Lonely Tower to the City of the White Wolf.'

'Aye. This is a fast ship, is it not?'

Intellectually Felix had already grasped this point but now he realised that emotionally he had not. Nor would he, really, until he saw the narrow, winding streets of Middenheim below him. It was all very well calculating in your head just how fast the airship was moving. It was another thing entirely experiencing it.

'It is one of the wonders of the age,' Felix said with feeling.

Borek stroked his beard with gnarled fingers and limped over to a seat. It was a huge, padded leather armchair, built to accommodate dwarfs. It was fixed to a short column, atop of which it swivelled, and there was a harness for strapping the occupant in which at the moment lay loose on the floor.

Gratefully the old dwarf slumped into his seat, took out his pipe and lit it. He fixed Felix with one bright eye. 'That it is! Let us hope that it is good enough for our purposes. For if it fails, there will most likely never be another.'

Lurk levered open the packing case and steeled his courage to the sticking point. Slowly, stealthily, he clambered out onto the mass of packing cases. He realised at once that the Horned Rat had smiled upon him. If the case in which he had taken refuge had been on the bottom of this mass, he would never have been able to get free. The weight of all the other cases packed above him would have left him trapped to die of slow starvation.

He paused, nose twitching and sniffed the air. He could detect no scents of anyone close to him. His eyes probed the darkness. They were well adapted for this task. The skaven were a race of tunnel dwellers. Although their vision was poorer than that of human eyes in full daylight, they could see much better in the gloom. There was no sign of anybody in the hold either. To most people the cargo space would have been in total darkness. Lurk guessed this most likely meant that it would be night outside.

The first thing he needed to do was shift his refuge. If any dwarf looked into the case, they would find it suspiciously empty and stinking of his musk and droppings. It would not take them long to work out that they had a stowaway aboard ship and start a search. The very thought made Lurk's musk glands tighten.

As it turned out, the empty case was light enough and he had little difficulty lifting it and placing it further back in the rows of similar cases. Perhaps he should look for something to put in it, so that anyone lifting it would not notice its suspicious lightness. For the life of him he could not think how to do this, though, so he abandoned consideration of the problem and gave thought to something else. He was hungry!

Fortunately he could smell food. Nearby were sacks of grain. He gnawed the corner of one and plunged his muzzle in deep, chewing and swallowing frantically to assuage his hunger. In the far corner he now noticed hundreds of cured hams hung from a steel rack. Surely no one would miss one, and he knew that meat would satisfy his stomach far better than grain. He grabbed a haunch of meat and gobbled half of it greedily. It was just too bad it wasn't fresh and raw, but then he supposed you couldn't expect the Horned Rat to provide everything. He stuffed the rest of the joint inside his tunic for later.

Now it was time to set about his mission for the grey seer, to carry out Thanquol's orders and search the ship.

Slowly, using all the stealth he had learned in long years of ambushes and sneak attacks, he stalked forward. His natural posture caused him to slouch forward and he had little difficulty moving on all four paws. Actually, had the floors not been metal and had he not been surrounded by the presence of his enemies, he would have felt quite at home here. These low wide corridors reminded him oddly of a skaven burrow.

He fought down feelings of nostalgia. Ahead of him was a metal ladder fixed into the walls. He scampered up it easily and prowled on down a long corridor. All around him he heard the sound of snoring, from where the unsuspecting dwarfs lay asleep. If only he had a squad of his stormvermin now, he thought, he could take the entire ship. Unfortunately he did not, so he scurried on.

Ahead of him he heard the sound of pistons moving up and down and dwarfish voices shouting above the din. Slowly, heart pounding, he poked his head through a doorway and looked within. Fortunately the chamber's occupants had their backs to him. He glanced around. The room was filled with huge machines. Cogs turned, pistons pumped and two enormous crankshafts ran out through the walls, rotating as they went.

Some buried instinct told Lurk that he had found the engine room. If only he could sabotage this machine he could bring the whole ship to a halt. He had no idea what good this would do him, but he felt that he'd best report the fact to Grey Seer Thanquol.

Not wanting to push his luck, he ducked backwards and scampered along his scent trail back towards the hold. He still had not found what he was looking for and from portholes along the side of the ship he could see the sun was starting to peak over the horizon. He wanted to be back in his hiding place before the crew came fully awake.

Glancing out through the porthole, he suddenly realised he had the answer to the grey seer's question. In the distance he could see a mighty peak rising out of the forest. That peak was crowned with the towers of a human city. He knew that city.

For long years he had been part of the skaven garrison which dwelt in the tunnels below the peak, ready at a moment's notice to infiltrate the metropolis of their hated enemies. The airship was heading for the place humans called Middenheim, the City of the White Wolf.

* * *

Felix's eyes snapped open. He had fallen asleep in one of the armchairs in the control room. He noticed at once that the sound of the engines had altered and that the craft was juddering slightly as it lost height. He rose up, and only at the last second remembered to stoop before he banged his head on the ceiling. He shuffled slowly over to the window and saw distant towers silhouetted against the rising sun. It was a sight of considerable beauty, for the buildings rose out of a mighty fortress that occupied the heights of a great peak. They had reached Middenheim more or less on schedule.

Even as he watched, he saw a large creature starting to rise from within the citadel and fly towards the airship. He fervently hoped that it had no hostile intent.

EIGHT
MIDDENHEIM

As Felix watched in rapt fascination, he could see that the creature was a winged horse, one of the fabled pegasii. Its rider wore the long robes and intricate headpiece of a sorcerer. A globe of fire encased one hand, and Felix knew that the mysterious rider could unleash it with a gesture. He had seen the wizards of the Empire on the field of battle and knew the awesome power they wielded.

The wizard directed his great flying steed alongside the airship. Its mighty pinions moved rhythmically, keeping the creature abreast of the airship with ease. The mage looked over and Borek rose from his chair and hobbled over to the window. He waved to the man, who answered him with a look of recognition. He applied spurs to his steed and hurtled forward, gesturing for them to follow.

Makaisson took over the wheel and began to make minute adjustments to their course. The airship moved in response, losing speed and altitude swiftly as they descended towards the spires of the city.

Looking down, Felix could see that the cobbled streets were full of people. They stared upwards in amazement, craning their necks for a better view of the vessel passing overhead. On some faces was written wonder, on others merely fear. In a way, Felix realised, whether they knew it or not, those people down there were looking on the passing of their way of life.

For thousands of years their city had rested secure and impregnable in its rocky eyrie. The only approach was up a long, narrow, spiral-ling path in the cliff-side or via a cableway that ran from the villages below. In its entire existence, no invader had ever managed to con-quer this place. It was a location where ten men could easily hold off a thousand, and often had. There were relatively few pegasii, wyverns or other flying steeds – and certainly no great armies of them.

The *Spirit of Grungni* changed everything. It could carry an entire company of soldiers in its hold. A fleet of such ships could deliver an army on to this spire. The odd-looking cannons he had noticed in the ship's side could bombard those cobbled streets and shale roofs from afar in a way no besieger could ever have managed before. In an odd way, today was the beginning of a new era, and he wondered if anybody except he himself realised it.

They passed over the steep and winding streets. The tall narrow tene-ments of the city rose towards the central heights of the peak which were dominated by the twin masses of the Elector Count's Palace and the mighty Temple of Ulric, Lord of Wolves. The two enormous struc-tures glared at each other across the highest square of the city and it was over this open space, with a clear view of the maze of rooftops and chimneys spread out beneath them, that the airship came to rest.

For the past few minutes Felix had wondered how this operation was going to be achieved and now he watched in fascination as it was revealed to him. Clearly they were expected. A group of dwarfs had mustered in the square, where great metal rings had already been driven into the stones of the plaza. Makaisson threw one of his con-trol levers backwards and the noise of the engines altered.

'Reverse engines,' he called. 'Brace yersels!'

Felix had a few moments to realise what he meant before the airship slowed to a stop. Makaisson then moved the lever to a neutral posi-tion and the noise of the engines died almost completely.

'Anchors awa'!' A group of engineers stood by the hawser cables. They hit release catches and the cables spun out dropping their attached lines. When the cables dropped like anchors, the dwarfs below were ready. They grabbed the lines and swiftly attached them to the hooks. In a matter of moments, the airship was made fast. Felix was still not sure how they themselves were going to get down, though. His curiosity on this point was soon satisfied.

It was a long way down. They were in the very bottom level of the gondola, looking at a massive hatch that an engineer had just thrown open. As Felix watched, a rope ladder was unrolled and dropped through the hatch. Still unfurling as it fell, it soon reached the ground below. One of the dwarfs in the square grabbed it and attempted to brace it but, for his pains, began to swing backwards and forwards.

Gotrek looked down through the hatch, grabbed the rope and swung himself out into space. He began the long descent, as agile as an ape. He used only one hand, fearlessly clutching his enormous axe in the other.

'After you, Felix,' Snorri said.

Felix looked down. It was a long drop but if he ever wanted to get his feet on solid earth again he was going to have to use the ladder. He swung himself outwards and down, feeling a moment of sick fear as his feet kicked in empty air before contacting the rope. Next he grabbed the top rung with his hands and began his descent, clinging on desperately as the wind tore at his cloak and brought tears to his eyes.

The rope ladder was not at all stable. It swung back and forwards in the breeze. Felix wished he had worn gloves, for the rope was digging into his fingers painfully. He forced himself to put one foot down and then the other. Having learned from his experiences when boarding the airship he did his best not to look down. At the level of the rooftops he was surprised to see people hanging out the windows and waving to him. In the distance he could hear cheering.

A dizzying sense of vertigo overtook him as he glanced down for the source. He saw that the square was surrounded by a throng of people being held back only by the count's elite guard of Knights of the White Wolf. It slowly dawned on him that the people were cheering for him. He was the first and only human to have descended from this airship and they assumed that he was some kind of hero. So as not to disappoint them he waved. Losing his grip almost overbalanced him and the ladder lurched to the right, nearly sending him tumbling to the cobblestones below. Hastily he gripped the ladder once more and continued his descent.

He doubted there was ever a man happier than he was when his boots touched the ground.

A group of heavily armoured and richly-dressed men strode out of the palace to greet them. Their robes were of the finest cloth, their heavy fur cloaks of mink and sable pelt. On their tabards was the wolf-head emblem of the Elector Count of Middenheim. They presented a sight that was at once redolent of wealth and strangely barbaric. Felix knew this was in keeping with the reputation of the city of their origin, for, in many ways, the Middenheimers were a people apart. The dominant faith in this city was the cult of the berserker god Ulric, and the priesthood of Sigmar, patron deity of the Empire, was more tolerated than revered. It was a source of abiding tension within the Empire but such was the wealth and military might of this powerful city-state that it was free to carve out its own path. Felix knew that this was a rare thing in a land where religious dissent had often been the cause of bloody civil strife.

It seemed that these men had been sent to welcome the dwarfs and usher them into the presence of Elector Count Stephan. Felix noticed that they were looking at him with something like surprise in their eyes. Quite obviously, whatever else they had been expecting, having a human descend from the great airship had not been included. Nonetheless they bowed to him in a courtly manner and informed him that the count requested his company. Felix returned their bows and allowed himself to be led into the palace, not quite sure whether he was a prisoner or a guest.

The palace was old and sumptuous. Great tapestries covered the walls, depicting scenes from the city-state's long, proud history. As he walked Felix recognised scenes from the Battle of Hel Fenn, and the wars with the vampire counts of Sylvania. He saw wolfskin-cloaked warriors engaged in battle with green-skinned orcs. And depictions of the hideous hordes of Chaos, which had besieged the city two hundred years ago during the time of Magnus the Pious.

The palace was huge, carved from the same stone as the peak by craftsmen who had obviously been stupendously skilled. Above each doorjamb, gargoyle heads leered down and the arches themselves were carved with the most intricate of frescoes. Carpets from Tilea, Araby and distant Cathay covered the heavy flagstones. In each hall a massive fire burned, keeping the chill of the heights at bay. Even in the daytime, lanterns burned in those halls furthest from the light, shining out in the gloom.

Here and there massive burly palace guards moved around on missions for their master, and every so often richly garbed councillors paused to gape at the dwarfs and those that accompanied them. So it was, spreading a strange silence in their wake, that Felix and his companions entered the throne room of the Elector Count of Middenheim, and confronted the lean, powerful figure sitting erect on the Wolf Throne.

Felix could see others grouped around the throne. Most were old, bearded men who he assumed were councillors, but two figures stood out. One leaned forward and whispered something in the count's ear. He was a tall and slender man, garbed in robes of sumptuous purple. The robes were trimmed with gold cloth inscribed with symbols which Felix had come to recognise as mystical signs. An ornate headpiece rested on his brow, of all things it resembled most a tall, conical elvish helm, only fashioned from felt and cloth-of-gold. Rings containing precious stones glittered on the man's fingers. An intangible aura of power hung over him, and made Felix uneasy. It was the pegasus-riding wizard and in the past his dealings with wizards had rarely been pleasant.

The other figure was equally intriguing. She stood just below the count's dais, a tall woman and perhaps a lovely one, but it was difficult to tell. Felix guessed that she was almost his height. She was not dressed in a court gown as the other ladies present were. She wore a sleeveless jerkin of leather over a white linen shirt. Her leather britches were cinched at the waist with a studded leather belt. High riding boots encased the thighs of her long legs. Her ash-blonde hair was cropped short almost to the scalp. Two swords were sheathed at her narrow waist. She stood straight-backed, with her chin tilted back. There was an air about her of far lands and distant places. Feeling his eyes upon her, she turned and glanced back in his direction.

The dwarfs bowed before the count's throne and began making florid introductions. Count Stephan cut them short politely enough, but with the manner of a military man who had no time for long-winded speeches. Felix was brought forward to stand beside Gotrek and Snorri and gave the best courtly bow he knew how. He saw interest flicker in the eyes of the count when he noticed a human in the dwarf party, before the ruler returned his full attention to Borek.

'Our chancellors have prepared the substances you requested for transfer to your vessel,' Count Stephan said.

By the look on Olger's face, Felix guessed that whatever those substances were, they must have cost a pretty penny. The miser looked as pale and miserable as a man who had undergone amputation.

'I thank you, noble lord, and welcome this affirmation of the ancient friendship among our people.'

The count smiled as if he and Borek were old friends and he had only been too pleased to make the gift. Felix looked up and was startled to find himself looking directly into the blue eyes of the woman on the dais. She was about the same age as he was, he realised. Unlike the noblewomen, her face was tanned. She had high cheekbones and wide lips, which lent her a decidedly exotic beauty. Felix guessed that she was not from anywhere within the Empire. She cocked her head to one side and examined him. Felix was unused to such direct and appraising scrutiny from a woman but he forced himself to hold her gaze. She smiled at him challengingly.

'Now you must tell me of your unique vessel and your mission,' Elector Count Stephan was saying.

Borek looked around the chamber meaningfully. 'Gladly, your Excellency, but some things are best discussed in private.'

The count surveyed the vast audience hall, the crowds of lackeys, guards and hangers-on. He nodded to show he understood and clapped his hands.

'Chamberlain, I would speak to noble Borek in private. Have food and wine brought to my apartments.'

The chamberlain bowed and without further ceremony Count Stephan rose, descended from his dais and offered Borek his arm to lean upon. Before Felix had even realised it, the audience chamber began to clear. In moments, he and the remaining dwarfs were left alone in the suddenly empty chamber.

Felix turned to Varek. The young dwarf shrugged.

'Who were the wizard and the girl?' Felix asked.

'I think they might be our passengers,' Varek replied.

'Passengers?'

'I'm sure either they or my uncle will tell you more when you need to know.' Varek seemed to realise that he had said more than he ought to and scuttled swiftly out, leaving Felix alone with Gotrek, Snorri, Olger and Makaisson.

'I'll be leaving the expedition here,' Olger said suddenly. 'Much as I would like to stay with you, I have clan business to transact here in Middenheim. Good luck and bring back the gold.'

He bowed and stumped away.

'Good riddance,' Gotrek jeered.

'Snorri thinks the old skinflint is scared,' Snorri said.

And why shouldn't he be, thought Felix? He was beginning to suspect that the miser was the most sensible dwarf of all he had ever encountered.

'Let's find some beer,' Gotrek said.

Felix stopped to purchase a pastry from a street vendor. He paused and looked around the street, happy to be in a human city once more, enjoying the teeming throngs all around him. Overhead the tall tenements of Middenheim loomed. People filled the narrow winding streets. Jugglers tossed multi-coloured balls. Acrobats tumbled. Gaudily garbed men on stilts towered over the crowd. Drums beat. Pipers played. Ragged beggars stuck out grubby hands. The smells of roasting chicken, cooked pies and night soil filled the air.

Felix kept one hand on his purse and the other on the hilt of his sword, for he was familiar with the perils and predators of urban life. Thieves, cut-purses and armed robbers were all too common. Dirty-faced children watched him with predatory eyes. Here and there warriors in the tabards of guardsmen moved through the crowds.

'Hello, handsome. Want a good time?' Painted women waved to him from the doorways of shabby houses. One jiggled her hips in a parody of lust. From the narrow windows above, others blew him kisses. Felix turned his eyes away and pushed on past. Briefly he wondered about the woman he had seen back in the palace, but he pushed the thought aside. There would be time enough to get to know her as their journey continued.

A drunk staggered from the door of a tavern and reeled against Felix. Felix smelled the man's beer soaked breath and then felt fingers fumbling for his purse. He brought up his knee, jabbed it into the would-be pickpocket's groin. The man collapsed, groaning.

'Quickly, this poor fellow has been taken ill,' shouted Felix and stepped over the prostrate body. Like wolves on a sickly deer, the street people descended on the fake drunkard. Felix vanished swiftly into the crowd before the guards noticed the disturbance.

He smiled. It felt good to be back in civilisation, surrounded by his own people. It felt good to have some time to himself. He was glad that he had been given the day off while Borek talked with the count, and the dwarf engineers loaded the barrels of black stuff aboard the airship. Gotrek and Snorri had headed off to a tavern in the lower levels but Felix was in no mood for an all day drinking session. The memory of his last appalling hangover was still too fresh in his mind. Instead he had decided to take a wander round the city and meet up with the Slayers later. He was sure that the Wolf and Vulture tavern would be an easy one to find. He did not have to return to the airship until dawn tomorrow. There would be plenty of time for carousing later, if he decided that was what he wanted to do.

Felix shook his head ruefully. Somewhere, somehow, during the flight to Middenheim he had obviously made up his mind to accompany the dwarfs. He was not entirely sure why, for it was certain to be dangerous. On the other hand, perhaps that was the reason. If he had wanted a calm, safe life he would doubtless now be working in the counting house of his father's business back in Altdorf. At some point during his wanderings with Gotrek he had come to enjoy the life of the wandering mercenary adventurer, and he doubted now that he could return to his old life even if he wanted to.

This quest was taking on a momentum of its own. There was an excitement about simply being aboard the airship which genuinely thrilled him. By daylight, in this teeming city, even the prospect of the Chaos Wastes was not so daunting. In fact, it represented a chance to see a place which few sane men had ever visited and returned to tell the tale. And of course, there was his oath to accompany Gotrek and record his doom as well.

Of course, he knew he was kidding himself. He could pinpoint exactly where his decision to remain with the airship had taken place. And it had nothing to do with oaths or adventure or the thrill of travel. He had made up his mind to go on when he had discovered that the woman in the throne room was also going to be a passenger.

And there was nothing wrong with that, he told himself. Providing it didn't result in his death.

From the edge of the city, Felix looked down on the forest below. He had followed the winding alleyways all the way down to the great outer walls, where a short climb had taken him up to the battlements. From here he could see the cableway that brought merchants and their goods up from the small township below. As he watched, the last carriage of the day crawled up the cables towards its terminus in the walls.

Looking further afield he saw the woods and the river stretching away to the horizon, and he appreciated the fact that the inhabitants of Middenheim had almost as good a view as the one he had got through the portholes of the airship. He wondered at the ingenuity and determination that kept this vast city supplied. According to the books of legend that he had read, the City of the White Wolf had started life as a fortress, its heights giving shelter to those who fled the constant tide of warfare that flowed below.

Down through the long centuries a fair-sized community had grown up on the heights, clustered around the fortress and the monastic temple of Ulric. The township had begun as home to the nobility and their garrisons, but had grown to include the merchants who provided them with luxuries. Of course, all food and goods were more expensive here, for they had to be hauled up the cables from below, but the nobles controlled vast estates out there in the hinterland and were not short of a gold piece or two. The cost was more than made up for by the increased security they enjoyed on their lofty perch. And, of course, there were the mines below the peak, a source of much wealth.

And other darker things besides. Felix had heard Gotrek talk of those mines and of a vast labyrinth of tunnels which extended below the peak. The mines were patrolled by dwarf soldiers and human guards, for it was rumoured that skaven had established a lair down there. Felix cursed suddenly, wondering if he was ever going to be out of reach of the accursed rat-men. Probably not. Somehow he knew that if the airship turned its nose towards the steaming jungles of legendary Lustria, they would arrive to find skaven already scuttling through the undergrowth.

The sun was starting to set. A bloody glow spread across the clouds as it descended below the horizon. Lanterns flickered to life on the watchtowers along the walls, and looking back Felix could see lights appearing in the windows of the tenements and taverns of the city. Soon he knew the lamplighters would be emerging and lantern-toting watchmen would start tolling the hours in the streets.

He knew it was time to go back. He had taken the last glimpse of Imperial society that he might ever have, and he felt strangely relaxed and contented, as if by making his decision to accompany the dwarfs on their quest, he had somehow absolved himself of all fear and doubt. It was better to have the thing decided, he thought, than to writhe in an agony of uncertainty. His way was clear now and he was relieved to find that he was not unhappy about it. He turned and started back up the long, cobbled path towards the palace, wondering whether he was imagining things when he thought he heard scurrying over the rooftops behind him.

NINE
BEYOND THE SEA OF CLAWS

As the airship cast off, the crowds stared up in awe. Makaisson turned the wheel and pulled the levers to alter their course a fraction. Narrowly avoiding the great spire of the Temple of Ulric, they set off northwards.

Felix relaxed in one of the armchairs on the command deck. There was plenty of room. Most of the dwarfs were sleeping off hangovers, leaving only a skeleton crew to man the bridge.

To tell the truth, Makaisson himself looked a little worse for wear. The little groans he emitted from time to time, combined with the way he squinted at the horizon through sore eyes, were not reassuring. Felix was not at all sure that he should be flying the ship.

'Can I help you?' he asked the chief engineer.

'What dae ye mean, young Felix?'

'Perhaps I can take the controls while you rest.'

'Ah dinnae ken. It's a highly technical job.'

'I could try. It might prove useful to have somebody else on board who can fly the ship, in case anything should happen to you. I mean you are a Slayer, you know.'

'The other engineers ken hoo to dae it... still, ah suppose ye hae a point. It woudnae dae onnie herm to hae an extra pilot – just in case.'

'Does that mean you'll do it.'

'Ah shouldnae really. It's against guild regulations tae teach onybody but a dwarf hoo to dae these things, but then again, this whole bloody thing is against guild regs, so whar's the herm, ah ask ye?'

He beckoned for Felix to come over and stand where he was standing. 'Tak the wheel, Herr Jaeger.'

Felix had to bend his knees to stand at the same height as the dwarf and he found the position fairly uncomfortable. The wheel felt heavy in his hands. He did his best to hold it steady but it felt like it had a life of its own, exerting pressure first this way and then that, so that Felix had to constantly fight to hold his position.

'That's the air currents,' Makaisson said. 'They tug at the rudder and the ailerons. Take's a while tae get used to it. Ye got it?'

Felix nodded nervously.

'Look doon a wee bit and tae yer left. Ye'll see a wee gadget there. It's a compass.'

Felix did so. He could see a compass that swung on a complex arrangement of gimbals so that the needle in its centre always pointed north.

'Ye'll notice that we're heading north-north-east at the moment. That's oor course. If ye turn the wheel a wee bit, we'll shift the course. Joost jink aroond a wee bit and bring the course back to north-north-east,'

Felix did as he was told and moved the wheel as gently as he could. Outside the window, the horizon seemed to spin slowly. He moved the wheel the opposite way and they spun back onto the correct heading.

'Weel din! Nithin' tae it, eh?'

Felix found that he was grinning back at Makaisson. There was something exhilarating about being in control of so massive and swift a thing as the airship.

'What next?' he asked.

'See that row o' levers next tae yer right hand?'

'Yes.'

'OK, the first yin is fur speed. Dinna dae onything till ah tell ye tae, right, but when ye push it forward the engines pick up speed. When ye pull it back the engines lose speed. When ye pull it ah the way back, ye gan backwards, intae reverse. Ye follow me?'

Felix nodded again.

'Noo there's a dial in front ye, marked in increments. Ye'll see that it's marked in different colours as weel.'

Felix saw the indicated gauge beside the compass. Right now the needle was in the green zone at the tenth increment. It was about five increments short of the red zone.

'While the needle is in the green, ye're fine. That's the zone o' tolerance for the engine. Move it forward – but keep the needle in the green.'

Felix leaned forward on the lever. It resisted his efforts, so he pushed harder than he had originally intended. As he did so the needle moved forward and the drone of the engine altered to a higher pitch. The ground seemed to unreel faster below them, and the clouds drifted by more quickly on either side. Suddenly Felix felt Makaisson's hard hand on top of his. Fingers like steel bands closed and he found the lever was being pulled back.

'Ah said keep it in the green, ye unnerstan? The red is for emergencies only. Ye run the engine in the red and ye'll gaun much faster but ye'll burn it oot after awhile, maybe even explode it. That's no such a guid thing at this height.'

Felix saw that he had accidentally run the needle into the red zone. He tried to pull his hand away but Makaisson's held it in place for a moment. 'Dinnae tak yer hand off the controls until ah tell ye. Keep yer hand on the speed stick the noo, alright?'

Felix nodded and the engineer freed his hand. 'Dinnae worry. Ye're no daein' too bad. So, the next stick on the right controls the fins. Try tae no get the two sticks mixed up, it could be messy!'

Felix was beginning to wish he had never suggested that he might learn this. It seemed that there were many possibilities for disaster that he had never thought of. 'In what way?'

'Well, the fins control oor height above the ground. When ye pull that lever back the fins on the tail change attitude and we gaun up. When ye push it forward we gaun doon. That's all ye really need tae ken. The actual reasons are a wee bit technical and ah doobt ye'd understand them.'

'I'll take your word for it.'

'Right, pull the lever back. Gently! We dinna want to wake onybody up. Now ye'll notice a wee gadget next tae the speed gauge. That's yer altitude. The higher the increment, the higher we are. Yince mare, dinna gaun intae the red zone for ony reason. That could be fatal because we'll be flying too high. An' try no to lay the thing get doon to zero either, coz that means we'll hae hit the ground. Now, slide the lever back to the neutral position. Ye'll feel a wee click when ye dae. That means we'll hae levelled off.'

Felix did as he was told. There was an odd buzzing in his ears, which vanished when he swallowed. He took his hand off the altitude lever and pointed to a smaller row of stubby levers attached to a panel at the height of his left hand. 'What do these do?'

'Dinna ouch ony of them. They control different functions like ballast, fuel and ither stuff. I'll tell ye aboot them anither time. Right noo, ye ken ah ye need to fly the ship. Noo, keep headin' north-north-east. An' see that clock there? In two hours' time wake me up. Ah'm ganne hae a wee kip. Ma heed's a bit sare fae ah the booze yesterday.'

'What if something goes wrong?'

'Joost gae me a shout. Ah'll be in this chair here.'

So saying, Makaisson sat himself down in the chair, and soon his snores filled the bridge of the airship.

For the first few minutes Felix felt a certain nervousness guiding the craft but as time wore on he gained confidence that nothing was going to go wrong. As time went on, some of the engineers came onto the bridge. Some glanced at him in amazement but seeing Makaisson slumbering nearby let him be. After a while, it became quite relaxing to watch the land and the clouds unroll beneath them.

'Are you the pilot then?' The soft voice stirred Felix from his reverie. It was a woman's voice, husky and with more than a trace of a foreign accent in it. At a guess he would have said Kislevite.

Felix shook his head but did not turn to look at the woman. He kept his attention focused on where they were going, just in case anything unexpected came their way. 'No. But you could say I am training to be one.'

A soft laugh. 'A useful skill.'

'I don't know. I doubt that I can base a career on it. There are not too many vessels like this in the world.'

'Only this one, I think. And given its mission, I doubt there will be another.'

'You know where we are going, then?'

'I know where you are going, and I do not envy you.'

Felix had to fight to keep his eyes fixed ahead and not to look round at her. He remembered what he had sworn to Borek back at the Lonely Tower. He did not really know this woman, and it was possible she was quizzing him for information.

'You know where we are bound?'

'I know you are headed out into the Wastes and that is enough for any sensible body to know. I do not think you will be coming back.'

Felix was discouraged to hear an assessment which so closely concurred with his own. He was also disappointed to learn that the woman had no intention of coming with them on their quest.

'I take it you are familiar with the place then?'

'As familiar as anybody can be who is not sworn to the Ruinous Powers. My family estates border the Troll Country which is as close as any mortal dare dwell to the accursed lands. My father is the March Warden there. We have spent much time battling the followers of Chaos when they try to infiltrate the lands of men.'

'It must be an interesting life,' Felix said ironically.

'You could say that. I doubt that it is any more interesting than yours though. What brings you aboard this vessel? I must admit I was astonished to see a human, and a good-looking one, where I expected only to find Borek and his people.'

Felix smiled. It had been a long time since anyone, particularly an attractive woman, had told him he was handsome. He did not let his guard down though. 'I am a friend.'

'You are a Dwarf Friend? You must have performed some epic deeds then. Ulric knows there have been few enough of those in history.'

Felix wondered whether this was true. He had always assumed that it was simply a polite form of address. Now it appeared that it might actually be some form of title. He was about to reply when Makaisson interrupted from behind them.

'Och, the lad has stood beside Gotrek Gurnisson on many an occasion, lassie. And he had a hand in the cleansing of the Sacred Tombs of Karak Eight Peaks. If that is nae grounds for namin' him a Dwarf Friend ah dinna ken what is! Onyway, noo that ye've woke me up wi yer chatter, ye may as well gimme that wheel. Ah'll tak iver noo.'

Makaisson stumped over and elbowed Felix from his position at the controls. He gave Felix a broad wink. 'Noo you and the lassie can talk tae yer heart's content.'

Felix shrugged and turned to smile at the woman. 'Felix Jaeger,' he said, bowing.

'Ulrika Magdova,' she said, smiling back. 'I am pleased to make your acquaintance.'

There was a formality about the way she spoke the words which showed she was unaccustomed to them. They were like a polite formula she had been taught for dealing with people from the Empire. He thought that in her own land the greeting would be somewhat different.

'Please, take a seat,' he said, feeling a certain stupid formality he wished he could have avoided. They both slumped down with their legs stretched out in the overstuffed dwarfish chairs. Felix could see that his earlier guess was correct and she was almost as tall as he. Looking at her face, he revised his earlier opinion of her appearance.

It went from merely beautiful up to stunningly beautiful. His mouth felt suddenly dry.

'So what are you doing on this craft?' he asked, just for something to say. She gave him a glance of languid amusement, as if she could read his thoughts exactly.

'I am travelling home to my father's estates.'

'I cannot imagine Borek simply letting somebody on to this ship as a passenger for no reason.'

She raised her right hand to her mouth and stroked her lip with its forefinger. Felix could see the fingers were callused like a swordsman's, the nails pared very short. 'My father and Borek are old friends. They fought together on many occasions in my father's youth. He helped guide Borek's last expedition to the edge of the Wastes. He looked after him and your friend Gotrek when they staggered back with the survivors. He was not surprised. He had warned them not to go. They would not listen.'

Felix stared at her. He had not imagined that any humans had been involved in that last expedition. 'That does not surprise me,' Felix said ruefully. He possessed considerable experience of just how stubborn dwarfs could be.

'Some things about it surprised even my father. He had not expected anybody to return from that doomed mission. Few indeed, save the followers of Chaos, ever do.'

'How long ago was this mission?'

'Before I was born. Over twenty winters ago.'

'They have waited a long time to go back then.'

'So it would seem. It also seems that they have prepared well. Indeed it was a message from my father to say that he had done what they asked which brought me to Middenheim.'

'What do you mean?'

'Borek asked my father to make certain preparations on our estate. To collect the black water. To build a tower. To stockpile certain supplies. At the time, they did not make sense, but now that I have seen this ship I think I understand.'

'The dwarfs have built a base, a way-station, on your father's land.'

'Aye. And paid for it in good dwarfish steel.'

Seeing Felix's quizzical look she smiled at him, and unsheathed one of her swords, pulling it part way from its scabbard. Felix noticed dwarf runes along the blade. 'We have little use for gold along the Marches of Chaos. Weapons suit us better and the dwarfs are the finest armourers in the world.'

'You came a long way from Kislev to Middenheim. That is far for a beautiful young woman travelling on her own.'

'Better, Herr Jaeger! I had despaired of ever getting a compliment from you. Men are more forward about such things in Kislev.'

'Women too, it seems,' Felix said in mild surprise.

'Life is short and winter is long, as they say.'

'What does that mean?'

'Are you so obtuse?'

Felix could not help but feel that this conversation was moving out of his control. He had never quite met a woman like this Kislevite before and he wasn't sure he liked it. Imperial women did not behave in quite this way, except perhaps for camp followers and tavern girls, and Ulrika Magdova certainly did not have the manner of either. Or perhaps, he was simply misunderstanding her manner. Maybe this was just the way women behaved in Kislev.

She spoke to fill the silence. 'I did not travel to Middenheim on my own – although I could have. I came with a bodyguard of my father's lancers. They departed northward and I waited to return with Borek.'

For the first time, she did not meet his gaze. He sensed that she was hiding something and he was not sure what. Certainly there was more going on here than met the eye. Also, for the first time, he started to suspect that she was not quite as confident as her beauty and her boldness had led him to believe. That suddenly made her more approachable and, in a way, more attractive. He smiled at her again and she smiled back, a little ruefully this time. Then she glanced over his shoulder, smoothed her britches with both her hands, and rose to her feet, all the while keeping him fixed with that dazzling smile.

Felix looked over in the direction of her gaze and saw that their other passenger, the sorcerer, had just entered the bridge area. He was looking at them in a puzzled, and Felix thought, perhaps resentful manner. If that was the case, he soon regained control of himself. A look of languid amusement passed over his lean handsome features and he advanced into the room. Ulrika Magdova sauntered past him, pausing only to give him a mildly disdainful glance.

'Good day, Herr Schreiber. A pleasure talking to you, Felix.'

'Good day,' Felix said weakly, rising just as she vanished from view. The magician threw himself down in the chair she had left.

'So,' he said, 'you've met the fair Ulrika. What do you think, eh?'

It was an impertinent question from a complete stranger, thought Felix, but then he had heard magicians could be somewhat odd. Then he noticed that the man was smiling and shaking his head like someone enjoying a private joke. White teeth showed against his tanned skin, the animated expression taking years off the wizard's age. Felix guessed that the mage could not be more than ten years older than himself. Suddenly, impulsively, the man stuck out his hand.

'Maximilian Schreiber, at your service. My friends call me Max.'

'Felix Jaeger at yours.'

'Felix Jaeger. That's a name I've heard before. There was quite a promising poet of that name. Are you any relation? I read some of his verses in Gottlieb's anthology several years before. Rather liked them, actually.'

Felix was pleasantly surprised to find that the stranger had heard of him. He cast his mind back to his student days when he had written verse and contributed to various anthologies. That all seemed to have happened to someone else, a long time ago.

'I wrote those,' he said.

'Excellent. A pleasant surprise. Why did you stop writing? Gottlieb's chapbook must be at least three years ago.'

'I ran into some problems with the law.'

'What were those?'

Something about the mage's smooth manner was starting to set Felix's teeth on edge. 'I was expelled from the university for killing a man in a duel. Then there were the Window Tax Riots.'

'Oh yes, the riots. So, in addition to being the poet Felix Jaeger, you are also the notorious outlaw Felix Jaeger, henchman to the infamous Gotrek Gurnisson.'

Felix went white with shock. It had been a long time since he had encountered anyone who had put those two facts together or even known he was an outlaw. The Empire was big and news travelled very slowly. It had been such a long time since he had been anywhere near Altdorf, the scene of that terrible slaughter during the riots. The wizard obviously noticed his expression. His smile became a grin.

'Don't worry. I am not about to turn you over to the law. I always thought it was an unjust and foolish tax myself. And to tell the truth, I sympathise with your predicament at the university. I was booted out of the Imperial College of Magicians myself, albeit a few years before you began your career of insurrection.'

'You were?'

'Oh yes. My tutors believed that I showed an unhealthy interest in the subject of Chaos.'

'I would have to agree with them, I think. It's a subject in which any interest is unhealthy.'

A gleam had come into the wizard's eyes and he leaned forward eagerly in his seat. 'I cannot believe that you think that way, Herr Jaeger. That's the kind of short-sightedness I would expect from the wizened greybeards at the college but not from an adventurer like yourself.'

Felix felt compelled to defend his point of view.

'I believe I know something of the subject. I have had more experience of fighting Chaos than most.'

'Exactly! I, too, have fought against the Dark Powers, my friend, and I have found its minions in some unlikely places. I do not think that I am wrong when I say that it is the greatest single threat to our nation, nay, our world, that currently exists.'

'I would agree with you there.'

'And that being the case, can it be wrong to study the subject? In order to fight such a powerful foe we must understand it. We must know its strengths and its weaknesses, its goals and its fears.'

'Yes, but the study of Chaos corrupts those who engage in it! Many have started down that path with the finest of intentions, only to find themselves enthralled by that thing they sought to fight.'

'Now you really do sound like my old tutors! Has it occurred to you that, if you were a servant of Chaos, you would use exactly that argument to discourage any investigation into your works?'

'You're not seriously suggesting that your tutors at the Imperial College were–'

'Of course not! I am just saying that the servants of Chaos are subtle. You have no idea how subtle they can be. All they would need to do was put the idea into books, spread the rumour, encourage its belief. And, of course, Chaos does corrupt. If you work with warpstone, it will change you. If you perform dark rituals, your soul will be tarnished. I admit there is some truth to this line of argument. However, I don't think that this should stop us from examining Chaos, trying to find ways to prevent its spread, to detect its followers, to blunt its terrifying power. There is a conspiracy of silence which permeates our entire society. It encourages ignorance. It gives our enemies shadows in which to hide, places in which to lurk and plot.'

Felix had to admit there was something in what Schreiber was saying. To tell the truth, he had often had similar thoughts himself. 'You might be right.'

'Might be? Come now, Felix, you know I am right. And so do many other people. Unfortunately, I made the mistake of publishing my opinions in a small pamphlet. The authorities decided that it was heretical and...'

639

'You too became an outlaw.'

'That more or less sums it up.'

'Why are you aboard this ship?'

'Because I continued my researches. I moved from place to place fighting against Chaos where I could, compiling information when I found it, hunting down wicked sorcerers. I have made myself into something of an expert on this subject, and in the end found a refuge at the court of Count Stephan. He is more far-sighted than many of our nobles.

'He and the Knights of the White Wolf have helped fund my researches. Five years ago I met your friend Borek when he visited the library in the temple. He was most interested when he found out that I believed I had found a way to protect against the worst affects of Chaos. He enlisted me to help protect his airship on its voyage.'

Suddenly Felix began to understand the scale of the planning which had gone into their quest. It was of an order of magnitude that he had never encountered before. Not only had Borek overseen the building of the vast industrial complex at the Lonely Tower, he had employed Ulrika's father to build an advance base and discovered and engaged this wizard to ward them against Chaos. The old dwarf had not been exaggerating when he claimed this was his life's work. Felix began to wonder what other feats of planning would be revealed as the trip progressed. Still, he was not entirely convinced by Schreiber's claims.

'You have found a way of protecting this airship against the effects of Chaos?'

'There are a number of them ranging from simple runes, to protective enchantments, to basic precautions such as ensuring an adequate supply of uncontaminated food and water. Believe me, Felix, I would not have agreed to aid you unless I believed that there was a good chance you would be safe.'

'You are not coming with us then?'

'Only to Kislev. Not all the way to Karag Dum.'

Felix looked at the wizard in surprise.

'I told you, Felix, I am a scholar. This is my field. I have studied all I could find on this subject. I was quite capable of working out for myself why an expedition of this magnitude is being prepared by a dwarf like Borek. It came as no surprise to me when he told me his goal.'

Schreiber rose from the chair. 'Speaking of that long-bearded scholar, I must go and discuss some things with him now. But I hope to have a chance to talk more with you before this voyage is complete.'

He bowed and walked away, but at the doorway he turned. 'I'm glad there is an educated man aboard. I thought I might have to spend this voyage simply chasing the delectable Ulrika. It will be nice to have some enlightened conversation as well.'

Felix wasn't sure why he found this remark so offensive. Perhaps, he told himself, he was simply jealous. And then he wondered, why did he already feel that way about a woman he had only just met?

KOSTER

TEN

KISLEV

Thanquol's palanquin hustled northward along the great tunnel of the Underways. This section of the mighty road that ran beneath the spine of the Worlds Edge Mountains was almost totally empty. Normally Thanquol would have been nervous, travelling these dangerous corridors with his much reduced bodyguard. He could easily be attacked by orcs, goblins or dwarfish raiding parties, trying to reclaim some part of their ancient domain. However, at this moment, the grey seer was too upset to be nervous.

He gnawed his tail in despair. He knew from his lackey, Lurk, that the airship had departed from Middenheim and headed northeastwards. The snivelling wretch had managed to report that they had passed over water, before making landfall again, and that the land below them was starting to look emptier and bleaker all the time. Fortunately for Thanquol, he was a far-travelled skaven of considerable knowledge, and he recognised that the airship's destination could only be the land known to humans as Kislev.

He had no idea what those foolish dwarfs could possibly want in that barbarous place. Perhaps they had heard rumours of gold or ancient treasure. Although dwarfs were not the race he had made his deepest studies of, Thanquol knew enough about them to guess that this was their most likely goal. Unfortunately he had no idea where this might eventually take them, and he also knew that the airship

had travelled much further and much faster than he was capable of
pursuing by normal means.

He was almost tempted to order Lurk to find some means of
sabotaging the airship to give him time to catch up. Only one thing
prevented him from doing this. In his considerable experience, a dolt-
ish lackey like Lurk would do something wrong and either get himself
killed or destroy the very airship that Thanquol so desperately wanted
to possess. No – giving such an order was the option of last resort,
and Thanquol decided that he would have to be desperate indeed to
try it. Before then, he would exhaust every other avenue open to him.

He considered his options. Perhaps he could contact the Lords of
Clan Moulder. Their mighty fortress, Hell Pit, was located in northern
Kislev and was the nearest skaven stronghold to the airship's probable destination. To a lesser intellect than Thanquol's, this might
have seemed like a wise plan. Potent as he undoubtedly was, even the
grey seer was forced to admit capturing the airship single-pawed was
almost certainly beyond him. He was going to need help, even if it
meant going with downcast tail to the Beastmasters of Clan Moulder.
But the thought had also occurred to him that it might not be wise to
give them all the details of his scheme, for they might try to seize the
airship by themselves. Being the blundering fools they were, they too
would doubtless fail without his guidance.

No, he decided, the best he could do was to scurry north as quickly
as possible and hope that something would arise to delay the dwarfs
until his arrival. He leaned out the palanquin's window and chittered
at his bearers to redouble their efforts. Fearing their master's righteous
wrath, they scuttled along more quickly, groaning beneath the weight
of their burden and all his sorcerous equipment.

Felix had always thought of Kislev as a land of ice and snow, where
winter never lifted, and the folk wandered around constantly wrapped
in furs. The land below contradicted this impression quite mightily.
It consisted of rolling plains of long grass set amidst thick forests of
pine. A moment's consideration told him that this had to be so, for
Kislev was a land famed for its horsemen, and it would be difficult for
them to be that way if they lived amid endless snowdrifts.

Felix had to admit that, if anything, the sun shone even more
brightly than it did on the Empire at the moment. The Kislevite summer might be brief but it was also intense. Felix wondered if this,
too, was part of Borek's plan, to come northward before the stormy
winds of winter could threaten the airship's progress. It would not

have surprised him to discover that this was the case. The ingenuity and skill with which this expedition had been planned was a far cry from his haphazard wanderings with Gotrek. During their travels they had simply decided to go as the whim took them, with only whatever they happened to be carrying at the time to aid them. Obviously this was not typical dwarfish behaviour, except perhaps where Slayers were concerned.

Below the airship he could see a herd of caribou, startled by the airship's vast shadow, begin to bound away. Hunters rose from their crouches and shaded their eyes to peer up in wonder at the passing vehicle. One of them, braver or more frightened than the rest, cast his spear up at them but it fell a long way short of the vessel and fell point first to stand quivering amidst the long grass.

They were flying beneath the clouds for a good reason. Watchers peered from every porthole and through the large windows of the command deck. They were nearing their destination and all of them had been ordered to keep their eyes peeled for Ulrika's father's mansion. Makaisson's navigation had brought them to the general area. Now they quartered the landscape seeking the exact spot where they would make their final landfall before heading into the Chaos Wastes.

So far all they had seen was the occasional hunter and the odd village where smoke drifted lazily skyward from holes in the turfed roofs of the peasants' log huts. Their presence had sent the villagers scurrying away from their harvests to huddle within the village walls, doubtless convinced that the airship was some new manifestation of Chaos come to trouble their land.

Felix was still amazed at how swiftly they had made the trip. A journey that would have taken months overland looked like it was going to take them only a few days at most, and much of that time had been spent searching for the Boyar's mansion in this sea of grass. Truly this engineering of the dwarfs was a most potent form of magic.

'There!' he heard Ulrika shout and turned to see her pointing to something in the distance. It lay in the shadows of a distant range of dark and threatening mountains. Felix realised her eyes must be keen. All he could see was a vague smudge of smoke.

Makaisson's hands shifted on the wheel, and the nose of the airship swung around in the direction the woman had indicated. He pushed the altitude lever and they swung down lower and faster, sending flocks of startled birds flapping out of the long grass. As the mountains approached, Felix kept his eyes pinned to the direction Ulrika had indicated. Slowly he saw a large, long hall come into view. To his surprise, beside the mansion house, within the compound's massive walls, was a tall tower, a smaller wooden version of the steel monstrosity which had loomed over the Lonely Tower.

This, then, was the place where they were going to land. This might well be the last human habitation he would ever see.

Ulrika's father was huge, a head taller than Felix and burly as a bear. His beard was long and white, but his head was shaved except for a single topknot. His eyes were the same startling blue as his daughter's; his teeth were yellow. A thick leather tunic encased his torso. Coarse cloth trousers covered his lower body, except where high riding boots covered his legs. A longsword and a shortsword hung from his thick leather belt. A dozen amulets jingled on the iron chains around his neck.

He strode out to where the dwarfs waited at the foot of the tower. Behind him a row of warriors presented their weapons with ritual formality. He loomed over Ulrika and clasped her to his mighty chest then swept her off her feet and whirled her round and round as if she were a child.

'Welcome home, daughter of my heart!' he bellowed.

'It is good to be here, father. Now put me down and greet your guests.'

The old man's gusty laughter boomed out and he stomped over to where the crew of the airship stood waiting. He stopped short of embracing the dwarfs. Instead he bowed low in the dwarfish fashion, showing surprising flexibility for a man of his age and enormous girth.

'Borek Forkbeard! It is good to see you. I trust you will find all as you requested it.'

'I trust I will,' the old dwarf said, bowing just as low.

'Gotrek Gurnisson, I bid you welcome also. It has been a long time since you honoured my hall with your presence. I am pleased to see you still carry that axe.'

'I am pleased to return, Ivan Petrovitch Straghov,' Gotrek said in his least surly manner. Felix guessed that the Slayer was almost pleased to see the Kislevite.

'And who is this? Snorri Nosebiter? I must see that a bucket of vodka is left at your table. Welcome!'

'Snorri thinks that would be a good idea.' One by one all the dwarfs were greeted or introduced and then Ulrika led her father over to where Felix and the wizard stood waiting.

'And, father, this is Felix Jaeger of Altdorf.'

'Pleased to make your acquaintance,' Felix said, extending his hand. Straghov ignored it as he loomed over Felix, hugged him in welcome and then kissed him once on each cheek. 'Welcome! Welcome!' he bellowed in Felix's ear, loud enough to threaten deafness. Before Felix could respond, he had been dropped and the old man was doing the same to Schreiber.

'I thank you for the enthusiasm of your welcome, sir,' the wizard said when he had regained his breath.

Felix exchanged glances with Ulrika, then looked in wonder over at the row of warriors who lined their way to the hall. Ivan Straghov might look and behave like a barbarian but there could be no doubt that he was a mighty warlord in his own land. A hundred riders stood by as an honour guard. All had hard faces and cold eyes, and all looked like they could use the well-honed weapons they presented to the dwarfs. According to Ulrika there were nine hundred more of these fierce riders who had sworn allegiance to her father. Being March Boyar was obviously an important post. Since it commanded the first line of defence against the hordes of Chaos, Felix guessed that it ought to be.

'Now we eat!' boomed Straghov. 'And drink!'

Huge tables had been set up inside the mansion's walls. Minor functionaries from all around had been invited to feast and marvel at the dwarfish airship. Caribou had been roasted on spits over great fire-pits. Plates were heaped with coarse black bread and cheese. Great flasks of fiery spirit which Snorri identified as vodka were put beside each plate. As promised, a bucket of the stuff was put beside Snorri.

Felix followed the example of the locals and tossed back his tumbler in one swift gulp. It felt like he was swallowing molten metal. A cloud of something acidic seemed to burn the lining of his throat and make its way up to his nostrils, bringing tears to his eyes. He felt like he ought to be breathing fire and it was all he could do to keep himself from spluttering. He guessed that such behaviour would not be good form here however.

He was glad that he had not done so when he noticed that all eyes watched him to see how he reacted to his first taste of the spirit.

'You drink like a true winged lancer!' Straghov bellowed and all the table banged their glasses on the table in agreement. Their host insisted that everyone fill their glasses, then shouted: 'To Felix Jaeger, who comes from the land of our allies, the Empire!'

Of course, Felix could do nothing less than pledge a return toast to the ancient friendship between his folk and the folk of Kislev. Before long, the dwarfs were joining in too. Felix noticed that a pleasant warmth had settled in his stomach and that his fingers felt slightly numb. The vodka certainly got easier to drink the more glasses he tossed back, and soon he ceased to feel like it was burning his throat.

Great mounds of food were devoured. Toast after toast was made. Great speeches of welcome and friendship were spoken until darkness fell. Somewhere during the course of the afternoon, Felix lost track of events. His head swimming from the vodka, he was only dimly aware of eating far too much, drinking far too much and joining in the singing of songs whose words he did not know. Some time during the evening he was sure he danced with Ulrika, before she whirled away to dance with Schreiber, and then sometime after that he wandered off to be sick beside the stables.

After that his mind blanked completely and great chunks of memory were lost to the vodka and Kislevite hospitality. For the rest of his life he was not sure quite who he spoke to or what he said or how he got to the chamber that was allocated to him. Forever afterwards, however, he was grateful that he did.

Felix awoke the next day feeling like a horse had kicked him in the head. Perhaps one had, he thought; he checked his face for bruises but could find none. He looked around the room and saw that the floor was of packed earth. The mattress was filled with straw and someone had thrown a thick quilt over him. During the night he had drooled on his pillow and a patch of wetness was evident where his head had been. At least, he hoped it was just drool.

He pulled himself to his feet, and wondered whether at some point during the previous evening he really had challenged Snorri Nosebiter to a wrestling match. He seemed to have a vague recollection of some such thing, or maybe he had just dreamt it. His limbs certainly felt twisted enough for him to have engaged in such a foolish pursuit. Maybe he had.

That was the worst thing about a really hard drinking session. You could never quite remember what you had said, who you had insulted and to whom you had issued foolish challenges. You simply engaged in insane behaviour. At that moment, he wondered if perhaps it was true that alcohol was a gift from the Dark Gods of Chaos intended to make men mad, as some of the temperance minded cults in the Empire claimed. Right now he didn't care. He just knew that he never, ever intended to drink again.

A knock sounded on the door. Felix threw it open and blinked out into the harsh daylight.

'Amazing,' Ulrika said by way of a greeting. 'You are on your feet. I would not have thought it possible after the amount of vodka you consumed last night.'

'That impressive, eh?'

'All were impressed. Particularly by the way you climbed the airship tower while reciting one of your poems.'

'I did what?'

'I am only joking. You only climbed the tower. Most people thought you would fall and break your neck, but no...'

'I really climbed the tower?'

'Of course, don't you remember? You bet Snorri Nosebiter a gold piece that you could. At one point you were going to do it blindfolded but Snorri thought that was an unfair advantage because you would not be able to see the ground and would not be quite so afraid. That was just after you'd lost a silver piece arm wrestling him.'

Felix groaned. 'What else did I do?'

'When we were dancing, you told me I was the most beautiful woman you had ever seen.'

'What? I'm sorry.'

'Don't be! You were very flattering.'

Felix felt himself starting to blush. It was one thing flattering a pretty woman. It was another having no memory of having done so.

'Anything else?'

'Is that not enough for one night?' she smiled.

'I suppose so.'

'So you are ready to go riding then?'

'Eh?'

'You told me that you were a great horseman, and you agreed to go riding with me this morning. I was going to show you round the estate. You were very enthusiastic about it last night.'

Felix pictured himself drunk and talking with this extremely pretty woman. He guessed that if she had offered to show him her father's pig-sties in his inebriated condition he would have shown a creditable amount of enthusiasm for it.

Actually, he was certain he would have managed to be enthusiastic about it in any condition except his present one. His hangover made even Ulrika Magdova look less ravishing than the prospect of going back to sleep.

'I am looking forward to seeing you on horseback. It should be quite an impressive sight.'

'I might have exaggerated about my horsemanship.'

'You can ride?'

'Er-yes.'

'Last night you told me you could ride as well as any Kislevite.'

Felix groaned again. Had some daemon taken over his tongue while he was under the influence of the vodka? What else had he said? And why had he drunk so much?

'Ready to go then?'

Felix nodded. 'Just let me have a wash first.'

He strode out into the courtyard. Snorri Nosebiter lay, still slumped over the table, his head encased in a bucket. Gotrek lay snoring by the smouldering remains of one of the fire-pits, his axe clutched comfortingly in his hands. Felix walked over to the water pump, put his head below it and began to work the lever. The cold stream sent a shock jarring along his spine. He puffed and blew and continued to pump, hoping to drive the hangover away by inflicting still greater pain on himself.

Had he really said all those things or was Ulrika Magdova kidding him? He found it all too easy to believe that he had told her she was beautiful. He had thought it often enough over the past few days. He knew how much he had a tendency to run off at the mouth when he was really drunk. On the other hand, it scarcely seemed possible that he had climbed the airship tower while so drunk he could not remember it. It was an act of mad recklessness. No, he decided, it was simply not possible. She had to be joking.

Snorri took his head from the bucket. He looked blearily over at Felix. 'About that gold piece Snorri owes you?'

'Yes,' said Felix uneasily.

'Snorri will pay you when we get back from the Chaos Wastes.'

'That seems reasonable,' Felix said and hurried off towards the stables.

Felix leaned back in the saddle and rolled his head around to clear the stiffness out of his neck. He looked down from the top of the rise to where the small streams cut across the rolling plain. The land was somewhat marshy down there, and bright birds flickered in and out of the reeds. He thought he saw some frogs splashing into the water. Dragonflies flickered past his face, as did other larger insects which he did not recognise. Some of them had bright metallic coloured carapaces, far more striking than those of any insect he had ever seen before. Was this perhaps some evidence of the nearness of the Wastes, he wondered?

He looked over at his companion and smiled, glad at long last to be here. At first the ride had seemed like a peculiarly refined form of torture, with the motion of the horse sending spasms of protest through Felix's queasy stomach. He had cursed the woman, his mount, the fresh air and the bright sun, in roughly that order. But the exercise and the sunlight seemed to have at long last worked their spell on him, and sent his hangover back into the dim, dark recesses of his skull. He had found himself beginning to take an interest in the landscape, and even to enjoy the sensation of speed, of the wind on his face and the sun on his skin.

Ulrika rode easily, as if born in the saddle. She was a Kislevite noble, so of course she had been riding virtually since she could walk. She had not said a word since they had set out, seemingly content to race along beneath the vast, empty sky until at last they had reached this small hillock and by wordless agreement come to a halt.

Beyond the stream, in the distance, the dark mountains marched threateningly towards the horizon, their huge bulk seemingly carved from the bleak bones of the earth. They looked more desolate than any place he had ever been. No snow marked those rugged peaks, but there was a hint of something else, of an oil-like film whose colours shifted and shimmered in the light of the sun. There was a sinister, threatening air about the mountains, hinting at the fact that beyond them lay the outriders of the Chaos Wastes.

'What is that pass?' Felix said, pointing north to the enormous gap which looked as if it had been hacked out of the mountain barrier by some giant's axe.

'That's Blackblood Pass,' Ulrika said quietly. 'It's one of the major routes down from the Wastes, and the reason why the Tzarina has placed this outpost here.'

'Do the Dark Ones pass this way often?'

'You can never tell when they will come or even what they will be. Sometimes they are huge riders in black plate mail. Sometimes they are beastmen, with the heads of animals and the weapons of men, but sometimes other twisted deformed things that are even worse. There seems to be no rhyme or reason to it. It does not matter whether it's high summer or the depth of winter; they can come at any time.'

'I have never been able to fathom the way Chaos works. Perhaps you should talk to Herr Schreiber about it.'

'Perhaps but I doubt that even Max's theories could explain it. Best just to keep weapons sharp and the beacons manned, and be ready to fight at any time.'

'Beacons?'

'Aye, there is a system of beacons stretching back from the pass. When they're lit all the villagers know to flee to their villages and lock the gates, and all the lancers know to muster at my father's house.'

'Smoke by day, fire by night,' Felix murmured.

'Yes.'

'You live in a frightening land, Ulrika.'

'Aye, but it is also beautiful, is it not?'

He looked at her and the land beyond and nodded his head. He noticed that her pupils were large in her eyes, and that her lips were slightly parted. She was leaning slightly towards him. Felix knew a cue when he heard one.

'That it is. As are you.' He leaned towards her. Their hands met and fingers interlaced. Their lips touched. It was as if an electric shock had passed through Felix, and almost as quickly as it had happened, it was over. Ulrika broke away, and reined her horse about.

'It's getting late. I will race you back to the mansion,' she said and turned her mount suddenly and took flight. Feeling more than a little frustrated, Felix set off in pursuit.

Lurk scurried along the top of the gondola. He was happier than he had been in a long time. It was dark and the skeleton crew left on the airship were mostly asleep, except for the dwarf on the command deck. The others were down below, drinking and laughing and singing their foolish human songs. There was plenty of food in the hold, and so far no indication that his presence had been noticed. Now that he was starting to feel more relaxed he could indulge the curiosity which was another Skaven trait. He had slunk around the airship, exploring all the nooks and crannies and he had discovered some very interesting things.

There was a flexible metal tunnel that ran up into the big balloon overhead. It passed right through the body of the gasbag and came out on a small observation deck on top. There was a hatch which led out onto the top of the gasbag. The whole thing was covered in webbing to which you could cling.

At the very rear of the airship was a chamber containing one of the small flying machines which had helped rout the skaven force during the Battle of the Lonely Tower. There was a huge doorway and a ramp that looked like they were designed to let the flying machine out. If only he knew enough to fly the thing, he could have stolen it and made his way back to Skavenblight a hero. The urge to get behind the controls and start flicking switches and pulling levers had been almost irresistible. He had given the notion serious consideration – but the grey seer had been very specific during their last communication.

Lurk was to do nothing and touch nothing without Thanquol's express instructions. The grey seer's words had been quite insulting, implying that Lurk was an idiot who would most likely do something disastrously wrong without Thanquol's guidance. It was just as well for Thanquol that he was who he was, Lurk decided. Only a sorcerer of Thanquol's ability could get away with talking to Lurk that way.

No, he was just going to have to sit tight and do nothing until he got his orders. There was nothing more to do except wait.

ELEVEN
NORTHWARD

Felix joined the crowd of peasants in the courtyard and stared up at the airship. Provisions were being placed aboard the craft, a reminder of the grim fact that all too soon they must leave this place.

From the courtyard of the mansion he could see crates, cases and large leather sacks being winched up the tower and then heaved across the gangplank and into the vessel. It looked like the dwarfs intended to take plenty of vodka aboard to supplement their casks of ale, for, as Snorri had pointed out, you could never be too careful about such things. Mostly, though, the provisions were of a more basic nature: smoked and sun-dried caribou meat, hundreds of loaves of black bread, and as many huge round cheeses. Whatever else might happen, Felix doubted that they would starve, unless they spent a very long time in the Chaos Wastes. Of course, starvation was the least of his worries.

He had noticed the dwarfs were making modifications to their craft. Fine mesh screens had been fitted over the ventilation holes that allowed air to enter the cupola. This was supposed to filter out the mutating dust which rose from the deserts of the Chaos Wastes. Dwarfs in elaborate cat's cradles hung over the side of the airship and made last minute modifications to the engines and rotors.

Other preparations were being made. For the past three days, Max Schreiber had retired to a small tower near the mansion and engaged in some arcane ritual. By night, Felix could sometimes see an eerie glow illuminating the tower windows, and feel the strange prickling of the hairs on the back of his neck that told him magic was being worked. If this bothered any of the others they did not show it. Presumably, Borek had told them it was the wizard's role to help them ward off the evil influence of Chaos, and he appeared to be doing just that. Schreiber himself had told him that this had been left until the last moment because the magic lost its potency over time. The nearer to their final goal he cast the spell, the more time it would last over the Wastes. Felix saw no reason to doubt the magician's expertise in this.

Even as Felix looked up, he could see the engineers clambering along the meshwork on the side of the huge balloon, attaching things that must be jewelled amulets judging by the way they sometimes glittered when the light caught them. He knew that the eyes of the figurehead had been replaced with two oddly glowing gems for he had been up on the bridge of the *Spirit of Grungni* once or twice to take more lessons from Makaisson in how to fly the airship.

Felix had come to enjoy these lessons and he believed that in an emergency he could most likely pilot the vast airship, although he was still uncertain whether he could land the thing if he was forced to. The banks of smaller levers had turned out to fulfil a multitude of purposes. One of them would release ballast, causing the ship to rise swiftly at need. Another sounded the horns which alerted the crew to some upcoming danger. A third would jettison all the black stuff in the fuel tanks in case of a fire, an eventuality that Makaisson assured him would be just about the worst thing that could happen to the airship.

He had found himself gaining a great respect for the chief engineer. Makaisson might well be as crazy as Gotrek claimed, but he obviously knew and loved his subject and he had supplied Felix with simple answers to even his most technical questions. He now knew that the airship flew because the gasbags were filled with a substance that was lighter than air, and had a natural tendency to lift up. He knew that black stuff was highly inflammable and might even explode if lit, and that was why it would have to be vented in an emergency.

Still, for the most part life on the Boyar's estate in these warm summer days had been idyllic, and there had been times when he could almost forget the danger which awaited them on their departure. Almost.

A hand fell on his shoulder and a low laugh sounded in his ear.

'There you are. Tell me, can you use that sword, Herr Jaeger?' It was Ulrika.

'Yes,' he said. 'I've had some practice.'

'Perhaps you would care to give me a lesson.'

'When and where?'

'Outside the walls, now.'

'You're on.'

Felix was not quite sure what he expected when he got outside. Ulrika had already unsheathed a blade and was making a few practice cuts in the air. Felix cocked his head to one side and watched her. She moved well, feet wide apart, right foot forward, keeping her balance as she advanced. The sabre gleamed brightly in the sun as she slashed at some imaginary foe.

He stripped off his cloak and jerkin, and unslung his own blade. It was a longsword, and it had greater length and weight than her weapon. It hissed through the air as he made some practice swipes. Felix moved confidently forward. He was good with a blade and he knew it. In his youth he had excelled in his fencing lessons, and as an adult he had survived many fights. And the Templar's blade he used was the best and lightest he had ever handled.

'Not with that, fool! With that,' she said, nodding in the direction of another blade, which lay in a wooden case by the wall.

Felix strode over to where the other sword lay against the wall. He unsheathed it from its scabbard and inspected it. It was another sabre, long and slightly curved. The cutting edge had been dulled which made sense if this was a practice weapon. He tested the weight and balance. It was lighter than his own sword but the grip felt unfamiliar in his hand. He tried a few experimental passes with it.

'Not what I'm used to,' he said.

'Excuses, excuses, Herr Jaeger. My father always said in a fight, you must be able to use whatever weapon comes to hand.'

'He is correct. But usually I make sure that the first weapon that comes to hand is my own sword.'

She merely smiled at him mockingly, head tilted back, lips slightly open. He shrugged and moved over towards her, the blade held negligently in his right hand.

'Are you sure you want to do this?' he asked, staring directly into her eyes, and wondering exactly why they were doing this.

A few of the guards must be thinking the same thing he guessed, for a small crowd had gathered to watch them from the walls.

'Why do you ask?'

'People can get hurt.'

'These are practice blades, deliberately blunted.'

'Accidents can still happen.'

'Are you afraid to fight me?'

'No.' He was going to say he was afraid that he might hurt her, but something told him that this would be the wrong thing to say.

'You should know that in Kislev we fight to first blood. Usually the loser comes away with a scar.'

'I already have many.'

'You must show me them some time,' she smiled.

While Felix was still wondering what she meant by this, she lunged. Felix barely managed to leap aside. As it was a slice was taken out of his shirt. Reflex action let him parry the next blow, and before he could even think about it, the action sent his counter hurtling back towards her. She blocked the blow easily, and suddenly their blades were flickering backwards and forwards almost faster than the eye could follow.

After a few moments they sprang apart. Neither was breathing hard. Felix realised that the woman was very, very good. Realistically, with his own blade in his hand, he was probably the better swordsman. But fighting at these speeds was mostly a matter of reflex, of a trained response which had been drilled into the fighter so often as to be automatic. In this kind of lightning-fast combat, things happened too quickly for any conscious response. The lighter curved blade was throwing his timing off and giving her the advantage. And that was the last chance he had to think about it for a while, as Ulrika pressed forward with her attack. The guards on the wall cheered her on.

'Did I tell you I have beaten all my father's guards at sabre practice,' she said, as he just managed to get his guard up in time to block her swipe. She wasn't kidding about fighting to first blood either. This was not like the sporting duels of his youth, where you fought to display your skills. This was much more like real combat. He supposed it made sense in a way. In a place as deadly as Kislev you did not want to acquire reflexes that would cause you to pull your blows. He knew, for it had taken him many real fights to completely overcome that conditioning.

'If you had, we wouldn't be doing this,' he muttered, slashing back at her wildly.

'And I have beaten all the local noblemen as well.' Her blow ripped the chest of his shirt and severed a button. Felix wondered if she was playing with him. The guards above jeered at him. 'Since I was fifteen no man has beaten me with the sabre.'

Felix very much doubted that they had let her win simply to curry favour with her father either. He had fought many men, and she was a lot better than most. His face was flushed and he was panting with effort. He was starting to feel a little angry about the way the guards were applauding his humiliation. He forced himself to concentrate, to keep his breathing easy, to keep to his stance as he had been taught.

He realised now that he faced another disadvantage. Most of the fighting he had done had very little to do with this formalised style of combat. It had all been in the rough and tumble of melee combat, where you killed your foe in any way that you could and style counted for nothing.

Realising that he would inevitably lose if he continued to fight in this manner, he decided to change his tactics. He blocked her next blow and pushed forward. As they were face to face, he reached forward and grabbed her left arm with his. Using all his strength he jerked hard, and pulled her around. As she went off-balance, he managed to strike her blade from her hand. He let her go and she fell backwards and he brought his blade down so that the point was against her throat.

'There's a first time for everything,' he said. The slightest drop of blood trickled down her throat.

'So it would seem, Herr Jaeger. Best of three, perhaps?' He saw that she was laughing, and he laughed too.

Felix lay down by the stream near the mansion, looking out across the rolling grasslands, lost in reverie, wondering what was going on between himself and Ulrika. The woman herself stood nearby, holding a short Kislevite composite bow. She stood for a moment, with the bow tensed, in a posture which could not help but reveal her excellent figure, then sent another arrow flashing one hundred strides into the direct centre of the target. It was her third bulls-eye.

'Well done,' Felix said.

She looked over at him. 'This is easy. It would be a far more difficult shot from the back of a galloping horse.'

Felix wondered if she was trying to impress him. It was hard to tell. She was very different from the other women he had known. She was more forward, more accomplished in the arts of war, more direct. Of course, this was Kislev, where noblewomen often fought alongside their menfolk in battle. He supposed they had to be able to, for this was wild frontier country with the Darkness to the north and wild untamed lands full of orcs to the east. This was a harsh country where every blade was needed. She seemed interested in him, in the way men and women always are interested in each other, but whenever he had pressed his suit she had backed away. It was most frustrating. He felt like the more he saw of the woman, the less he actually understood her.

A shadow fell across him and a hand tapped him lightly on the shoulder. Felix looked up, his train of thought disturbed. Varek stood there, peering short-sightedly into the distance towards Ulrika.

'What is it?' Felix asked.

'My uncle asked me to tell you that our preparations are complete. We will leave tomorrow at dawn.'

Felix nodded to show his understanding. Varek bowed low to Ulrika and then backed away.

'What was that?' she asked.

Felix told her. A cloud passed across her face.

'So soon,' she said softly and reached out to touch his face, as if to reassure herself that he was still there.

The sun sank beneath the horizon. In the darkness, Felix stood on the wall and looked towards the distant mountains. It was still early and a warm breeze blew across the grasslands. The two moons had yet to rise. A strange shimmering glow was visible beyond the northern peaks. The sky was filled with dancing lights, the colour of gold, silver and blood. It was a strange sight, at once captivating and frightening.

From below came the sound of musicians tuning their instruments, and cooks bellowing to each other as they prepared the evening feast. Judging from the number of cattle slaughtered and flasks of vodka being produced, Straghov was preparing to give them a right royal send-off.

A slight noise to his left attracted Felix's attention and he realised that he was not alone on the battlements. Gotrek stood there too, gazing into the distance. He seemed rapt and a look of concentration creased his face.

'That glow – is it the light of Chaos?' Felix asked at last.

'Aye, manling, that it is.'

'From here it looks almost beautiful.'

'You might think so now but if you went through Blackblood Pass and marched under that sky you would think differently.'

'Is it really so bad?'

'Worse than I can make it sound. The sands of the deserts are all of strange colours, and the bones of huge animals gleam in the light.

The wells are poisonous, the rivers are not of water but other stuff like blood or mucous. The winds drive the dust everywhere. There are ruins that once were the cities of men, elf and dwarf. There are monsters and enemies without number, and they are not troubled by fear or by sanity.'

'You lost a lot of people, the last time you were there.'

'Aye.'

'What are our chances then?' Felix wanted to add 'of surviving', but he knew that would be a meaningless question to ask a Slayer. 'Of reaching Karag Dum?'

Gotrek was silent for a long time. From behind them rose the sound of singing. From the grass beyond the manor house came the sound of night insects. It was so tranquil that Felix found it hard to believe that this was a land on the frontier of an endless war, and that tomorrow they would be passing over the Chaos Wastes, through a country from which they might never return. Standing here in the warm night air, Felix felt like he was going to live forever.

'In truth, manling, I cannot say. If we went on foot, there would be no chance whatsoever, of that I am certain. With this airship of Makaisson's we might be able to make it.'

He shook his head ruefully. 'I do not know. It depends on how accurate Borek's maps are, and how potent Schreiber's spells prove, and whether the engines break down or we run out of fuel or food, or warpstorms...'

'Warpstorms?'

'Monstrous tempests filled with the power of the Darkness. They can make stone flow like water and turn men into beasts or mutants.'

'Why do you want to go back?' Felix turned to lean against the battlements so that he could get a view of the courtyard behind them.

'Because we might get to Karag Dum, manling. And if we do, our names will live forever. And if we fail, well, it will be a mighty death.'

After that Felix asked no more questions. Looking down into the courtyard and catching sight of Ulrika in a long bright dress, he did not want to believe that it was possible that he could die.

Felix made his way to the edge of the courtyard. Behind him he could hear the sounds of drinking and dancing. Pipers tootled on instruments which resembled miniature bagpipes; other musicians banged away rhythmically on their hide-covered wooden drums. The smell of roasting meat filled his nostrils, warring with the sharp acrid taint of vodka. From somewhere outside came shouting and grunting and cries of encouragement as the warriors egged on two wrestlers.

He was not hungry and he was stone cold sober, for he had decided that he could not face another night of drinking, even if it was to be his last night on earth. He was looking for Ulrika but she had vanished earlier, accompanied by two of the peasant women who appeared to be either her maids or her friends, he was not sure which. It was all a bit anti-climactic. Here he was, dressed in his freshly washed and mended clothes, his hair combed and his body washed – and he could not even find her to steal a kiss. He felt surly and miserable, and more than a little confused. Didn't the girl even care that he was leaving tomorrow? Wouldn't she even talk to him? He was in no mood for the gaiety behind him. He was going to return to his room and sulk. He smiled bitterly as he went, knowing he was being childish and not wanting to do anything about it.

At the half-open door he paused. His chamber was dark and there was a quiet sound from within. Felix's hand reached for his sword, wondering if this was a robber or some servant of the powers of Chaos which had slithered in from the night under the cover of the merrymaking.

'Felix, is that you?' asked a voice that he recognised.

'Yes,' he said in a voice suddenly so thick that he had difficulty forcing the words out of his mouth. A light flickered and a lantern was lit. Felix could see a bare arm protruding from beneath the coverlet.

'I thought you were never going to show up,' Ulrika said and threw the quilt aside to reveal her long, naked body. Felix rushed to join her on the bed. The scent of her filled his nostrils. Their lips met in a long kiss and this time she did not break away.

The light of dawn and the crowing of the cockerels woke Felix. He opened his eyes to see that Ulrika lay beside him, propped up on one elbow, studying his face. When she saw that he was awake she smiled a little sadly. He reached up and ran his hand across her cheek, feeling the soft skin of her face beneath his fingers. She caught his hand, and turned it over to kiss the palm of his hand. He laughed and reached out. He drew her down to him, feeling the warmth of her body, happy to be there, happy to be holding her and feeling her heart beat against his naked flesh. He laughed from sheer pleasure, but she shuddered and turned away from him as if she was about to cry.

'What's wrong?' he asked.

'You must go,' she said.

'I'll be back,' he blurted foolishly.

'No, you will not. No man ever returns from the Wastes. Not sane. Not untouched by Chaos.'

He realised then why their lovemaking of the previous evening had possessed such desperate urgency. It was a one night thing, a gift from a woman to a warrior she thought she would never see again. He wondered if that happened a lot here. His happiness vanished but he held her anyway, stroking her hair.

A heavy knock sounded on the door.

'Time to be away, manling,' came Gotrek's voice, and it sounded like the voice of doom.

TWELVE
THE CHAOS WASTES

Felix felt sadness settle on him like a cloak as he watched the Straghov mansion fall away below the airship. The tiny waving figures slowly receded into the distance and then faded from view entirely as the *Spirit of Grungni* picked up speed. The mansion dwindled until it was lost in the endless immensity of the rolling grass-covered plains. Felix paced the metal deck restlessly.

He wondered if he would ever see Ulrika again. She plainly didn't think so, and she was in a better position to know about these things than he was, having lived on the borders of the Chaos Wastes all of her life. It was odd but already he missed her, strange considering he had never even met the woman until a few days before.

For a swift, dreadful moment, he felt like going to Makaisson and asking him to turn the airship around. He wanted to say that there had been a terrible mistake and he did not want to leave. He found himself wishing he had stayed behind with her, but things had happened so quickly and he had been swept up suddenly once more by the momentum of the dwarfs' quest. Everyone, including her, had seemed to believe he was going, and so he had gone, despite having no real inclination to do so.

It was typical of how things went in his world. Small events took on a life of their own, and before he knew it, he was caught up in wildly unlikely occurrences far beyond his control. He wondered if everybody's lives were like that and not just his. Did everyone pile tiny decisions upon tiny decisions like a child piling pebbles, only to realise at the last moment that they had built a shifting unstable mountain beneath themselves, and that there was no way off without causing an avalanche?

He knew that he could not go to the chief engineer and ask him to turn back for a number of reasons. The first and simplest was that Makaisson might not do it, and he would forfeit the respect and good-will of the crew without gaining anything. The second reason was that he had no idea what reception he would get even if he did turn back. Perhaps what had attracted Ulrika to him was the belief that there was something heroic about his part in the quest, and abandoning it now would mark him as a coward. He knew that the people of this harsh land would want no truck with cowards.

And maybe, he was forced to admit, part of him wanted to go on anyway, to see this new place, to find out how it would all end, to measure his courage against a wilderness that caused dismay even to Gotrek. Maybe the way he felt other people might judge him was the way he judged himself. If he abandoned the *Spirit of Grungni* he would be abandoning his heroic view of himself and retreating into being just like everybody else. Maybe part of him really wanted the fame that the dwarfs aboard the airship craved. He did not know. There were times when his motives confused even himself. They seemed to vary with his moods or his hangovers.

He just knew that he felt terrible right now – and that he wanted to see Ulrika again. The mood of gloom seemed to have infected the whole airship. All the dwarfs were quiet and their expressions were pained. Perhaps they felt this unaccountable sadness as well. Or maybe they were simply hungover, for last night every last one of them had drunk like a Marienburg sailor on a spree or, to be nastily exact, dwarfs confronted by a lake of free booze. Felix had to admit that the airship was currently no place for those with a hangover. The deck vibrated visibly and occasionally the whole gondola shook as they passed through clouds and patches of turbulence.

He pushed his way towards the command deck and saw that it was mostly empty, save for the basic crew needed to fly the ship. He paced moodily over to stand beside Makaisson and looked out the window. The vast stone bulk of the mountains loomed ever closer. He could see that they were headed for Blackblood Pass. It yawned in front of them like the mouth of some great daemon.

Soon they were in the pass itself with the mountains looming all around them, and the lowest of the strange glittering peaks level with the airship. Felix studied them but the glowing, shimmering substance that capped them seemed strangely hard to look at. The eye slid along it like a man tumbling on ice, and he found that he could not really focus on the peaks close up. It was his first indication of how strange Chaos could be. He was sure that it would not be his last.

The pass itself was rocky and bleak. Here and there oddly shaped boulders had been placed alongside the track, and Felix felt sure that strange, outlandish runes had been carved into them. Noticing that some of them gleamed white, he borrowed a telescope from Makaisson and focused it on them. To his horror he saw that what he had taken to be a chalked symbol was in fact a deformed skeleton chained to the rock. Were they human sacrifices left here by warriors of Chaos, he wondered, or warning markers left by the Kislevites? Either seemed perfectly possible.

Varek appeared beside Felix and maintained an awe-struck silence for a few minutes. Felix knew that the young dwarf shared his mood.

'Schreiber thinks these mountains shield all of Kislev,' Varek said eventually.

'What do you mean?'

'I talked with him back at the manor house. He has a theory that says that if it wasn't for this range of mountains, the wind would blow all the warpstone dust down from the Chaos Wastes and infect the population with mutation. He says that they would all change and become deformed and subject to the mad whims of the Dark Gods.'

'I thought there already were mutants in Kislev. Sigmar knows, I've fought enough of them in the Empire. There cannot be fewer here!'

Varek looked at Felix and smiled sadly. 'In Kislev they kill anyone who shows the slightest stigmata of mutation – even babies.'

'They do the same in the Empire,' Felix said, but he knew that wasn't really true. Many parents hid their mutant children and people shielded their mutant relatives. He had encountered such cases in his wanderings. Mutants were not bad people, he thought; they were just suffering from an illness. He shook his head bitterly, knowing that no dwarf and most likely no Kislevite would agree with that conclusion. It was indeed a terrible world.

'Schreiber claims it would be much worse without these mountains, that they are a natural barrier which prevents most of the dust reaching the lands of men. He says that the strange stuff on the peaks is congealed Dark Magic, the pure stuff of Chaos.'

'He has many interesting theories, Herr Schreiber,' Felix said sourly.

'He says these are not just theories. He has conducted experiments on animals using warpstone dust.'

'Then he is mad. Warpstone is an evil substance. It drives men mad. I have seen it.'

'He says he is very careful and shields himself with magic, and all manner of protective substances. My uncle believes his theories. It is one reason why there is a layer of lead foil within the hull of this airship.'

'I think no good will come to Herr Schreiber in the end.'

'I am inclined to agree, Felix, but all the same he could be right. My uncle says it fits with dwarfish lore. Some claim that our people first started building their cities underground during the first great Chaos incursions long ages ago and that the rock shielded us from the taint of Chaos which has affected all other races.'

He seemed embarrassed as he said this, as if unsure how Felix would respond to the accusation that his folk were touched by Chaos. From his own experience of travel within the Empire and beyond, however, Felix found it only too easy to believe that it was the case. Humankind gave itself over all too easily to the worship of the Darkness. It was a depressing thought.

'When we pass beyond these mountains we will be on the very edge of the Realm of Chaos,' Varek muttered darkly.

'Do you think that the spells Schreiber wove around the airship will protect us?' Felix asked.

'I know nothing of magic, Felix. It is not a subject that many dwarfs know about. My uncle believes that it will, and he is considered wise in these matters.'

'A strange man, Herr Schreiber. You know, he asked me to record my impressions of the Wastes in case we made it back.'

'Me too. He says it will help with his researches.'

'Let us hope then that we return to present him with useful material.'

Varek smiled. 'Indeed, let us hope so.'

Lurk was worried. Ever since the human wizard had come aboard the airship and begun casting his spells, he had been unable to contact Grey Seer Thanquol. It was a terrible thing, for he knew the skaven sorcerer would blame him for it, whatever the real cause. He wanted to do something, but he knew nothing about sorcery. A feeling of helplessness surged in him. With it came a desire to rend and tear, to exorcise his fears by killing something, preferably something weak and helpless.

Unfortunately there had been no likely candidates for his fury. The airship was full of well-armed and equipped dwarfs, and Lurk did not have a dozen of his packmates with him to encourage his righteous skaven wrath.

He had known that he needed to find this outlet for his pent-up energies. He had found it in exploring the airship while most of the dwarfs slept. Once again he had found himself at the promising tunnel opening in the topmost level of the gondola.

Slowly, carefully, he turned the massive handle and felt the lock click open. He pushed upwards with all his strength and saw a ladder running upwards. Wind tugged his fur for a moment and he realised he stood atop the gondola. Looking up he saw the ladder disappeared into a circular opening in the fabric of the gasbag. He pulled himself up through the opening and was immediately surrounded by what appeared to be a mass of monstrous balloons. They were fixed in long rows within the gasbag by fine wires.

Quickly he scurried up the ladder, leaping upwards with the natural agility of a skaven, reassured by the pressing closeness of the gasbags all around him. His keen nostrils twitched and his whiskers bristled. He recognised a faint acrid tang to the air that no human or dwarf would have noticed. He recognised this scent! He had caught hints of it down below in the gondola but that was not where he knew the smell from. No, he had encountered it in the great marshes around Skavenblight where the ratfolk factories poured their chemical by-products into the mud and quicksand. Sometimes huge bubbles would form where the effluent was piped, and when those bubbles broke the surface and popped this particular smell was emitted.

Was it possible that the dwarfs had trapped this gas in these thin balloon-like sacks, and that it was these thousands of sacks which lifted this vessel into the sky? Could it be that the means to create airships was already within skaven paws? Should he tell Grey Seer Thanquol of his suspicions?

He considered the thought for a moment and then decided against it. It was a ludicrous theory! Surely only the most powerful of sorcer-ies could keep this vessel aloft. That must have been what the human sorcerer was doing back at the human surface-burrow! He must have been recharging the spells that let the airship fly. These gasbags must serve some other purpose. Perhaps they were weapons, like poison gas globes. That, too, seemed unlikely, however, for he had never heard of the marsh gases giving anybody anything worse than a bad headache.

He scampered all the way to the top of the ladder, noting that various rope walkways ran through the massive balloon to allow access to its innards. This would make a good hiding place if he had to abandon the cargo hold below. When he reached the top of the ladder he emerged into an open crow's nest atop the ship. It seemed to be a kind of observation deck, about the size of a rowing boat. Various strange meters and gauges were set into a large metal box. Heeding Thanquol's words, he did not dare touch them. Standing on a large tripod beside them was a telescope, mounted above a large, multi-barrelled weapon which reminded Lurk of the organ guns he had faced in his battles with humans and dwarfs. Doubtless the weapon was meant to protect the airship in case of attack from above.

Overhead he had a perfect view of the sky. The chill wind whipped his fur, and he sniffed the air. By the Horned Rat! It contained the faintest hint of warpstone! Lurk's fur bristled. If he could find a source of that fabled substance he would be rich beyond his wildest dreams of avarice – provided Thanquol let him keep some. Perhaps best not to mention the precious Chaos rock to the grey seer before it was absolutely necessary. After all, he could be wrong.

A walkway ran away along the top of this massive structure to other crow's nests at the front and rear of the ship. He realised that he was looking at a row of defensive emplacements similar to this one. It looked like the dwarfs were taking no chances. Was it possible that those rope walkways within the balloon itself led to other weapons in the sides of the airship? He would have to investigate.

He looked through the eyepiece of the telescope and scanned his surroundings, taking careful note of the enormous mountains with their glittering peaks, and the odd traces of colour in the northern sky. He suddenly felt enormously exposed. This was not the place for a tunnel-dweller like himself. There was too much sky, too much fresh air and the horizon was too far away. He had best return below.

There you are! The thought was so powerful it truly startled him. Lurk shot bolt upright and his tail stretched to its fullest extent. *Where have you been?*

Nowhere, most understanding of Overlords. Lurk thought carefully. *In the airship, as you commanded.*

Then our foe-fiends have shielded their ship with sorcery. Incompetent fool-slave, they must have detected your presence!

It was a terrifying thought, which Lurk prayed most devoutly was not true. He swiftly explained to the mighty voice thundering in his head about the presence of the human sorcerer on the ship, and about how he had enshrouded the cupola in mysterious spells. The silence which followed was so long that Lurk started to believe that Thanquol had lost contact. Just as he was offering up his thanks to the Horned Rat, though, the commanding voice spoke again.

The man-wizard must have put shieldspells on the shipcraft to protect it from something. The spells are only on the vessel below not where you are. Come to where you are now at the same time each day and I will contact you.

Yes, most potent of potentates, Lurk thought back.

Lurk hastily scampered back down the ladder. Only on his way back down did he wonder whether the grey seer understood the danger. Perhaps the crow's-nest would be occupied. Perhaps he would be unable to carry out this order. It was a frightening thought. Lurk wished he had a few underlings present to bully and relieve his frustrations. On the way back down he settled for slashing a few balloons with his claws. They burst, sending rushes of foul but familiar gas into his nostrils.

Only when he was safely back in his crate did Lurk start to worry what would happen to him if any of the dwarfs noticed the balloons he had burst. Perhaps they would suspect his presence. On the other paw, his natural skaven curiosity also made him wonder what would happen if he burst all of the balloons.

Felix continued to survey the ground beneath them, as he had done for hours. They had reached the very beginnings of the Chaos Wastes now. Below them he could see the first dunes of odd, multicoloured sand beginning to mingle with the bleak rocky plain. The sky ahead was turbulent, filled with shifting clouds of unusual metallic shades. The sun was rarely visible and when it showed its face it looked larger, and redder. It was as if they were not only crossing into a new land, but into an entirely new world. The gems in the eyes of the ship's figurehead glowed brightly, as if whatever spell had been placed upon them was now fully activated.

Once again the sheer speed of the airship filled Felix with appalled wonder. In the past few hours they had passed over towering mountains, then rolling plains. Those plains had not looked too different from the grasslands of Kislev – except that when you looked more closely you could see charred ruins where the stones had apparently flowed like water into new and bizarre shapes, and the ponds and lakes shimmered with odd pinks and blues as if tainted by strange chemicals.

After the plains had come marshland and then the tundra. The temperature had dropped noticeably and sometimes flurries of crimson snow had battered against the windows, before melting and running down the glass in red droplets which reminded Felix uncomfortably of blood.

Eventually these bleak lands had also given way, to a place where nothing grew, a stony plain littered with towering boulders that reminded Felix of ancient menhirs. It seemed to him unlikely that these could have been raised by men, but then you never knew. Sometimes they had passed over small bands of beastmen who had beat their chests and bellowed challenges up at them. On other occasions they had flown above clusters of foraging men, who scattered at their approach. Through the telescope Felix saw that all of them bore the stigmata of mutation. How did they survive in this unhealthy land, he wondered – trying not to consider the dark tales of cannibalism and necrophagy that were told of the cults of Chaos.

Now they had left even those bleak lands far behind them and were looking down on the shimmering desert. Felix heard the click of Borek's stick on the stone floor as the old dwarf approached, then felt the touch of a leathery hand on his sleeve.

'Take this amulet and put it on,' Borek said. 'We have entered the Chaos Wastes proper now, and it will shield you against their influence. Try to keep it at all times against your flesh, for that will transfer its power to you and ward you against the warping emanations of the Dark Magic.'

Felix accepted the amulet and held it up to the light. A silver chain and casing held a gem the exact shape and colour of a piece of ice, the sort of frozen stalactite he had often seen in winter hanging from the eaves of his father's house. It was a crystal of a type he had never seen before, and as he looked within it he thought that he caught sight of a faint glow.

He touched the stone, half-expecting it to be frozen, but if anything it felt slightly warm.

He cocked his head suspiciously and looked down at the old dwarf.

'This was made for you by Herr Schreiber, wasn't it?'

Borek beamed gnomishly up at him. 'You do not trust him, do you, Herr Jaeger?'

Felix shook his head. 'I trust no wizard who has dealings with Chaos.'

'That is commendable, I suppose, but also a little foolish.'

'I have had some experience of magic and of Chaos.'

Borek glanced out the windows and smiled ruefully. 'As have I. And let me tell you, I trust Maximilian Schreiber with my life.'

'Good! Because it seems to me that is exactly what you're doing.'

'You are stubborn. We dwarfs find that an admirable quality. Yet you are wrong about the wizard. I have known him many years. I have talked with him and travelled with him. I have saved his life and he has saved mine. There is no taint in him.'

The quiet tone of authority in the loremaster's voice was more convincing than his words. He felt that the dwarf was probably right, but still… Felix had grown up in a land where magic and Chaos had often been regarded with horror, and he had some terrible experiences at the hands of sorcerers. It was hard to put aside a lifetime of prejudices. He said as much.

The loremaster shrugged and then gestured at the gondola that surrounded him. 'Even dwarfs can change, Herr Jaeger, and if anything we are far more bound by tradition and by prejudice than you. This whole airship goes against the traditions of one of our strongest guilds. Yet we have put aside our prejudices because our need is great.'

'And you think my need for this amulet is great.'

'I think it will be your best protection against Chaos, Herr Jaeger, while its magic lasts. And believe me, you will need protection against Chaos.'

He turned and shouted something in rapid dwarfish to Makaisson. It came as a shock to Felix to hear him speaking that harsh guttural tongue. During their travels together all of the dwarfs around him had spoken Reikspiel. At first Felix had thought it was out of politeness, because he was a foreigner and could not understand, but later he had come to realise that it was really down to the peculiarly suspicious dwarfish mind. Yes, they were being polite, but they also regarded their tongue as sacred and secret, and did not want outsiders to learn it unless they were completely trustworthy. Of all the humans he knew, only the higher ranks of the priesthood of Sigmar were proficient in the language and they taught it only to their own priests after ordination. Felix guessed that Borek's decision to speak now meant that he had crossed some barrier and that the old dwarf trusted him. He felt obscurely pleased.

'I was just telling the pilot to take the craft down towards those ruins. I thought I recognised them,' Borek said.

Felix followed the direction indicated by the loremaster's pointed finger. There were tumbled down buildings and other things among them. He raised the telescope to his eye and saw that they resembled wagons of metal, totally enclosed with only crystal window slots out of which drivers could see, and four more slots in the side through which weapons could be poked. There was a peculiar arrangement of funnels at the back and no yokes to which any beast of burden might be harnessed. Something about them reminded him of Imperial war wagons that had been completely roofed over, and also of the Imperial steam tanks he had once seen in Nuln.

'This was our last expedition's first campsite in the Wastes,' Borek said. 'See where those rusting hulks are? Those were our vehicles. We were attacked here by an enemy warband and drove them off only with great losses. Those cairns there were raised over our dead.'

Felix realised that the airship had come to a halt over the ruins and that the other dwarfs were crowding the windows and portholes to gaze down on it. They looked down at it with the sort of awe that Felix had seen human pilgrims display when they entered a shrine. In a way, it was worrying evidence of the dangers of the Wastes. In another, it was reassuring, in that it showed that people had come this way before, and that things were not a complete unknown here.

He looked down on the abandoned vehicles and the empty tombs, and his earlier sadness returned redoubled. Those things had stood there for nearly twenty years and the only other eyes that had looked upon them were those of Chaos worshippers and monsters. He truly wished that he had not come here.

'Near here are the caves where Gotrek found his axe,' Borek said softly.

'Is that so? Was the failure of your expedition the reason why Gotrek became a Slayer?'

'No. That happened later…'

Borek smiled sadly then looked at him, opened his mouth as if to speak, and then, as if realising that he had already said too much, closed it again. Felix wanted to ask more but it came to him that if the old dwarf didn't want to speak there was no way to make him do so.

Felix noticed that he still held the amulet negligently in his hand. The thought struck him that it was undoubtedly true that the old dwarf knew more about these things than he did, and that perhaps he should heed the loremaster's words. He looped the silver chain around his neck and let the stone dangle down inside his shirt. Where it touched his flesh he felt a strange tingling. A shiver passed through him and then was gone, leaving only a warm glow that in no way reassured him.

Borek patted him on the back. 'Good,' he said. 'Now you are better protected than we ever were in the old days.'

Felix looked up towards the horizon and offered up a prayer to Sigmar for the souls of the dwarfs down there, and for his own safety. A sudden premonition of doom came to him and did not leave, even after the airship's engines roared to life once more and they began to move forwards, deeper into the Chaos Wastes.

THIRTEEN
WARPSTORM

Felix pressed his nose against the cold glass of the window and for the first time felt truly terrified. The horns calling the crew to battle stations had just sounded, and all the dwarfs ran to take up their positions at the guns and engines, leaving Felix to stand idly by, a helpless spectator in this time of fear. He looked down on the eerie landscape below.

The desert had a wild and terrible beauty. Enormous rock formations towered over the glittering sand like wind eroded statues of monsters. An emerald lake glittered greenly under the crimson sky. By its shores two enormous armies marched towards each other in a tide of flesh and metal.

Felix wondered at his fear. The warriors of Chaos advancing below seemed not at all concerned with the airship overhead. They were far too intent on each other. Only occasionally would a beastman or a Chaos warrior look up at the sky and brandish a weapon. None of the missile weapons they carried appeared to have the range to hit the airship. Makaisson had sounded the alert just to be on the safe side, however, and Felix could not blame him. The numbers and the insane ferocity of the crowd below them were terrifying.

These were both mighty forces, perhaps the largest armies he had ever seen. Thousands of beastmen surged below, like a sea of hoofed and horned animals grown upright into twisted parodies of men. Felix had fought these followers of Darkness before, but now something about the sheer numbers here made them seem far more terrifying than ever before. Huge banners rose from the midst of the forces, each a twisted parody of the heraldic emblems of his distant homeland. Monstrous men garbed in incredibly ornate black armour marched at the head of each force or rode at its flanks on mutated steeds which dwarfed even the largest of human war-horses.

There were thousands upon thousands of warriors present. Felix wondered at that. How could this barren landscape support such vast regiments? Obviously there was sorcery at work here. Looking down on these immense armies he recalled the descriptions he had read of the previous incursions of Chaos, during the time of Magnus the Pious, when Praag had been besieged and it seemed like the forces of the Dark Gods were about to sweep away the entire civilised world. They had always seemed faintly unreal to him, with their lurid depictions of daemons, and their enormous hordes of twisted feral things but those armies down there made those hellish visions seem all too plausible. He could easily see those mighty forces crashing through Blackblood Pass and smashing through the lands of men. For the first time he started to truly understand the power of Chaos, and he wondered why it had not yet devoured the world.

With a roar Felix could hear even above the racket of the airship's engines, the armies closed the distance between them. Felix trained the telescope, focusing on those distant figures, turning them from tiny marionettes into living breathing warriors.

A huge figure garbed in armour of black iron, on which was inscribed redly glowing runes charged his barded war-horse towards a mob of beastmen. This foul knight brandished an enormous battleaxe in each hand. The horse's trappings were fantastically ornate. Its head was shielded by a moulded mask that gave it the features of a daemonic dragon. The armour on its body was segmented like that of a centipede and on each section were numerous discs, carved in the shape of leering daemon masks. The mounted warrior rode full pelt into a band of beastmen. His axe decapitated a foe with each swing. His horse's hooves dashed out the brains of another, and it continued onwards trampling the bodies of the slain into bloody mush. Behind the knight his fellows charged with maniacal fervour towards packs of beastmen that outnumbered them more than twenty to one. They seemed fearless and uncaring of whether they lived or died.

In another part of the battlefield, monstrous minotaurs armed with axes the size of small trees hacked their way through all that opposed them. They towered over the beastmen the way adults tower over small children, and it seemed to Felix that a beastman had about as much chance of overcoming one as a child had of overcoming a full grown man. Even as Felix watched, one of the bull-headed giants caught a goat-headed thing on its horns and lifted it kicking and screaming from the ground. With a shake of its head, the monster sent its gored victim flying twenty paces to land atop its comrades. The impact sent half a dozen of them sprawling onto the bloody sand. But then, even as Felix watched, the rest of beastmen swarmed over the minotaur, striking with spears, clambering up its legs, harrying it the way a pack of wild dogs would savage a bear. The massive creature fell and disappeared in a cloud of dust, to be trampled under the beastmen's hooves and impaled on their spears.

Winged humanoids with daemonic features rose like a flock of hideous bats and wheeled over the battlefield. At first Felix feared that they were going to attack the airship and his hands reached for the hilt of his sword but then the hellish flock gave out a hideous, ear-piercing shriek and descended down onto the beastmen hordes. They lashed out with taloned claws and ripped their victims limb from limb with a strength that seemed supernatural, before being lopped into pieces themselves by their frenzied foes.

In the centre of all this howling madness loomed a gigantic figure clad in the most fantastically ornate armour Felix had ever seen. Every piece of it appeared to moulded with grinning skulls and leering gargoyle faces. The warrior was mounted on a skeletal steed which seemed barely able to sustain its great weight and yet moved with a speed like the wind. In his right hand, the Chaos champion held an enormous scythe; in his left, a banner depicting a throne of skulls whose empty eye-sockets wept tears of blood. The warlord gave instructions to his followers with great sweeping gestures of the scythe and hordes of lesser, black armoured warriors leapt to obey, running to their deaths or to dispatch their foe with a strange savage joy.

Felix had to admit that they were terrifying. He watched aghast at the sheer frenzy with which the combat was fought. He had never seen such insane hatred as these two forces seemed to possess for each other, and suddenly it came to him that here was the reason why the followers of Darkness had yet to overwhelm the world. They were as divided amongst themselves as the nations of men were; more so, in truth. Perhaps then the rumours of rivalry between the Ruinous Powers were true. For this Felix was profoundly grateful, for here was a force that inspired respect and fear.

There was something disturbing about all this as well. What if the powers were somehow to put aside their rivalry and turn their faces towards the world? What if some mighty warlord was to arise among the forces of Chaos and unite them in one invincible horde? Then the uncountable hosts would march down on Kislev and the lands beyond. Suddenly Straghov's fortress and his thousand lancers seemed pitifully few.

In a matter of minutes the airship swept over the battle and it dwindled away behind them, lost in the enormous immensity of the endless desert. No matter how vast the warring armies were, this landscape could reduce them to less than the significance of ants. A vast dark gloom obscured the northern horizon. The very sight of it filled him with foreboding. Felix let out his breath in a long sigh and returned to his cabin to sleep.

The shaking of the airship woke Felix unhappily from a dream of Ulrika. He pulled himself upright just as an enormous crash echoed through the steel corridors, and the whole vessel vibrated as if struck with an enormous hammer. His stomach lurched as the lantern on his wall swung, sending shadows flickering across his chamber. In that brief instant he felt certain he was going to die.

He pulled himself upright and glanced through the porthole. Outside all was roiling murk. Then there was a flash of incredible green lightning, multiple forks flickering down from above and losing themselves in the gloom. After a few seconds the voice of thunder spoke and the whole ship shook once more. The vibrations cast Felix from his bed and sent him rolling to the floor. As he leapt upright, he banged his head against the low ceiling. The pain sent lights dancing before his eyes and he reached a hand out to grasp the wall and help keep his balance. To his surprise it felt warm.

Struggling to keep his balance on the rocking floor, he shuffled out into the corridor and headed towards the control room. His ears rang with the sound of thunder, and he could barely control the terror which clawed at his guts. This was far worse than any earlier turbulence. It was as if a giant had grasped the airship in its enormous hand and was trying to wrestle it to the ground. He could hear the roar of titanic winds hurtling past the hull. Any moment he thought the vessel would be split like a ripe melon hit by a hammer, and he and everybody else in the vessel would fall tumbling through a thousand strides of storm-tossed air to splatter on the ground below.

It was the sense of helplessness that was so frightening, the knowledge that there was nothing he could do to prevent any of this happening. There was no way off the *Spirit of Grungni* except clambering out through the hatches in the roof and leaping to certain death. At least in battle he could do something, wield a sword, smite a foe. Here and now he could do nothing save pray to Sigmar, and he doubted very much, given where they were currently located, that there was anything the God of the Hammer could do to save them. The twenty strides to the control room seemed to take a lifetime and Felix confidently believed that each step might be his last.

Arriving at the control room at last, he saw the dwarfs clutching at their control stations like it was their last hope of life. Gotrek stood in the centre, his axe held negligently in one hand, looking almost relaxed, riding the rolling deck with slight adjustments of his stance. No fear showed on his face, just a fixed grin of the sort he normally only revealed in combat. Felix noticed that the runes on his axe-blade were glowing redly. Makaisson wrestled with the control wheel, his enormous muscles straining, huge sinews standing out like cables beneath his tattooed flesh. Old Borek was strapped into one of the armchairs, while Varek huddled behind him, a look somewhere between fear and wonderment inscribed on his face. Snorri was nowhere to be seen.

'What's going on?' Felix shouted, struggling to make himself heard over the echoes of thunder, the roar of the wind and the scream of the engines. The whole ship shook once more and there was a sickening sensation of being dropped, as if the airship had suddenly lost buoyancy and was falling like a stone towards the earth.

'Warpstorm, manling!' Gotrek bellowed. 'The worst I've seen!'

Eerie green lightning flickered once more, the flash illuminated the whole cabin intensely, elongated Makaisson's shadow until it filled the floor, then vanished. The bolt appeared to have flickered only a few hundred yards away. Felix noticed that in its aftermath particles of shimmering dust, like a cloud of strangely coloured fireflies, filled their field of vision as far as the eye could see. Then the blast of thunder almost deafened him and the ship began to drop once more. After a moment the sensation of falling stopped and the airship righted itself like a ship cresting a wave.

Felix scrambled over to the window and looked downwards. Through a gap in the clouds, in the flickering of the lightning, he thought he caught sight of the ground below. It was only a few hundred paces beneath them, dunes of glittering sand rising and tumbling, being driven before the titanic winds like foaming breakers on a storm-tossed sea. The wind shook the huge airship like a terrier shaking a rat. Felix knew that in a few dozen more heartbeats they were going to be driven into the ground, and the vessel was going to buckle and break like a toy boat thrown against a wall by a vicious child.

'Malakai! We're going to crash!' he shouted. 'We're almost at the ground!'

'Then come ivver here and gae us a hand, laddie. Pull on that altitude stick for all ye're worth. An' keep yer eyes peeled. The instruments hae stopped workin' in this storm.'

Felix rushed over to stand beside the engineer and pulled on the lever. Normally it would have moved easily but now it appeared to be stuck. Felix braced both his legs and heaved with all his might but still it would not move. The cold metal refused to be shifted. A vision of the airship impacting on the rocky desert below filled Felix's mind and he pulled once more, putting all the strength of fear into his efforts. Sweat ran down his brow. His muscles felt like they were going to erupt through his skin, and he knew that if he kept this up much longer he would burst a blood vessel. It was no use; still the cursed lever would not move.

'I can't shift it!' he called.

"'Tis the wind on the ailerons, laddie. It's fightin' ye. Keep trying'. Dinna gae up!'

Felix kept tugging and still nothing happened. He knew they must be mere seconds from disaster and still there was nothing he could do. He offered up a prayer to Sigmar for his soul, knowing that his life was about to end here in the Chaos Wastes. Then suddenly Gotrek was beside him, lending his massive strength to the struggle with the lever. And still it did not move.

Gotrek's beard bristled. The veins stood out on his forehead, and then something gave way. At first Felix feared that they had simply bent the stick out of shape but no, it was moving slowly, surely, inexorably backwards. As it did so, the nose of airship tilted skywards. Then it seemed like the airship was being thrown backwards like a galleon caught by a huge breaker. The deck rocked and he and Gotrek lost their footing, and were sent tumbling backwards towards the rear cabin wall. There was a sickening sensation in Felix's churning innards as the airship began to leap uncontrollably skyward and then was dashed downwards again.

'Hold on tight!' bellowed Makaisson. 'This is gannae be rough!'

* * *

Lurk squirted the musk of fear. He felt his glands void until they were empty and still they tried to keep on spurting. The wind tugged at his pelt, riffling it with a thousand daemon fingers. Glittering warpstone dust filled his mouth and threatened to choke him. He had already swallowed a fair amount of the stuff and a warm glow filled his stomach. His fur stood on end. The roar of thunder almost deafened him. Tears filled his eyes from fear and constant irritation of the onrushing wind. He clutched the rails of the crow's nest with all four paws; his tail was looped round the rails to anchor him in place. He fought to keep himself low within the observation post, yet still the wind threatened to tear him from his place and send him tumbling to his doom. It was almost too much to be borne.

He cursed the day he had ever left his nice warm burrow in Skavenblight. He cursed Grey Seer Thanquol for his stupid orders. He cursed the stupid dwarfs and their stupid airship and their stupid journey. He cursed everyone and everything he could think of – except the Horned Rat, towards whom he remembered to send the occasional prayer for his deliverance.

Only a few minutes ago it had all seemed so quiet. He had climbed from his hiding place in the hold up to the crow's nest to make his daily report to Grey Seer Thanquol. The ship had been vibrating a little but Lurk had become used to its little motions and had paid no attention. But by the time he had reached the observation deck, the movements had become larger, the whole ship was bucking in the air like a crazed horse. But it was only when he had poked his snout through the upper hatch into the crow's nest proper that he noticed that the ship was surrounded by the strangely glowing cloud and its bizarre, multi-coloured lightning flashes.

Sound skaven prudence had told him that he should retreat below but he had been held in place by one thing: the tingling taste of warpstone dust on his tongue. It held him in place, fascinated. It was the source of much of the grey seer's much-feared power, and quite possibly the source of all magic. He had thought that maybe if he tasted some he, too, might acquire magical powers, but so far there had been no sign of them. By the time he had tried to return below, the accursed dwarfs had sealed the hatches and there was no way he could open them from above. They were locked.

In frantic fear he had scrambled around inside the gasbag but the strangely shifting balloons had spooked him and he had grown tired of hanging from the ladder. So he had clambered back up to the crow's nest and there the wind had grabbed him. He had only just been able to save himself by seizing the railings and now there was nothing he could do except wait and pray while the airship rocked below him like a raft in a typhoon.

Another series of thunderclaps made Lurk look up. He saw a series of lightning flashes marching across the sky, coming ever closer. Their unholy brilliance dazzled him. He shut his eyes firmly but he knew beyond a shadow of a doubt that they were about to hit the airship.

He remembered to send a final curse in the general direction of Grey Seer Thanquol.

Felix, too, saw the line of lightning bolts exploding directly in front of the airship. Makaisson twisted the wheel instinctively trying to avoid being hit, but it was too late. The greenish bolts pummelled the airship. In the instant before the tremendous glare blinded him, Felix had time to notice that the gems on the ship's figurehead blazed bright as the sun. Then the ship shook as if it was about to fly apart and for a long moment Felix saw no more. For a heartbeat the terrible fear that he had been blinded filled him but it passed as his vision slowly returned, and he noticed that everything in the command deck was surrounded by a swiftly fading halo of green.

The amulet on his chest felt almost hot enough to burn and he felt like ripping it off until the thought struck him that this might not be wise, and that perhaps it was protecting him from the magic of Chaos which had so obviously been contained within the lightning. He saw that the amulet on Gotrek's bare chest was glowing a furious green as it absorbed the halo about him. Then suddenly the ship stopped shaking and the sky around them was clear.

Felix picked himself up and limped over to the window of the command deck. He could still see the green-black clouds of the warpstorm boiling below them. Occasionally the clouds would flash brightly with a glow of witch-light as the lightning sparked again and again. It was like looking down on a peculiar chaotic sea and Felix half-expected to see some enormous monster rise up out of its depths and try and swallow the airship in its jaws.

It took him a few moments to realise that the drone of the engines had changed. The sound slowly died away, until they made no noise at all. The clouds slowly passed beyond the airship. It began to gently rotate this way and that in the breeze.

'We've lost power,' Makaisson muttered. 'This isnae guid.'

Snorri chose that moment to appear in the cabin. He was yawning widely. 'What was all the noise?' he asked. 'It woke Snorri up.'

FOURTEEN
THE RUINED CITY

Felix listened unhappily as the engineers reported back to the command deck in turn, each bearing a tale of woe. It appeared that the warpstorm had caused a great deal of damage. There were rips in the gasbag, the engines had stopped working properly, the rotor blades were bent out of shape and there was some structural damage besides.

'We'll joost hae tae stop fur repairs,' Makaisson announced calmly. Looking down through the windows Felix wished he shared the dwarf's confidence. The storm had finally cleared and the sky was its usual overcast mixture of strangely coloured clouds.

Below them lay the ruins of an enormous city, with not a soul visible in the streets. Such desolation was eerie. The wind whistled mournfully as it stirred the shifting sands which drifted through the abandoned buildings.

Then Felix heard a much more cheering sound: somebody, somewhere had managed to get one of the engines working. Gleefully Makaisson took control of his craft again. He nursed the airship down until it was only a hundred strides above the buildings.

'We'll moor here. Draup they lines.'

Mooring lines dropped. Felix saw the grapnel hooks on the end of one snag on a tumbled stone wall. It was enough to hold the drifting airship in place.

'Right, get doon there and secure they hooks! I'll try tae haud her steady up here.'

'Wait,' Felix said. 'It might be dangerous.'

'Och, yer right, laddie. Gotrek, Snorri, Felix, off ye go and make sure that there's nae wee beastmen lurkin' aboot doon there.'

Felix wished that he hadn't opened his mouth.

From the ground the ruins looked even more vast and forbidding than they had from the air. The buildings seemed immeasurably ancient. Huge blocks of stone had been placed atop of each other without the use of mortar. Originally their weight and the precision with which they had been positioned held them in place. It was a style that Felix had seen only once before – in the ruins he had seen above the ancient underground dwarfhold of Karak Eight Peaks. He said this out loud.

'This isn't dwarfish workmanship, manling,' Gotrek sneered. His voice was muffled by the scarf he had wrapped round the lower part of his face to keep out any warpstone dust that might be in the air. Both Snorri and Felix had done the same thing. It seemed descending into madness and mutation did not fit in with the Slayer ideal of a heroic doom. 'Looks like it. Maybe it was copied or perhaps the builders had dwarf advisors but this was not dwarfish work. Stonework is shoddy. The alignment is less than perfect.'

Felix shrugged. His mail shirt felt heavy on his shoulders but he was glad it was there. In this strange place, the more armour he had the better. Right now he wouldn't have minded a complete suit of plate mail. He glanced around him. The street on which they stood was paved with huge flagstones. On each stone was inscribed an outlandish rune. The wind whispered eerily through the desolation. It was cold and he had the uncanny feeling of being watched. 'I have never heard of any human cities this far north, and it does not look like elvish work.'

'Elvish work!' Gotrek said contemptuously. 'A contradiction in terms: elves don't work.'

'I doubt this was built by beastmen or the warriors of Chaos. It seems too sophisticated for them, and it looks very ancient.'

'Looks can be deceiving here in the Chaos Wastes.'

'What do you mean?'

'There are all manner of illusions and mirages, and it is said that deep in the Wastes, the Great Powers of Chaos can create and destroy things at their whim.'

'Then we'd best hope that we are not so deep in the Wastes.'

'Aye.'

An eerie wailing call echoed through the ruins, like the shriek of a soul in torment or the cry of a mad thing wandering lost and forlorn through an endless wilderness. Felix span around and ripped his sword from its scabbard.

'What was that?' he asked.

'I do not know, manling, but doubtless we will find out if it comes closer.'

'Snorri hopes it does!' said the Slayer almost cheerily.

Felix glanced at the rope ladder hanging from the airship's side. He had not enjoyed clambering down it, and he did not look forward to the prospect of climbing up it again, but it was good to know that it was there, just in case they needed to beat a swift retreat. The bizarre call sounded again, closer now, but it was hard to tell exactly.

With the echoes in these ruins it could be coming from leagues away. Felix consoled himself with the thought that at least it had not been answered. He fingered the amulet on his chest, but it gave no sense of warmth. Perhaps there was no Dark Magic at work here; perhaps it had become overloaded in the warpstorm. He had noticed that none of the gems on the airship's sides were glowing now. That might mean something good or it might mean something bad. Felix did not know enough about magic to be able to tell.

Varek was gesturing them from the opening above. He seemed to want to know whether they were about to secure the airship. Felix shook his head, trying to indicate that the folk above should do nothing till they had ascertained what was making this hideous racket.

'Should we investigate the shrieking?' Felix asked.

'Good idea, manling,' Gotrek said nastily. 'Let's go wandering through these ruins and see how far we can get from the airship. Maybe we should split up too. That way we can cover more ground!'

'It was just a suggestion,' Felix said. 'There's no need to be sarcastic.'

'It sounded like a good plan to Snorri,' the other Slayer said.

Just then, from amidst the ruins, a figure limped into view. It looked like a human but it was so filthy, ragged and unkempt that Felix wasn't sure if this was the case. Around him he sensed a change in the attitude of Snorri and Gotrek. Without them visibly changing position, they seemed to become more wary, ready to strike out in any direction at a moment's notice.

Felix heard a clinking from behind them, and turned his head momentarily – to see that the grapnel at the end of mooring line had come loose. The airship was drifting free on the breeze. The vessel's engines chose that moment to sputter and die. He cursed silently to himself as the rope ladder rose out of his reach, then he turned his head and forced himself to concentrate once more on the advancing figure.

He could see that it was indeed a man. He walked in a shuffling crouch. His hair was so long that it reached his waist. His beard was filthy and dragged almost to the ground. Weeping sores covered his hands and arms where they were exposed. He limped wearily up to where they stood and let out another long wail. He was leaning on a staff that looked like it had been made by lashing together a number of human bones with sinew. A blank-eyed skull glared from its tip.

Felix stared at the man, and met a gaze full of melancholy madness.

'Begone from my city or I will feed you to my beasts,' the stranger said eventually. He fingered one of the many verdigrised copper amulets which hung from a chain around his neck. Felix could see that it had been carved into the likeness of a screaming skull.

'What beasts?' said Gotrek.

'Snorri thinks you're a nutter,' Snorri said.

Listen to who's talking, thought Felix.

'The beasts which fear and worship me,' the man said. 'The creatures to whom I am a god.'

Felix looked at the man and felt a surge of fear, knowing that he was mad. On the other hand, he did not want to simply slay the man out of hand just because he was mad. He had obviously been here for some time and it occurred to Felix that the man might have useful knowledge. He thought he had nothing to lose by humouring this lunatic.

'What is your name, oh mighty one?' Felix asked, hoping the others would have wit enough to play along with him. It was, he knew, most likely a forlorn hope but he thought he might as well try. The stranger appeared to consider this for a moment.

'Hans, Hans Muller – but you can call me the divine one.'

'And what are you doing here, Divine One?' Felix asked softly. 'You're a long way from anywhere.'

'I got lost.'

'Take a wrong turning back in Kislev, did you?' Gotrek asked sarcastically. Felix saw that the Slayer's axe was held ready to strike. There was a faint glow along the runes of the blade. This was usually a very bad sign.

'No, short one. I am a magician. I was experimenting with certain spells of translocation and something went wrong. I ended up here.'

'Short one?' Gotrek said, a note of menace in his voice.

'Translocation?' Felix asked hastily. The fact that the man was a wizard was not making him feel any easier. He had never much cared for sorcerers, having had several bad experiences with them.

'A method of moving between two points without traversing the lands in between. My theories were at least partially correct. I moved. Fortunately I moved too far and ended up here where the natives recognise my godhood.'

'Tell us, oh Divine One, what do you know of Karag Dum?' Felix asked.

'The great daemon has returned there,' Muller said instantly.

At the mention of daemons, Felix shuddered. In the Chaos Wastes it seemed all too likely that such sinister entities could be present.

'Daemon?'

'The daemon told of in the Prophecy. The Great Destroyer. It awaits only the coming of the Axe Bearer to fulfil its prophecy and its destiny!'

'Tell us more,' Felix said, shuddering.

Seeing Felix's reaction, a strange, furtive look came into the mage's eye. He licked his lips with the tip of a thin pinkish tongue. He looked twisted and cunning and suddenly Felix did not trust him at all.

'My beasts must be fed,' the mage said, then made a strange gesture. His hand moved through the air and seemed to gather oddly glowing energies to it. A shimmering sphere of light suddenly surrounded his hand. Even as he made to cast it, Gotrek's axe flashed and severed the hand at the wrist. The sphere of light fell from Muller's outstretched fingers and hit the ground. There was an explosion. A blast of warm air passed over Felix. His flesh tingled and he felt an odd dizziness.

In a moment he had recovered and the flashing before his eyes calmed down. He was grateful to see that Gotrek and Snorri were still there too, although the wizard had vanished.

'That was not a very destructive spell,' Felix said. 'He could not exactly have been a powerful wizard.'

'I'm not so sure, manling,' Gotrek said.

'What do you mean?'

'Take a look around.'

Felix did so. The first thing he noticed was that the airship was gone. Then he noticed the roof, the walls, and the peculiar patterns arrayed on the flagstoned floor.

'Next time we meet a sorcerer, manling,' said Gotrek, 'let's kill him first and ask questions later.'

* * *

They stood in an oddly shaped chamber, in the centre of a large pentagram. At each point of the pentagram was a human skull and within each skull something glowed. A greenish light leaked from the eye-socket of every skull. Overhead was a massive stone roof. The walls of the chamber were carved from the same stones as the rest of the city. Odd-looking luminous moss grew in the cracks between blocks.

'Where are we?' whispered Felix. There was something about the atmosphere of this place which made him want to be extremely quiet. An aura of watchfulness, a sense of something old and evil waiting for something to happen. His words echoed away. Under the shadows of the roof something rustled and stirred and Felix sincerely hoped that it was only bats.

'Snorri has no idea,' said Snorri loudly. 'Somewhere underground, maybe.'

'Let us go and find out,' said Gotrek, striding towards the edge of the pentagram. As he did so, the chalked lines on the floor began to gleam brightly. The hair on the back of Felix's neck stood on end.

'No! Wait!' he shouted.

Gotrek strode blithely on. As his foot touched the edge of the pentacle, sparks flew up and he was surrounded by the brilliant glow. The smell of ozone filled the air. In an instant the Slayer was thrown backwards into the centre of the pentagram. It did not even slow him down. He threw himself at the barrier once more – and once again was tossed back.

As this happened, Felix watched closely what was happening. Each time the spell took effect, the eyes of the skulls blazed brighter; after Gotrek was thrown backwards, the illumination dimmed.

'You could try smashing one of those heads,' Felix suggested. Gotrek did not respond but stomped over to one of the points of the pentacle. His axe flashed downwards, the runes on the blade blazing. The skull smashed into a thousand fragments. A cloud of ectoplasmic vapour rose above it. There was a long, shrieking wail, as of a soul that had been set free after centuries of imprisonment. As the cry subsided, the remaining skulls went dark. Gotrek stepped outside the pentagram easily this time.

A quick inspection revealed that there was only one way out of the chamber. It led down a long ramp into a maze of gloomy corridors. The whole area was lit by glowing gems set in the ceiling. Felix had seen their like before, beneath Karak Eight Peaks.

'Those do look like dwarf work,' he said, as they marched down the shadowy corridors.

'Aye, manling, they do. Maybe the folk of Karag Dum traded with this city.'

'Or maybe Karag Dum was plundered by the people here.'

'That is an evil thought but it is also a possibility.'

Once more they fell silent. Gotrek led them easily through the maze, always moving with confidence, never having to retrace his steps. Felix was amazed by the certainty that the dwarfs showed here, for he knew that if he had been on his own, by now he would have been hopelessly lost.

The watchful stillness had once more settled over the labyrinth. Felix's flesh crawled. Every so often he stopped to glance back over his shoulder just to make sure that there was nothing coming up behind him. He felt as if a blade might be plunged into his unprotected back at any moment.

As they hurried on, Felix wondered where the other dwarfs were. He hoped that they had not left without them. The situation at the moment did not look good. The three of them were trapped in a huge maze, without food or water and with no knowledge of exactly where they were. If they made it to the surface, and they were still in the ruined city, then they might be able to attract the attention of the airship. But if it had already gone, then their prospects were bleak. Felix did not look forward to a long trek through the Chaos Wastes in an effort to get home. From what he had witnessed on the journey so far it seemed unlikely that they could survive.

He pushed these thoughts aside and forced himself to concentrate on his surroundings. The corridor had opened up into a long hallway. Light filtered in from high overhead. Glittering particles of dust shimmered in the beams. The hall itself was many storeys high. On each level was a gallery. A huge ornamental pool, filled with scummy water, took up most of the ground floor of the chamber. In the centre of the pool stood a fountain which had long since ceased to flow. It was a statue carved in the shape of an armoured warrior. The warrior looked human enough, save for the fact that he had an additional arm in which he held some sort of staff.

Felix walked to the edge of the pool and looked in. The water was murky except where little flecks of green light glowed in, like trapped stars. He had seen this stuff before and knew it was warpstone.

'We won't be drinking this water,' he muttered, and the thought immediately made him thirsty. And as he thought this, he noticed a distorted reflection in the water. A huge winged shape which grew larger behind him even as he watched.

'Look out!' he shouted and threw himself backwards away from the pool. Razor-sharp talons slashed the air where he had stood mere moments before. Felix had the fleeting impression of a hideous winged humanoid, much like the ones he had seen flying over the battlefield earlier. Then there was a huge splash as the creature tumbled into the waters of the pool.

Felix had a moment to recover himself and look up. A horde of the winged creatures were emerging onto the galleries set into the walls high above them and throwing themselves into the air. He could hear the flap of their wings and the snapping of their pinions as they took flight. These creatures were not flying silently. The one which attacked him must have glided down from a long way above.

'Harpies!' Snorri shouted. 'Good!'

Gotrek looked grim as he brandished his axe. Snorri grinned like a maniac and capered on the spot at the prospect of impending violence. Felix glanced back over at the water where the winged fiend had vanished. There was a great splash and droplets of water soaked his face as the creature broke surface and flexed its water-logged wings. As it attempted to take to the air, it gave an unearthly shriek as a huge tentacle, as thick as a cable and covered in suckers, enfolded the mutant thing and dragged it back below the water. Felix was suddenly very glad that he had not disturbed the water, and then he had no more time for thinking.

The hellish flock descended. Felix was surrounded by flapping limbs. Their wingbeats drove the awful charnel stench of the creatures everywhere. He ducked a slashing talon, lopped off the attached hand with his counterstroke and caught a quick glimpse of a hideously contorted shrieking face. Quickly he slashed all around him, clearing an area in which he could fight. The dwarfs' battle cries rang in his ears along with the infernal croaking of the harpies.

He twisted his head trying to see where the Slayers had got to, intending to fight his way towards them. As he did so, he felt a sharp piercing pain in his shoulders. The whole world performed a cartwheel. The thunder of wings filled his ears and the smell of rotten meat filled his nostrils. He had been grabbed by a harpy and was being borne aloft, like a field-mouse being taken back to an owl's nest to feed its fledglings.

The thing's acceleration was awful. He glanced down and caught a quick glimpse of the battle below. Snorri and Gotrek stood in the eye of a storm of wings. All around them lay the mutilated bodies of dead harpies, but many more came on. Gotrek reached up and grabbed one by its leg, pulled it down and crushed its head with the blade of his axe. Next to him Snorri smashed another's shoulder blade with his hammer. As the crippled beast flopped to the ground, the Slayer beheaded it with his axe.

In the pool, the water boiled and churned as something truly huge rose to the surface. The thrashings of the entangled harpy died away as more and more tentacles enshrouded it and crushed its life out. An enormous head broke surface. The sight of a circular leech-like maw filled with needle-sharp teeth distracted Felix from his predicament. He had been about to stab upwards at the Harpy and hope that the water below broke his fall – but now it seemed like that would simply be a case of jumping out of the cookpot and into the fire.

Snorri, seeing what was happening to Felix, cast his hammer straight up at the harpy. Felix flinched as it flew straight and true. There was a sickening crunch as the weapon impacted and suddenly Felix was tumbling downwards towards the pool.

'No! You idiot!' he shouted as the turbulent waters grew beneath him and the air whistled past his ears. The thing in the pool looked up with huge, almost human eyes. In that moment it occurred to Felix that the creature might once have been a man warped by the hideous mutating power of Chaos. Then he saw the head turn upwards and the leech like mouth gape wide and in that instant he realised that he was going to die. If the fall didn't kill him then he would be grabbed by those hideous slimy tentacles and dragged into that vast mouth.

He knew a brief flicker of despair and then an eruption of something like a berserker's fury. If he was going to die, he was going to take the monster with him! He twisted his body to get his feet below him and as he impacted on the monster he drove his sword downward into the creature's rubbery flesh. All the force of his long fall, all of the weight of his body and all the strength of his arms powered the enchanted Templar's blade home. It cut through flesh and speared right into the creature's brain. The tentacles went limp instantly

The impact drove all the breath from Felix but he did not feel anything break. The beast's rubbery mass and enormous soft bulk had broken his fall. He swiftly sprang upright and leapt from the thing's head to the edge of the pool, taking great care not to touch the water. Even as he did so, he noticed that Gotrek and Snorri had routed the harpies. The majority of the surviving flock had taken to the air and were swiftly flapping their way out of the Slayers' reach. A glance behind him confirmed that the thing in the pool was already slipping back beneath the surface of the fetid waters.

693

Snorri bent down and picked up his fallen hammer. He looked up at Felix and grinned. 'Good throw, huh?' he said.

Felix restrained himself from striking the dwarf with his blade.

'Let's get moving,' Gotrek said. 'We don't have all day to waste.'

Felix stopped and rubbed his shoulder. The bruising was painful and the area was tender. Fortunately for him the harpy's claws had not penetrated his flesh, although they had burst some of the chain links and driven the points through the armour's leather under-jerkin and into his arm. They were more like scratches than real wounds. Normally he would have paused to wash and dress them but here in the midst of these Chaos haunted ruins he had no desire to stop – and even less desire to remove his armoured shirt. To tell the truth, he had not seen any water he would trust here either.

While Felix had paused, Gotrek and Snorri had continued onwards up the seemingly endless stairs. He rushed to catch them up, not wanting to be left on his own. The brooding stillness of the place had only intensified since the harpies' attack and he wondered what wicked thing they could possibly encounter next.

His legs were aching from the constant climbing of steep stairs. They had risen about ten levels. The pool was still visible below them. He stumbled suddenly. A warped skull, humanoid but with goat horns, rattled away from his foot. It had been stripped of all flesh. Felix stooped and picked it up. It was light and cold, dry in his hands. Looking inside he saw score marks along the crown. An image flickered through his mind and he saw one of the harpies reaching inside the severed head to scoop out the brain and devour it. Hastily he tossed the skull away. It fell and clattered among the bones which lay strewn about the gallery.

They had obviously reached the area where the harpies nested, for there were bones everywhere, cracked for marrow and stripped of all flesh. The skeletons of beastmen, mutants and humans lay mingled with each other. Many of them were fouled with light brown excrement and the stink was awful. Even through the scarf wrapped over his mouth it made Felix want to gag. He wondered how much longer these galleries could go on for, and whether he could go through even one more without vomiting. Why had Muller made his lair here, he wondered? And how had he survived among all these ferocious monsters? Had his magic prevented them from attacking him? Or had he come to some arrangement with the creatures? Felix was forced to acknowledge the fact that he would never know, and in truth, he was not sure he really wanted to. The pacts and alliances that must be needed to survive in a place like this did not bear thinking about – and that was before you came to consider the question of food and drink.

Perhaps Muller had even been sane when he came here, but had been driven mad by a diet that must have consisted of tainted flesh and warpstone-corrupted water. Felix did not want to consider that this might be the only option open to him and his companions too, if they did not find a way out of here soon. At the moment, death seemed preferable to such an existence but who could tell? Perhaps it would become easier as your brain degenerated and warpstone-inspired madness consumed the mind. Perhaps you might even come to enjoy it. Once more he forced the thought from his head – and as he did so he realised that the staircase had finally come to an end.

Up ahead Gotrek stood in front of a massive archway. The lintel was covered in a mass of carved daemon heads. They smiled mockingly, bared monstrous fangs, stuck out their tongues. Their expressions were crazed and debauched and full of madness and Felix wondered at the minds which could have carved such things. The archway itself was sealed by an enormous slab of stone inscribed with the twisted characters that Felix had come to associate with the followers of the Dark Powers of Chaos. It was becoming increasingly obvious that this part of the ruined city, at least, had long been home to the slaves of Darkness.

Gotrek reached out and pushed the stone but nothing happened. The slab did not budge. Slowly the Slayer applied more and more pressure until the huge muscles swelled and rippled all along his back and arms. Sweat beaded his forehead and his breathing came in ragged gasps. Snorri joined him but even their combined strengths had no effect on the archway. Felix did not even bother to try and help them. There was not enough room for him to squeeze in between them, and anyway, he doubted that his efforts would count for much compared to the amount of force the two dwarfs were bringing to bear.

Eventually Gotrek gave up. He stood back and scratched his head with one massive hand. He picked up his axe and looked as if he was considering swinging it at the door but then he simply grinned and reached out to touch one of the leering daemon heads carved on the lintel. He pushed down on the tongue. It moved and as it did so the archway swung open, sending the still-straining Snorri sprawling through it to land flat on his face on the dusty flagstones beyond.

'No damage done. He landed on his head,' Gotrek muttered and strode through. With a last glance at the galleries behind them, Felix hastily followed.

They emerged onto a wide flat space open to the sky. Ahead of them was a walled barrier like a battlement. Behind them was a massive wall. Felix strode forward to the barrier and looked down. At once he realised that they were on the penultimate level almost at the very top of a massive ziggurat, for below them were all the lower steps. Close by was a flight of monstrous stairs leading all the way back down to the ground. The stairs also led up to a peak of the pyramid, and Felix hastily climbed them. At the top was a great open ledge. It was old and crumbling and it extended out over a wide expanse of empty air. Felix gingerly walked to the edge and looked down.

A long way below him was the pool in which the monstrous thing had dwelled and all the galleries in which the Chaos harpies had nested. There were chains and manacles along the walled edges of the ledge, and a slow realisation of the platform's function came to him. This was a place of sacrifice. Living victims had once been brought here and then thrown screaming from the ledge to tumble into the pool below, where the dweller in the murky water devoured them. It must have been an unpleasant fate, and Felix wondered about the sanity of those who had devised it.

Had this whole vast ziggurat been built purely with this function in mind? Or it had it once served a different purpose and become corrupted as the foul power of Chaos spread across this ancient land? Was it even possible, as Gotrek had suggested earlier, that this whole structure had been created by whim of one of the Dark Gods or their daemonic servitors?

None of his thinking was going any way towards finding salvation, Felix decided. They had found the open air but they had no idea where the airship was or how they could locate it. And if they failed to do that they were doomed.

He turned back from the vertiginous drop and scanned the horizon. Surely, he thought, if the airship was still over the city, it would be visible. He squinted in the strange light filtering through the clouds and tried to concentrate, wishing all the while that he still had the telescope that he had left on the ship. All he could see was the cloud of harpies circling high above them.

Then, to his amazement, far off in the distance, he saw a small dark speck that seemed to be moving in their direction. He prayed fervently to Sigmar that it was the *Spirit of Grungni*. Then he raced over to the outside edge of the ziggurat's uppermost level and shouted for the dwarfs to come and join him. But even as he did so, he noticed that an enormous horde of beastmen had emerged from the nearby buildings far below and were racing along the streets towards the ziggurat. Over their heads fluttered two harpies, screaming in their foul tongue.

Doubtless they were the things which had attracted the beastmen's attention. Before he could throw himself flat, one of the bestial Chaos worshippers noticed him, for it brandished its spear in the air and pointed with one outstretched arm towards Felix. The whole disgusting horde let out a howl of triumph and began to hurry up the long stairway towards them. Felix cursed his luck and went to join Snorri and Gotrek.

The two Slayers seemed profoundly indifferent to the fact that several thousand beastmen were racing towards them, too many for even such formidable warriors as themselves to slay.

'The stairway is a good point to make our stand,' observed Gotrek. 'Narrow. Not too many of them can get to us at once. Good killing.'

'Hardly seems fair,' Snorri said. 'They'll be tired by the time they get to us. All that running and then all those stairs. Maybe we should go down and meet them halfway.'

'They're spawn of Chaos. I will do nothing to oblige them.'

'Fair enough. Snorri sees your point.'

Felix shook his head in despair. He was going to die, and he was going to die in the company of two maniacs. It was too much. He had survived evil magic, the attacks of a tentacled monster and a flock of mutant harpies only to be brought down at the last by a horde of shambling, misshapen monsters, beasts that wore the shape of men.

He turned his head to the heavens to ask blessed Sigmar to simply smite him down and get it over with when he noticed that the dot in the distance had swollen into the definite outline of the airship. It was heading directly in their direction. Felix looked down the ziggurat again. The beastmen were almost halfway up it. He glanced back at the airship. It was much further away than the beastmen, but it was moving much faster. He hardly dared hope that it would reach them in time.

The beastmen were well up the steps now, an onrushing tide of twisted flesh, brandishing spears and howling war cries. Felix could distinctly hear the clatter of hooves on the stone stairs. His heart raced. His mouth felt dry. This was almost worse than certain death. Now there was a faint hope that they might get away.

The airship swept low over the beastmen. Felix could see that the outside had been cleaned and all the engines were working. The rips in the gasbag had been repaired. He would not have believed that it was possible for so much work to be done in so short a time. The dwarfs had certainly been busy. He could see now that the doorways in the side of the ship were open as was the hatch in the bottom. Someone had thrown open the portholes as well, and a rain of black spheres was descending on the onrushing horde. One of them burst in the air sending shrapnel everywhere. Beastmen howled in agony. Felix realised that the dwarfs on the ship were dropping bombs!

More and more fell tearing great holes in the ranks of the beastmen. The foul Chaos things stopped and howled and shook their weapons at the sky. One or two threw their spears but they fell short, then dropped back into the tightly pressed mass of beastmen, impaling their comrades. For a moment Felix dared to hope that they would be routed by their fear of this awesome apparition above their heads. Then a larger leader-type emerged from the milling throng and shouted at the rest of its force to advance, and the beastmen came on once more. Still, the precious moments of confusion had given the airship time to sail forward until it was almost overhead. Felix could see Varek in the hatchway above him, uncoiling the craft's beloved rope ladder. He let out a long sigh of relief, knowing that he was safe.

Then the airship passed on by him, taking the rope ladder with it. What were they playing at, thought Felix, risking a glance down at the oncoming ranks of beastmen? This was no time for stupid jokes! Then he realised what had happened. The airship still had momentum from its rush to save them. The howling of the engines above him revealed that Makaisson had thrown the craft into reverse and was killing his vessel's speed expertly.

The *Spirit of Grungni* now hovered directly over the well in the centre of the ziggurat. Felix turned to the Slayers and bellowed; 'Come on! We must find Karag Dum! That is your destiny!'

The Slayers looked at him as if he were mad. He realised that they did actually want to throw away their lives in this pointless battle against superior numbers. Inspiration struck him. 'There is a daemon at Karag Dum! It pollutes sacred dwarf soil. It is your duty to kill it!'

Well, he thought, he'd done his best to talk the Slayers out of their folly. Now it was time to go. Without looking behind him, he raced up the stairway and out onto the ramp from which sacrifices had been thrown. The ladder dangled right out in the middle of the great central well – far too far for him to jump out and reach it. Behind him he could hear the roaring of the beastmen. They seemed to be almost upon him. He risked a glance over his shoulder and saw Snorri and Gotrek brandishing their weapons defiantly. He knew that it could only be a matter of moments before the horde was upon him.

He glanced back and saw that the rope ladder was coming back in his direction. Instantly he made his decision. He sheathed his sword, took a flying leap and made a grasp for the ladder. For a moment, he had a dizzying sense of the enormous drop beneath him, then his fingers were clutching the rope. The impact felt like it was going to tear his arm from its socket, and sent a surge of agony shooting through the shoulder that the harpy had bruised earlier. Somehow, he managed to hold on and then to grasp the swaying ladder with his other hand and begin to pull himself up.

He risked a glance down and saw that they were running in the direction of the ramp's edge.

'Snorri! Gotrek!' he shouted to encourage them.

Just beyond and below them he could see the first of the onrushing beastmen come into view. The Slayers looked up and almost as one reached up and made a grab for the ladder. Both managed to catch hold of it as it went flying by and were pulled off the ziggurat and into the air. Felix caught a view of the great mass of bestial faces glaring up at him as they went soaring past.

A rain of stuff was dropping from the ship now, and Felix realised that Makaisson was jettisoning ballast to enable them to gain height quickly. The sludge and pebbles dropped on the Chaos worshippers. They responded by casting their spears. Reflexively he closed his eyes as the missiles whizzed past his ears, then the beastmen were left far behind on the sacrificial ziggurat and the airship was gaining altitude fast.

Looking back to where they had been he saw an awful thing was happening. Before they had realised their danger, the leaders of the charging beastmen had gone running right off the edge of the ramp and were tumbling out into space. A few of their followers had time to realise what was happening and to give out roars of horror and fear. However, pushed on by the press of bodies behind them, they were being forced off the edge of the ramp and out into the abyss beneath them.

Felix offered up a prayer of thanks to Sigmar for his deliverance and began to pull himself, hand over hand up the ladder and into the *Spirit of Grungni*. Once safely there, he turned to reach down and helped pull the pair of Slayers up into the airship.

'Missed a good fight there,' Snorri said. 'Pity they got the drop on us.'

Felix gave Snorri a penetrating look. Was it actually possible that the idiot was making a joke, he wondered. In the distance he could still hear the screams of the falling beastmen.

'How did you find us?' Felix asked Varek as the ruined city faded into the gloom behind them.

'After you vanished, we finished the repairs and all the crew we could spare manned the telescopes,' Varek said. 'We were lucky. We saw a great flock of those winged things rising over the ziggurat in the centre of the city and decided that something must have attracted their attention. We thought even if all we found was your corpses it was worth the effort.'

Felix realised exactly how lucky they had been. The same thing that had attracted the horde of beastmen had also brought the attention of the airship's crew. He shuddered to think of what might have happened if they had fought with the creatures during the night. They would never have been found.

FIFTEEN
THE HORDES OF CHAOS

Lurk felt peculiar. His skin tingled. His fur itched. He was hungry all the time. Ever since he had been exposed to the warpstone dust during the storm, an odd sickness had convulsed him. He had taken to stealing more and more of the dwarfs' supplies away, and he devoured them all in great orgies of consumption where he simply could not stop himself until all the food was gone. He was just thankful that someone had eventually opened the hatch back into the ship before he started to eat his own tail.

The effects of all this consumption were starting to show. His muscles had swollen, his tail had grown thicker and he was getting bigger. His head hurt a lot and he found it difficult to think straight. He prayed to the Horned Rat that he had not caught some sort of plague. He remembered his fear when he had fallen sick in Nuln and how that had almost ended his life. If the plague returned now, he had none of the herbal medicines Vilebroth Null had used to preserve his life.

Slowly he pulled himself up the ladder to the crow's nest so that he could make his daily communion with that wretched Thanquol. He was heartily sick of that nagging voice within his head, babbling foolish orders and telling him what to do. Part of his mind knew that he should not be thinking this way, that it was most unwise but he could not bring himself to care. His body ached all over. His vision was blurring and his fur was beginning to fall out in places where monstrous boils were erupting. He decided not to bother about contacting the grey seer. He would return to his burrow and sleep. First though, he would need to eat. He was starting to feel a hankering for a nice bit of plump dwarf flesh.

Felix knocked on the door of Borek's cabin. The metal echoed beneath his knuckles.

'Come in,' the dwarf said. Felix opened the door and went in. Borek's cabin was larger than his. The walls were lined with crystal-fronted cabinets containing many books. A table was bolted to the floor in the centre and on it was laid out an ancient map, held in place by four strange looking paperweights of black metal.

Noticing Felix's curiosity, Borek said, 'Magnets.'

'What?'

'Those paperweights are magnets. They stick to iron and steel. It's some odd philosophical principle, akin to the one that keeps compass needles pointing northwards. Go ahead: try to pick one up.'

Felix did as he was told, and felt a resistance that he had not expected. He let go of the metal and it seemed to leap from his hand and adhered to the table with a click. It was typical of the dwarf's attention to detail, he thought, that they had managed to find a way of keeping maps in place even on such an unstable platform as this airship. He mentioned this fact.

'It's a power that has been known for a long time. It's used by our navigators on the steamships out of Barak Varr.' He smiled. 'But I suspect that you are not here to discuss the finer points of furnishing a vessel's cabin...'

Felix agreed that he was not and he began to speak, telling Borek about what had happened with the sorcerer and his mention of the daemon. The encounter with Muller had made him think. For the first time, he had really begun to take seriously the dreadful possibility that such a thing might exist at Karag Dum. The old dwarf listened, nodding occasionally. When Felix finished, there was a short silence while Borek filled his pipe.

'How can this be?' Felix asked. 'How can daemons exist here and not outside the Wastes?'

Borek looked at him long and hard. 'They can and do exist outside the Wastes. According to our records, many have fought against the armies of the dwarfs.'

'Then where are they now?'

'Vanished. Who knows why? Who can truly explain the workings of Chaos?'

'But surely you have a theory?'

'There are many theories, Herr Jaeger. As far as we know, raw magical energy flows much more strongly through the Wastes. It seems most likely that daemons feed on this energy and need it to exist. Beyond the Wastes they can manifest for only a short time before vanishing because magic is weaker. Here in the Realm of Chaos they can manifest themselves for much longer periods because there is more power for them to draw on.'

'Why is that?'

'Schreiber believes there is some sort of disturbance at the very centre of the Wastes which is the source of all magic. According to him, it also warps time and distance in some manner. Many scholars claim that time flows at different rates in different parts of the Wastes, you know. And that the further you go into the Wastes, the more pronounced this effect becomes.'

'Why are the fiends not swarming all over us now then?'

'Perhaps because we have not gone far enough. I doubt that it is possible for a daemon to exist for long out here, so close to the edge of the Wastes, but I do not know for certain that this is the case. There is a lot I do not know about these matters.'

'But you think a daemon still dwells in Karag Dum?'

Borek laughed grimly. 'It is all too possible. Even as I left there were dire rumours that some dread thing had been summoned and King Thangrim Firebeard and his runemasters marched to meet it. It may be it was trapped there or never left. I do not know. I and my kin escaped the city before those final battles.'

'It is not exactly a pleasant thought.'

'No, but it is one that we will soon know the answer to. We should reach Karag Dum within the next day or so.'

'What then?'

'Then we will see.'

'Faster! Quick-quick!' Grey Seer Thanquol chittered. He was tired and restless from being constantly cooped up inside his palanquin. Such confinement went against all his skaven instincts to get up and scuttle about, but he really had no choice. For the past few days he had done nothing but use communications spells and ride relays of palanquins through the subterranean roadways of the Under-Empire, stopping only long enough to change bearers and palanquins, eating all his meals as he moved on. He had blisters on his rump from sitting so long and he felt like his back was going to be permanently curved.

His bearers whined their complaints and Thanquol considered blasting one or two apart just to make an example of them, but he knew it would be counter-productive. All he would achieve would be to slow himself down until they reached the next way-station, where he could acquire a change of slaves. Still, he promised himself, once they were there, these whinging lackeys would suffer!

That is, if he could find the strength. The grey seer felt drained by the strain of having to expend so much power to communicate with Lurk over so long a distance. And now the buffoon was not even responding to his calls. It was so frustrating! He had no idea what had happened. Was Lurk dead? Had the airship crashed in some hideous accident? Was this long chase all for nothing? Surely it could not be, but ever since he had seen that accursed Jaeger, Thanquol had felt a sinking feeling. Where the human and his wretched dwarf companion were concerned, Thanquol was always prepared for the worst. The two of them seemed to have been born only to thwart him.

He cursed the engineers of Clan Skryre. Why could they not bend their accursed ingenuity to building some improved means of transport through the tunnels of the Under-Empire? Surely they could think of something more effective than simple relays of slave-borne litters! Did they always have to spend their days working out bigger and better weapons? Why not warpstone-powered chariots or traction engines, Thanquol wondered? Or some long-range version of the doomwheel? Surely such things could not be beyond them? If he remembered, he would mention his ideas to the Council of Thirteen in his next report.

'Faster! Quick! Go-go!' he urged, his throat hoarse. He needed to get to the northlands soon, he knew, and find out what had happened to that wonderful airship. If only he could get his paws on that, he would never again lack for swift transportation.

And when he got there, he vowed, someone was really going to pay for the discomfort he had endured.

Felix lay on the bed in his cabin, staring at the metal ceiling. His head spun with all the things he had learned this day concerning the Realm of Chaos. The world was a great deal more complex than he would ever have thought possible, and it was increasingly obvious to him that his own people still had a lot to learn from the Elder Races.

He closed his eyes but sleep would not come. He felt tired but also restless. His shoulder still pained him, despite the healing salves which Varek had applied. He knew the area was going to be tender for some time to come. Still, his mail had been repaired by one of Makaisson's apprentices, and it looked better than new.

Cursing his lot, he rose from the bed and pulled on his boots. Leaving his chamber, he walked to the airship's rear observation turret. The rearmost bubble of the turret was small and housed an organ gun mounted on a swivel platform. Felix slumped down into its seat and worked the foot pedals that sent it turning first to the left and then to the right. He found the motion oddly relaxing, reminiscent of swinging in a hammock or being in his grandfather's rocking chair.

He reached up and grasped the handles of the organ gun. This was another of Makaisson's unusual designs. It had grips like a pistol and was fired by pulling a trigger. The whole mechanism of the gun was balanced on a gimbal and could be swivelled up or down, left or right, almost without effort. Felix did not know what the dwarfs expected to attack them flying at such an altitude, but they were obviously taking no chances.

He gazed out over the land over which they had passed. The sky had darkened into some semblance of night. At least, the clouds were darker above them and there was no suggestion of a sun above. Felix wondered about that. They had reached an area where it seemed no matter how high they climbed the sky was always obscured. He had decided that it was either some form of potent magic or simply that somewhere in the distance, great masses of warpstone dust were being thrown high into the air and driven upwards by powerful winds. The only illumination came from huge fire-pits set in the rough terrain below, craters resembling the bubbling mouths of volcanoes around whose glowing openings twisted figures capered.

As the airship passed over the fire-pits, it shuddered slightly, caught by the rising current of warm air. This did not frighten Felix as it once had. He had come to find gentle turbulence actually rather soothing. It was strange. The more he flew, the more he had come to regard the sky as being something akin to the sea. The winds were its currents, the clouds something like the waves.

He wondered if the sea, too, had currents at different levels, the way the winds appeared to move at different speeds at different heights. There was much here for a philosopher to study, he thought yawning, and slipped gently into sleep.

Lurk pulled himself slowly and stealthily down the corridors of the ship. The hunger in his stomach was like a living thing clawing and trying to escape. It caused him actual physical pain. Ahead of him, he sensed prey. It did not have the scent of dwarf but of humanity. Lurk did not care. He simply wanted to feel hot red blood gush into his mouth and gorge on chunks of raw, warm meat and a human would suit his purposes just as well as a dwarf.

He entered the rear chamber and heard the snoring of the figure in front of him. Good! His foolish prey was completely unaware, lost in a swinish slumber the like of which no skaven would ever allow itself to fall into, even if there were no obvious threat of danger. The human's blond-furred head was thrown back, and his neck was bared, as if inviting Lurk's fangs.

Lurk tip-toed forward and loomed over the human's sleeping form. Saliva filled his mouth at the prospect of fresh meat. All it would take would be one bite to sever the artery! He would lock his jaws on the human's neck to smother his screams. Another few paces and he would be in a position to strike.

Suddenly Lurk heard footsteps on the ladder leading down from the deck above. Someone was coming! He cursed quietly, knowing that if he attacked now, he would be discovered before he could consume his prey, and that the alarm would be given. Some spark of self-preservation buried deep in his mind told him that this would not be a good idea, so he padded swiftly back down the corridor, returning the way he had come.

Felix woke suddenly at the sound of wary footsteps on the ladder. He was glad to be woken, for he had been having a nightmare in which a giant rat-like thing stalked ever closer to him down a dark, mist-shrouded tunnel. Doubtless it was a bad dream inspired by the beastmen he had seen today. Sigmar knew, they had been monstrous enough to inspire a lifetime of nightmares.

He looked up to see Varek lowering himself onto the observation deck. He carried his book in one hand and his pen in the other, and he looked a little disappointed to find someone else present, as if he had desired to be alone here.

'Good evening, Felix,' he said, forcing a smile.

'Is it evening?'

'Who can tell,' the dwarf shrugged. 'It's as good a term for it as any in this foul place. The sky is darker and the land is obscured so I suppose it might as well be.'

'Then good evening to you, Varek,' said Felix. 'What are you doing here?'

'I came here to write up my notes. It's difficult to do when you're sharing a cabin with Gotrek and Snorri.'

'I can imagine.' Felix was suddenly glad that his height and the fact that he was a human had qualified him for his own cabin. It was one of only three single rooms on the entire airship, and Borek and Makaisson had the others. 'What were they doing?'

'Gotrek claimed that Snorri had beaten him on a technicality in their last head-butting contest. They were having quite an argument about it. Snorri wanted to have another contest right there and then to settle the matter but I talked them out of it.'

'How?' Felix couldn't imagine this soft-spoken young dwarf talking the pair of Trollslayers out of anything at all.

'I reminded them that it usually takes about three days for the loser to recover from a head-butting bout and that's assuming nothing serious is broken – and if that happened one of them would miss out on our arrival in Karag Dum. Assuming that we would arrive on time, of course. That seemed to do the trick. When I left them they were having a vodka drinking contest instead. Hopefully by the time I get back they'll have knocked themselves out with that instead.'

'I wouldn't bet on it,' Felix said.

Varek smiled sadly.

'Nor would I.'

'Don't mind me,' said Felix. 'I was just taking a nap.' He made to settle back once more.

'Before you do, could I just ask you to go over all the details of today's events. I want to make sure I get it all exactly right.'

'Of course,' Felix said, and began to go over the story once more, with only slight exaggerations.

Felix woke later, still in the gunnery chair of the organ gun to find one of the engineers sweeping the decks around him. Yawning and stretching, he pulled himself up and decided to go get some breakfast. As he rose he noticed that there was a small band of mounted warriors directly below them, apparently riding in the same direction as the airship was flying.

'Are they following us?' he asked, knowing it was a foolish question even as he asked it. While he watched, the black-armoured riders had fallen far behind the swiftly-moving airship.

'No,' replied the dwarf, 'but something is surely up. All morning we've been passing over war-bands moving in the same direction. It's almost as if they know where we are going and are moving to intercept us.'

'That isn't possible,' said Felix, but in his secret heart he was unsure. After all, who knew what the forces of Chaos were really capable of.

'It's getting worse,' Varek said, continuing to focus the telescope out the window of the command deck. 'There are hundreds more. Now there seems to be more of them ahead of us than there is behind.'

Felix was forced to agree; even with the naked eye it was obvious. All day they had been passing over bands of beastmen, Chaos warriors and other wicked things. The further they travelled, the more frequent the sightings had become. And all of the followers of Darkness were streaming in the same direction the airship was moving in. It was as if a secret signal had been given and an army was being gathered.

'I don't like this at all,' said Felix. 'Can they really know what we're doing? Are they waiting for us?'

'I don't think that is very likely,' Borek said, a little testily. He had slumped back into one of the padded leather command chairs and sat there, stroking his beard meditatively with the fingers of one gnarled hand. 'There is no way they could be aware of our coming. We have no traitors aboard this ship. No one could have known our plans until we set out, and even if they did, they surely could not have sent word faster than we have travelled.'

The old dwarf sounded as if he was trying to convince himself. Felix had no difficulty finding flaws in any of his arguments. Schreiber had known about their goal, as had Straghov and any number of his followers. Sorcery could transmit a message even faster than the airship could fly. More simply still, perhaps the Chaos followers had visionaries in their midst who could foresee the future. It sometimes appalled Felix how quickly and easily he could find the dark side of things.

'And we're assuming they are concerned with us,' Borek continued. 'There is no proof of that either. Perhaps they have their own reasons for gathering along this route.'

'And what could those be?'

'I don't know but I'm sure that if it's the case we will find out soon enough.'

As the airship flew on, the warbands became larger, as many of the smaller mobs of Chaos worshippers met and banded together to form larger units. In some bands up to a dozen banners could be seen fluttering in the wind.

Grotesque creatures were becoming more common among the creatures below. Felix saw strange warriors, part man, part woman with enormous crab-like claws. They were mounted on loping two-legged creatures with long protruding tongues. As he watched through a telescope from high above, this troop of daemonic cavalry chased down a scattered band of mutants. Their foul steeds shot out their long sticky tongues, grasped their victims and reeled them into their masters' – or mistresses' – claws the way certain jungle lizards were supposed to capture flies.

Odd, brightly coloured creatures whose hideously exaggerated faces appeared to emerge directly from the middle of their torsos capered through the bright desert sands. They waved up at the passing airship as if greeting a long lost kinsman and then clutched their sides, rolling around in insane daemonic mirth.

One enormous black-armoured rider led a pack of twisted hounds across the rocks. His animals had enormous reptilian crests and their skins glowed a bright metallic red. At times Felix felt like he was looking down into scenes dragged from some madman's nightmares, but he could not stop himself from watching all the same.

Ahead of them a range of hills rose out of the desert. As they approached, Felix saw that the foothills were merely outriders of a much larger range of towering peaks, tall as anything in the Worlds Edge Mountains. These hills shimmered with unnatural colours. And for the first time Felix saw something in the Wastes that resembled vegetation.

A forest of monstrous slimy fungi bloomed on the hillsides. Each of the mighty mushrooms was as large as the tallest tree and its canopy was huge enough to shelter a small village. Each was a slightly different sickly shade – jaundiced yellow, bone white, nausea green – and each rose towards the sky as if fighting with its fellows for every scrap of light and every inch of space. Some of the fungi had multiple caps, each branching from a central stalk. A vile mucous enshrouded the flesh of the fungal trees and dripped poisonously onto the ground below. All suggested something unnatural and evil, a life that should not exist in any sane world.

Here and there one of the mighty fungal trees had fallen – or been deliberately felled – and beastmen and mutants crawled over it, like ants on a rotted log. They consumed the corrupt flesh of the fallen giant and drank its slime. After they ate it, they shouted and fought and engaged in orgies of unspeakable activities, as if the dead thing's substance contained some strange and intoxicating drug.

As the hills rose before Felix's rapt gaze, they became cleaner and devoid of the unnatural vegetation. Instead more ruins became evident. He spied small forts made from little more than accumulated boulders. Intricately crafted castles with walls shod in steel and brass. Palaces carved from the living rock of the hills. There was no rhyme or reason to it. Near every structure lay skeletons and unburied corpses or gallows from which dangled dead beastmen. The smell of burning and death rose from the hillside. This was an area that had obviously seen a lot of fighting but was now deserted, and as they flew on, it became obvious why.

Over the hills warriors moved en masse, flowing like a turbulent stream down into the roads which passed through the valleys, joining the torrent of Chaos worshippers who travelled on the dusty roads. They rode, they limped, they marched, they crawled, they hopped, they flopped obscenely but they all moved – and they all had one destination in mind. There could be no doubt now that all the worshippers of Chaos were heading in the same direction that they were themselves – the distant mountains.

Hours went by. The airship passed over a flat plain in the shadow of the hills and still the endless flow moved beneath them. In the centre of the plain, Felix could see that four enormous boulders had been carved into monstrous parodies of the human form. At first he had thought it was a trick of the light, a mirage brought on by the odd shape of the rocks and his own tired eyes but after a while he had realised that this was not true. Each of the mighty stones really had been carved into the shape of what he assumed was one of the Dark Gods of Chaos.

As he came closer he began to get some idea of the scale of these monumental statues. Each was loftier than the mooring mast at the Lonely Tower. He had heard that some of the peaks on the elves' Islands of Ulthuan had been carved into enormous statues but this was work that must surely dwarf even that. Some awesome magic had been used to reshape the very bones of the earth into these mocking images, and in a moment of wonder and terror Felix came to some understanding of the true might of the Powers of Chaos.

One of the statues was a huge squatting thing, its sides blotched with boils and cankers. Its leering image spoke of a million years of pestilence and death. Somewhere in the back of his mind, a voice whispered to Felix the name of Nurgle, Daemon God of Plague.

Another was shaped into something bird-headed, with enormous wings enfolded round its body. Eerie and unnatural light played around the head, a crown of mystical energy that transmitted the thought that here was an object sacred to Tzeentch, the Architect of Fate, the Changer of Ways.

The third statue was carved in the shape of a creature not quite man and not quite woman, posed in an attitude at once both lascivious and mocking. Huge caves made blank empty eye sockets. Felix shivered, for somehow he knew this to be a depiction of one of the many aspects of Slaanesh, Lord of Unspeakable Pleasures. He had encountered this Daemon-God's worshippers many times in the past.

The last took the shape of a massive warrior, bat-winged, armed with sword and whip, face masked by a helmet that obscured all features. There was something in the stance that suggested a creature at once shambling and ape-like, but possessed of enormous physical power. This must be Khorne, the Blood God, Lord of the Throne of Skulls. Felix shivered. Khorne's was a name which had inspired terror since the dawn of time.

Around the feet of these titanic effigies a few worshippers prostrated themselves and threw down offerings but most simply saluted and moved on. Felix had given up on any attempt to count the Chaos worshippers. They numbered in the thousands now. It was like watching an army of ants on the march, and the motives of the horde seemed just as incomprehensible and just as threatening. He was only glad that they were marching away from the lands of men, deeper into the Wastes, although he realised that it would take only one order to turn this great army around and send it scything southward, if a powerful enough leader were to arise.

The command deck behind Felix was silent save for the throb of the engines, and Felix knew that all the dwarfs present were thinking the same thoughts as he was. All of them had been overcome by the terrible majesty of the army gathered below them.

The foothills climbed beneath them and now ahead of the airship loomed the true peaks of the range. Beneath them the land looked almost normal, with streams and trees and what might have been goats leaping along the ridges. Was it possible that some parts of the Waste had remained untouched by the warping influence of Chaos? Did some counter-balancing force still strive against its effects? Or was this some trick of the Dark Powers, an innocuous veil drawn over a secret thing even darker and more terrible than anything they had yet witnessed?

Makaisson let out his breath in a long, slow whistle as he pulled levers and turned the great wheel, sending the airship soaring through a long valley which sliced between the brooding black peaks. He had to make constant small adjustments to the controls as he fought against crosswinds and turbulence while threading a path through the winding valley.

The airship turned almost ninety degrees to the right and ahead of them lay a long vale teeming with the followers of Chaos. Wisps of smoke rose from their cooking fires to form a dark cloud that threatened to obscure their vision. Tens of thousands of beastmen looked up at them curiously. Thousands of Chaos warriors were drawn up within a crazy maze of earthworks. The airship droned steadily down the valley towards the deepening darkness that filled its far end.

Enormous chariots pulled by hideous mutant beasts larger than elephants rose above the mass. Here and there some had tumbled down, some had melted, some had simply been smashed as if by a superior force. Huge t-shaped crosses had been placed among the ranks of tents and blockhouses, and each bore a crucified figure. Some were fresh; others had been reduced to skeletons by the carrion birds.

Ahead of them loomed a singularly enormous mountain. Its huge bulk blocked the end of the valley. Its sides were covered in row upon row of broken fortifications. The ground on the mountain's lower slopes was covered by a white plain of bones. The fortifications rose to a citadel atop the mountain's very peak, and it was obvious that a battle had been fought here – and recently, for smoke still rose from burning buildings and black-armoured warriors moved among the corpses of the recently dead.

A tense silence filled the command deck of the *Spirit of Grungni*. All of the dwarfs appeared to be holding their breath in amazement and horror. Eventually Borek spoke and his voice came out in a harsh croak.

'Behold the peak of Karag Dum,' he said.

SIXTEEN
KARAG DUM

'Look out!' Felix shouted. From amidst the teeming hordes below them, one of the Chaos worshippers – a tall, lean figure robed in black, covered in amulets and wearing a silver helm with curved goat's horns – had raised an ornate staff to point at them. Sizzling energies crackled around the staff's tip and a bolt of blood red lightning leapt from the ground to the airship. His fellow sorcerers gathered to add their power to the attack, and the fury of the assault intensified until the blaze hurt the eye and the roar of the thunder threatened to deafen Felix.

Lightning flashed and crackled all around the *Spirit of Grungni*. The burnt tin stench of ozone filled the air. It was as if they were trapped in the centre of a thunderstorm all of their own. The gondola trembled and shook. The gemmed eyes of the figurehead blazed and Felix felt the amulet on his chest grow warm. Makaisson wrenched the wheel and tugged the altitude lever and they headed skywards towards the low, overhanging clouds.

The airship shivered and bucked like a frightened horse, and Felix feared that their magical protection was going to be overcome. Then, as suddenly as the attack had started, it ceased.

Not a moment too soon, as far as Felix was concerned. He looked down on the encamped Chaos army. It seemed that they had crossed some boundary, come too close and so had been attacked. It seemed possible, therefore, that as long as they kept their distance, they would be allowed to fly above the army unmolested. Perhaps the Chaos worshippers had feared an attack from above, thought Felix. Or, just as likely, they were simply mad.

An appalled silence filled the control room. The dwarfs exchanged shocked glances. Felix crouched down by the window and watched them. Eventually Borek spoke in a low croak.

'This is not what I expected,' he said, and the weight of his years showed in his voice. He shook his head. 'This is not possible.'

Gotrek was pale, though whether with fury or some other suppressed emotion Felix could not tell. 'Does the citadel still stand? Are our people still down there?'

Borek looked up at him with one rheumy eye and shook his head. 'Nothing could withstand the forces of Chaos for two centuries. There can be no one left alive down there.'

Gotrek's knuckles whitened as his grip on his axe tightened. 'Then why is that huge army down there? Why do they lay siege to the dwarfhold? Who are they fighting, if not our kinsfolk?'

'I do not know,' Borek said. 'You saw that army. You saw the devastation in the vale. The dwarfhold could not have withstood such an attack for so long.'

'What if they have? What if there are still dwarfs alive down there? It means we have abandoned our kinfolk to the mercies of Chaos for well nigh two centuries. It means we have forsaken our old treaties of alliance with them. It means our nations have not kept faith.'

Borek picked up his walking stick and tapped its tip on the steel floor. It was the only sound audible save for the hum of the engines. Felix considered their argument. He had to agree with Borek. It seemed hugely unlikely that any citadel could have held out for nearly two hundred years against a siege by the ravaging armies of Chaos, even one held by such tenacious defenders as the dwarfs. Another possible explanation struck him.

'Isn't it possible,' he ventured, 'that Karag Dum fell to the forces of Chaos and some warlord of the Dark Powers took it over and used it as his citadel? Perhaps the Chaos worshippers fight among themselves for possession.'

He saw that all eyes were upon him. On some faces was written understanding, on some disappointment. It struck him that some of the dwarfs had hoped to find their lost kinsfolk down there, Gotrek included.

'That seems the most likely explanation,' Borek said. 'And, if it is true, then there is very little for us to do here. We would be as well to turn this airship around and go home.'

Again Felix sensed disappointment in the control room, this time greater than before. These dwarfs had come a long way, made great sacrifices in order to get here, and now their leader was telling them it might all have been in vain. Even so, the dwarfs all nodded their agreement. Except Gotrek.

'But it is not the only explanation,' the Slayer said. 'We do not know it is the case for certain.'

'True, Gotrek, but what would you have us do?'

'Land someone in the citadel! Conduct the expedition into the depths we came to mount. Find out if any of our people yet live down there.'

'I take it you are volunteering to do this.'

'I am. We can wait until it's dark and then descend on the peak. If I remember your maps, there is a secret passage down from the cliff face. I can enter there and make my way down to the Underhalls.'

'Snorri will go too,' said Snorri. 'Can't let Gotrek grab all the glory. Good chance to smash some Chaos warriors as well.'

'I will go too, uncle,' Varek said suddenly. 'I would like to look upon the home of my ancestors.'

'I suppose I'd better go as well. You'll need someone with half a brain down there,' said another voice. Felix was shocked when he recognised it was his own.

'Before we do anything, let us take another look at what is going on below,' said Borek. 'Perhaps then we will have a clearer idea of what is happening.'

They took the airship down to just below cloud level and moved in a wide sweep round the mountain. As they did so, it became obvious that it was surrounded by not just one but four enormous armed camps.

Each camp was dedicated to one of the great Powers of Chaos. Over the nearest fluttered the blood red pennants of Khorne. Over another hung the luminous banners of Tzeentch. Over the third, the polychromatic flags of Slaanesh pulsed and changed hue. The slime-dripping flags of Nurgle erupted from the pestilent horde at the fourth camp.

As they watched, it became obvious that the followers of the powers were wary of each other. Each camp was surrounded by a ditch, not just facing the peak but all around, as if the armies feared attack by each other. Here and there, along the boundaries, Felix was sure that he saw sporadic skirmishes being fought between some warriors.

He also saw that these camps were the final destination of all the Chaos worshippers which they had seen out in the deserts. They were arriving from all points of the compass and found their way to one or other of the camps. Felix was willing to bet that they were each seeking the camp of their own faction, and going to swell its ranks.

He supposed there was a certain warped logic to it all – if the four powers were all rivals and fought with each other as much as they did with anyone else. Given the friction that must exist between their followers it made sense to segregate them and minimise tension. Somehow, though, he could not help but feel that he was missing something.

Then, even as he watched from the safety of the airship, he saw the army of Khorne muster along its border with the army of Slaanesh, and, with a mighty roar, fling itself into battle. It was plain these armies were here to fight with each other, as much as they were to besiege Karag Dum.

'We will wait for you for as long as we have food and then we will go,' Borek said solemnly. 'We'll fly high and watch the peak through our telescopes. If you discover anything, make your way back up and fire one of Makaisson's green flares. We will come and get you as quickly as we can.'

Felix nodded and not for the first time checked the flares he had stuck in his belt. They were still there, along with the other equipment the dwarfs had given him: a compass, an ever-burning lantern that used one of their precious glowstones for illumination, several flasks of water, and another of vodka. He had a small sackful of provisions over his shoulder. He wore his mail coat once more and was glad of it.

And not for the first time, too, he asked himself why he was doing this, and once more he discovered that he could not quite formulate a reason. It made much more sense to stick with the airship. At least that way, he could get home even if Gotrek and the others failed. Yet there was more to this than common sense. He and Gotrek had faced countless perils together, and despite the Slayer's quest for death they had always survived. Felix suspected that there was more than luck involved, some kind of destiny even, and that he would have a better chance of escaping alive from the Chaos Wastes in the company of the Slayer than on his own. At least he was trying to convince himself that this was the case.

And at the end of the day there was his oath. He had sworn to follow the Slayer and record his doom, and he suspected that enough of dwarfish culture had rubbed off on him for him to take his promise very seriously. He glanced out of the window. Below them he could see the fires of the Chaos camps, and the shadowy figures which moved around them. Occasionally, too, he could hear the sounds of weapon on weapon as a brawl broke out.

It was night, or what passed for it here in the Wastes. They had waited many hours for the sky to darken and eventually their patience had been rewarded. The airship too was dark, all the lights having been extinguished so as not to give away their position. The engines were being run with minimum power so as to make as little noise as possible. Ahead of them loomed the shadowy bulk of the peak. He hoped that Makaisson knew what he was doing, and that they weren't going to smash into the mountain. Intellectually he knew that dwarfs could see much better in the dark than humans, but there was a difference between possessing that knowledge and believing it with all his heart, particularly at a moment like this, when his life was at stake.

'If you discover people still alive and want us to come for you, fire a red flare,' Borek said. 'Understand?'

'I understand,' Felix said. It would have been difficult not to have. Borek had explained it all to them a dozen times during the long wait. The flares were another of Makaisson's inventions, a variant of the basic rocket which would leave a brilliant trail of a chosen hue behind itself.

The airship juddered to a halt. Felix knew that this was their signal to go. Gotrek led the way, swinging himself out of the hatch and down the ladder. Snorri followed him, humming happily to himself. Next came Varek. He paused in the opening and gave Felix a nervous grin and then he, too, vanished through the hatch. He had a sack of bombs strapped to his chest and Makaisson's strange gun slung over his shoulder. Felix wished he owned one of the weapons and knew how to use it, but it was too late to learn now. He took a deep breath, exhaled and let himself out onto the ladder.

The night wind bit into his flesh. It was cold in a way that he would never have expected in the middle of a desert. He told himself to be sensible. They were somewhere far to the north of Kislev. It was bound to be chilly. The ladder swung a little under the weight of the climbers and Felix's stomach lurched.

Sigmar, what am I doing here, he asked himself? How did I end up dangling from a flying machine designed by a maniac, hovering over the sides of a mountain on the slopes of which are camped a great army of thousands of Chaos warriors. Well, if nothing else, he told himself, it will be an interesting death. Then he gathered all his courage and continued the descent.

The four of them stood on a ledge close to the peak, under the shadow of a protective wall. Felix glanced up to see the ladder being rolled back into the airship, and the vessel lifting skyward once more out of range of the Chaos horde's sorcerers. He strained his ears to see if he could pick up the sound of any sentries giving the alarm. All he could hear was Snorri humming.

'Stop that, please,' he whispered.

'Sure,' Snorri said loudly.

Felix fought down the urge to hit him with his sword.

'This pathway should lead us to the Gate of Eagles,' Varek murmured.

'Then let's get going,' Gotrek said. 'We don't have all night.'

They stopped by a monstrous statue of an eagle carved in the face of the rock. Gotrek reached down between the talons of its right claw and depressed a hidden switch. A small opening, just large enough for a dwarf to scramble through, opened in its base. They hurried through. Felix heard another switch click and the dim light of outside vanished behind them.

He felt Varek tug at his sleeve. They had already agreed that they would not shine any lights until they knew their way was safe. That way there would be nothing to give them away in the darkness. It was all right for the dwarfs, Felix realised, for they really could see in the dark but this plan left him blind and utterly reliant on them for guidance. Perhaps this had not been such a great plan after all. He reached out with his left hand to feel the cold stone of the wall, and then he followed where Varek led.

'There are many such secret escape routes out,' Varek whispered. 'They were used as sally ports during sieges.'

'What if traitors used them to break into the city,' Felix asked.

'No dwarf would ever do such a thing,' Varek said. Felix could hear genuine shock in the young dwarf's voice that anyone could even suggest such a thing.

'Quiet back there,' Gotrek said. 'You want to attract the attention of every beastman and Chaos thing on the mountain?'

'That's not a bad idea,' said Snorri. There was a noise that sounded suspiciously like Gotrek's fist connecting with Snorri's head, then there was silence.

* * *

Lurk grinned. The pain was over. The long days of sweating and writhing in his makeshift burrow had ended. He no longer felt the pulsing ache in his skull and the wracking agony of every bone in his body being stretched. He had been purified by pain, reshaped by agony. He had been chosen by the Horned Rat, blessed by the Lurker in Unknowable Darkness, the Scurrying Lord of the Pit.

He knew instinctively that he had changed and that these changes were a sign of his master's favour. The warpstone dust had been merely a catalyst, an agent of change that carried the blessing of his god. He was bigger now, too big to fit into his crate, so large he had to hunker down to squeeze through the corridors. And he was strong. His shoulders were as broad as a rat-ogre's. His chest had become a barrel of muscle. His arms were now thicker than his legs once had been and his legs were pillars of pulsing power.

He felt like he could bend steel bars with his bare paws and rip through granite with his fangs.

His teeth were much longer and sharper now. His lower canines protruded like tusks and made it difficult for him to keep his mouth properly closed. Saliva dribbled constantly from the corners of his mouth.

His skull was heavier and it felt like the bones had erupted through his cheeks to create a mask of hard armour. Large, ram-like horns had emerged from his forehead. At the time they had caused him a splitting headache but now he could see that it was a mark of the Horned Rat's favour, a sign that he had truly been chosen, a blessing that marked him as different, special, superior. All his life he had known he was better than other Skaven, and now, at last, was the proof.

Look at his tail so long, so sleek, so supple and crowned with four spikes, a veritable mace of bone. Look at his claws – so much longer, so much sharper, each the size of a poniard. He had become a living engine of destruction fuelled by the hatred and hunger burning in his heart. He had nothing to fear from a non-entity like Thanquol. When he returned to Skavenblight it would be in absolute triumph. The Council of Thirteen itself would grovel at his feet. He would lead the assembled armies of skavenkind and crush everything that got in his way. The whole world would tremble and be conquered by the invincible, omnipotent Lurk.

But now he was hungry, and it was time to hunt. He could hear dwarf feet approaching. After listening for a moment, he realised that there was more than one of them. A deep rooted instinct told him that superior numbers were only a good thing when they were on your side. It was not sensible to attack a group of foes. Perhaps, he decided, he would wait a little longer, until there was just the one, and then… then he would reveal his awesome power.

Felix heard the deep rumble of stone on stone as Gotrek pushed another switch. A gust of foul air passed his face and he guessed that the dwarf had opened another secret door. They moved swiftly forward and Felix heard the opening shift back into place behind them. He was not sure how it was done. He had not heard a second switch being thrown. Perhaps the mechanism was timed. Perhaps there was a pressure plate underfoot. He knew he should wait to ask another time. He might have to find his way back this way on his own, if he became separated from the others.

There was light up ahead, a dim and distant glow. It was subdued and occasionally it faded, only to return to brightness once more. It was not like the light of a torch, more like that of glowstone or a spell. By its faint illumination, he could now see the squat outlines of the dwarfs ahead of him.

Gotrek held up a hand to indicate that they should remain where they were and then moved forward silently alone, with a stealth that Felix would not have guessed he was capable of.

He was glad that the Slayer seemed to be taking their mission so seriously. It appeared that his need to learn the fate of the inhabitants of Karag Dum was overriding even his desire for a heroic death. And why not, Felix asked himself? The two were not mutually exclusive. If Gotrek wished to be remembered in dwarfish history, surely there would be no better way than being recalled as the saviour of these lost kinsfolk? Or did he have another, more personal motive? Felix knew he would never dare to ask.

He took another deep breath to calm himself. The air smelled fusty, and there was a hint of rot and something else in it. It was the same sort of scent he remembered in the harpy's lair back in the ziggurat, the rank odour of Chaos beasts. He heard Snorri sniffing and knew that the hammer-wielding Slayer had noticed it too.

Gotrek had reached the junction ahead and beckoned for them to follow. They hastened forward until they reached the opening and emerged into another long corridor.

The flickering light came from glowgems set in the ceiling. Some had been smashed, others removed. Those which had been left behind were cracked and worked only intermittently, sending shadows skittering away into the gloom.

The stonework reminded Felix of the dwarf architecture he had marvelled at in Karak Eight Peaks. The walls were supported by hewn blocks of basalt. Massive arches supported the high, arching roof. Each was a work of art. The nearest were carved with the likeness of two kneeling dwarfs, facing each other across the corridor, lifting the roof on their backs.

They must have been beautiful when they were made but they had been vandalised. The faces had been chipped off and parts of the stonework had been scored with blades. It angered Felix that someone could have defaced something into which an artist had placed so much labour.

As they crept down the corridor, he saw that the destruction was no isolated incident. Every last arch had been ruined in some way. Many had been blackened by fire or scorched by spells. Some looked as if they had been eaten away by acid.

Slowly it dawned on Felix that he was not looking at mere wanton vandalism, but rather the evidence of a battle. A bitter conflict had been fought out in this corridor using all manner of weapons, natural and supernatural. They started to pass skeletons, still clad in armour and clutching weapons in their bony fingers. Some belonged to dwarfs, some to hideously mutated beastmen.

'Well, we know that the followers of Chaos got in,' Varek murmured.

'Aye, and were met with cold steel by stout-hearted dwarfs,' said Gotrek.

'But are any of them left alive now?' Felix muttered.

The corridors carried them deeper and deeper into the depths. Some sloped downwards. Others brought them to steep stairwells. Everywhere there were signs of old battles. Mummified corpses lay everywhere. An aura of evil brooded over everything. Somewhere in the depths lurked a terrible presence. Felix fought hard to control the fear which had started to gnaw at him, the certainty that – round the next bend or at the bottom of the next flight of stairs – they were going to encounter something malign, supernatural and terrible.

Gotrek paused in one long hall, lined by titanic statues. Bodies were strewn everywhere but none of them belonged to dwarfs. All were of beastmen or Chaos warriors. One pair of bodies lay with swords through each other's ribs. They had killed each other with simultaneous strokes.

Gotrek gazed down on them thoughtfully. 'Here there was a blood-letting between the foul ones.'

'Perhaps they fell out over the division of spoils.'

'So where is the treasure, Felix?' Varek asked.

'Carried away by the victors?' Felix replied. He looked closer at the corpses and noticed that their insignia were different.

'Perhaps they followed different powers or rival warlords. Perhaps there was some kind of squabble between the victors.'

'Perhaps,' said Gotrek.

'Why is it so quiet here?' Felix asked. 'There was an entire army outside, but we have seen no evidence of anyone since we got in here.'

Gotrek laughed. 'This is one of the ancient dwarfholds, manling. It extends for leagues under the earth. There are hundreds of levels. The total length of the corridors and halls must come to thousands of leagues. You could lose an army the size of the one outside in a small corner of this city.'

'Then how are we going to find any survivors which might be here?'

'If any dwarf lives on down here, there are certain places where they will be, and we are heading there,' Varek said.

With that, they pushed on into the darkness.

In many more places it was clear that the battles had not been fought between dwarfs and Chaos worshippers but amongst the followers of the Dark Powers themselves. Only occasionally did they come across signs that dwarfs had been involved in any of the warfare. It became increasingly evident from the bodies they found that there had been a war between the forces of Chaos. Here they found signs that the warriors of Slaanesh had fought against the berserk followers of Khorne. There they found evidence that the worshippers of Tzeentch had struggled with the plague-ridden servants of Nurgle. In one large hall, they came across a place where the followers of all four powers had fallen out and slaughtered each other.

Felix found the gloom oppressive. It was depressing to wander through these endless, battle-scarred corridors and find the remains of old battles. He thought of that vast army camped outside. Who did they represent? What were they waiting for? It seemed senseless. He shrugged. Then again, why did that surprise him? The followers of Chaos were not sane as he measured sanity. Perhaps they fought for the unknowable amusement of their Dark Gods. Perhaps they fought for the amusement of the evil thing he sensed down here. Perhaps they, too, were only being allowed to proceed by some whim of whatever thing lurked down here. He wondered if the others felt this same uneasy sense of presence. He could not find the courage to ask them.

As they passed through gallery after echoing gallery, and chamber after high-ceilinged chamber, it became obvious that Gotrek was right. There was certainly room enough in here to house a dozen armies even if they were all the size of the forces gathered outside. He wondered what it must have been like to dwell here in an underground city like this in its heyday. Even before the followers of Chaos came, it must have been near-empty, for he knew the dwarfs were a dying race and had been so for millennia. Still, there must have been a time when these streets were filled with dwarfs buying and selling, laughing and crying, loving and living and going about their daily business. Now it seemed like a tomb, and the dead bodies of interlopers everywhere seemed like a desecration.

Gotrek knelt beside the goat-headed corpse before which he had suddenly paused. It was not like the others they had seen – it was still warm! Flesh still clung to its bones. Warm black blood formed a pool under it. Nearby lay other beastmen, all just as dead.

Felix squatted for a better look. In life the beastman had not been pretty, and death had not improved its looks. It had the great head of a goat and the body of a man. Its furry legs ended in hooves. Its brow had been branded with the mark of Khorne. Its strange liquid eyes were glazed in death. They stared blankly up at the towering ceiling high overhead. A crossbow shaft protruded from its chest; another stuck out from its gut. One hand still clutched at the missiles which had killed it. The hand was beautifully formed, more like that of a monk than a monster, and Felix thought of how incongruous it looked on that bestial form. The beast stank of wet fur and the excrement and urine that it had released when it died.

Gotrek tugged at one of the crossbow bolts. It came free with a hideous sucking sound and a thin trickle of black blood oozed forth from where it had been. Gotrek turned the missile back and forth in his hand, studying it closely with his one good eye. Felix could not see what fascinated him so much about it. It looked well made but hardly any different from any other crossbow bolt he had seen.

'This is a dwarf weapon,' Gotrek said eventually, and there was something which might even have been triumph in his voice.

'How can you tell?' Felix asked.

'Look at the manufacture, manling. No human ever made a point that fitted so well, or feathered a bolt so perfectly. Also, there are dwarf runes on the tip.'

'So you're saying that these beastmen were killed by dwarfs?'

Gotrek shrugged and looked away. 'Maybe.'

'Perhaps the beastmen found one of the armouries,' Varek suggested tentatively. He plainly didn't want to contradict Gotrek, and Felix could see that he hoped he was wrong. He wanted for there to be dwarfs down here and still fighting.

'When have you ever seen a beastman armed with a crossbow?' Gotrek asked.

'It might have been a dark warrior.'

'Or such a warrior armed that way, for that matter?'

It was a fair point. In all of his encounters with the followers of the Dark Powers, Felix had never met one which used such a sophisticated weapon. Of course, that didn't mean there couldn't be a first time. He decided to keep that thought to himself. Instead he asked: 'How will we find these dwarfs then?'

'Maybe Snorri should ask those beastmen,' Snorri suggested from behind them.

Felix's heart skipped a beat when he heard Snorri's words. He turned to look in the direction that the Slayer had indicated. Sure enough, there stood a band of at least twenty beastmen. For a moment, they looked just as surprised as Felix but then they recovered from their shock and raised their spears for the attack.

'Or maybe we should just kill them,' Gotrek said, lowering his head and charging.

'No! Don't!' shouted Felix – but already it was too late. Varek had started to turn the crank on his strange looking gun. A hail of bullets tore into the beastmen, killing two and dropping another pair. Howling with rage and frothing with berserk fury, the beastmen charged forward. Felix knew there was nothing for it now but to fight and most likely die in a futile skirmish with the Chaos worshippers. Snorri had obviously decided the same, for he had raised his weapons and begun to move forward as well. With the two Slayers blocking his line of sight, Varek started to move to a new position, hoping to out-flank the beastmen and pour fire into the side of their formation.

Felix drew his blade and raced forward to aid Gotrek and Snorri. Before he could get into action, before the two sides had closed to within twenty strides of each other, a new hail of crossbow bolts hurtled out of the dark and scythed into the beastmen. The missiles fell like a dark rain. Felix saw one dog-headed monstrosity tumble with a bolt through its eye, tears of blood running down its cheek. Its chest was pin-cushioned with bolts even as it dropped. Another clutched its heart and fell, to be trampled below the hooves of its brethren. The beastmen's rush faltered as more and more of them fell. The survivors halted and looked around, desperately trying to see where the attack was coming from.

Gotrek, Snorri and Felix crashed into them and went through their line like an axe through rotting wood. Felix felt a shock run up his arm from the impact, then something warm and sticky was running over his hands. He pulled his blade free, kicked his chosen beastman to the ground and stabbed another. His sword took the surprised beastman in the shoulder, glanced up and lopped off an ear. Not waiting to draw his weapon back, he smashed the pommel into his foe's face and felt teeth break in its mouth. The beastman bellowed in pain, before Felix clubbed it down and stabbed it through the heart.

Almost before it had begun, the fight was over. Overwhelmed by the fury of their foes, the last surviving beastmen turned and fled. Felix could see that Gotrek had slaughtered four of them; their sliced remains lay at his feet. Snorri was jumping up and down on a corpse, happy as a child playing in a sandpit. A burst from Varek's gun chopped down the surviving beastmen even as they fled.

Felix looked around, panting more with reaction to the sudden short combat than from the effort. He wanted to see whoever it was who had aided them and thank them.

'Be very still!' said a deep, guttural voice. 'You are inches away from death.'

SEVENTEEN
THE LAST DWARFS

Felix froze. He tried not even to blink his eyes, let alone breathe. He had no doubts that whoever was lurking in the shadows meant what they said, and he had no desire to find his body bristling with crossbow bolts.

'Are you dwarfs?' Varek asked, with what Felix thought was more curiosity than common sense.

'Aye, that we are. The question is: what are you?'

A massively broad-shouldered dwarf strode into view in front of them. He was garbed in leather armour, huge metal shoulder pads protected his upper torso. A winged helm with cheekguards shielded his face. Slung over his shoulder he carried a crossbow. A heavy warhammer dangled from a loop on his belt. He removed the helmet to peer at them and Felix could see that his face was craggy and his eyes were feverishly bright. His beard was long and black shot through with silver. There was an unnatural leanness about his face such as Felix had never seen in a dwarf before.

He sauntered around the four of them and inspected them with a casual air that was almost insulting. Felix could tell that Gotrek and Snorri had their tempers barely under control and if something was not done soon, murderous violence would ensue.

'Two of you look like Slayers,' the newcomer said. 'One of you has the look of Grungni's folk. The other, the human, must die.'

Almost before Felix realised that the dwarf meant him, the newcomer had unslung his crossbow and pointed it directly at his chest. Felix found himself staring at the glittering point of a crossbow bolt. As if in slow motion he saw the stranger's finger begin to squeeze the trigger. He knew he could never throw himself aside in time but his muscles tensed for the attempt.

'Wait,' Gotrek said softly and there was such a note of command in his voice that the newcomer froze. 'If you harm the manling, you will surely die.'

The other dwarf laughed harshly. 'Those are brave words for one who is in no position to back them up. Tell me why should I spare him?'

'Because he is a Dwarf Friend and a Rememberer, and if you kill him your name will live long in infamy and will be recorded in the Book of Grudges as a fool and a coward.'

'Who are you to speak of the Great Book?'

'I am Gotrek, son of Gurni, and if you cross me in this matter I will be your death.'

There was cold certainty in the Slayer's voice that commanded belief. Gotrek added something in dwarfish, which caused the newcomer's face to flush and his eyes to widen.

'So you speak the Old Tongue,' he said.

Felix heard a shocked murmur from around the hall, and suddenly realised how many other dwarfs were watching them.

It seemed inconceivable that such a large force could have moved through the tunnels with such stealth. He risked glancing around and saw that several score of lean, weary looking dwarfs had emerged from the gloom. All of them had weapons pointed at the party, and seemed prepared to use them. He could see that their wargear all had the same look, as of something that had been patched and reused many times over.

A brief spirited debate followed in dwarfish between Gotrek and the newcomers. Felix looked over at Varek. 'What is being said?'

'These dwarfs think that we are agents of Chaos. They wanted to kill us. Gotrek has told them that we come from outside and that we can help them. Some of them don't believe it and say it is a trick. Their leader says that he cannot risk killing us and that it is a matter for his father, the king himself, to decide.'

To Felix this seemed like a very bald summary of what was obviously an impassioned debate. Voices were being raised. Harsh guttural oaths were being sworn. Both Gotrek and the dwarfish leader had spat on the ground in front of each other's feet. It was an odd sensation to know that his very life hung in the balance and that he could neither say nor do anything to influence the decision. He was reminded of being on the airship during the great warpstorm. All he could do now was remind himself that they had survived that, and might survive this.

Varek continued to mutter: 'It is only the fact that we speak the Old Tongue which keeps them from killing us out of hand. They do not want to believe that any follower of Chaos could have learned it. Certainly no dwarf would teach them.'

'That's reassuring to know,' said Felix.

The argument ended. The dwarf leader turned and spoke to Felix in strongly-accented Reikspiel.

'I do not know if this tale of flying ships and other wonders is true. I only know that this is too grave a matter for me to decide. Your fate is in the hands of the king, and he will pass judgement on you.'

'I still say it's a trick, Hargrim,' said one of the other dwarfs, an old, miserable-looking fellow with deep set eyes and a beard of pure grey. 'We know that the world outside is ruled by Chaos. There are no other dwarfholds left. We should kill these interlopers, not lead them deeper into our realm.'

'You have had your say, Torvald, and my decision stands until the king himself overturns it. If the world has not been overrun by the forces of Chaos, this is indeed momentous news. It may be that we are not the last dwarfs.'

'Aye, Hargrim, and it may be that we are fools and dupes of the Dark Powers. But as you say, you are our captain and on your head be it. There will be time enough to kill these outsiders soon, if they prove false.'

'The king will know,' Hargrim said. 'Come! Let us go. We have wasted enough time and I would not want to be caught in these halls if the Terror comes. Bind them and take their weapons.'

A group of dwarfs broke away from the main body and moved towards them. As they did so, Gotrek stepped forward menacingly.

'You will take this axe from my cold, dead hands,' he said softly and with such menace in his voice that the dwarfs froze on the spot.

'That can be arranged, stranger,' Hargrim said just as quietly. Gotrek raised his axe and the runes on the blade flashed in the dim light. The closest dwarfs gasped.

'He bears the weapon of power!' Torvald gasped, and his voice held horror and wonder. 'It is the Prophecy. Those are the Great Runes. The

Terror has returned and the axe of our ancestors has come back to us. The Last Days are upon us.'

A look of shock once more passed over Hargrim's face and he advanced towards Gotrek, his eyes fixed on the blade of the axe. As he read them, a great look of wonder appeared in his eyes.

'Where did you get this blade?' the dwarfish captain asked, then added something in dwarfish.

'I found it in a cave in the Chaos Wastes many years ago,' Gotrek replied slowly in Reikspiel. He appeared to be considering whether he should say more, then thought better of it.

'If you are truly a dwarf then you are favoured by the Ancestor Gods,' Hargrim said. 'For that is a mighty weapon.'

Gotrek grinned nastily and scratched one of the Trollslayer tattoos on his shaven head meaningfully. 'If the gods favour me, they have shown no great sign of it,' he said dryly.

'Be that as it may, such a weapon does not find its way into anyone's hands by chance. You may keep your weapons for now, until the king declares differently.'

Hargrim looked at Gotrek for a long time, and what might have been a thin smile creased his lips. 'It may be as Torvald says, Gotrek Gurnisson. It may be your coming was foretold. The king and his priests will know.'

He turned to his troops. 'Come. We have far to go before we can rest, and we do not want to be caught abroad while the Terror stalks the Underhalls.'

He glanced back at them over his shoulder. 'Come with us,' he said. The four comrades moved into place behind him and marched off into the gloom.

'We will rest here,' Hargrim said, holding up his hand to indicate that they should halt. At first Felix had no idea why the dwarf captain had chosen this spot. It seemed to be just another ruined hallway, like so many others they had passed through. Eventually, though, he noticed that there was a rune carved low in the corner of the wall, and a jet of water sprayed from the wall into a large cistern. This, at least, would be a place where they could drink.

Hargrim barked an order to one of his warriors and the dwarf moved forward. He produced a stone from his leather satchel and dipped it in the water. For a few moments, he stared into the cup and then nodded his head.

'The water is clear, captain,' he said.

Hargrim noticed Felix's curious glance. 'Sometimes the outsiders poison the wells. Sometimes it contains Chaos stuff that causes madness and mutation. Mikal's runestone contains old enchantments that warn of such things.'

'A useful thing to have,' Felix said.

'No. An essential thing to have. Without it, sooner or later, we would all die.'

'What is this Prophecy of which you spoke?' Felix asked, determined to at least try and get an answer.

'It does not concern you,' Hargrim said bluntly. 'It is for the king to test its truth. Best get some rest while you still may.'

Wearily, the dwarfs threw themselves down to rest, except for four sentries who took up positions at each entrance to the room. Felix noted with approval the four exits from this chamber, so hopefully if danger threatened from any direction they would always have a line of retreat. He walked over and sat down beside Gotrek, Snorri and Varek.

All three of his companions seemed strangely elated. Felix thought he understood why – they had found their lost kinsfolk. There were still dwarfs alive in the Underhalls of Karag Dum. In defiance of all probability, a few still lived, even after two hundred years of isolation in the Chaos Wastes.

He lay on his back and stared at the ceiling, thinking of the journey they had made to get to this isolated place. It had not been easy. They had made their way further and further into the labyrinth of tunnels beneath Karag Dum.

During the trip Felix had counted the number of dwarfs around him; there were nearly fifty. All of them wore leather armour and were lightly armed and armoured, very unlike the traditional dwarfish warriors he knew of. It seemed they travelled light and quickly through the halls of what once had been their city, and relied more on stealth and surprise for victory than on the strength of their arms. Tunnel fighters, Varek had called them.

As they travelled further, Felix came to understand why they were so lightly armoured. They passed through areas where the presence of Chaos was evident and signs of open war between the powers were visible all around. It looked like an insane and ferocious struggle was being fought here in the ruins of the dwarf city. He had asked Hargrim about this, but the dwarf had not replied. There were mysteries here, that was clear. He just needed to find someone who could explain them to him.

Well, there was little sense in worrying about it now. He lay back and stared at the ceiling, wondering what Ulrika was doing now. In moments, he was asleep. The last thing he heard was the scratching of a pen, as Varek recorded the day's events in his book.

An eerie howling woke Felix from his sleep. It echoed down the great hallways and had penetrated his dreams, jerking him awake. There was something unnatural about the noise, something that evoked primal terrors. The mere sound of it sent shivers of fear running down his spine, and made his legs feel weak.

All around him the dwarfs had come awake. He could hear the clamour as they reached for their weapons. He glanced around and saw his fear was echoed on every face, save Gotrek and Snorri's.

'What is it?' he asked. 'The Terror?'

'No,' Hargrim said. 'It is the hounds.'

'What are they?' Varek asked.

'You will soon see,' Hargrim said. He turned and spoke to his followers. 'I want ten volunteers to hold the hounds off, while the rest of us try to win clear.'

It was obvious from the expressions on their faces that the dwarfs thought he was asking for volunteers for a suicide mission. Still, more than twenty of them stepped forward.

'I will stay,' Gotrek said.

'Snorri too,' said Snorri.

'You cannot. I must get you away. King Thangrim must hear your story.'

'It might be too late for that,' Felix said glancing over his shoulder at the northernmost entrance. An enormous beast had leapt through the entrance. Before anyone could react, it ripped off the nearest sentry's arm with a single snap of its jaws and pulled another to the ground and disembowelled him with its claws. The beast moved so swiftly, with almost supernatural grace, that Felix was barely able to follow its actions.

Through the doorway several more huge beasts bounded. They resembled monstrous dogs with strange reptilian ruffles around their heads and great iron collars around their necks. Their flesh glistened, the colour of blood. Each was bigger than a man. One of them opened its mouth and bayed. As it did so, its mouth distended widely like that of a snake. It looked like it could take off a man's head with a single bite. Something about the daemonic creature made Felix want to turn and flee, screaming for help. He forced himself to stand his ground.

He knew that if he ran the beast would simply overtake him and rend his flesh as it had the sentries'.

'Flesh hounds of Khorne,' he heard Varek gasp. 'I thought they were only legends.'

'Fire at will,' Hargrim ordered. A hail of crossbow bolts hurtled towards the ravenous beasts. They opened their mouths and bayed mockingly. Most of the bolts simply ricocheted off their flesh and fell to the floor. As far as Felix could see only one had bit home. Varek fired and his bullets had no more effect than the crossbows. The hounds bounded forward, loping with a deceptively long easy stride which covered the ground faster than a horse could run.

'Stand back,' Gotrek said and paced out to meet them. None of the dwarfs disobeyed. Felix could tell that they were just as affected by the creatures' supernatural aura as he was. Only Gotrek showed no sign of dismay. Felix noticed that the runes along his axe blade were glowing brighter than he had ever seen them do before. Even so, Felix wondered whether the Slayer would survive. The creatures were so fast and strong. They were upon him almost before he had a chance to realise it. Their huge jaws widened. Their metallic teeth glistened. Their triumphant baying reached a crescendo loud enough to wake the dead.

Gotrek's axe flashed forward like a thunderbolt. The first hound's armoured skin smoked and burned where the blade touched. The beast seemed almost to explode as the axe swept though it, cutting it in two, sending innards erupting all over the floor. The Slayer's next stroke impacted on a second hound's collar. Sparks flew as metal met metal. There was a hideous grating screech. The runes on Gotrek's axe glowed as bright as red-hot coals and the collar gave way. The flesh hound's head and neck parted company. The corpse flopped to the ground, molten ichor spilling out onto the floor. Another stroke cleaved a third flesh hound down the middle lengthwise, revealing skeleton and spine and ruptured organs.

Surprised by the fury of the Slayer's attack, the remaining pack pulled back, snarling like wolves at bay. Then, with an eerie intelligence, they returned to the fray. Two flesh hounds attacked the Slayer simultaneously, one from each side. Gotrek dashed one's brains out with the axe and caught the other by the throat even as it leapt. Almost without effort the dwarf held the monstrous creature at arm's length, then he lifted it so high that its hind limbs scrabbled for purchase on empty air. He dropped it. Before it had touched the ground he has smashed through its ribs with the axe.

The last beast had circled right behind the Slayer and was about to leap on his back. 'Look out!' yelled Felix but Snorri had already tossed his axe. It bounced from the creature's shoulder but the force of the blow distracted the flesh hound. It gathered its legs beneath it for the spring but even as it took to the air, Gotrek half turned and sent his axe slashing through a bloody arc which crunched through the creature's ribcage and ended in its stomach. The force of the blow flattened the flesh hound into the ground. Gotrek stomped on its neck. There was a hideous sound of grinding vertebrae and then the axe fell once more, ending the monster's unnatural life.

The corpses of the Chaos creatures started to bubble where they lay. For a moment flesh and bone melted and ran, evaporating like boiling water. Even as Felix watched, they turned into wisps of foul looking vapour which rose towards the ceiling, then disappeared. It was like they had never been there.

For a moment there was silence, and then the dwarfs burst into cheering and applause. After a few moments they seemed to remember who they were applauding and fell silent.

'If ever I doubted that was the Axe of Valek, I do so no longer. That was a fight worthy of King Thangrim himself,' Hargrim said.

'It was easy,' Gotrek said and spat upon the floor.

'We'd best be moving,' Hargrim said. 'If the hounds were here, their foul master may be near, and however mighty you are, Gotrek Gurnisson, against that you cannot prevail.'

'Bring it on and we'll see.'

'No! Now more than ever I must bring you before the king. He must hear your tale.'

After the fight with the flesh hounds, Felix noticed a change in the dwarfs' attitude. They seemed to be more accepting of the four comrades, and less suspicious. Even old Torvald contented himself with only an occasional suspicious glance in their direction. They marched on through the endless silent corridors and even Felix could tell that they were descending all the time now. He wondered how long this could continue. After several more hours it seemed to him that they would keep going down until they reached the world's fiery heart but it was not to be.

Instead they stopped in the middle of a long and seemingly featureless corridor. While his troops shielded him from view Hargrim manipulated a hidden switch which opened a small secret doorway. An opening appeared in the wall where none had been before. The dwarf gestured for the four comrades to enter, his face stern.

'Tread very carefully now. You are on sacred ground and we will kill you at the first sign of treachery.'

EIGHTEEN
FIREBEARD

Warily, Felix stepped through the entrance. This corridor seemed no different from the rest, save that the glowstones all functioned and the air smelled slightly cleaner. The rest of the war-band hastily pushed in behind and the door swung shut behind them. Felix noticed that the dwarfs of Karag Dum relaxed visibly; conversely, Gotrek, Snorri and Varek appeared more excited. He could not tell why. Perhaps because they felt they were getting closer to their goal. It was not a feeling he shared. The long trek through the Underhalls had made him tense and nervous and he just wanted to find a place to lie down and rest.

This new corridor led into a winding maze of passageways. Every now and again Hargrim stopped and pressed a panel in the wall. He gave no explanation as to why, he simply did it and moved on.

Felix looked at Varek to see if the young dwarf could tell him what was happening.

'Deadfalls. Pit traps. Defensive works of some sort, most likely,' the dwarf said quietly, but was silenced by a nasty look from their guardians.

They passed maybe a dozen sentries at their posts, all of whom looked amazed at the sight of strangers from the outside world. Eventually they entered a monstrously long hall which was plainly inhabited by the dwarfs. This was a huge place with many exits. A well had been sunk deep into the floor in the far end of the chamber. The ceiling was low, with none of the vaulting of the magnificent halls they had passed through en route. A forest of enormous squat pillars propped up the roof. On each pillar was inscribed a strange symbol which hurt Felix's eye when he tried to read it.

'Runes of Concealment,' Varek breathed from beside him. 'No wonder this place has survived so long.'

'What's that?' Felix said.

'These runes protect the halls from magical seekings, just as the concealed entrances protect it from normal sight. This place would be all but impossible for one who was not a dwarf to find unaided.'

Felix could see hooded and cowled dwarf women working at their chores. A few priests strode backwards and forwards, speaking words of comfort and reassurance, patting heads, invoking blessings. There were many warriors, a good number of whom were crippled. Some had hooks. Some stumped around on the wooden legs. Some had bandages over their eyes indicating that they were blind. Felix had never seen so many maimed people together in one place before, not even on the beggar-filled streets of Altdorf. It certainly looked like these people had come out on the losing end of a war. Nowhere did he see any children in evidence.

'So few,' Varek muttered. 'This was once a great city.'

'Welcome to the Hall of the Well. Wait here,' Hargrim said. 'I will bring news of your coming to the king.'

The captain strode off through a huge archway and vanished somewhere into the recesses of the city. Many of those who had been working stopped and stared frankly at them. A few of the crippled beggars came over. One reached out and touched Felix disbelievingly.

'You are the first human ever to set foot in this citadel,' he croaked.

'I am honoured.'

'Ha! You may soon be dead,' the crippled warrior said and turned away. The rest of the crowd moved in. One of the cowled women asked a question in dwarfish. Varek responded. The crowd emitted a collective gasp. One of the women burst into tears.

'They asked where we had come from,' said Varek in answer to Felix's unspoken question. 'I told them we had come from across the Wastes, from the kingdom of the dwarfs.'

'I don't believe you,' said another greybeard, and turned and stalked away. It looked like there were tears in his eyes. As they waited, the crowd did not disperse. It surrounded them and stared until Hargrim returned, accompanied by a group of fully armoured warriors, each of

whom carried a rune-engraved weapon. The eldritch symbols burned
with a mystic light. Felix knew enough about dwarfs by now to tell
that these were powerful magical weapons. These longbeards were
the best equipped dwarfs Felix had seen since entering Karag Dum.
They marched with a precision that would have shamed the Imperial
Guard in Altdorf. Their armour gleamed, and they moved with pride
and discipline.

'The king will see you,' Hargrim said. 'Now you will be judged.'

'So we are to meet the legendary Thangrim Firebeard after all,' Varek
said. 'Who would have thought it?'

Gotrek laughed nastily.

'I have never seen so many rune weapons,' Varek murmured to Felix.
'Every one of those warriors carries one.'

'We collected them from the dead,' Hargrim said coldly. 'There have
been so many dead heroes here.'

King Thangrim's hall was vast. Huge statues of dwarf kings stood like
sentries against each wall. More of the heavily armoured dwarf warriors stood immobile between the statues. The four newcomers were
surrounded by an escort of the king's guard. They were taking no
chances of this being an assassination attempt. Their weapons were
drawn, and they looked as if they knew how to use them.

A raised dais dominated the far end of the chamber. On the dais was
a throne bearing a powerful and majestic figure wearing long robes
over heavy armour. Two priests flanked the king. One was a priestess of Valaya. Felix could tell that by the fact that she carried a sacred
book. The other was armoured and carried an axe, and Felix wondered
if he was a priest of Grimnir, the warrior god.

As they came closer to the dais Felix got a better look at the dwarfish
king. He was old, as old as Borek, but there was nothing feeble about
him. He looked like an aged oak, gnarled but still strong. The flesh
had fallen from his arms but still there were massive knots of muscle
there, and his shoulders were broader even than Snorri's. His hair was
long and red, although striped through with white. His beard reached
almost to the floor and it, too, was white in places. Piercing eyes glittered in deep-set sockets. Felix knew that this dwarf might be ancient
but his mind was still keen.

The weapon that sat upon the king's knees drew Felix's attention. It
was a massive hammer, with a short handle. Runes had been cut into
the head and something about them compelled the eye to look. He
knew without being told that this was a weapon of awesome power,

the legendary Hammer of Fate, which they had come all this way to find.

The guard parted in front of them to leave a path leading only to the throne. The four comrades advanced. Varek went down on one knee, making florid and elaborate gestures with his right hand. Gotrek and Snorri lounged arrogantly beside him, making no sign of obeisance. Felix decided to err on the side of caution; he bowed low, then knelt beside Varek.

'You are certainly impertinent enough to be Slayers,' said the king. His voice was rich and deep and surprisingly youthful coming from that ancient throat. He laughed and his mirth boomed out through the chamber. 'I can almost believe that the cock and bull story you told Hargrim is true.'

'No one calls me a liar and lives,' Gotrek said. The flat menace in his voice caused the guards to raise their weapons in readiness.

The king raised a mocking eyebrow. 'And few indeed threaten me in my own throne room and live. Still I ask your forgiveness, Slayer, if that is what you be. We are surrounded by the servants of the Dark Powers. Suspicion is only wisdom under such circumstances. And you must admit that we have cause to be suspicious.'

'That you have,' Gotrek admitted.

'You have come to us claiming that you have voyaged here from the world beyond our walls. I would hear your tale from your own lips before I pass judgement. Tell it to me.'

'I claim more than that,' Varek said suddenly. 'I claim kinship with the folk of Karag Dum. My father was Varig. My uncle was Borek, whom you sent out into the world to seek aid.'

King Thangrim smiled cynically. 'If what you say is true it took a long time for Borek to send aid, and you do not represent much of an army. Still, tell your tale.'

The king listened attentively while Varek spoke, stopping occasionally to ask confirmation from Gotrek. He told the tale simply and well, and Felix was astonished at the power of his memory. He also noticed that as the dwarfs spoke the priestess of Valaya's eyes never left them, and he remembered that the priestesses were supposed to have the gift of knowing the truth. At the end of the tale, the king turned to the priestess.

'Well,' he said.

'They speak true,' she replied. There was an audible gasp from the warriors in the chamber. The king raised his hand and scratched his chin through his fine long beard. He considered them for a moment and then smiled grimly.

'Now tell me, Slayer, how you came by the Axe of Valek,' said the king.

Gotrek's answering smile was as grim as Thangrim's. 'Its owner had no use for it, being dead, so I took it. Do you have a claim upon it?'

'The person who carried that blade from here was my son, Morekai. He sought to cross the Wastes and find out if anyone still lived there.'

'Then he is dead, Thangrim Firebeard. His corpse lay in a cave on the edges of the Wastes. It lay surrounded by the bodies of twenty slain beastmen.'

'There was no one with him? He left here with twenty sworn companions.'

'There was only one dwarf. I buried him according to the ancient rites, and being in need of a weapon at the time, I took this one. If it is yours, I will return it to you.'

The old king looked down and grief entered his eyes. When he spoke again he sounded as old as he looked. 'So he died alone at the end.'

'He died a hero's death,' Gotrek said. 'He paved his road to the Iron Halls with the bones of his foes.'

Thangrim looked up once more and his smile was almost grateful. 'Keep the blade, Slayer. Such a weapon is not owned. It has its own doom, and it shapes the destiny of its wielder. If it is in your hands now, it is there for a reason.'

'As you say,' Gotrek said.

'And you have given me much to think on,' Thangrim said wearily. 'And my apologies for doubting you. Go now. Rest. We will talk again later.'

'Prepare apartments for our guests,' he shouted. 'And feed them of our finest.'

Felix could not help but notice that there was a note of bitter irony in the king's voice.

Felix stared at the fish suspiciously. It was large and it looked well-cooked, yet there was something odd about it. After a few moment's consideration he realised that it had no eyes. The meat smelled good and everyone else was eating it, yet he kept thinking of the things he had seen in the Wastes, of the mutants and beastmen, and of all the things he had been told about warpstone dust. He just could not bring himself to eat a mutant fish, and he knew there was good reason for this.

By all accounts it was possible for mutation to be passed on through eating mutated food. It was said that the worst mutants were always cannibals who fed on other mutants. He had no desire to put this theory of mutation being contagious to the test.

'It's blindfish, manling,' said Gotrek from across the table. Felix realised that the Slayer must have seen the look on his face and understood what was going through his mind. 'It is naturally this way. Dwarfs have feasted on it since long before the coming of the Darkness. You can eat it.'

'It's a delicacy, actually,' Varek added. 'In the dwarfholds we breed them. They dwell in the deep cisterns. We feed them on mushrooms and insects.'

Somehow this knowledge did not make the fish seem any more appetising. Unaware of the effect he was having, Varek continued to speak. 'They live in darkness. Some loremasters think that is why they have no eyes. They don't need them. Try some.'

Felix speared some on his knife and lifted the flesh up for examination. It was white and tender looking and when he tried it, it was delicious. He said so.

'It can be monotonous,' said Hargrim, who was sat on the other side of him. 'We live on mushrooms and bugs and blindfish. There are times when I wish I could have something different.'

Felix dug into his pack and produced a strip of beef jerky. Hargrim looked at it just as suspiciously as Felix had inspected the fish. 'Try some,' Felix said.

Hargrim took some and began to chew. Eventually he managed to swallow. 'Interesting,' he pronounced carefully.

Snorri laughed. 'Now the blindfish doesn't taste so bad after all, does it? Here try some of this to wash it down.'

Snorri handed over a flask of Kislevite vodka. Hargrim swigged it down. For a moment, he looked like he might actually cough but then he recovered and smacked his lips and took some more. 'That's better,' he said.

Felix emptied his pack onto the table. There was waybread and cheese and more jerky. It added to the mushrooms cooked in blindfish oil, the blindfish itself and the jugs of water. 'Help yourself,' he said.

Hargrim did so.

With the speed the provisions disappeared Felix was glad that Hargrim was the only one of the local dwarfs who had joined them at their table.

Felix looked around the room. It was richly furnished with thick but worn carpets and drapes, fine dwarfish statuary and a merchant's ransom in silver and gold. It was one of the royal apartments. Each of the comrades had been given a similar one. Felix supposed that was one good thing about the casualties the dwarfs had suffered: there was plenty of room. He pushed the thought aside as unworthy and realised that he was getting drunk.

'I still cannot believe that we have strangers here,' Hargrim said. From the flush on his face, Felix could tell that the captain was inebriated as well. 'It astonishes me. For so long we thought we were the last dwarfs in the world. We thought Chaos had overrun everywhere else. We sent out messengers and scouts into the wilderness but they never returned. It all seemed so hopeless and now you arrive and tell us that there is a whole world beyond the Wastes, that Chaos was thrown back, that the Empire and Bretonnia and all those other places of legend still exist. It hardly seems possible that others have survived these past twenty years without us knowing it!'

'Twenty years?' spluttered Felix and Varek almost simultaneously.

'Aye! Why do you look at me that way?'

'It has been two hundred years since the last incursion of Chaos!' Felix said.

Hargrim looked at him in astonishment. 'That cannot be!'

'Time flows strangely in the Chaos Wastes,' Varek reminded them.

'Strangely indeed,' said Felix, remembering what Borek had told him of the odd powers of the place. Could the Dark Powers warp even the flow of time, he wondered, or was this some strange property that the Wastes themselves possessed?

'Believe me,' Varek said to Hargrim, 'Here in Karag Dum only twenty years may have passed but beyond the Wastes it has been centuries, and there Chaos was thrown back.'

'How did it happen?'

'Magnus the Pious rallied men and dwarfs to his cause, and broke the hordes of Chaos at the Siege of Praag, in Kislev. Eventually the followers of the Dark Ones were driven back to beyond Blackblood Pass.'

'And yet no one ever came to relieve us,' said Hargrim, and he sounded almost bitter.

Felix did not know what to say. 'Everyone thought Karag Dum had fallen. The last reports were of the city being overrun by the hordes of Chaos.'

Gotrek surprised him by speaking. 'No one knew what had happened. The Chaos Wastes had retreated but they had still advanced beyond where they once had been. They always do. Karag Dum was cut off. No one could find a way through. It was tried, believe me.

Borek sought long and hard for a way to return.'

'I do believe you, Gotrek, son of Gurni, for I have seen the Wastes, looked out from our highest towers, and I know they stretch as far as the eye can see. I have fought the warriors of Chaos and know they are as uncountable as flakes of snow in a blizzard. We have so few warriors that we soon stopped trying to get messengers out. Many were captured and hideously tortured.'

'How have you survived?' Varek asked – somewhat tactlessly, Felix thought. Still he was glad the young dwarf had asked the question. He wanted to know the answer himself. Hargrim shook his head.

'With great difficulty,' he said at last and smiled wearily, 'But that is not a fair answer my friends. The answer is that our foes are divided and we hide and fight them as we may.'

'What do you mean?' Gotrek asked.

'Tell Snorri about the fighting,' said Snorri.

'After the last great siege, when the forces of the Enemy used terrible sorcery to break our walls, we retreated deeper and deeper into the mines, determined to sell our lives dearly and make them pay for every inch of dwarfish territory with blood. Our people divided up into their clans and hosts and made their way to the secret fastnesses we had prepared against such a day.'

'Like this one,' Felix said.

'Precisely. We retreated under the earth, to places shielded by runes of power, and we emerged into the debated halls to raid and fight and we discovered a strange thing...'

'What was that?' Gotrek asked.

'We found that the forces of Chaos had fallen out with each other. We did not know then but we found out from captured prisoners that their supreme leader, Skathlok Ironclaw, had been drawn away to a battle in the south, and that his lieutenants, each of whom followed a different power, had fallen into dispute over the spoils.'

'When was this?' asked Varek.

Hargrim gave a date in dwarfish which meant nothing to Felix.

'It was the Imperial Year 2302,' Varek translated. 'At about the time of the Siege of Praag.'

'If this was the case, why did you not drive them from the city?' asked Gotrek. Hargrim laughed and there was no mirth to his laughter.

'Because there were still so few of us left, son of Gurni. After the Great Siege we numbered less than five thousand warriors, and those were split between five hidden citadels. Even with the majority of their warriors gone, our foes numbered ten times that and divided though they were, we knew they would unite to fight against us if we emerged in strength. So, over the years, we learned to sally forth in small groups and pick away at our enemies. It was not a good strategy, as we later learned.'

'Why?' asked Felix.

'Because for every one of their warriors who fell, another one would appear. For every war-band we destroyed, two more would come in from the Wastes. But when we lost a warrior we could never replace him. We may have killed twenty for every stout-hearted dwarf we lost, but in the end we had no way of replacing our losses, and they did.'

'I can understand this,' said Felix. 'There are many warriors out in the Wastes, and this is a worthy citadel and would provide them with shelter.'

Hargrim shook his head sadly. 'You do not understand the followers of Chaos at all well, if that is what you think, Felix Jaeger. They came here because there was treasure here – gold and dwarf-made weapons, and most of all the black steel they covet for the making of their armour and the forging of their foul weapons. They came here because they knew they would find others to fight of their own kind, and thus win glory in the eyes of their insane gods. This place has become a kind of testing ground for the warriors of Chaos, where they can find others to slaughter in order to advance themselves.'

Hargrim's words made sense to Felix. He had occasionally wondered where the Chaos warriors got their weapons. He had seen no sign of foundries or factories or any kind of manufacturing since they entered the Wastes, yet the followers of the Dark Powers must get their gear from somewhere. He had simply assumed that it was the product of sorcery or bartered from renegade human smiths but now he saw another answer. Here at Karag Dum was ore and all the equipment produced by dwarfish industry. If some of the things he had heard were true, this one hold could produce more steel than the whole Empire. He voiced his suspicions at once.

'You are correct, Felix Jaeger. We tried to destroy all the forges and furnaces and anvils we could not dismantle and carry into the hidden places, but we did not have enough time to get rid of them all. Some were seized by the followers of the Ruinous Powers. Some were repaired using black and incomprehensible magics. Now the mines are worked by hordes of beastmen and mutant slaves, and mage-priests oversee the manufacture of weapons and armour.'

'If this place could be retaken, it would be a terrible blow to the powers of Chaos. For where else would they get their weapons?' Felix said in drunken excitement.

'Perhaps. Perhaps not,' Hargrim said. 'The Chaos worshippers must have other mines and other foundries now and empty as Karag Dum now seems it is still well held.'

'What do you mean?'

'It is not now as it was in the early days. Many warriors of Chaos have come here and hold their own small fiefdoms. There are entire towns in the Underhalls now which are dedicated to the worship of one of the four Powers of Darkness. They each have their own liege lords and armies. They trade ore, weapons and armour to those outside. They exchange swords for slaves, spearpoints and arrowheads for their disgusting food, armour for magical devices.'

'You said there were other dwarf fastnesses in Karag Dum,' Varek said.

'Gone now,' Hargrim said. 'Over the years, they have been wiped out. Those of their people that survived made their way here. Most did not. Many have been hunted down by the Hounds of Khorne as they fled. Others would not come here lest they led the followers of the Terror to our last haven.'

'The Terror?' Felix said.

'Of that it is best not to speak,' said Hargrim. 'For it is our doom. When first it came it took the lives of hundreds of stout warriors. Our runemaster gave his life to drive it off. Now that it has returned I doubt that anything can stop it – although your axe gives me some hope, Gotrek Gurnisson.'

Felix's heart sank as he saw Gotrek and Snorri exchange glances. He knew that Hargrim had aroused the Slayer's professional interest. Hargrim saw this too and shook his head.

'Tell me: what do you think King Thangrim is thinking about?' Felix asked, just to change the subject. 'Do you think it likely that he will send messengers to the outside world.'

'I do not know, Felix Jaeger. I think it likely that we will all die here.'

After that there was silence for a minute, and then Gotrek spoke: 'I wish to know more of this creature known as the Terror.'

'This does not surprise me,' Hargrim said, looking up and inspecting the dwarf's tattoos. 'You wish to hunt it?'

'I do.'

'That would not be wise.'

'It is not a question of wisdom. It is a question of my doom.'

'And Snorri's,' said Snorri.

'Spoken like true Slayers,' Hargrim said. 'Very well. I will tell what I know of this fell creature. It is a daemon of Chaos, potent and deadly. It was summoned by Skathlok in the last days of the siege and he treated it not as a master treats a servant but as a warrior treats his king. It came upon us at the south-west gate after that was thrown down and none of us could stand against it. It slew a dozen heroes armed with potent rune weapons. It almost slew King Thangrim himself when he faced it in the Hall of Shadows. They exchanged blows for mere moments but it had the mastery. He could not believe its strength.'

Gotrek reached down and grabbed his axe. A gleam had come into his eye. 'It must be strong indeed to withstand the Hammer of Fate.'

'Stronger than anything it is, Gotrek Gurnisson. More fell by far than the three orc chieftains of the Red Fang. More dangerous than the three ogre mages of Ventragh Heath. Deadlier even than the dragon Glaugir, for all its poison breath. I speak without boasting when I say I have stood beside my liege as he measured himself against mighty foes, but this vile thing was by far the mightiest. I doubt that in the full pride of his youth, even so great a warrior as Thangrim Firebeard could have overcome it.'

'How then was it beaten?' asked Felix, licking his lips nervously. 'How did you survive to tell us this tale.'

'It was not beaten, it was driven off when our high Runesmith Valek smote it with the sacred axe you carry, then invoked the Rune of Unbinding. Such a wound it was that anything but a creature so great would have died instantly. This thing merely withdrew into the deepest depths of the mountain, near its fiery heart. It must have brooded down there for many years, recovering its strength, for now it has returned. As it prophesied.'

'Prophesied?'

'Even as it disappeared, it told us it would return to be our doom. It told the king that one day it would return and tear out his heart with its claws and devour it before his still-living eyes, and he told Thangrim that this was his doom. And all of us who heard it believed this prophecy, for there was a flat truth in its voice.'

'It was a daemon,' Felix said softly. 'Daemons have been known to lie.'

'Aye, but this one gloated as it spoke and we knew that it intended to work our ruin in its own time and way. Some of the warriors even suspect that this is why we have been allowed to survive for so long. And our Runesmith Valek also spoke a prophecy before he died. He told us to fear not, for his axe also would return to us when the Last

Days came. Many of us wondered about this prophecy, for how could the axe return to us when it was destined to remain hidden in our fortresses. Then the king's son took the axe and we thought it lost. And lo, you have returned it to us but a score of days after the Terror returned.'

He looked meaningfully at Gotrek's axe. 'You can see why your coming has disturbed the king.'

'How did Valek invoke this Rune of Unbinding?' Gotrek asked.

'I know not. He was a runesmith and knew many secrets. I only know that he summoned its power and it killed him, consuming his life even as it banished the daemon. The axe you bear is old and potent beyond all reckoning. It passed from runesmith to runesmith from the most ancient times. Its full history was passed only from bearer to bearer, but with Valek's death the tale was lost. His son and apprentice fell before him in that final battle. The king's son, Morekai, took it from the runesmith's smouldering corpse and bore it away with him when he tried to cross the Wastes.'

'Then without the Rune of Unbinding this creature cannot be beaten?' Felix asked.

'Who can say. That weapon is potent indeed even without the Rune of Unbinding. Perhaps in the hands of a warrior sufficiently strong…'

'Describe this daemon,' Gotrek said.

Hargrim leaned forward drunkenly and rested his chin on his fist. For a moment, he smiled a smile empty of all humour. Then he sank into reverie and gazed off into the distance, as if looking once more on a sight he would rather not see.'

'Huge it was,' he said eventually. 'More than twice the height of a tall man. Vast were its wings. Vast and bat-like, and when it unfurled them there was a crack like thunder. In one hand it bore a terrible whip. In the other an axe emblazoned with evil and eldritch runes that hurt the eye to look upon. Its eyes burned with infernal fire. Horns crowned its bestial head. On its brow was the mark of the Blood God.'

As Hargrim spoke, a silence and a chill spread across the chamber. Felix began to have a terrible suspicion that he knew what the dwarf was describing. It was a creature that was hinted at in the old books he had read about the time of Chaos. It was indeed a creature worthy to be known as the Terror.

'A Blutdrengrik,' said Gotrek quietly.

'The Bane of Grung,' Varek mumbled, tugging nervously at his beard.

'A Bloodthirster of Khorne,' Felix whispered, and felt the cold hand of fear touch his spine. He had just named the deadliest, most violent and implacable creature ever to emerge from the nethermost pits of Hell. A daemon second only to the Dark God it served in its mythical powers of destruction. A being which even the mightiest would fear to face.

'Let's go and kill it,' said Snorri.

'Let's have another drink first,' Felix said, hoping to dissuade the Slayers from this foolish quest for as long as possible.

Felix awoke with that same feeling of disorientation which he had become quite familiar with over the years. He was in a strange place, looking at a strange ceiling and he felt somewhat nauseous. It took him a few moments to get his rebellious mind and stomach under control and to work out where he was. When he managed to do so, he wished he had not.

He was deep underground in a chamber in a ruined dwarf citadel, somewhere deep in the Chaos Wastes. And he had a hangover. Surely there were few worse fates that could befall a mortal man, he told himself. He pulled himself up off the sumptuous but rather fusty smelling and too short bed, pulled on his boots and strode out into the corridor to find something that would settle his stomach. As he did so, he was greeted by one of the king's armoured guards who informed him that his presence was required in the throne room. Immediately.

Felix realised that he had indeed found a worse fate. Not only was he stuck in this terrible place but he had to face an old and irascible dwarfish tyrant on an empty stomach. Stifling a groan he followed the guard.

'We cannot leave this place,' said King Thangrim Firebeard. 'There are too many of us. According to what you have told me there is not enough room in your ship for more than an extra dozen people at most. There are several hundred of my people here. It would be unfair to chose some to go and some to stay.'

Felix had to admit the old dwarf had a point. He had arrived in the ruler's chamber only to find the others already being grilled by the old despot. Apparently Varek had suggested that the people of Karag Dum should leave their ancestral home. Thangrim had raised a few cogent objections.

'It would only be a temporary measure, your majesty,' Varek said. 'Once we had flown those people back to the Lonely Tower we could return with a skeleton crew and take more. We could continue to ferry them back until we had taken everyone. It is possible.'

'Maybe. But you have told me that even flying across the Chaos Wastes is perilous. Perhaps your ship will crash.'

'Surely, your majesty remaining here with the forces of Chaos pounding upon your doors is more perilous. It is only a matter of time before you are hunted down and destroyed.' Varek was becoming impassioned and flustered. His eyes were large and round behind the lenses of his glasses.

'You do not understand, youngling. We have here wives and wounded. We cannot simply abandon them or send them away with but a small escort. You know how perilous the halls are. You have seen them. It would take many warriors to guard them, and there is not enough room on your ship for them and the escort.'

'The escort could return to your halls,' Varek said. 'They are warriors. They have done this before.'

'Your point is a fair one but eventually we would have to move our ancestral hoards. These are no small treasures, and not a gold piece or trinket will I leave behind for the despoilers.'

Felix spoke up for the first time. 'But surely gold means nothing when the lives of your people are concerned, your majesty.'

Every dwarf present looked at him as if he was either deranged or profoundly stupid. No one even bothered to answer him. Felix wished the floor would open up and swallow him. He should have known better than to try and make such a rational argument to dwarfs when gold was being discussed.

'Could we carry away our father's treasures on your one small ship?' Thangrim asked.

'From what I have heard about your hoard, may it ever grow and prosper, I doubt it.'

'Then how can you expect us to leave this place while we have blood left in our veins?'

'Perhaps we could return with more than one airship, great king,' Varek said. 'Perhaps we could return with enough craft to carry all your people and all your hoard.'

'If you could, I would see that you were suitably rewarded. Let me think on what you have said. You may go.'

Varek rose to go and Felix moved to join him. He felt a vague sense of relief at being about to leave the king's presence – and at the prospect of getting some food.

'Thangrim Firebeard,' Gotrek said. 'I crave a boon.'

'Tell me what it is, Gotrek Gurnisson.'

'I wish to seek out this creature you call the Terror, and either slay it or find my doom.'

King Thangrim smiled down at Gotrek and appeared to consider his request.

At that moment, however, a distant horn sounded. A few heartbeats later a dwarf raced through the entrance of the throne room and advanced at once to the king. Thangrim gestured for the messenger to come closer and then listened to his whispered words. When the new arrival had finished speaking, his face looked grim indeed.

'It appears it will not be necessary for you to seek the monster out, Gotrek Gurnisson. It is coming here now – and it brings with it an army.'

Wonderful, thought Felix, and I haven't even had a chance to grab my last meal.

BLOCKBUSTER

NINETEEN
BLOODTHIRSTER

'The hordes of Chaos come again,' King Thangrim said. 'Sound the war-horns. We muster for battle.'

The king raised himself from his throne and lifted his great war-hammer up high. In that moment Felix could see a glittering aura like lightning playing around the head of the weapon. The air was filled with the smell of ozone.

The king's guard cheered heartily but Felix sensed a deep uneasiness behind their show of courage.

'This is good,' Gotrek said.

This is very bad, thought Felix, contemplating the oncoming hordes of Chaos, led by a daemon of unspeakable power. He wondered how he could ever have thought things were bad when he got up this morning. All he had to worry about then was a hangover. Now he had much worse things to concern himself with.

The king strode down the steps accompanied by his priests, and made his way out into the hall. His guards fell into step behind him. Outside in the Hall of the Well, dwarf folk were hastily assembling. Warriors rushed out of every entrance. Some buckled on shields and weapons. Others had breastplates half-strapped to their chests and were hastily tightening fastenings as they assembled. As Felix watched, he saw one old warrior jam a helmet onto his head, spit on the floor and make a few practice swipes with his axe. Seeing Felix looking at him, he gave him a thumbs-up sign.

Out of the corner of his eye, Felix saw Hargrim assembling his tunnel fighters. They too were strapping on heavier dwarfish armour. It seemed that the time for stealth was over and now they wanted the heaviest protection they could get. Felix did not blame them. His own chainmail shirt suddenly seemed woefully inadequate when he remembered the vast mass of bestial warriors he had seen during the approach to Karag Dum, and when he thought of the legendary deadliness of the Bloodthirster.

But what else was there to do but fight? He drew his own enchanted blade from the scabbard and strode over to where Hargrim stood. 'How did they find us?' he shouted to make himself heard over the din of dwarfs preparing for battle.

'I know not. Perhaps they found the place where we killed its hounds. Mayhap others of his foul pack found our scent. What does it matter? It is the Prophecy. The Last Day is upon us.'

'Try not to be so cheerful,' Felix said, and glanced around to see where Gotrek, Snorri and Varek were. He could see the Slayers standing near the king. Varek was nowhere to be seen. Felix wondered where he had gone. He realised that whatever happened in this battle, his place was beside his companions. If nothing else, he knew he had no chance of finding his way out of these halls on his own. Any of the others could probably manage it blindfolded.

On the other hand, he was probably being far too optimistic imagining there would be any chance of escape whatsoever. Snorri and Gotrek would never leave while the Bloodthirster was present, but he doubted that even those two formidable warriors could prevail over so mighty a daemon.

'Good luck!' he shouted to Hargrim and raced over to where the Slayers stood.

'May Grungni, Grimnir and Valaya watch over you, Felix Jaeger,' Hargrim said and returned to bellowing orders to his troops.

Now from out of the access tunnels came the sounds of battle: the brash echo of horns, the clash of weapons, and the bellowing of something hideous echoed down the corridors. The dwarfs had finished their dispositions and their line of battle was drawn up across the Well Hall. There were certainly more dwarfs here than had defended the Lonely Tower, but that was not a reassuring thought. Compared to the numbers their attackers could summon, they were pitifully few.

Felix looked up to where King Thangrim stood, carried on a shield held by four bearers. 'They have breached the outer gate,' said the king. 'Our sentries will hold them for a while.'

Looking beyond Thangrim, Felix could see that the women and those too aged and wounded to fight were disappearing through an entrance he had not seen before. Once the last one had gone through, the doorway was sealed behind them, and it was done so cunningly that no sign of the hidden exit remained.

'They go to the vaults with our hoard, to wait out the final battle,' Thangrim said. 'If we are victorious they will be freed. If not, they die.'

'What do you mean?'

'The vaults can only be opened from the outside,' Gotrek said. Felix was suddenly glad he had not tried to flee through those doors. He could think of nothing worse than huddling in the gloomy vaults, waiting to die of suffocation or starvation while the battle raged outside. At least out here, he would have some control over his fate, and when death came it would be quick. He hoped.

He could see Varek returning now. The young dwarf had Makaisson's gun strapped to his chest and carried a bag full of bombs. He moved with a purposefulness that Felix had never seen in him before as he raced up and came to a stop beside Felix.

'Hold this for a moment,' Varek said to Felix and handed him the gun. Felix sheathed his sword and took it, surprised by how heavy it was, and by the ease with which Varek had handled it. Varek produced his book and pen, and began to inscribe a few notes on its pages. Seeing Felix's astonished look, he said: 'Just a last explanation. In case someone comes upon this later. Well, we can but hope, eh?'

Felix forced himself to smile, but it came out shakily. 'I suppose so.'

In the distance the clamour reached a peak and then there was a bestial roar of triumph. Felix guessed things had not gone well for the dwarf sentries.

Thangrim had started to shout in dwarfish. Felix could not understand a word he was bellowing but the dwarfs seemed to like it. They cheered him mightily, even Gotrek and Snorri. Only Varek did not add his voice to the resounding chorus, for he was too busy writing.

Felix kept his eyes glued to the doorway through which he knew their foes would come. He knew that several hundred crossbow-toting dwarfs were doing the same thing. But still this did not reassure him. He had an oppressive sense of approaching doom. Fear gripped his heart. A shadow lay on his soul. He knew that something terrible was approaching.

'Bet Snorri kills more beastmen than you, Gotrek,' said Snorri.

Gotrek grunted derisively. 'The manling will kill more beastmen than you,' Gotrek replied.

'Want to bet on that, Felix?' Snorri asked.

Felix shook his head. His mouth was too dry for him to form a response. Terror had started to take root in his mind, a paralysing fear that shook the foundations of his sanity and made him want to find a dark corner in which to hide himself and whimper. Part of his mind told him that this was unnatural, that he should not feel such fear, but it was still hard to fight against it. There was something in that hideous roaring that turned his blood to water.

'Just remember, Snorri,' Gotrek said. 'The daemon is mine.'

'Depends if Snorri gets to it first,' said Snorri with a grin.

Felix found he could not bear to look at the entrance anymore so he glanced at Gotrek and Snorri. Even the Slayers were tense, he could tell. Gotrek's knuckles were white from gripping the haft of his axe so tightly. Snorri's hand trembled a little where he clutched his axe. Seeing Felix looking at him, he grinned. He appeared to make an effort to calm himself, and the trembling stopped.

'Snorri's not worried,' Snorri said. 'Much.'

Felix grinned back, knowing how unnatural he must look. He felt like the skin of his face was too tight and as if all his hair was trying to stand on end like a Trollslayer's crest. He was probably pale as death too, he thought.

Suddenly, just for a moment, everything fell silent. In the eerie stillness all Felix could hear was the scratching of Varek's pen. Then even that stopped and Felix felt a tug on his arm and realised that Varek was asking for his gun back. Felix gave it to him, and unsheathed his sword once more.

The roar which shattered the silence was so loud and so terrifying that Felix almost dropped his blade. He looked up and fought down the urge to soil his britches. The most frightening thing he had ever seen had entered the hall and behind it he could see the leering heads of hundreds of beastmen.

As he gazed on the creature in wonder and in terror, Felix thought: this is what a daemon looks like. This is the incarnate nightmare which had bedevilled my people since time began.

He knew now that there was something magical about the terror the thing inspired. It was the unnatural aura of something which had crept forth from the nethermost pits and which no mortal being could help but sense and respond to. In some ways it hurt the eyes simply to look upon the Bloodthirster. Its very appearance told you it was made from no natural substance. The charnel stink of the thing was worse than anything he could have imagined. It reeked of rotting meat and congealed blood and other less describable and far more loathsome things.

It looked as Hargrim had described it. It was far taller and far heavier than Felix. Vast bat-like wings flexed on its shoulders. It was as muscular as a minotaur. In one hand it held a great coiled whip, in the other a terrifying axe larger than a man's body. Its skin was ruddy red and its face was savage and bestial. And yet of all the Bloodthirster's features, it was its eyes which Felix knew he would never forget.

They were like pools of infinite darkness out of which a malign and ageless intelligence gazed. Somewhere in those unknowable depths flickered red fires of savage hatred, an insane ferocity that would overthrow the order of the entire Universe if it could, in order to try and sate a bloodlust that could never be satisfied. Here was a creature that had looked upon the birth and death of worlds, and might look out on the death of everything. Compared to its life, his own existence was less than the life of a mayfly. Compared to its strength and savagery and cunning, he was less than nothing.

And yet looking on, Felix felt his fear start to drain away. After all, embodied terror that it might be, it really was not as bad as he had imagined it would be. It could never be as fearful as the nightmare thing his own brain had been conjuring up mere heartbeats before. It was awe-inspiring, mystical and potent to be sure but he felt now that he had seen it, he could fight it, and glancing at the others he knew that they felt the same. In a way, he was not too sorry to look upon the thing, even if it caused his death. He knew he had now seen something that few men ever would, and there was a certain satisfaction in that. He knew also that he could confront this ultimately fearsome thing and in the end, not be completely daunted.

Then it spoke and the fear returned, redoubled: 'I have come to claim my blood debt, King Thangrim, as I said I would.'

Its voice was like a brazen horn, and yet there was something in it that suggested the void, and a cold so chilly that it burned. It was as loud as thunder and yet so perfectly pitched that every word carried exactly the minutely calculated freight of hatred that the daemon intended it to. It was the voice of an angry and vengeful demi-god. Felix could tell that the daemon was not speaking in Reikspiel and yet he could still somehow understand its meaning perfectly, and not for a moment did he doubt that the same was true for the dwarfs.

'You have come to be cast into the pit once more,' King Thangrim said. His voice was clear and deep and resonant but, compared to the Bloodthirster, he sounded like a rebellious child shrieking defiance at an adult.

'I will tear out your heart and eat it before your still-living eyes, just as I promised,' the thing replied. 'And not all your little warriors will save you. For every moment of every hour of every day of every year of my waiting I have looked forward to this day, and now it has arrived.'

As the daemon spoke more and more beastmen and black-armoured warriors filtered into the room behind it, yet not a single dwarf fired a bolt or raised a weapon. There was something hypnotic about the creature and something unbearably fascinating about its confrontation with the ancient dwarf king. Felix wanted to shout a warning, to tell the dwarfs to attack, yet he did not. He was held enthralled by the same spell as held them all, while more and more followers of Chaos flowed in. Thangrim looked as if he wanted to reply, but could not. He looked old and weary and beaten before he started.

'You have lost none of your arrogance, little one, but you are old and feeble now and I… I am stronger than ever I was.'

'You certainly smell that way!' Gotrek roared suddenly.

The daemon's burning gaze shot towards the Slayer and Felix quailed as for a moment the thing's eyes rested upon him. It was as if Death itself had looked on him from out of its bony sockets. Felix was astonished that the Slayer managed to hold the daemon's gaze but somehow he did. After a moment he even managed a feral grin and brandished his axe. The runes along the blade blazed brighter than ever Felix had seen them. Gotrek took his thumb and ran it along the blade. A single bead of blood appeared and the Trollslayer flicked it contemptuously in the direction of the daemon.

'Thirsty?' he inquired. 'Try that. It will be all you get today.'

'I will drink every drop of your blood, and I will crack your skull and devour your few brains, and as I do I will consume your soul. You will learn the true meaning of terror.'

'I am learning the true meaning of tedium,' Gotrek said and laughed a grating laugh. 'Do you intend to bore me to death with your speeches or do you want to come over here and die?'

Felix was amazed that the Slayer could say anything with that soul-blasting gaze upon him, but somehow Gotrek had managed to speak. And in doing so he had heartened the whole dwarf army. Felix could sense the dwarfs throwing off the influence of the daemon's presence and readying their weapons to fight. Thangrim straightened and raised his hammer and as he did so lightning crackled once more about its head.

Amazingly the daemon smiled, revealing long fangs and a mouth that looked like it could swallow a horse. 'A moment of defiance earns you an eternity of torment. You will have aeons to reflect on your folly. And before you die, consider this. It was you who led me to this secret place.'

Seeing that Gotrek refused to rise to the bait, the daemon continued: 'That axe and I are linked. Since it wounded me I have always been able to sense its presence, no matter how well it was hidden. I followed its spoor to this place. I thank you for the service you have done me, slave.'

Felix looked at Gotrek to see how he was taking this. No emotion save implacable hatred showed on the Slayer's face. Felix wondered how Gotrek managed it. His own mind whirled. It seemed that their whole long quest, all the ingenuity which Borek had expended to bring them here, all the dangers they had overcome, had served only to lead this daemon to its final goal. It was a maddening thought that all their efforts had come to this, that they had been caught up in an intricate web of prophecy and doom of which they had known nothing, that they were simply pawns in an aeons-long game played by the Ruinous Powers.

Looking across the narrow gap which separated the two armies, Felix once more felt the sick certainty of defeat. Ranks upon ranks of crooked horned beastmen were drawn up beside the daemon. Row upon row of Chaos warriors stood ready to attack, awesome mystical blades held ready for slaughter. Packs of their terrible hounds bayed hungrily, as if demanding the souls of their prey.

Ranked against them was a dwarf host which looked pitifully weak. Around the king's fluttering banner was his guard, all finely decked in the best armour and armed with potent weapons. Between King Thangrim and the daemon stood a line of mighty warriors, each armed with glittering rune-carved blades. Beyond the king, the army's right flank was hidden from him but Felix knew it was made up of units of crossbows and hammer wielders. Here on the left flank were rank upon rank of long-bearded veterans armed with hammers and axes. Among them stood Gotrek, Snorri, Varek and himself. Felix offered up a prayer to Sigmar of the Hammer. If the deity heard he gave no sign.

Instead the daemon raised its blade and gave the signal to advance. In a cacophony of drums and braying, brazen horns the Chaos Horde began to advance. The lean hounds loped ahead of the foot troops ready to rend and tear. The daemon watched with an expression of hideous satisfaction. As the beastmen came on, the dwarfs opened fire with their crossbows, carving a bloody swathe through their inhuman foes.

Felix was almost deafened as Varek opened fire with his gun. The blaze of the rotating muzzles underlit the young dwarf's face as he sent a stream of hot lead out to mow down the oncoming brutes. In the flashes, Varek's twisted face looked no less daemonic and hate-filled than the creatures they faced.

King Thangrim raised his hammer, lightning bolts flickered around it, gigantic shadows flickered away to the edge of the chamber. He whirled it around his head and it seemed to gather power and light as it did so. The runes blazed dazzlingly. Blue sparks rained down all around it. The smell of ozone cut through the stench of the daemonic host.

The dwarf king released the Hammer of Fate. It hurtled towards the Bloodthirster like a comet, trailing sparks and streams of lightning. Where these fell beastmen fell also, their skin blackened, their fur standing on end. The great warhammer flew straight and true and impacted on the daemon with a sound like a thunderclap. The Bloodthirster bellowed in anguish and stumbled. The dwarf host roared mightily. To Felix's amazement the weapon hurtled back across the chamber, causing beastmen to flinch and duck. The king stretched out his hand and his weapon flew back, like a hawk returning to a falconer's glove after hunting.

For a moment Felix hoped that the awesome and terrible weapon might have downed the Bloodthirster. But when he dared look his hopes were dashed. Drops of blazing ichor dripped from a wound in the daemon's side and vanished into puffs of poisonous looking smoke where they hit the floor, but it still stood, immensely strong and immensely terrible gazing mockingly at the dwarfs. Its fiery glance silenced their cheers in a moment.

'If it will not come to us, we will just have to go to it,' Gotrek said and charged forward to meet the onrushing Chaos horde.

'Snorri thinks this is a good idea!' said Snorri, racing after the other Slayer.

'Wait for me,' Felix said and loped along cursing beside them. With his longer stride it was easy for him to keep up with the running dwarfs and still have some time to glance around at what was happening. Around them, he could see the whole dwarf army was advancing to meet their oncoming foe.

Tactically Felix knew that this was a mistake. The dwarfs should have kept their distance and hammered their foes with crossbow bolts until the last moment. Now they seemed caught up in the general madness of the daemon's presence, overwhelmed by a lust to get to grips with their enemy, hand to hand, breast to breast, to rend and tear and kill at close range. Felix could not blame them. After so many years of being hunted through what had once been their home, they were filled with blazing hatred. In gratifying that hatred, Felix saw they were throwing away their one small tactical advantage.

Still, perhaps it did not matter. They were going to die anyway, and so it might just be best to get it all over with. He gripped his sword with both hands as the first wave of beastmen swept over them, and then there was no more time for thought, only for killing.

A shock passed up Felix's arm as his blade embedded itself in the chest of a dog-headed beastman. The sickening stench of blood and wet fur filled his nostrils as the creature fell against him. He kicked it away and chopped out at another of the foul creatures, severing an artery in its throat. As the thing reached up to try to press the wound shut, Felix worked his blade under its ribcage and up into its heart.

Around him Gotrek and Snorri hacked and chopped and slew. Every time Gotrek smashed down with his axe, a mangled foe fell clutching the bloody ruin of its chest, the amputated stump of its limbs, or tried to staunch the flow of blood that simply could not be stopped. From the corner of his eye, Felix saw Snorri smash forward with a simultaneous blow of both axe and hammer that caught a beastman's head between them. The top of the creature's skull came away, sheared off by the axe and its brains erupted forth in a pulpy grey jelly driven out by the force of the hammer blow.

A deafening bang followed by howls of bestial agony told Felix that Varek had lobbed one of his bombs. A moment later a cloud of acrid smoke filled his field of vision and brought tears to his eyes. He coughed and the sound attracted the attention of another beastman. A monstrous axe shrieked towards him from out of the smoke and he had only just time to raise his blade and parry before it hit. The shock sent tingles of agony shooting up into his shoulder. A moment later a huge hand came out of the gloom and grabbed him by the throat. Sharp nails driven by iron-sinewed fingers bit into his neck. Beads of blood ran down his windpipe.

As the smoke cleared he saw he had been grabbed by a monstrously muscular beastman. From the corner of his eye, he saw one of the beastman's disgusting brothers running closer with spear levelled.

Everything started to happen in slow motion. He knew that he was about to die. Frantically, he tried to pull himself clear but the beast-man was too strong, and was already drawing back its axe for the killing blow. The tip of its comrade's spear glittered as it came closer. With those awful fingers round his neck Felix could not even call for help from Gotrek or Snorri.

Any second he expected the spear to burst through his ribs or for the axe to descend with skull-smashing force. Knowing he had only moments to live filled Felix with desperate strength and ferocious cunning. Instead of trying to pull away, he suddenly relaxed and stepped forward. His unexpected movement threw his captor momentarily off-balance. Taking advantage of this, Felix swivelled on the spot and threw all his weight into the move, swinging the beastman round and to the side. The Chaos worshipper grunted as the spear which had been aimed at Felix drove right into its back. Its muscles spasmed in agony and its fingers loosened around Felix's neck. Felix stepped back, took careful aim and lopped off its bestial head with one swing.

The sightless goat's head rolled onto the floor. Black blood gouted towards the ceiling from the stump of the neck, rising in powerful spurts which weakened even as the body tumbled forward onto the floor. The second beastman stood there, holding its newly freed spear, blinking in stupid astonishment as if it could not quite believe that he had just killed its companion. Felix took advantage of his momentary confusion to stab it in the groin and then send his blade ripping upwards, slicing the belly and sending ropy entrails looping to the ground.

For a moment, he stood in the eye of the storm, surrounded by a swirling vortex of incredible violence. Dwarf fought with beastman. Axe smashed against spear and club. Over to his right he could see Gotrek engaged in combat with two Chaos warriors. The black-armoured giants raced forward, hoping to take the Slayer from either side so that one could strike him while the other held his attention. Gotrek raced towards them, striking the first as he passed, caving in the warrior's breastplate with a blow of astonishing power. The armour did not quite give way, but the blood leaking through the armpits and joins at the waist told of a fatal blow. Instead of halting, the Slayer swept on past, leaving the second warrior to strike uselessly at the spot where he had been. As he did so, Gotrek struck downwards and backwards at his attacker taking his foe through the back of the leg, hamstringing him. As the warrior toppled Gotrek caved in his head and glanced around for more prey without a second thought.

The Slayer was covered in blood and looked as if he had been work-ing in some hellish butcher's shop. Felix realised that he looked no better. His hands were red and slimy stuff covered his boots. He shook his head and noticed that the Slayer was gesturing a warning to him. Just in time he turned and ducked beneath the blow of a monstrous black armoured figure. His new opponent's sword was enormous and odd runes blazed redly along its length. Felix brought his own blade smashing forward but it rebounded off the man's armour. Demented laughter pealed forth from inside the man's face-concealing helmet. It was as if Felix had merely tickled him. The man slashed forward once more and Felix sprang backwards, out of reach of his blade. Seeing an opening, he hit the man's blade as it passed, adding to its momentum and sending his foe spinning round. As he did so, Felix leapt forward in a shoulder charge, sending his off-balance opponent tumbling to the floor. Before the man could rise, Felix pulled back his helmeted head and ran his blade along the man's leathery throat, severing an artery and leaving the dying Chaos Warrior flopping on the ground like a fish stranded on dry land.

He had no time to enjoy his triumph. He sensed rather than saw a blow descending on his own exposed skull and tried to leap to one side. His foot slipped on the blood-slick stone and he was only partially successful. A massive club clipped his head and sent him sprawling to the ground. Stars danced before his eyes. Even that glanc-ing blow had come close to driving consciousness from his head. He tried to pull himself to his feet but he suddenly had no control over his limbs. They flopped wildly instead of obeying him. He was vaguely aware of a misshapen figure towering above him and a huge club being raised to dash his brains out.

A sudden weariness overcame Felix. All sound seemed to die away. He was too tired to care and he was not afraid to die. There was noth-ing he could do now. The club would descend and his life would be over. There was no sense in struggling. Best just to lie back and sur-render to the inevitable.

For a moment only, he felt so helpless. Then he gathered all of his willpower to make one final futile attempt at movement. He knew it was impossible, that in his weakened state he could never get out of the way in time. His shoulders tensed and at any moment he expected to feel agony smash through his brain as the fatal blow connected.

It never came. Instead, his foe toppled away from him, blood exploding from his back. Gotrek bent over, gripped him by his chain mail vest and hauled him to his feet.

'Get up, manling. There's still killing to be done!' The Slayer swung his axe and dropped a beastman with one blow. 'You cannot die till you have witnessed me kill a daemon!'

'Where is it?' Felix asked, still dazed.

'Over there,' Gotrek said and pointed with one blood-covered finger.

Felix looked in the direction he had indicated and through a gap in the fury of battle witnessed a scene of momentous courage. Snorri steamed headlong at the daemon and lashed out at it with his axe and hammer. The daemon looked down and laughed mockingly as Snorri's attacks bounced off its hide.

'Snorri, you idiot!' Gotrek bellowed. 'Only rune weapons will affect the accursed thing!'

If Snorri heard, he gave no sign. He continued to lash ineffectually at the mighty monster, launching a whirlwind of blows that would have dropped a dozen oxen, yet left the daemon unscathed. At last, as if tiring of watching the antics of a jester, the Bloodthirster lashed out almost languidly with its axe. Snorri tried to block, crossing both weapons in front of him, but he had no chance. The haft of his axe and his hammer splintered, and the sheer force of the daemon's blow sent him hurtling across the chamber like a stone launched from a catapult. He went tumbling through the air to land at the feet of King Thangrim, splashing the old dwarf's beard with blood.

The Bloodthirster ploughed on through the warriors of King Thangrim's elite guard. Its weapons flickered almost too fast for the eye to follow and every time one struck, a dwarf warrior fell. It seemed like no armour could resist those hell-forged weapons. In mere moments, brave warriors were reduced to mewling, dying piles of ragged flesh. Proud armour was rent asunder. Even as Felix watched, the Bloodthirster smashed through a row of dwarfs with its axe, leaving only mangled corpses in its wake. Yet the great daemon was not having things all its own way. The rune weapons of the dwarfs had bitten its flesh in a few places. Smoking ichor dribbled onto the floor as it advanced.

Rage blazed in King Thangrim's eyes. His beard bristled. He raised his hammer once more as if in answer to the daemon's challenge and cast it to smash on the daemon's breast. Once more the ancient weapon bit home. Once more daemonic blood spurted forth. Once more the hideous thing staggered – then grinned and came on with redoubled fury.

Nothing could stand in its way. It ploughed through the dwarf king's guards like a battering ram through a rotting doorway. Felix saw that one warrior managed to ram a runic blade into its back before it was aware of him. The blade stuck fast, protruding out from the Bloodthirster's shoulder blades before it turned and lashed out with its whip. Felix had no idea what that infernal lash was made from but it cut through dwarf-forged armour with ease and flayed its targets to the bone. Felix saw skin and muscle part as if slashed with a cleaver, white bone and yellow cartilage suddenly exposed in the dim, guttering light. The whip lashed forward again, spinning its shrieking victim like a top and tugging more flesh from his carcass. Another dwarf strode forward and smote the daemon with a rune-etched hammer. The impact caused the daemon some discomfort, but the swing of its axe decapitated its attacker. All the while it kept lashing its victim. In heartbeats, a bloody, skinned carcass that was not recognisable as a dwarf lay at its feet.

'How much longer will you hide behind your warriors, little king?' asked the daemon, and such was the dreadful magic of its voice that the words were audible where Felix stood even above the clamour of battle. The king threw his hammer once more but this time the daemon threw down his whip and caught it with one outstretched claw. The runes blazed along the hammer's head and where it held the weapon the daemon's hand blackened but it reversed the weapon and sent it hurtling back towards the king.

There was a crack like thunder and the hammer flew too fast for the eye to follow. It crashed into the dwarf king and sent him sprawling to the ground. A groan came from the dwarf army as they saw their leader tumble and fall. The daemon bellowed in triumph. Insane laughter rumbled above the fray and echoed through the hall. The host of Chaos fought on with redoubled fury and everywhere seemed to gain the upper hand over the dwarfs.

The Bloodthirster strode through the dismayed throng, slaying right and left as it went. The priest of Grimnir went forth to meet it and was disembowelled with a slash of its claw even as his warhammer buried itself in the daemon's flesh. The old priestess of Valaya stood before it. She raised her book as if it were a shield. A glow leapt from the pages and for a moment the daemon paused. Then it laughed once more and brought its axe arcing down, cleaving through the book and the priestess both. Her bisected form fell in two pieces to the floor and the daemon strode forward in triumph to stand above the dying king.

'Come, manling. Now is the hour of my doom,' Gotrek said, and made to stride towards the daemon. Nothing could stand in the Slayer's way. Anything that tried to do so died. He was now as much an engine of destruction as the daemon had been. As he moved towards his goal he struck left and right and everywhere he struck beastmen and Chaos warriors fell, cloven by the power of the axe and the arm that drove it.

With a shrug, Felix strode along behind, resolved to his fate. His head still rang from the glancing blow he had taken, and the scenes of nightmarish carnage all around had taken on an unreal quality. There now seemed nothing unlikely about the Slayer's mission. It did indeed seem inevitable that Gotrek would fight with the daemon, and die his heroic death, and that Felix would witness it and die in turn himself. There was no other possibility. Looking around the hall Felix could see that the dwarfs were beaten. Their foes had the upper hand, and the fall of King Thangrim had demoralised them utterly. There was no sign of Snorri or Varek. Felix knew that he was not going to leave this battlefield alive. He might as well do as the Trollslayer wished. He owed the dwarf his life once more, and this was the way to pay the debt.

The Bloodthirster stood over the recumbent form of the old dwarf king. It drove its axe blade deep into the ancient flagstones so that the weapon stood there quivering. Then it reached down and picked up Thangrim Firebeard with both its claws, as gently as a man might pick up a small child.

Felix ducked the swing of a beastman's axe, lopped his attacker's hand off at the wrist and kept running, leaving the amputee falling to his knees and clutching a bleeding stump. Three Chaos warriors came between Gotrek and the daemon. His axe smashed through the neck of one, opened the stomach of another and buried itself in the groin of a third. The backward swing of the axe toppled them to the floor and left Felix with a clear view of what happened next between the king and his tormentor.

The Bloodthirster peeled away Thangrim's armour like a man might strip away the peel from an orange. The dwarf managed to lean forward and spat in his tormentor's face. The spittle mingled with the ichor that ran down the daemon's brow and evaporated with a sizzle. Grinning widely, the Bloodthirster pushed its claws into the king's exposed flesh and began to pull outwards. The dwarf's ribcage cracked and flew open like the shell of an oyster, revealing the exposed innards. Blood sprayed across the Bloodthirster as it kept at its unholy work.

It raised the body to the level of its eyes, holding him easily with one hand. With the other it reached out and tore Thangrim's still-beating heart from his chest, raised it so that the king's wide eyes could see what it was doing. It squeezed the heart. The meat was crushed with an audible squelch. Blood gushed forth and sprayed down into the monster's mouth. Then, like a Bretonnian epicure devouring the flesh of an opened shellfish, it threw back its head and let the heart slide down into its open mouth. All this the king watched with wide, appalled eyes.

The daemon's throat swelled as it swallowed the whole heart and then it opened its mouth and gave an enormous belch of satisfaction. It let the heartless, now dead thing which had once been the proud king of Karag Dum flop to the floor and turned to bellow its triumph to its assembled followers.

Felix had a perfect view of the whole thing, for at that moment he and Gotrek had almost reached the Bloodthirster.

'I hope you enjoyed your last meal, daemon,' Gotrek said. 'Now you die.'

The daemon looked down at him and smiled. 'Your brain will be my desert,' it said with terrible certainty.

For a moment the Slayer and the daemon stood frozen facing each other. Gotrek held his blazing axe poised to strike. A look of near-berserk fury transformed his face into something almost as terrifying as the daemon. The Bloodthirster flexed its wings with an audible snap and gestured mockingly for Gotrek to advance. Felix looked from Gotrek to the daemon to the corpse of Thangrim. He had heard that the brain could still live for moments after the heart ceased to beat. He knew that in Thangrim's case this was true, for it was what the daemon had willed in order to fulfil its unholy oath. Suddenly he was very angry, at the senseless cruelty of the daemon and the insane malignity of all of Chaos. He wanted to take his sword and plunge it into the daemon's breast.

The long frozen moment ended. Gotrek bellowed his war cry and charged. His axe flashed forward and down and buried itself in the daemon's chest. Blazing ichor belched forth, scorching the dwarf and sending him reeling backward for a moment. He recovered himself well and launched another blow. The Bloodthirster raised its claw to block it and another huge gash appeared in its arm. For a moment, Felix thought that in his fury Gotrek might overwhelm it, but the Bloodthirster stepped back out of the Slayer's reach and made a grasping gesture.

Its huge axe sprang up out of the ground and flew into the daemon's hand in the time it took to blink. For a moment the daemon stood there. Felix could see that it had taken damage. The dwarf guard's sword still protruded from its back. Thangrim's hammer had left deep welts in its flesh, through which broken bones showed. Gotrek's axe had left two gaping wounds from which ichor dripped, smouldering to the floor. From its entire body rose a foul vapour like smoke. At times its outline seemed to waver and go out of focus as if it were not quite there. Then it snapped into being once again, becoming hard-edged and distinct.

And it launched itself at the Slayer.

There was a flurry of blows much too fast for the mortal eye to follow. Felix had no idea how Gotrek survived the encounter but he did, reeling backwards with a great gash across his forehead and claw marks all across his chest. The Bloodthirster bore another great rent on its arm but appeared less damaged than the Slayer.

'I see you've had enough,' Gotrek gasped defiantly.

The daemon laughed and prepared to spring forward once again. Felix steeled himself, knowing now that what he was about to do was suicide. He was going to die. It did not matter, Felix knew that if the Slayer fell, the daemon would overpower him in heartbeats, so he decided to get in his blow while he could. He sprang forward and struck with all his might at the daemon. The Templar Aldred's enchanted blade bit deep into the daemon's flesh. Felix pulled back the sword and tried for a second blow. The daemon turned to face him at the last second and sent him sprawling backwards with a mere buffet of its arm that nearly knocked the life from Felix.

As its claw made contact, something exploded against Felix's chest, sending a surge of pain flickering right through him. The Templar's blade was sent spinning from his hand. As he fell, he landed on something hard and heavy, and the wind was knocked from his lungs. He could hear what might have been a howl of unearthly agony coming from the Bloodthirster.

Gotrek took advantage of the distraction to spring forward and for a moment Felix thought the Slayer was going to be able to take the Bloodthirster. His axe flashed through a ferocious arc and almost connected but the Slayer's wounds slowed him and the daemon leapt aside and avoided the stroke which otherwise would have beheaded it. There followed another flurry of blows that were too fast for the eye to follow. They ended with Gotrek's axe being knocked from his hand. As the dwarf stood there, staggering, barely upright, the Bloodthirster smashed down with a mighty fist, slamming the Slayer to the ground. Gotrek fell prostrate at the daemon's feet. All hope fled from Felix's heart.

He reached down and tried to push himself upright. Looking down he could see the smouldering remains of Schreiber's amulet on his chest. The daemon's fist must have caught it when it struck him. The amulet had exploded, overloaded by the daemon's sheer power. Still, thought Felix, perhaps it had saved his life. Something had robbed the Bloodthirster's blow of much of its force. He was certain that it should have killed him – yet it had not.

He could not find his sword but his fingers clutched something hard and heavy. He realised that it was the Hammer of Fate. He tried to lift it but it would not move. It was not simply that it was too heavy, it was that some force kept it locked in place on the ground like the magnet which held maps in place on the airship.

Felix cursed. They had come so close. The daemon was moving slowly now, breathing hard, ichor dripping from great rents in its flesh, barely able to maintain its form. One more blow would finish the thing, of that he was certain. He heaved until he thought his muscles would crack and still the accursed hammer would not move. It was a magic artefact, intended to be wielded only by dwarf heroes, and it was beyond the strength of mortal man to overcome its magic.

The Bloodthirster had bent down now over Gotrek, as it had over Thangrim. It reached down and enveloped the fallen Slayer's head with one mighty hand. Slowly it lifted him upwards.

Felix knew what was coming next. The daemon would squeeze the dwarf's head until his skull shattered like a melon, then it would consume his brain and eat his immortal soul. Behind the triumphant daemon he could see the beastmen were crushing the last of the dwarfs' resistance. Varek stood at one of the pillars. The scholar had armed himself with a hammer from somewhere. A wave of frenzied beastmen closed in.

'Help me, Sigmar of the Hammer,' Felix howled with a fervour which he had not felt since he was a frightened child. 'Help me, Grungni! Help me Grimnir! Help me, Valaya! Help me! Help me, damn you!'

At the invocation of the gods' names, the runes on the hammer flickered and fire leapt back into them. Felix felt the weapon begin to come free of the ground. It was heavy at first but weighed progressively less as he lifted it, as if some other force was lending him the strength to overcome its vast weight. A burning pain shot through Felix's hand where he held the warhammer. He felt sparks scorching his sleeve. The taint of ozone filled his nostrils. The pain almost made him drop the thing. He fought to keep a grip on it while every nerve ending in his hand shrieked with agony. Somehow, he managed to maintain his hold.

Felix knew he would only get one chance. He drew the hammer back for the cast. The daemon sensed the gathering of energies behind it and turned to face him, the Slayer held negligently in one hand, the way a man might hold a broken doll. The terrible eyes rested on Felix and for a moment he felt another surge of that familiar terror. He knew the daemon was about to spring, to rend him limb from limb and he would not be quick enough to stop it. He wrestled down his fear, smiled shyly and decided to try anyway.

The Bloodthirster dropped Gotrek and sprang, both claws outstretched, its mouth wide open, its fangs bared. Eyes through which hell looked out upon the world glared directly into Felix's soul. Its hideous odour filled his nostrils. The heat of its body radiated across the closing gap. Felix flung the sacred warhammer forward and released it. It hurtled forward like a falling meteor, trailing a comet tail of blazing lightning. It smashed directly into the daemon's head with a noise like a clap of thunder. The force of the impact stopped its headlong rush. It toppled over backwards but only for a moment. The Hammer of Fate glanced off it and flew into the gloom.

Slowly the daemon pulled itself upright. Felix knew now that there was nothing he could do to stop it. Its victory was inevitable. He had done his best, and it had not been enough. He barely had the energy to stand, let alone flee from the creature. His chest was scorched. His hand felt like the flesh was peeling off the bone.

The Bloodthirster staggered forward, grinning evilly. The look in its ancient eyes told him that it knew what he was thinking and that it mocked his despair. Its enormous shadow fell across him. It flexed its wings, pulling the rune-carved blade free from its back and sending it flying across the chamber. It drew back its claws for the killing blow.

'Oi! You! I haven't finished with you yet!' roared Gotrek's voice from behind it.

The monstrous head of his great, ancient axe suddenly protruded through the Bloodthirster's chest. As it did so, the daemon began to come apart, in a shower of red and gold sparks which transformed into stinking vapour. The thing started to vanish, like a fire burning down before their eyes. Through the fading mist Felix could see the bruised and battered form of the Slayer, barely able to stand upright. Slowly the Bloodthirster faded from view.

But Felix could still see the daemon's blazing eyes and its last words still echoed inside his head: *I will remember you, mortals, and I have all eternity in which to take my vengeance.*

Wonderful, thought Felix, that's all I need. The enmity of the favoured of Khorne! Still, his heart had lifted. The daemon was gone and the terrible fear that its presence had inflicted had vanished like morning mist in the light of the rising sun. Felix felt a weight fall from his shoulders that he had not even known was there, and a vast sense of relief filled him.

Gotrek reeled over to where the Hammer of Fate lay and picked it up. This time the weapon lifted easily and as it did so something strange started to happen. Bolts of lightning flickered between the hammer and the axe, creating a searing electrical arc. As they did so, the Slayer seemed to swell with barely contained power. His crest stood on end above his head. His beard bristled. His eyes blazed with an odd blue light.

'The gods mock me, manling!' he roared in a voice that was as audible as a thunderclap. Bitterness twisted his face. 'I came here seeking my doom, and instead brought doom upon this place. Now, someone is going to pay.'

He turned and walked back into the fray. The Hammer of Fate left a blurred trail of light behind it as it struck. His ancient, daemon-slaying axe smashed through a Chaos warrior and took a huge chunk out of one of the pillars behind him. An aura of fear surrounded him now, like the one that had surrounded the daemon, and the Chaos worshippers began to back away.

Gotrek let out a mighty battle cry and leapt into their midst, and a terrible slaying began. Filled with god-like power by the awesome weapons he held, the Slayer was invincible. His axe sheared through armour and flesh effortlessly; no weapon could stand against it. The hammer sent bolt after bolt of terrifying power out to lash the Chaos warriors like a daemon's whip.

Felix watched appalled at the carnage the Slayer wrought until he saw his blade lying on the floor, forced his hand to grip it, and rushed down into the fray himself. In moments it was over. Dismayed by the fall of their leader, unable to withstand the invincible power of the angry Slayer, the remnants of the Chaos horde turned tail and fled.

TWENTY
AFTERMATH

Felix surveyed the Hall of the Well wearily. Corpses lay everywhere, evidence of a battle fought with insane ferocity on one side and unyielding dwarfish determination on the other. Dried blood carpeted the floor. The stench of death filled his nostrils.

He looked down at where Gotrek lay, pale and still, propped up against one of the pillars which supported the ceiling's roof. His entire chest was swathed in bandages and one arm was held immobile in a sling. Bruises covered the Slayer's head, evident even beneath his tattoos. The grip of the daemon had not been gentle. The fight with the Bloodthirster had come very near to killing the Slayer and the combat afterwards had not helped any. The Slayer's chest barely moved, as he struggled on the borderland between life and death. Not even Varek could say whether he would live or die.

The young dwarf looked up uncertainly. 'I have done my best for him. The rest is in the lap of the gods. It is a wonder he lives at all. I suspect only the power of the Hammer of Fate kept him alive as long as he was fighting.'

Felix wondered whether the time had finally arrived when he would have to record the Slayer's doom. It had certainly been an epic battle, all that Gotrek could have wanted for his end. The dwarfs had rallied at the sight of the daemon's banishment. The Chaos horde had lost all heart for the fight as the berserk Slayer ploughed through their midst, armed with his invincible weaponry, violent and deadly as some ancient divinity of war. Such was the slaughter Gotrek had wrought, it must have seemed to the Chaos worshippers that their vile gods had turned against them. In the end, demoralised and panicking, they had turned and fled the hall, leaving the dwarfs triumphant. Only then had Gotrek collapsed.

Such a victory had been bought at a hideous cost. Felix doubted that more than a score of the dwarfs survived and most of those had been hidden in the Vault when the fighting was on. If not for the power of the hammer and Gotrek's skill with the axe, he doubted that any of them would have lived. And it seemed that the Slayer might yet pay the ultimate price for their victory.

Snorri limped through the dead, favouring his right leg. He did not look much better than Gotrek. His chest had been stitched together with whipcord. It was probably testimony to his awesome dwarfish toughness that he was still alive at all. No human could have survived the Bloodthirster's blow or the loss of blood which followed. A make-shift turban of bandages wrapped round his head made him look like a very short, very broad, and very stupid native of Araby. He whistled happily to himself as he surveyed the red ruin all around. But even he lost some of his cheerfulness when he looked down at Gotrek's recumbent form.

'Good fight,' he said softly to no one in particular. Felix was about to disagree. He wanted to say that, in his opinion, there was no such thing as a good fight, there were only those you won and those you lost. Fighting was a dirty, messy, painful and dangerous business, and on the whole he had decided it was something that he would rather avoid.

Yet even as he thought this, Felix knew that he was trying to deceive himself. There was a bizarre elation in survival and awful joy to be found in victory, and he was not immune to it. And when he considered the alternatives to victory he found he was forced to agree with Snorri.

'Yes, it was a good fight,' he said, though he wondered whether any of those lying dead on the cold stone floor would agree, were they able to speak.

The effort of talking made his own body ache. He inspected his hand. It was stiff and scorched from where he had held the Hammer of Fate as it discharged its lightning bolts. Even the opiate salves that Varek had applied could not dull the pain entirely. He wasn't entirely sure what magic had protected Thangrim from this sort of thing, but it obviously did not work for humans. Still, it had done its work and he shouldn't really complain about the sloppy way in which the gods had answered his prayers.

Looking at the bandages which bound his hand, he now wondered how he had ever managed to keep fighting – but really he knew the answer. In the heat of battle, a man could endure pain that would floor him under normal circumstances. He had once seen a man continue to fight for some minutes after taking a wound that eventually killed him. Looking at his hand, he wondered if he would ever be able to wield a blade again. Or even the pen that would be needed to record the Slayer's death.

Varek had assured him that he would, in time, but right now he was not so sure. Still, he supposed, he could always learn to wield a blade left-handed. He tried to draw the Templar's sword from the scabbard with his left hand but it felt all wrong. Still, there was time enough to learn.

His whole body ached and he wanted simply to lie down and sleep, but there was still much to do. Hargrim and the other dwarfs finished their discussion and strode over to him. Hargrim held the Hammer of Fate in his right hand. Felix noticed somewhat sourly that it had not burned him.

'We owe you a debt we can never pay, Felix Jaeger,' Hargrim started. 'You have saved the honour of our people and prevented the sacred warhammer of our ancestors from falling into the hands of our foes.'

Felix smiled at the dwarf. 'You owe me nothing, Hargrim. The Hammer of Fate saved my life. There is no debt.'

'Nobly spoken. Nevertheless, what we have is yours.'

'Thank you, but I just want to go home,' Felix said, hoping he did not sound ungrateful.

'We will leave together,' Hargrim said. Felix raised an eyebrow.

'There are too few of us now to defend this place, and the Dark Ones surely now know of its location. It is only a matter of time before they return. It is time to take our Book of Grudges and the hammer and what we can carry of our hoard, and leave.'

'I believe there is enough room on the *Spirit of Grungni*, Felix,' said Varek. He looked on Felix respectfully, as if seeking his approval for the decision. Obviously wielding the Hammer of Fate had given him some status among the dwarfs. 'There are only twenty-two dwarfs of Karag Dum now and if we clear the hold and double up in the cabins there will be space enough.'

'I am sure you are correct,' Felix said.

'It is imperative that we get the sacred warhammer away from here. And as much of the dwarfhoard as we can carry.'

'Of course it is,' Felix said, looking at the chests the dwarfs were bearing out of the hidden vault. 'But I worry about how we are going to get everything out. We have to find our way through the Chaos worshippers. And we are too weak and too few to fight.'

Hargrim grinned. 'Do not worry about that, Felix Jaeger. There are still many secret paths through Karag Dum which are known only to the dwarfs.'

Felix looked over at the recumbent Gotrek, who looked far too pale and feeble to be moved. 'What about Gotrek and the other wounded?' he said. Perhaps they should wait for the Slayer to die and bury him here in the vault along with the other heroes of the battle.

'When I'm too weak to walk, manling, I will be too weak to live,' came a voice from the Trollslayer. Gotrek's one good eye slowly opened. They all hurried over as he forced himself upright.

'Then, by all means, let us get going,' Felix said happily.

The Slayer looked around at the field of battle. 'It seems my doom has eluded me yet again,' he said sourly.

'Don't worry,' Felix said. 'I'm sure some other doom awaits!'

Thanquol pulled back the curtain of his palanquin and blinked as the unaccustomed light crashed into his retina. He had just emerged from the Underways into the day. The bright summer sun of northern Kislev glared down on him like the watching eye of some pitiless god.

He looked out into the awesome crater of Hell Pit. Beneath him he could see the enormous fortress of Clan Moulder. A sense of satisfaction filled him. He had driven his exhausted bearers for days to reach his goal.

'Move quick-quick!' he ordered the panting slaves. 'We still have a great distance to go!'

Slowly the bearers stumbled down the slope.

Eerie echoes erupted from the oddly sculpted towers. Great beasts roared. The smell of monsters and warpstone made Thanquol's nostrils twitch.

Here he knew he would find the allies he needed to capture the airship and take his inevitable revenge on Gurnisson and Jaeger. Already he could see skaven warriors accompanied by misshapen shambling beasts coming to greet him.

Now, if only he could re-establish contact with his minion Lurk

Snitchtongue, things would be well. He wondered what Lurk was up to right now.

Lurk was not quite sure what those stupid dwarfs were up to, but he knew that soon the time would be right for him to act. He felt strong and certain that the Horned Rat was with him. Now, he waited only for his opportunity to strike. If the situation called for action, he would not wait. Oh no. He would spring out and overwhelm his foes.

Maybe.

Provided there weren't too many of them.

OTHER TALES

A PLACE OF QUIET ASSEMBLY

John Brunner

'You'll have a comfortable trip,' the landlord of the coaching inn assured Henkin Warsch. 'There are only two other passengers booked for today's stage.'

Which sounded promising enough. However, before they were even out of sight of the inn Henkin was sincerely regretting the maggot that had made him turn aside from his intended route and visit a place he had last seen twenty years before. One of his fellow-travellers was tolerably presentable, albeit gloomy of mien – a young, bookish type in much-worn clothes, with a Sudenland cloak over all – and Henkin might have quite enjoyed chatting with him. But the third member of the party was a dwarf, reeking of ale and burdened with a monstrous axe, who thanks to his huge muscle-knotted arms took up far more room than might have been estimated from his stature. Worst of all, his crest of hair and multiple tattoos marked him out as a Slayer, self-condemned to seek out death in combat – a most discomforting fellow traveller!

If only I could pretend I don't speak Reikspiel, he thought.

The inn's bootboy, however, had put paid to any chance of that. While hoisting Henkin's travelling bag to the roof of the coach, he had announced for the world to hear, 'This here gentleman hails from Marienburg! I'll wager he can report much news to help you pass away the miles!'

Presumably he hoped the flattery would earn him an extra tip. It failed. Scowling, Henkin handed him the least coin in his pocket and scrambled aboard.

Whereupon the ordeal commenced.

It wasn't just that the road was hilly and potholed. He was expecting that. But somehow the dwarf – fortunately in a jovial mood – had taken it into his head that no one from the Wasteland had a proper sense of humour. Accordingly he launched into a string of what he thought of as hilarious jokes. They began as merely scatological; they degenerated to filthy; and at last became downright disgusting.

'…and there he was, over ears in the privy! Haw-haw!' Naturally, Henkin's disinclination to laugh served, in his view, to prove his original point. So he tried again, and again, and yet again. Mercifully, at long last he ran out of new – one should rather, Henkin thought, say ancient – stories to tell, and with a contemptuous scowl leaned back and shut his eyes, though keeping a firm grip on the haft of his axe. Within moments he began to snore.

At which point his companion murmured. 'I must apologise for my friend, mein herr. He has had – ah – a difficult life. Felix Jaeger, by the way, at your service.'

Reluctantly Henkin offered his own name.

'Well, at least the weather is fine,' the other went on after a pause. Glancing out of the window, he added, 'We must be approaching Hohlenkreis, I suppose.'

Against his will Henkin corrected him. 'No, we haven't passed Schatzenheim yet.'

'You know this part of the world?' Felix countered, his eyebrows ascending as though to join his hair.

Henkin, in his turn, started at the landscape. The road, cut from the hillside like a ledge, was barely wide enough for the coach. Here it wound between sullen grey rocks and patches of grassy earth. Higher up the slope were birches, beeches and alders, last outposts of the army of trees that occupied the valley they were leaving. Towards the crest of the pass they would cede place to spruce and larch. That was a haunt of wolves…

'There was a time,' Henkin said at length, 'when I knew this area better than my own home.'

'Really? How so?'

Henkin shrugged. 'I was sent to school near here. To be precise, at Schrammel Monastery.'

'That name sounds familiar…' Felix frowned with the effort of recollection, then brightened. 'Ah, of course! Schrammel is where we're due to put up for the night. So we shall enjoy your company at the inn also?'

Henkin shook his head. 'No, by the time we arrive there should be an hour of daylight left. I'll walk on to the monastery – it isn't far – and invoke an ex-pupil's traditional right to a meal and a bed. Yesterday, on impulse, I decided that being so close I shouldn't miss the chance.'

'Hmm! Your teachers must have left quite an impression!'

'They did, they did indeed. Inasmuch as I've succeeded at all in life, I owe it to their influence. I don't mind admitting it now, but I was an unruly youth.' As he spoke, he thought how oddly the words must strike this stranger's ears, for today he was portly, well dressed and altogether respectable – 'to the point where our family priest feared there might be some spark of Chaos in my nature. It was his counsel that led to my being sent to a monastery run by followers of Solkan to continue my studies. At Schrammel I was rescued from danger that I didn't realise I was in. I often wish I'd been able to complete my education there.'

'You were withdrawn early?' Felix inquired.

Henkin spread his hands. 'My father died. I was called home to take over the family business. But – well, to be candid, I wasn't cut out for it. Last year I decided to sell up, even though I didn't get anything like a fair price.' An embarrassed cough. 'My wife had left me, you see... If only my teachers had had time to reform my character completely, cure me of my excessive capacity for boredom... At first I hated the place, I admit, because the regime was very strict. How I remember being roused in winter before dawn, having to break the ice in my washbowl before morning prayers! And the sound of a hundred empty bellies grumbling in the refectorium as they brought in the bread and milk – why, I can almost hear it now! As we boys used to say, it made nonsense of the monastery's watchword – "A Place of Quiet Assembly"!'

He gave a chuckle, and Felix politely echoed it. 'Of course, they had to be strict. Unvarying adherence to routine: that was their chief weapon against the threat of Chaos – that, and memorising. Memorising! Goodness yes! They stocked my head with lines I'll carry to my dying day. "Let loose the forces of disorder – I'll not quail! Against my steely heart Chaos will ne'er prevail!"'

'Why!' Felix exclaimed. 'That's from Tarradasch's *Barbenoire*, isn't it?'

Henkin smiled wryly. 'Yes indeed. They made me learn the whole thing, word-perfect, as a warning against arrogance. I forget what I'd done, but I'm sure I deserved it... I'm impressed that you recognise it, though. I thought Tarradasch was out of fashion.'

'Oh, I can claim nodding acquaintance with most of the great works of the past. To be candid, I have ambitions in that direction myself. Oddly enough, that's partly why I'm travelling in such – ah – unlikely company.'

'Really? Do explain!'

Felix obliged. After detailing the agreement whereby he was to immortalise his associate's valiant deeds in a poem, he described a few of the said deeds – thereby causing Henkin to cringe nervously away from the slumbering dwarf – and eventually turned to a general discussion of literature. Thus the time passed pleasantly enough until with a grating of iron tyres on cobblestones the coach drew up outside Schrammel's only inn, the Mead and Mazer.

'I'd advise you,' Felix murmured, 'to get out first. Gotrek may resent being woken up... Will you return from the monastery to join us for the rest of the journey?'

'That's my intention, yes,' he said with a grimace. 'I shall be roused in plenty of time, I'm sure.'

'I look forward to seeing you then. Enjoy your – ah – sentimental visit.'

Having arranged for his heavy luggage to be looked after at the inn, Henkin set off cheerfully enough with a satchel containing bare necessities. The weather at this hour was still clement, though ahead he could see wisps of drifting mist. He remembered how clammy it used to feel on his fair skin when he and other malefactors were sent on a punishment run. The prospect of being enshrouded in it dampened his spirits. Moreover the passage of time seemed to have made the path steeper than it used to be, and he often had to pause for breath.

Nonetheless, the sight of old landmarks encouraged him. Here, for example, was the gnarled stump of an oak which his school-friends had nicknamed the *Hexengalgen* – witches' gallows. Its crown was gone, felled no doubt in a winter gale, but there was no mistaking its rugose bark, patched now with fungi that he recognised as edible. Seeing it reminded him how hungry he was, hungry enough to be looking forward even to the meagre victuals on which the pupils at the monastery survived: coarse bread, watery bone-broth and a few sad vegetables. But the teachers ate the same, and they'd seemed hale enough.

Of course, he was accustomed to finer fare these days. He hoped his digestion would cope...

The way was definitely steeper than he had allowed for. The distance from the oak-stump to the next landmark – a moss-covered rock known as Frozen Dwarf because it bore a faint resemblance to one of that quarrelsome and obnoxious race – seemed to have doubled. How different it had been when he was seventeen!

Nonetheless he plodded on, and the sun was still up when he breasted the final rise. Thence he could survey a peaceful view he once had hated, yet now had power to bring tears to his eyes.

Yes, it was unchanged. There were the buildings he recalled so clearly, ringed with a forbidding grey stone wall. Some were veiled by gathering mist, but he could identify them all. There was the dormitorium, with its infirmary wing that fronted on neat square plots planted with medicinal herbs as well as vegetables for the pot. The kitchen where the latter were cooked was a separate building, separate even from the refectorium, for its smoke and, in summer, the hordes of flies it attracted to the scent of meat, made it a noisome neighbour. Over there was the schola, which as well as study-rooms contained the library... He wondered who now had charge of the great iron keys that used to swing from the cord of Frater Jurgen's brown robe, keys that granted access to the locked section where only the best and most pious students were admitted, there to confront revolting but accurate accounts of what evil the forces of Chaos had accomplished in the world. Jurgen, of course, must be long dead; he had been already stooped and greying in Henkin's day.

Then there were the byres, the stables, the sheds where wandering beggars were granted overnight shelter – and finally, drawing the eye as though by some trick of perspective every line of sight must climax with it, the temple, where worship was accorded to the God of Law and none other, the most dedicated and vindictive of Chaos's opponents. Unbidden, lines from a familiar hymn rose to Henkin's lips:

'Help us to serve thee, God of Right and Law! Whene'er we pray to Thee for recompense, Avenge our wrongs, O–'

That's odd! The name was on the tip of his tongue, yet he could not recall it. Surely it would come back if he recited the lines again? He did so, and there was still an infuriating blankness. Yet he'd known it when talking to Felix in the coach!

'Oh, that's absurd!' he crossly told the air. 'I must be getting senile before my time!'

Annoyed, he slung his satchel more comfortably and descended the path that led to the tall oak gate, surmounted by a little watchtower, which constituted the sole means of passage through the encircling wall. Darkness deepened around him at each step. On the hilltop the sun had not quite set, but before he reached the valley floor night had definitely fallen, and chilly shrouds of mist engulfed him even as he tugged the rusty bell-chain.

The dull clang was still resounding when there was a scraping noise from above – a wooden shutter being slid back in the watchtower – and a cracked voice demanded who was there.

Remarkable, he thought. *That sounds exactly like Frater Knoblauch who kept the gate in my day! Oh, I suppose each gatekeeper must copy the mannerisms of his forerunner...*

Stepping back, tilting his head, unable to make out a fact but discerning the glimmer of a lantern, he called out an answer.

'Henkin Warsch! I used to be a pupil here! I claim by right a meal and a bed!'

'Henkin Warsch!' the gatekeeper echoed in astonishment. 'Well, well! That's amazing! I'll unlock in a trice!'

And he was as good as his word, for the heavy panels swung wide before Henkin had drawn two more breaths. There in front of him, unmistakable in the faint yellow gleam of his lamp, was Frater Knoblauch in person, wheezing with the effort of hurrying down the narrow stairs.

'But – no, it can't be!' Henkin exclaimed. 'You can't possibly be Frater Knoblauch!'

'And why not?' the old man riposted.

'I thought... I mean: I left here twenty years ago!'

'So you expected me to be dead, is that it?' the other said caustically. 'Well, I suppose to a boy anyone over fifty seems an ancient. No, here I am, as hale and hearty as anyone may hope at my age. Our way of life is a healthy one, you know – we don't rot our bodies with drink or waste our vitality by wenching! Come in, come in so I can shut the gate. A bed you can certainly have, but if you want food you'll have to make haste. It's after sunset, you know, and we still keep the same hours.'

Henkin's stomach uttered a grumble at the prospect of going supperless to sleep, bringing back to mind the joke he had repeated to his travelling companion.

'But I don't think they'll have started yet,' Frater Knoblauch added reassuringly, and set off at a clumsy scuttle towards the refectorium.

He led Henkin through an entrance reserved for teaching staff, which as a boy he had been forbidden to use, and time rolled back as he found himself on the great dais where he had never before set foot save to sweep it free of crumbs, looking down on the dim-lit hall. There, just as in the old days, ninety or a hundred drawn, pale boys sat unspeakingly before bowls of stew and lumps of coarse black bread. Those whose turn it was to dish out this exiguous repast were returning tureens and ladles to shelves along the wall and darting back to their places on wooden benches the sight of which brought recollected aches to Henkin's buttocks.

'You're in luck,' Knoblauch murmured. 'Grace has not been spoken. Wait here. I'll inform the prior.'

Henkin followed Knoblauch with his gaze. Even if the gatekeeper was the same, the prior certainly couldn't be: Alberich had been over seventy. But it was the custom for the staff to eat with their cowls raised, to discourage even an exchange of glances that might infringe the spirit of the absolute rule against conversation at table, so the man's features were invisible. Listening to Knoblauch, he nodded gravely, indicated with a finger that the visitor was to be shown to a seat and food brought for him – in precisely the way Alberich would have.

No, that is impossible, he thought. He must simply have schooled himself into a perfect imitation of the former prior!

One of the senior boys was signalled and came at a fast walk, never of course a run. Having received instructions, he approached Henkin, looking dazed, as though he could not believe anyone would voluntarily return to this place once released. He ushered him to the last unoccupied chair at the high table, and delivered the same stew and bread as served all the company. Then he made for a lectern halfway along the left-hand wall, whereon reposed a large leather-bound book, and stood waiting, eyes on the prior.

Ah! It's all coming back, all coming back! During the main course there was always a reading, some kind of homily or moral tale! How I used to hate my turn for duty, not just because I read so badly but because it meant going hungry for still a while longer, until I was allowed to wolf down cold leftovers before rushing to catch up with the others...

The prior rose and spoke in a reedy but resonant voice, as much like Alberich's as were his movements – and, as Henkin now perceived, his stature, too: Alberich had been unusually tall. Instead of reciting the expected grace, however, he made an announcement.

'Fraters! Boys! Today we witness a singular event. We share our repast with a former pupil. Fleeing the hurly-burly of the world he has rejoined us in our place of quiet assembly. I bid you all to welcome Henkin Warsch.'

He turned his head towards Henkin, but the cowl so shadowed his face that no expression was discernible. At a loss, Henkin did what he would have done at home: rose from his chair, bowed awkwardly first to the prior and then to the body of the hall, and resumed his seat.

Apparently nothing more was expected, for the prior proceeded to intone the grace. At once there was a susurrus of gulping and chewing and swallowing, as though the great room were full of ravenous hogs incapable of squealing. To his own surprise – for the stew looked and smelled even less appetising than he had expected – Henkin found himself tucking in just as eagerly. Bland and flavourless the food might be, not to mention half-cold, but it was filling, and his long trudge from Schrammel town had bequeathed him a ferocious appetite.

Having waited until the first frantic mouthfuls had been consumed, the boy at the lectern raised his voice. Henkin failed to catch his introductory words because he was chomping down on another hunk of bread–

And, speaking of missed words: that grace. It includes the name I couldn't remember just now: the name of – of...

He shook his head, confused. He hadn't heard it.

At least, however, it didn't matter that he had missed the title of the reading. He recognised the opening line, having heard it countless times, and read it too.

'The Hate Child,' he whispered soundlessly. 'Yes, of course.'

He composed himself to listen to the familiar tale, not certain whether he was actually hearing it, or whether it as well was emerging from memory.

'In the distant past, in a province of Bretonnia, there ruled a noble count named Benoist, surnamed Orguleux for his great vanity. It was his ambition to have his own way in all things, and for that he was a mighty man, of body large and of nature determined, rare were the times when he was disappointed. None, though, may stand against death, and it came to pass that his wife, whom after his fashion he may have loved, died in confinement with their first child, and the baby also shortly after.

'Distracted by fury and sorrow, he went forth among the villages and hamlets of that land, begging or stealing his food, sleeping in barns and ditches, until he looked to a passer's glance like a common vagrant.

'It so fell out one evening that he crossed a woman of surpassing fairness, feeding geese beside a river when the moons were full. Smitten by her countenance, he made himself known, saying, "I am Count Benoist, your lord and master. My wife is dead. It is you I choose to be my new consort, and to seal the bargain I shall take you now." Though he had seen himself reflected in the pools he drank from, and so knew that he was dirty and unkempt, he was used to his own way in everything.

'Now the beauteous woman, who was called Yvette, was versed in arcane lore. She understood he made no empty boast. Curtseying, she said, "My lord, this is an honour to me and my family. But you must not take me now. It is the Night of Savage Moons, a time when the forces of Chaos are drawn tidewise from the Northern Wastes, and warpstone dust, it's said, blows in the wind. Come for me tomorrow instead, and I shall willingly consent to be your bride."

'Enraged, Count Benoist threw her to the ground and used her as he would, despite her warnings. So cruelly did he whelm her that she fainted, and after he was done he slung her on his shoulder and bore her unaided to his castle, where he commanded servants to attend her.

'On the morrow when she woke, she said to him, "I keep my word. Summon priests that they may marry us." He did, for she was very beautiful. But he did not know she married him for punishment. Perhaps she too was unaware. It had happened on the Night of Savage Moons.

'In the fullness of time she bore a son and called him Estephe. He grew up tall and comely, a fit heir. But there was in him a certain moody wildness, so that now and then he and his youthful companions fell to riotous carousing, while at other times black misery held him in thrall and he would speak to none, but walked alone and muttered curses.

'It chanced that on the day he turned eighteen, by when he overtopped his father and was nimbler with a sword, he was in the grip of such despair. That day his mother told him how he had been got on her against her will. So presently he sought the count and ran him through, and on the battlements he played at kickball with his father's head, wherefore all held him for accursed, and rightly so.

'Thus may it be seen how we must always be on guard, for the subtlety of Chaos knows no bounds.'

The reader closed the book. The slowest eaters among the boys gobbled their last frantic scraps of food. All rose as the prior pronounced concluding grace – and once again Henkin missed being reminded of the name of the God of Law, for a frightening idea distracted him.

Why, he thought, there was something of that boy in me, and traces still remain! Thank goodness Father sent me here, for otherwise... I had just such bouts of depression, and I too ran amok and thought it funny to break windows or rob peasants on their way to market! Besides, my mother never welcomed her husband's physical attentions, which is why I was and am an only child... Was Estephe, too? The story doesn't say.

But there was no time to wonder. The boys were filing, quickly but silently, towards the dormitorium, bar those whose task it was to clear away the bowls and sweep up crumbs. He was expecting the prior and the rest of the staff to approach, ask questions, find out why he had decided to pay this visit, allow him to express the gratitude that had suddenly filled his heart as the moral of Count Benoist's fate sank home. But nothing of the sort happened. Nodding to him solemnly in turn, they too left the hall, and in a moment he found himself alone but for another of the older boys, this one carrying a candlestick, who confided in a whisper that he was to guide Henkin to his room. So at least he was permitted to sleep alone, instead of on one of a hundred hard platforms covered with bracken-filled bags by way of mattress, no pillow, and just a single threadbare blanket such as he had shivered under in the old days. However, the staff's quarters he was shown to were only marginally more luxurious...

He hadn't retired at such an early hour in years. At first he was sure he wouldn't be able to sleep. In a way he welcomed the prospect. As though some vestige of his youthful self had returned, he looked forward to brooding over his annoyance at this cold reception. Then, even as he closed the wooden shutters against the now-dense mist, he was overcome by a vast surge of weariness. Yawning so hard he felt his head might split, he tossed aside his boots and outer clothing, rinsed his mouth and splashed his face with water from a cracked ewer, blew out his candle and lay down. He was asleep before he could draw the blanket over him.

He woke to midnight darkness. But not silence. The stones enclosing him, the very air, were resonating, to the boom of a vast and brazen gong...

Even as he prepared to be angry at this premature arousal, a thrill of anticipation permeated his entire body. With it came a clear and penetrating thought, more naked feeling than mere words. Yet it might be glossed as:

I forgot this! Only now do I remember it! How could it have escaped my memory, this which offered compensation for the cold and hunger, this which made it worth my while to spend so many agonising months in quarters barely better than a prison? This is the summons to the Quiet Assembly!

He was on his feet, feverishly snatching at his boots and cloak, aware of stirrings beyond the walls on either side, in the dormitorium below, even above the roof where owls were circling, and doubtless bats, the soft pat of their wings adding to the wonderful reverberation of the gong. Fingers a-tangle with excitement, he finally contrived to tie his laces, and rushed to the landing.

He instantly checked his pace. Of course. It must be slow and solemn, like everything here. Recollection seized him as he saw the pupils emerging one by one onto the stairs ahead of him, moving as though they were still lost to sleep, but surely, and with implacable intent.

At their rear he fell in, and found as he would not have expected when he arrived, but now thought was perfectly natural, the prior himself standing beside an open door admitting curls of mist. Hood thrown back, he was flanked by two attendants handing lit torches to the boys. Still cowled, they bore remarkable likeness to Frater Jurgen the librarian, iron keys and all, and Frater Wildgans who had been Henkin's chief instructor. But he was of no mind to let such matters trouble him.

Yes: the prior was Alberich. And seemingly no older. And now confronting Henkin as he descended the last cold tread of the stone flight, and bowing to him. Bowing! Saying nothing – yet his action was more eloquent than words.

Henkin's heart began to pound in perfect unison with the gong, while his paces, and the pupils', likewise kept time to it. Conscious that this ceremony was the honour due him for his decision to return, he followed the triple line of torch-bearing boys. 'Jurgen' and 'Wildgans' fell in beside him, and the prior himself took up the rear.

They were, of course, being summoned to the temple.

Ah! This is how it was, he thought. This is the way we used to be brought face to face with the elemental essence of Law and Right! Not by dull rote learning, not by memorising moral tales and masterworks, not through obedience to the discipline impressed on us with bread and broth – and, occasionally, necessary stripes – but by being brought from slumber at the dead hour when the random fretful forces of the body are most sluggish, least subject to the whims and wilfulness of daylight, and shown the unbearable fact of the god whom otherwise we knew as nothing more than words…! This is what saved me, thanks to the selfless dedication of the teaching fraters. How could I never have thought of it from then till now? How could I have overlooked for twenty years this sensation of the marvellous, this drunken joy?

He felt himself swaying, so tremendous was the charge of expectation that imbued his being. No other prospect of high events had matched it: not his wedding, not the birth of his children, not his first coup in the trade he had inherited from his father, then in the others he had turned to as his early interest waned; nor this first (of many) undetected love affairs – nor even the last which had been detected and cost him his marriage and his former livelihood. This had no parallel. This was what had made life here endurable, and now he was to experience it again.

He wanted to cry out in gratitude, although his tongue seemed tied, exactly as it had been when he strove to recall that thought-to-be familiar hymn.

Ah, it didn't matter. Within the hour, within minutes perhaps, a name would spring to his lips and set the seal on his destiny. He needed only to utter it aloud, and he would be accepted, in some way he did not yet comprehend, but he would. Oh yes: he would, when it was time.

Here at last was the entrance to the temple. Knoblauch stood on guard. Passing him, the boys drew up in serried ranks to either side, facing a high and distant idol. The torches they bore cast but wan illumination on the rich hangings that lined the walls, for mist had gathered within the temple, too, as though wafted indoors by the wings of the circling bats and owls. The idol itself, so tall that its raised arms reached the roof, was scarcely visible. It didn't matter, though. Henkin knew with comfortable assurance what god was honoured in this fane: the one whose law upheld not only roof but sky, to whom he was already dedicated, and who had drawn him hither after two decades.

Ah! How few among all humankind can boast they have held steadfast for so long to a pledge undertaken in youth!

Henkin started. He was curiously uncertain whether the thought had sprung unbidden to his mind, or whether Prior Alberich had uttered the words – which, oddly, had been followed by what sounded like a chuckle. He made to ask, but was forestalled. Knoblauch swung the heavy doors shut with a thud, and in the same instant the gong – which had become almost deafening – ceased to boom.

Amid an air of total expectation, Henkin found himself advancing along the central aisle of the temple, the boys on either side as still as rocks, even when a splatter of wax dripped from a torch and landed scalding on the back of a bare hand, staring with indescribable longing towards the mist-veiled idol. Henkin remembered that longing now, how it ached, how it festered, how it could only be assuaged by such a ceremony as was now in progress.

Yet there was no chanting of anthems, no procession of gorgeously attired acolytes, no incense, no heaps of offerings, none of the trivia to be found in almost any other temple. Of course not. This rite was unique.

It was, after all, the Place of Quiet Assembly.

Of their own accord, his feet ceased to move. He stood before the statue. If he glanced up, he would be able to recognise it, and the name that hovered on his tongue would be spoken. The fruit of his education would ripen on the instant. He would become a perfect servant of the god's cause – which, ever since his schooldays, had been what he wanted most.

Wondering why he had not returned here long ago, to join Alberich and Knoblauch, Jurgen and Wildgans and the rest, he glanced from side to side seeking approval. He met an encouraging smile from the prior.

At least, he forced himself to believe it was a smile. It involved lips parted over a set of teeth remarkable for so elderly a man, and there was a glint of expectation in his eyes, so...

Deciding not to look too long, Henkin clung to the remnants of the delight he had felt on the way hither – now, for some strange reason, it had begun to dissipate – and boldly threw his head to stare directly at the image of the god.

And froze, caught between adoration and astonishment.

For those were not arms that reached to the roof. Arms there were, ending in monstrous hands, and legs with vast broad feet. Towering above them, though, sprouted by a hideous head, were – horns? No, tentacles! They flexed! And each one ended, as it curved towards him, in a gaping pseudopod-coronaed face...

It spoke – from which of its three mouths, Henkin could not tell. It said, in a voice like the grating of rocks against rocks when spring floods undermine a hillside and presage landslides in a valley:

'Speak my name. You only need to speak my name and life indefinite awaits you. Live forever!'

Almost, the name emerged. Yet, somewhere in the inmost depths of Henkin's awareness, something rebelled. Some part of him complained, its mental tone no better than peevish – like his mother's when his father had offended her by winning an argument – a sense, one might say, of obstinate conviction.

That's not the God of Law, he thought. It looks more like the one I've striven against throughout my life!

For what felt like half eternity, Henkin stood transfixed with puzzlement. He knew the name he was supposed to speak. He was quite unable to recall the other one. It followed, by the twisted logic that held him in its grip, that he should utter the one he could.

On the other hand, if he did, there was some kind of penalty... or something... or... Raising his hands to his temples, he swayed giddily, gathered his forces, licked his lips, prepared to make a once-and-for-all commitment–

And there came a thunderous crash at the oaken door, as of a monstrous axe shattering its timbers like the flimsy partitions of a peasant's cot.

Which turned out to be exactly what it was.

Slowly, like a fly trapped by the resin that in a thousand years would be more profitably sold as amber for embalming it, Henkin turned. At the far end of the aisle something was moving so fast he could barely follow it. Also his ears were more assaulted than they had been by the gong.

The moving thing was the axe. He could not see its wielder. But it was the wielder he was hearing. He had been told, he had read, how terrible was the war cry of a dwarf in berserk state. Not until it blasted back in echo from the arched roof of the temple was he able to believe its force. Gotrek's first victim, after the door, had been Frater Knoblauch, whose head, staring at his body on the stone flags, bore an expression suggesting it felt it should, but couldn't quite, recognise the nearby carcass.

At that sight the boys, screaming at the pitch of their lungs, broke and ran, trampling the fraters who tried to stop them, hurling their torches aside, heedless of whether they landed at the foot of the hangings. Flames leapt up. Smoke mingled with the mist. Alberich and his companions, cowls thrown back, turned snarling to confront the intruder, Henkin for the moment forgotten.

'Hurry! Warsch, run! This way, you fool!'

Still bemused by the grip of enchantment, Henkin stared towards the speaker, waving frantically from near the door. He ventured muzzily, 'Is that you, Felix Jaeger?'

'Of course it's me!' Felix shouted. He had a sword in his hand, but such work was better left to his companion. 'This way! *Move!* Before Gotrek brings the roof down on our heads!'

Sluggishly, Henkin sought mute permission from the prior – he felt he had to. Or from Jurgen, or Wildgans. But the attention of all three was on the dwarf. Drawing themselves up within their cowled robes, they seemed tree-tall compared with him. Magical auras flashed as they mustered for a counter-attack. 'Poor fool!' Henkin heard distinctly, in Alberich's voice. 'To think he imagines a mere axe can slay one who has lived a thousand years!'

They stretched out their arms. Horrors indescribable assembled at their conjunct fingertips.

Ignoring the other fraters and the fleeing boys, Gotrek ceased his bellowing. Poised on the balls of his feet, brandishing his axe, he looked far more terrifying than before: no longer dancing with the ecstasy of blood-lust, but gathering himself into himself, eyes gleaming with mad joy… Shaking from head to toe, Henkin realised what he was watching: a Slayer on the brink of conviction that here might be the end of his quest.

As if to confirm it, the dwarf began to sing – not shout his war cry, not utter threats, nor curses, but to chant in dwarfish. Surely, thought Henkin in wonder, it was the ballad of his family's deeds: that family who must all be dead, for else he'd not have taken to his lonely road.

Sneering contempt, Prior Alberich and his companions mustered all their magic force, prepared to cast–

And in exactly that brief moment when they had no power save what was being drawn into their spell, Gotrek hurled his axe.

He threw so hard it carried him with it, for he did not let go. Was it a throw or a leap? Or was it both? Dazed, Henkin could not decide. All he could tell was this: such was its violence, the flying blade *mowed* Alberich and his companions like corn beneath the harvest-scythe. The dwarf, who had spun clear around, landed on his feet before the idol. Panting, but still gasping out his song, he raised the blade anew, this time menacing the statue itself.

Where had the spell-power gone? Into the axe, Henkin abruptly realised. It must have! For what he had taken for arms upholding the temple roof – what turned out to be half-horn, half-tentacle – they were descending, their hideous fanged mouths like flesh-eroding lampreys closing on the stubby form of Gotrek. His singing, now the boys' screams had faded, was not the only noise to be heard. Suddenly there were menacing creaks and grinds as, its support removed, the building began to sag and sway…

'*Move*, you fool!' thundered Felix, seizing Henkin's arm, and dragged him away on quaking ground to the music of snapping timbers, tumbling stones and crackling flames, amid the destined downfall of Schrammel Monastery.

Abruptly it was bitterly cold, and they were very weak, and time seemed to grind to a stop.

Henkin wished the moving earth would do the same.

It was dawn. Dew-sodden, Henkin forced his eyes open and drank in the sights revealed by the returning sun. He saw mounds of rubble, the line of the fallen wall, smoke drifting from what had been the temple and now looked more like a tent propped up by broken poles – but no other movement save seekers of carrion come cautiously to glean the ruins. Plus a stir amid the smouldering wreckage, as though a trace of Chaos lurked there still, shifting and wriggling.

Of neither fraters nor pupils was there any sign.

Nor, come to that, of Gotrek.

Wrapped in his red wool cloak, Felix sat brooding on a nearby rock. Without preamble Henkin demanded, 'Where's the dwarf? He saved my life!'

Felix gave a dour shrug. 'It looks as though he's achieved his ambition. The temple collapsed with him inside. I only just dragged you out in time… Well, it's what he's always wanted. And I suppose I should be glad to be released from my pledge at last.'

'But how did it all happen?' Henkin sat up gingerly. 'Perhaps warpstone dust? In the air, the food, our very blood?'

'That, or some like manifestation. At any rate, for centuries this monastery has functioned as a tool for–'

'Tzeentch!' Henkin blurted. That was the word he had been tempted to utter, the name of the power his family's priest had feared already held him in his grip. And the name of the God of Right and Law came back to him, too.

Soberly, Felix nodded.

'Indeed. How better might the servants of the Changer of the Ways disguise their work than by pretending to serve Solkan? It must have cost them dear to adopt such a static guise, but in the long term I suppose they felt it worth the effort to plant so many converts in staid, respectable families.'

Scrambling to his feet, Henkin said bitterly, 'If only my father and our priest could have known what a fate they were condemning me to! I did want to follow in my father's footsteps – I swear it! I wanted to build up our business, make it the wealthiest in Marienburg, and instead my life has been a *mess!* Here I am entering middle age without a wife, without a career, without anything my family hoped I would enjoy! And all because my father was duped into sending me here because I was so unruly and the monastery was called "A Place of Quiet Assembly"!'

'Quiet it wasn't,' roared a distant voice. 'Not last night, anyway!'

Startled, Felix and Henkin glanced around. Gotrek was emerging from the wrecked temple, axe over shoulder. He must, Henkin reasoned, have been the cause of what he'd mistaken for simple subsidence.

And the dwarf did not look pleased in the least.

Faintly Henkin caught a whisper from Felix: 'Oh, *no*...'

But there were things he still needed to know. Urgently he demanded, 'How did you find out? And why did you come after me? You too could have been ensnared!'

Resignedly, Felix explained.

'We discovered over dinner that everyone at the inn knew about the monastery – "the Monstery", as they call it. With that, we forgot all thought of food.'

'You mean the landlord could have warned me?' Rage boiled up in Henkin's throat.

'Of course he could! But he looked forward to inheriting your luggage.' Brushing dust from crest and eyebrows, the dwarf sat down beside Felix and inspected his axe, cursing under his breath.

'Why, the–'

'Save your breath,' Felix cut in. 'Gotrek made him a promise. He knows what's going to happen to him when we get back if he's so much as laid a finger on your belongings.'

'When...?' Henkin had to swallow hard. 'But, herr dwarf, were you expecting to return?'

Felix drew a hissing breath, as in alarm.

There was a long silence. Eventually Gotrek shrugged. In a tone so different from the one Henkin had heard during yesterday's coach-ride that it was hard to credit the same person was speaking, he said gruffly, 'Last night didn't pay off, but it was one of the likeliest chances to come my way. For that, I'd even forgive someone who lacks a sense of humour! If I hadn't picked up such a charge of magic... In the upshot, though,' he said, glowering, 'all it's landed me with is another verse for Felix's poem and another doom cheated from me!' He lifted his axe as though to strike Henkin out of his way.

Henkin hesitated. Within him, he now knew, Tzeentch the Changer of the Ways held sway but had not yet conquered. Very well! If Tzeentch's disciples could control their mutable nature long enough to delude the world into imagining they served the rigid Solkan, could he not govern himself at least for one brief moment, do and say the right and necessary thing? One did after all know a little about Slayers...

Resolved, he drew himself to his full height.

'Gotrek,' he said, daringly. 'I heard you sing as you confronted them!'

The huge-knuckled fists tightened on the axe; the muscles of the shoulders tensed; the glare intensified.

'Herr dwarf! I'm aware how rare a privilege that is! I'll treasure it!'

The massive hands relaxed, just a trifle.

'Of course, I shall never, so long as I live, mention the fact to another living soul! Not until your companion has completed his poem – the great work that will immortalise your deeds.'

From the corner of his eye Henkin noticed that Felix, visibly surprised, was nodding.

'I'm only sorry, *herr dwarf*, that my unworthy self could not after all be the means of your attaining your ambition!'

Had that gone too far? By now he was practically gabbling.

'If you'll accompany me back to the inn, although we must have missed the morning coach, I promise you we shall pass the time until the next most pleasantly, with abundance of food and ale at my expense, and you may tell me all the jokes you wish and I'll applaud the verses Felix makes about your deeds here today!'

For a moment Henkin imagined he might have won Gotrek over. But then the dwarf shrugged again, rising. Words could not portray the mask of misery he wore.

'What's the use? You humans care only about your own miserable lives. When Felix composes his account of what happened here, he'll miss the point, as usual... Ah, never mind. It was a good fight, at least. So I'll take you up on the ale. It does beat water. All right, let's get on back to Schrammel.'

Felix failed to suppress a groan.

But, since there was no better bargain to be had – and since last night not merely a life had been saved, but a soul – Henkin and he fell in behind the dwarf and duly trudged back to the Mead and Mazer.

BLOOD SPORT

Josh Reynolds

The screech echoed across the peaks of the Grey Mountains. It was a sound of raw, animal agony that set the crows to flight and the horses to pulling at their tethers. The echo of the screech faded and the cockatrice slumped, serpentine tail lashing, its unnatural ichors staining the harsh soil. A hoof stamped down, pulverising the dying beast's skull and its writhing body abruptly went still.

The hippogryph shook itself and snapped its beak angrily. It reared up on its hooves, flapping its wings as it clawed at the air with the talons on its forelimbs. It squalled at the cheering crowd and Felix Jaeger heard the raw hatred in the beast's voice and shuddered. 'Nasty beast,' he said.

'Aye,' Gotrek Gurnisson grunted, his one good eye locked on the hippogryph.

'Are you sure about this?'

'Aye,' the dwarf said again. The Slayer's tattooed frame trembled with what might have been eagerness and his pace, never very swift, had nonetheless become inexorable.

'We don't need the money that badly, Gotrek,' Felix said, following the dwarf down through the rickety stands. The arena attached to the mountain trading post was made of convenient stones and hastily assembled planking and it groaned from the weight of the crowd. They were a mix of the worst from either side of the Gisoreux Gap, and there were accents from as far north as Kislev and as far south as Tobaro. The arena itself was simply a great crater of stone and wood with a thick woven net mounted over it.

Gotrek turned and glared at Felix. 'It's not about the money, manling,' he rasped. The haft of his axe creaked as his grip tightened. Felix stepped back.

'Gotrek, this–' he began. Gotrek turned and stamped away, his fiery crest of hair marking his path as effectively as a shark's fin. His massive hands, elbows and shoulders cleared his way through the crowd.

'Is perhaps not the wisest course,' Felix finished lamely. He looked down at the betting slip in his hand and shrugged. If the Slayer was determined to pit himself against the beast, there was little the poet could do to stop him.

They had been on their way to Bretonnia when the first stories of the so-called 'King of the Gap' had reached them. Beast-baiting, distasteful as it was, was quite common on both sides of the Gap and the longevity of the beast in question was measured in days, if not hours.

The King of the Gap had survived for three years.

The hippogryph squalled again and leapt into the air, striking the net that kept it trapped. It was a magnificent beast, despite the chaotic amalgamation of equine, avian and feline qualities. Old scars covered its once-glossy coat and the vibrant crimson plumage was dulled by age and grime. It dropped low and drove a massive shoulder into the heavy boards that separated it from the stands, snarling and squawking.

Long hunting spears were jabbed through the boards, driving the beast back. It sank to the arena and galloped around the circumference, trumpeting a challenge. That cry was answered by the blast of a hunting horn as the wooden portcullis was raised and Gotrek stalked into the ring.

Hippogryph and Slayer eyed each other for a moment. Gotrek raised his axe. The beast broke into a gallop. Gotrek dodged to the side, far quicker than his heavy frame would seem to allow, as the hippogryph's claws gouged the stone. A wing snapped out, nearly bowling the dwarf over. Gotrek's axe chopped down, shaving a tuft of hair from the monster's tail. A hoof shot out, catching Gotrek on the shoulder and Felix winced as he heard an audible 'pop'. The crowd bayed.

Gotrek grabbed his dislocated shoulder and snapped it back into place with barely a glimmer of effort. The hard-faced guards who worked for the trading post began to look unhappy. The outcome wasn't in doubt, but Felix wondered whether he and Gotrek would live to collect their winnings. The beast had made the owners of this trading post money for three years. They weren't going to be happy when Gotrek butchered it. He loosened his sword in its sheath.

The hippogryph shrieked and spun, lunging for the Slayer. Again Gotrek ducked, throwing himself between its legs. He popped up behind it, and Felix tensed. This was it.

Except that it wasn't.

Gotrek grabbed a handful of the hippogryph's feathers and jerked himself up onto its back. It began to thrash and buck, screaming wildly. Gotrek clung tightly to it. The crowd didn't seem to know what to make of it. Neither did Felix. His heart leapt into his throat when the hippogryph thrust itself into the air. Its wings beat like thunder as it rolled upwards. Gotrek held on with stoic determination.

The creature smashed itself into the nets and began to squall. Gotrek, trapped between the beast and the net, struggled to free his axe. The betting slip crumpled in Felix's hand and his mouth was dry. Gotrek's axe sprang free... and sliced through the net.

The crowd gave a collective moan as the hippogryph hurtled into the sky with a triumphant scream. Gotrek tumbled to the arena floor. Felix drew his sword and sliced through the boards separating it from the stands. He leapt down, rushing forwards as the Slayer struggled to his feet. The crowd was in chaos as the guards struggled to regain control, and a number of the latter were hurrying towards them, murder stamped on their faces. It looked like all bets were off.

'Gotrek, what did you do?' Felix said, as he and the dwarf faced the approaching guards.

'We should all be free to seek our own doom, manling.' Gotrek ran his thumb across his axe and squeezed a drop of blood from his thumb, flicking it at the approaching guards as he grinned wildly. 'Now, let's go help these fools with theirs, eh?'

KINEATER

Jordan Ellinger

An outraged shriek pierced the chill night air, and Felix looked up from where he sat by the caravan's cook-fire. From the pitch of the shriek, he guessed it was Talia, and not her older sister. The two Kislevite women had been at each other's throats since their carriage joined Zayed al Mahrak's caravan in Skabrand.

Anya flung open the carriage door and stormed into the snow. Slim as a rail, and with none of the feminine curves Felix had come to associate with northern women since his time with Ulrika, Anya was only slightly less beautiful than Talia, who pursued with her hands outstretched almost into claws, her face twisted into a snarl.

Anya stomped away from her sister, then lost her footing on the icy ground and nearly fell. Picking herself up, she suddenly noticed the ring of drovers and guards who regarded her from around the fire, many cradling wooden bowls filled with an aromatic Arabyan stew. Most stared, but big Akmal – no stranger to the serving wenches and harlots of Pigbarter – hooted lewdly. Embarrassed, she straightened and assumed a regal pose only to be bowled over moments later by her sister.

'This should be interesting,' muttered Gotrek from where he sat next to Felix. Much to old Zayed's distress, the dwarf had broached a half-keg of Pigbarter ale – a brew that the Slayer had pronounced weak but palatable – and was well on his way to finishing it.

It was good to see him take an interest in anything beyond the bottom of his stein, thought Felix. They had seen virtually no action since Zayed had hired ogre mercenaries as additional escorts in Skabrand, and Gotrek had fallen into something of a depression. Notorious places like Deathgate Pass and the Fallen City had passed without so much as a goblin raid, and the Slayer had begun to believe that the gods were conspiring against him. As much as Felix was embarrassed for the two Kislevite noblewomen who howled and scratched at each other like alley cats, he was glad to see his friend shake the cloud that had been hanging over him.

'How dare you write that, you bitch,' cried Talia, wrestling with her sister like a common street urchin. She gathered a double handful of snow from the ground nearby and mashed it into Anya's face. 'You daughter of a whore!'

'She's your mother too, you drunken fool,' Anya sputtered. Sliding on the snow, she shoved her sister aside and then regained her footing.

Talia clumsily rolled to her feet, swaying slightly. Apparently, Felix mused, Gotrek was not the only one deep in his cups. The younger sister's cheeks were as red as those of a brewmeister at the Festival of Sonnstill. She cursed richly in the Kislev language, then snatched up several wooden bowls from the food table and made as if to throw them.

Anya had come to her feet nearly as fast as Talia, but instead of shielding herself, she paled and simply stared open-mouthed at the mountainous shadow which loomed behind her sister.

Noting her surprise, Talia turned as well.

Vork Kineater, one of the few ogres that Felix could identify on sight, watched them from the shadows just beyond the firelight. A mountain of flesh nearly ten feet tall, he dwarfed a nearby caravan wagon. Thickly muscled arms bristling with coarse hairs were folded over his chest. A plate of crude metal the size of a man was secured to his torso by leather straps that girded his grossly distended belly. Kineater was apparently the leader of the ogre mercenaries, a position Felix suspected he'd earned through sheer bulk.

The brutes hadn't been with the caravan long, and old Zayed had given them strict orders to camp well away from the wagons so that they would not be tempted by the thought of a midnight snack of horseflesh. That an ogre – their leader no less! – had approached this close was a dangerous sign.

Felix rose, his hand instinctively finding Karaghul in its sheath, and sent a quick prayer to Sigmar that the ogre had merely wandered into this area of the camp by mistake. He was about as willing to fight an ogre as he was to have a double helping of Zayed's stew.

Kineater chuckled deep in his throat, an action that made his belly bounce like a tub of cheese curds. Arrogantly, he rolled his hand, as if he were watching gladiators and not noblewomen. 'Keep fighting,' he said, the words mashed by the yellowing tusks that jutted out from his protruding lower jaw.

Talia darkened like a storm and screeched, upending the bubbling stew pot with a two-handed push. The effort unbalanced her and she stumbled backwards, hitting Kineater's prodigious belly, and collapsed. She coughed once, and then retched all over the ogre's sandaled foot.

Nearly every man present winced. No one made a sound.

Kineater backed away, a confused expression on his face. He lifted his foot and shook it, unable to see beyond his gut plate, but clearly feeling the warm vomit slide between his toes. Another of the mountainous creatures had come up behind him, and Kineater turned, pointing at his foot.

'She shared food!'

Anya rushed to her sister's aid. The ogre turned back towards them, leaning down with a snot-encrusted face, a string of saliva hanging from his grizzled jaw. To her credit, Anya stood steadfastly before him, supporting her sister with an arm around her waist. Her refusal to cower before him seemed to anger Kineater.

'She shared food!' he roared.

'Enough!' Gotrek snatched up his axe and stomped across the campfire until he was standing in front of the ogre. The dwarf was many times smaller than the huge brute, but a tattooed Slayer with axe in hand was intimidating enough to give an avalanche pause. 'How can a dwarf drink with all this noise? You're souring my ale!'

Felix sighed, then drew his sword and joined the Slayer. It was rare for Gotrek to display a sense of chivalry; rare enough that Felix suspected that the Slayer was merely using the women as an opportunity to test his mettle against an ogre. Of course, even if Gotrek defeated Kineater, the rest of his troops would seek revenge and the Slayer could not fight them all.

What a way to end an epic! Gotrek Gurnisson, Slayer of daemons, killed by a hired ogre in the middle of nowhere. Of course, Felix wouldn't have to worry about writing said epic, since he would probably suffer the same fate.

Kineater's gaze darted between Talia and Gotrek. For a moment he tensed in readiness for combat, but seemed to think better of it. He struck the ground with his club, then turned and disappeared into the darkness with the rest of his band at his heels.

Felix let out an audible breath and lowered his blade. Around the Slayer, even mealtimes could be deadly. He looked over at the two sisters, but Anya was already halfway to her carriage, her sister's arm draped around her shoulders. Some thanks, but Felix had to admit that, with the state Talia was in, it made sense for Anya to hustle her back to their carriage as soon as possible.

Gotrek glared at the retreating ogres, and spat on the ground in disgust. 'Come, manling,' he said, returning to his spot by the fire. 'That ale won't drink itself.'

Felix had difficulty sleeping that night. The possibility of dying in a pointless brawl had reminded him how far he really was from home. Gotrek was obsessed with driving ever eastwards and Felix was honour-bound to follow, but he had never once thought his quest might take him as far as the Kingdom of the Dragon. The thought of leaving the Empire behind, perhaps never to return, was disquieting.

Mannslieb rode high in the night sky, and the full moon provided adequate light for writing, so he rose from his cot and stepped into the cool night air with his journal tucked under one arm. He found a spot near the fire, now no more than glowing embers in a pile of ash, and nodded to Hansur, the dark-skinned man from southern Ind who'd drawn first watch. The rest of the guards slept under dark woollen blankets, as close to the fire as they could get, so Felix picked a spot near the edge of the circle to avoid disturbing them. He had just opened his precious vial of iron gall ink and sharpened his quill when a shadow fell across his page.

'My thanks to you and the Slayer for standing up to Kineater,' said Anya. She raised her voice and looked meaningfully at Hansur. 'Especially when none of these dogs would.'

Hansur shrugged dismissively, then wandered off towards the rear of the camp, leaving them alone. A few of the men snored or turned in their sleep, but Felix was not surprised that, after a hard day's slog, they did not awaken.

'It was nothing,' he replied. Indeed, Gotrek had been the one to intervene. Felix had merely covered the Slayer's back, as he always did. On the other hand, none of it would have been necessary had Anya's sister not gone berserk. 'Your sister is quite... spirited.'

Anya made a sour face, then crossed her arms and looked towards

the fire, though Felix got the impression she was staring at something
far away.

'Spirited is not the word for it, I'm afraid. She's a real hellion. Some
years ago, she fell from the balcony of our rooms at the Golden Horn.
She had deep bruising around her temples and blood ran from her
eyes and ears. My family's *doktors* claimed that, though there was no
sign of mutation, the Ruinous Powers had claimed her. Her behaviour, much the same as you saw tonight, seemed to bear out those
suspicions.'

Anya shuddered and drew her shawl close around her shoulders. 'I
had heard of a small sect of Cathayan monks who were said to special-
ise in just such injuries as my sister suffered. Rather than give her up
to damnation or the pyre, I volunteered to bring her to them. Perhaps
they can help her to master whatever daemon possesses her, and my
sister will be returned to me.'

Felix had experience with the doktors of Praag, when he and Gotrek
had helped to defend the walls during the great siege. If they had failed
to treat Talia, he saw little chance that Cathayan monks would succeed. Still, were he in Anya's place he too might have grasped at straws.

'Please, join me,' he said with a polite smile. He dragged another
log close by, anchored it in the snow and then brushed it off with his
sleeve. 'I don't think we've been introduced. My name is Felix Jaeger.'

She held out a hand. It was a formal gesture, but the corners of her
mouth curled into a smile.

'Anya Nitikin.'

Felix's eyes widened. 'Nitikin? *The* Anya Nitikin? Author of *Call of
the South*?'

'The same.'

Felix rose quickly, embarrassed to find himself still seated. He had
never expected to meet one of the finest writers in the Empire; though
she was Kislevite, Anya Nitikin wrote in Reikspiel and not Kislevarin,
and the people of the Empire had come to think of her as one of their
own.

'I'm sorry, I had no idea. We used to study your work in Altdorf. I
thought–'

He stopped himself quickly.

'...that I would be older?' she said, completing his sentence. 'I've
heard that before.' She tucked her dress under her legs and sat, then
adjusted her pleats. 'You used to study my work?' she asked. 'Are you
a writer?'

'A poet actually, though it's been years since I've published.' He realised he was still holding his quill, and blushed. 'Please excuse me while I put these things away.'

She nodded, so he quickly stoppered the ink vial and placed it alongside his quill in the velvet case that, after Karaghul, was his most treasured possession.

'Why did you stop publishing?' she asked.

Felix smiled wryly. 'I swore an oath to record the death of an unkillable dwarf in an epic poem.'

'Unkillable?'

'So far.' He shrugged, looking over at Gotrek. In spite of the cold, the Slayer slept bare-chested on top of his bedroll. He snorted in his sleep, then rubbed the side of his nose and turned over. 'It has been years,' Felix continued. 'I fear that whatever promise I might once have shown has long since faded.'

'Is that your work?' asked Anya, indicating the small, leather-bound journal he had set aside. 'May I read it?'

'It's just notes, really,' said Felix. 'After so many years I feared that I was forgetting some of the important details of the Slayer's journey.'

She held out her hand. 'I would love to take a look.'

Reluctantly, Felix handed her the journal. It was prose, not poetry, and rough at that... But on the other hand he hadn't thought about literature in so many years that he found himself looking forward to a little recognition from a fellow artist.

'Well,' said Anya dryly, after leafing through a few pages, 'I didn't expect that. It's really nothing more than a penny dreadful.' Her finger stabbed down onto a page. 'Here, you have a giant six times the height of a man, despite the fact that any such creature would collapse under its own weight. And "ratmen"? They're nothing more than a myth!'

Felix stiffened.

A penny dreadful? From his lofty perch as a poet in Altdorf he'd looked down on those books, filled as they were with nothing but lurid stories, scandalously illustrated on cheap paper. Now Anya Nitikin, one of the most popular authors in the Empire, was looking down on *him*. His cheeks burned with shame and he snatched back the journal.

'They're just notes...' he muttered.

Any further artistic debate they might have had was cut short by a distant scream, followed by a deep and rumbling belch. Several more belches echoed from elsewhere in the middle-distance, deep and loud enough that not even Gotrek on his drunkest day could have produced them.

The ogres were signalling to each other.

His anger forgotten, Felix hastily slid the journal into his pack and pushed Anya behind him. There were very few reasons for ogres to signal in the dead of night: either something was attacking the caravan, or it was the ogres themselves who were attacking.

A hunk of twisted flesh and rags flew over the stacked barrels at the edge of the clearing, landing in the embers of the fire. Felix knew, even before the reek of scorching hair reached him, that it was Hansur. 'Gotrek!' he cried. 'The ogres are attacking!'

As he turned, a dark shape loomed up behind the barrels. Roaring a challenge, an ogre emerged into the flickering light of the campfire and uprooted a dead tree with a single tug. Swinging it like a club in an almost casual arc, he struck the stack, and a heavy barrel bounced through the campsite, crushing two men before they'd even had a chance to rise from their cots.

The ogre followed the barrel into the clearing, leading with its prodigious gut. It was not Kineater, the one who'd laughed at them earlier – this ogre wore a leather mask over its face that left only its beady eyes and gaping maw visible. A necklace of dried heads adorned its neck, their hair woven together into a cord. It might have been smaller than the first ogre, Felix thought, but not by much.

It smashed a dazed guard, still struggling from his bedroll, then rounded on Felix, raising its club for an overhead blow. 'Humans die!'

'Run!' Felix yelled over his shoulder to Anya, before diving out of the way of the mighty club. The tree trunk smashed into the ground where he'd stood, breaking up the frozen sod and flinging clumps of snow to either side.

Felix drew Karaghul and stabbed at the mounds of flab and muscle that hung from the creature's arm, but he barely drew blood. Nevertheless the ogre howled, and spun with amazing speed, heaving itself forwards. Its metal belly plate, adorned with crude toothy glyphs, loomed in Felix's vision and once more he was forced to hurl himself aside or be crushed.

Elsewhere in the camp the caravan guards were fighting back, but Felix could see at least four more ogres stomping between them, swatting left and right with their clubs. Further away, horses screamed in their pens as an ogre slaughtered them mercilessly.

More dark and looming shapes attacked the wagons, and for a moment, Felix thought he saw Talia standing on top of her carriage, defending herself against a howling ogre with a large kitchen knife.

The only spot of real resistance centred on Gotrek. The Slayer's red mohawk and tattooed chest were clearly visible in the moonlight as he faced down a huge brute that carried a club ringed with iron bands. Rusted chains encircled both its arms, running up its shoulders to a metal collar that was barely visible under folds of flab at its neck.

The Slayer's axe whirled before him, but there was precious little he could target. Much like the ogre Felix faced, this one wore a metal plate on its stomach, and it kept this between itself and Gotrek's axe. The ogre's armour was impenetrable... But Felix wondered, what held the armour to the ogre?

Adrenaline surging in his veins, Felix ducked under the masked ogre's next swing and sprinted towards Gotrek. He slid to a stop just behind the massive chained ogre and swung his blade – not at the beast itself, but at its belly straps.

Leather parted and then snapped. Gotrek whooped as the belly plate sagged and then fell to the ground. The Slayer hewed out with his axe and opened a wide cut in the ogre's gut, spilling its steaming innards into the snow.

'Good work, manling!' Gotrek yelled over the howls of the dying ogre. 'Now stay out of my way!' With that the dwarf charged the ogre with the leather facemask, who was rapidly closing the distance between them.

Working together, Gotrek attacking from the front and Felix slicing the leather straps on the ogre's flanks, they dispatched it too in short order. By the time it had collapsed to the ground, the battle was over.

The ogres had retreated.

The campsite was a mess. Men moved between their fallen brethren, tending to the wounded and putting those with crushed limbs or staved-in chests out of their misery with merciful blade strokes. Some of the soldiers carried torches out into the frozen darkness, seeking to corral wagon horses that had broken their traces and fled in panic.

Zayed al Mahrak, the caravan's diminutive Arabyan master, had emerged from whatever hole he'd found in which to hide during the battle, and was now inspecting the damage to his merchandise. He moved from shattered crate to shattered crate, stepping gingerly to avoid patches of red, blood-crusted snow.

'Where's Anya?' Felix asked Gotrek. He'd lost track of her, but hoped that she'd found a safe place to wait out the fighting. Or did he? He remembered her look of scorn when she'd read his journal. He was surprised at how much it had stung – more than any review he'd received for his poetry in the past.

The Slayer cleaned his axe with a handful of snow, and strapped it to his back. 'You know women. She'll probably return with the horses,' he said with a shrug.

Felix didn't see her amongst the wounded, so he guessed she'd fled to her carriage. He knew he should check on her, but he didn't feel that he could face her just yet. A sudden thought occurred to him. 'Gotrek,' he asked. 'What do *you* think of my poetry?'

The Slayer looked utterly bemused, but before he could answer, Anya Nitikin strode out of the darkness, cursing richly. She swept past Gotrek and Felix, and slapped Zayed on the cheek. Hard.

'This!' she said, her teeth clenched. 'This is how you spend our good Kislevite gold? On mercenaries? Your ogres have taken my sister and it is your fault!'

'My fault?' responded the old man, rubbing his cheek. Anya had left a red mark on his dark skin. 'Ogres are the most loyal mercenaries gold can buy. Kineater is himself a Tyrant, responsible for the reputation of his tribe. If the recent attack on Middenheim by the forces of Chaos had not disrupted almost all trade between the Empire and Cathay, I could not have hired him at any price.'

'Any merchant who'd trust an ogre with his goods deserves what he gets,' said Gotrek. 'No dwarf would attack the caravan he'd pledged to guard.'

'That may be, but I'd already employed every dwarf in Pigbarter,' Zayed shot back. Of course, there had only been one dwarf in the trading town – Gotrek himself.

'Obviously, something has given this "Kinita" cause to disregard Goldtooth's order.'

'No, lass, it's *Kineater*,' said Gotrek gruffly. 'He probably ate his whole family to earn that name.'

'I care not.' Anya's gaze swept over the nearby guards, who suddenly busied themselves with various mundane tasks. She rounded on the caravan master with eyes of iron. 'Gather your men. We launch a rescue mission at first light.'

'That is impossible,' Zayed said with a sigh, 'Can you not see the carnage around you? My men are injured and our horses slaughtered. Without our escort, we are at the mercy of bandits and worse. As soon as we are able, we make for Cathay by the safest roads.'

Anya's cheeks reddened. It was obvious she had no patience left. 'No. You will not leave my sister in the hands of those brutes.'

As much as Felix abhorred the idea of leaving Talia to Kineater's mercy, he saw Zayed's point. 'Only a madman would track a tribe of ogres into the Mountains of Mourn on the faint hope that they won't eat their captive at the first stop,' he said. 'Even if your sister is still alive, we're simply too few to pose any serious threat to them.'

'Hold your tongue, Jaeger!' Anya's hand cut the air like a knife. 'My sister is alive. If Kineater's lot were looking for food they would have taken the horses, not slaughtered them,' said Anya. 'This is a kidnapping, not a robbery or a hunt.'

Zayed only spread his hands helplessly. 'Nevertheless...' he mumbled.

Anya would not be dissuaded. 'If you won't help me,' she said, 'then at least allow me to recruit volunteers from amongst your men.'

Zayed's eyes hardened and he crossed his arms. 'You are welcome to ask, but you won't find anyone foolish enough to volunteer for such a mission.'

Felix's jaw tightened at the sound of Gotrek's voice.

'I'll bring your sister back.' The Slayer's eye glittered in the torchlight. 'My axe thirsts for Kineater's blood. The coward waited until I was in my bed to attack and if there is one thing here that I object to, it's meeting my doom in my sleep.'

Anya waited for more volunteers, but not even one of the hired men would meet her gaze. At last, she sneered at them and turned back to the Slayer. 'Thank you, Gotrek Gurnisson. If there is even a shred of truth in the stories Herr Jaeger records in his journals, you two will more than suffice.'

To Zayed's distress, Anya had suggested that they ride, but in order to forestall any confrontation with Gotrek, Felix had quickly pointed out that riders would make an easy target for ogre hunters. Better to follow on foot and remain hidden as long as possible.

He regretted that suggestion now.

Though they followed a wide swathe of compacted snow and chewed horse bones left by the ogres, a thin crust of ice had settled on the ground, making the journey treacherous. Worse still, without horses they were forced to carry their supplies on their backs – and, as no one had any idea where the ogres were heading, that meant several days of rations and enough wood to start a fire in a blizzard.

Even Anya carried a pack, showing surprising strength for such a slender woman. She trudged stoically behind them, wrapped in furs cut in the latest Kislev fashion. When she spoke at all, it was in short, breathy utterances through a purple scarf that covered the lower half of her face.

As the sun sank towards the mountaintops, Gotrek slowed his pace until he trotted along beside them. 'We're being followed, manling,' he said gruffly, keeping his gaze on the path ahead of them.

Felix had to consciously resist looking up into the hills. Could Kine-ater have left sentries behind? Surely he could not have expected a rescue mission. Felix hadn't expected it himself.

'Ogres?'

Gotrek grunted. 'No. Even you with your dim eyes would have spotted an ogre.'

Felix ignored the jibe. 'One of Zayed's guards, then?'

'A goblin.'

'A *gnoblar*,' Anya corrected him, keeping her voice low. 'Cousins of the grobi, to be certain, but a separate race. They are both food and slaves to the ogres. If this one has fled the cooking pot, it could very well be our ally.'

'No dwarf would ally himself with a goblin,' said Gotrek, vehemently.

'Our prisoner then,' said Anya.

'How do you suggest we capture it?' asked Felix.

'The caravan guards call them "magpies" because they dart up and down the length of a caravan, stealing anything that's not nailed down. Theft is a racial obsession for them. I suggest we camp here for the night,' she said, unshouldering her pack and letting it thump to the ground. 'I have a plan.'

The moon had not even risen when Felix heard a stealthy presence creeping into the clearing. Anya had 'forgotten' a hunk of dried beef just at the edge of their campsite. To sweeten the trap, she'd unclipped her jade earrings and placed them in a compartment of her backpack, being as obvious as possible about it.

At the sound of icy rustling nearby, Felix cracked an eyelid. A small green creature, slightly larger than a goblin, fumbled with the knot Anya had tied in her backpack. It froze as Gotrek shifted in his cot, waiting patiently until the dwarf's breathing steadied once more before resuming its work.

With Anya's earrings clutched in its tiny fingers, it turned to scurry back into the night. Felix tensed, but waited until it came within arm's reach before hurling himself bodily at it.

Its reactions were lightning fast, and he barely caught hold of one of its arms. Though nothing but skin and bones, the gnoblar displayed surprising strength, squealing and gnashing at its captor. It had almost freed itself when it caught sight of Gotrek, who'd hurled his blanket aside almost as soon as Felix had made his lunge. The creature's struggles ceased as it became paralysed with fear. Still, Felix had no doubt that if he relaxed his guard for even a second, it would slip off into the darkness and disappear.

Anya knelt in front of the creature, keeping well away from its claws. 'Who is your ogre, gnoblar?'

'Let Cabbage go and Cabbage will tell you,' it whined.

'Cabbage?' asked Felix.

Anya looked up at him. 'Gnoblars are a superstitious bunch. They tend to pick names for themselves that might dissuade an ogre from eating them.'

'Cabbage?' Felix asked again.

'Why eat Cabbage when tasty granite lies nearby?' squealed the gnoblar. Anya laughed and even Gotrek smirked a little. Felix had never minded the taste of a nicely boiled *kohl*, but he knew that Gotrek hated it with a passion.

Without warning, the gnoblar twisted in Felix's grasp and bit down hard on his wrist, just beneath the cuff of his mail. Felix yelped and jerked his hand away, accidentally giving Cabbage just enough leeway to pull free. In a heartbeat, he had darted past Anya towards the darkness at the edge of the camp.

Only Gotrek stood between Cabbage and freedom, but he had a Slayer's reflexes. He lunged out, snatching the gnoblar by the scruff of his neck and shaking him. A mad smile curled his lip. 'Bite me, gnoblar, and I'll pull your head off.'

Cabbage gulped and went limp. Gotrek shook him once more for emphasis then set him down well inside the range of his axe.

'I no run,' Cabbage said, looking contrite.

'Could have fooled me,' responded Gotrek.

'Let's hear him out,' said Felix, massaging his wrist where Cabbage had bitten him. It was tender, but thankfully the skin was unbroken. Judging from the size of Cabbage's incisors, he could have easily inflicted real damage had he intended to.

Cabbage nodded furiously. 'Yes, yes. Gutsnorter want Cabbage find tasty-mens...' He paused, scratching his bald head. He grunted and snuffled to himself in what Felix assumed was the ogre tongue. Surprisingly, Anya responded with a similar series of barks, and his little eyes lit up. 'Lady speak ogre?'

Anya nodded and knelt in front of the creature, and they began to converse in the gnoblar's odd language.

As the conversation went on, Felix had more and more difficulty hiding a smile. He'd never heard the language spoken by a human before: coming from Cabbage, it sounded halfway natural; from a distinguished noblewoman like Anya Nitikin, it sounded like she was trying to talk while slurping cold soup. On several occasions, she burped mid-sentence and Felix had to stifle a laugh. He hated himself for his childish sense of humour, but by the end of the conversation, even Gotrek had let out a few throaty chuckles.

'Cabbage did indeed seek us out,' said Anya at length, not noticing Felix and Gotrek's poorly disguised mirth. 'His master is one of Kineater's remaining relatives named Gutsnorter. Gutsnorter claims that Kineater has gone mad.' Anya paused, a bitter expression on her face. 'He wants to marry my sister.'

Gotrek let out an incredulous laugh. 'An ogre marry a human? That's like Felix marrying a sliced ham.'

Felix blinked, about to interject, but Anya beat him to it. 'I'll thank you not to compare my sister to a sliced ham,' she said, regarding the Slayer coldly. 'Kineater is a Tyrant, and though one of the other ogres could challenge him for leadership of the tribe, he's too powerful.' Anya stood and stepped away from Cabbage. 'They say that no ogre worth his salt can see past his own belly. When he steps on a splinter, he must have a gnoblar remove it. This is how Gutsnorter thinks.'

Felix scratched his head. 'So in Gutsnorter's mind, your sister is the splinter and we are the gnoblars.'

Gotrek grunted in disgust. 'I'd like to put my axe in Gutsnorter's mind.'

'Gutsnorter,' continued Anya, ignoring the interruption, 'is especially devious for an ogre, and has come up with a plan for us to rescue my sister.'

At this point Cabbage chimed in. 'Cabbage take tasty-mens through secret ways. We sneaks through kitchen and meets Gutsnorter. He steals nasty-bride from Kineater, then tasty-mens takes her away.'

Felix sighed. 'That's the plan? The food is supposed to break into the kitchen?'

Anya shrugged. 'For an ogre, it's brilliant.'

Cabbage's 'secret ways' turned out to be an old cave-bear dwelling near a scree-covered escarpment at the foot of a mountain. The cave had a wide mouth, clogged with the remains of its former occupant as well as shreds of fur and bone, rotten planks of wood, and even half a caravan wheel. Moisture dripped from the tips of stalactites onto piles of detritus.

The smell of mould and mildew was powerful enough that Anya retrieved a silken handkerchief from her pack, daubed it with fragrant oil, and held it over her mouth and nose. It appeared that they were entering the ogres' kitchen through the waste chute.

Cabbage had no problem clambering over the piles of refuse, but Gotrek grumbled, muttering words to the effect that 'only an ogre would befoul a perfectly good tunnel'. Anya followed the Slayer and Felix took the rear, eyeing the shadows uneasily. Cabbage couldn't be the only gnoblar who knew about these tunnels, and he half expected to see one of the scrawny green creatures dart out of some hidden nook screaming an alarm to its masters.

The tunnel soon sloped upwards towards a half-circle of light far above them. The floor became slick with some foul sludge whose origins Felix tried hard not to guess. At first, Anya hiked up her skirt to keep it out of the muck, but as they trudged ever upwards and balance became more precarious, she gave up and let the hem drag in the gunk.

Felix followed close behind her, his thoughts as dark as their surroundings. Anya's almost casual dismissal of his journal had affected him more than he cared to admit. For the first time since his university days, he found himself questioning his own abilities as a writer. Anya was smart, beautiful, spoke at least three languages with ease, and her books were famed from Wissenland to Ostermark. Felix was... well, he'd enjoyed some small success in Altdorf, but surely after all this time he had been forgotten.

He winced to think of how arrogant he'd been to claim Gotrek's epic for himself. The Slayer deserved someone better. He deserved someone like Anya.

'Anya,' he said. 'I–'

'Quiet, tasty-mens,' Cabbage hissed out of the darkness, 'or Rumble-belly will hear us.'

Gotrek clutched his axe tightly, his face twisted into a snarl as he trotted along beside Felix. 'If he calls me a man one more time, I'll feed him to my axe.'

The tunnel levelled out, broadening into a dimly lit chamber that reeked of peppery spice and spoiled meat. Dozens of dark shapes hung from chains around a large oven that Felix was glad to see was empty; there was no telling what horrors might have been cooking within, otherwise.

Cabbage darted across the room then waited for them at the far entrance. Caught off guard by the gnoblar's haste, Felix hurried to follow, bumping into one of the hanging shapes and recoiling in disgust. A fleshy, bloodshot eye stared back at him; it was the corpse of a caravan horse. He shuddered, and then caught up with Cabbage.

It quickly became apparent that the 'kitchen' was actually a cave halfway up the mountain slope. Spread out in the valley below them was the ogre settlement.

It was one of the largest collections of tents and shacks Felix had seen outside of an army camp. They carpeted the valley floor: huge triangular structures made from the crudely cut skins of giant mountain beasts. The snow around them had been trampled into a disgusting yellow-brown slurry spotted with unidentifiable lumps of bone, or worse.

Near the edge of the settlement was a fenced-off area where junk piles were sorted by material – iron with iron, wood with wood – and a wild contraption that resembled nothing more than a catapult rose from between the stacks. The hide of something that looked disturbingly like a dark-skinned man was stretched as tight as a drum on an elaborate structure made of bone and sinew. A gnoblar was painting it with a sticky substance that might have been a kind of dye.

The only permanent dwelling was a haphazardly constructed rectangle of boulders roofed with a ship's mast and a patched sail, despite the fact that the closest body of water was hundreds of leagues away. A team of shaggy rhinoxen was yoked outside, grunting and snorting at any gnoblar unlucky enough to pass too close.

'No guards?' said Gotrek, surveying the surrounding peaks.

'If they mean to hold the ceremony tonight, they will be dozing in their tents,' said Anya.

As they watched, an ogre emerged from one of the tents. Greasy black cords of hair hung from its balding pate, and it wore a white apron in a crude mockery of an Altdorf chef.

'Rumblebelly,' whispered Cabbage with a shiver.

Most of the gnoblars apparently gave Rumblebelly a wide berth, being especially careful of the notched steel cleaver he carried, but a dozen gnoblar minions followed close behind him carrying various foodstuffs, cracked dishes and bent utensils, and slabs of meat large enough that two together had to carry them on their backs.

But that was not what drew Felix's attention. Several gnoblars near the back dragged a prisoner in their wake.

'Talia!' Anya cried softly. The gnoblars led the younger Nitikin sister by a leash of thick hemp rope which bound her wrists together. Talia was not giving them an easy time of it. She seemed to be especially fond of lulling them into complacency and then tugging sharply on the rope to jerk them off their feet. Though the gnoblars cursed her roundly, they dared not lay a finger on the Tyrant's future bride.

Eventually, they disappeared into a large tent at the edge of the camp. Judging from the crimson stain in the snow just outside, it had been only recently vacated by its former occupant.

Rumblebelly moved towards several rough-hewn tables which surrounded a deep pit in the centre of the camp. Felix guessed the pit would play a part in the ceremony, since most of the activity was centered there. Already the feasting tables were stacked high with putrid dishes.

Anya noticed his fascination. 'That pit is a tribute to the ogre god, the Great Maw. Any ogre may challenge Kineater for control of the tribe, and such challenges are frequent at events such as this. Challengers have merely to descend into the pit and face him, unarmed and unarmoured, in single combat.' She paused to swallow, her face grim. 'The winner eats the loser.'

'Where's your ogre, grobi?' asked Gotrek, impatiently. The Slayer sounded almost hopeful that Gutsnorter would abandon them and they would be forced to hack their way through the camp.

Cabbage blinked short-sightedly and shielded his eyes from the sun. 'Can't see mighty Gutsnorter.'

'Fine then,' said Anya. 'We'll rescue Talia without him.'

Felix winced. To even get near Talia, they would have to sneak through a swarm of gnoblars, not to mention bypassing the infamous Rumblebelly. 'Are you sure that's wise?' he asked.

Anya pushed herself from their rocky perch and headed back into the kitchen.

'Of course. I have a plan of my own.'

Felix crouched behind the boulders at the base of the slope that led to the kitchen. A gnoblar sentry – if it could even be called that – sat on a nearby rock, watching the preparations not five paces in front of him. It yawned, its enormous nose rising skywards, then scratched its rear and flatulated almost silently. Felix thanked Sigmar that the filthy little creature was more interested in what was going on inside the camp than outside of it.

A few paces away, Anya placed a bag of red powder into Cabbage's hands, whispering to him in the ogre dialect while Gotrek looked on, disgusted.

'Any plan that relies on a gnoblar isn't fit for a dwarf,' he grumbled, but remained where he was.

Privately, Felix agreed with him. He didn't trust Cabbage, and he disliked the fact that the gnoblar's vaunted patron, Gutsnorter, had apparently disappeared. Anya had explained that any gnoblar without an ogre patron usually ended up in the cooking pot. As time had passed and Gutsnorter still did not appear, Cabbage had grown visibly nervous. Now, the gnoblar seemed to disagree with the set of instructions he was receiving and shook his head vigorously, pushing the bag back into Anya's hands.

Suddenly all of the rage and impotence Felix had been feeling since the attack on the caravan, and all of the frustration and resentment towards Anya for insulting his work, boiled to the surface. He pushed himself close to Cabbage until he was eye-to-eye with the terrified creature.

'Listen, you filthy little scallywag,' he hissed, barely restraining himself to a venomous whisper. 'You led us into this mess, and you'll lead us out again. You think being eaten by an ogre is bad? When I'm done with you, there won't be enough left for an appetiser.'

Cabbage snivelled loudly, his dark eyes wide with terror. For a moment, Felix thought he might forget the plan entirely and run, squealing, into the camp, but instead the gnoblar snatched up the bag and stepped out into the open.

'Scallywag?' asked Gotrek, arching his eyebrow.

Felix said nothing. He was a little embarrassed by his outburst. Throwing tantrums wasn't his department – it was Gotrek's.

Shivering like a beanpole in a high wind, Cabbage proceeded into the camp, clutching the bag to his chest. He skirted the feasting tables and the oblivious Rumblebelly with his cleaver, instead heading towards the pair of shaggy white rhinoxen. Though he drew a curious eye from some of the other gnoblars, Rumblebelly ignored him.

It occurred to Felix that despite sending Cabbage on his way, he had no idea what was in the bag, so he asked Anya.

'Just some noxious powder I found in the kitchen,' she said with a grin. 'Ogres may be stupid, but they take their meals seriously enough to recognise a good spice when they loot one.'

'What good will that do?' asked Felix.

Anya smiled mischievously. 'Watch.'

Cabbage now stood directly under the flaring nostrils of the closest rhinoxen. It shook its shaggy head and a long pink tongue snaked out to lick at its own snout. It smelled the spice, and didn't like it. Cabbage looked back towards them nervously.

Gotrek grinned evilly and ran a thumb along the blade of his axe.

Cabbage immediately deflated and Felix didn't blame him. The blood of brave men ran cold when the Slayer bared his teeth.

The gnoblar turned back towards the rhinoxen, shrugged, and then swung the bag in a wide arc right at the beast's nose. Red powder exploded into the air, swirling around them both, and Cabbage scampered out of sight.

The beast and its mate bellowed and reared up into the air, then leapt forwards, straining at their harnesses. The chain that stretched from their collars to the central mast-pillar of the storage building pulled taut, and the crack of splitting wood rent the air – the pillar shifted, bringing the building's patched-sail roof canopy collapsing down. The crash of the mast hitting the ground only goaded the rhinoxen to new levels of terror, and they stampeded straight towards Rumblebelly and his tables full of food.

The massive ogre merely grunted and casually tossed one of the tables aside, then set himself to receive the charge. In a feat of strength the likes of which Felix had never seen before, Rumblebelly grabbed one of the charging rhinoxen by the horn and forced its head down into the icy ground, and then cupped his fists together and brought them down hard upon the back of the other beast, snapping its spine in one blow.

'Stay here,' Felix shouted to Anya, struggling to be heard over the commotion. She nodded, stepping back under cover.

Once she was safe, Gotrek and Felix dashed over to the tent where the gnoblars had taken Talia, and Felix drew Karaghul as he approached the entrance. He reached for the flap, but Gotrek beat him to it, lowering a shoulder and barreling right through the opening.

A dozen gnoblars awaited them, screeching in alarm as the Slayer burst in. Gotrek laid about himself with his axe, felling four of the diminutive creatures in a heartbeat.

Assuming his traditional position just behind the Slayer, Felix stabbed out, disembowelling a screaming green body and then batting aside another gnoblar's primitive club with a quick parry. A third enemy assailed him, its face covered in greasy pink powder that he supposed could only have been makeup. Felix parried a dagger thrust and returned with one of his own, and the gnoblar reeled backwards, its eye a wounded wreck. He quickly put it out of its misery.

'Is that all?' asked Gotrek. He stood atop a small heap of dismembered gnoblar bodies with blood spattered up and down his naked chest, darkening his fiery red beard.

Talia was gagged and lashed to a chair on the far side of the hut. Her dress was torn and she was smeared with the same awful smelling substance the pink gnoblar had worn. As ridiculous as she looked, there was still fire in her eyes.

Felix quickly crossed to her and pulled down her gag. 'Can you walk?'

'I walked here, didn't I?' she snapped.

Obviously, anger was Talia's way of coping with a stressful situation, and after years of dealing with Gotrek, Felix had developed a thick skin. Still, he struggled to hide his annoyance as he undid her bonds. If she was this scathing in the midst of a rescue, how would she be on the long walk home?

Gotrek stood at the entrance, peering out into the settlement. 'We're too late, manling. Kineater's finally hauled himself out of his den.'

As Rumblebelly had set about the fallen rhinoxen with his cleaver to the hooting delight of his gnoblar assistants, their rescue attempt had gone completely unnoticed. But now ogres had begun streaming out of their tents to gather for the ceremony, enormous slabs of fat and muscle armed with bone clubs and metal scimitars the size of a man.

Kineater had emerged from the largest tent, a head taller at least than any other ogre. The Tyrant cursed when he saw the destruction and waddled towards Rumblebelly, who stood over the rhinoxen corpses. If Gotrek and Felix didn't hurry, their escape route would be cut off.

'I'll hold them back while you get the girl to safety.' Gotrek's single eye gleamed madly and he ran a thumb along the edge of his axe, drawing blood.

'The girl?' asked Talia sharply.

Felix ignored her. The Slayer was thinking of a glorious death, but even he couldn't hold off the entire tribe. He cast a quick look out of the tent flap. It might just be possible to stick to the edge of the camp and keep as many tents between them and Kineater as possible. If they were quick enough perhaps they could manage an escape without being seen.

'I know what you're thinking, manling,' Gotrek growled. 'And I'm telling you, no dwarf should steal out of camp like a common thief.' He followed up with a Khalazid curse for good measure.

'You swore to return Talia to her sister,' Felix argued, appealing to Gotrek's sense of honour. The Slayer had never broken a vow in his life and Felix gambled that he wouldn't start now. 'I'm certain there will be enough glorious doom for all of us, should the ogres choose to pursue.'

Gotrek glared at him balefully for a long moment, then spat on the floor. 'Fine. We'll do this your way. But I'll remember this, manling.'

Most of the ogres were already engaged in bullish shows of strength and bravado among themselves, and so the three of them were able to pass through the camp without raising a cry of alarm. On the single occasion that they were spotted by a squeaking gnoblar sentry, Talia had slit its throat with Felix's dagger before he'd even been aware that she'd taken it.

After what seemed like a fraught eternity, they reached the edge of the line of dwellings. Anya had come much closer to meet them, and now crouched behind a large rocky outcrop a dozen yards away. Felix surveyed the open ground between them – cover was sparse, and if any member of the tribe so much as glanced in their direction, they would be seen.

'There's nothing for it,' he said grimly. 'We run.'

'You first,' the Slayer sulked.

Felix shook his head. 'We all go together.'

Just as they began their mad dash for Anya's hiding place they heard a high-pitched screech of rage and horror. Food dishes still lay scattered around the pit in the centre of the settlement, and Cabbage stood amidst them, gibbering incoherently.

Felix strained to see what the gnoblar was looking at, and then cursed under his breath.

It was a boiled ogre head. Now they knew why Gutsnorter hadn't met them.

Cabbage blinked and then looked around, shoulders hunching in fear. Felix remembered what Anya had told him about gnoblars without a patron. He felt a brief moment of pity as Cabbage cast frantically about himself. Then their eyes met, and the gnoblar lifted a finger, stabbing in their direction.

'Tasty-mens! Tasty-mens steal Tyrant's bride!'

Caught in the open halfway between the tents and the rocks, there was nowhere to hide. Rumblebelly's head swung up from his work, and his cleaver followed. Kineater bellowed in rage and stomped towards them, his belly swaying left and right as he charged.

'I'll deal with them,' said Gotrek, wheeling around. 'Get Talia and Anya back to old Zayed's caravan.' He took a step towards the charging ogres and banged the flat of his axe against his chest. 'Come feel the bite of my axe, grobi-lovers!'

Not even the Slayer could prevail against a whole camp of ogres, but he might be able to hold them off long enough for Felix and the Nitikin sisters to escape. Ogres were dangerous, but slow. Even in the mountains, Felix was confident he could reach Zayed's caravan before Kineater and his warriors did, especially if Gotrek was able to bring down the Tyrant first. That would provoke a leadership contest which would–

Felix's eyes widened, and he stared at the pit.

A plan, a plan so insane that Cabbage himself might have come up with it, flared in his mind. If this didn't work, Anya would be the only one left to write Gotrek's epic, because Felix would be as dead as his companion. But there was no alternative. He had to try it.

Steeling his courage, he stepped in front of Gotrek.

'What are you doing?' demanded the Slayer.

Felix couldn't suppress a mad grin. It wasn't often that Gotrek was surprised. Then the reality of what he was about to do hit him, and it was all he could do to keep his voice from quavering.

'Gotrek Gurnisson challenges Vork Kineater to a guts-out pit fight for leadership of the tribe!' shouted Felix.

'What are you doing, manling?' asked the Slayer again.

In the bluster of their charge, the ogres didn't hear him, so he shouted again at the top of his lungs. This time, he had an effect.

Kineater slowed his run as the meaning of Felix's challenge penetrated his thick skull. Several more ogres stomped up, including Rumblebelly. Suddenly Gotrek and Felix were surrounded by a sea of flab and muscle and tusks. Felix came up no further than the belly of the shortest ogre. He felt childish and weak, and it was all he could do to keep from bolting in fear.

'Do you accept the challenge?' he yelled, doing his best to sound fearless.

Kineater put a hand on his hips and laughed deep in his belly. It was an avalanche of sound, like rocks grinding over each other. Finally he glared down at Gotrek. 'You wanna wrestle Kineater?' he asked incredulously.

Gotrek glared at Felix suspiciously. 'Aye.'

Kineater's eyes narrowed thoughtfully. Felix could tell that the Tyrant had some experience with dwarfs, perhaps with the Chaos dwarfs who had once been rumoured to have burrowed beneath these very mountains. Kineater had not ascended to the position of Tyrant by brute force alone.

'Little dwarf cannot challenge Kineater,' he said, looking at

Rumblebelly for support, 'cause he got no ogre blood in 'im.'

Grunts of agreement sounded from the mass of ogres, and one or two of them burped hungrily.

Gotrek raised his axe and assumed a fighting stance. 'Nice try, manling.'

Felix's mind raced. His eyes fell on a nearby dish. Not allowing himself time to think about what he was doing, he snatched up a morsel of food from the ground and gave it to Gotrek. 'Eat this.'

'By Grungni's beard, manling, have you lost your mind?' Gotrek exclaimed. 'I could smell the rot on this "banquet" from halfway up the mountain!'

Felix gulped, and looked up at the assembled ogres. Their confusion had kept Gotrek and Felix from being eaten thus far, but soon that confusion would give way to anger, and then a fight would be inevitable.

'Gotrek,' he begged. 'Please. Trust me.'

Reluctantly, the Slayer took the morsel and bit into it. 'Ach, it tastes foul. What is it?'

'Gutsnorter's finger,' Felix mumbled. He hastily turned back to the assembled ogres, half expecting to feel Gotrek's axe in his back. 'There! He's got some ogre in him, so accept the challenge, you cowardly heap of rhinox dung.'

'Guts out' meant that neither participant in the challenge could wear armour of any sort. Four gnoblars stripped Kineater down to his leathery skin, leaving nothing but a sweaty loincloth which appeared to have been torn from the same sail as the fallen tent canopy. Gotrek, dressed in only his breeches, was allowed to fight as he was, but before he descended into the pit Rumblebelly demanded his axe.

'You can pry it from my cold dead hands,' growled Gotrek, glaring with his one eye at the ogre Butcher.

'Tyrant get axe as prize,' said Rumblebelly, his face twisted into a scowl. 'You win, you get it back. You lose, you don't need axe.'

It was a stunning bit of logic for an ogre, and Felix's estimation of the Butcher's intelligence rose several notches. Even Gotrek seemed impressed, but he handed over the axe only reluctantly, as though he were parting with an old friend and not a deadly weapon. Perhaps, thought Felix, Gotrek thought of the axe more as the former than the latter.

As Rumblebelly turned to place the axe upon one of the feasting tables, Gotrek drew Felix aside. Though he'd thought it a necessity at the time, Felix felt terrible for tricking the Slayer into eating cooked ogre. He deserved Gotrek's wrath and he braced himself to take whatever punishment the Slayer doled out. If he demanded that they part ways, well, Felix would accept that too.

But instead of being angry, Gotrek seemed unusually cheerful. 'Well done, manling. This will be a grand doom indeed.'

Relief flooded into Felix. Far from being offended, Gotrek was actually pleased that Felix's trick had resulted in a more epic death – single combat, unarmed, with an opponent four times his size? In his dwarf mind, his admittance into Grimnir's halls would be assured.

Felix watched the Slayer descend into the Great Maw from the lip of the pit. Nearby, Talia glared evilly at Rumblebelly from where she'd been tied to the leg of a feasting table – Felix found it difficult not to like her indomitable spirit. His father was rich enough that he'd met plenty of spoiled children in his day, and even counted some among his friends. When those sheltered fledglings finally emerged from the nest of privilege, one or two brushes with the real world was usually enough to cure them of their arrogance. Talia, on the other hand, might have fought Kineater herself, if she'd had the chance. If the Cathayan monks didn't manage to tame her, she'd make a fine soldier in the fight against Chaos.

Anya stood beside Felix, having also been betrayed by Cabbage. The gnoblar had evidently earned a position of respect for his actions. Rumblebelly himself had gnawed off a section of Cabbage's ear which, Felix understood, meant the gnoblar had a new patron.

'That was a brave thing you did,' Anya said, 'but Gotrek cannot possibly hope to win.'

'I've learned over the years never to bet against the Slayer. We've faced down larger creatures than this before,' Felix responded, keeping a brave face. The roars and cheers of the assembled ogres had reached an unsettling new high as Rumblebelly began some vile gastric ritual.

It was true that Gotrek and Felix had slain all manner of beasts in their travels, but always before, the Slayer had been armed with his trusty axe. He was as strong as any dwarf Felix had ever met, and they were already a hardy breed. But he could not hope to match Kineater's strength. The ogre was just too big.

'I've been meaning to talk to you about that,' said Anya. 'The Slayer... well, he attracts trouble, does he not. Surely you do not need to exaggerate in your journal in order to craft a compelling story about him?'

Felix started. Exaggerate? He had recorded their adventures as plainly as he could, meaning to add poetic language later, when he crafted his epic. Did she think his journal was full of nothing but lies?

Before he could respond, a new roar erupted from the crowd of ogres. The fight was about to begin.

Gotrek stood on one side of the pit, his chest and arms rippling with corded muscle. As he flexed, his tattoos seemed to dance across his skin. Facing a man, the Slayer was a short but fearsome opponent. Next to Kineater, Gotrek looked like a deformed child.

The ogre stood opposite him, a mountain of flesh with a protruding gut that overhung his feet.

On the lip of the pit, Rumblebelly belched loudly and struck his cleaver along one of the great sharpened stones that Felix supposed represented the teeth of the Great Maw, scattering a few dull sparks from the metal onto the combatants below.

Taking his cue, Kineater bellowed and charged the Slayer, leading with his gut. Obviously, he intended to crush Gotrek under his titanic weight.

For a moment, the Slayer disappeared under a sea of flesh, only to emerge on the other side of the ogre, punching at his thighs and kidneys. Hope fluttered in Felix's chest – nearly every opponent a dwarf ever faced was taller than himself. Gotrek might look over-matched, but he was in his element.

Kineater, on the other hand, was used to wrestling ogres. Enraged, he swept his arm around in a wild haymaker, but he'd aimed for a taller opponent and Gotrek was able to slip underneath the blow. Seeing an opening, the Slayer leapt towards Kineater and battered the ogre's kneecap. Bones snapped and the Tyrant howled in pain. He stumbled and toppled to the ground. Gotrek jumped free, like a lumberjack dodging a falling tree, but unfortunately Kineater lashed out with a meaty paw, catching Gotrek around the waist and pinning his arms to his side.

The Slayer flexed, trying to break the ogre's hold, but Kineater shifted his weight and bore him down to the ground.

'He'll be killed,' gasped Anya.

Without conscious thought, Felix's hand fell to the pommel of his sword. It did look bad. The Tyrant rained hammer-fist after hammer-fist down upon Gotrek. How long could he resist such punishment? At times, the Slayer's endurance seemed inhuman, but even he had his limits.

Felix stood on the very lip of the Maw, on the edge of one of the tooth-stones. The pit was fifteen feet deep: shallow enough that an ogre could climb out of it without assistance, but deep enough that

Felix couldn't jump in without fear of injury. Furthermore, Gotrek had explicitly told him not to intervene. If Felix were to rob him of his doom, the Slayer might never forgive him. Reluctantly, he stepped away from the edge and turned his attention to the crowd of ogres and gnoblars.

The pit was ringed by the dark, fleshy bodies of dozens of ogres who grunted and bellowed encouragement to their Tyrant in a mixture of broken Reikspiel and their own guttural language. Several brave gnoblars had pushed their way to the front of the crowd, where they squatted on the edge of the Maw.

As Felix watched, one of the ogres snatched up a gnoblar and popped the squealing creature into its mouth. It crunched once, twice, and then pushed a twitching, spindly arm into its maw and began to chew. Even this did nothing to distract the rest of the ogres. Apparently, the occurrence was common enough that not even the gnoblars squatting directly in front of the offending ogre so much as shifted positions. Indeed, it was probably the safest place for them, since that particular ogre's hunger was already sated.

In the pit, Kineater pinned the Slayer under his massive bulk. Gotrek freed a hand, but could do little more than fend off the ogre's blows. The Slayer's face was a bloody mess and his eyepatch had been torn aside, exposing his ruined eye.

Leering in victory, Kineater leaned in close until he was nose-to-nose with his opponent.

'I'm 'unna eat your face, little tasty-man!'

Gotrek's expression darkened and his cheeks reddened in anger.

'Don't call me a man!'

Roaring with anger, Gotrek curled his free arm around Kineater's massive neck and, pulling his face even closer, bit down hard on the Tyrant's nose.

The ogre's eyes widened and he reared up, instinctively recoiling from the pain. Blood poured from the wreck of his face, matting the greasy black hair on his chest.

Now free from the ogre's grip, Gotrek climbed to his feet and spat out a lump of gristly flesh. He wiped Kineater's blood off his lips with the back of his hand, and then crouched once again and waved the ogre forwards. 'Come on, you sorry sack of flab. Let's finish this.'

Kineater's confident swagger had been replaced by cold fear. For the first time, apparently, he realised that he *could* be beaten. Felix had no idea how long Kineater had been Tyrant, but given his size and the relative lack of challengers amongst his tribe, he guessed it was a very long time. All of that might be now about to end – at the hands of a dwarf no less.

Enraged, Kineater turned and reached up the side of the pit, freeing one of the Maw's tooth-stones from its moorings. He advanced on the Slayer, swinging it before him as an improvised club.

On the lip of the Maw, Rumblebelly's brow pulled low over his beady eyes. He grunted out a word in the ogre language that Felix could understand despite the language barrier: Kineater was cheating. Worse, in his quest to defeat the Slayer he had quite literally extracted one of their deity's teeth. Rumblebelly barked again, and beat his chest with his free hand. Several other ogres began to growl and hurl scraps of rubbish into the pit, while all around them gnoblars gazed up in horror at the sky, as if they expected swift retribution to rain from the heavens.

Down below, Kineater charged at Gotrek, wielding the great tooth-stone. At the last moment, the Slayer hurled himself aside, the club passing a hair's-breadth over his head.

Luckily Kineater had swung too hard and overextended. Gotrek seized the opportunity, kicking at the same knee he'd attacked before. Once again, Kineater fell, and this time Gotrek was there to hammer home a vicious blow to the Tyrant's ruined nose. In spite of the damage, the blow brought him inside Kineater's range, and the ogre lashed out once again with the tooth. The stone hit Gotrek with rib-shattering force, smashing him into the wall.

Felix cursed. Kineater had obviously committed some kind of grave insult against the Great Maw, but by the time these ogres were done with all their bellowing and teeth gnashing, the Slayer would be dead. He knew that he should use the distraction to disappear with Anya and Talia, but somehow he couldn't bring himself to leave Gotrek. Perhaps, like the gnoblars, years of living in fear of one enemy or another had dulled its bite? Or maybe he simply felt an overwhelming urge to see how his epic would end. If he left now, he would never know what had passed in the Slayer's final moments. He stepped back to the edge of the pit.

Gotrek had regained his footing and faced Kineater. His eyepatch was gone completely, and his face was livid with bruises. A long, bloody wound skirted the top of his cheekbone, dripping dark red into his fiery beard.

Kineater had fared no better. Blood ran freely from his wounded nose and he could barely hobble forwards on his buckled knee. Yet still he advanced, swinging the tooth-stone in huge, deadly arcs before him.

But the Slayer had had enough.

He faced down Kineater, jaw set, a kind of madness glimmering in his eye. 'Do your worst, you pig-skinned mountain ape!' he yelled, his fist raised in the air.

Kineater purpled with rage, and charged. He brought the tooth-stone in an overhead arc that should have squashed the Slayer flat, but at the last minute Gotrek – who only a moment before had looked unmovable – stepped aside and let it impact upon the churned earth.

As the Tyrant shifted his weight to retrieve the stone, Gotrek seized the tooth and yanked it forwards, using the ogre's weight against him. Overbalanced, Kineater stumbled, releasing his grip on the weapon.

The tooth was several feet in length and tapered to a brutal point, and Felix guessed it must weigh upwards of three hundred pounds. Nevertheless, Gotrek yelled a battle cry, heaved it overhead and then brought it crashing down on Kineater's skull. The Tyrant's head caved under the blow, spraying blood and brain matter everywhere.

A few spasmodic twitches later, Vork Kineater lay dead.

The Slayer stood over the Tyrant's corpse, breathing raggedly, his fists clenched at his sides. He did not celebrate. To a Slayer, each victory was also a defeat, because he had not yet found his doom and would be forced to seek it elsewhere. After a long moment, he stepped away from the corpse and climbed the wall of the pit.

Silence descended over the camp like a burial shroud.

Felix stirred uneasily, wondering if he should draw his sword. Several ogres glared at Gotrek stupidly, while others scowled, chewing their spit. Not one of them had seriously expected the Slayer to beat their Tyrant; it had all just been great sport. Now that the unthinkable had come to pass, they were too stupid to know how to react. Not even the gnoblars made so much as a sound.

The only movement was from Anya who edged closer to her sister. She had drawn a dagger, ready to cut Talia's bonds if they needed to make a sudden escape.

The Slayer put one bloody hand over the rim of the pit, then hauled himself over the lip and got to his feet.

'My axe,' he said to Rumblebelly. 'Now.'

The butcher considered Gotrek grimly. Felix sensed that Rumblebelly held some sway in the absence of the Tyrant, much as a warrior priest might issue commands in an Imperial army if the general were to be disabled. He was the key to all of this. His word would be law among the tribe.

The ogre held up both arms and turned towards the crowd. 'The

Great Maw is pleased! The dwarf is new Tyrant!' He looked back down at Gotrek and passed him his axe, his cleaver gleaming wickedly in the cold afternoon sun. He jerked a thumb at the pit. 'Now, eat 'im.'

Felix paled. Anya had mentioned that the winner of a pit fight ate the loser, but he'd assumed that was a formality and not a mandatory requirement. In truth, his plan had ended when the fight began. He certainly hadn't expected Gotrek to win. There was no way the Slayer was going to devour Kineater. The last thing he'd want was to be their Tyrant.

But maybe that was the answer.

'Your Tyrant,' Felix called out to the surrounding ogres, 'decrees that the ogre who eats the most Vork is the new Tyrant.'

It took a moment for the crowd to process the concept, but one especially bright ogre caught on and leapt down into the pit. Another followed, seizing the first by the back of the neck and hurling him against a wall. Soon there were enough ogres in the pit to shake the earth.

Rumblebelly's brow furrowed. 'No! That is not the way!'

But even those ogres closest to him had waded into the fray. The lure of power was too great for their simple minds. Disgusted, he turned back towards Gotrek and Felix, his metal cleaver in hand.

Gotrek stood his ground, daring the butcher to try something. His skin was already mottled with bruises, and he blinked away blood from his swelling eye as he glared up at Rumblebelly. The Slayer lifted his axe and, with a trembling hand, drew his thumb along the blade, drawing blood. Slowly, his bruised face cracked into a smile that showed his missing teeth.

Rumblebelly stared down at the Slayer in disbelief. His gaze darted from Gotrek to Felix, to the Nitikin sisters, and then back to Gotrek. At last, he shook his head and spat on the ground. 'Go. You are painful meat. Not worth eating.'

Not worth eating. Felix could think of no finer compliment for an ogre butcher to bestow upon them.

Rumblebelly had greatly disappointed Gotrek by refusing to obstruct their escape – preferring instead to watch the struggle for leadership unfold – but the dwarf did not seem to let it affect him unduly. He spent much of the hike back to the caravan talking with Talia. Normally taciturn, the Slayer didn't seem to mind the Kislevite woman – Gotrek knew a thing or two about having a foul temper, and shared his wisdom with the younger Nitikin.

'Do you think she'll go back to her former ways?' Felix asked Anya. They'd fallen a few paces behind Gotrek and Talia.

Anya looked up at her sister appraisingly. 'I'm afraid her daemons won't be banished so easily. However, I'm sure that being judged to be so ill-behaved that an ogre thinks you're beautiful is an eye-opening experience indeed, for a woman of her station.'

Ahead of them, Gotrek had drawn his axe and was showing Talia how to keep the edge keen. She watched with rapt attention.

'Of course,' admitted Anya, 'it could be that her temper has simply become more... focused?'

Felix chuckled. It was difficult to imagine a woman of Talia's slender build wielding an axe like Gotrek's, but he could certainly picture her with a rapier. That mental image provoked a thought of Ulrika and he felt his heart twinge. Maybe it was time to deal with the other matter.

'*Boyarina*–'

'Why the formality?' Anya asked, lightning quick. 'Even if we're not old friends, we have at least shared in an adventure.'

Felix paused, unsure of how to continue. Flattery would never work on a woman like Anya, nor would deception. She already suspected he was about to ask for some favour, so he might as well spit it out. 'I want to ask you if you would take up my duties. You proved yourself level-headed in the fight today, and of course, your literary talents are beyond question.'

Anya paused. Her gaze fell to the ground, and then back to Felix. 'Is this because I compared your journal to a penny dreadful?'

He sighed. 'Partly. It has been years since I've been published, and the life of a vagabond leaves little time to polish my prose–'

Anya cut him off, her tone harsh and impatient. 'I said nothing about your prose. Your prose is beautiful. It is obvious that you are a poet, and a fine one at that. My complaint was not with the quality of your journal, but with its content.' Here, she blushed and lowered her gaze, then brushed an intruding lock of hair from her eyes. 'I thought you'd made your stories up. Now, having seen what I've seen, I... I feel quite foolish. Who would have thought a dwarf would be named an ogre Tyrant?'

Felix gaped. Anya Nitikin, one of the Empire's foremost authors, thought his prose was beautiful? It was the finest compliment he'd received in years, and from an author of her calibre no less. 'I-I...' he stuttered, unable to find the words. 'Thank you,' he said at last.

'And as for handing me your duties, there is no one quite as suited to them as you are. No one else could follow the Slayer for all these years, enduring his insults by day and fighting at his side by night.' She smiled and put her hand on his arm sympathetically. 'I'm afraid, Herr Jaeger, that the gods have already chosen your destiny for you, and it is to pen one of the world's great epics.'

Felix held his head up high. He'd thought himself cursed to live as a wanderer, chasing after a doomed warrior on a futile quest. But Anya saw him as a warrior-poet, an artist who had deliberately chosen the bohemian life for his art. Perhaps he had at last found in prose something he'd been searching for in poetry. Perhaps now he had found his purpose.

'Have you thought of a title for your epic?' she asked curiously.

'Years ago I had a vision of a book labelled *My Travels with Gotrek* in gold print,' Felix confessed. 'But I have been struggling to find names for each volume.'

Anya chuckled to herself. 'The dwarf is a Trollslayer, is he not?'

Felix nodded.

'It seems that might make a good title for your first volume,' she said.

Felix tapped his chin with a fingertip. 'Of course. In our second adventure we fought the ratmen in Nuln. I could take a minor liberty with Gotrek's moniker and call that volume *Skavenslayer*, in their strange tongue.'

Anya's eyes danced with barely suppressed mirth. 'You realise that one day you may run out of new monsters to slay?'

An ironic smile graced Felix's face. 'I do indeed. In fact, I look forward to it.'

MIND-STEALER

C. L. Werner

The sharp stench of solder and melted copper made Thanquol's whiskers twitch. The grey seer's body shook as his nose rebelled against the smell and his body was wracked by a terrific sneeze. The little bells fixed to his horns jangled discordantly as he tried to cleanse the odour from his sinuses.

'Fast-quick,' the grey-robed ratman snarled, spitting each word through clenched fangs. His paw clenched tighter about the heft of his staff, the icons and talismans tied about its metal head clattering against the scarred wood. Never a particularly patient skaven, Thanquol's temper was coming to a boil.

The object of his ire didn't seem aware that messy sorcerous death was hovering just over his shoulder. The brown-furred skaven continued to fiddle with his spanners and hammers, sometimes reaching into the pockets of the leather apron he wore to fish out some strange tool or instrument. The stone slab which was serving as his workbench was littered with a confusion of metal gears and copper wire, ratgut tubes and little slivers of refined warpstone. The sickly glow of the warpstone was reflected in the thick goggles the skaven wore, making it seem as though his eyes had been replaced with hellish flames.

'Soon-soon,' the brown skaven chittered. 'No worry-fear,

Great-Mighty Thanquol! Krakul Zapskratch is good-smart warlock-engineer! Best-best in Under-Empire!'

Thanquol scowled at the magnitude of Krakul's boasting. Only an empty-brained slack-wit would spew such an outrageous lie and expect his betters to believe him! To think that any warlock-engineer with real ability would be wasting his life as an itinerant tinker-rat wandering from burrow to burrow, selling his services to whatever three-flea warlord he could find! Just for daring to make such a bold-smelling lie, the grey seer was tempted to call down the wrath of the Horned One upon the fool-meat and burn him to a cinder!

Of course, there was a very good reason why Thanquol couldn't do that. Krakul Zapskratch might be a loathsome, lying, sneaky ill-smelling braggart, but he was also the only warlock-engineer in Greypaw Hollow. Kill the tinker-rat, and there was no one else in the miserable, misbegotten warren capable of making the repairs Boneripper needed.

The grey seer's eyes narrowed as he glared down at the enormous body lying stretched across the stone slab. Had it been standing, the creature would have been three times the size of its master, a towering construction of steel, bone and wire fuelled by a warpstone heart and driven by the arcane mechanics of Clan Skryre's techno-sorcery. In shape, it retained a morbid resemblance to a living rat-ogre, and the warlock-engineers had even used the bones of Thanquol's first Boneripper when assembling their creation. The skeletal automaton had been a gift-bribe by Kaskitt Steelgrin, meant to buy the grey seer's services in a crooked scheme to ransack the treasury of Bonestash while the skaven were busy fighting the dwarf-things of Karak Angkul.

Thanquol lashed his tail in amusement. Kaskitt had paid for his treachery and presumption. Boneripper belonged to him now, without any obligations to a wire-chewing scrap-rat and his larcenous schemes. Even the control valve the warlock-engineers had hidden among Boneripper's gears, designed to shut the rat-ogre down should it be ordered to attack any skaven of Clan Skryre, was gone, disabled by dwarfish pistol-fire. The grey seer had impressed upon Krakul what would happen to him if he so much as thought about repairing that particular mechanism.

Of course, that didn't keep Thanquol from watching every move the warlock-engineer made. It didn't matter if he had no idea what Krakul was doing with all his strange gizmos. The only important thing was for Krakul to *think* the grey seer knew what he was about. There was, after all, a chance that Krakul wasn't the mouse-brain he seemed.

Krakul frittered around with a nest of corroded wires and punctured tubes situated behind Boneripper's metal chestplate. Thanquol could hear the tinker-rat tutting under his breath as he removed the damaged mechanisms. There was a distinctive green glow about the wires, and Krakul was careful to handle them only with a set of insulated tongs.

Thanquol's ears sank back against the sides of his skull, his head crooking back in a glowering gesture. He wasn't about to listen to Krakul chide him about having Boneripper lug a large quantity of warpstone for days on end. The corrosion could have been caused by anything! Maybe some of the smelly fluids Clan Skryre used as coolants, or the warpfire projector built into Boneripper's third arm. The lummox had suffered enough damage from bullets and boulders that almost anything could have leaked down inside its chest. The green glow emanating from the wires didn't mean anything!

Agitated squeaks rose from the tunnel outside Krakul's burrow. Thanquol pulled aside the man-hide curtain which separated the workshop from the main tunnel. Across the narrow corridor, he could see other skaven faces peering out from their holes. He followed the direction of their gaze, his nose twitching as the smells of blood and fear-musk excited his senses. Greypaw Hollow sat beneath a forest and it wasn't unusual for Warlord Pakstab to send groups of clanrats out to scavenge the wilderness for food and materials.

What was unusual was for one of these expeditions to return in such a sorry condition. Thanquol could see the miserable little ratkin, their fur bloodied, their eyes wide with fright. Several of them bore ugly gashes and deep wounds, hobbling about on broken legs and hugging broken arms to their chests.

Thanquol clapped a paw against his ear to stifle the shrill, wheedling voices of the scavengers as they reported their misfortune to a furious Pakstab. Whatever had befallen the fool-meat, whether they had scurried right into a troll hole or been stamped by a herd of cattle, it was Pakstab's problem. Another petty inconsequence that was far beneath the dignity of a grey seer to notice. Thanquol had more important things to occupy himself with.

He was just turning his head to return to Krakul's workshop when a particular whine froze him in his place. Thanquol felt a tingle of fear squeeze at his glands and a cold hand close about his heart. It was a shaking paw that drew the rat-skull snuff-box from his robe.

The grey seer felt an intoxicating rush of warmth course through his body as he sniffed the pulverised weed, burning away the fear and allowing hate free reign. Thanquol gnashed his fangs, spinning about and marching out into the tunnel. Skaven heads vanished back into their holes as the enraged sorcerer stalked past.

Had he heard right? He would find out! He would find out if these flea-spleened maggots had really seen what they had seen!

The few skaven bold enough to emerge from their burrows to investigate the curious squeaks and smells of the returned scavengers quickly scurried out of Thanquol's way as the sorcerer marched up the corridor. Even the armoured stormvermin, their claws wrapped about the hafts of hatchet-headed halberds, cringed when they saw the intense hatred blazing from the grey seer's eyes and sniffed the murderous aggression in his scent.

Grey Seer Thanquol brushed past Pakstab as though the warlord wasn't even there. His paw trembled with rage as he closed his fingers around the throat of one of the scavengers. The little ratman's eyes boggled in terror as Thanquol pulled him close.

'What did you smell-see?' Thanquol hissed. 'Speak-squeak! Quick-quick!' The only sound the crippled ratman could make was a wet rattle as the grey seer throttled him. Absently, Thanquol released his choking clutch, glaring as the dead skaven toppled to the floor. The temerity of the worm-fondler to die when the mighty Thanquol had questions to ask him! Out of spite, the grey seer kicked the corpse in the head, then turned his attention to the other scavengers.

'You!' the grey seer pronounced, pointing a claw at one of the rat-men, a portly creature missing an ear, half his tail and most of one paw, each of the injuries so fresh that black blood leaked from his wounds.

'Mercy-pity!' the ratman whined, awkwardly falling to his knees and exposing his throat in a gesture of submission. 'No-no hurt-harm, most merciless of priests, great gnawer of–'

Thanquol ground his fangs together, in no mood to be flattered by this fool-meat. 'What did that to you?' he snarled, jabbing the end of his staff into the scavenger's mangled paw. The wretch squealed in agony, quivering on the floor. Thanquol lifted his head, casting his eyes across the other scavengers.

'We smell-track man-things in forest,' one of the scavengers hastily spoke up. 'Many-few man-things carrying many-many strange-meat in wheel-burrow. We try-fetch food-fodder from wheel-burrow.'

Thanquol's eyes narrowed with impatience. He didn't care a lick for any of this. 'What kept you from stealing the food?' he demanded, smacking the quivering skaven on the floor with his staff. The fresh squeal of pain had the desired effect. The other scavenger couldn't finish his story fast enough.

'Breeder-thing see us!' the scavenger cried. 'Call-bring much-much man-thing! Fight-kill much-much! Many-many die-die from one-eye and dwarf-thing!'

Thanquol swatted the quivering skaven again as he slowly strode towards the talkative scavenger. 'A man-thing and a dwarf-thing did this to you?' he growled. He raised a claw to emphasise his next point. 'With one eye?'

The scavenger's fright had risen to such a state that he couldn't speak, simply bobbing his head up and down in a desperate effort to appease the fearsome sorcerer.

Gotrek Gurnisson and his mangy man-thing, Felix Jaeger! By the malicious malevolence of the Horned One!

Vengeance boiled up inside Thanquol's black heart. The grey seer rounded upon Pakstab, pointing a claw at the startled warlord's nose. 'Get-fetch your battle-rats!' the enraged sorcerer snarled, foam dripping from his mouth. 'Great enemies of skavendom have hurt-harm your valiant scouts! I will avenge their injuries upon these heretic-things with your army!'

Pakstab blinked in confusion. His whiskers trembled, his eyes narrowed with suspicion. Thanquol could read the warlord's thoughts. He wanted no part in fighting whoever had savaged his scavengers. He certainly wanted nothing to do with Thanquol's vengeance.

Hissing a curse, invoking one of the thirteen forbidden names of the Horned Rat, Thanquol gestured with his staff at one of the injured scavengers. An emerald glow suffused the metal icon fitted to the top of the staff. The same green glow surrounded the doomed scavenger. The ratman had time to shriek once before his body collapsed into a pool of steaming green mush.

'We march-kill enemy-meat now!' Thanquol screamed, turning his blazing eyes back upon Pakstab. The warlord nodded his head with an eagerness that was obscene. That was the beauty of a gratuitous display of destruction magic: there was never a need to repeat it.

Thanquol turned away to leave Pakstab to gather his warriors. He could be confident that Pakstab would marshal his forces quickly. After all, the warlord would be right there beside Thanquol when they made the attack. Anything that happened to the grey seer would happen to Pakstab too.

Worse, Thanquol promised, if Gotrek and Felix slipped through his paws! What he would do to Pakstab would be such a horror that his screams would be heard in Skavenblight!

As the grey seer stalked back down the tunnel towards Krakul's workshop, he barked orders at the tinker-rat, using a bit of his magic to magnify his words so that they carried into the farthest corners of the burrow.

'Fix-finish Boneripper, wire-nibbler! I want my rat-ogre on its feet and ready to kill-slay!' Thanquol brushed aside the curtain, fixing his imperious stare on the warlock-engineer. Krakul's eyes might have been hidden behind his goggles, but there was no mistaking the frightened posture and smell of the tinker-rat.

Thanquol reached into his robe and removed a little sliver of black cheese from his pocket. He stared at it for a moment, then glared at Krakul. 'You have until my third nibble to fix Boneripper,' the grey seer pronounced. 'After that, I will burn off one of your fingers every time I take another bite.'

Krakul was an eccentric, scheming scrap-fondler, but he had the good sense to know when a sorcerer was making an idle threat. With almost unseemly haste, the warlock-engineer leapt back to the stone slab, tools clattering against Boneripper's metal chassis, as he hurried to finish the repairs.

The confusion of smells emanating from the caravan threw each of the skaven into a state of anxiety and excitement. The good, familiar odours of oats and wheat, the appetising scents of horses and oxen, the reek of human sweat and the stink of iron and bronze; these all mixed in a single aroma that tantalised the skaven, made their bellies growl and their paws itch. The promise of full bellies and a bit of plunder was one that every ratman dreamed about.

Still, there were other smells teasing the keen skaven noses. There was a heavy, greasy stench one old crook-eared ratman said was troll. There was a musky, reptilian fug none of the skaven could identify. There was a sinister coppery smell that reminded Thanquol of the abominations Clan Moulder kept in Hell Pit, though he wasn't about to offer that insight to any of his yellow-spleened underlings.

The other smells didn't matter, because Thanquol had detected the scent he was looking for. It was that vile mix of tattoo ink and cold steel, animal starch and cheap beer, all wrapped around the dirt-stench of a dwarf.

Gotrek Gurnisson! He was travelling with the caravan, and if he was there, then that damnable Felix Jaeger was with him! Thanquol didn't know what trick of fate had thrust his two most hated enemies into his clutches, nor did he care. It was enough that the Horned Rat had smiled upon him and bestowed this delectable gift upon him. Before he was through with them, he'd offer the human's two eyes and the dwarf's single, blood-crazed orb as a burned offering to the Horned One by token of gratitude. Maybe he'd even teach them how to pray to the Horned One for mercy.

Not that it would do them any good.

When the humans made camp. That would be the time to do it. Their horses would be grazing, their wagons unhitched; at least some of their number would be sleeping. The skaven could set upon them and slaughter half the company before they had a chance to blink!

Yes, it was a good plan. The audacity of Pakstab's weasel-tongued track-sniffer Naktit to try and take credit for developing such a plan! Because the scout-rat had mentioned something of the sort first, he had the temerity to believe the same idea hadn't already occurred to Thanquol! Why should a grey seer share his innermost thoughts with the sort of verminous rabble Greypaw Hollow dared call warriors? It had been sorely tempting to let Boneripper smash the creeping little nuisance into paste for his arrogance.

But that would have been the petty, spiteful reaction of a lesser skaven. Thanquol was grand enough to be gracious and forget the failings of his underlings. With Gotrek and Felix nearly in his grasp, he felt magnanimous enough to ignore the stupidity of lesser ratmen. The Horned One had granted him a mighty boon; surely Thanquol could allow similar beneficence. Yes, he'd let Naktit keep his worthless little life.

Unless something went wrong! If that happened, he'd have Boneripper squeeze the creepy little tick-tracker until his eyes popped out of his skull.

It was early morning when the skaven started trailing the caravan, slinking through the dense thickets and close-set trees, always keeping out of sight while maintaining a clear view of the trail. The wagons were unusual, the sort of thing that even Thanquol with his vast experience and study of humans had never seen before. Their sides were painted in bright, garish colours, flags and pennants waving above them, bold words emblazoned on their sides. The horses and oxen which pulled the wagons were similarly arrayed, bright plumes fastened to their bridles and garlands of flowers tied about their necks. The men driving the wagons were also dressed in bright, gaudy clothing, sporting billowy breeches and vibrant vests and headscarves.

Most perplexing of all were the half-dozen cage-carts. These followed behind the other wagons, their contents hidden beneath tarps. The smells rising from them and the brief view of bars afforded by the trailing edge of the tarps, left no doubt that each cage held some living beast. Low growls, sullen snarls or angry howls rose from some of the carts. Most of the sounds were new to the skaven, though a few of the cries were familiar enough to send shivers down their spines. The old crop-eared ratman started whining about trolls again – at least until Boneripper stepped on his head. Fear was a useful thing, but only when the ratkin knew what they should be most afraid of.

Thanquol peered through the bushes, trying vainly to spot his hated foes, but there was no sign of either Gotrek or Felix. The grey seer concluded the two were inside one of the wagons. It would be in keeping with their perfidious natures to hide themselves away.

Taking a pinch of warpstone snuff, Thanquol resisted the burning desire to launch the attack immediately. He didn't care that more of Pakstab's clanrats would die in such an impulsive raid than in a carefully planned assault. It was the possibility that Gotrek and Felix might escape that stayed his paw. However much it vexed him, he would have to wait. Naktit insisted the time to attack would be when the caravan settled down to camp and it was Thanquol's experience that humans, with their pathetic vision, wouldn't travel at night. He could wait.

As it transpired, however, he didn't have to wait that long. Thanquol blinked in bewilderment when, just a little past noon, the caravan came to a halt. He watched in wonder as the wagons moved into a wide clearing and the men driving them began to unhitch their teams. There were still a good six hours of daylight left, a fact each of the light-sensitive skaven appreciated quite keenly. Surely the humans weren't stupid enough to squander…

Thanquol grinned, turning his eyes to the ground at his feet, envisioning the deep, dark burrow of the Horned Rat. Truly his god was favouring him! First to deliver Gotrek and Felix to him, then to make the stupid humans stop well before nightfall. The skaven could rest and recuperate from their forced march through the forest.

The only thing Thanquol didn't like was the size of the clearing. Every skaven was agoraphobic and the clearing elicited a feeling of unspeakable dread. The forest had been dense enough to be almost comforting, but all the open sky above the clearing was another thing entirely. It would be a bit better at night, but even so, the thought of all those stars glaring down at them like so many hungry eyes was something to make the glands clench.

A few of the humans were sent away on horseback, galloping off down the trail. Thanquol dismissed them from his thoughts after snarling an order to Pakstab that no opportunistic sword-rat should bother them. He didn't want the humans breaking camp when their outriders failed to return and they became uneasy. He wanted the stupid creatures to think themselves perfectly safe and alone until the very moment of the attack.

For the second time, Thanquol blinked in disbelief. The humans that remained in camp were removing poles and an immense roll of canvas from one of the wagons. While he watched, they spread the canvas out across the clearing, then began to prop it up from beneath with the poles. It was unbelievable, but the humans were constructing some kind of massive tent, effectively placing a roof over the clearing! Truly the Horned One had decided to recognise and reward his selfless and valiant servant!

Gratitude to his god died on his tongue when Thanquol spotted two figures climbing down from one of the wagons. One was a tall human with long blond hair, the other was a stocky dwarf, his head shaved except for a single strip of ginger fur running down the centre of his scalp. Flecks of foam dribbled from Thanquol's mouth as he glared at his hated enemies. His fingers closed around a nugget of warpstone hidden in the seam of his robe.

It would be so easy! Bite down on the warpstone, draw its sorcerous energies into his body and unleash a spell of such devastation that the two blood-ticks would burst into a thousand gory fragments! All the humiliation and disgrace that these two had brought upon him would be avenged in one moment of sadistic violence!

Thanquol let his paw fall empty at his side. It was too easy. Too easy for Gotrek and Felix. All the times they had meddled in his affairs... No, they wouldn't get off so easy! For them, there would be no quick death.

'Pakstab!' Thanquol snarled. The warlord scurried forwards, his posture displaying a submissiveness rooted in fear, but his fur bristling with a far less docile resentment. The grey seer bared his fangs at Pakstab until the warlord was well and truly subdued.

'Keep your tree-rats quiet,' the grey seer hissed. 'We wait until nightfall and the man-things sleep.' He jabbed a paw towards the wagon where his enemies stood. 'I want those ones alive!'

Dismissing the warlord from his mind, Thanquol returned his

attention to the clearing. Soon it would be dark and then the humans would go to sleep. That was when he would lead Pakstab's brave warriors into combat.

He only wished there was a way to make Gotrek and Felix understand they had only a few hours left to live!

Thanquol reached over and snatched the far-eye from Krakul's hand, an effort made easier since the warlock-engineer was short a few fingers. The grey seer ground his fangs together in a fit of anger.

Crickets chirruped, owls hooted, bats flittered about the trees. It was night, as black and welcoming as the tunnels of Skavenblight.

Why, then, were the humans still awake! Even worse, there were more of them! The outriders had returned after only a short time, but it wasn't long after that more humans began to trickle into the camp. These weren't so brightly dressed as the ones from the caravan, and they stank of dirt and manure: typical odours of the slavelings humans used to grow their crops and tend their flesh-beasts.

Thanquol didn't care who they were or where they came from. What he wanted to know was what they were doing! By the horns of the Horned One, none of it made sense to him! The field-humans, obviously a lesser clan than the brightly dressed ones, had wandered about the camp as though they each of them were a fangleader inspecting a new burrow. The caravan humans hurried about, performing every sort of bizarre labour at the slightest command of the field-humans.

The grey seer was still scratching his ears at some of the things he had seen. There was a gangly human who could spit fire and another one that was able to stick a sword clear down his throat without skewering himself! He saw a grungy little man-thing in voluminous robes engaged in the rather despicable antic of biting the heads from live chickens. As he would soon spit out the chickenhead, Thanquol could make absolutely no sense of this particular activity. There was a pair of breeders who capered about on a thin rope stretched between two poles, displaying an agility that would have impressed even a murder-adept of Clan Eshin. He watched another human gallop around the camp on a horse, flipping and jumping all around the animal, making the grey seer wonder if some saboteur had slathered grease across the horse's back.

None of it made any kind of sense! The field-humans would slap their hands together in moronic fashion, howling loudly and baring their teeth at the caravan-humans. Yet the threatening display only excited the caravan-humans to new efforts.

Thanquol removed the spyglass from his face long enough to scowl at Naktit. So, the humans would go to sleep once it was dark, would they!

The grey seer's nose twitched as a new smell reached him. It was the odour of magic, crude but powerful. Forgetting Naktit for the moment, Thanquol swung back around and directed the spyglass upon the source of the aethyric energy.

What he saw made his glands tighten. Some of the brightly-clad humans were opening the door to one of the cages. Locked inside was an enormous troll! As soon as the door was open, the brute lurched out into the clearing, roaring and thumping its chest! Thanquol could only scratch his ear in disbelief. The humans were insane to let such a monster loose!

The field-humans screamed and started to scatter, but before they could get far a caravan-human wearing a broad-brimmed hat called out to them, ordering them to stop. He turned and faced the troll, drawing from the crimson sash he wore not a sword or axe or blunderbuss but a slender flute. Before the amazed grey seer's eyes, the troll stopped, its dull eyes staring down at the little man.

Expecting any sort of horrific violence to follow, Thanquol's wonder increased when the man began to play his flute. The troll lifted up its huge feet and began to dance!

Thanquol scowled as he heard the field-humans screeching and slapping their hands together. He focused his attention not on what he could see, but upon what he could feel. Sniffing the patterns of magic in the air, he could follow the slender strands of energy emanating from the troll. One strand led back to one of the wagons where a bound human lay hidden, his mouth tightly gagged. As he struggled, his movement struck Thanquol as peculiar, more like an idiot's fit than the resistance of a grown man-thing.

The other strand of magic led to a dark little pavilion set aside from the main tent. Just visible at the entrance of the pavilion was an old breeder, her flesh withered, all the meat shrivelled by age. Thanquol could tell at a glance that the breeder-thing was a mage by the grey hue of her hair. It was easy to forget that human breeders sometimes developed such abilities, a sure sign of their inferiority to the skaven whose breeders' only purpose was to make and nurse more skaven.

The breeder-witch was doing something, weaving her magic between the idiot-flesh and the troll. Whatever she was doing, it gave her control over the troll, control more perfect and precise than any cave-lurking goblin chief had ever dreamed of.

The presence of a sorceress made Thanquol reconsider the wisdom of the planned attack. It was always dangerous to risk the powers of an unknown wizard, even if it was just a breeder-thing. If he had an apprentice to send out to cast spells and draw the witch's attention, he would have felt better.

A cruel smile flashed upon Thanquol's verminous face. Lowering the spyglass, he turned towards Krakul. Few among the warlock-engineers had true magic, and he rather doubted that Krakul was one of those who did. However, many of the contraptions crafted by Clan Skryre mimicked magic in their effects. Surely enough to trick a stupid breeder-witch!

'Brave-wise Krakul,' Thanquol said. 'I give you the honour-glory to lead the attack.'

Krakul looked like he'd swallowed one of his own spanners. The warlock-engineer looked about him, as though hoping there was some other skaven named Krakul standing nearby.

'Great and holy Thanquol the Terrifying!' Krakul squealed. 'I am not worthy of such distinction. I am only poor-small tinker-rat–'

'Stop whining,' Thanquol snapped. 'You're going.' He drew upon the smallest measure of his sorcery, causing his eyes to take on a ghoulish green glow. 'Or would you rather stay?' he hissed. Krakul didn't have any real magic, but Thanquol certainly did. It was perhaps wise to remind him of that fact.

'Take the clanrats and attack from the right,' Thanquol ordered. 'Naktit's scouts will come from the left. Once you have the man-things' attention, Pakstab will lead the stormvermin and strike the centre.'

'Where will you be, invincible one?' Pakstab asked, his tone not quite as servile as it could have been.

Thanquol smoothed his whiskers. 'I will stay here and ensure nothing goes wrong with your plan.' Now that so many unforeseen complications had become part of the situation, Thanquol felt it was time to distance himself from responsibility for organising the attack. After all, these were Pakstab's warriors. Why shouldn't the warlord shoulder the responsibility if they couldn't adapt to changes on the battlefield?

Pakstab glared murderously at the grey seer, his fingers twitching about the hilt of his sword. The warlord glanced past Thanquol at the imposing hulk of Boneripper. Grinding his fangs together, Pakstab relented. Turning away, he began squealing orders at his underlings. If he was expected to lead the attack, he was going to make sure there were plenty of skaven around him to do the brunt of the fighting. It was exactly the sort of cowardly, selfish scheming Thanquol had come to expect from a greedy, grasping thug like Pakstab. It was unfortunate for Greypaw Hollow that there was no leader of Thanquol's calibre ruling the warren, a leader with the cold resolve and iron self-control to set aside his own desires for the betterment of all skavendom.

The grey seer drew a sharp intake of breath as his eyes fell upon one corner of the clearing. Most of the field-humans had gathered to watch the dancing troll, giving Thanquol a better view of the rest of the space. Now he could see a burly dwarf standing beside a pile of boulders, an immense hammer in his thick hands. Judging by the broken stones around him, the braggart had been showing off his brainless physique, smashing rocks for the entertainment of the field-humans, glutting his drunken ego on the empty-headed praise of buffoons and churls!

Gotrek Gurnisson! Well, this was the last time he would interfere in Thanquol's affairs!

Spinning around, the enraged grey seer snapped commands at Boneripper. 'Kill-burn-slay!' Thanquol shrieked at the skeletal rat-ogre, the warp-tooth fitted to the sorcerer's ear pulsing with power as it transmitted his fury to the hulking automaton. Without hesitation, Boneripper reared up and charged out from the forest, hurtling towards the clearing like a warp-fuelled avalanche.

Squeaks of shock and dismay rose from the bushes and underbrush. The creeping skaven warriors of Greypaw Hollow weren't in position yet. They wailed against losing the element of surprise when Boneripper charged past them, bemoaning the squandered opportunity for massacring the humans without a fight. Many of them turned tail, ready to scurry back to their dark burrows.

Thanquol dissuaded the warriors from their cowardly retreat with a show of force. Summoning the might of the Horned One into his body, harnessing the aethyric currents around him, the grey seer pointed his staff at the closest of the fleeing ratmen. A crackle of green lightning leapt from the head of the staff, coiling about the retreating stormvermin, cooking him inside his armour. As the smouldering ratman crashed to the ground, Thanquol's magically magnified voice thundered over the clearing.

'All-all fight-kill!' Thanquol roared. 'Kill much-much or suffer-die!'

The threat turned the frightened skaven around. By now Boneripper had reached the clearing. The carnage it was causing among the hapless humans helped to further bolster the fragile courage of the ratmen. Squeaking their war-cries, the verminous horde descended upon the caravan.

Thanquol lashed his tail in frustration. That idiot Boneripper! Stupid, brainless oaf of a scrap-heap! Couldn't it tell when he wanted it to do what he said and when he didn't? The brute had spoiled the ambush by its moronic interpretation of its master's outburst!

But was it Boneripper's fault? Might that treacherous tinkerrat Krakul have done something to the rat-ogre, changing it from Thanquol's clever, loyal, unquestioning bodyguard into a lumbering dolt with only the vaguest semblance of intelligence? Yes-yes, that certainly sounded probable! It wasn't so long ago that Ikit Claw had unreasonably developed some paranoid ideas about Thanquol and tried to kill him. It was more than coincidence that Krakul was of the same clan as the Claw!

Thanquol yipped in alarm as another idea came to him. Hiking his grey robe up above his knees, he dashed towards the clearing. The timing of Krakul's treachery had spoiled the perfect ambush, opening the possibility that Gotrek and Felix might escape! And now it occurred to him that this might be Krakul's real purpose. Thanquol had long known that there had to be someone using the two insufferable interlopers against him. Neither one of them was clever enough to continually be interfering in the grey seer's schemes. There had to be a traitor, a villain from the lowest dregs of skavendom whose pride and arrogance couldn't abide the greatness of Thanquol's genius. It was another skaven who kept thrusting the pair in his way!

It was up to Thanquol to see that his enemies were taken alive, that they might confess who it was that had...

Again the grey seer yipped in alarm. The mangled body of a stormvermin went flying past him, almost bowling him over as it went tumbling into the bushes. A second body crashed to earth almost at his feet.

Thoughts of traitors and vengeance abated as Thanquol began to appreciate his surroundings. In his haste, he'd scurried well ahead of the main body of Pakstab's warriors. He was in the clearing, under the tent, with a frightened mob of humans rushing about, screaming and wailing in abject terror.

Unfortunately, the troll wasn't frightened of the skaven. It had stopped dancing, too. Instead it had lumbered out and intercepted the boldest and most eager of the stormvermin. With decidedly untroll-like deliberation, the monster brought its scaly fists pounding into one ratman after another, each powerful blow smashing a furry body into ruin.

Thanquol froze as the ugly brute turned towards him. The musk of fear spurted from his glands as the troll opened its jaws wide, roaring at the grey seer. The monster's hand tightened about the squealing clanrat it held, breaking every bone in the skaven's body. The fearful display forced Thanquol into action. Drawing upon his sorcery, he pointed his staff at the troll, sending a blast of malignant magic full into the monster's face.

Wisps of black smoke rose from the troll's head as the spell crackled across its flesh. But the brute didn't fall. As the smoke cleared, it glared at Thanquol. The scaly, blackened skin of the monster's face may have been scorched by his magic, but already the incredible regenerative powers of the troll were undoing the damage. Before Thanquol's eyes, the burned skin began to heal. Snorting and huffing, the troll lumbered towards the skaven sorcerer.

'Boneripper!' the grey seer squeaked as the troll swung at him. The monster's tremendous fist smashed into the ground Thanquol had been standing on before making a frantic leap for one of the posts supporting the tent. He wrapped his limbs about the post, clinging to it as though it were the mast of a sinking ship. A sideways glance showed him the troll using its other hand to pull its fist from a crater that had punched clear down to bedrock. His glands spurted fear-musk as he considered what such a blow would have done to him had it landed.

'Boneripper!' the sorcerer shrieked again. He wasn't certain if his bodyguard heard him; the range of the warp-tooth which controlled the rat-ogre had never been explained to him. Worse, there was the possibility that Krakul had done something to limit Thanquol's control. He should never have trusted that snivelling scrap-rat!

Something else heard him, however. Turning its head upwards, the troll glared at Thanquol. There was a chilling intelligence in the monster's eyes, a keenness of hate that he'd never seen any troll exhibit before. Frantically, Thanquol pawed at his robe, seeking a piece of warpstone to fuel another spell – a spell strong enough to overcome the troll's regeneration.

Bellowing its rage, the troll charged towards Thanquol's post. The grey seer squeaked in terror, the sliver of warpstone slipping from his jaws. He watched as the glowing green stone hurtled downwards, seeing his last hope of survival falling with it.

Suddenly, Boneripper's skeletal bulk was between Thanquol and the oncoming troll. The rat-ogre's piston-driven arms closed about the troll's enormity, crushing it in an embrace of steel and sinew. The troll flailed about in Boneripper's grip, trying to tear its way free.

The two monsters might have stood there all night, immovable object against irresistible force. But Thanquol had other ideas. Baring his fangs, glaring at the troll's ugly visage, he snarled an order at Boneripper: 'Burn-slay!'

Obediently, Boneripper lifted its third arm, pressing the nozzle of the warpfire projector against the troll's skull. There was a tremendous flash of light, a resounding boom and a thunderous crash that knocked Thanquol from his perch. The grey seer smashed to earth, moaning as the impact rattled his bones.

When his head stopped ringing, Thanquol darted a look over at the troll. It was dead now, only a smoking stump of neck rising from its shoulders. Boneripper's warpfire had burned the monster's head off! The threat to himself vanquished, Thanquol looked for his bodyguard. The explosion had thrown Boneripper to the ground, its third arm nothing but a jumble of twisted metal and shattered bone. The rat-ogre didn't move, even when Thanquol snarled an order at it to do so.

Wonderful! The slack-witted dolt had destroyed itself! Surely it should have understood not to use its warpfire at such close quarters! By the Horned One, what could have possessed the lummox... But, of course, it was Krakul and his treacherous meddling with Boneripper's mechanisms! When Thanquol got his paws on the filthy maggot-chewer...

The grey seer forgot about Krakul when he spotted two figures rushing at him from across the clearing. Thanquol's empty glands clenched as he recognised the hated Gotrek and Felix! His paw drew another shard of warpstone from his robe, popping the sorcerous rock into his mouth, sending magical energy coursing through his veins. He could cast a quick spell that would get him a hundred miles away, far from Gotrek's murderous axe and Felix's flashing sword!

Only... the dwarf wasn't carrying his deadly axe. He was still lugging around that huge hammer. It was the human who was brandishing an axe, but a far smaller one than the weapon of Gotrek Gurnisson.

It was a trick! That was why they weren't using their usual armaments! That was why Felix had grown so tall and muscular, why the dwarf had changed his tattoos and added a ring of metal studs across his brow! They knew the mightiest sorcerer in the world, the most favoured disciple of the Horned Rat, a genius so insidious that even the Lords of Decay trembled in his presence – they knew that there was no hope of resisting their unconquerable foe! They had taken these stupid measures to try and disguise themselves, as though anyone could hide from Thanquol's wrath!

Thanquol stretched forth his paw, the malignity of his magic erupting in a blast of terrific force. The pulsation of raw aethyric energy sizzled across the clearing, causing grass to wither and cloth to burst into flame. The head of the human's axe dripped to the ground in a molten mess, the wooden heft of the dwarf's hammer became a mass of fire. Thanquol chittered in triumph as his hated enemies stopped their crazed charge and stared stupidly at their ruined weapons!

'Die-die now-now!' Thanquol hissed, unleashing a withering blast of green fire against his foes. Their screams fell silent as their bodies boiled beneath the fury of his sorcery. The grey seer cackled wildly as he watched his enemies writhe and twist in the malignant flames.

He had dreamed of this moment for so long! There was no restraint now, no thought of interrogation and torture, just utter destruction – the extermination due to these low creatures who had dared trifle with his greatness! He grinned savagely as he watched the agony blazing in the eyes of his dying enemies.

And then cold, hateful realisation forced itself upon Thanquol in his moment of triumph. Looking into the eyes of his enemies, he couldn't escape the observation that the dwarf had two and the human only one! His mind went back to the wounded scavenger-rat's report. What Thanquol had heard was 'one-eyed dwarf', but what the scout had said was 'one-eye and dwarf'. The grey seer was prepared to believe many things, he might even accept that Felix would put out one of his eyes in an effort to hide from Thanquol's wrath, but the one thing he couldn't believe was that Gotrek had similarly been able to grow a new eye. As loathe as he was to admit it, these two weren't his hated arch-foes!

Outraged fury caused Thanquol to send another blast of magic into the twitching bodies. His enemies in Greypaw Hollow were behind this, goading him into this foolish attack! He'd see that they paid for playing upon his selfless drive to exterminate the enemies of Skavendom!

Before the grey seer could visit further destruction upon the corpses, a roar sounded from behind him. Thanquol spun about, staring in horror at a gigantic beast. The thing was bigger than either Boneripper or the troll, so large that there was something absurd about it as it crawled out from its cage, about the idea that something so enormous had been able to fit inside so small a space.

Where the troll had been a scaly brute, this creature was a shaggy monstrosity, its body covered in greasy, black fur. Four arms projected from its muscular torso, two of them terminating in great bony blades like the pincers of a tunnel-mantis. The beast's head was like that of a goat, three spear-like horns thrusting outwards from its forehead. For all its monstrousness, there was a terrible gleam of intelligence in the beast's eyes, the same expression of hate and determination he had seen in the troll's eyes.

Once again, Thanquol could smell magic in the air, tendrils of energy that drifted between the beast and a human who was flailing against three others who were trying to bind him with chains. Again, the grey seer followed the coils of energy back to the aged breeder-witch. She stood, glaring back at him, her wrinkled face drawn back into an expression of loathing.

'Keep Abela's body safe!' the witch shouted at the men trying to chain the lunatic thrashing about on the ground. 'We must give him time to use the ghorgon to destroy the underfolk!'

The ghorgon, for such Thanquol decided the four-armed beast must be, lost no time trying to follow the witch's orders. The creature came charging forwards, swatting aside those skaven unlucky enough to get in its way, slashing them with its bony blades or clawing them with its powerful hands. One stormvermin, driven mad with fear, tried to gut the monster with a pole-axe. For his efforts, the ratman was knocked to the ground and pulverised beneath the ghorgon's hoofed feet.

The air was heavy with the musk of fear now, Pakstab's craven warriors fleeing before the ghorgon's assault. Thanquol could hear the warlord's weasely voice calling off the attack, enjoining his weak-spleened vermin to retreat. The traitor-meat had no compunction about abandoning his confederate and spiritual advisor on the battlefield, even after all the generosity and beneficence Thanquol had showered upon Greypaw Hollow!

The ground trembled under his feet while Thanquol stared after his vanished allies. Spinning back around, the grey seer squeaked in fright. Barrelling down upon him, each of its four arms raised to visit murderous death upon him, was the ghorgon! Without any of Pakstab's cringing ratkin to slaughter, the beast had made incredible time crossing the clearing.

Thanquol's own terror saved him. Where a second of thought or deliberation would have doomed him, instinct rose to his rescue. Pointing his claw at the charging ghorgon, the grey seer unleashed the full force of the spell he had conjured.

A sheet of crackling green lightning crashed into the ghorgon. The beast howled in agony as its fur burst into flame, fingers of warp-lightning searing through its flesh and blackening its bones. The smouldering carcass of the monster crashed to earth, its momentum propelling it onwards. Staggered by the reckless release of such a mighty spell, Thanquol couldn't even muster the energy to dash aside as the huge bulk came sliding towards him. Even dead, the ghorgon was massive enough to smash the grey seer into paste.

Thanquol sighed with relief when the sliding body came to rest almost at his very feet. That relief ended with a shrill screech that made him jump.

'You've killed Abela!' the breeder-witch wailed, pointing her withered hand at Thanquol. 'You've killed my son!'

Thanquol could smell the currents of magic gathering about the old witch as she summoned the aethyric powers to her with vengeful abandon. Before he could raise his own defences, he felt the unleashed fury of the witch wrap itself about him in an invisible coil. He could smell the thread of energy writhing back to the witch. Worse, he could sense the thread working its way across the clearing, closing upon a little cage suspended near the troll-wagon. A small, wiry green creature moped about in the cage, its long arms dangling between the bars.

Fear thundered in Thanquol's heart. He understood the magic of the breeder-witch. She had placed the mind of her whelp into the ghorgon, and she had done the same with the troll and another human. Now she intended to force Thanquol's mind into the loathsome body of a snotling!

Panic seized the grey seer. He struggled frantically against the hag's curse, pawing at the air, trying belatedly to raise a magical barrier against her spell. Bit by bit, he could feel the magic taking hold of him, could sense his inner being ripped from his flesh, sent drifting towards the cage.

'Boneripper!' Thanquol yelled, crying out to his bodyguard to save him, forgetting for the moment the brute's collapse after destroying the troll.

The rat-ogre seemed to have forgotten as well. Awkwardly, Boneripper rose up from the ground, its shattered arm still smoking. The automaton swung about, facing towards Thanquol, obediently waiting for further orders, oblivious to the stream of magic winding past its towering bulk.

Before Thanquol could call out to the rat-ogre to order it to kill the witch, he felt the last vestiges of his essence drawn out from his body. His spirit, his mind, was sent hurtling across the clearing. A flash of unspeakable cold, a confusion of whirring light and sound, and then there was only darkness.

It took a tremendous effort of willpower to vanquish that darkness, an effort that Thanquol found almost beyond him to make. Only the thought of all the enemies and traitors who would outlive him sustained him in his moment of despair. Feeling as though a thousand daggers pierced every corner of his being, as though a great fire had been sent raging through his chest, the grey seer fought his way back to consciousness.

The first thing that struck Thanquol was the almost complete absence of smell. What little he could discern were the aroma of old bone and the stink of metal, both underlaid with a tantalising hint of warpstone. The next thing which impressed him was his vision. It was much sharper than before, but everything had a strange, unworldly green hue to it. There was no sensation of touch: he couldn't feel the bars of the cage or even the floor under his feet. He couldn't even feel his heart beating in his chest!

Terror flooded through Thanquol's mind as he considered the only possibility. The spell had been too much for the snotling's fragile body to endure. His spirit had been hurled into a corpse! Any moment now his essence would be sent on its long journey to the burrows of the Horned One, there to answer for his failures and mistakes!

Thanquol shivered in horror at that fate. The Horned Rat knew he existed only to serve the vicious god of the skaven, that there was no more loyal or steadfast priest to enter the Order of Grey Seers! Yet, even in the afterworld there might be spies and traitors, filling the Horned One's ears with lies about Thanquol's devotion.

For a second chance! Thanquol would give himself utterly to the Horned One, devote himself purely to service to his god if only the Horned Rat would give his humble priest another opportunity to serve him!

In his terrified grief, Thanquol raised his hand to cover his eyes. It wasn't the fact that the arm of what should have been a corpse moved when he willed it to move that shocked Thanquol. It was the shape of that arm. Not the leathery green limb of a snotling, but the massive, bony arm of a skeletal colossus!

Something had gone wrong with the breeder-witch's spell!

Thanquol swung his body around, feeling the immense power of his new form. He glared down at the witch, savouring the terror gripping her features. The hag had not brought about his destruction, but her own. The transfer of Thanquol's spirit into the body of the snotling had been intercepted, blocked when Boneripper lurched up from the ground. Instead of being cast into the fragile body of a greenskin runt, Thanquol had been invested into the mighty frame of a rat-ogre!

The grey seer opened his skeletal jaws and chittered malignantly, the sound crackling like lightning across the clearing.

The witch turned aside, glaring towards Thanquol's real body. Her voice cracked as she shouted orders to the other caravan-humans.

Thanquol watched the humans go racing towards his old body. Let them have it, the weak, puny husk of rat-flesh! What need had he of a body of fragile flesh when his genius was enshrined in a hulk of bone and steel, merged with the pinnacle of Clan Skryre engineering!

He raised his skeletal paw, intending to send a spell searing down into the witch's body. Thanquol cringed when nothing happened. He couldn't feel any magic coursing through his new body. Worse, he couldn't sense the aethyric emanations around him! He tried sniffing at the witch, but couldn't discern even the faintest whiff of magic!

Suspicion flared through Thanquol's mind. If he couldn't smell magic, he could see confidence, and the witch was much too confident now. Somehow, in some way, Thanquol sensed he was still bound to his old body. He remembered the care the humans had taken with the bodies of their kinsmen when the witch cast their minds into the monsters.

Howling in panic, Thanquol charged across the clearing, the skeletal claws of the rat-ogre swatting aside the converging humans as though they were flies. He didn't waste the time to savour the havoc, but sprang for the horned ratman standing alone and vulnerable. Invested with Boneripper's mind, Thanquol's old body stood unmoving, gripped by the idiocy that required commands from its master to give it motivation.

Thanquol tried snarling at his old body, to get Boneripper to flee, but without the warp-tooth, he had no way of commanding the stupid brute. Instead, he resorted to scooping up his body and tucking it under the rat-ogre's arm. Without further hesitation, Thanquol dashed into the forest, leaving the clearing and the caravan behind.

He needed time to understand what had happened to him, time to study the effects of the witch's curse. Then, once he was master of this condition, he would come back and settle with the witch and his hated enemies Gotrek and Felix!

Thanquol spent almost an hour lurching through the gloom of the forest before he found the other skaven. He cursed the dim-senses of his new body. With a proper nose, he would have been able to find the fools quickly. Instead, he had been forced to grope about in the brush looking for tracks.

After deserting him, his duplicitous allies had retreated to a shadowy patch of scrubland a league or so from where the caravan had made camp. Thanquol could hear them arguing amongst themselves, trying to concoct some lie that would make their abandonment of skavendom's greatest hero believable when Skavenblight sent its representatives to Greypaw Hollow.

Thanquol listened to the vainglorious squeaking of Warlord Pakstab for a full minute. It was just as well Boneripper's body didn't have a stomach, because it surely would have turned hearing the weak-spleened maggot-nibbler touting his brave effort to reach the embattled grey seer. Only the arrival of three gigantic beast-things had driven him away. He knew that the noble Thanquol wouldn't have wanted Greypaw Hollow's valiant warlord to throw away his life needlessly.

Snorting with contempt, Thanquol lumbered out from the trees. The sudden appearance of the skeletal rat-ogre brought squeals of fright from the skaven. Thanquol lashed his bony tail in amusement. Unable to smell, he'd been forced to judge the wind by sight alone, but he'd managed to prevent Boneripper's scent from betraying his presence to the treacherous ratmen. Surprise was his, and he intended to use it to the fullest.

'Pakstab-meat,' Thanquol snarled. The skaven were doubly horrified to hear the grey seer's voice thundering at them from Boneripper's jaws. 'Stop-speak, before I ring your neck!'

The warlord fell to his knees in shock. 'Terrible Thanquol… is-is that you?'

The rat-ogre loomed over Pakstab, swatting him across the muzzle with a bony claw. The blow sent the ratman tumbling through the scrub. 'Next stupid question?' Thanquol growled, turning his skull-like visage so he could stare down at each of the skaven in turn.

'What-what happened?' Krakul asked, the warlock-engineer's eyes boggling excitedly behind his goggles.

Thanquol took a shaking step towards the tinker-rat. 'You should have stayed quiet,' he warned. He lifted Boneripper's massive claw, intending to swat the treasonous little scrap-licker. As he did so, however, he felt a cold pain in his side. His entire body shivered to a stop.

Krakul clapped his paws together, chittering maliciously. The reason was obvious to Thanquol: the faithless weasel had repaired the safety valve, making it impossible for Boneripper to hurt a skaven of Clan Skryre.

Boneripper, however, was a being without mind or will of its own. Thanquol possessed the finest mind in the Under-Empire and a will-power that could resist the wiles of gods and daemons alike. Snarling against the cold pain, Thanquol reached down to his side, clawing at his back until he ripped Krakul's gizmo from its fastenings. Holding the device between his skeletal talons, he glared down at the warlock.

'This belongs to you,' Thanquol hissed, hurling the gizmo down at Krakul. The warlock-engineer shrieked once as the heavy bronze safety valve struck him, shattering his skull into a pulpy mess.

The other skaven wailed in horror, falling to their knees, exposing their throats in submission. It was sorely tempting to annihilate every one of the vermin, but Thanquol knew he needed them. He'd had time to do a lot of thinking while hunting for his disloyal underlings. He didn't like the conclusions he'd reached.

Strong and powerful, mightier than any vessel of flesh and bone, the rat-ogre's unliving body was nevertheless cut off from the aethyr, denying Thanquol access to the divine power of the Horned Rat and the black sorcery which emanated from such power. For a grey seer, being denied this was even more terrifying than the diminished sensory stimulation offered by Boneripper's mechanical senses.

There was another aspect which chilled Thanquol to his very marrow and made him feel very small and timid despite his new brawn and bulk. How many Bonerippers had there been? Each of them dying in some spectacular and gruesome fashion? There was something hideously unlucky about rat-ogres, something that was positively fatal to them. Thanquol didn't like the idea that he had inherited the current Boneripper's ill fortune when he'd switched bodies with the brute. He felt as though he were scurrying about a drain, fighting against time and current before he was sucked down to a horrible doom!

No! He had to get back into his own body – and he had to do it quickly. The only way to do that was to force the breeder-witch to undo her curse. She had to know the secret of such magic, she must have used it many times with the beasts of her carnival!

'Hear-listen!' Thanquol growled at the grovelling skaven. 'All of you obey! Find-seek breeder-witch! Don't hurt, only find!' Thanquol could see the scheming wheels turning in the brains of his underlings, so he decided to add a threat to his command.

'Hurt-harm breeder-witch and I will go to Greypaw Hollow!' Thanquol snarled, rearing up to the rat-ogre's full height. He thumped both bony claws against his chest, recalling how formidable the troll's performance had been. The effect was only somewhat lessened when he dropped his real body to the ground.

'I will kill your breeders, crush your whelps and take your warpstone!' Thanquol threatened. 'I will make Greypaw Hollow the lowest of thrall-clans! You will all be fodder-meat for the snake-maggots of Clan Verms!'

The dire threat brought renewed promises of fealty and obedience from the skaven, their whines and squeaks echoing through the forest. They could be counted upon to do what Thanquol demanded of them. His threat would keep them in line.

Of course, after all he had suffered, Thanquol intended to carry out every part of his threat, whether the simpering ratkin obeyed him or not.

Thanquol stared down at the little village, cursing for the umpteenth time Boneripper's lack of smell. With a proper nose, he'd be able to pick out the breeder-witch's scent from the air. He could tell in an instant if Naktit was lying to him and punish the track-rat accordingly. The only thing that made him dubious of such treachery was the fact that the other skaven had no way of knowing about this particular infirmity. As far as they knew, Thanquol could smell as keenly as any of them.

Unless, of course, that filthy tinker-rat Krakul had said something before he died.

Flexing the massive arms of the rat-ogre, Thanquol glowered at his underlings. The scouts had been gone only a short time before reporting that the caravan had been abandoned. There were signs of a fight that must have happened after Thanquol's... withdrawal. From the evidence, the fighting had been between two groups of humans. The scouts couldn't say which of the humans had won, but they had been able to follow the witch's scent back to this village.

Thanquol ground his fangs in annoyance. Naktit said that the witch had been taken to the biggest building in the village. The grey seer knew that sort of structure; it was one of the god-burrows the humans built to worship the confusing pantheon they followed. This particular one had a big hammer on its spire. Thanquol knew that particular cult quite well – the followers of Sigmar had a positive mania for burning any wizard or witch they could get their hands on. If he didn't act fast, the breeder-witch would be dead and the secret of her curse lost with her!

He couldn't let that happen! More and more, Thanquol felt the gnawing dread that something dire would happen, that the same fate which had overtaken six other Bonerippers would soon befall this one! To save himself, he had to save the witch from the witch hunters!

'You are sure-certain there is a tunnel?' Thanquol snapped at Naktit.

The scout bobbed his head in frantic eagerness. 'Yes-yes, Horrible One! Man-thing temple-place always have tunnel! Use to hide-flee when man-thing gods make war!'

Thanquol reached a huge claw to his face to brush his whiskers, only belatedly remembering that Boneripper didn't have any. It was true enough that the different priests of the humans sometimes made war against each other. The first thing they would do in such a war would be to burn down the houses of other gods. But would humans have enough brains to build an escape tunnel?

The rat-ogre's skull twisted about, craning downwards to regard the horned ratman standing at Thanquol's feet. There was such a look of dull idiocy on the grey seer's face that Thanquol felt a gnawing horror crawl through him. Whatever happened, he had to return to his own body. He couldn't abandon it to the mindless Boneripper. He had to be back inside his own fur, feeling blood coursing through his veins, a heart pounding in his chest! He had to restore his connection to the Horned One's power! More, he had to get a sniff of snuff. His nerves, or whatever he had in the rat-ogre's body, were on edge for lack of a pinch of warpsnuff. It didn't do any good to dump the stuff into the rat-ogre's nasal cavities; it would only burn up in the automaton's furnace.

Yes, they would attack the human village. Pakstab would lead the majority of the skaven in an assault against the village walls, drawing the humans away from the temple. While the humans were occupied with Pakstab's diversion, Thanquol and Naktit's scouts would use the tunnel to sneak into the crypt beneath the temple. Humans had a tendency to lock their captives underground, so he was hopeful the breeder-witch would be there.

If not – well, every last ratkin in the expedition knew what Thanquol would do to them if anything went wrong!

Thanquol snarled as his metal shoulders brushed against the ceiling of the tunnel, sending a cascade of debris raining down upon him. Belatedly, he remembered to shield the horned body strapped to his back, twisting about awkwardly so the rat-ogre's metal chest took the brunt of the rubble. After all he had gone through, it would be a cruelty beyond imagination to have his real body mangled before he could return to it.

Or was that the point? He glared suspiciously at the narrow tunnel and at Naktit. Had that been the scout's scheme, to lure Thanquol down here where the rat-ogre's ridiculous size would prove disadvantageous? Where Boneripper's very bulk threatened to bring the entire hole crashing about his ears?

Thanquol bit down on his suspicions. As much as it galled him, he had to trust Naktit. He had to trust that the breeder-witch was where the scout said she was. He was a bit reassured by Naktit's presence – surely the tracker would know he'd be the first casualty if Thanquol found out he was lying.

Eventually, the tunnel wormed its way beneath the stone foundations of a building. So far, it appeared Naktit's report was accurate. The only building in the human warren large enough to warrant such ponderous foundations was the temple. Thanquol began to feel a bit more optimistic. When this was all over, he might even allow Naktit to live.

Human voices, low and distorted, began to filter into the tunnel. Ahead, Thanquol could see a heavy stone wall with a ring set into it. This, as Naktit hurried to explain, was the entrance to the temple. On the other side was the crypt.

'...confess, woman, while you still have a tongue to do so!' The voice was harsh and cruel, almost skaven-like in its vicious inflection.

'You will torture me anyway, templar, so what use are my words?'

The second voice set Thanquol's jaws clacking together. It was the breeder-witch! From her tone, she sounded weak, possibly wounded. Maybe dying? Thanquol fought down the panic that threatened to overwhelm him. He had to wait, let Pakstab draw away the other humans. Then he could safely step in and snatch the breeder-witch.

'By Sigmar's hammer, you will confess all your evils!' the witch hunter snarled. 'You will confess that you are in league with the creatures of Chaos, that you lured the people of this community to your encampment in order to feed their flesh to your hideous masters!'

'The Strigany are no servants of the Old Night,' the witch spoke, her voice weary. 'The monsters you speak of attacked my people as well as yours.'

'Evil will always turn upon itself,' the witch hunter snapped. He might have said more, but the sound of frantic voices and hurried steps interrupted him.

'Brother Echter! The monsters are attacking the village!'

'They have come to save their infernal mistress,' the witch hunter swore. 'Rally the militia! These abominations must not be allowed to reach the temple!'

The sound of rushing feet faded as the humans raced upstairs. Thanquol gave them enough time to be well and truly gone before telling Naktit to open the secret door. Pakstab's warriors would keep the humans occupied while they slipped in and stole the breeder-witch.

Naktit and his scouts tugged at the iron ring, slowly pulling back the block that sealed off the tunnel. Thanquol bristled at the delay. Lumbering forwards he seized the top of the stone with his claws and dragged the ponderous obstruction aside. Glaring at the skaven, he motioned for them to hurry onwards into the crypt.

The room on the other side of the wall was long and narrow, its sides lined with deep niches. Within each niche reposed the mouldering bones of some long dead human, the remains sealed away by an iron gate. A set of stone steps rose up into the ceiling, blocked by a trapdoor.

Except for the skaven, there was only one other living occupant in the crypt. The breeder-witch was locked inside one of the niches, her arms bound to her sides with heavy leather straps, her face disfigured by a heavy wax seal marked with the sign of the twin-tailed comet.

Thanquol brushed aside the scouts, rushing to the witch's niche. The hag groaned in terror when she saw the ghastly rat-ogre peering at her through the bars. Then a cackle of amusement wracked her aged body.

'Not liking your new home, rat-fiend?' she laughed.

Thanquol's claw lashed out, pounding against the gate and denting its iron bars. 'Fix-change!' he snarled at her. 'Away-take curse-hex or I smash-kill slow-slow!'

The witch peered at him with hateful eyes. 'Kill me and you'll never get back,' she threatened, pointing her chin towards the horned rat-man lashed behind the rat-ogre's shoulders.

Thanquol recoiled at the witch's words. He crouched lower, trying to assume a meek posture. It was difficult to manage with a body as massive as Boneripper's.

'Fix-change,' he repeated, trying to keep his voice low and pleasing. 'Save-help me and I save-help you. Other man-things not hurt-harm.'

Again the witch laughed. 'Help me? Can you give me back my sons who you and your vermin slaughtered?'

Thanquol smashed his fist against the ceiling, bringing a trickle of dust down upon his head. Of all the times for a human to start acting stupid! Here he was offering this one a chance to escape torture and slow death, and all she could talk about were her dead whelps!

A sound behind him caused Thanquol to turn. Running feet in the temple above, people rushing towards the trapdoor. The humans were coming back!

Another sound drew Thanquol's attention to the far wall. Naktit and his scouts were back in the tunnel, pushing the block back into place. At once the enormity of Pakstab's treachery was apparent. The warlord had led the attack only long enough to make Thanquol think everything was going according to plan. As soon as the grey seer had time to get into the crypt, the coward had called off the attack. Now Naktit was closing off the only route of escape! Once again, the traitors of Greypaw Hollow were leaving him to face the humans alone!

Thanquol lurched towards the closing tunnel, then turned back around. What use to escape if he left the witch behind? He needed her to break the curse! If he left her behind, the priest-humans would kill her and then he'd be trapped inside Boneripper for the rest of his life. Which, given the durability of rat-ogres, wasn't likely to be long.

The trapdoor was being pulled open even as Thanquol turned back towards the witch's cell. The harsh voice of the witch hunter shouted from the top of the stairs.

'Behold! The heretic's creatures have come to save her!'

Brother Echter's statement was punctuated with a pistol shot. Thanquol could dimly feel the bullet crack against the rat-ogre's back. From past experience, he knew it would take more than that to slow down Boneripper. However, there was just a chance that the human would reach the same conclusion and start shooting at Thanquol's body.

Turning around, protecting the body lashed to the rat-ogre's back, Thanquol roared at the frightened men clattering down the stairs, pounding his claws against his chest. The display appeared to impress the humans just as much as it had Pakstab's skaven. The men following the witch hunter cried out in despair, then turned and fled back up the stairs.

'You'll not frighten me, mutant!' Brother Echter swore, undaunted by the defection of his followers. Boldly, he drew a second pistol from his belt.

Thanquol was in no mood for such nonsense. Lunging forwards, he brought Boneripper's massive claw slashing down, tearing deep furrows through the witch hunter's flesh. The mutilated man screamed through the tatters of his face and crashed to the floor.

The skeletal rat-ogre turned back towards the witch's cell, shaking his bloody claw at the obstinate hag. 'You will suffer much-much unless you fix-change!' Thanquol growled.

'You killed everything I cared for,' the witch told him. 'And if you kill me, you'll never get back!'

Thanquol clenched his bony hands, shaking with frustration. How could he threaten something that didn't care if she lived or died? Worse, how could he threaten something that in dying would doom him as well?

Before he could work out the dilemma, the crypt echoed with the explosive report of a pistol shot. The hag's gloating countenance became twisted with pain, a bright bloom of blood springing from her breast. Wailing in horror, Thanquol brought Boneripper's giant foot smashing down upon the mangled witch hunter. Vengefully he stomped out the lingering spark of life that had enabled Brother Echter to shoot the witch.

Filled with despair, Thanquol went back to the cell. The breeder-witch was lying upon the floor, bleeding out from her wound. If he had had his magic, he could have helped her, much as it offended his senses. But the hag's own curse made this impossible. He could only watch helplessly as the witch died, and in dying sealed his own fate.

Thanquol railed against the injustice of it all! To be doomed to such a cruel end because of the crude magic of a filthy breeder-thing, and all because a bunch of slack-witted fool-meat had led him to believe his mortal enemies were near! If he had the chance again, he would kill every last rat in Greypaw Hollow for goading him into this useless flea-hunt! By the Horned One, they should suffer for doing this to him!

As Thanquol bemoaned his fate, as he watched the witch die, a strange sensation came upon him. A flash of unspeakable cold, a whirring blur of light and darkness...

The grey seer fought against the darkness, though this time the struggle was far less than it had been before. When he could see again, it was with the clear vision of skaven eyes. A thousand smells rushed into his nose, a hundred sounds trickled into his ears. He could feel the blood flowing through his veins, the heart pounding in his chest. For good measure, he twitched his whiskers.

He was back in his own body! Again he could feel the aethyric forces flowing about him, the glory of the Horned Rat waiting to shape itself at his command. Thanquol couldn't understand how the curse had been broken. Some final, desperate effort to gain the grey seer's aid on the part of the witch?

Thanquol struggled to peer over Boneripper's shoulder to see into the cell. Irritably, he snarled an order at his bodyguard, telling it to turn around. With its usual slavish obedience, the rat-ogre shifted its position.

The witch was dead, there was no mistaking that smell! Thanquol ground his fangs together as the solution to his deliverance came to him. The hag had been toying with him! She had told him if she died he would never break the curse when it was her very death that had ended the enchantment! How he wished she was alive so he could wring her neck!

For the moment, however, he had more pressing problems. The humans would recover from their fright soon, and when they did, they would come back to the crypt in force. It would be best for him to be far away when they did.

Then there was the small matter of Greypaw Hollow and the treachery of its denizens. Thanquol would teach those rats the price for betraying him!

But first he'd have one of them cut him loose. The idea of travelling all the way to Skavenblight tied to Boneripper's back wasn't exactly appealing.

He'd spent more than enough time around the rat-ogre.

EDITOR'S NOTE

We have included the previously untitled short story Death and Glory! *out of historical interest. Its first and only appearance was in the first edition of the Empire army book, way back in 1993. While it is not the first published G&F story (we believe the honour of this lies with* Geheimnisnacht, *also included in this collection) it is one of the very earliest, and dates back to when William King was employed by Games Workshop as a staff writer. Eagle-eyed readers will notice that a well-known character appears to die at the end of the story; is this a huge continuity glitch? Well... maybe! We don't actually see him die, though his death is strongly implied. Maybe this battle has yet to happen, or may or may not happen – Gotrek & Felix see some pretty strange things as they pass through the Paths of the Old Ones in the novel* Giantslayer.*

Finally, when we recovered the file from our archives, we were surprised and delighted to find that the story had a last line, which was somehow missed off the original typeset. So here in all its glory, is the Empire story, restored to its former glory, complete with final line!

DEATH AND GLORY!

William King

'Repent! This is your last night on earth! The end of the world is coming,' the flagellant cried.

Felix Jaeger cursed the dark destiny that had dragged him into these terrible events. He should be at home in his father's mansion, not listening to the ranting of some deranged maniac on the eve of what must surely be the one of the largest battles in the Empire's history. This was no place for an aspiring poet.

Why did he have to be here? And where was Gotrek? The last time he had seen him the Trollslayer had been wandering off to booze with his fellow outcast dwarfs. What bad luck – they spend six days in the mountains hunting for trolls and when they return they find the Imperial army camped outside the walls of Hauptmansburg and all able-bodied men called to serve. All Felix had wanted was a decent meal and a comfortable bed, not a pitched battle with the hordes of orcdom.

'Cast off your worldly goods! Dispose of your chattels! They will profit you not! The end is coming!' the flagellant ranted.

Felix inspected the zealot with some distaste. The flickering firelight revealed an appearance that was most disturbing. His scrawny body was naked except for a loincloth and the tattered remains of a jerkin. Old scars criss-crossed his chest and legs. Fresh red blood dripped from a weal on his shoulders. Festering open sores marred his face and abdomen. Mad blue eyes glared out from his starved fanatic's face. In one bony hand he clutched an oak club driven through with rusty nails. Some of the puncture marks on his body were obviously self-inflicted.

'Easy for you to say, father. You don't have a copper pfennig to your name! Me – I'm well paid to fight,' shouted Eusebio. His fine linen shirt lent an air of truth to his words. Felix had seen noblemen less well-dressed than the foppish young Tilean mercenary.

'Too well paid,' called Sergeant Lothar to loud laughter from the gathering crowd. 'All you have to do is stand back and fire your cross-bow at those green-skinned devils. It's we halberdiers who'll have to get to grips with them. Doubtless while our noble lords and masters stand back and applaud themselves for winning yet another battle.'

Eusebio gave an eloquent shrug. Obviously he thought that if Lothar wanted to risk his life in the press of the melee then more fool him.

'Aye, laugh!' thundered the flagellant. 'Laugh while ye can. Smile as skulls smile! Tomorrow the grave yawns for you all!'

Felix shuddered and drew his tattered red cloak tighter about his body although it wasn't cold. The hundreds of blazing campfires and the press of thousands of bodies kept the night chill at bay. All around the soldiers fell silent. They were a superstitious lot and tomorrow they would be fighting for their lives. The fanatic's words held a harsh core of truth. Sensing that he had the attention of the warriors the flagellant pulled himself up to his full height. He pointed an accusing finger at Eusebio.

'You, Tilean! You're so proud of your appearance! How will that fine shirt look tomorrow all rent and stained with blood? Better to look like me. Prepare your body for the wounds of the morrow.'

Eusebio made the sign of the hammer across his chest like a peasant warding off the evil eye. The Tilean had obviously been in the Empire long enough to look to its patron deity, Sigmar of the Hammer, for protection. There was some muttering among the crowd now. An archer with the guttural accent of a native of Reikwald forest agreed with the fanatic. Felix heard a Stirlander Greatsword say that such words would bring ill-luck. The Stirlander fingered the hilt of his mighty blade meaningfully. A less religious or a more sane man than the fanatic would have shut up. That blade was almost as tall as Felix, and Felix was a tall man.

The flagellant warmed to his theme. A grinning young pistolier pulled faces behind his back and gestured to his fellows to indicate that the zealot was mad.

'From the north, Chaos comes. The minions of the four Great Powers ride forth, clad in black and bronze. In their left hand is fire. In their right hand is the sword. Darkness is behind them. Destruction to the fore. Their castles are built of skulls! Their garments are woven from the flayed skins of women! They will trample the cities of men beneath iron-shod hooves. In the woods lurk beasts that walk like men. They gather now that the last days are near.'

He looked directly at Morrslieb, the lesser moon. 'They have allies. Men who have sold their souls to the darkness. Mutants and foul creatures tainted by warpstone in their blood. Fat merchants who seek the meaningless trappings of power and wealth!'

There was a commotion at the edge of the crowd. Felix could see a man in the shining armour and plumed helmet of a Reiksguard knight. He had come all the way from the silk pavilions of the nobility to investigate the disturbance. Sweat stood out on the flagellant's brow now. His eyes were glazed. A fine trickle of drool leaked from the corner of his mouth. His hands shook. Felix was reminded of a man in the grip of a terminal fever.

'From the mountains of the east come the orcish hordes: green-skinned savages with the hearts of beasts and the fury of madmen. They will cast down the kingdoms of men and dwell in the ruins before the last day dawns and Chaos swallows the world. Tomorrow you will face them. Tomorrow Morr will reach out for you with his bony claw.'

'You there, that's enough of that talk!' The powerful voice of the Reiksguard cut through the babble. 'Tomorrow we will face the orcish scum and will triumph, as men have done since the time of Sigmar!'

The fanatic stared at the knight. He looked as if he were about to argue but then he shrugged. 'There are none so blind as those who will not see!'

He stalked off towards the camp's edge where a huge band of his brothers waited. The crowd parted round him and no one would meet his gaze.

'The rest of you get some sleep. You have to fight a battle tomorrow. The Empire needs you all well rested!'

The crowd dispersed. Felix threw himself down next to the nearest fire, and pulled his cloak tight about him. The frenzied wailing of the flagellants echoed through the night. Even as Felix drifted into sleep he thought it an evil omen.

* * *

With a clatter of armour the Knights Panther rode past. Felix stepped from the road and let them go by. Only a fool would have stood in the way of those massive armoured men on their mighty metal-clad steeds. From the helmtop of one knight the eyeless head of a great cat stared sightlessly toward the battlefield.

'You there! What are you doing wandering about like a dazed half-wit. Get to your company!'

Felix looked around. A burly man with the bull-head insignia of Ostland on his shield was bellowing and gesturing furiously with his spear. It took Felix a moment to realise that the man was talking to him. He was tempted to tell the man to go to hell but he squared his shoulders and marched purposefully on, determined to find the Trollslayer before the battle began. He was bound by his oath to record the slayer's doom in an epic poem so he felt he should at least be present to witness the conflict.

He walked to the brow of the hill near the Imperial guns. Everywhere artillery men and siege engineers were busy. A captain of cannon leaned on the barrel of his weapon measuring ranges and consulting a small book of charts. Muscular gunners, stripped to the waist, hastily piled cannonballs beside their massive cast-iron weapons. Small sweating lads puffed on firepots to keep them alight.

From this vantage point the entire field of battle was visible. In the distance Felix could see the green horde, a vast seething mass of scrawny hunchback goblin infantry and bellowing orcs. Great trolls loomed over the press of bodies. He saw the long skirmish line of wolf riders in the van of the enemy army. The blood-chilling howl of those giant beasts sent shivers down Felix's spine. He had faced wolf riders before and it had not been a pleasant experience. On the far right flank orcs strained to pull back the arms of huge, crude catapults. Near them, strung out along a low narrow ridge, was a unit of orc crossbowmen. There were far too many greenskins to count.

Felix had heard dark rumours of the size of the orc horde. If anything, these had been an underestimation. The Imperial force was seriously outnumbered.

The soldiers of the Emperor were ranged between two small hills. On the the hill where Felix stood were two great cannon. On the other hilltop was the dread Helblaster volley gun and a third cannon. Both hills were protected by a screen of missile troops. On the slope below Felix were the Tilean crossbowmen. Eusebio turned and gave Felix a cheerful wave.

Reikland archers protected the volley gun. To the left, at the foot of the hill, was the great frenzied warband of the flagellants. They howled and lashed each other. Felix didn't know whether the sound scared the enemy but it certainly frightened him.

Between the two hills lay the main body of the Imperial troops. They were laid out in a checkerboard pattern. The forward troops alternated between units of cavalry and units of infantry. Felix saw the Knights Panther take up position beside a block of Reiksguard foot knights. The Knights of the White Wolf brandished their great two-handed hammers and exchanged cheery insults with the Middenheim halberdiers. Behind them were spearmen from the provinces, the dark red tunics of Carroburg contrasting with the black tabards of Nuln. In front of the whole army was a long skirmish line of Kislevite horse archers.

Felix saw the proud figure of the young Emperor Karl-Franz himself. He had just finished addressing the troops of the centre. He leapt into the saddle of his pegasus, Northwind, and took to the sky in a sweep of white wings. A great roar of acclaim rose from the Imperial troops as his steed carried him cloudwards.

With a loud clanking of tracks and chuffing of pistons a steam tank rolled into position in the Imperial centre. The air vibrated with the thrum of its engine. The acrid smell of its smoke filled Felix's nostrils.

The troops parted to let the steam tank through. Its massive armoured bulk was an awesome sight. Felix had heard of these products of the Imperial School of Engineering but he had never seen one. Thinking that the cheer he had heard was for him the tank commander doffed his plumed hat in recognition of this tribute. A wave of catcalls was the soldier's response.

Suddenly the Imperial army was silenced. From out of the orc ranks something huge emerged. With a flap of leathery pinions it pulled itself into the sky. Felix saw that it was a wyvern, and on its back was a huge orc. He tried to estimate the span of the creature's wings but gave up. It was huge. The wyvern opened its draconic maw and let out a huge bellow. A hush fell on the Imperial soldiery. Every man present felt terror in his heart.

'Send that big lizard over here!' roared a voice that Felix recognised. 'I haven't had breakfast yet.'

Felix turned to look back down the hill. A group of dwarfs limped wearily up the slope. They looked a forbidding bunch: all had huge crests of dyed hair, all were covered in strange, intricate tattoos and all brandished mighty battle axes and warhammers. They were marked as members of the cult of Slayers, that strange band of doomed brethren sworn to seek death in battle. Their leader was an enormously muscular dwarf with one eye covered by a great black patch. It was he who shouted at the wyvern rider.

'That's Gotrek Gurnisson.' Felix heard one of the gunners say. 'He's a nutter. I saw him drink a whole keg of ale last night.'

As if in answer to Gotrek's challenge, the wyvern roared again. Its bestial call rolled over the battlefield. Once more the Imperial force fell silent.

'Come down here and say that,' shouted Gotrek. The flagellants let out a mighty wail.

'And you lot shut up,' bellowed the Trollslayer. 'Can't you see Snorri Nosebiter here has a hangover?'

If the flagellants heard the dwarf they chose to ignore him. In the distance the Orc army had begun to move.

'Morning, manling,' said Gotrek as the dwarfs made it to the crest of the hill. He took a deep breath and grinned to reveal his missing teeth. As he always did when the prospect of carnage beckoned he appeared obscenely cheerful. 'Looks like a good day for it.'

'For what?' Felix asked. He was obscurely relieved to see the Trollslayer. He wasn't sure why. There was nothing reassuring about a demented dwarf with a big axe.

'For dying.' Gotrek pointed a powerful stubby finger at the advancing horde. He looked like a child given a particularly good present on a high feast day. 'Look Snorri, Trolls!'

The Slayer beside Gotrek shook his head and nodded blearily. Were those three studs really driven into his forehead, Felix wondered?

'Snorri thinks you're right, Gotrek,' said Snorri, and he gestured towards the trolls with his huge warhammer. 'Snorri thinks we should go and have a word with them.'

The dwarfs raced down the hill as fast as their short legs would carry them. Briefly Felix debated with himself as to whether he should follow. Then he heard the howl of dismay from the gunners. From the corner of his eye he caught sight of something huge hurtling towards him. He threw himself flat. The air was displaced by an enormous mass and the sudden breeze rippled his hair. The ground shook with a tremendous impact. Looking around Felix saw a massive boulder that hadn't been there moments before. Two legs protruded from beneath it. Blood splattered the stone and a trickle of red leaked from below the giant rock.

The howling of the flagellants increased in volume, competing with the distant bestial grunting of the orcs. If Felix hadn't known better he would have sworn the greenskins were counting down. That couldn't be it... no orc could count past three.

Suddenly the orcs stopped chanting. The arm of the great catapult sprang forward. Another huge boulder arced towards the hill. Felix watched it come in. There was an appalling feeling of helplessness about the whole situation. He wanted to run and take cover but he had no idea what direction to run in. Perhaps if he moved he would simply position himself under the path of the boulder, like the poor devil behind him.

There were audible gasps of relief as the boulder swept on over the hill. Seeing the orcs hastening to reload their machines, Felix risked a glance at the battlefield. A horde of goblin archers had moved forward. They were small, stunted creatures garbed in black. Night goblins! He had heard dire rumours of their noxious drug-induced frenzies and the dread fanatic cultists they produced. The goblin archers opened fire but their missiles fell far short of the jeering Imperial line. The giant wolves loped forward easily despite the weight of the riders on their backs. Disciplined ranks of huge orc warriors marched forwards. The impression of an invincible host was only spoiled by the fact that two units in the rear had stopped to shout insults and catcalls at each other. Three huge trolls loomed over the squabble and watched the fracas with baffled bemusement.

What was that over there? Surely it couldn't be! It was. Felix shuddered. Way off on the left he could see a huge spider scuttle forward. On its back was a gibbering goblin shaman. The goblin mage brandished a staff of bone around which played a glowing nimbus of light. The shaman pointed the staff at the hill on which Felix stood and the hair on the nape of Felix's neck stood on end. He felt a strange tingling on his skin. No, he thought. Not vile sorcery too. He was going to die.

Before anything more could happen Felix heard the sound of a spell being recited nearby. A tall man in a grey cloak raised his hands and made a short chopping gesture with the flat of his hand. The surge of mystical energy around him subsided as quickly as it had come into being.

With a roar the Imperial army surged forward. Kislevite horse archers raced towards the night goblins. Slightly behind them trotted the Knights Panther and the White Wolves. The steam tank rumbled toward the enemy, juddering slightly on the uneven ground. With disciplined precision the formations of halberdiers and spearmen marched forward ready to close any gaps in the Imperial line. The proud banner of the Empire fluttered right in the middle of the force.

'Quickly, silence those catapults,' shouted the captain of artillery. The ground shook and a great cloud of black smoke billowed forth. The air within Felix's lungs seemed to vibrate and the sound of the blast temporarily deafened him. The whistle of a cannon shot filled the air. The ground near the orc chukkas erupted. Clods of dirt were thrown twenty feet into the air.

'Not a bad shot, commander of the second cannon. But this is how it's done. Hans – alter the angle to the right by two degrees!'

'Two degrees right. Yes, sir.' After the sweating gunners had heaved the cannon round the captain took a lighted taper from the boy with the firepot and touched it to the fuse. The fuse fizzed and sputtered and then went out.

'Yes, that's the way it's done alright. Brilliant,' said the first gun's commander.

On the far hill the cannon roared. Smoke billowed down and obscured the Tileans from sight. In the distance a catapult flew to pieces, timbers splintered by the impact. Felix saw the orc who had been loading the thing hurled into the air as the arm was suddenly unleashed.

'Good shot,' said one of the gunners nonchalantly. The archers and the crossbowmen opened fire. A hail of arrows and bolts rained down on the foe. Orcs fell clutching wooden stalks that had suddenly sprouted in their chests like obscene plants. The air shimmered now as spell and counterspell flickered between the two armies. A hail of iron bolts leapt from the brow of the grey-cloaked mage and pierced several wolf riders, the rest fell back towards their own line while their leaders frantically tried to rally them.

A giant boulder landed in the middle of the Knights Panther. Two brave men died instantly. The knights' banner was snapped like a twig. The hideous whickering of broken-backed horses filled the air. The rest of the knights continued stalwartly forward towards the jeering orcs and goblins. A shattering wave of crossbow bolts fell onto them from the orcs. One rider went down with an arrow through the eyeslit of his helm. With a bolt through its chest, one of the steeds rolled over, trapping another rider beneath its thrashing bulk. Foam spewing from its mouth, the terrified last steed fled the battlefield, taking its rider with it.

The Kislevites raced forward at the night goblins. From the midst of the black-garbed mob three figures emerged, whirling frantically. They all carried great ball and chains. Swiftly their whirling achieved near unstoppable momentum and the weight of the balls dragged them towards the horse archers.

The riders frantically stopped short, horses rearing as they tried to avoid whirling steel doom. Two fanatics ploughed by them but one made it right into the middle of the cavalry. The great ball wreaked terrible havoc. Blood and brains splattered everywhere. Men and horses fell, bones shattered and flesh pulped. Felix averted his eyes from the destruction.

The cannons spoke once more. This time their shots tore right through the second stone thrower, smashing it utterly. The gunners cheered excitedly. The captain of the first gun punched his fist into the air in triumph. Felix felt a little like cheering himself, he was so relieved at the prospect of not having rocks fall on his head.

The remaining Kislevites raced across their front to the enemy line. More fanatics were tempted forth by the easy targets presented. Felix watched two of the whirling maniacs collide. Their chains became hopelessly intertwined as the wrecking balls hurtled around in an ever decreasing spiral till they smashed their hapless bearers between them.

From the right there was a crash as the volley gun essayed an experimental shot. Even at this long range it cut a bloody swathe in the green line. The crossbowmen fired again, killing two of the fanatics. At this range that was good shooting. A cloud of arrows disposed of the remainder.

'For Sigmar and Karl-Franz!' The warcry went up from the Imperial line. The orcs chanted their bestial battle cries. A howling green wave broke on the steel wall of the Imperial line. A swirling melee erupted covering nearly half a league of ground.

Felix's keen eyes scanned the battlefield, looking for Gotrek. There! He could just see the frenzied dwarfs cutting a path of bloody ruin through the goblins towards the trolls. Gotrek's great axe rose then fell in a bloody arc destroying everything in its path. He was causing barely less havoc than the steam tank as it rolled forward, crushing everything in its way. Around the tank men and greenskin clashed in furious conflict. The White Wolves surged into a band of bellowing orcs, sending them fleeing in utter confusion.

Having silenced the enemy artillery the cannons were now free to wreak havoc on the rear of the enemy formations. Looking down into the howling maelstrom of conflict Felix was glad of his safe position on the hill. Down there the casualties were horrendous. Many of those who were not killed outright would die later from their wounds. Many more would live on in the half-life of the terribly maimed. Down there he could see spearmen and halberdiers breast to breast with steel-thewed orcs. In the tight press of bodies there was barely room to swing a weapon. Many would die beneath the trampling feet of their comrades as the melee swept backwards and forwards.

Felix congratulated himself on the fact that for once he was in the right place at the right time. For once he had avoided the brutal hand-to-hand fighting. With the enemy stone throwers gone he was safe and in a position to observe the fighting. Now all that was needed was for the Imperial army to carry the day. Well, the cannons could see to that now.

Suddenly a wail of terror went up from the nearby gunners. Felix followed the pointing hand of the gun-captain. In the sky a small dot was swiftly expanding as it descended towards them. It was the wyvern! By Sigmar, no! This couldn't be happening.

With a snap the wyvern opened its mighty pinions, slowing its meteoric descent. All around the gunners turned to flee in abject fear. The grey-clad wizard looked up and began to chant a spell. He was too late. The thing descended on him crushing the mage beneath its ponderous bulk.

Too numb to move, Felix stood frozen on the spot. It grew suddenly cold as the wyvern loomed over him. He stood in the titanic shadow of those leathery wings. The musty leathery smell of the beast filled his nostrils. The creature's long scaly neck snaked round and a head nearly as large as a man looked down on Felix. He stared upward into cold reptilian eyes. The creature gave its croaking roar and its snarl revealed teeth as large as daggers.

By Sigmar, the thing was big. As it reared upright it was nearly five times as tall as Felix. It lashed a tail as thick as a battering ram. The whip-like crack was as loud as a musket going off. Poison dripped from the barbed stinger. As the droplets touched the ground the grass blackened and died. A long tongue, glistening with mucous, flickered out and Felix flinched.

Enthroned on the monster's back was the largest orc Felix had ever seen, obviously the general of this warhost. In his left hand he held a scimitar that probably weighed as much as Felix. In his right he brandished a bizarre daemon-headed staff. He glared down at Felix with yellow hate-filled eyes. Felix knew he was going to die.

Swift as a thunderbolt the wyvern's head snapped forward. Mighty jaws gaped. A blast of stinking breath seared Felix's face. Instinctively he leapt backward and the jaws snapped closed right in front of his face. He was reminded of a beartrap closing. Felix turned, filled with an urge to put something big between him and the monster. Swiftly he vaulted the cannon, feeling the thing's cold breath on his neck with every step. Now he turned at bay, knowing there was no way he could out run the monster. It was too late for that. In a futile gesture of pointless bravado, he drew his sword, determined to at least go down fighting.

A sweep of the wyvern's giant claw knocked the cannon over. Felix barely had time to spring clear. He fell back into a defensive posture as his fencing masters had once taught him. It was a reflex drilled into him by long hours of practice.

'Now you die!' grunted the orcish chieftain in bad Reikspiel.

'Come down here and say that,' shouted Felix with more bravery than he felt. The wyvern's jaws gaped. Now, thought Felix. One good thrust and he could ram his blade right down the wyvern's throat, maybe punch up through the soft inside of the jaw into the thing's tiny brain. The beast's death-throes would probably kill him but what else was there for him to do? He was going to die anyway.

Everything seemed to slow down. He felt everything with utter clarity, sensed his own movements with utter precision. In the distance he could hear the cries of the embattled and the screams of the dying. The smells of blood and gunpowder and fear filled his nostrils. Cold sweat ran down his back. Any second now the thing would strike, and, like a dying scorpion stinging, Felix would strike back.

A shadow fell on the wyvern. Mighty pinions beat the air. A white thunderbolt fell. A golden-armoured warrior struck. A titanic hammer swung in an irresistible arc. The head of the orc general was knocked clean off his shoulders. The wyvern turned, whining. A green fountain of blood spurted from the orc's neck and the body toppled forward from its throne. With its rider's weight gone, the wyvern bellowed once and leapt into the sky, free to seek out its mountain home.

Felix found himself facing the Emperor Karl-Franz over the corpse of the orc general. The Emperor opened his visor and gazed down on Felix with keen, far seeing eyes.

'That was the bravest thing I've ever seen,' said the Emperor.

'It was nothing,' said Felix, then reaction swept through him and he fainted clean away.

* * *

William King

The huge red sun set over the battlefield. By its ruddy light the scene was like a picture of hell. Mauled bodies lay everywhere. Imperial soldiers heaped the corpses of dead orcs on great pyres for burning. The cries of the wounded and the dying drifted up like the pleas of damned souls. The frenzied howling of the flagellants mocked any pretence of victory. Felix passed a dying man who begged him for water. Not having any, Felix averted his eyes and walked on.

He found Gotrek on the cold hillside. The Trollslayer was tamping down the last clods of earth on a gravesite. He didn't look up as Felix approached, seemingly lost in his own inhuman and bitter thoughts.

'Evening, manling,' Gotrek muttered. He leaned forward on the handle of the spade and turned his head to survey the scene of the carnage. Suddenly he looked very old and very tired. He gestured to the grave with his broad right hand.

'Snorri Nosebiter lies there. He killed three trolls.' The Slayer laughed bitterly. 'The last one fell on him.'

'I met the Emperor Karl-Franz today. He saved me from the wyvern. I thought I was going to die.'

In the distance the steam tank hauled the bodies of the barded horses from the field. Sparks flared from its chimneys, and glittered like fireflies in the gathering darkness.

'We're all going to die, manling. It's the manner of our going that's important.'

'We won, Gotrek. The White Wolves broke the savage orcs. The cannons smashed those big goblin units. Even those flagellants played their part by taking the gobbos in the flank. Or so Eusebio told me.'

Felix flushed. He had already decided not to mention the embarrassing fact of his fainting in front of Karl-Franz.

'Another great victory over the forces of evil,' Gotrek said mockingly. He shook his head. The golden chain that ran from his nose to his ear jingled. 'By Grungni, even when we win, we lose. There is no end of orcs and Chaos warriors and other enemies. One day they will sweep through the Kingdom of Dwarfs and the Empire of Men and all will end in blood and darkness.'

'You're beginning to sound like a flagellant,' said Felix. He was still alive when he had expected to be dead. He found it hard to share the dwarf's gloomy thoughts. 'We won here. We turned back the orc army. The Empire is saved.'

'For now, manling. For now.'

A GOTREK & FELIX GAZETTEER

A

Adolphus Krieger
A vampire. He was one of von Carstein's most trusted minions but vanished after the battle of Hel Fenn and von Carstein's defeat, only to resurface in Praag centuries later. Tall, dark and thin, he speaks with a noticeably foreign accent. He will also stop at nothing to get his hands on the Eye of Khemri, a deceptively powerful artefact.

Alberich
Prior of the Schrammel monastery.

Albericht Kruger
The Mutant Master. He was a mild-mannered mage who attended Altdorf University at the same time as Felix Jaeger but he has now become corrupted by the Dark Arts he practises.

Albion
Reputedly a land of perpetual rain and mists, very little else is actually known about it, mainly because it has always been surrounded by spells of great potency intended to ward it from the eye of outsiders.

Aldred Keppler
Known as 'Fellblade', a knight of the Order of the Fiery Heart. He journeyed to Karag Eight Peaks to retrieve the blade Karaghul.

Aldreth
One of the oldest servants of Teclis and his brother.

Altdorf
Greatest city in the Old World, Capital of the Empire, and seat of the Emperor Karl Franz II.

Anya Nitikin
A Kislevite woman, author of *Call of the South*, said to be one of the finest writers in the Empire. She is taking her

younger sister Talia to the Kingdom of the Dragon searching for a cure for her out-of-control behaviour.

Arek Daemonclaw

A formidable Chaos Warrior who has succeeded in uniting the four different factions of the Dark Powers to march down from the Chaos Wastes and lay siege to Praag. He is superstrong, superfast and near invulnerable.

Axe of the Runemasters

Also known as the Axe of Valek. An ancient artefact of immense power, previously wielded only by the High Runemasters of Karag Dum.

B

Baldurach

A member of the Council of Truthsayers in Albion.

Barak Varr

'Torrent Gate', the dwarf port lying on the mouth of Blood River. Being not only a lowland fortress but a haven for ocean-going vessels, more traditional dwarfs consider the locals a little touched.

Belegar

Nominal ruler of Karag Eight Peaks, he led the expedition to reclaim the lost stronghold.

Bjorni Bjornsson

Bjorni is a squat, muscular, repulsively ugly dwarf with a gruesome collection of warts on his face and a particularly huge and hairy one right on the end of his nose. He is crude, lewd and tells some exceptionally tall tales about his sexual conquests, though admittedly he does enjoy surprising success with women, a fact which never ceases to amaze Felix

Jaeger. He is first encountered by Ulrika at Karak Kadrin and introduces himself by propositioning her. Though she rejects him, he joins the party on their quest anyway and is one of the seven slayers who go to confront the dragon Skjalandir in its lair.

Black Coach

Unmarked coach that travels the Bögenhafen road on Geheimnisnacht, said to be driven by daemons.

Blind Pig, The

A tavern on Commerce Street, Nuln, owned by Heinz. Gotrek and Felix were employed as bouncers and it is here that the gutter runners stage their daring attack.

Blutdorf

A small and particularly squalid village located between Fredericksburg and Nuln.

Blutdorf Keep

Rundown castle overlooking Blutdorf, inhabited by the wizard Albericht Kruger.

Boneripper

Thanquol obtains a succession of unfortunate rat-ogre bodyguards from Clan Moulder, at great cost. Finally, he has a mechanical version constructed by a warlock-engineer, but even this proves unreliable.

Borek the Scholar

Also known as Borek Forkbeard because he has a huge forked beard which reaches all the way to the floor before being looped back up into his belt

He is the ancient dwarf scholar who organises an expedition to the Chaos Wastes to try and find the lost citadel of Karag Dum. It was Borek and his brother Vareg, who brought the last message from Karag Dum before it was swallowed by the Wastes, and though he tried to return at the time, the first mission failed and he was one of only three survivors.

Bounty Bay
Location where the combined fleets of Estalia finally defeated Redhand's pirate fleet. Redhand is believed to have escaped.

Bran Mac Kerog
The bear-like chieftain of the mountain men of Carn Mallog whose main passion seems to be greed.

Brocht
Huge circular stone tower.

Broken Pickaxe, The
Inn situated in the small town of Gelt. Gotrek, Felix and their party stay there en route to the Dragon Mountain.

C

Cabbage
A gnoblar in the service of the ogre Gutsnorter.

Captain Ahabsson
Captain of the *Storm Hammer*. He has a hook to replace his lost hand, and a letter of marque from Barak Varr.

Carn Mallog
A settlement of brochts on a ridge top and home to Bran Mac Kerog's mountain men. They are massive structures designed to resist siege and are engraved with runes similar to the tattoo patterns which adorn the faces of the warriors.

Caspian Rodor
Former grandmaster of the Order of the Black Bear. When he died, Rodor had his body sealed up in a cask of Wynters XVI. On the anniversary of his death, it became the tradition for every man in the order to take a ceremonial drink from his grave-cask.

Cauldron of a Thousand Poxes
A hideously powerful artefact for brewing diseases. Reputedly stolen from a temple of the Plague God, Nurgle and reconsecrated to the service of the Horned Rat.

Chang Squik
Of Clan Eshin, the assassins. Trained for years in the delivery of silent death. 3rd Degree adept in the way of the Crimson Talon and black belt in the Path of the Deadly Paw. Pupil of the infamous skaven assassin, Deathmaster Snikch.

Chaos Wastes
A hellish land to the far north beyond Kislev and Blackblood Pass. The armies of the four ruinous powers of Chaos reside there.

Count Andriev
Ulrika's distant cousin, a collector of antiques and curiosities. He hires the slayer and his companions to protect his collection and in particular, the Eye of Khemri.

Countess Gabriella of Nachthafen
A beautiful woman of indeterminate age. Sister-in-law to Rudgar. She also appears to have a mysterious connection to Krieger.

Count Hrothgar
Nobleman and member of the Order. He wants the Children of Ulric dead.

Crannog Mere
A strange floating village built in the middle of a lake. The somewhat primitive

houses appear to be either on stilts or situated atop small artificial islands and are linked by causeways of mud and logs. The only way of getting out to them is by way of a narrow, winding causeway, cunningly concealed just below the waterline so that it can only be seen from close at hand.

Culum

A massive and extremely well muscled Albion tribesman who challenges Gotrek to an arm wrestling competition. He is related to Murdo MacBaldoch in some way and married to Klara.

Cult of Slayers

Dwarf cult which has its spiritual home in Karak Kadrin, where the Shrine of Grimnir is located.

D

Darkstone Ring

Stone circle lying between Blutroch and the Standing Stones Inn, to the north of the Bögenhafen road.

Detlef Sierck

Greatest playwright in the Empire, and known associate of the vampire Genevieve.

Dieter

A stern, grey-haired man, who looks after the von Diehl entourage. He employs Gotrek and Felix as mercenaries.

Dog and Donkey, The

A tavern in Guntersbad, and the scene of Gotrek and Snorri's epic drinking contest.

Dragon Crag

Another name for Karak Azgal.

Dragon Mountain

Under this peak, in an extensive cave system, is where the dragon Skjalandir has made his home.

Dragon Vale

The valley leading to the Dragon Mountain, which has been devastated by Skjalandir since it has made its home there.

Drakenhof Castle

A huge castle in Sylvania, it is said to be built on a particularly ill-omened site, a nexus of terrible dark energies, and is a sacred place to the Arisen.

Drexler, Doktor

A physician and scholar in Nuln. He studied medicine in Kah Sabar, Araby. Felix is referred to him by his brother when he starts displaying what could be possible symptoms of the Plague.

E

Echter

A witch hunter Thanquol locks horns with when his mind is temporarily trapped in Boneripper's body.

Elissa

Barmaid at the Blind Pig in Nuln and Felix's love interest for awhile.

Emperor's Griffon

Tavern in the Human quarter of Karak Kadrin.

Enrik Kozinski

The Duke of Praag. A middle-aged man with greying hair, his tendency to see the works of Chaos around him has led to rumours that he shares his father's insanity. His curt manner and fiery temperament belie a gentle and caring manner.

Eye of Khemri

A small, oval-shaped pendant carved from obsidian with a central eye surrounded by odd pictograms of animal-headed people. The stone itself is gripped in a silver hand setting with pointed talons. Found in the rubble of Khemri and also known as the Eye of Nagash.

Eye of the Lord

A magical artefact, kept by Kelmain and Lhoigor. A gigantic crystal orb encased in metal, it is used to predict the future.

F

Faragrim

A senile dwarf prospector who Gotrek and Felix bump into in the Border Princes.

Fedrich Gerlach

Innkeep at the Skewered Dragon, Middenheim.

Felix Jaeger

Born the younger son of a wealthy Altdorf merchant, Gustav Jaeger and his wife Renata, Felix Jaeger always had dreams of becoming a famous poet and scholar. Unfortunately, his promising career was cut short when he found himself expelled from University after accidentally killing a fellow student in a duel. He then became involved in the infamous Window Tax Riots where he met Gotrek Gurnisson under somewhat fortuitous circumstances, when the slayer pulled him out from under the hooves of one of the mounted cavalry officers sent in to break up the fray. Unfortunately, the slayer then took exception to nearly being trampled himself, so set about breaking a few heads. Unsurprisingly,

both soon found themselves wanted by the authorities.

Later that evening in the Axe and Hammer tavern, Felix heard of the slayer's quest to find a worthy doom, and being slightly worse for wear at the time, swore a blood oath to follow the dwarf and record his demise in a suitably epic poem, never dreaming just what this would entail.

The duo's adventures have seen them journey extensively throughout the Empire, battling the forces of Chaos wherever they find them. Felix acquired the mystical dragon-hilted blade, Karaghul, in a troll's treasure hoard under Karak Eight Peaks and has used it to great effect against the numerous enemies he has fought since, particularly the dragon Skjalandir. Since teaming up with the slayer, he has also thwarted a skaven invasion, an assassination plot and a great Chaos incursion, and battled true Terror in the lost dwarf city of Karag Dum. He has also found time to meet and fall in love with Ulrika Magdova Straghov, though the affair has been a bitter-sweet experience.

Tall, broad-shouldered and blond, probably the most notable thing about Felix's handsome features is the long, thin scar which mars his cheek, a legacy of his student duelling days. He wears a tattered, red Sudenland wool cloak and though his clothes are of good quality, they have all seen better days; much like the poet himself, in fact.

Forgast Gaptooth

A slayer acquaintance of Snorri who killed a troll in a most unusual way.

Fort von Diehl

Settlement founded by the von Diehl family and their retainers, following their exile from the Empire.

Frau Winter
Sorceress, part of the von Diehl entourage, and mistress to Kirsten.

Fredericksburg
Town in Averland, near Blackfire Pass.

Fritz von Halstadt
Head of Nuln's secret police and a chief magistrate. A tall, gaunt man, von Halstadt is a deadly swordsman and obsessed with the Elector Countess he serves.

G

Garg Gorgul
Huge ogre encountered by Gotrek and Felix below Karag Eight Peaks.

Geheimnisnacht
'Night of Mystery', considered extremely unlucky by citizens of the Empire. Both moons are full on this night.

Gnoblars
These malicious little greenskins are related to goblins, and indeed rather resemble them. They can be mostly found living alongside ogres, where they serve as servants, soldiers and (more often than they would like) food.

Golden Brotherhood
A secret order devoted to seeking Chaos and destroying it. Max Schreiber is a member.

Golden Gull
Katja Murillo's ship, sunk by Uragh Goldtusk while she was searching for Redhand's treasure.

Golden Hammer, The
An upmarket restaurant in Nuln which Otto Jaeger takes Felix to, and where

Felix sees and recognises Fritz von Halstadt.

Gospodar Muster
A force of 5,000 mounted warriors, led by the Ice Queen herself, that go to aid Praag in its fight against the forces of Arek Daemonclaw.

Gotrek Gurnisson
Gotrek, son of Gurni was born and raised in the corridors of Karaz-a-Karak and like all citizens of the King's Council, did his military service in the depths below the Everpeak as a youth. Details of the intervening years between then and his meeting with Felix Jaeger are vague, though it is known that he was part of the first ill-fated attempt to find the lost city of Karag Dum. One of only three survivors to return from the Chaos Wastes, when he did so, he was carrying the awesome starmetal rune axe which never leaves his side.

After swearing blood kinship with Felix Jaeger and making him his Rememberer, the pair set out on their travels, the slayer actively seeking his doom, the man simply there to record it. Losing his eye in an epic battle against some greenskins at Fort von Diehl has been perhaps the most noticeable injury the slayer has sustained and though there have been a few close calls, much to his chagrin, Gotrek inevitably lives on to fight another day.

A typical slayer, Gotrek sports the bright orange crest and numerous tattoos which mark him as such. He is huge by dwarvish standards and though he only comes up to his companion's chest, he outweighs him by a substantial margin, all of it muscle. A gold chain runs from nostril to ear and a leather patch covers his ruined eye. He can drink almost as well as he can fight, which is saying something indeed, and he hates trees, boats and elves with a vengeance.

'...there was no denying that the trollslayer presented a formidable appearance. Although Gotrek only came up to Felix's chest, and a great deal of that height was made up of the huge dyed crest of red hair atop his shaved and tattooed skull, he was broader at the shoulders than a blacksmith. In one massive paw, he held a rune-covered axe that most men would have struggled to lift with both hands. When he shifted his massive head, the gold chain that ran from his nose to his ear jingled.'

From *Trollslayer*
by William King

Gottfried von Diehl
Baron of the Vennland Marches, exiled after a conflict with their Sigmarite neighbours. He leads his people on a doomed expedition out of the Empire south into the Border Princes.

Green Man, The
A fortified inn on the road to Drakenhof.

Greypaw Hollow
A small skaven settlement located under a forest.

Grimme
A dwarf slayer, first encountered by Felix in the Shrine of Grimnir. He speaks very little, seeming to be too overwhelmed by some personal grief to allow any kind of connection with others. He is one of the seven slayers who go to beard the dragon in its den.

Gulf of Araby
Expanse of water lying between the southern coast of Araby and the Southlands.

Grume of the Night Fang
A massive and foul-smelling Khorne warlord who is in league with the Tzeentch sorcerers, Kelmain and Lhoigor. He wants to kill Gotrek and claim his axe for his own, and carries the fearsome Skull Mace of Malarak to help him achieve his goal.

Guntersbad
A small town on the road to Talabheim.

Gurag
A monstrously obese orc shaman who pits his powers and his wits against Teclis, with surprising results.

Gutsnorter
An ogre, and relative of Vork Kineater.

H

Hall of the Well
The main hall housing Thangrim's people in Karag Dum. The settlement is protected by Runes of Concealment.

Hammer of Fate
The mighty magical warhammer used by King Thangrim, said to be one of the artefacts bequeathed to the dwarfs by the Ancestor-Gods.

Hanged Man, The
Inn located in Blutdorf, just as unpleasant as the rest of the village.

Hans Muller
The Divine One. A filthy, unkempt and quite, quite mad mage whose Spell of Translocation went wrong so he ended up the Ruined City in the Chaos Wastes where he meets Gotrek, Felix and Snorri.

Hargrim
Son of Thangrim Firebeard, a massive broad-shouldered dwarf and leader of the Tunnel Fighters at Karag Dum.

Hate Child, The
A parable told by the monks of the Schrammel monastery. It concerns a noble count called Benoist, and the consequences of his liaison with a woman called Yvette.

Haunted Citadel
An abandoned slann fortress in the swamps near Crannog Mere.

Heart of Fire
A magical gem secreted in the depths of the temple where Redhand's treasure was hidden. It was believed to control the eruptions of the island's volcano.

Hef (i)
Trapper, hired by the von Diehl family to guide them across the Border Princes. Felix first encounters him in the trading post where Hef is harassing Kirsten.

Hef (ii)
One of two twin sewerjack knifemen who work with Gotrek & Felix in the Nuln sewers (see also Spider).

Heinz
Owner of the Blind Pig and old mercenary friend of Gotrek. He spent ten years as a Halberdier and rose to the rank of captain during Karl Franz's campaigns against orcs to the East. Sports a bad leg after being stamped on by a Bretonnian charger at the Battle of Red Orc Pass.

Henkin Warsch
A traveller who crosses paths with Gotrek & Felix at Schrammel, near the infamous monstery there.

Henrik Richter
A bandit chief who has forged the bands of outlaws together in a bid to defeat the invading horde led by Ugrek Manflayer.

Heskit One Eye
Master Warp Engineer of Clan Skyre, he leads the attack on Nuln's College of Engineering in an attempt to steal a steam tank.

Hieronymous Ostwald, Count
Secretary to Her Serene Highness, Countess Emmanuelle. Friend of Drexler's.

Hippogryph
A fabulous beast with the forequarters of a griffon, and the rear quarters of a horse, found in the wildest reaches of the Old World. They are occasionally captured and forced to fight in arenas, or tamed for use as riding beasts.

Holdborn, Sergeant
An officious dwarf sergeant at Karak Azgal.

I

Indestructible
Malakai's first flying ship. Big as a sailing ship, the fuselage was over a hundred paces long and the ship itself could fly at ten leagues an hour. It crashed and was destroyed utterly.

Iron Door, The
Tavern in Karak Kadrin. A reputed hangout for slayers, renegades, and other lowlifes.

Ivan Stragov
Ulrika's father. A huge burly man with a long white beard and a shaved head except for a top knot. He is a Kislevite March Warden, in command of a thousand men.

Ivan took care of Borek, Gotrek and Snorri on their return from the Chaos Wastes on their first mission to find Karag Dum and thus earned their respect and friendship.

Ivory Road

A long trading road that runs between Barak Varr, the dwarf sea port, and Cathay, far to the east. It is a dangerous trip, not be undertaken without an armed escort.

Ixix

Goblin shaman, serving under Ugrek Manflayer, considered mad even by greenskin standards.

Izak Grottle

Obese Clan Moulder Packmaster, Grottle's appetite for food is rivalled only by his appetite for power.

J

Johann Zauberlich

A wizard and companion to Aldred Keppler. When not adventuring, he is a lecturer at the University of Nuln.

Jules Gascoigne

A Bretonnian scout originating from Quenelles. He was hired by Aldred Keppler to guide their party to Karag Eight Peaks.

Jurgen, Frater

Librarian of the Schrammel monastery.

Justine

A Chaos Warrior of Khorne, leader of the beastmen that destroyed Kleindorf.

K

Karag Dum

Lost dwarfhold in the Chaos Wastes and formerly one of the greatest dwarf cities, the mightiest in the northern lands in fact. Lost during the last great incursion of Chaos before the reign of Magnus the Pious.

Karaghul

Magic sword, originally wielded by the Templar Raphael. It was discovered by Felix, in Thulgul the troll's treasure hoard.

Karak Eight Peaks

Ancient dwarf stronghold that fell to the goblins three thousand years ago.

Karak Kadrin

'Slayer Keep', a dwarf stronghold that overlooks the Peak Pass in the Worlds Edge Mountains. Karak Kadrin has never fallen, partly due to the presence of the Shrine of Grimnir which attracts slayers from across the Old World.

Karak Varn

A Dwarf steamship that sank in a tale told by Urli aboard the *Storm Hammer*. Nobody knows why it sank.

Karl-Franz

Leader of the most powerful human nation in the Old World, the Empire, he leads fearlessly leads his armies into battle against their enemies – greenskins, beastmen, and worse.

Kat

A young girl with a distinctive white streak in her black hair. She was found by Gotrek & Felix in the ruins of Kleindorf.

Katja Murillo

Captain of the *Golden Gull*, and captive of Uragh Goldtusk when she first meets Felix. Tall, with raven-black, curly hair that falls to her shoulders, and with a low, husky voice. Despite being somewhat attracted, Felix cannot help but be suspicious of her.

Kelmain Blackstaff

An albino Tzeentchian sorcerer of immense power, he is also the identical twin of Lhoigor. Both he and his brother served as advisors to Arek Daemonclaw and also had a hand in the corruption of the dragon, Skjalandir. Kelmain carries a staff of ebony and silver, which he found in ruins in the Chaos Wastes. He and Lhoigor are also responsible for opening the Paths of Old Ones and unwittingly putting the whole of the Old World in jeopardy by doing so.

Kingdom of the Dragon
A mysterious land – possibly mythical – rumoured to lie far, far to the east.

Kirsten
Indentured to Frau Winter, part of the von Diehl entourage. Felix rescues her from the attentions of Hef, Kell and Lars in the trading post and she becomes his first love.

Kislev
Reputed to be a land of ice and snow where winter never lifts. In actuality, it is a land of rolling plains and thick forests of pine which has a brief but intense summer and a long, cold winter. Famed for its horsemen.

Klara
Culum's pretty and somewhat inquisitive wife. Her attempt to wheedle information out of Felix only succeeds in earning him the enmity of her husband.

Kleindorf
Small village on the Flensburg road, deep in the Drakwald.

Knoblauch, Frater
Gatekeeper at the Schrammel monastery.

Krakul Zapskratch
An itinerant warlock engineer who at one time passes through the skaven

outpost of Greypaw Hollow. It is here where he takes on a job for Grey Seer Thanquol – constructing a mechanical Boneripper.

> 'Had it been standing, the creature would have been three times the size of its master, a towering construction of steel, bone and wire fuelled by a warpstone heart and driven by the arcane mechanics of Clan Skryre techno-sorcery. In shape, it retained a morbid resemblance to a living rat-ogre, and the warlock-engineers had even used the bones of Thanquol's first Boneripper when assembling their creation.'

> From *Mindstealer* by CL Werner

Kregaerak
The location near where the *Karak Varn* was washed up.

L

Lars
Trapper. Felix manages to enamour himself of Lars by smashing his teeth during a fight in the trading post.

Lhoigor Goldenrod
A tall, vulpine albino sorcerer of immense power, he is evenly matched with his identical twin, Kelmain. Both Lhoigor and his brother come from the strange Weirdblood tribe and from birth they were marked by the favour of the Changer of Ways, by being born with teeth and claws so they could have meat as their first meal. Lhoigor carries a gold-sheathed staff which was unearthed in the Ruins of Ulangor in the Chaos Wastes.

Lonely Tower
Built on top of an old coal mine, this is the secret location where Malakai

and his engineers build the Spirit of Grungni. It comes under attack by Grey Seer Thanquol and his minions as they try to steal the airship.

Lord of Dragons

One of the Undying Ones, ghostly elven wizards who sacrificed themselves in order to save Ulthuan and their people. He and his brethren are mighty mages, responsible for maintaining the web of spells that keeps the island continent of Ulthuan afloat and it is he who brings the danger facing the island to Teclis's attention.

Lothar Kryptman

Alchemist, living in Fredericksburg. A weirdroot addict, he assists Gotrek & Felix after their encounter in the Sleeping Dragon.

Lothern

Great elvish harbour city where the Phoenix King holds court. Teclis and his brother Tyrion have a mansion built on the side of the highest hill overlooking the city.

Lurkers Within

Ancient spider daemons who guard the Haunted Citadel in Albion. They are naturally resistant to magic.

Lurking Horror

A fantastic beast that is rumoured to be quite fantastical.

Lurk Snitchtongue

Thanquol's henchling and a former Clawleader. He has a warpstone powered communication amulet hammered into his skull by his master and sneaks aboard the Spirit of Grungni at his master's command. An encounter with a warp-storm while onboard leaves him somewhat changed though.

M

Magda Freyadotter

Cleric of Valaya, member of Belegar's expedition to Karag Eight Peaks. She warns Gotrek and his party of the dangers awaiting them beneath the Peaks.

Magdalena

Mysterious silver-haired girl with golden eyes, a captive of Count Hrothgar.

Magrig One Eye

The fearsome guardian of the Temple of the Old Ones. He was the mightiest of the giants of old before his brain became clouded and he acquired the lust for manflesh. He lost an eye in a ferocious battle to the death with his brother and is worshipped as a god by the local orc tribes.

Magritta

City-state on the southern coast of Estalia. Built upon the Bay of Quietude, it commands one of the greatest fleets in the Old World, much to the chagrin of its Tilean neighbours.

Malakai Makaisson

Thought to be the best engineer who ever lived. He was drummed out of the Guild of Engineers after the first airship fiasco and became a slayer. He built the Spirit of Grungni and is responsible for devising many other ingenious munitions and weapons also.

He is another shaven-headed dwarf, with the customary red dyed crest and a short white beard. When flying the airship, he wears a short leather jerkin with sheepskin collar, a leather cap with long ear flaps and a cut-out for his crest to fit through and thick optical lenses engraved with crosshairs.

Malakai appears to have been a prolific inventer, and well travelled, with devices allegedly invented by him turning up all over the Empire and the dwarf realms. The powered skiff used by the dwarfs of Wynters Breery being a case in point.

He is originally from Dwimmerdim Vale, way up north – an isolated place, which is thought to account for his somewhat odd accent.

Malgrim
Chief engineer of the *Storm Hammer*.

Manfred von Diehl
Nephew and heir to Gottfried von Diehl, considered a brilliant, if blasphemous playwright among the cognoscenti of Altdorf.

Maximillian Schreiber
Max is a powerful mage and as such, he has become an invaluable ally to Gotrek and Felix in their recent adventures. He was expelled from the Imperial College of Magicians for showing an unhealthy interest in Chaos but found a sympathetic sponsor for his research in the form of the Elector Count of Middenheim. A tall, good-looking man with a well-trimmed beard, he is about ten years older than Felix. He and the other man also share a mutual interest in the same woman, Ulrika Straghov, and this has led to a few complications recently. Max is also a member of the mysterious Golden Brotherhood, an order dedicated to fighting Chaos, though the details are vague.

Mead and Mazer, The
Schrammel's only inn.

Megalean Chain
A group of islands lying in or near the Gulf of Araby.

Middenheim
The City of the White Wolf. The central heights of this mountain top city are dominated by the Elector Count's Palace and the mighty Temple of Ulric. It started life as a fortress but then a fair sized community sprung up around the heights as well.

Migrunsson, Engineer
Dwarf engineer involved in the fight to reclaim Karak Azgal from the orcs.

Mikal's Ford
Site of the mustering of the Kislevite forces.

Mobi
Dwarf marine aboard the *Storm Hammer*. He is short even for a dwarf, and very wide.

Morakai
Thangrim Firebeard's other son who died out in the wastes in the cave surrounded by the bodies of the twenty beastmen he'd killed.

Morrslieb
One of the two moons of the Old World (the other being Mannslieb). Morrslieb is smaller than its brother, and characterised by a sickly green glow. It is generally considered to be a sign of ill omen.

Murdo MacBaldoch
The old but surprisingly tough chieftain of Crannog Mere. He is also a member of the Order of Truthsayers of Albion and a canny man. He wears trews and a pleated cloak of a tartan colour that blends into the undergrowth and sports the same strange tattoos that all his people do, tattoos that bear a marked resemblance to some of the engravings in the Paths of the Old Ones.

N

Naktit

Scout-rat in the employ of Warlord Pakstab.

Narli

Ancient dwarf marine aboard the *Storm Hammer*. His face was like a diseased prune and his beard came almost to his feet.

Nuln

Large city-state in the southern Empire and former capital. Ruled by Countess Emmanuelle von Liebewitz.

O

Ogham Rings

Great stone circles, which attract dark magical energy in Albion and somehow render it harmless.

Olaf

Cultist sent to kill Felix in Praag. A short, stocky man with a high rasping voice. He accompanied Sergei and was considered the brains of the pair.

Old Ones

A race of gods older than the gods. Some claim they created the world, others that they never existed at all.

Olgar Olgersson

Also known as Olgar Goldgrabber because of his miserly tendencies. He funds the expedition to the Chaos Wastes.

Oracle of Truthsayers

A tall woman, sharp faced but still beautiful. She is a respected wise woman throughout Albion and lives with her guardians in sacred caves up in the mountains. She has been gifted with visions though had to pay a heavy price for the power. Teclis is told to seek her out and ask her advice on how to close the Paths of the Old Ones.

P

Pakstab, Warlord

The leader of the skaven settlement of Greypaw Hollow.

Paths of the Old Ones

An ancient network of strange interdimensional corridors with nexus points in places all over the world. A very dangerous place indeed.

Pavel

Tzeentchian cultist, sent to assassinate Enrik.

Pigbarter

A filthy little port city on the estuary of the River Ruin, whose primary is currency is swine.

Praag

City in northern Kislev on the River Lynsk. Kislev's second most powerful City State.

Q

Quadira

Citadel on the Gulf of Araby, where Gotrek and Felix board the *Storm Hammer*.

R

Ranagor

A renowned breeder of gryphons who raised Teclis's beast from an egg she found on the slopes of Mount Brood.

Red Rose, The
Large brothel in Praag, visited by Felix, Gotrek and the other slayers during their 'investigations'.

Redhand
Pirate captain and former scourge of the southern seas. At one time, Redhand's fleet sailed as they pleased and even stormed the walls of Magritta. Redhand's fate is unknown.

Rememberer
Someone who travels with a slayer to record the heroic manner of his death. For reasons that can only be guessed at, they are usually human.

Roche
Adolphus Krieger's hulking, pock-marked henchman. His family has served Krieger for generations.

Rodrik
A huge, golden-maned knight and body-guard to Countess Gabriella. Son of Rudgar.

Rudgar
Count of Waldenhof. A tall, florid aristo-crat and brother-in-law to the Countess Gabriella.

Ruined City
An ancient city in the Chaos Wastes where everything is built on a giant scale. There is a massive ziggurat in the middle of it which is home to harpies and something far worse.

Rumblebelly
An ogre 'chef'.

S

Schrammel
A small village somewhere in the iso-lated wildness of the Empire.

Schrammel Monastery
The site of this monastery – now in ruins – lies an hour's walk from the village of Schrammel, somewhere in the Empire. Supposedly run by the followers of Solkan, the God of Law, in reality the monastery's allegiance lay with a darker master.

Sergei
Cultist sent with Olaf to kill Felix in Praag. A tall, heavily built man with a deep voice. His lack of wits make him no less dangerous.

Shienara
One of Teclis's female companions. She and her twin, Malyria, are courtesans.

Shrine of Grimnir
Located in the dwarf hold of Karak Kadrin, this shrine is dedicated to Grim-nir, the most bloodthirsty of the dwarf ancestor gods. Once a dwarf has taken his slayer oath, his name is carved into the great pillar in the temple – the pillar of woe – so all will know of their pass-ing from life.

'You say Grimnir is bloodthirsty,' Ulrika asked. 'Does he accept living sacrifices then?'

'Only the lives of his slayers. He takes their death in payment for their sins. And their hair.'

Borek must have noticed the star-tled look pass across Felix's face, for he added: 'Most slayers take their vow before the great altar of Grimnir down there, that is where they shave their heads, then they burn their hair in the great furnace. Outside is the street of the skin artists, where they have their first tattoos inked into their flesh.'

From *Dragonslayer* by William King

Siobhain

One of the Oracle's Guardians and an accomplished warrior. She is almost as tall as Felix and tattoos cover her face and arms in the style of her people.

Skabrand

An ogre settlement located in the southern reaches of the Mountains of Mourn.

Skewered Dragon, The

A bar in Middenheim.

Skitch

Izak Grottle's henchling. A hunchback who wears glasses, Skitch is reputed to be the best ratmaster of his day.

Skjalandir

A huge and ancient dragon, it is first encountered by the Spirit of Grungni whilst travelling to Kislev. Its long sleep had been disturbed by Kelmain and Lhoigor, who drove warpstone charms into its flesh, corrupting it. Skjalandir made its nest in a system of caverns below the Dragon Mountain along the Old High Road.

Skull Mace of Malarak

A weapon wielded by Grume of the Nightfang. Made of some odd metal, its head is shaped like the skull of a daemon and the empty eye-sockets glow with an infernal light. It freezes the limbs and chills the hearts of those who face it.

Sleeping Dragon, The

Tavern in Fredericksburg.

Snelli

Dwarf marine aboard the *Storm Hammer*. He volunteers to join the party that search for Redhand's treasure.

Snorri Nosebiter

Snorri is a massive, well-muscled and immensely stupid slayer. His trademark 'crest' is made up of nails, which have been painted different colours and driven into his skull and this may account for his lack of wits. His beard is cropped short and his nose has been broken so many times that it's shapeless. One ear is cauliflowered, while the other one is missing altogether, leaving only a hole in the side of his head. He has a huge ring through his nose and is heavily scarred and tattooed.

He is one of only three survivors of the first ill-fated mission to find Karag Dum, and at some point in the past, there has been a tragedy involving a dwarf woman and child, which has led Snorri to take the Oath.

Snorri fights with a hammer and axe and enjoys the simple things in life – drinking and killing, and he is very good at both!

Sonnstill

The festival of the summer solstice, observed in and around the Empire and the surrounding lands.

Sphere of Destiny

Strange apparatus Teclis found in the ruins of an ancient Cathayan city nearly two centuries ago. A massive sphere of bronze, engraved with strange runes, he uses it to augment his powers when performing a particular spell of viewing.

Spirit of Grungni

The second airship built in secret by Malakai, it is even bigger than its ill-fated predecessor, the Indestructible. It is made up of two main parts: a massive, many skinned balloon full of lift-gas cells, and a smaller, heavily armed and armoured cabin suspended beneath it. There are weapons cupolas embedded into the fuselage of the main ship and it has many portholes and a massive glass window at the front helm to allow a good view from the command deck. Powered by 'black water' engines and a massive propellor at the stern, the airship is capable of flying over two hundred leagues per day. Malakai wanted to call it the *Unstoppable* but much to the relief of the many dwarfs who serve onboard, he was persuaded against it!

Spider

One of two twin sewerjack knifemen Gotrek and Felix work with in Nuln. He is distinguished from his brother by the spider tattooed onto his cheek (see also Hef II).

Standing Stones Inn

Coach house on the Bögenhafen road.

Steg

Dwarf slayer, met by Felix and Gotrek in the Iron Door tavern. His shame lies in being caught as a thief, though he seems little concerned about further tarnishing his name.

Stew

The sewers beneath Nuln where Gotrek, Felix and the other sewerjacks patrol. The tunnels themselves are of Khazalid workmanship with high vaulted ceilings more reminiscent of a cathedral than a sewage system.

Storm Hammer

Dwarf steamship which Gotrek and Felix take passage on to escape Araby.

Sulmander's tomb

Gotrek & Felix ransacked this tomb whilst in Araby.

T

Talia Nitikin

A Kislevite woman, younger sister of Anya. Following a fall, her behaviour has become so erratic and aggressive that she is danger of being labelled a follower of Chaos.

Tasirion

An elf mage who broke elvish law by unlocking the Paths of the Old Ones. The venture ended in his ultimate madness and his fate is considered a warning to others who might attempt to do the same. He has left some documented accounts about the Paths which Teclis consults.

Teclis

A mighty elven arch-mage and twin to Tyrion. In his youth, he was frail and sickly but then he learned to strengthen himself with spells and potions so now the only visible legacy of this former weakness is a slight limp in his left leg. He bears the War Crown of Saphery and the staff of Lileath, artefacts of considerable power.

His first encounter with Gotrek Gurnisson is within the Paths of the Old Ones and it is not an auspicious one.

Temple of the Old Ones

A massive stepped pyramid in Albion with seven huge levels, each level marked with ancient runes.

Terror

The Great Destroyer, a Blutdrengrik, the Bane of Grung – a bloodthirster of Khorne!

A daemon of Chaos summoned by Skathloc in the last days of the siege of Karag Dum. Huge, more than twice the height of a man, it is winged with ruddy red skin and has the mark of the Blood God on its brow. It is armed with whip and axe.

Thangrim Firebeard
The leader of the dwarfs at Karag Dum. An old but still powerful dwarf with long red hair and beard striped with white, he carries the Hammer of Fate.

Thanquol
A skaven magelord and master schemer whose cunning plans always seem to be thwarted – usually by his own paranoia! Pre-eminent among the Grey Seers, the feared and potent skaven magicians who rank just below the Council of Thirteen itself, Thanquol is a mighty mage indeed, especially when he augments his powers by liberal use of the powdered warpstone snuff he keeps in a manskin pouch at his belt.

Pale-furred with pink, blind-seeming eyes, he sports the horns which signify his calling, and the favour of his master, the Horned Rat. Thanquol loathes and fears Gotrek Gurnisson in equal measures, and holds the slayer and his human companion entirely responsible for all his recent setbacks. Still, he is determined to have his revenge, no matter how long it takes!

Thulgul
A hideously mutated troll, the guardian of the lost hoard of Karag Eight Peaks.

Tobaro
Tilean city-state on the western coast of the Tilean Sea. Built upon ancient Elven ruins, the city is protected both inland and along the coast by rugged natural defences.

Tobi
Young dwarf marine aboard the *Storm Hammer*.

Trollslayer's Doom
The alternate name Felix considered for his 'My Travels with Gotrek' journals.

Truthsayers
The order of wizards of Albion. The formation of the order of Truthsayers apparently dates back to the legendary times when the Old Ones walked the earth.

Twisted Paths
Spoken of by Tasirion, they are said to be where the work of the Old Ones intersect with bubbles of pure Chaos.

Tyrion
Teclis's twin brother. A handsome warrior and consort to the Everqueen. The deadliest elf warrior in twenty generations.

Tzarina Katarin
'The Ice Queen', ruler of Kislev. An accomplished mage and warrior, her nickname derives from her cool demeanour as well as her mastery of Ice Magic.

U

Ugrek Manflayer
A massive orc, who has united the greenskin tribes near Karak Kadrin. He is known as far as Altdorf, such is his reputation. He is said to skin his captives and make the skins into cloaks. He wields a magical cleaver.

Ulgo
A witch hunter and member of the Cult of Ulric. He accuses Gotrek & Felix of conspiring with Chaos.

Ulli Ullisson
A dwarf slayer, who joins Felix and Gotrek's quest to slay the dragon Skjalindir. His freshly shaven head suggests that he is only a recent convert to the slayer cult, and his manner is that

of a nervous braggart rather than a truly brave warrior.

Ulrika Magdova Straghov
A beautiful, blonde Kislevite and an expert swordswoman. Her father is March Warden of an estate bordering the troll country and she is the love of Felix Jaeger's life for a while.

Ulthuan
The island continent of the elves, raised and held above the sea by potent magic.

Ungrim Ironfist
Slayer-king of Karak Kadrin. Due to the vow taken by his ancestor Baragor, Ungrim is bound both by his oaths as king and slayer, and tries to balance both as best he can.

Unsinkable
Malakai's famous steamship and the biggest one ever seen. Two hundred paces long and weighing overfive hundred tons, it could sail at over three leagues an hour and had steam-powered gatling turrets for protection. It hit a rock and sank.

Uragh Goldtusk
Orcish captain, and the most feared pirate in the Gulf of Araby. Remarkably agile and intelligent for an orc, he wields twin cutlasses.

Urli
Marine sergeant aboard the *Storm Hammer*. Known as Ugli Urli to his comrades, his face has been pock-marked by shrapnel.

V

Varek Varigsson
Son of Vareg of the Clan Grimnar and nephew of Borek Forkbeard.

Plump and civilised looking, his well-groomed beard reaches almost to the floor and he wears thick glasses. A scholar like his uncle, he diligently keeps a diary of all the events that take place. He is equipped with bombs made by Malakai, and the engineer also taught him how to fly a gyrocopter, a skill he uses to great effect against the dragon

Van Niek's Emporium
Shop in Nuln that specialises in rare and exotic books and other artefacts. Reputedly, it also serves as a government front as well.

Vermak Skab
Warlord of Clan Skab and Lurk's distant cousin. Sent to lead the attack on Nuln but tragically meets his end in a terrible accident involving a loaded crossbow and an exploding donkey!

Vilebroth Null
Low Abbot of the Plague Monks of Clan Pestilens who tries to bring about the downfall of Nuln by using the Cauldron of a Thousand Poxes to spread the plague.

Villem Kozinski
Younger brother of the Duke Enrik. His diplomatic manner makes him a more suitable candidate for the throne than his brother, and he acts as a foil to Enrik's abruptness.

Voorman
Count Hrothgar's pet wizard and a member of the Order of Tzeentch.

Von Diehls
An ancient Empire family line, rumoured to be cursed.

Vork Kineater
Leader of the ogre mercenaries

employed in Skabrand by Zayed al Fahruk to protect his caravan. It's possible his name came from eating all his family. Kineater kidnaps Talia Nitikin, intending to marry her, an act which inflames the other ogres of his tribe against him.

W

Waldenschlosse
Castle which sits above Waldenhof and home to Rudgar, Count of Waldenhof.

Warlord Pakstab
Warlord of the skaven settlement Greypaw Hollow.

White Boar, The
A tavern in Praag where Gotrek, Felix and the rest stayed during the Siege of Praag.

Wildgans, Frater
An instructor at the Schrammel monastery.

Witch
Grey seer Thanquol suffers an unfortunate consequence when he angers an unnamed strigany witch in a forest.

Wolfgang Krassner
Man killed by Felix in a duel, resulting in his expulsion from university.

Wolfgang Lammel
Decadent fop and Slaaneshi cultist. His father owns the Sleeping Dragon in Fredricksburg, where he hangs out with his equally unpleasant friends.

Worlds Edge Mountains
Immense range of mountains that mark the eastern boundary of the Empire and the Old World, believed in ancient times to be the edge of the world itself.

Z

Zayed al Mahrak
An Arabyan caravan master who plies his trade between the Empire and far Cathay.

Zarkhul
A prophet and the uniter of the orc tribes of Albion. He intends to lead them into the great Waaagh to reclaim the Temple of Old Ones.

ABOUT THE AUTHORS

William King was born in Stranraer, Scotland, in 1959. He is the author of the Tyrion & Teclis trilogy and the Macharian Crusade, as well as the much-loved Gotrek & Felix series and the Space Wolf novels. His short stories have appeared in many magazines and compilations, including *White Dwarf* and *Inferno!* Bill currently lives in Prague.

John Brunner (1934 – 1995) was a prolific British author of science fiction novels and stories. His career spanned over four decades and won him many accolades. His 1968 novel *Stand on Zanzibar,* about an overpopulated world, won the 1968 Hugo Award for best science fiction novel. It also won the BSFA award the same year. *The Jagged Orbit* won the BSFA award in 1970.

Jordan Ellinger is a recent first place winner in the Writers of the Future contest and a Clarion West graduate, and his work can be seen in numerous anthologies across the science fiction and fantasy genres. When he is not writing, he is a freelance editor attached to such projects as Every Day Fiction and Raygun Revival.

Author of the novels *Knight of the Blazing Sun*, *Neferata* and the forthcoming *Gotrek and Felix: Road of Skulls*, **Josh Reynolds** used to be a roadie for the Hong Kong Cavaliers, but now writes full time. His work has appeared in various anthologies, including *Age of Legend* and several issues of the electronic magazine *Hammer and Bolter*.

C. L. Werner's Black Library credits include *Time of Legends: Dead Winter, Mathias Thulmann: Witch Hunter, Runefang,* the Brunner the Bounty Hunter trilogy and the Thanquol and Boneripper series. Currently living in the American south-west, he continues to write stories of mayhem and madness set in the worlds of Warhammer and Warhammer 40,000. He claims that he was a diseased servant of the Horned Rat long before his first story was ever published.

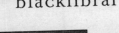